To Decide Our Destiny

PRELUDE TO GLORY

To Decide
Our Destiny

A NOVEL BY

RON CARTER

BOOKCRAFT

SALT LAKE CITY, UTAH

Library of Congress Catalog Card Number: 99-96498

ISBN 1-57008-695-8

First Printing, 1999

Printed in the United States of America

This series is dedicated to the common people
of long ago who paid the price.

★ ★ ★

America was discovered, colonized, and made into a great nation so that the Lord would have a proper place both to restore the gospel and from which to send it forth to all other nations. As a prelude to his coming, and so the promised work of restoration would roll forward, the foundations of the American nation were laid.

—BRUCE R. MCCONKIE

This volume is dedicated to
Gary, Eric, Tom, Jeff, John, Kris, Karen,
Shannon, and Joe. My children.

To Decide
Our Destiny

"My brave fellows, you have done all I asked you to do, and more than could be reasonably expected; but your country is at stake, your wives, your houses, and all that you hold dear. You have worn yourselves out with fatigues and hardships, but we know not how to spare you. If you will consent to stay only one month longer, you will render that service to the cause of liberty, and to your country, which you probably never can do under any other circumstances. The present is emphatically the crisis which is to decide our destiny."

George Washington
DECEMBER 30, 1776
ADDRESSING THE SOLDIERS
WHOSE ENLISTMENT EXPIRED
DECEMBER 31, 1776

PREFACE

★ ★ ★

The reader will be greatly assisted in following the *Prelude to Glory* series if the author's overall approach is understood.

The volumes do not present the critical events of the Revolutionary War in chronological, month-by-month, year-by-year order. The reason is simple. At all times during the eight years of the conflict, the tremendous events that shaped the war and decided the final result were happening in two, and sometimes three, different geographical areas at the same time. This being true, it became obvious that moving back and forth, from one battle front to another, would be extremely confusing.

Thus, the decision was made to follow each major event through to its conclusion, as seen through the eyes of selected characters, and then go back and pick up the thread of other great events that were happening at the same time in other geographical areas, as seen through the eyes of the characters caught up in those events.

The reader will recall that volume I, *Our Sacred Honor*, followed the fictional family of John Phelps Dunson from the beginning of hostilities between the British and the Americans in April, 1775, through the Lexington and Concord battles, and then moved into the experiences of Matthew Dunson, John's eldest son, who was a navigator in the sea battles later in the war. In volume II, *The Times That Try Men's Souls*, Billy Weems, Matthew's dearest friend who was nearly killed at the Lexington battle, experienced the terrible defeats and the misery of the Americans as they lost battle after battle in and around New York before the army ultimately retreated in the early winter of 1776 to the frozen banks of the Delaware River in Pennsylvania.

Now, in volume III, *To Decide Our Destiny*, Billy Weems and his friend Eli Stroud suffer alongside their fellow soldiers as they struggle to survive the bitter winter and the even more bitter realization that the Revolution itself is in jeopardy. They watch as General George Washington rises to the challenge and takes the initiative. Billy and Eli willingly follow his heroic leadership across the Delaware River in a terrible storm on Christmas night, and then into battle at Trenton and again at Princeton. These two battles are hailed by historians and military experts as being important turning points of the war and classic examples of Washington's military genius and strength of character.

Volume IV will continue the events of 1777 as the British prepare for the battle of Saratoga under the leadership of General John Burgoyne. Subsequent volumes will follow the campaign in the Southern states, the Constitutional Convention, the drafting of our Constitution, and beyond.

And again, rest assured those two sweet youngsters, Matthew and Kathleen are doing well and the conclusion of their story is coming soon. Also, Eli Stroud and Mary Flint are facing surprises, as are Billy Weems and Brigitte Dunson.

CHRONOLOGY OF IMPORTANT EVENTS
RELATED TO THIS VOLUME

★ ★ ★

1775

April 19. The first shot is fired at Lexington, Massachusetts, and the Revolutionary War begins. (*See volume 1*)

June 15. The Continental Congress appoints George Washington of Virginia to be commander in chief of the Continental army.

June 17. The battle of Bunker Hill and Breed's Hill is fought, which the British win at great cost, suffering numerous casualties before the colonial forces abandon the hills due to lack of ammunition. (*See volume 1*)

1776

February–March. Commodore Esek Hopkins leads eight small colonial ships to the Bahamas to obtain munitions from two British forts, Nassau and Montague. (*See volume 1*)

March 17. General Sir William Howe evacuates his British command from Boston. (*See volume 1*)

July 9. On orders of General Washington, the Declaration of Independence (adopted by the Continental Congress on July 4) is read publicly to the entire American command in the New York area, as well as to the citizens. (*See volume 2*)

Late August–Early December. The British and American armies clash in a series of battles at Long Island, Kip's Bay, Harlem Heights, White Plains, and Fort Washington. Though the Americans make occasional gains in the battles, the British effectively decimate the Continental army to the point that Washington has no choice but to begin a retreat across the length of New Jersey. He crosses the Delaware River into Pennsylvania and establishes a camp at McKonkey's Ferry, nine miles north of Trenton. (*See volume 2*)

September 21. An accidental fire burns about one-fourth of New York City. (*See volume 2*)

October 11. General Benedict Arnold leads a tiny fleet of fifteen hastily constructed ships to stall the British fleet of twenty-five ships on Lake Champlain. Arnold delays the movement of thirteen thousand British troops from moving south until the spring of 1777 and essentially saves George Washington's Continental army. (*See volume 1*)

December 10. Benjamin Franklin travels to France to persuade the French government to support America in the Revolution.

December 14. General William Howe closes the winter campaign, and the British troops retire into winter quarters. Howe stations General James Grant at Princeton with a small force of British soldiers. Colonel Carl Emil Kurt von Donop is given command of three thousand Hessians along the Delaware River opposite the American camp, and he quarters fourteen hundred of his men in Trenton under the command of Colonel Johann Gottlieb Rall.

December 22. John Honeyman, an American spy posing as a British Loyalist, is under orders from General Washington and makes a reconnaissance journey to Trenton, is later "captured" by the Americans, and reports his findings to Washington directly.

December 25. Washington's three-point attack of Trenton begins as he and his army cross the Delaware River at McKonkey's Ferry at night and during a raging blizzard. General James Ewing attempts a crossing at the Trenton Ferry, and General John Cadwalader moves into position at Dunk's Ferry.

December 26. The battle of Trenton is fought to a dramatic conclusion.

December 29. Benjamin Franklin meets with Comte de Vergennes to discuss French aid for the Americans.

December 31. Enlistments for the majority of soldiers in the Continental army are due to expire at midnight.

1777

January 2. General Charles Cornwallis leads a British force of 8,000 men out of Princeton with orders to destroy what is left of Washington's army. Colonel Edward Hand and a small force of 600 Pennsylvanian riflemen are dispatched to stop the British before they can reach Trenton.

January 3. Washington and his army of over four thousand men endure a midnight march out of Trenton and into Princeton, where they surprise British colonel Charles Mawhood's command shortly after sunrise. The battle of Princeton is fought with surprising results.

January 7. The Continental army establishes winter quarters in Morristown, New Jersey.

February 25. As the political relationships between England, France, and America tighten, Comte de Vergennes receives news regarding the outcome of the battles of Trenton and Princeton and plans a course of action for France.

May 6. British general John Burgoyne arrives in Canada to begin his campaign down the Champlain-Hudson region.

1779

September 23. Commodore John Paul Jones, aboard the *Bonhomme Richard*, engages the larger British man-of-war *Serapis* off the east coast of England in the much-celebrated night battle in which Jones utters the now-famous cry, "I have not yet begun to fight!" (*See volume 1*)

Part One

★ ★ ★

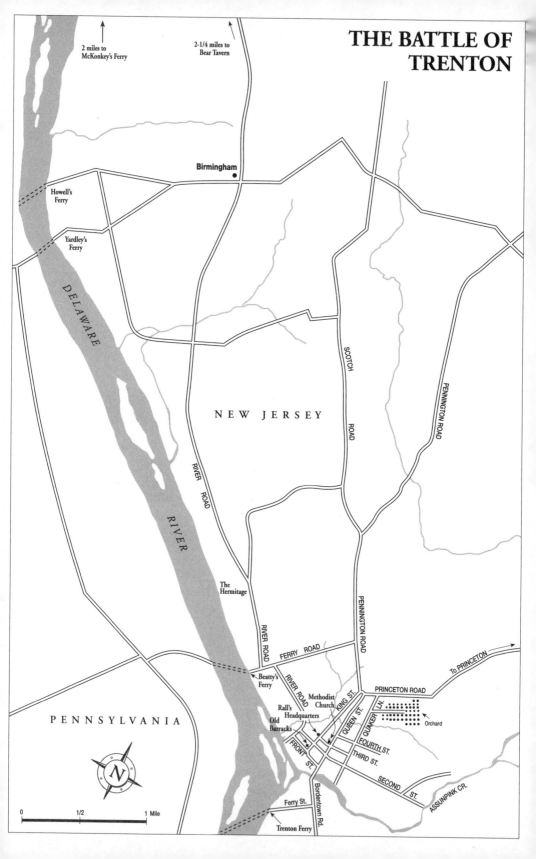

THE BATTLE OF TRENTON

2 miles to
McKonkey's Ferry

2-1/4 miles to
Bear Tavern

Birmingham

Howell's
Ferry

Yardley's
Ferry

DELAWARE

NEW JERSEY

SCOTCH ROAD

PENNINGTON ROAD

RIVER ROAD

RIVER

The
Hermitage

RIVER ROAD

PENNINGTON ROAD

FERRY ROAD

To PRINCETON

Beatty's
Ferry

RIVER ROAD

PRINCETON ROAD

Methodist
Church

KING ST.

QUAKER LN.

Rall's
Headquarters

QUEEN ST.

Orchard

Old
Barracks

FOURTH ST.

THIRD ST.

PENNSYLVANIA

FRONT ST.

SECOND ST.

ASSUNPINK CR.

Bordentown Rd.

Ferry St.

Trenton Ferry

N

0   1/2   1 Mile

The Delaware River, Trenton, New Jersey

December 7, 1776

CHAPTER I

★ ★ ★

*T*hey came streaming from the east on the ice-covered roads or through snow-choked fields and orchards, freezing in rags and tatters, feet wrapped in strips of raw beefhide or tarp or ancient threadbare blankets that left blood on the frozen snow and ice. Their eyes were sunken, cheeks hollow, beards clogged with matter from sores that would not heal. Most of them walked hunched over from starvation cramps in their empty bellies, and from dysentery and fever and battle wounds. No longer were their drums banging and fifes shrilling proudly as they plodded on wordlessly with but one thought.

Run. *Run.*

This was the Continental army that had caught the British by surprise at Lexington and Concord in April of 1775, and again at Bunker Hill in June, and had beaten them, humiliated them, and then put Boston under siege to drive them out, southwest to New York. Jubilant, heady with their spectacular victories, they had gathered at Long Island in June of 1776 to finish their annihilation of the British army. None brought winter clothing—there was no need. They would drive the redcoats back into the sea and then return to their farms and ships and businesses and homes in time for the fall harvest, well before the storms and snows of winter would require warm clothing.

They were more than twenty thousand gathered around New York under the command of General George Washington. He dug in part of them on the high ground of Long Island and faced General William

Howe as he led his British and Hessian army against them in the sweltering heat of August, but none of the Americans had been prepared for the holocaust that followed. Five times the British wreaked Armageddon on them—Long Island, Manhattan Island, White Plains, Fort Washington, Fort Lee—and five times the Continental army ran in a blind panic to save itself. In the wild retreat they had abandoned most of their gunpowder, muskets, cannon, blankets, food, tents, cartridges, medicine, and wounded.

No one knew the number of men remaining. All they knew was the entire Continental army was fragmented under a divided command, scattered, shamed, emaciated, sick, strung out across the state of New Jersey from the Hudson River to the farmlands southwest of the village of Princeton, where General Washington had led scarcely six thousand of them. Of those missing, no one knew how many had been killed or taken prisoner in the nightmare of battles or abandoned when sickness or their wounds would not let them run. Nor did anyone know how many had crept away in the night to become deserters—sometimes entire regiments—rather than face one more day of the unending torture.

Officers and soldiers on the outer edges of the moving mass paused at the neat farmyards to seize hastily what they could of anything in the granaries or barns or root cellars that could be eaten. They dumped it—grain, turnips, cabbages, pigs, chickens—into their moving wagons and gave the sullen farmers Continental scrip or scrawled promissory notes or anything they had in exchange. If they had nothing to give, they took it at bayonet point and moved on, constantly glancing over their shoulders at the skyline, never stopping, afraid to linger for fear of the British somewhere behind. What they got from the farms was gone within minutes—never enough, never enough.

"Move on, keep moving," General Washington had urged as he rode among them on his big bay gelding. "Trenton is over the next rise and the Delaware River just beyond. Boats are waiting. We'll be safe when we've crossed into Pennsylvania. Keep moving."

They heard his brave words, but in their hearts they knew. The British were just hours behind them, and crossing the Delaware was their last desperate hope to hide behind something, anything, that would halt the relentless pursuit by the redcoats. If the half-frozen river did not stop the redcoats—if General Howe or General Cornwallis followed them across the Delaware—there would be nothing standing between the British army and the Second Continental Congress convened at Philadelphia forty miles south, least of all the shambles of the Continental army.

The Marblehead Massachusetts Regiment under Colonel John Glover led the army west towards Trenton on the old Princeton Road, and crested the gentle rise with the mid-afternoon wintry sun in their faces. Glover, a scant five feet four inches, stout, sandy-colored hair, finely-chiseled features, fearless, was respected and beloved by his Marblehead Regiment as no other. Corporal Billy Weems of Company Nine of the scattered Boston Regiment, who had survived the horror of the bloody, catastrophic defeats, marched stoically in the front ranks of Glover's men. Barrel-chested, thick legged and armed, strong, plain face, bearded, it was Billy who turned from time to time to raise a beckoning arm and call to those plodding behind him. "Keep up the pace! Keep up! The river's just ahead."

They squinted to point at the white church steeple in the distance, rising above the barren oak and maple trees that lined the streets of the village on the banks of the Delaware, and raised their arms to beckon to those behind as they trudged on. They descended the gentle incline past the apple orchard on the left, to the junction of Princeton Road with the three major streets at the north end, and the leaders paused a moment in surprise. Every door, every window was closed. Smoke rose from chimneys, but the streets were vacant. No living thing moved except for the black ravens that perched on the lifeless tree branches to study the intruders and squawk their protest as the incoming soldiers swung their muskets from their shoulders and checked the powder pans, ready, and started south through the town.

Billy led twenty men down the street furthest west. They walked warily in the eerie quiet, eyes constantly moving, searching every home, barn, building, and window for a musket barrel or a cannon muzzle that might mean ambush. Curtains moved, and faces disappeared from windows, but no door opened, and no one called or challenged. They passed the square white church and turned east at the big, stone Old Barracks building, cold, empty, to meet with those who had come down the other two streets. They gathered at the south end of the village to cross the bridge that spanned the frozen Assunpink Creek three hundred yards from where it emptied into the great Delaware River. Across the creek they followed the road six hundred yards further south to the cutoff that led west, over a small rise, then down to the crusted snow on the open, frozen ground east of the Trenton Ferry, with the army gathering behind them.

Colonel John Glover turned to face his Massachusetts Regiment, Billy among them, and raised both hands.

"Halt!" He waited while they quieted, then pointed across the river. "Pennsylvania's over there. That's where we're going."

Every Marblehead fisherman in the regiment had spent his life on the water, fresh and salt, summer and winter, bright sunlight or the blackest night. Great or small, there was no vessel or craft designed for the water they did not know. Sail, oars, poles—it was all the same to them. For a moment their eyes left Glover to narrow as they studied the river, more than four hundred yards wide with ice thirty yards from each shore outward towards the black channel that ran fast in the center, choked with chunked ice. They read it all and accepted it and turned back to Colonel Glover.

He wasted not one word or one moment. "Officers Hampton and Maxwell have freight boats from the Durham iron works up at Riegelsville collected on the far side. They got rid of all other boats on the river for thirty-five miles each direction, so the British can't follow us unless they build more boats. The ferry's over there, too. We'll have to pull it back."

The Marbleheaders leaned on their muskets as he continued.

Glover's voice rang with intensity as he spoke the single truth that hung like a great, evil cloud over the entire army, riding them heavy every moment, day and night. "The British are just hours behind us, moving this way. If they trap us here against the river, we'll have no chance. If they catch us on the water, their cannon will have every boat on the bottom within minutes. So there will be no stopping."

The men shifted their feet, but there was not one murmur.

"We work until we're on the far side. Men, baggage, cannon, livestock—all of it." He waited and watched for a moment until he knew his men understood and had accepted it. Then he turned, drew out his telescope, and for half a minute studied the far riverbank, searching for the big, flat-bottomed Durham boats. They were there, twenty yards from shore on higher ground, turned upside down, covered with willows and brush. He brought the glass back to the ferry for several seconds, then turned to his men.

"We'll have to break the ferry out of the ice on the far shore. The first fifty of you men give a hand on the rope."

The few that had blankets or knapsacks set them on the snow and ice that covered the frozen ground, leaned their muskets across them, and fifty men, Billy with them, walked down to the ferry landing, their wrapped feet crunching the snow and ice that covered the great, black timbers. They studied the six, two-inch hawsers, and the huge three-foot cast-iron pulley, then lined up, twenty-five men on each side, and grasped the lower rope. The man nearest the water glanced back over his shoulder into the faces of those waiting, nodded once, and began.

"Cap'n says we *heave!*"

"First Mate says we *heave!*"

"Bosun says we *heave!*"

"The cook says we *heave!*"

"We *heave!*"

"We *heave!*"

Each time the word *heave* rang out all fifty men threw their backs into the rope and strained.

The cadence was established. Glover watched the hawser jerk tight as the men pulled, then relaxed, and then he raised his telescope once more to watch the ferry, holding his breath to see if they could break it out of the ice that locked it against the dock on the Pennsylvania side. Half a minute passed, then a full minute. No one on the shore behind Glover realized they were all holding their breath, hands clenched, leaning slightly forward, and then straightening each time they heard the shouted word *heave*.

And then suddenly the icy rope moved, the big pulley groaned and turned, the ferry lurched forward, and they heard the great cracking sound as a shelf of ice separated from the far shore. The ferry was free, moving towards the channel. A shout arose from two thousand voices behind Glover while the fifty men on the rope held their cadence.

Every man on the Trenton riverbank watched in silence as the ferry moved into the open channel, and they held their breath as the floating ice chunks slammed crashing into the upstream side and began to pile up, forcing the ferry downstream. Tons of pressure jerked the towrope singing tight and the men increased the cadence, pulling desperately.

The big, rectangular, flat-bottomed craft creaked as it moved onward through the ice, and then it was at the halfway point, and then it was nearly to the ice shelf on the Trenton side. It rammed into the thin leading edge, and the crushed ice stacked up against the square bow of the ferry while the great chunks that had piled against the upstream side were pushed back and away and quickly drifted into the main channel. Every man on shore released pent-up breath while those on the rope continued their relentless rhythm, and the ferry cut a channel through the ice on the riverbank as it came crunching into the dock.

Glover didn't hesitate. "You Marbleheaders board the ferry until it's full."

Minutes later the loaded ferry pulled away from the Trenton dock with ninety men and their muskets on board, Billy with them, shoulder to shoulder. Half of them pulled the rope while twenty others lined both sides with great oak and maple poles and started their rotation. Standing at the front of the ferry, facing the rear, they drove their poles to the bottom of the river and then walked towards the rear, pushing with all their weight on the poles to drive the ferry onward before they returned to the front of the line to repeat. Those on the upstream side were battling the big ice chunks to keep them from piling up as the others worked with their poles.

The late afternoon sun was casting long shadows eastward when the ferry thudded into its dock on the Pennsylvania side. Wisps of vapor rose from the channel of black water where the ferry had broken its way out and then back in, as seventy of the Marbleheaders lowered the short ramp on the front of the ferry and walked onto the timbers of the landing, then angled north to trot upstream to the hidden Durham boats. The twenty men left on the ferry waited until those at the boats turned to wave before they reversed the ferry and started once again for the Trenton side.

Billy was with the second crew of ten as they threw aside the brush and willows that hid the great boats and for a moment Billy paused to look in amazement. Shaped roughly like a gigantic flat-bottomed canoe, they ranged in length from forty to sixty feet, eight feet wide at the beam, built from black, heavy oak, thick hulled, tough, capable of loading fifteen tons burden, and constructed with a notch at either end to receive a tiller for steering.

The boats had been hidden upside down to avoid being filled with snow and ice. Without a wasted moment or movement the tattered Marbleheaders, steam rising from their bearded faces, lined up in crews of ten to seize one side of the great boats and heave with all their strength to roll them over onto their bottoms with a great, hollow boom. Poles, paddles, and a tiller were tied inside, and Billy watched the faces of the Marbleheaders as they jerked the knots from the ropes and laid the equipment rattling in the bottom of the boats.

Freezing, starving, their blue jacket and white pants uniforms in tatters, feet wrapped in rags, the dreaded British army just hours away and coming to annihilate them, the Marblehead fishermen still grinned at the sight of a solid boat and what they needed to make it work. They were men of the sea, and for them nothing in the world compared to the sight of a solid, seaworthy boat. Billy saw it and he found himself grinning with them as they grasped the gunwales, five men on each side, and threw their weight against the heavy boats to skid them on the crusted snow and ice down to the river.

They pushed out onto the shore-ice and kept their legs driving until they felt the ice beneath their feet begin to give. They vaulted into the boats as they slid like great sleds on the river-ice, then broke through to throw ice shards and river water high on both sides. The crews seized the long poles and started their rotation as the suck and pull of the current seized the boat. The man at the tiller pushed it left and the boat nose swung slightly upstream. Billy worked his position, waiting, watching for the first great ice chunk to slam into the side of the heavy boat, and then it was there. The man on the tiller pushed hard left and swung the bow of the boat further upstream at an angle to the ice chunk, while the men on the upstream side of the boat caught it on the end of their poles as it came in. They did not try to stop it, rather, they let it come, but leaned all their weight onto their poles to push it towards the rear of the boat. It collided with the angled boat five feet from the stern, slid down the side, and was gone without so much as rocking the vessel. The Marbleheader on the tiller brought the boat back onto course, eyes riveted on the incoming ice chunks, waiting for the next big one. Billy released held breath and his shoulders slumped. The Marbleheaders glanced at him and smiled, and Billy grinned back at them through his beard as they continued poling for the Trenton shore, just above the Trenton ferry landing.

In the glow of a sun touching the western rim, the blunt bows of the seven boats plowed grinding into the shore-ice to cut their own channel for twenty feet, then slowed and stopped as the ice thickened. Soldiers on shore threw stiff, frozen ropes to waiting hands that tied them to the tiller uprights in the bow of the boat, and a hundred men on shore dragged the great boats up onto the ice, sliding, until their bows were touching solid land.

Glover was waiting. "Fill the boats," he ordered his men, and within minutes all seven of the first Durham boats were filled with nearly four hundred Marblehead fishermen who knelt with their muskets while the crews dropped the towropes, moved the tillers from one end to the other to set them thumping into their notch, launched the boats back into the channels they had cut coming in, and began poling the boats back across the river.

Once on the Pennsylvania side, the men quickly stripped back the brush and willows from the remaining boats and within minutes had them sliding on the river-ice, then into the main channel, poling back for the Trenton side through the ice chunks and freezing water. Again waiting hands threw ice-slick ropes from the shore and men dragged the heavy boats until their bows hit thumping on the frozen ground, and again Glover was waiting. He turned to the front ranks of the waiting army.

"Load onto the Durham boats and kneel or sit down. Take your muskets and knapsacks. When you reach the far side, start big fires and keep them going until we're finished. We'll need the light to land and unload and to keep men from freezing to death. The livestock and cannon will cross on the ferry just as soon as you've started. When it gets there, unload it and string rope picket lines in the trees for the horses and mules."

While the fishermen held the boats steady, the first ranks climbed in and worked their way forward to kneel or sit on their knapsacks until they were jammed in with only enough room for the crews to man their poles.

A Marbleheader touched Billy's shoulder and Billy turned as the man nodded to him. "You've done your fair share. This is fishermen's work. You'll be needed on the Pennsylvania shore. I'd be obliged to take the pole." He paused, then added, "You get tired of soldierin', you come join us. You got the makin's of a proper fisherman."

Billy's face reddened at the rare praise as he glanced at the other men in the crew of his boat and they all gave him a nod of their heads. It was thanks enough, and Billy handed his pole to the man and took his place with those crouched in the boat as it moved away from shore.

In the gathering gloom of dusk the soldiers still remaining on the frozen Trenton riverbank peered north over their shoulders, past the town, anxious, fearful, watching for the first glimpse of red-coated soldiers

Glover saw their faces and raised his voice. "General Washington is with a company that fell back towards Princeton to tear up bridges and block roads to slow the British. He'll get here before the British do, so we'll have warning. Until that happens, we keep working. When your turn comes, load and unload as fast as you can. Don't stop moving."

He watched while the great boats moved out into the main channel and grim pride showed in his face as his men held them on course through the fast-moving water and the floating ice chunks that slammed into them. He turned on his heel and walked down to the big, cumbersome ferry to his crew waiting there.

"The horses and mules are coming with the cannon. Take the horses first, then the mules while there's still a little daylight. The cannon can wait until after dark."

"Aye, sir."

From behind them came raised voices and the sound of shod hooves and heavy wheels on frozen ground, and he turned to see the first of the horses being led down the slight incline to the ferry landing, while men labored with the spokes and the trails of the cannon, moving them down with the horses. Glover raised a hand to stop them, then shouted. "Hold the cannon back until the horses and mules have crossed. Get restraining ropes on the guns and block the wheels."

The cannon stopped and ropes were tied to the trails and staked down while numb hands shoved blocks against the front of the wheels and frozen feet kicked them to wedge them into place as men led the winter-haired, haltered horses onto the ferry landing, hooves thumping hollow on the black timbers. The horses threw their heads high against the halter ropes as they were led up the ramp and onto the ferry, nervous, stuttering their feet, eyes white-rimmed, distrustful of being in a strange boat on an ice-clogged river in fading light. Behind them, the larger, heavier mules stood waiting, growing restless. Glover turned north to return to the waiting army when he stopped dead in his tracks.

The frantic shout came right on top of the rumble.

"*Loose gun! Loose gun!*"

Glover glanced up the incline and gasped. A cannon had pulled the stakes on its restraining ropes and rolled over its wheel blocks. Men dived to grasp the loose ropes but could not stop or turn the two-ton gun as it gathered speed, rumbling down the incline, directly towards the mules above the landing. The men holding the mule halters instantly broke left or right, jerking the halter ropes, shouting at the mules to move. The great animals reared back in panic, not understanding the ominous sound or the ground-vibrations coming from behind, nor the sudden, unexpected, frantic jerk on their halter ropes and the panic in the men around them. Ahead of them, the horses partially turned and half of them reared, fighting their halter ropes, jamming together while the men battled to hold them. The huge gun gained speed and bounced crazily as it bore down on the clustered mules, and it flashed in the minds of the men clinging to their halter ropes—*no chance—no chance.*

They dropped the ropes and sprinted, diving away and there was nothing anyone could do as the great gun gained speed, careened sideways and tipped. The muzzle dropped as the wheel on the uphill side left the ground, and the gun rolled, ripping into the snow and ice to throw great clods of torn frozen earth high as the wheels and trails went over the top, then underneath, and back on top again. It plowed into the hindquarters of the nearest frenzied mule and those men closest heard the sharp cracks as both back legs broke at the knees and the fifteen-hundred-pound mule went down in a heap, throwing its head to scream out its terror and pain while the gun came to rest leaning on its hindquarters, one wheel up, turning slowly.

For a split second no one moved and then everyone moved. Two men grabbed their muskets and trotted to the front of the mule and shot it in the forehead. The head dropped and the carcass shuddered and then relaxed as the sounds of pain stopped. Twenty others grabbed the cannon and heaved it back onto its wheels as John Glover came running, wide-eyed.

"Is anyone hurt?"

Half a dozen men shook their heads, and Glover turned to trot up the incline to where the remainder of the cannon were tied, shouting as he came, face flushed, arm raised and pointing. "Tie off those cannon! Double the restraining ropes! That could have killed ten soldiers."

Humiliated men scrambled for ropes while others shoved poles through the spokes of the wheels to lock them in place. Glover paced among them long enough to be certain the cannon were tied down before he trotted back down to the ferry where the dead mule had been pulled to one side, the cannon to the other, upright and undamaged. The ferry was jammed with horses, with forty head waiting on the landing along with twenty-four mules. Glover's fishermen were locking the endgate and picking up their poles to push off.

He cupped his hands to call to them. "Shove off. Get back as soon as you can."

In the freezing afterglow of a sun already set the ferry moved away from the dock and Glover turned back to the dead mule, surrounded by a cluster of men staring at the carcass. They glanced at Glover, then back at the carcass, and he read their faces and spoke quietly.

"Move it fifty yards downstream and get the head downhill and cut the throat. I'll send word across to get ready. Load it with the first cannon."

"Aye, sir."

On the water, Billy watched the Trenton shore fade in the deep dusk and then it was gone. The fishermen struck flint to steel to light lanterns and men held them high at both ends of the boat while Billy pondered how the fishermen at the tillers knew what course to steer with no fires on the Pennsylvania shore to give them a bearing. The soldiers in the boats peered up and down the river in awed silence at the strange, ethereal sight of fifty pairs of yellow lanterns in a line moving in the darkness, reflecting off the black, ice-filled water, showing ghostly men plying the black shapes of the low boats, while they listened to the hollow, booming sound of ice chunks slamming into the hulls.

In full darkness the boats rammed into the frozen Pennsylvania riverbank and instantly the fishermen in the bow leaped to the ground to keep the rope tight while the soldiers systematically unloaded. The moment their boats were empty the crews clambored back in and jammed their poles against the frozen bank to push off, then began their rotation, poling the boat back towards the open channel, each with their two lanterns held high. Across the river, on the Trenton side, tiny points of light flickered, then caught and grew until huge fires spread from the Trenton ferry landing five hundred yards upstream.

On the frozen ground of the Pennsylvania side, the first load of soldiers just landed dropped their knapsacks and thrust frozen fingers in their mouths until the warmth brought feeling, and then they fumbled to strike a spark from flint and steel and light what few lanterns they had among them. They held them high to peer about in the feeble yellow light, and Billy's eyes widened. In full darkness, guided by something unknown to Billy, the Marbleheaders had put them ashore at exactly the place they had left.

The temperature had dropped ten degrees since sundown and was going lower with every passing minute. The bitter cold cut into them, and the emaciated soldiers grimly set their jaws in the stark realization they must build fires or be dead before morning. They took the few axes they could find in the piled equipment and trudged away from the river to the trees, and with their lanterns casting surreal shadows they sought out the dead windfalls to cut branches and drag them back to the riverbank. They broke and stacked small twigs and lighted them from their lanterns, then added larger branches and limbs until the fires were high, sending millions of sparks spiraling into the black heavens to glow and disappear.

Bone-weary, they slumped down to sit on anything they could find, or the frozen ground if there was nothing. With their hands and frozen feet to the fire, they squinted against the heat, not knowing or caring where their camp gear was in the growing pile. They only knew there would be no rest until more than five thousand men still on the Trenton side of the river had been brought across. They said nothing as they stared into the firelight, noses running in the heat, ice in their hair and beards melting, dripping on the front of their ragged shirts and frayed coats while steam rose from the wet, icy rags and blanket strips bound to their feet. Heads nodded and chins dropped. Men slowly toppled onto their sides to move for a moment, then settle, unable to fight off sleep and other men reached to move their feet to keep them out of the fire.

They heard the ferry crunch into the landing downstream and Billy rose to look for the lights. The heavy sound of the ramp dropping onto the frozen landing came echoing and then the faint voices of the men and the staccato stamping of nervous horses' hooves as they began unloading. Billy drew a deep, weary breath and spoke.

"We've got to get picket ropes strung in the trees."

Those who could picked through the tangled heap of camp equipment for ropes, then followed Billy down to the trees near the ferry. Quickly they strung one-inch hawsers to oak trunks while men brought the horses to tie them, then return to the ferry for the trip back to the Trenton landing for the next load.

The lights of the fifty incoming Durham boats were approaching as the soldiers returned to their fires for a moment's warmth, and once again they walked down to the riverbank to cast ropes to the fishermen crouched in the bow. They held the boats steady while the soldiers jumped to the frozen ground and kept moving to make room for those behind.

From the north came the clank and rattle of the great black cooking kettles and the heavy, twelve-foot iron tripods from which they hung, and Billy straightened to look, puzzled at why a boat had landed with equipment and not men. A voice came piercing, "Hallooooo . . . we need help."

With his boat empty and moving steadily back towards the Trenton shore, Billy and half a dozen others trotted north to find men wrestling the big iron cook pots out of a Durham boat onto the riverbank while others struggled with the heavy tripods and chains. The dim lantern light at both ends of the boats showed the shadowy shapes of a dozen more of the round kettles upside down in the boat. The men were straining to unload them over the bow of the boat onto the riverbank, one at a time, frustrated by the rise of the gunwales at the front of the boat. Billy studied them for a moment, then picked up a rope and threw one end to the men farther back in the boat.

"Tie it to the handle of one of the kettles and dump it overboard," he called, and the men on the boat slowed to watch. Billy motioned to four other men standing near him and they waited while a man on the boat quickly looped the rope through the thick, heavy handle and tied it off before three other men seized the rim of the kettle and the stubby legs and heaved it over the side. Water and ice flew ten feet in the air and the great black pot sank out of sight as Billy and those with him on shore grasped the rope, set their feet, and backed up. The cook pot broke the surface three feet from shore and ten seconds later was twenty feet inland, upside down. Billy and those with him walked back to the boat and again Billy threw the rope, and others threw their ropes, and moments later the heavy kettles hit the water, and the boat was emptied within minutes, riding high in the water.

Billy walked to the man who was setting the tiller in the slot on the near end of the boat.

"You didn't bring men?"

The man shook his head in the firelight. "Colonel Glover's orders. He sent word with some officer on one of the boats farther down the line that there's fresh meat coming on the ferry with the first load of cannon and he wanted those cook kettles set up over the fires and half-filled with water."

Fresh meat! Never had the thought of fresh meat reached inside Billy as it did at that moment, and then his forehead wrinkled. "Fresh meat? How did he get fresh meat?"

The man wiped at his frozen beard and weighed his answer. "Mule. An accident. Broke both hind legs. You heard those musket shots earlier?"

By half past nine the three-legged tripods straddled thirty fires and each of the fifty-gallon cook kettles was hanging from the heavy chains and filled with thirty gallons of river water. By half past ten, wisps of steam were rising from the kettles, and men peered at them in disbelieving anticipation. *Fresh meat. Fresh meat. Fresh meat.* It ran through their brains like a chant.

A sliver of crescent moon arose a little after eleven o'clock in a clear sky, with the temperature hovering at ten degrees above zero. The fires reflected rose and gold and blue from endless frost crystals on the riverbank and in the woods as the men established a rhythm with the incoming and outgoing boats. Knapsacks and gear were carried back from the riverbank and dumped haphazardly into unsorted piles to make way for the next incoming load. In the minutes when no boats were unloading, the shaking men returned to the fires to stand near the flames, first facing, then with their backs to the warmth while they waited for feeling to come once again into their hands and feet.

At half past eleven the ferry thumped into its dock with the first load of cannon and a hundred men walked downstream, past the horses picketed in the trees, to unload. Two men tied a rope to the ends of each of the long trails on the cannon, while two others took their places at the brass handholds. Two more men took positions, one on each of the big wheels, and on signal, the eight men rolled the cannon up the ferry ramp onto the landing, backwards, muzzle toward the ferry, and tilted down. Two other men walked beside with long poles, ready to jam them between the spokes if anyone slipped, or a rope broke, or for any reason the men lost control of the heavy guns. They moved the cannon away from the landing and turned them sideways to the slope so they would not roll, and they blocked the wheels and staked the restraining ropes.

With the last cannon rolling forward on the thick, frozen deck of the ferry, half a dozen men went to the far end and stopped, gazing downward at the carcass of the dead mule, black and unreal in the dim lantern light. They wasted no time. A rope was looped around the two broken hind legs and they turned their backs to the dead animal to drag it off the ferry, onto the landing, and up the incline.

A little past midnight, with a fire on both sides for warmth and lanterns held high to cast yellow light, a dozen men tipped the mule onto its back and braced it from both sides with sticks. One man slit the hide, vent to throat, without opening the cavity. Two men removed the head and took it to one side, while two others began at a foreleg on either side. They skinned out and disjointed the leg at the knee and continued downward, laying the hide on the ground as they went. They worked back towards the hindquarters, skinned them out, and disjointed the tail, handing the bones and the tail to waiting men as they went. One man carefully opened the cavity between the hind legs, inserted his hand into the opening with his knife blade upward, and carefully moved the knife forward, opening the cavity from vent to brisket, smoking. Carefully they let the carcass roll onto one side and the viscera, paunch, and contents of the chest cavity rolled out onto the hide and they turned their heads for a moment, away from the stench and the rising vapors. They disconnected it all from the carcass and left it lying on the hide to once again roll the carcass onto its back. A man stepped forward with a broadaxe and split the brisket to the throat, then to the hindquarters to chop through the pelvis bone, and the two halves of the carcass sagged away from each other.

The men down by the river working the incoming Durham boats turned from time to time, watching the group gathered around the carcass, swallowing at the thought of hot broth and meat. They turned back to the boats, to glance over their shoulders again and again.

Four men knelt on the hide, frozen stiff, and began removing great chunks of meat from the neck back to the shanks on the hindquarters, and dumped it in waiting wooden tubs. The head was stripped to the bone, the tongue removed, and the brain removed with a broadaxe while a man cut through every joint in the tail, and others diced the great chunks of meat into tiny pieces and dumped the mix back into the wooden tubs. With the skeleton exposed, they began disjointing it and piling the disjointed bones on one side of the hide. Others took the bones and set them on rocks and smashed them with sledges to expose the rich marrow, then put the shattered bones back into the tubs.

They washed the liver, tongue, heart, kidneys, and brain in the river, then set them in the glowing embers of a fire to roast. They dragged the paunch down to the river to split it open and dump the contents into the frigid water, then wash the empty belly as best they could and bring it back dripping, ice forming. They laid the intestinal tract on the frozen hide, stripped out all the connecting tissue, then slit the intestine lengthwise and took it to the river to wash it clean and bring it back. Then they diced the lungs, empty intestine and paunch, and the connecting tissue and dumped it all into the wooden tubs.

A little before three o'clock they lifted the heart, tongue, kidneys, liver, and brain from the coals of the fire and chopped them fine, then lifted the tubs and walked from fire to fire, portioning it into twenty-eight of the thirty boiling cook kettles. They put the shattered bones in the last two; thirteen hundred pounds of meat and bone boiling in nine hundred gallons of river water. The only things that escaped the cook pots were the hide and the hooves, and before morning the hide would be thawed out and cut into strips to wrap frozen feet. Someone walked from pot to pot with a ten-pound canvas bag of salt, sprinkling a handful into each while the men stood by the fires, silent, looking at the pots, struggling to believe that sometime in the morning they would have a bowl of hot broth and meat. No man among them could remember anything so sweet as the stench of a dead mule simmering in the big iron kettles in the black of night, ten degrees below zero, on a frozen riverbank hundreds of miles from home.

At four o'clock twelve men lifted the two kettles filled with boiling bones from their chains, set them on the frozen ground, and used three-gallon dippers on five-foot handles to sift out the bones. They dipped the broth, rich and nourishing with the bone marrow, along with the shred and scraps of meat into five-gallon buckets and portioned it out among the remaining twenty-eight kettles. Strong hands lifted the great smoking kettles from their chains and set them on the frozen ground while the soldiers found anything that would hold the steaming mixture and lined up. They were all given their fair portion, holding back enough for those yet to come from the Trenton side of the river. They walked back to the fires to sip at it, not caring that it seared their mouths, feeling the rich broth and the warmth hit their empty, cramped bellies and spread, pausing with closed eyes to feel it, savor it, aware only that they could remember nothing they had ever eaten which meant so much as the dead mule. When the broth was gone they picked the pieces of chunked meat from the bottom of the bowls and slowly chewed them for a long time, then wiped the bowl clean with their fingers and licked them. They washed the bowls in the river and returned them to wherever they had found them, and turned back to the incoming boats.

By five o'clock they knew they would still have men on the Trenton side at daybreak, and growing desperation drove them on. They peered across the river into the blackness beyond the village, searching for a line of distant lights moving towards them, and listening for the faint sound of fife and drum setting the cadence for soldiers' feet, and the rumble of moving cannon. More boats hit the shore and the waiting soldiers forced frozen hands and feet to move as they unloaded men and baggage, then dragged the great, heavy craft inland, over the rise and among the trees to tip them over and cover them with brush and willows away from British eyes and cannon. They walked stiff-legged back to the fires by the river to peer anxiously eastward, again searching for the first flash of lights and the sound of a distant marching army while they watched the lanterns on the water move steadily towards them.

Imperceptibly, the blackness to the east became deep purple and then gray. Dawn came bleak in the bitter cold with the last of the boats still on the water, their exhausted crews holding them on course against the pull of the current and the slamming jolt of the heavy ice chunks, while the tattered soldiers on shore stood by the fires, vapor rising from their bearded faces, waiting for them to land, and to see if the Revolution lived or died on the banks of the Delaware.

Billy stood among them, bone-weary, hands raw from pulling frozen hawsers half the night, shivering in the coat he had made from two gray, threadbare, abandoned blankets, and the trousers he had fashioned from half-burned sailcloth he had found on the banks of the Hackensack River in a time he could now hardly remember. He looked about at the chaotic stacks of equipment scattered for half a mile among the cannon. Driven by the fear of being caught by the British on the Trenton side, or on the water, where they would have been chopped to pieces by British grapeshot, they had hastily dumped it where they could and kept working through the night.

The sun rose to flood the frozen world with light and Billy held his outstretched hands towards the fire while his clothing steamed and his nose dripped. Steam rose from his round, plain face, and for a moment his thoughts went back to the shock he had felt two days ago when he had seen his own reflection in a bucket of water dipped from the Assunpink Creek south of Trenton. He had stared in disbelief at a man he did not recognize: sunken eyes, hollow cheeks, and heavy beard and eyebrows clogged with ice. Shocked, he had stood stone-still peering down at his body, and was stunned when the realization struck into him that he was a scarecrow, dressed in rags, beard and hair unkempt, his stocky, robust body shrunken, skin loose and sagging.

He pushed the memory away and licked at his cracked, bleeding lips and closed his eyes to avoid the smoke from the fire. He reached to wipe his dripping nose and the ice melting from his beard, and looked at the men milling around, disorganized, exhausted. Those who arrived in the last boats were wandering, searching through the piled knapsacks and rolled blankets for their own, turning every few minutes to peer across the river, watching for a glimpse of red on the distant skyline or on the flatlands approaching the river, or in the village of Trenton. Billy narrowed his eyes and held his breath to stop the vapor while he carefully studied the town and what he could see of the land beyond. There were no red-coated British or blue-coated Hessians.

He turned back to the fire, ringed by men who had little left to give, standing silent, staring into the flames. A man of average size moved in beside Billy, and Billy glanced at him. He was dressed in a heavy winter coat and scarf, thick-soled shoes, and a fur cap. His face showed no trace of the ravages of war. Billy could see an artist's sketch pad bound in leather stuffed inside his coat, and he saw the shock and disbelief and sick revulsion in the man's eyes as the man stood rooted, mouth hanging open, looking up and down the riverbank at what was left of the Continental army.

Billy spoke. "Newspaper?"

The man answered while still looking at the havoc around him. "No. Artist. I heard about this and thought someone should come make sketches for the world to see. I came in this morning on the backroads from Philadelphia." He swallowed hard, then turned his eyes to Billy. His face was white, eyes glazed in shock. "It's not possible. I've never seen anything so hellish in my life. I've never known men could look like this."

At that moment, across the fire a man sat on an upside-down wooden bucket with the bottom cracked. His bearded face was a mass of open sores, crusted, cracked, bleeding, so thick he could not clean them. He wore no shirt, only a filthy, frayed blanket jacket above his waist. His legs were bare and he was huddled close to the fire barefooted, shaking violently. Suddenly he raised his face and he called to the man standing next to Billy, voice high, cracking.

"Charles! Charles Peale! Is that you?"

The man beside Billy flinched at the call of his name and turned his face to peer at the stranger, drawn by something familiar in the voice. He narrowed his eyes to study the stricken face, the matted hair, the sunken eyes, and suddenly he started. His head jerked forward and he stammered—"James? James?"—voice thick in disbelief.

"Yes! It's me—James!" Instantly Charles Peale was on his knees beside his brother, whom he thought had been killed at the battle of Long Island when Clinton's ten thousand redcoats had used the Jamaica Road to flank the Americans and the battle had become a wild, bloody rout—a nightmare of blasting muskets and cannon and lunging bayonets.

"Oh, James, James," he said, and sobbed openly as he tenderly wrapped his brother inside his arms and held him close. James reached both arms around his brother's neck and clung to him, weeping, murmuring, "Charles, Charles." A time passed before Charles leaned back to look into the eyes of his brother, and he gently touched the oozing eruptions on the thin face. He turned his eyes upward to the men standing in the circle, and shaking hands pulled blankets from rounded shoulders and helped wrap them around James's exposed legs and feet. Charles carefully lifted his brother into his arms and started north, up the riverbank, carrying him like a child, calling for a doctor.

The men circling the fire watched him go, and they swallowed hard and avoided meeting the eyes of each other as the brothers disappeared in the milling throng. A shouted order brought their heads up and they saw the gold braid on the tricornered hat of a major striding towards them through the litter, and they fell silent to listen as he cupped his hand to his mouth to shout again.

"General Washington just arrived! Move back! Get away from the river, over the rise. The British will be in Trenton in one hour with cannon. Back! Move!"

Every eye moved up and down the riverbank looking for Washington, but he was not to be seen in the chaotic disarray of six thousand soldiers and their gear and weapons, and the shoulders of every man on the riverbank slumped. Enough British cannon on the far bank could cut them and everything they had to pieces in half an hour.

Billy drew a great breath and brought his head up. "Let's get at it. Muskets and blankets first. We can't fight without muskets, or if we're frozen dead."

One man, bearded, dark, surly, his tattered light summer jacket hanging from thin shoulders, raised his face. "You an officer?"

Billy shook his head. "No. Corporal Billy Weems, Boston Regiment, Company Nine."

The man shook his head and tried to speak, but could not, and he tried again. "Can't go no farther." Suddenly a sob racked his body and he turned on Billy, his voice rising hysterically as he spoke. "You got no right givin' orders—no right—I'm from North Carolina and you got no right—" Suddenly his hand was under his coat and then it was raising a knife and, wild-eyed, he lunged at Billy.

Billy's movement was a blur as he caught the upcoming hand just behind the wrist and his fingers closed like a vise. He reached with his other hand to take the knife from the numb fingers and throw it into the snow. A high, thin, choking whine came from the man as he jerked to free himself, and he raised his other hand to tear at Billy's throat. Billy caught it and stood there, face-to-face with the man, who wrenched his body to break away. Billy stood solid, holding both hands, waiting while the man slowly settled, and his head tipped forward, and his whole body began to shake, racked with silent sobbing.

Those nearest had backed away, startled, staring wide-eyed, and they watched as Billy slowly lowered the man's hands and let them go. Billy reached to pick up the knife from the snow, and he slipped it back into the belt sheath and straightened the filthy, ragged coat. He picked up a rolled blanket and tucked it under the man's arm, then caught the straps on three knapsacks, and quietly spoke to the man who stood beaten in body and soul with tears frozen on his cheeks and in his beard.

"Come on," Billy said quietly. "I'll help."

Billy lifted the man's arm around his own shoulders, slipped his free hand around the man's waist, and started west, through the crusted snow, half carrying the man who clutched the blanket under his arm and stumbled along beside Billy. The others followed, and the south end of the camp was moving. They dropped the baggage in the snow behind the low rise that hid it from the river, and returned for the next load, eyes searching across the river for the British.

On the third trip back to the riverbank, Billy walked to the nearest cannon and gave some hand signals and nine men came and they lined up, five on each side. Two grasped the handles on each of the carriage trails and lifted, while two more seized the spokes in each of the five-foot wheels, and the last two grasped the barrel. On Billy's signal they turned the big gun around and started west up the slight incline when a nasal voice came twangy in the frigid air.

"All right, you lovelies, let's hide these guns in the trees on the rise and get ready to give the British a welcome."

Billy stopped dead in his tracks and turned. "Turlock? Sergeant Turlock?" He stood with his mouth gaping open as he stared, searching in the throng, and suddenly the bandy-legged, feisty little sergeant was there. Bearded and hollow-cheeked, his long hair was held back by a leather thong. His head was thrust through a hole in a blanket that was tied at his waist with rope, and his feet were bound in rags. The little man stopped to stare back at Billy, and suddenly his eyes opened wide.

"Weems! Billy Weems!" Billy heard the warm sound of recognition in the voice, and the men handling the cannon set the carriage trails on the ground. Billy strode quickly to Turlock and impulsively seized the little man by the shoulders.

"Sergeant! I thought . . . you're not dead? Long Island?"

Turlock's grin showed through his long, matted beard and his sunken cheeks crinkled as he grasped Billy's arms. "No. Taken prisoner. You?"

"Crossed over to Manhattan with the army and been with it since. Captured? You got away?"

Turlock nodded. "Seen any of the rest of Company Nine?"

"No. Lost track of the whole regiment when we made our run from Fort Lee."

"Where's your friend? The Indian?"

Billy shrugged. "Eli? He's not Indian, just raised by them. He took his rifle and left a few days ago. Doing something for General Washington—couldn't say what. Hasn't come back yet."

Turlock backed up a step. "Looks like you missed a few meals, and forgot your winter clothes."

Billy shook his head. "This is as bad as anything I ever saw. You've missed some meals yourself."

Turlock shrugged. "Soldierin' ain't what it used to be." He looked at the men waiting by the cannon and spoke to Billy. "Let's get that thing set up. The British'll be across the river before long."

"You got orders?"

Turlock shook his head. "Can't find an officer that'll listen. If we hide ten or fifteen guns in the trees right at the crest of the rise to the west, and cut willows to cover them, we can stop the British long enough to buy an extra hour or two. Save some men and some of the baggage and food, what we have of it. If some officer doesn't like it, I'll talk to him."

Billy turned back to the crew waiting at the cannon. "We're going to move it up there"—he pointed—"right at the crest of the little rise and turn it towards the far bank of the river and cut willows to hide it. That way we can fire at them and pull it back where they can't hit it."

While they worked the heavy gun through the trees and snow to the crest of the incline, Turlock turned and barked orders to men near the next cannon, and minutes later it was moving west, while he moved on to the next gun. Half an hour later they had fourteen cannon spaced ten yards apart on the rim, wheels blocked, nearly hidden with cut willows and brush, each with a crew, hugging themselves for warmth, blowing on numb hands. Turlock set the sighting quadrant in the first barrel, motioned to Billy, and Billy twisted the heavy elevation screw at the rear of the cannon to lower the muzzle. Twenty minutes later they had all fourteen guns sighted in for eight hundred yards. Turlock shouted to the crews and they gathered behind the center cannon.

"Corporal Weems takes the cannon on the south end of the line, I take the one on the north. The rest of you stay with the one you're assigned. I got them all sighted in to clear those islands in the river and hit the far bank up high, where we'll first see their cannon. When you see them on the far bank, shout to clear our men from our field of fire so we don't have to shoot over their heads. The idea is to let the British get their guns out in the open, and then we got to scatter their crews before they can get set or loaded. It's too far for grapeshot, but not for cannister, so load with cannister. When you run out of cannister, load with solid shot and try to hit their guns. Don't shoot until I do, and then pick your targets and load and fire as fast as you can. And don't forget to sponge after every shot. We don't need any dead or one-armed cannoneers."

The gun crews walked back to their stations and stood peering in silence across the river, waiting, watching, calculating how much longer it would take to get all the equipment moved inland past the rim and into the woods, where British guns could not reach it. It seemed the

American soldiers around them were moving at half-speed, and the gun crews found themselves mumbling under their breath, "Move. Move. Hurry!" while their eyes never left the far riverbank, and they continued making time calculations.

One more hour. Just one more hour.

At that moment the sound of a thousand voices rising along the riverbank brought their heads around, searching, and they saw General George Washington riding a long-legged bay gelding south at a canter, towards the ferry. The men had stopped for a moment to open a way for him, and he was calling to them as he rode, but he was too far from the cannon crews for them to understand the words. The men raised their fists in the air and answered, and he moved on, down to the ferry and stopped, then turned and retraced his path back to the north end of camp while all the officers broke away and trotted after him, gathering around him for orders.

The soldiers heard the British before they saw them. The sun was two hours high, turning the countless frost crystals on tree branches and willows into diamonds, when the militant sound of fife and drum came drifting across the Delaware. Instantly Billy and the other men on the fourteen cannon leaped forward shouting to the soldiers in front of them, "Clear out! Get out from in front. We're going to open fire with cannon from here!"

It took ten seconds for the startled army to understand, and then they instantly grabbed what baggage they could and scattered, working west into the trees and timber, behind the cannon.

The first flash of brilliant red showed from across the river, and then the British were there on the southwest edge of Trenton, mixed with the blue-coated Hessians, wheeling their horse-drawn cannon forward to form a line on high ground away from the riverbank, where their shot would clear the low islands in the river. Turlock crouched behind his cannon, smoking linstock in hand, waited two seconds, then smacked the spark onto the touchhole. One second later the big gun bucked and roared, and three seconds later the other thirteen remaining guns thundered, and a pall of white smoke drifted into the clear blue winter sky. Turlock held his breath and watched long enough to see the spread of hundreds of one-inch lead cannister balls kick snow and dirt all around the cannon and British crews. For a moment the British army stood stock-still in astonishment as men groaned and staggered backwards, stumbling, falling, and a dozen horses went to their knees.

"Reload!" screamed Turlock, and fourteen wet sponges plunged down the cannon barrels to kill all lingering sparks, followed by the powder ladle, dried grass, and the next open-ended metal cannister tube stuffed with one-inch lead balls. Once again the smoking linstocks hit the touchholes, and the cannon roared and the shot whistled across the river to rip into the stunned British. They turned and scrambled back from their guns, looking for anything they could crouch behind to escape the onslaught.

Billy watched long enough to be certain the British crews had left their guns, then loaded a solid shot cannonball and crouched behind his cannon, lining it on a British gun carriage. His first shot plowed into the frozen ground twenty feet short, throwing snow and black frozen earth forty feet in the air. The second one smashed a wheel off the gun carriage, and the cannon dropped at a crazy angle and then came to rest on its side, muzzle buried in the snow and dirt. The other American gunners loaded solid shot and three more British gun carriages jumped and then settled, useless, axles or wheels broken and splintered.

While they were reloading, they saw the British roll more guns into sight. The Americans jammed cannister shot into their own barrels as they watched the white smoke billow from the cannon across the river, and then the British were straining desperately to pull their guns back, out of sight to reload and fire again.

The thought flashed in Billy's mind—*too fast, they didn't have time to aim*—and the Americans shoved their linstocks against the touchholes, and their own cannon roared as the incoming British cannonballs plowed into the frozen ground at the river's edge, fifty feet short of the nearest Americans still moving their baggage and food stores inland. It threw clods and ice shards high, and then the sound of the cannon came rolling past.

The American cannon crews were standing bolt upright, holding their breath to see if their own cannister would reach the British before they could roll their cannon back out of sight, and in that instant the cannister shot struck. For a moment the British guns and crews disappeared in a shower of snow and dirt while all up and down the line red-coated men stumbled and dropped while others abandoned their guns and sprinted for cover. Billy and the American cannoneers were not aware they had thrust clenched fists into the air, nor did they realize they had raised a shout of defiance that reached across the river, and that it was swelled by the voices of hundreds of men who had paused in their frantic work long enough to watch the hated redcoats go down under the hail of cannister shot.

Billy glanced down the incline at the scrambling Americans and made an instant calculation—*fifteen more minutes and our men will be clear*—and at that moment Turlock's high voice came cracking.

"Reload! Keep firing!"

They hit a rhythm, and the heat waves rose from the gun barrels into the frigid morning air. The British retrieved enough guns to fire sixty rounds, half of them cannister. One cannonball hit one of the great, empty stew kettles with a resounding clang and blew it wide open. One charge of cannister shredded an old, frayed tent, while one errant lead ball ripped through the coat of an American to leave a gray welt across his back, but it did not draw blood. There were no other injuries or damage as the last of the Americans scrambled over the low rise to safety.

"All right, you lovelies, cease fire and get these guns back!"

The gun crews grabbed their rammers and sponges, slammed the ammunition boxes closed, jammed the lids on the budge barrels of powder, grabbed the handles on the gun carriage trails and the spokes of the great wheels, and threw their backs into moving the big guns backwards, crunching through the snow, over the crest of the low rise, out of sight of the river and the British cannon beyond. They stopped and dropped their gear and slumped into the snow, fighting for breath as they lay on their backs, eyes closed, exhausted. Their breathing slowed and they sat up, all heads turning north at the sound of an incoming horse.

The rider reined in his horse, stiff-legged, slipping on the frozen ground and snow. He wore the gold braid of a major on his tricornered hat. His cape covered his shoulder epaulets. He held a tight rein on his horse, vapor rising from its nostrils as it worked its feet, wanting to run in the cold.

"Who fired the cannon? Colonel Knox wants to know. So does General Washington."

Turlock was on his feet. "I was responsible, sir."

"You an officer?"

"No, sir. Sergeant Alvin Turlock. Boston Regiment."

Billy rose to stand beside Turlock as the major continued.

"Colonel Henry Knox is in command of those cannon. You knew that?"

"I didn't know who was in command, sir. I lost track back at Long Island."

"Lost track? How?"

"Captured. I just caught up yesterday."

The major looked at the gun crews, exhausted, filthy, ragged, staring at him, waiting. He counted the cannon and straightened in his saddle, and Billy saw the surprise in his face. "Only fourteen?"

"That's all we had time for, sir."

"Against more than sixty?"

"We weren't counting, sir."

The major looked past the cannon, at the remains of the Continental army, sitting on their baggage or in the snow, trying to find the strength to rise and start fires and search to see if their blankets and knapsacks were among those that got over the rise. He looked back at Turlock.

"Who gave you orders?"

"No one, sir. Things was pretty mixed up and I couldn't find no officer to get orders, so I just gathered some men, and we covered our soldiers with the cannon while they got off the riverbank."

The major hesitated and wiped at his mouth. "Colonel said to tell you next time get permission first."

Turlock's eyes were steady. "Sir, next time I'll see if I can talk the British into waiting while I come find him."

A faint smile flitted across the major's face. "Maybe he'll forgive it just this once." His eyes dropped for a moment while he made up his mind. "General Washington said well done. Carry on, sergeant." He reined his horse around and was gone. Turlock watched him ride out of sight before he turned back to Billy.

"Officers," he grunted, and turned to the cannon crews. "You did good. Saved some men and gear. Get on back to your companies if you can find them." He turned back to Billy.

"We better get firewood and . . ."

He got no further. Sixty British cannonballs tore crashing through the treetops above their heads, and men for five hundred yards dropped to the snow as the balls whistled on past to plow into the frozen ground one thousand yards farther west. Shattered tree limbs and branches came falling like rain, and then the sound of the big guns rolled over the rise while the echo rang up and down the river. Everyone remained on the ground motionless, peering up at the shattered treetops, and thirty seconds later the second volley came ripping to fall harmlessly more than a half mile distant, followed by the roar and the rolling echo.

Turlock recovered from the shock and stood, safely hidden by the rise in the ground. "Wastin' powder and shot to try to scare us." He shook his head.

Five more times the big British cannon blasted, and the trees above the heads of the crouched Americans shook as the heavy balls sent white shards and branches and even whole limbs showering. Then the heavy guns fell silent and Turlock moved to the rim to peer cautiously, Billy by his side. They watched as the red- and blue-coated soldiers across the river seized the trails and spokes of the gun carriages and moved the cannon away from the river, out of sight. They backed away from the rim before he rose to pound the snow and dirt from his coat. He studied the scattered litter of broken branches and limbs, and a wry grin showed in his beard as he looked at Billy.

"Well, we got firewood."

Billy lowered his face and shook his head as he grinned, and the man nearest him suddenly chuckled. The chuckles spread among the men, and despite being dirty, sick, and starving, the men rose from the frozen earth to gather wood. They built fires and huddled about them, waiting for orders that did not come. The sun reached its zenith, and the ragged army made one last hurried trip over the rise to the riverbank to gather quickly what baggage and supplies remained, then scrambled back over the rim to the safety of the woods beyond, with the sound of the Hessians shouting insults across the Delaware.

Their orders came shortly after two o'clock: remain where they were for the night. They would organize a camp tomorrow. They waited with bowed heads to hear something—anything—about food rations, but there was nothing. They stared silently into their fires for a long time before they rose to search through their knapsacks or their blankets one more time for anything they could eat. In fading light they erected an iron tripod over a fire and melted snow in a black pot. They added what little they had found in their knapsacks—half a cup of Indian corn-meal scraped off the bottom, dried peach pits, a crust of bread, a hand-ful of dried peas, a forgotten corncob, a shriveled wild turnip, a chunk of rancid pork—and they boiled it and gathered around to ladel it out into wooden or pewter bowls and stand near the fire to try to choke it down while their noses dripped from the heat, and the ice in their beards and hair melted.

They had no tools to cut trenches in the frozen ground for a place to sleep, so they gathered brittle, snow-covered leaves from the woods and lay on their sides by the fires with their feet to the heat, and pulled the thin cover of leaves over themselves for what little protection it pro-vided against the frost that would settle in the night.

Turlock sat on a log by the fire waiting while the others laid down for the night, shaking with the cold. A sickly quarter moon rose to hover above the black skyline, and silence settled over the camp, save for the sound of hardwood knots popping in the fires and of starving men trying to sleep on the frozen ground. From a distance came the haunt-ing song of a wolf, and then another, and then they were silent.

Quietly Billy sat down beside him, palms stretched towards the fire, and for a time they both stared into the dancing flames and glowing embers in silence, each caught up in a strange, unexpected reverie of thoughts and memories that came at random, on their own terms. The flames dwindled and the charred wood crumbled to send a column of sparks towards the black dome overhead, and the two men laid fresh wood on top. They watched it begin to smoke, and then catch, and the flames climbed.

Staring into the ever-changing flames, Billy was suddenly in the square, austere, orderly parlor of his home in Boston, watching the fire in the big stone fireplace. Cooking pots hung on arms bolted to the sidewalls, and the rich, pungent aromas of ham and custard filled the room. He saw his mother's face, round, plain, as it had ever been, filled with the pain of a husband lost at sea, and her selfless love for her children and her home. Trudy was there, beginning the magical change from a child to a woman, with her two new front teeth too large and her knees bigger than her legs.

And then his thoughts were with Matthew, tall, serious, with whom he had grown up sharing everything, the brother he never had. And Kathleen, who had loved Matthew for as long as Billy could remember, and whom Matthew loved with all his heart. He saw Brigitte, the ever-present tagalong younger sister of Matthew, spirited, outspoken, and his breathing slowed as he remembered leaving Boston with the regiment, when she had impulsively thrown her arms about him and held him with tears in her eyes. He allowed himself to recall the shocking realization that the child had become a woman—strong and beautiful. He released held breath as he remembered she had given her heart to a British captain, tall, striking, good, and he set his jaw as he remembered once again that he was stocky and plain. He pushed his thoughts back into their private chambers in his mind, to be brought out again at a quiet time and remembered with a gentle reverence.

The quiet words of Turlock brought him back to the frozen camp of starving, freezing men. "Home? Thinking of home?"

Billy nodded.

"Where?"

"Boston."

"Family?"

"Mother. Sister." He paused for a moment. "You?"

Turlock shook his head. "No home."

Billy turned his head to look, and the firelight showed yellow in Turlock's small, craggy face, and lighted his dark, gray-streaked beard. "No family?"

Again Turlock shook his head.

"Where are you from?"

Turlock drew and released a great breath and vapor rose into the darkness. It was as though he needed to tell a story that had been too long locked up inside. He kept his face forward, towards the fire.

"Somewhere up near Falmouth. I don't know, exactly. My mother died birthing me. No one ever told me about my father—who he was. The midwife kept me for a few months and then gave me away. The new family put me in an orphanage. When I was nine, they gave me to a sea captain. I was on the sea with him for a time but he was mean—only wanted me for a free cabin boy. His name was Ulysses Edwards. I ran away to join the British army. I learned cannon and muskets, and fought the French and Indians. I was there when Fort Duquesne fell, and General Braddock was killed. General Washington—he was Braddock's aide-de-camp then—was right there at his side. I remember Washington tried to save him but couldn't. He buried him in the middle of the road and made us all march over the grave so the Indians couldn't find the body and cut it. I remember that."

He wiped at his dripping nose with a grimy sleeve.

"No schooling or money—no chance to be an officer. I stayed with the army until I seen the British meant to hold the colonies down, and then I quit them and joined the militia to fight them. I was there the night we threw the tea in Boston harbor—three hundred forty-two chests of it."

Billy sat unmoving, startled, caught up in the poignant story.

"I heard about General Washington, and I came to Boston to join with him." Turlock paused for a time, staring, lost in his memories.

Billy waited, then spoke. "Married?"

For a moment a faraway expression stole into his eyes, and Billy saw his pain. "Who'd want me?"

"Couldn't you find any of your family? Your mother's people?"

He shook his head. "Her name was Angela. That's all I ever knew. I spent some time looking. I finally took the name Turlock because I heard there was a priest by that name who was kind." Again he shook his head. "All the family I ever knew was the army."

Billy remained silent for a minute before he asked, "You were captured on Long Island?"

"When the British flanked us and our boys ran for the swamp I tried to get ahead and turn them, but I couldn't. The Hessians took me."

"But you escaped."

For a full minute Turlock did not speak. Billy saw the sick look in his eyes, and waited.

"They put me on a prison ship off Long Island. I never seen nothing like it. We was kept below decks. The smell of dead and rotting bodies . . ." His voice trailed off and he did not finish the sentence. "Every morning they dumped ten, twenty bodies overboard and took on ten, twenty new prisoners. I lost fifteen pounds in a week and I was dying. I told them I was a gunnery sergeant and I could be useful helping train their troops to the cannon and musket. They sent me to a Hessian regiment that didn't know nothing about cannon. I taught 'em for a few days, while I watched for a chance to sneak out at night, but none came. I realized they'd send me away if they believed I was crazy, so I convinced 'em."

"Convinced them you were crazy? How?"

A wry smile crept over the leathery face. "Ate dirt. Grass. Talked to bushes. Hugged a tree. Sang hymns all night." He chuckled for a moment. "The morning I hooked up two oxen to a cannon backwards, they'd had enough. They turned me out of camp and said don't come back. I came here."

Billy couldn't surpress a grin. "You hugged a tree?"

Turlock nodded his head. "Right in front of a colonel. Scared him."

They looked at each other, and laughed in the frozen silence. It passed and they settled down again.

"You've served your time in the army. Why did you come back?"

For a long time Turlock stared into the fire. "A feeling. I can't hardly explain it, even to myself. A feeling like there's something holy about this war. Like religion. Like it would be a sin if I didn't." He turned his eyes to Billy, and Billy saw the deep need for understanding, affirmation. "You understand?"

Billy spoke quietly. "I do. That feeling's what's holding me here."

In that moment something happened between the two men—one old and battered, wizened by his hard world, the other young and inexperienced in his sheltered world. Neither tried to put it to words because they could not, and they both turned their faces back to the fire and peered at the flames.

Turlock broke the silence. "Coming here I heard about the retreat across New Jersey."

Billy slowly shook his head while a haunted look stole into his eyes. "I never knew such a thing could happen. The pain . . ."

Turlock murmured. "I figured this is where I belonged."

Billy remained silent, staring into the flames as the images of starving men eating from the pig troughs of the farms they passed danced before his eyes, and of men using their belt knives to cut off toes that were frozen black and putrid.

Turlock continued. "When I was coming here I heard some things. Congress sent Ben Franklin to France a while back. You heard about it?"

Billy shook his head.

"They figured we need help, and France is our only chance, and that Franklin's our last hope for getting it."

"I thought France surrendered to England a long time ago."

"In '63, but she's never got over it. If she could find a way to sting the British, she would."

He pursed his mouth for a time in deep thought. "I wonder if Franklin really went over there. And if he did, I wonder what's happening. Do you suppose he can persuade the king to get into this war on our side?"

Notes

One of the more accepted authorities on the Trenton campaign is Richard M. Ketchum, whose book *The Winter Soldiers* provides the foundation for the factual support for most of this volume.

As the Continental army approached Trenton, New Jersey, General Washington returned with a command of men to meet General Sterling at Princeton, but upon hearing Sterling's report of a British advance, Washington began a controlled retreat back to Trenton, tearing up the bridges to slow the British (see Ketchum, *The Winter Soldiers*, p. 201).

The Americans began crossing the Delaware River late December 7, 1776, continued through the night, and finished early in the morning of December 8, 1776. They had scarcely finished when the British appeared on the New Jersey side of the river and began shelling the Americans with cannon. On December 14, 1776, General William Howe declared the British campaign for 1776 concluded, and left for winter quarters in New York City (see Ketchum, *The Winter Soldiers*, pp. 202–3).

Charles Willson Peale, a famous artist of the Revolution, visited the American camp at that time. He passed his brother, who was seated on a log, sick, half-naked, and emaciated beyond recognition. It was only after James called his name that he looked directly at him and recognized him. Charles recorded the condition of the American army at that time as "the most hellish scene I ever beheld" (as quoted in Ketchum, *The Winter Soldiers*, p. 204).

The inhuman conditions on the British prison ship, as described here in the novel by Sergeant Alvin Turlock, are accurate (see Leckie, *George Washington's War*, pp. 182–83).

CHAPTER II

★ ★ ★

*V*apor trailed from their flared nostrils, and steam rolled from the hides of the two old brown horses as they threw weary legs and listened to the rumble of the ancient coach behind. For four hours the driver had pushed them on, alternating from a walk to trot, then an easy lope, then a walk, pacing them, saving them so they would not break down in the middle of the oncoming night. The dirt road was rutted and pitted from the fall rains and early December snow. The old coach had been built fifty years earlier, sturdy but with no springs. The passenger van was slung to the frame on great leather straps that kept it swaying constantly but did little to soften the unending shocks that wrenched the coach and shook the silent passengers inside.

Before boarding the battered old coach in the small French coastal fishing village of Aunoy, the driver had shoveled hot, glowing coals from the tavern stove into a metal box and two men had set it on the floor inside the van. With an old, frayed wool blanket over their legs to hold the heat, the passengers had kept their feet warm as they made their way towards the town of Nantes, to the southeast, until the coals cooled. They kept the blanket over their legs and feet to hold in what little warmth remained, and clasped their hands in their laps away from the biting cold. The sun had settled behind the flat coastal skyline, and the world was slipping into a stark, frigid, wintry twilight. The mud in the road was firming, and spidery veins of ice were forming in the puddles and on the ponds near the road as the coach moved on, creaking and complaining.

Inside, Benjamin Franklin bit off a groan and shifted his weight to relieve the pressure on his back and legs. He glanced across the gap between the facing seats at his two grandsons, William Temple Franklin, nearly seventeen, seated opposite him, and seven-year-old Benjamin Franklin Bache, next to William. Both stoically bore the biting cold and the lurching jolts in determined silence.

Forty-four days earlier, on October 27, 1776, the three of them had boarded the light, sixteen-gun American sloop *Reprisal* at Marcus Hook in Pennsylvania, commanded by Captain Lambert Wickes. The ship was loaded with indigo, to be sold in Europe at as high a price as possible. Two days later, October 29, they cleared Cape May and set a course north and east into the teeth of the deadly winter storms of the North Atlantic, and it was then Captain Wickes opened and read his sealed orders from Congress. His jaw dropped as he realized for the first time that perhaps his cargo, and his mission, were other than indigo and the markets in Europe.

"The Honourable Doctor Franklin being appointed by Congress one of their Commissioners for negotiating some publick business at the court of France, you are to receive him and his suite on board the *Reprisal*, as passengers, whom it is your duty and we dare say it will be your inclination, to treat with the greatest respect and attention, and your best endeavours will not be wanting to make their time on board the ship perfectly agreeable."

The balance of his orders were firm and blunt. If he were pursued by any ships, he was to escape if at all possible. Fight only if it were absolutely unavoidable.

What Captain Wickes had not been told was that the appointment under which Congress was sending Franklin to France was not as a simple commissioner conducting some unnamed public business with the French. The truth was that one year earlier a terrified Congress had suddenly faced the monstrous absurdity of the notion the American colonies could meet and beat the most powerful nation on the face of the earth in an all-out war, without help. The few American foundries and factories could never build the cannon or manufacture the gun-powder sufficient to wage such a war, and without them their cause was lost absolutely. In desperation Congress had flailed about for some way to get the help they must have to survive.

France! The French were still seething inwardly from their humiliating defeat in 1763 by England in the Seven Years' War. Would the deep need for revenge and redemption drive France to hurt the British by helping the Americans? And if they could be persuaded to help the Americans, how was it to be done? Open for the world to see, or clandestine, hidden? And who had the stature and the skills to go to France and make such arrangements.

Quickly Congress formed the Secret Committee of Congress and appointed Thomas Willing as chairman, with Benjamin Franklin, Thomas Lynch of South Carolina, and Benjamin Harrison of Virginia as members. Then, in short order, Congress formed a second committee, the Committee of Secret Correspondence, to which committee they appointed Benjamin Franklin, Thomas Johnson, John Dickinson, John Hay, and Benjamin Harrison. No one save a few members of Congress, and the men appointed to the committees knew of the committee's existence, or their mission, which was to make whatever deals were required, on whatever terms they could, to get the munitions and supplies upon which the American Revolution, so bravely begun and now so desperately in need, depended.

The Secret Committee contacted Arthur Lee, an American businessman of longtime standing in London and requested he make it his business to learn secretly the attitude of the British towards the French. At the same time they sent Congressman Silas Deane of Connecticut to France to gauge covertly the possibility of making undercover deals to get the war supplies from the French.

By early October of 1776, with General George Washington and the Continental army reeling from the catastrophic beatings they had sustained at the hands of General Howe's forces in and around New York, Congress understood one thing. Help had to come soon or the Revolution was doomed. In their darkest hour they turned to the single man in the entire American population whose years of experience among the hierarchy in England had established him as a world-recognized figure, blessed with native intelligence and uncanny wisdom that uniquely qualified him to meet as an equal the political manipulators and career assassins of the courts of the kings in Europe.

They called Benjamin Franklin.

Born in Boston, January 17, 1706, Franklin was seventy years of age, frail, plagued with gout that could disable him for two weeks at a time, and a rash that covered part of his body and most of his scalp. He had a high forehead with long, receding gray hair, jowls that were beginning to sag, and eyesight that required bifocals to see or read. He had long since retired from the arena of business with enough wealth to see him comfortably through life, and given his last years to matters in which he had a personal interest, including public service. He had listened carefully to the urgent plea from Congress and responded with his usual sagacity.

"I am old and good for nothing," he had said to Doctor Benjamin Rush seated nearby upon hearing the announcement, "but as the storekeepers say of their remnants of cloth, I am but a bolt end, and you may have me for what you are pleased to give."

Those who knew him understood the profound message behind his self-effacing, witty response. In his own homespun colonial style he had silently declared to the world that history had brought a suffering humanity to the threshold of a new day. It remained hidden to those who refused to see, but those who had the eyes saw the hand of the Almighty immutably moving mankind towards a dawn that was glorious beyond anything ever dreamed.

The steady gaze in Franklin's half-closed eyes, and the set of his chin silently said what Franklin had not. *I am ready and I will go, and I will do whatever I can as God gives me strength and inspiration, and we shall see who is standing and who has fallen at the end of the day.*

With his usual foresight, he had brought along his two grandsons, William because he was old enough and clearheaded enough to be used as a confidential courier, and Benjamin because he was young enough that being exposed to an education in France and the affairs in Europe would serve him well in the world that was coming.

Franklin heard the shouted command, and felt the horses answer to the pull on the reins as they stiffened their forelegs and set them slipping in the hardened mud to slow the coach and bring it to a rocking stop. He peered out the coach window into the deep gloom of late twilight searching for a reason for the stop, but there was nothing—no lights, no town, no approaching coach, no one in the roadway.

The driver clambered down from his box and opened the coach door, vapor rising from his face as he spoke. "We will rest the horses for a few moments while I light two lanterns on the coach. That will give a little light to show the road for the horses, but not enough to be seen far." His face was long and serious as he pointed ahead. "A band of robbers infests the woods just ahead. A fortnight ago they stopped a coach such as this near this very spot and murdered the travelers and stole their money and baggage." He paused, then added, "I will move through the woods quickly and I will stop for nothing."

A wry smile passed over Franklin's face as a thought flickered through his mind. *How considerate of the driver to deliver such a joyous message on this side of the woods.*

Minutes later the coach jerked into motion and the driver raised the horses to a gallop and held it for five minutes while Franklin and his two grandsons clung to the sides as it bucked and jumped over the ruts and pits in the road. The coach broke out of the woods onto an open plain and slowed. Again Franklin shifted his weight, wincing at the pain. During the sea voyage his teeth had proved too weak to tear and chew the flesh of the fowl in the ship's food stores. The only meat on board Franklin could chew was the salted beef, which alone had sustained him through the rough voyage. The result was an eruption of painful boils on his neck and back, and sitting had become a matter of enduring the sharp pain of the pressure on the red, angry eruptions.

A frosty quarter moon rose as the coach jostled easterly along the narrow, twisted road, and Franklin's high forehead wrinkled and his shoulders sagged for a moment at the unbearable weight that had been placed on his tired, aging body by a Congress that knew if Franklin failed, the Revolution failed with him. He drew a great breath, coughed at the bite of the cold in his lungs, and began gathering his thoughts, organizing them, sorting out the answers he must have almost instantly on his arrival in Paris, and he groped for a plan to get them. He reached back in his memories.

Where did this all begin—the events that now found him riding in an old coach in the dark of a frigid winter's night on a backcountry road in France, bound for Paris with the ludicrous hope of persuading King Louis XVI, the young monarch with a rather limited grasp of both politics and power, to join hands with a loosely gathered, untutored, unproven collection of colonies half a world away in a do-or-die effort to take on and defeat the greatest army on the earth?

Was it 1757? Did it begin in 1757 with his first officially ordered voyage by Governor Denny of Pennsylvania to London to seek parliamentary approval of Franklin's compromise bill to settle grievances between the disgruntled Penn family—the political leaders in the colonies—and the Crown? No, it began farther back.

A smile tugged as he remembered the earliest prominent appearance of his name in French society. In early May of 1752, in a walled garden in the small village of Marly-la-Ville, twenty-five miles north of Paris, the French natural philosopher Thomas-François Dalibard had erected a strange apparatus that included a long metal rod set upright into the sky and a wire insulated in a bottle, according to the directions found in the writings of Benjamin Franklin of Philadelphia in British North America. Dalibard waited impatiently for three days for a thunderstorm to provide the necessary lightning, and when nature failed him, he explained the crude machinery to a close group of enthralled friends and made his way back to Paris.

Then, on May 10, 1752, with a thunderstorm approaching, a fearless, retired French dragoon named Coiffier who understood something about the Dalibard experiment, grasped the wire and waited. The storm rolled in, Coiffier touched the wire to the rod, sparks flew, and the smell of sulfur was everywhere. Sulfur meant the Devil, and Coiffier instantly sent a runner sprinting to get M. Raulet, Prior of Marly, to use his priestly authority to dispel the powers of evil. The storm had worsened and hail was slanting when Prior Raulet arrived, grasped the bottle with the wire and touched it to the rod six times. Each time sparks flew and the sulfur smell became overpowering. Then Prior Raulet touched the rod with his hand. The shock stood his hair on end and threw him back, hand and arm numb, eyes popping from his head.

Prior Raulet sent a full account of the historic experiment to Dalibard in Paris, and Dalibard prepared a report for the Royal Academy of Sciences. Franklin, the unlettered colonial, with no formal education beyond the second grade, and a printer by trade, had indeed proven that lightning was electricity and could be caught and stored. The name Benjamin Franklin began appearing first in one place, then another.

Shortly the name became more—a household possession in every kitchen in every hamlet in France, and his history and achievement were discussed over back fences, in pubs, schools, churches, inns, wherever people gathered. Franklin—the fifteenth child of a tallow chandler—apprenticed to his brother in Boston as a printer at age twelve, left at age seventeen for Philadelphia to seek his fortune, and find it he did. A master printer, essayist, journalist, author and publisher of the world renowned *Poor Richard's Almanack.* Inventor of street paving and streetlights, the Franklin stove, bifocal glasses, the lightning rod. Founder of the first circulating library, a hospital, the first fire insurance company, the American Philosophical Society, and an academy. Writer of scientific research on eclipses, whirlwinds, ants, and the Gulf Stream.

Retired from business at age forty-two, he became a civic leader, then a leader in the colonies, then in the affairs of the world. With his second-grade education, he received honorary degrees from Harvard, William and Mary, Yale, and finally a doctorate degree from the University of Edinburgh. Forever after he was addressed as "Doctor Franklin." With it all, he remained a simple man from the colonies. He moved quickly into the dress and manners of the English political hierarchy, and developed an uncanny ability to blend into the people and circumstances wherever he found himself, sharing incomparable wit and seeming to enjoy immensely whatever he happened to be doing at any moment.

The sound of a wolf mourning the moon came clear in the night, and Franklin leaned forward in the rocking coach to stare into the darkness. There was no light, no movement, nothing, and he settled back and tucked the blanket over his legs. He sobered and his eyes narrowed as he once again picked up his thoughts.

A somber feeling crept through him as he recalled. If 1752 was the beginning, 1775 was the end. He stared unseeing into his lap as the bright images flickered in his mind. The great, cold, opulent halls of Parliament in London, the crossroads of the civilized world and the fountainhead of political power, corruption and intrigue—the statesmen and the knaves, the brilliant and the foolish—the lessons each had taught him in his unparalleled rise to prominence in the politics of London, and the world, representing the House of Representatives of Massachusetts Bay as its agent to England.

He set his jaw at the remembrance of the jealousy it evoked from Arthur Lee when it was Franklin and not Lee who received the appointment, and the resulting confrontation that wintry morning of January 16, 1771, when Franklin called on Lord Hillsborough, who had become England's secretary of state for the colonies, to announce his appointment. Lord Hillsborough had denied Franklin's announcement, bluntly telling him that Governor Thomas Hutchinson of Massachusetts had refused to give assent to the necessary bill confirming the appointment and had in fact written to Hillsborough to make the refusal official. Shocked, Franklin had told Hillsborough no bill was necessary for the appointment and asked to see the letter from Governor Hutchinson, which Hillsborough did not produce. It was later that Franklin puzzled over a letter written by Governor Hutchinson to Hillsborough wherein the governor took the confusing position that "The Council have renewed their choice of Mr. Bollan and the House have chosen Doctor Franklin" as the official representative, which he, Governor Hutchinson could not condone since two agents were not needed. Hutchinson would prepare legislation to remedy the problem and notify Hillsborough upon its approval. The legislation failed when the Council and the House each refused to change their appointment, and Governor Hutchinson refused to confirm Franklin as the official representative, and so informed Hillsborough in 1772.

Once again Franklin felt the sick rise in his stomach as he concluded that there was something more than Hutchinson's letter behind

Hillsborough's refusal to acknowledge him, and although he showed no hint of his fear, the episode had left him with the growing conviction that somehow, for reasons he could not dream, he had suddenly fallen out of favor with the entire English ministry.

Was it his plan to create and populate a new colony in America, west of the Alleghenies? One million two hundred thousand acres to be wrested from the great Ohio valley wilderness and populated to serve as a western defense for the colonies already in place on the Atlantic seaboard, and bring to the Indians the blessings of civilization. He had dreamed the plan and worked out the details by 1763, but no one, either in England or the colonies, had shown the slightest interest. His own dogged determination had kept the plan alive until 1769 when Samuel Wharton and William Trent of Pennsylvania arrived in London to support the plan and move it along.

It was expanded from 1,200,000 acres to 20,000,000 acres, and soon attracted Lord Hertford, the lord chamberlain, Lord Camden, the lord chancellor, and Lord Rochford, secretary of state for the northern department, all of whom became shareholders in what was formally named the Grand Ohio Company. They selected three alternative names for the new colony, one of which would finally be selected according to the political winds at that future time. Indiana, Pittsylvania, or Vandalia, the latter name because Queen Charlotte was said to be a descendant of the royal line of the Vandals.

The plan stalled when Virginia and Pennsylvania, as well as the Indian tribes living in the wilderness, contested the land claims of the Grand Ohio Company, and once again Franklin stubbornly refused to let it die. Finally in 1772, a formally drawn petition was considered by the English Board of Trade, but it was denied by none other than Lord Hillsborough! The Privy Council was advised of the denial, following which Lord Gower and other prominent English shareholders in the Grand Ohio Company contested the denial and persuaded the Privy Council to hear evidence against the decision of the Board of Trade and Hillsborough.

Franklin's breathing slowed at the memory of June 5, 1772, when he, Thomas Walpole, and others interested in the plan, appeared before a committee of the Privy Council in the Cockpit at Whitehall, that historically famous chamber where great matters of the kingdom were subjected to the intense, intimidating scrutiny of the political denizens of the British Empire. With frowning eyes the council had listened in stony silence and left the chamber.

Their decision had stunned Franklin. The Privy Council had overturned the Hillsborough ruling and agreed to forward the petition, and the prospects for the Grand Ohio Company leaped. Hillsborough was devastated, and Franklin would never forget the day Hillsborough resigned rather than remain in office, beaten by the colonial, Benjamin Franklin.

In the near total blackness of night, Franklin reached to close the curtains on the coach windows to stop the flow of freezing air, then settled back into his seat and tucked the blanket, and continued laboring with his thoughts.

Too late he had realized that by beating Hillsborough, he had provoked powerful political enemies in high places, and slowly, surely, seemingly insignificant things began to occur. Individually they meant little until one day Franklin began to put them all together, and he could still feel the shock.

Following the British Stamp Act of 1765, and the Townshend Act of 1767, Britain had sent troops to quiet the growing restlessness in the colonies. In 1770, a mob of Boston colonials forced a confrontation with a small British patrol, and in the face of snowballs and sticks being thrown at them, the frightened soldiers levelled their muskets and fired. Five colonials died, and the cry went out from Boston, "Massacre!" It reverbrated in the corridors of Whitehall in London, and Franklin still remembered the confused feeling of speaking out again and again in an attempt to explain and reconcile the Americans to the English and the English to the Americans.

And he vividly remembered the guarded glances that soon began among the British political powers that plainly bespoke their silent, unanswered questions. Where does Mr. Franklin stand in this widening void between England and her colonies? How long can he remain with one foot firmly planted in England and the other in America?

Franklin stopped to cough and shift his weight once more, wincing from the pain of the boils down his back. For long moments he pondered before he once again opened the door into his memory where he had carefully locked away the most catastrophic episode of his political career in London.

It was the winter of 1772 when a British gentleman of some political standing had been in private conversation with Franklin regarding the use of British troops in the colonies. When Franklin stated that in his opinion the sending of troops to control the colonies seemed to suggest something less than parental regard on the part of England, the unnamed gentleman had taken exception. He replied that if blame were to be laid, it would have to be on the Americans themselves, since it was *their* leaders who had suggested the British take harsh measures. Astonished, Franklin demanded proof. Shortly thereafter, this same unnamed British gentleman delivered to Franklin letters written by Thomas Hutchinson, governor of Massachusetts, to Thomas Whatley in the British Parliament. If the letters were read from the British point of view, they could be construed to mean that Hutchinson was urging the British to take stronger measures against his own constituents in Massachusetts.

Riding in the ancient coach in the middle of a freezing night, on an unknown back road in France, Franklin felt again the rise of his gorge at the awful weapon that had been placed in his hands. This was the same Governor Thomas Hutchinson who had flatly refused to recognize Franklin's appointment by the Massachusetts House of Representatives as its agent to England! Caught in seditious correspondence with Whatley in England! What would happen if these letters were made public in Massachusetts? Who would believe Franklin had exposed Hutchinson out of a sense of patriotic duty, and not out of revenge for what Hutchinson had done to him?

Days turned to weeks while Franklin agonized. How well he knew the unspoken rules of the game of political intrigue and character assassination. It was standard British practice that none of his mail arriving from America, and none of his correspondence leaving London, was forwarded without agents of the British government first opening the envelopes with chemicals that left no trace, and carefully reading all of the contents. He also knew that if he so much as suggested the practice publicly, the outcry of innocence and righteous indignation would be instant and thunderous. Gentlemen simply did not read other gentlemen's mail, let alone make the contents public.

He remembered the date of December 2, 1772, when he sent the clandestine letters to Thomas Cushing in Boston. Despite Franklin's specific directions to Cushing regarding strict limitations on the use of the letters, by June 2, 1773, they had reached the floor of the House of Representatives of the Massachusetts legislature, where Sam Adams had them read into the house minutes and moved for a Committee of the whole House to consider them. Franklin was appalled! He had only meant to inform the proper persons of the ambivalence of Governor Hutchinson. In fact, he had sewn a political whirlwind that was instantly out of his control. The House voted 101 to 5 that "the tendency and design of the letters . . . was to overthrow the Constitution of this Government and to introduce Arbitrary Power into the Province." They thereupon drafted a resolution that "if His Majesty in his great Goodness, shall be pleased to remove His Excellency Thomas Hutchinson Esq., and the Hon'ble Andrew Oliver Esq., from the Offices of Governor and Lieutenant Governor, it is the humble opinion of this Board, that it will be promotive of His Majesty's Service, and the Good of his loyal and affectionate People of this Province."

June 26, 1773, Hutchinson drafted his response to the actions of the Massachusetts House petition, in which he denied the entirety of the charges, flatly accused Franklin of the heinous political crime of intercepting and reading private mail, and demanded action on the matter. The resolution of the Massachusetts House and the response by Governor Hutchinson both crossed the Atlantic on the same boat and arrived in London in mid-August.

It was Franklin's duty as agent for the Massachusetts House to present the petition to Lord Dartmouth in London, secretary of state for the colonies, which he did immediately. However, he did not reveal to Dartmouth that it was himself who had forwarded the explosive Hutchinson letters to Boston in the first instance. For reasons never revealed, Lord Dartmouth did not resolve the matter quietly, as was his option. Rather, he wrote emollient, sympathetic letters to both Hutchinson and Franklin and stated that he would lay the matter before King George III "the next time I shall have the Honor of being admitted into his presence."

The matter began its journey through the ponderous political processes of English politics and in late fall appeared to have stalled. Then, December 11, 1773, William Whatley, brother of the late Thomas Whatley, accused John Temple, the former surveyor general of the customs in Massachusetts, of being the villain who had revealed the Hutchinson letters to the Massachusetts newspapers. Temple reared back in anger and denied it, and did what was required of a gentleman wrongly accused of such an act. He challenged Whatley to a sword duel, which took place in Hyde Park, and resulted in Whatley being injured twice, Temple injured not at all, and neither man satisfied. The duel would have to be fought again, to the finish.

The lurching of the coach slowed and stopped, and Franklin raised the curtain on the window to see the driver scramble down from the box. He glanced up at Franklin.

"Resting the horses for a minute while they drink."

Minutes later the driver climbed back into the box and the coach once again jolted into motion, and Franklin heard the splash as the wheels rolled through a shallow stream that crossed the road. They continued once again into the black of night.

Franklin shook his head at the remembrance of the trap he had laid for himself. He could not let two men try to kill each other over what he had done. December 25, 1773, he wrote a complete statement declaring that he, Franklin, was the one who had delivered the Hutchinson letters to Boston, and thus he alone should bear the consequences. He had his statement published December 27 in the London newspaper, *The Public Advertiser.*

January 8, 1774, Franklin was informed that in three days' time the Lords of the Committee of His Majesty's Privy Council for Plantation Affairs would be considering the Massachusetts House's petition to remove Governor Hutchinson and Lieutenant Governor Oliver; his attendance was required. Less than twenty-four hours before the hearing, Franklin learned that Hutchinson and Oliver had secretly obtained leave to have the hearing conducted by private counsel, and not by the members of the Privy Council. When he learned whom they had selected as private counsel, he knew in his heart he was finished. Solicitor General Alexander Wedderburn was to examine Franklin. In all the British Empire there was no practitioner of law more detested, or whose principles and practices had sunk lower than Wedderburn's. Before a judicial tribunal he knew no restraints, no limits to his savage, brutal, despicable conduct.

At Franklin's request, a delay was granted until February first, and in those three weeks, two events occurred. Franklin hired John Dunning for representation before the Privy Council. And, news arrived in London that on the night of December 16, 1773, citizens of Boston dressed as Mohawk Indians had dumped three hundred forty-two chests of tea into Boston harbor to protest English taxes. The Boston Tea Party burst onto the London political scene like a cannon blast just days before Franklin was to appear in the Cockpit at Whitehall to be examined regarding his now infamous action of intercepting private mail and publishing it for political purposes.

Franklin leaned back in the coach and rested his head against the hard cushion. He let the scenes of the January 29, 1774 Privy Council proceeding in Whitehall run before his closed eyes as though they happened yesterday.

The clambering crowd spilling out into the courtyard and street—the thirty-six members of the Privy Council, including Dartmouth, Hillsborough, and Rochford, all seated at the long table that ran below the windows—the Archbishop of Canterbury—the bishop of London—high political figures from both sides of the Atlantic. He recalled being required to stand in the Cockpit facing the tribunal—the reading of the resolution of the Massachusetts House—Franklin's covering letter of the Petition—the letters from Hutchinson and Oliver—and then the moment Wedderburn rose to address the Privy Council.

For one hour his voice rang off the walls of the high-vaulted chamber, first insulting Franklin by quoting from Hutchinson's letters and then excoriating Franklin's literary reputation with his caustic "this man of letters." And then Wedderburn unleashed a tirade. He shouted, accusing Franklin of fraud, theft, malignant heart—having forfeited all right to move among honorable men by breaking the sacred trust inherent in politics and religion of respect for private correspondence. Mark him—brand him—a man without honor.

Franklin stood for the entire hour as though cut from granite. He moved not one muscle, uttered no word.

Wedderburn then declared he was ready to examine Franklin as a witness. Franklin denied Wedderburn his greatest hope in the entire matter, and stunned everyone within hearing distance, by simply refusing to submit to any such degradation. Wedderburn had already crucified him before one word of evidence had been taken, Franklin was not now going to give Wedderburn the satisfaction of picking his bones. The hearing adjourned. Before evening of that day the Privy Council announced their decision. All charges against Hutchinson and Oliver were declared false, groundless, and both men were exonerated of everything.

The following morning Franklin received official notice. The king had found it necessary to remove Franklin from his post of deputy postmaster for North America. With stoic calm Franklin accepted it, and for the following year he stubbornly remained in London, determined to rebuild his political image, but it was impossible. On March 21, 1775, in total anonymity, he boarded the *Pennsylvania Packet* with his grandson, and on May 5, arrived at the Delaware River off Philadelphia to the shocking news that sixteen days earlier—April 19, 1775—American militia had met British regulars at Lexington and Concord, and in the daylong battle that followed had all but annihilated the entire British column. The spark he had predicted, and feared, had been struck and it had ignited an explosion heard around the world. A state of war existed between the colonies and Britain.

On May 13, 1775, eight days after Franklin arrived in Philadelphia, the authorities in England issued a warrant for his arrest. He was an international fugitive.

Franklin flinched at the sound of the driver's voice calling commands to the horses, and then the coach slowed and stopped. William, opposite Franklin, yawned and raised the window shade as the driver walked stiff-legged from the horses. Vapor rose from his face as he spoke. "Stopping to let the horses rest." He pointed east, where the earliest light of dawn was separating the earth from the sky. "Nantes is just over there. We will arrive shortly after sunrise."

Franklin nodded and settled back to weigh the first and most critical question of his entire mission. All of France knew of his eighteen-year courtship with England—his rise—his unparalleled popularity—the Grand Ohio Company—his desperate, losing attempt to reconcile the English with their rebellious colonies in America—the Hutchinson letters affair—the wicked destruction inflicted on him by Wedderburn in the Cockpit at Whitehall—his flight in the night from England to America—the issuance of the English warrant for his arrest.

No one was more aware than Franklin of the fact that during all those years he was becoming the darling, and then the outcast of England, France had been seething with a need for national redemption for the losses they had sustained at the hands of the English when, in 1763, they ceded nearly all their rights and claims in North America to England at the French surrender following the Seven Years' War.

The first critical question Franklin had to answer was simple. With the history Franklin had of being a recognized figure in the British empire so despised by the French, what attitude would the French people have towards him now?

The second critical question was equally simple. What would be the attitude of the French government?

He heaved a great sigh and peered eastward towards the first streaks of sun on the undersides of the light skiff of clouds, and at the stark, leafless silhouettes of the trees on the rolling farmland between the coach and Nantes.

I'll have some of the answers in a few hours.

The Loire River, running west into the Bay of Biscay, was a golden ribbon in the frosty light of the winter sun as it passed near the southern reaches of the village of Nantes. The driver wheeled the rocking coach to a stop on a narrow cobblestone street in front of an inn near the center of the village and climbed down from the box. The carved sign above the door was written in French, with a figure above the letters of a blue pony prancing on a road. Franklin stamped his feet for a moment to raise warmth and circulation, then opened the door to the coach and fluently translated for his grandsons.

"The Blue Pony Inn. We are here."

William threw aside the old blanket and stepped from the coach, then turned to reach for the hand of his grandfather. Slowly Franklin made the steps down to the cobblestone and stood for a moment while his trembling legs steadied and took the load of his aging, frail body. His grandson Benjamin followed and the three of them turned to the driver, who spoke. "I will unload your baggage and then I must take care of the horses." He gestured to the tired team, heads down, steam rising from their sweated hides.

The door of the inn opened and a portly, middle-aged woman with a great shawl pulled tightly about her shoulders walked out to meet them. She spoke to the driver.

"You have guests for the inn?"

The driver turned to her, and stopped, then paused a moment to savor the announcement. "Clotilde, may I present Monsieur Benjamin Franklin of America, and his companions. They will need food and lodging for a time."

The woman froze in her tracks and her eyes popped as she shifted them from the driver to Franklin. She opened her mouth to speak, could find no words, and spontaneously turned on her heel to call in through the open door, "Marius, come at once! You are not going to believe!"

Marius gasped when Franklin returned his greeting in fluent French, and then Marius stumbled all over himself getting the baggage inside. Franklin paid in advance. The second floor room was small and spartan, but clean, and warmed by its own fireplace. While Franklin and his grandsons unpacked and washed, Clotilde set breakfast on the large table in the dining room by the great front window overlooking the street, and quietly hissed orders to her son. He threw on his coat and disappeared out the back kitchen door, and within minutes the town of Nantes was alive with the news. Benjamin Franklin is at the Blue Pony Inn. Yes! Benjamin Franklin of America.

The food was simple, basic, delicious, and served steaming in large bowls. No sooner had Franklin raised his fork than two small faces appeared just outside the window and two noses pressed against the glass. Wide-eyed, the children pointed, exclaimed, and ran away, only to reappear within minutes with several more.

Franklin raised understanding eyes to William and Benjamin and smiled. "We should soon see either the sheriff, the mayor, or the priest, depending on what the village of Nantes thinks of us."

They finished their meal, and Clotilde appeared at Franklin's elbow, gesturing, talking, making it clear she was urging. "Would you care for more? You must have more."

Franklin raised his eyes to hers, and his nose crinkled with his smile. "It is the finest breakfast I can remember. How I wish I could eat more, but I cannot. You must accept my great compliments and thanks. It was wonderful."

Clotilde did not realize she had just been captured by Benjamin Franklin. An uncontrollable grin crossed her face, her glance fell to the floor, and she blushed. "Sir, it was nothing."

Franklin stood. "After a night of winter travel, it was everything. May I ask a great favor?"

"Anything, sir."

"My grandsons and I are very tired. Could you arrange not to have us disturbed while we rest in our room?"

"Oh, yes, sir. I will."

Franklin bowed and turned towards the stairway to the second floor when the front door burst open. In thirty seconds the room was half-filled with wide-eyed children who stood gaping, wordless. Behind them came their parents, and behind the parents came a tall, gaunt man wearing a black coat and high-crowned hat.

Clotilde's mouth fell open, and she clacked it shut before she turned to Franklin. "Sir, may I present our mayor, the most honorable Monsieur Jerome DeClerc."

Instantly Franklin shifted to face the man squarely, and bowed deeply from the waist. "Sir," he said, "it is my most profound honor to visit your town. May I request your permission to remain for a few days."

The mayor stood anchored to the spot, dumbstruck. In his wildest dreams he had never conceived that Benjamin Franklin—*the* Benjamin Franklin—would grace the small village of Nantes with his presence, and it was beyond all belief that Franklin had now asked his permission to remain for a few days. All rules of political protocol left his mind like lightning, and he licked dry lips and stammered. "Stay here? In Nantes? You want to—" He suddenly realized what he was saying and cleared his throat, straightened his spine, and squared his shoulders. "May I extend an official welcome to Nantes. We would be honored if you were to remain here. The town is yours. If there is anything you wish, you have only to ask." He stopped, quickly reviewed what he had said, and bobbed his head.

Franklin smiled warmly. "It is a privilege. Thank you. If there is anything I can do to be of service, you would honor me by mentioning it."

The mayor stopped to consider, but the numbness had not yet left his brain. "Not at the moment."

"Then may I ask your permission to take my grandsons to our room? We have traveled all night and—"

The mayor cut him off. "But of course. Of course."

Once in their room, Franklin turned to his grandsons and smiled. "They sent the mayor, not the sheriff or the priest. Apparently they intend to welcome us, not to arrest us, or call us to repentance."

While Franklin and his grandsons sought the comfort of soft beds and down quilts, Clotilde and Marius spent the day quieting the unending stream of townspeople who appeared at the door, clambering for a glimpse of the mythical Benjamin Franklin, the man who had tamed lightning. In the late afternoon, a written invitation was delivered. The mayor would be most honored if Mr. Franklin would attend a great banquet that evening in his honor, in the chambers of City Hall.

The streets were filled, City Hall was jammed to the walls, and hastily made bunting and handmade welcome signs hung everywhere. Franklin was at his best, blending in, talking to high and low, modestly acknowledging his accomplishments when asked, inquiring in turn of the merchants about business, the schoolteachers about schools, the blacksmiths about horseshoes, the bakers about pastries.

In the midnight quiet of his room, with his grandsons asleep, Franklin sat on the edge of his bed and reflected deeply on the events of the day. Finally he nodded his head in conclusion, laid down in the dark, and pulled the great, down-filled quilt up to his chin.

I believe I have the answer to the first question. It seems the French people will accept me. As for the second question? the politically powerful? That is yet to be seen.

With the good food, his body gained strength and the painful boils began to heal. The coach he hired for the wintry ride northeast to Paris was drawn by four horses, had glass windows, and a recess in the floor for a metal box into which hot coals were placed each day. The road smoothed after they passed Le Mans, and they stopped for two days in Versailles, with the lights of nearby Paris showing dully on the underside of the clouds at night. On December 22, 1776, the driver halted the carriage before the Hôtel d'Hambourg in the Rue de l'Université in Paris, and Franklin and his grandsons helped unload their luggage onto the cobblestoned street. At the registry desk inside, Franklin quietly signed his name in the leather-bound ledger, paid for one week in advance, accepted the large brass key from the clerk, and smiled as he raised his eyes.

"I am advised you have an American, Silas Deane, registered here."

The clerk eyed him. "That is correct."

"Would you be so kind as to advise Mr. Deane that Mr. Franklin has arrived by appointment?"

The clerk nodded and began to turn, then stopped in his tracks. "Monsieur Franklin? Doctor Benjamin Franklin?"

Franklin nodded, bemused. "So I am told."

The clerk jerked the registry book around and read the signature, raised startled eyes to Franklin, and stuttered, "Y-yes, sir. At once, sir."

Minutes later Silas Deane—average height, slender, with thinning hair and slightly rounded shoulders—paused on the stairs until he identified Franklin waiting with his grandsons and baggage in the foyer, then descended the stairs rapidly. He seized Franklin's hand and shook it warmly, and Franklin sensed the tremendous relief as the man spoke.

"Doctor Franklin! Welcome! I am so profoundly gratified that you have arrived safely. Your presence here in Paris could hardly be more timely or more desperately needed. I trust your passage was acceptable?"

"It is my honor to be here with you, Mr. Deane. I survived the passage, though I dare not say by how much. I trust you are well—that you are getting along grandly with your work here."

Deane glanced about the foyer nervously. "Tolerable. I see you have not taken time to unpack your luggage."

Franklin nodded. "I preferred my first act in Paris to be meeting you. Would there be a later time convenient for us to talk? Perhaps after my grandsons and I have had time to unpack and take supper?"

At ten minutes past nine P.M. Franklin settled onto a chair in the privacy of Deane's room. He leaned back, one hand resting on the table between them. Deane, opposite him, drew a deep breath as Franklin spoke quietly, casually.

"May we speak freely in this room?"

"Yes. I'm certain of it."

"Is there anything of immediate importance that we should handle first?"

Deane shook his head.

Franklin pursed his mouth for a moment in thought. "I would very much appreciate developing a picture of how things stand presently. Would you care to give me your view, or would you prefer I ask questions?"

Deane considered for a moment. "Do you have questions?"

Franklin nodded and continued casually, quietly. "Is my coming here well known to the French people generally?"

"Very well known."

"What reaction?"

"From the common citizenry? Adulation."

"From the political powers?"

"King Louis?" Deane shook his head. "A bit of a dullard. He's turned the entire matter over to Comte de Vergennes, his foreign minister. I do not know his reaction."

"What instruction did the king give Vergennes? Do you know?"

"Vergennes has never said."

Franklin's expression and casual voice had not changed. "Do the French know of the loss of New York, and Washington's retreat to New Jersey? The pitiful condition of the Continental army now?"

Deane nodded. "Yes."

"What result?"

"Vergennes does not think the Continental army can survive it."

"Then why has Vergennes not broken off any dealings with us altogether? allowed you to remain here?"

Deane shrugged. "He's never said, and I've been afraid to ask. It's too critical, too heavy."

"Has France taken any steps to aid the Americans?"

Deane leaned forward, narrowed eyes glowing. "Yes. Have you ever heard the name Beaumarchais? Pierre Augustin Caron de Beaumarchais?"

Franklin dropped his eyes while he searched his memory. "The author? *The Marriage of Figaro?*"

"Yes."

"What is the current state of affairs with him?"

"Over a year ago, Beaumarchais saw the rebellion coming and went to Vergennes. He's well known, and Vergennes listened. Beaumarchais offered his services in secretly arranging aid for the Americans until they were strong enough to withstand the British. Vergennes took him to King Louis. Louis agreed. Louis saw to it that one million livres reached Beaumarchais. He also persuaded Spain to contribute another million, which Beaumarchais was ordered to use to set up a regular commercial company named 'Rodrique Hortalez and Company.' From all appearances it has nothing to do with King Louis or France. Since early this year, Beaumarchais has been shipping arms and ammunition undercover to the colonies. The British know about Rodrique Hortalez and Company, but they can't prove King Louis has anything to do with it. They're watching it. Closely."

"Does Stormont know this?"

"The British ambassador to Paris? Yes, he does. He smells the rat, but he can't find it."

"Does he know I'm here?"

"He knew about your coming before you arrived. He knows about the two Irish ships Captain Wickes took as prizes just off the Irish coast. He knows where you landed and when. He's already told Vergennes that if you set foot in Paris he's going to leave instantly and not return."

"What did Vergennes say?"

Deane grinned. "Vergennes agreed totally with Stormont. Told him he'd already sent a messenger to Nantes to stop you before you even started your journey to Paris. However, it was possible the messenger might miss you if you were already on your way, and if that happened he would try to find you and stop you before you ever reached Paris. And he added that of course if you actually got into the city without being detected, it would be a bit undesirable to turn you out because of the scandalous scene it would create for all of France if it were known that she neither abided nor respected the laws of nations, not to mention hospitality."

Franklin chuckled, then sobered. *Vergennes is to be reckoned with. Be careful.*

"What was Stormont's reply?"

"Nothing, yet. You've arrived and he's still here."

Franklin changed his train of thought. "You heard about those two ships we brought in with us at Belle Ile?"

Deane's eyebrows peaked. "Yes. I was surprised. Wasn't Wickes told to avoid battles? I have to tell you, if the British officer Sir Grey Cooper had been a bit more alert, he would have had a dozen British gunboats off the Bordeaux coast and found your ship and arrested you. They still have an active criminal warrant for you."

Franklin dropped his eyes and spoke through a grin. "I know about the warrant. One ship was Irish, the other British. Wickes turned to me when we saw them and asked me what to do. The man was all but bursting out in tears in his need to go after them. I told him to attack. He did. We took them both without firing a shot."

For several seconds a silent chuckle shook Deane's shoulders, and Franklin waited before he continued.

"Where's Arthur Lee, our third man? Still in London? Would Stormont trump up charges and arrest him and hold him hostage to force me out?"

Deane shook his head. "I saw that coming and I wrote to Lee. He's due in Paris in the next day or two."

Franklin relaxed. "Good. Has he ever gotten over that small problem of a few years ago about which of us was the actual agent for the Massachusetts House?"

Dean shrugged. "I didn't know about it."

"No matter. Does Stormont know Lee has left London?"

"Yes."

"Has he done anything about it?"

"Not that I know about."

"Is Stormont still talking with Vergennes?"

"Yes. Lately he's warned Vergennes against you. Told him that France could expect you to rise to political heights and then betray their trust through treachery in an attempt to bring France down in defeat, just as you did to England."

"What did Vergennes say?"

"He agreed totally. Said he would never trust you beyond what he could prove to his own satisfaction."

Franklin smiled, nodded, and for a time sat with his head slightly bowed, staring at the tabletop as he worked with the information Deane had delivered to him, putting it together, smoothing it, pushing to see the bigger dimensions of it. He raised his head.

"Is there anything else I should know?"

"Yes." Once again Deane leaned forward, eyes intense. "Nothing in the past decade has been as closely scrutinized as your arrival here for the American colonies. Every politician in London knows. Both Stormont and Horace Walpole have published articles in London newspapers that are accurate nearly to the last detail. Their network of eyes and ears now reaches everywhere, watching and waiting for the first mistake. They plan to bring down both you and France with the whole world watching."

Deane paused to order his thoughts. "The French people view you as the only person alive who can provide a way for them to revenge themselves against England. The government is another matter. I can only guess the mind of King Louis."

"Anything else?"

"Yes. I've made arrangements with Beaumarchais for two hundred brass cannon and thirty thousand fusees and gunpowder. They should be ready for shipment soon. We don't call them cannon and munitions in our dealings. We simply refer to them as commercial commodities. You'll hear more of this, and I tell you now only so you'll know if it comes up." Deane paused and pursed his mouth while he searched for words to express his last thought. "I'm a businessman. Not a politician. I can handle business arrangements, but I am poorly prepared to handle the intrigues we are getting into. I understand you are quite capable in that regard. You don't know the mighty relief I feel at having you here."

Franklin rose. "I'll do what I can. You've given me much of what I need." He walked to the door and turned. "I think we should meet Comte de Vergennes immediately. Could I prepare a document for our signatures tomorrow morning?"

"Absolutely."

At midnight, with his two grandsons asleep in their beds, Franklin silently lighted a lamp on a table and took quill in hand. For long minutes he worked with the words in his mind, then carefully wrote the required proper political salutation to Comte de Vergennes, and continued.

"We beg leave to acquaint your Excellency that we are appointed and fully empowered by the Congress of the United States of America to propose and negotiate a treaty of amity and commerce between France and the United States." He reread the lines with approval, and for more than half an hour he continued to write, pausing to select his words, rereading the message to be certain he had said what was intended.

The following morning he and Deane signed their names with a flourish, and Franklin turned to his grandson, William. "I would very much appreciate you delivering this to his Excellency, the Foreign Minister Vergennes. Mr. Deane can give you the address."

Hastily Deane wrote it out and Franklin read it, surprised. "He resides in Versailles?"

"Yes."

The next morning William was greeted by a clerk at the Foreign Office in Versailles. The balding, rotund little man stared at the youthful American with a condescending eye and glanced at the document. "Monsieur Gérard is absent today. I will deliver this to him upon his return."

William reflected for one moment. "May I inquire, since the document is for his Excelleny, Comte de Vergennes, why is it necessary to deliver it to Monsieur Gérard?"

The man raised his nose. "Monsieur Gérard receives all messages."

William nodded. "I see. And when will Monsieur Gérard return?"

The man tossed the document on his desk. "I do not know."

William smiled. "Well, sir"—he reached to pick up the document—"then may I wait and deliver this document to his Excellency myself?" His eyes narrowed slightly and his smile became wooden. "It is from representatives of the United States of America." He paused. "And it is urgent." He slipped the document back into his inside coat pocket.

The round little man's eyes opened wide for a split second. "America? From whom in America?"

William locked eyes with him. "Doctor Benjamin Franklin and Silas Deane."

The man's head thrust forward. "Franklin? Doctor Benjamin Franklin?"

William neither spoke nor moved.

"Please wait," the man stammered and disappeared through a door at the rear of the room to return in two minutes. "His Excellency has instructed me to accept the document and deliver it to him."

William drew the paper from his pocket and paused, smiling while his eyes took on a flinty spark. "I am most grateful for the offer, but sir, I will deliver this to his Excellency myself, if it takes all day."

The man clamped his mouth shut and once again disappeared. Within minutes he returned, followed by a rather small man dressed in a black coat, white shirt, and black bow gathered at his throat. The man's face was a blend of amusement and pique as he approached William.

"I understand you have a message from the representatives of the United States of America?"

"I do, sir. For his Excellency, the Foreign Minister, Comte de Vergennes."

"I am he."

William bowed. "I am honored, sir. I herewith deliver the message." He handed the document to Vergennes.

"Your name?"

"William Temple Franklin."

"Related to Doctor Franklin?"

"My grandfather, sir."

Vergennes smiled despite himself. "How interesting." He reflected for a moment. "I will want to study this in depth. Would you return tomorrow morning at nine o'clock for my reply? I shall try to schedule a meeting with Doctor Franklin in the next few days."

"It would be my privilege, sir. I shall take lodging overnight nearby."

Five days later Franklin and Deane hunched their shoulders against a drizzle of freezing rain and made their way to the Office of the Foreign Minister in Versailles. At ten o'clock Monsieur Gérard, sparse, hawk-nosed, immaculate in both dress and manner, appeared before them in the plush anteroom outside the office of Vergennes. "His Excellency will see you now."

The square room was not large, but every appointment, every fixture, was luxurious. The great, dark oak desk stood squarely before a floor-to-ceiling window with velvet draperies. A massive painting of King Louis XVI dominated the wall above the oak mantel on the marble fireplace.

Vergennes stood instantly as Deane walked through the door, Franklin following. "Accept my warmest welcome to France," he said in accented English as he strode across the polished hardwood floor. "I am the French Foreign Minister. I am honored to greet you and welcome you to France."

Deane bowed. "I am Silas Deane and this is Benjamin Franklin. We are most honored at your warm reception."

For a moment, Vergennes's eyes locked with Franklin's. "I trust your journey was reasonably acceptable."

Franklin smiled and replied in fluent French. "Shall we say, I survived it?"

Vergennes's eyes lighted. "I have heard stories concerning 'Admiral Franklin.' May I presume they are true? Your vessel—let me see—the *Reprisal* I believe—took two British prizes of war not far off the Brittany coast?" Vergennes's French was as smooth as glass.

Franklin chuckled. "It is true, but do not believe the propaganda about 'Admiral Franklin.' I simply nodded my head at the wrong moment and Captain Wickes misunderstood. That brave soul attacked without so much as a warning."

Vergennes laughed. "Please be seated, gentlemen."

As Franklin settled onto the velvet upholstered chair facing Vergennes's desk, he felt the old, familiar rise in his breast as every sense, every nerve in his being came to a fierce, intense focus on Vergennes, and what was to come in the next hour. He knew the rules of political exchange by which nations conducted their business at the highest levels. In times of war, the implicit was more critical than the explicit, the hidden more deadly than the revealed. You learned to maintain every requirement of absolute innocence and propriety while you sorted the truth out, or you went down. In what was coming with Vergennes, the sorting would have to be almost instantaneous.

Vergennes sat on his high-backed, intricately carved, velvet upholstered chair and turned to Franklin. "I was greatly impressed by your written inquiries of a few days ago—the ones delivered by your grandson. Extremely bright young man—great future—I'm sure you're very proud, as you ought to be."

Franklin smiled benignly. "William favors his father's side."

Vergennes smiled back. "May I address the questions you posed?"

"We would be delighted."

"You expressed concern about our French seaports. Rest assured, all our ports are, and will remain open to your ships of commerce. We are anxious to maintain the usual import-export relationship with all of the colonies, with our two peoples exchanging goods and merchandise according to the usual rules of sovereign states that enjoy friendly relations." He paused, then added as though by afterthought. "Of course, such exchange will be subject to such treaties as either of our countries might have with others."

"Excellent." Franklin leaned back in his chair. "I would be delighted to frame such a treaty for your consideration, or at least a document setting forth the general terms by which the merchants of both countries can be guided."

Vergennes raised his hands, palms up, eyebrows arched. "There is no need. The merchants have already established their own rules. The exchange is proceeding beautifully. May I suggest that a formal treaty or document would only serve to interrupt what is already the accepted practice."

Franklin nodded. "Should the Congress of the United States wish to obtain various items from the government of France—perhaps munitions—I presume we should make the request in writing through your good offices?"

"Of course. We would be delighted to consider it. Simply submit the requests in writing to myself, privately, from time to time according to your need."

Again Franklin nodded. "There is a rumor that a few such requests and acquisitions have already been made."

Vergennes leaned forward, his face a mask of surprise. "How interesting. I have heard no such rumors, nor am I privy to any such dealings. I am intensely surprised."

Franklin passed it off. "No matter." He cleared his throat and once again brought his eyes to Vergennes's. "There is some concern about the proximity of France to England. The channel is narrow. Shipping moves freely. Considering the current disaffection between the United States and England, may we understand that French ports will extend the usual courtesy of protecting our incoming ships once they have arrived in your ports?"

Vergennes nodded deeply. "Of course. All internationally

recognized courtesies will be afforded your incoming commercial vessels once they have reached waters considered to be a French port."

Franklin paused for a moment. "Would it be prudent for us to establish ourselves with any other offices of your government? Perhaps your Minister of Domestic Affairs?"

Vergennes shrugged. "I see no need. For the time, you would be best served to communicate with only this office. I will be most happy to give my personal attention to anything you may wish."

"You are most gracious. Is there anything you wish to inquire of us?"

Vergennes drew a deep breath, eyebrows arched. "Nothing of any moment." Then he suddenly raised one finger. "Except one thing. Reports have arrived concerning General Washington. Has he lately suffered some rather uh, serious setbacks? in or around New York?"

Franklin paused. "He has taken a terrible beating."

Vergennes waited. Franklin neither moved nor spoke. Vergennes broke the silence. "Where is he now?"

"At my last report, in New Jersey." As he spoke, Franklin's instincts rose. *He wants desperately to know everything I can tell him about Washington.*

Vergennes spoke. "In what condition?"

Franklin weighed his answer for a moment, then answered bluntly. "Terrible. He lost Long Island, New York, White Plains, Fort Washington, Fort Lee, and nearly half his army before he made a forced retreat across New Jersey. I believe he intends wintering in Pennsylvania. Most enlistments in his army expire the end of this month, and I presume a substantial part of his armed forces will leave. At last report they were sick, cold, and short of ammunition." He stopped. He locked eyes with Vergennes and slowly a smile formed, and he waited in silence for Vergennes's reaction.

For five seconds Vergennes did not move. His eyes bored into Franklin's reaching, searching, probing, and then he spoke quietly. "Will he recover?"

There it was! The prologue was ended. The stage was set. The political games had been played. They had finally reached the question on which the relationship between the United States and France finally came to rest, the greatest question Vergennes would face in his entire political career. If General George Washington could raise his ravaged army from the ashes of defeat to stop the British and drive them from America, then he, Vergennes was the man history had chosen to sense the right moment to join forces with the Americans to redeem the honor of France. His name would be remembered forever. Vergennes knew it, and now he knew Franklin knew it.

The air was charged. There was not a sound in the room as Franklin sorted out his answer. He leaned forward, reached to place one hand on the edge of Vergennes's desk. He spoke softly, with an intensity that came from the depths of his being. "He will, sir. He will."

Deane felt the hair on his neck lift. Vergennes's breathing slowed as the words drove deep, past his defenses, past his political foundations, deep into the core of the man. Slowly he recovered, and once again assumed the mask of complete control, prepared to play out the necessary political requirements. Franklin straightened in his chair, his face relaxed, and he was once again humble, affable.

Vergennes stood. "I hope you are correct in your judgment of General Washington. I extend my every hope for his success, and yours."

The interview was over.

As Vergennes stood at the window watching the coach rumble away in the rain-soaked street, his thoughts ran. *He is formidable. I did not find the bottom of him. I must watch—watch.*

Inside the coach Deane knocked rain from his hat, then raised his eyes to Franklin, seated opposite him. "I understood most of it, but my French is not as good as yours. What did I miss?"

Franklin raised his head thoughtfully before he smiled. "Would you care for my observations?"

Deane stopped all movement, waiting.

"Usual protocol requires him to hold a social event to announce our arrival, to which the political agents for every country with an ambassador in Paris would be invited. He hasn't done it and he has no intention of doing it. You will also remember that he referred to our *commercial* ships being welcome on the usual terms into French ports, and then refused my offer to reduce his offer to writing—a treaty. He conspicuously said nothing about our military ships, and it is clear he means to refuse them access to French ports."

Deane leaned back in his seat in amazement, and Franklin paused to give him time.

"I mentioned the rumors about munitions and he denied any knowledge of it, yet you have arranged for two hundred cannon and thirty thousand fusees. There is but one place that many cannon could be obtained, and that's from the French army. Vergennes not only knows about those cannon, he likely picked them out."

Franklin paused to glance out the rain-spattered windows at the people, wrapped to their throats in heavy coats and mufflers and hunched under umbrellas as they walked rapidly through the cold rain in the streets, hurrying to do their business.

"I inquired as to which other French government offices we should present our credentials, and his answer was instant and decisive. His office only, in private, and none other." Franklin shook his head briefly. "That brings us to a conclusion. Vergennes is afraid of England. He dare not give us formal recognition by arranging the usual social event for fear it would appear that France is both recognizing us as a sovereign and embracing us. And for the same reason he will not treaty with the United States. Either the social event or a treaty might provoke England to a war with France, which France cannot now win, and you may rest assured, England is watching every port, every ship, every foreigner who enters France. So, Vergennes wants us to remain under the exclusive, private control of his office, and no other."

Franklin stopped for a long time and Silas Deane did not move or speak.

"With all that, the most critical question raised was his. He had to know what we expect to happen with General Washington and the Continental army. There is nothing more critically important to him than that because he will become famous if he is able to sense the precise moment to join forces with us to defeat the British."

Franklin collected his thoughts. "So. It seems he granted that audience to give us a rather simple set of rules. Avoid all appearances that France and America are in combination. Deal with him only, and in private. Keep our warships out of French ports. Expect no treaties between our governments. He will make his move when he sees fit. In the meantime, we wait."

Deane drew and released a great breath, but said nothing.

Franklin raised his hand to stroke his chin thoughtfully. "Our good man Vergennes has effectively boxed us away from creating any open ties with the French government. However, I do not recall a single word that would prevent us from making some ties with the French *people*."

He smiled amiably at Deane. "Do you suppose you could acquire a calendar of the high social events to occur this season in Paris?"

Notes

In 1772, the English Privy Council supported Benjamin Franklin's plan for the Grand Ohio Company, overturning a previous ruling by Lord Hillsborough, who had become a political enemy of Franklin. Franklin's political demise in England came only a few short months later as the result of his involvement in the 1773 "Hutchinson Letters affair." Though Franklin felt it was his duty to make the private letters public, he had already had a political quarrel with Hutchinson in 1771 over the Massachusetts agent appointment to England— the same event where Franklin and Hillsborough clashed for the first time. When the letters with the information of how Hutchinson—an American governor—encouraged the English Parliament to pass stricter measures on the colonies were published, tempers flared, accusations flew, and eventually Franklin confessed his involvement to avoid William Whatley, an innocent man, from being killed in a duel. England had no choice but to bring Franklin before the Privy Council in the Cockpit at Whitehall where he was destroyed politically. Franklin struggled on in England for a year, trying to restore his good name, but finally left for America unnoticed. However, as one of Franklin's biographers, Ronald W. Clark, observes, "But for that [exile], it appears almost certain that he would have remained in Britain, probably for the rest of his life, with results which would certainly have affected the course of history" (*Benjamin Franklin*, p. 184). A detailed account of Franklin's political rise and fall in England can be found in chapter eight of Clark's *Benjamin Franklin*.

Indeed, it was only after his return to America that Franklin joined the Revolution at age seventy. Though his standing in England was gone, his acceptance in America remained strong. The American Congress placed him on both the Secret Committee and the Secret Committee of Correspondence, which was later known as the Committee of Foreign Affairs, and later still, the Department of State (see Clark, *Benjamin Franklin,* p. 280).

By the time the Americans needed to ask France for aid in the war, there was not another American better qualified than Franklin (see Clark, *Benjamin Franklin,* p. 281). And when Congress gave him the commission to go to France, Franklin stated to Doctor Benjamin Rush, "I am old and good for nothing, but as the store-keepers say of their remnants of cloth, I am but a fag end, and you may have me for what you are pleased to give" (as quoted in Clark, *Benjamin Franklin,* p. 297).

By then, France had already started smuggling supplies to America through Rodrique Hortalez and Company, a business front that had been organized by Pierre Augustin Caron de Beaumarchais, author of *The Marriage of Figaro,* and Arthur Lee (see Clark, *Benjamin Franklin,* pp. 294–95).

The facts presented in the novel surrounding Franklin's journey to France are accurate and are briefly outlined on pages 299–301 of Clark's work *Benjamin Franklin.*

The British practice of reading incoming and outgoing mail as described in the novel was indeed standard for the day (see Clark, *Benjamin Franklin,* pp. 224–25).

Franklin never did see the letter Hutchinson sent to Hillsborough denying support of Franklin's appointment as the Massachusetts agent in England, but the author included the scene for illustrative purposes in the novel (see Clark, *Benjamin Franklin,* p. 219).

For additional explanation of the political relationship between America, France, and England in the time frame of 1776–77, see Higginbotham, *The War of American Independence,* pp. 226–36; Leckie, *George Washington's War,* p. 228; Mackesy, *The War for America,* p. 104.

CHAPTER III

★ ★ ★

*T*he last arc of the setting sun slipped behind the western rim of the frozen world, and for a few moments the stark, lifeless trees became a delicate filigree against the colorless afterglow as dusk came creeping. Vapor trailed behind the head of John Honeyman as he followed the five black Angus steers, and the polled Scottish heifer, and the Guernsey cow down the lane, south from the pasture to the unpainted, clapboard milking shed, with the holding pen beside. Average height, muscled, prominent jaw, with two days growth of beard stubble, Honeyman breathed light in the frigid air to keep from freezing his lungs; his steps crunched softly as his boots broke the crusted snow and ice.

The Guernsey lagged and he reached to poke her hindquarters with the six-foot oak staff he carried, and he said, "Move, cattle cattle, move." The Guernsey flinched and lunged ahead for a moment, then slowed to a steady pace with the others as they moved down the lane between the two split rail fences.

In the distance a door closed, and Honeyman glanced at the small, square house beyond the shed. A thin wisp of smoke rose straight from the stone chimney to disappear in the still air, and the curtained windows glowed in the twilight; his wife had lighted the lamps, and supper was waiting. Hot mutton stew with fresh-baked bread and butter churned yesterday, and steaming coffee. He licked chapped lips in anticipation. Half a mile beyond his house the lights of Griggstown were winking on, and six miles beyond Griggstown, the lights of Princeton.

For a moment he stared at the rolling hills past Princeton, beyond which lay the great river, and Trenton, and his thoughts ran. *He's there. With his army. Or what's left of it.*

The cattle plodded into the small holding pen, and Honeyman swung the weathered gate closed and dropped the latch ring over the two posts. The steers and the heifer walked on to the feed manger and waited while Honeyman plowed through the black, crusted muck, ducked between two fence rails to reach the stacked, dry grass, and forked the feed manger half full. He waited for a moment to watch them bury their muzzles in the brittle stems, and he heard the grinding begin. He drove the wooden pitchfork back into the stack, ducked back between the rails into the pen, and spoke to the cow, waiting patiently beside the door into the small milking barn.

"I'm coming," he said to her. "Won't be a minute." Her udder was firm, full, and beginning to drip when he opened the door, and she walked into the darkness to the stanchion and again waited while he struck flint to steel. He caught the spark in tinder, blew softly, thrust a splinter of dry wood into the lick of flame, and lighted a lantern. He hung the lantern on a heavy wooden peg driven into the great center post that supported the ridgepole in the low roof and forked dry grass into the cow's manger. She thrust her head through the opening and began working the grass while he closed the stanchion and dropped the locking block into place.

Honeyman settled the heavy wooden milk bucket beneath the cow, sat down on the one-legged milk stool, and pulled a cloth from inside his coat. Quickly he wiped the tight udder, then thrust the cloth back into his coat. He blew on his hands to warm them, and settled into the rhythmic pumping, listening to the gentle hiss as the first streams of milk hit the bottom of the bucket. The smoking froth quieted those that followed. He leaned his forehead into the warm flank of the cow, hands working rhythmically, and watched the milk rise steadily in the bucket, yellow in the lantern light. Quietly, unexpected scenes and memories from long ago came, and he saw them and felt them, and he let them come.

Young, strong—being brutally forced into involuntary servitude in the British army—into the wilds of the north woods—ordered to kill the French and the Indians with them—rising to become personal bodyguard of General James Wolfe—the battle at Fort Quebec on the Plains of Abraham—Wolfe's daring strike—the insistence that his men form in ranks to fight the French at point-blank range—Wolfe mortally wounded by an unseen rifleman—the surrender of the fort—the end of the war—the regiment being mustered out—his growing rejection of the British and all they stood for—the treaty of 1763—the French surrendering all claims to North America—withdrawing.

He continued the rhythm of the milking while his thoughts moved ahead.

Meeting the Irish girl—their marriage—four children—building their small farm in Griggstown—establishing himself on a small farm as a weaver and a cattle dealer—watching the British slowly but surely begin to tighten their grip—the hot anger it stirred in his soul—the slow realization that he could not stand by and let them crush the colonies—waiting, watching for his chance—the appointment of General George Washington as commander in chief of the Continental army June 15, 1775, in Philadelphia—going to find General Washington—their private conference—his secret offer—the acceptance by General Washington.

The offer Honeyman had made, and Washington had accepted, was that he would pose as a hard-core Tory, loyal to the Crown, doing all he could to help the British. Speaking out hard and loud against the Americans, in church, in town hall—anywhere. Handing out British proclamations against them. Giving British soldiers lodging, food, drink, aid, support, comfort—selling them beef for their troops. Watching American movements and reporting harmless information to the British. Gaining their trust, their confidence—anything to gain their trust and confidence.

And all the while he was posing as a loyal subject of the Crown, he would be watching the British like a hawk. Memorizing troop movements—ammunition magazines—supply depots—the names and ranks of the officers—morale—fortifications—cannon placement—anything, everything. He would report his information directly to General

Washington. How? He would find a way. And if General Washington needed anything, he would send a secret message. No one other than Washington and Honeyman, either British or American, was to know of their arrangement.

What if the Americans came to arrest him or burn his farm? That was a risk he would take. The sole protection would be for Hannah and the children. General Washington wrote a letter, signed and sealed, to be held in secret by Honeyman's wife, ordering that no one was to harm or molest her or her children. She was told only that should anyone come threatening, she was to use the letter as a last means to protect herself, or the children, from harm.

So far Honeyman had been arrested by Tory-hating Americans twice, beaten once, and had hidden once for two days in the Bear Swamp south of Princeton from a mob that came at night with torches and tar and feathers. His terrified wife had gathered the children and faced the threatening mob in the light of the torches, but had told them nothing about her husband, using instead the letter for protection.

In the shadows cast by the lantern light, Honeyman stripped out the udder, rose from the milking stool, pushed it into the corner with his foot, and picked up the smoking milk bucket. He lifted the locking block on the stanchion and opened it, and left the brown-and-white spotted cow to finish the dried grass before she laid down in the straw for the night.

He cupped his right hand at the top of the lantern chimney to blow out the wick when suddenly the hair on his arms and the back of his neck rose with the sudden sure sensation that he was not alone. He shifted his right foot back a few inches for leverage to throw the bucket of milk, then, without moving his hand or his head, his eyes darted to the dark, shadowy corners of the small barn, searching.

The voice came quiet, low, from the sacked grain in the corner to his left. "Stand easy."

Honeyman flinched and tensed and his right hand dropped to grasp the bottom of the milk bucket, ready, waiting for a shape to emerge from the shadows.

"You Honeyman?"

Honeyman's breath came short. "Who wants to know?"

"Friend. You Honeyman?"

"Get out in the open where I can see you."

"I'll ask once more. You Honeyman?"

John Honeyman made an instant judgment and took a chance. "Yes. Get out where I can see you."

Without a sound, a tall shape was suddenly standing half-hidden in the light and shadow. Honeyman gasped at the sight of the wolf skin coat and buckskin hunting shirt, the moccasins with the Iroquois beadwork, the long Pennsylvania rifle, and the weapon belt with the tomahawk. It flashed in his mind—*Indian*—and then the voice came again and it was the voice of a white man.

"Set the bucket down. No need to waste the milk."

Slowly Honeyman settled the bucket onto the dirt floor and straightened and suddenly anger surged. "Who are you? You got a reason for being here?"

"Eli Stroud. Scout for General George Washington. He sent me."

Honeyman gasped and started. "General Washington? Is he all right?"

Eli stepped out into the full light and Honeyman saw the slightly hawked nose and the prominent chin with the scar on the left jawline; the blue eyes and brown hair of a white man. Eli weighed his answer.

"The general's all right, but his army's taken a beating. He sent me to deliver a message to you." He dug inside his coat and reached out with the folded paper. Honeyman grasped the paper and turned it to the lantern light scarcely breathing and read the brief, terse message. He read it once more, and carefully went over the signature again and again. Authentic. He raised anxious eyes to Eli.

"You read this?"

"No. General said only you."

"Know what it says?"

"No. He didn't tell me."

Honeyman read it once more, moving his lips silently with every word. Then he turned to the lantern, held the letter over the chimney until it curled and began to smoke, and then caught. He dropped the burning paper on the dirt floor, and the two men watched it burn to black ashes and crumble. Honeyman ground it into the dirt with his shoe heel.

Eli spoke. "Anything I should tell the general?"

Honeyman reflected. "Tell him I understand."

"That's all?"

Honeyman nodded. "That's all."

Eli nodded and started for the door, and Honeyman spoke.

"Stroud, I wish I could ask you to supper, but I can't. It's best if no one knows you came, not even my wife or the children."

Eli nodded. "Might want to put out that lantern before I open the door. You leave first. Don't know who might be watching."

Honeyman picked up the milk bucket and blew out the lamp. Eli opened the door and waited while Honeyman walked out into the night. Eli listened to the sound of Honeyman's boots in the crisp snow fade before he soundlessly closed the door. Behind Eli the Guernsey turned her head in the darkness, knowing something was different, and raised a quiet complaint. Eli counted one hundred breaths, opened the door, listened intently while he counted five more breaths, then slipped silently into the frigid, starry night.

Honeyman stopped at the root cellar near the back of the house long enough to set the bucket of milk on a shelf to chill overnight, climb back up the five stairs, and lower the thick plank door. He stopped to scrape the mud from his heavy shoes as Hannah opened the back door, and he blinked at the flood of light. He savored the warmth and the smells of supper and hot, spiced apple cider as he stepped inside. He hung his coat and unlaced and set his shoes thumping on the floor, then glanced at the table where the four children stood waiting.

While they watched in wide-eyed, respectful anticipation, he washed in the kitchen, ran a comb through his long hair, and returned to his place at the head of the table. They knelt while he said grace, and waited until he was seated before they took their chairs. The warmth of the stew and the freshly baked bread settled in and spread and they ate in silent gratitude. They tore chunks of bread to wipe their plates clean, and drank cold milk from the morning milking. Last, his wife poured a pitcher full of hot cider laced with cinnamon, and the children clutched their pewter mugs, eyes dancing as they waited for the special treat.

Honeyman packed his pipe and sought the large rocking chair while Hannah and the children cleared the table and finished the dishes. He rocked in silence, going over the message from Washington again and again, forcing the beginnings of a plan to take shape in his mind.

He started at the call from Hannah. "John, it's bedtime for the children." He glanced at the clock on the mantel, startled that it was well past eight o'clock. He rose and walked to the bedroom where he knelt with the family, nodded to Janey, their oldest daughter, who bowed her head and dutifully offered the evening prayer.

He had settled back into the rocking chair, toying with his cold pipe, when Hannah, slender, large eyes, blonde hair, round face, sat down near him.

"Something's happened."

He drew a great breath and looked her in the eyes. "Yes. I'll be gone for a day. Maybe more." For a moment Hannah's breathing constricted, then evened once again, and for a time neither of them moved or spoke. She had learned never to inquire about John's unexplained absences, but she had never learned to rise above the panic that surged in her heart each time he looked her in the eye and quietly said he would be gone. She could manage the house and feed the livestock and milk the Guernsey for a time, but she could not control the sick fear while he was gone. She had survived the arrests, the beating, the hiding in the swamp, but she could not bear the thought that one day a stranger would knock on her door, eyes downcast, hat in his hand and try to explain that John would not be coming home.

She rose in silence, mouth clenched, battling her fears. She had reached the door to their bedroom before John's voice stopped her.

"Hannah, it will be all right. All right."

She nodded and went into the bedroom and behind the closed door, slumped onto the bed. She buried her face in her hands and her shoulders shook with her quiet sobbing.

The morning star was dwindling as Honeyman walked out the back door into the gray, frost-covered world. He fed the beef animals, milked the cow, and with the first arc of sun igniting diamonds in every crystal of frost, walked back to the root cellar with a smoking bucket of milk. Vapor trailed behind his head and his face showed white spots from the deep cold. He left the fresh milk in the root cellar and took the chilled bucket from last night into the house. Hannah and Janey would separate the milk, feed the whey to the sow and her nine pigs, and make square pats of butter and round wheels of cheese from the butterfat to go into the root cellar for barter in Princeton on their next trip into town.

At the breakfast table, he poured thick milk on steaming oatmeal porridge, added honey, and reached for the bread.

"Janey, I'll be gone for a day or two. Got to sell some of the beef animals. You help your mother, and help your brother and sisters with their schoolbooks."

Janey nodded. "When will you be back?"

"Two trips. I'll be back tomorrow, but I'll need to leave again a couple days later."

Janey looked at Hannah from the corners of her eyes and saw the tight lines around her mouth and the forced concentration as her mother kept her eyes on her own bowl of porridge. Janey understood the signs, but not the reasons. She nodded her head without looking at her father and continued her breakfast.

Honeyman finished his breakfast, and without a word went to the bedroom. He took two coins from a box beneath the bed and put them in his pocket, then put on a wool sweater and picked a scarf from a wall peg. He walked back to the kitchen and put on his coat, then his old, black shapeless hat, and walked out the door. He put rope halters with twenty-foot lead ropes on two of the Angus steers and tied them to the fence before he opened the gate and let the other animals up the lane and out to the pasture. He saddled and bridled the big, heavy-footed plow horse with long winter hair hanging six inches from its belly, and walked back to the house.

Hannah and the children stood nearby while he wrapped the hand-knitted scarf high around his neck and tucked the ends inside his coat, then tugged on his mittens. She handed him a small canvas bag with bread and cheese and meat. He stood still for a moment, handling it, looking at it, before he raised his eyes to hers. They stood for a moment in awkward silence before he spoke.

"It's cold. Might give the sow a little grain."

She nodded.

"I'll be back sometime tomorrow—early afternoon—and then I have to go again."

She nodded her head and her eyes dropped.

He turned to the children. "No nonsense. Help your mother."

The sun was a chill, golden ball shining through the bare branches of the eastern trees as he tied the two lead ropes to the saddle and mounted the big sorrel horse. He pulled its head south and clucked it to a walk. The two Angus steers set their legs stiff against the pull of the rope, eyes rolling white as the horse dug its calked shoes into the frozen ground. The two steers tossed their heads, bawling their displeasure at being dragged away from the pen and feed.

Honeyman walked the big horse south on the dirt road that divided the small village of Princeton, past the tiny College of New Jersey, with its great Nassau Hall, watching for British soldiers, making mental notes of the homes and buildings where they were billeted. He marked well the British headquarters, where the arrogant General James Grant now commanded the light infantry of the British Second Brigade, with a troop of light horse under the command of Brigadier General Alexander Leslie. When General Charles Cornwallis was given leave to return to England to be with his gravely ill wife, General Howe had sent Grant to take command of the string of British outposts—Staten Island, Perth Amboy, Brunswick, Princeton, Trenton, Bordentown, Burlington. The command headquarters were at Princeton, near the middle of the eighty-mile spread. The same General Grant who had strutted like a peacock, bragging he could march from one end of the colonies to the other with but five thousand British regulars and the entire American army and militia could not stop him. He had declared loud and long that nothing was more disgusting than American soldiers—undisciplined, cowardly trash!

The road angled southwest and Honeyman's horse plodded faithfully on, across the Stony Brook Bridge and past Worth's Mill where the land flattened nearly level. With the sun approaching its zenith they crossed Eight Mile Run, and Honeyman stopped to loosen the saddle girth and let the animals drink. He ate bread and cheese and drank clear, cold water from the creek before he tightened the cinch, once again mounted the horse, and pushed on. In the early afternoon they crossed Shabbakonk Creek, and in the distance Honeyman could see the clustered trees, with stark, bare branches and limbs that marked Trenton. He pulled the horse to a stop and the Angus steers slowed and stopped, questioning. For a long time he sat the horse, vapors rising from his face, as he carefully studied the town of Trenton in his mind.

The village of Trenton was laid out nearly true to the compass. The south end of the town was very close to the Assunpink Creek, which emptied into the Delaware River at the southwest corner of the village, where the Delaware angled slightly to the right and continued southerly. Queen Street divided the town on a north-south line, with King Street one block west and Quaker Lane one block east. Queen was the single street that continued south to cross the Assunpink on the only bridge at the south end of town. Once across the Assunpink, Queen became Bordentown Road, leading south to Bordentown, Burlington, and Philadelphia.

Running east-west, starting at the south end of town next to the Assunpink Creek and working north, the first street was Front Street, then Second, Third, and Fourth Streets. Clustered among these crossroads of dirt streets were about one hundred homes, some shops and businesses, and the Trenton mills.

All three of the north-south streets—King, Queen, and Quaker Lane—ended where they connected to the Princeton Road. Thus, travelers coming to Trenton on the Princeton Road could choose one of the three streets, Quaker, Queen, or King, to turn south to enter the village.

Honeyman made his decision and clucked to the horse, and moved on. He sat loose and easy in the saddle, turning his head from time to time to check on the cattle he was leading. Coming to the first north-south road, Quaker Lane, he glanced casually to his left at the apple orchard and the cornfield, stark in the bright sunlight and the patchy snow. He turned left onto Quaker Lane, and worked south on the slick glaze where the direct sun had thawed the top of the frozen ground enough to make a watery surface. He nodded and tipped his hat to those who were in the streets, and who he knew to be avid Tories, while his eyes took in everything. He reached Second Street and turned west to Queen Street and paused. Standing tall in the stirrups, he studied the Assunpink Creek, then turned north, moving up Queen Street, once again tipping his hat and calling greetings to those whom he knew to be loyal to the Crown, and who knew him to be an outspoken Tory. At the top of Queen Street, where it ended at the Princeton Road, he turned left to King Street, and turned left once more, moving south on King.

He approached Third Street to his left, with the Methodist Church on the east side of the street, near the far corner. On the west side of King Street, was the large frame home of Stacy Potts. During the past year Honeyman had carefully cultivated the friendship of Potts, who was a declared Tory, faithful to the Crown. It was Potts who had welcomed the British with open arms and generously offered his spacious and comfortable home to them for their headquarters. General William Howe accepted the offer, but it was not British soldiers he sent to occupy Trenton. Howe gave overall command of the forces to German Colonel Carl Emil Kurt von Donop, who established his headquarters in Burlington, south of Trenton halfway to Philadelphia, and gave command of the Trenton post to German Colonel Johann Gottlieb Rall. Von Donop's entire command, including the soldiers assigned to Rall at Trenton, were the blue-coated German Hessians.

In the months since their arrival, Honeyman had quietly learned that neither von Donop nor Rall spoke English, nor did they intend to learn, and their failure to establish open, solid communications with the local Americans had created a sense of nervous unrest between the Hessians and the Americans, both Tories and Patriots. While von Donop had some modicum of regard for Americans as soldiers, Rall held them in utter contempt. He had led his command straight into the breastworks on Long Island and watched the Americans scatter and run in terror. He had led his Hessians into the battle for Fort Washington, and again watched the Americans throw down their muskets and run for the protection of the fort, and then surrender it, all within half a day. It was the Hessians who ordered the Americans to march out of the fort, stripped of all their clothing—the ultimate humiliation—and it was only the angry orders from General Howe himself that saved the Americans from the shame of doing it.

Since taking command at Trenton, Rall's daily patrols had reported the cowardice and disorganization of the Americans camped just across the Delaware River, and of the destitute, inhuman condition of their filthy camps, with sickness rampant, no food, clothing, pay, blankets, or tents, and daily desertions by the hundreds. Rall was absolutely unshakeable in his conclusion that he would beat the Americans by simply waiting for American stupidity and the hardships of a fierce winter to kill those who did not desert. It was ridiculous to order his men to dig trenches and build breastworks in the winter to defend Trenton when it was so clear that it was a senseless waste of time. He laughed at the suggestion the Americans might attack. "Let them," he had bragged. "We'll show them the bayonet. They can't stand the bayonet."

And Honeyman had learned one more thing. The German-trained Hessians brought with them from Europe the centuries-honored European tradition of the right of spoils. A conquering army was entitled to the spoils of their conquest, and the Hessians had stared wide-eyed at the wealth of the American colonies, lusting greedily to conquer and then strip everything they wanted from the homes and businesses of the colonists. Their mistake was they could not tell the difference between a subject loyal to the Crown, and a rebel, whom they were here to defeat. And, being unable to understand English, either spoken or written, they had no idea what the loyal Tory homeowners were shouting at them, nor could they read the written oaths of loyalty to the Crown and England the Tories thrust under their noses, nor did they care. They drove Tories and rebels alike from their homes at bayonet point, plundering at will, carrying off whatever they wished, including their women. General Howe had been appalled and issued harsh orders that the Hessians were to cease the barbaric practice, but the Hessians grunted and smiled and continued as though Howe had never spoken.

Thus it was that when the Hessians were ordered to occupy the beautiful and prosperous village of Trenton, many of the residents had abandoned their homes and businesses, and the Trenton mills, and the fourteen hundred Hessian soldiers had gleefully moved in to occupy the vacant buildings. They stabled their horses in some of the homes, tearing out walls to accommodate the animals. They threw the horse dung into the kitchen until it was filled, then knocked out the windows and threw it out into the gardens and the cultivated yards.

Honeyman dismounted in front of Rall's headquarters and tied the reins of the big horse to the large iron ring anchored in the stone post, then tied the lead ropes to the two cattle to a different post and walked to the front door. A picket stopped him.

"I'm John Honeyman. I have a contract to deliver beef. I've brought two." He gestured over his shoulder with his thumb towards the two steers.

The Hessian picket understood nothing, but he recognized Honeyman, who had delivered beef half a dozen times. He pointed down the street to the Old Barracks, and Honeyman nodded.

Five minutes later Honeyman turned the horse west off of King Street and led the cattle past the old, two-storied square stone building that stood at the bend in the road where King Street joined Front Street within sight of the Delaware River to the south. The Old Barracks had been built in 1758 to house three hundred soldiers during the French and Indian wars, and in need could accommodate over four hundred. Now it was filled with Hessians and a few Tory refugees. Cattle and livestock pens with feed and water had been erected behind it, and were used to hold British horses, and cattle to feed the troops.

Honeyman waited at the back door of the Old Barracks for the captain in charge of the livestock, then led the steers to the cattle pen furthest west. While he slipped the halters off the animals, he quickly counted the cattle in the pen. He coiled and tied the lead ropes while the captain issued his receipt, then remounted his horse. Five minutes later he again approached the picket stationed at the front entrance of the headquarters in the Potts's home, and held up the piece of paper.

The picket opened the door and gestured Honeyman inside.

Honeyman nodded and walked into the room that once had been the parlor, now converted to an office and waiting room. He took off his hat and approached the desk facing the door. The young lieutenant raised his head from a large ledger and waited for Honeyman to speak.

"I got a receipt for two more cattle."

"What price?" The German accent was thick.

"On contract. Same as always."

The lieutenant took the paper, checked the signature, and spoke to Honeyman without looking at him. "Wait."

Honeyman nodded and moved to a hard bench against the south wall, shoes sounding hollow on the hardwood floor. The bench creaked as he sat, and he waited until the young lieutenant was absorbed in working with quill and ink before he yawned and stretched, then leaned back. Casually he studied the large map on the wall behind the lieutenant, quickly memorizing names, locations, and numbers.

The lieutenant used a key to open a metal box in a desk drawer and laid the paperwork on his desk while he recalled the word he needed. "Sign."

Honeyman walked to the desk, briefly scanned the paper, signed his name, and waited. The lieutenant put the voucher inside the metal box, counted out four coins, locked and replaced the box, then opened a second drawer and studied the contract. He stood and held out the coins to Honeyman. "Pay." He took a breath while he struggled with the next words, hating the struggle of speaking in English. "More later?"

Honeyman put the money in a leather purse, stuffed it into his trouser pocket, and nodded, then held up three fingers as he spoke. "Three more."

"Good ones?"

"Angus. Good. More in January."

The lieutenant nodded. "Talk later."

Honeyman nodded in agreement, then tapped himself on the chest and pointed south. "Stay tonight. Same price?"

The lieutenant nodded, and Honeyman drew one of the two smaller coins he had brought from home from his pocket and handed it to the lieutenant, who dropped it into the money box and spoke.

"Tell Captain Schultz. You stay. Old Barracks."

Honeyman bobbed his head. "Thank you." He turned on his heel and walked out into the late afternoon sunlight, where the old sorrel horse stood at the hitching post, head down, half-asleep, one hind leg cocked. Honeyman smiled at the picket by the front door, untied the bridle reins and mounted, then paused for one moment as he realized that the only two cannon he had seen in town were the two now before him, in front of the headquarters building.

The horse plodded down King Street once more, past the Old Barracks building to the rear entrance, where Honeyman stopped at the door to knock.

"I stay. One night."

The sergeant nodded indifferently and pointed to the horse pens.

Honeyman led the horse into the nearest of the three large pens, stripped the saddle, blanket, and bridle, and watched the jaded animal wearily work its way through the herd to the water tank. He carried his gear back outside the pen, closed and latched the gate, and climbed the fence to peer over the top rail. With the practiced eye of a stockman he counted the horses by threes, in all the pens. One hundred eighty-eight head. He marked the number in his mind, walked to stow his gear in the tack shed, then climbed the stairs to the second floor of the barracks building and put his blanket and pillow on a bunk against the south wall, beneath a window.

Supper was boiled beef and cabbage with hard, dark bread. Finished, he followed some Hessian soldiers out into the frigid night air, up to the Oak Tree tavern. He used his last coin from home to pay for a pint of hot spiced cider, took his change and his steaming pewter mug, and settled onto a stool at a small table in the corner.

The soldiers ordered dark beer, and as the evening wore on, their tongues loosened with each succeeding pint. They became loud in singing the drinking songs of their homeland, then boistrous and profane in their cursing of the German army in general and their officers and current duty in particular. Honeyman nursed his hot cider, eyes half-closed, appearing to be absorbed in his own problems, while he listened intently, piecing together what he could of the half-German, half-English exchanges in the confusion of the tavern.

The daily patrols up and down the Delaware River ordered by Rall were stupid—the American patrols every morning and evening were cowardly—hiding behind trees, shooting from ambush—Rall moving the two cannon up and down King Street with fife and drum every day as a show of strength was utter idiocy—German girls were far superior to colonial girls—if Rall would spend as much time taking command as he did drinking half the night and sleeping it off in the morning they could do some soldiering—build fortifications—defenses for the village—the weather was bound to get worse—up north past Riegelsville a cold snap had frozen eighteen inches of ice on the river—military food wasn't fit—the German Christmas celebration was coming—holiday—no duty for a day—drinking—cards—carousing—a break from the misery and grinding monotony—a toast to Christmas—and another toast to Christmas.

The dregs in Honeyman's cider mug were cold when he followed the last German soldiers out of the tavern into the starry night, their boots crunching in the frozen mud and slush as they trudged back down King Street to the barracks.

The morning reveille drum came rattling in the six o'clock gray. At seven o'clock, with the skiff of high clouds in the eastern sky shot through with red and yellow from the rising sun, Honeyman turned his horse north on King Street. A little past one in the afternoon he reined the old sorrel in at the feed pen of his home, racked the saddle, bridle, and blanket in the milking barn, threw a forkload of hay into the manger, and walked to meet the children as they came running to throw their arms about his waist.

At seven o'clock two mornings later he stood in the kitchen, drew Hannah close and held her for a moment, then each of the children, before he walked out to the horse, already saddled and waiting, with the three Angus steers on lead ropes tied to the feed pen. At a little after eleven o'clock he stopped at Eight Mile Run to let the horse and the three Angus steers water while he ate cheese and meat and bread. At half past one he pulled the big horse to a stop less than one mile from the junction of Princeton Road and Quaker Lane. For a time he sat the old horse while his eyes scoured the orchard and cornfield ahead to his left, then the road straight ahead, as the three Angus steers milled about, throwing their heads against the restraint of the lead ropes. There was nothing moving on the road, or in the orchard or cornfield. He checked his pocket to be certain he had the usual two coins, and an old, crumpled copy of a receipt from cattle delivered to the Hessians six weeks earlier.

He moved past the junction of Princeton Road and Quaker Lane, on past Queen, then King Streets, and angled back to the northwest on the old Scotch Road, turned back to his left, southwest on the Ferry Road, down to the River Road that paralleled the Delaware. He turned right once again, moving northwest with the Delaware River in sight to his left. He passed the Hermitage on his left, continued one mile, and again pulled the horse to a stop and dismounted. He led one of the steers into the brush and trees and willows along the riverbank and tied it to a tree, then returned to the horse. Forty minutes later he rode past the Old Barracks building and stopped at the rear entrance and knocked on the door. A captain appeared and eyed Honeyman for a moment before he remembered him.

"Ja?"

Honeyman pointed and spoke, watching the Hessian's eyes to be certain he understood. "Two more beef. Lost number three. Down by the river, west. Leave two here, and go catch the third one. Now. Before dark."

He penned the steers and coiled the two lead ropes and tied them to the saddle, then rummaged through the tack shed until he found a whip with a five-foot stock and a twelve-foot lash. Three minutes later Honeyman raised the old horse to a lumbering, rough trot, headed west on Second Street towards the River Road with the whip clutched in his right hand. Once again, he passed the Hermitage and ten minutes later left the River Road, watching sharp as he plowed through the willows and brush that grew heavy as he approached the Delaware. He stopped the horse twenty feet short of the black steer and it lunged and bawled, the whites of its eyes showing as it set its legs stiff against the taut rope.

Honeyman dismounted, tied the reins together, and threw them back over the horse's head, then walked towards the steer. The big horse's head came up, startled, questioning at being left saddled, unhobbled, and untied. The steer bawled again and threw its head from side to side as Honeyman worked down the rope, talking low. He reached the halter and quickly released the jaw strip as the animal reared back and jerked free, backing up, not knowing what to do with its sudden freedom. Then it turned and kicked its hocks high as it plunged away from Honeyman, rattling the brush and thick willows.

Honeyman coiled the lead rope and halter and gave the animal a fifty-yard lead before he started after it, trotting, shouting, cracking the whip like a pistol shot in the fading light of late afternoon. The frightened steer turned away from the river and trotted out into the open, ears pricked, head high and swinging from side to side, lost, bewildered. Honeyman followed, stumbling on the uneven, frozen ground, whip popping as he called again and again. The steer crossed the River Road into an open field and Honeyman followed.

He was twenty yards past the road when he saw the mounted riders a quarter mile farther north, up the road, moving towards him at an easy lope. In the mid-afternoon sunlight he stopped to stare at them, panting from his run, vapor rising from his face. At one hundred yards he shouted to them, "Head that steer! I'll pay you!"

The riders smacked their spurs to their horses and came at him at a full gallop. At fifty yards he saw the muskets slung on their backs with the bayonets pointing upward, and he turned to run as hard as he could, slipping on the crusted, uneven ice and snow. They caught up to him, one on each side, and knocked him to the ground and one dived onto him, then the other. He got his knees under his body and threw them off and ran, and again they caught him. They threw him down and one quickly used the lead rope he carried to tie him, hand and foot, while the other one threw the whip away.

He strained against the ropes while the two men sat for a moment, panting to catch their breath, one licking knuckles that were torn and bleeding from being driven against frozen earth and ice in their brief battle, while the other one roughly went through Honeyman's pockets. He jerked out the two coins and the crumpled receipt. He smoothed the worn paper and read. He lowered the paper and raised his eyes.

"John Honeyman?"

Honeyman strained against the ropes, then turned hot on the man nearest him. "Who are you? Robbers? You want the money? Take it. It's all I've got."

The man rose to his feet, voice filled with anger. "You're under arrest in the name of General George Washington and the Continental army of the United States."

Honeyman's mouth dropped open for a second. "You're soldiers? Where're your uniforms?"

The man wiped a grimy sleeve across his mouth. "I lost mine at Long Island." He jerked Honeyman to his feet, still tied. "You're going across the river."

"Why?" he cried. "I'm a Patriot. I'm on your side."

The man paused and thrust his face close to Honeyman's, and his eyes were flashing as he thrust the yellow receipt under Honeyman's nose. "You're the Tory that's been delivering beef to feed the Hessians at Trenton—six or eight head this month, just like the one you were chasing today. There's a few men on the other side of the river that would like to talk to you before we hang you."

He loosened the lead rope from Honeyman's feet and cut it just below his bound wrists. He fashioned a noose and slipped it over Honeyman's head and handed the rope end up to the other soldier who had caught their horses and was now beside them, mounted.

He spoke to Honeyman as he mounted his own horse. "You can make a break any time you want and save us the trouble of hanging you later." He drew a pistol from his saddle holster and leveled it at Honeyman's head at near point-blank range. "And should the noose fail, I won't." He reined his horse around and started north, Honeyman forced to trot to keep up.

The sun was reaching for the western rim when they turned southwest towards McKonkey's Ferry and it was half-gone when the two soldiers docked their boat on the Pennsylvania side of the Delaware and walked their prisoner into the American camp. Five minutes later the two troopers were led by a captain to Washington's headquarters at the east end of camp in the two-story stone home of William Keith. The picket at the door stopped them, staring at Honeyman.

"For what purpose does the captain approach?"

"We've captured a Tory who has information about Trenton. The general will want to know."

The picket considered. "I'll advise the general's aide." He rapped on the door and waited, then rapped again, and seconds later it opened. A major in full uniform stood in the doorway, puzzled at the sight of Honeyman, clothing dirtied from the fight in the snowy field, hands tied. He waited for the picket to speak.

"Sir, the captain says this man is a Tory. Might know about Trenton."

The major looked at the captain. "You sure of this?"

"Yes."

"Does he have a name?"

"John Honeyman." He handed the Hessian receipt to the major.

The major read it and shrugged. "Wait here. I'll tell the general." He turned on his heel and closed the door against the freezing air and returned to open it two minutes later. "You will bring the prisoner in. The general wishes to speak to you."

The captain blinked in surprise. "All of us?"

"Yes."

The captain followed the major down the hall with Honeyman behind and then the two soldiers. Their boots clumped on the polished hardwood floor and the sound was strange in the silence of the building. The major stopped at a door, straightened his tunic, and rapped.

"Enter." The voice was restrained.

The major swung the heavy door open. "Sir, the prisoner is here with the men who captured him."

"Bring them in."

The major led and the five men lined up before Washington's heavy oak desk. The room was average sized, furnished with solid but not costly appointments, with a great stone fireplace behind Washington. His uniform was clean, proper, long hair pulled back and tied behind. Tall, sitting erect, his face was clouded, dark, chin set like granite, blue-gray eyes boring into Honeyman. He held up the crumpled receipt. "Is this yours?"

Honeyman's words came hot. "These men took that from me, and my money. They had no right!"

"You're John Honeyman?"

Honeyman clamped his mouth shut and stared defiantly back at Washington.

Washington shifted his eyes to the two soldiers, their tattered clothing still showing the dirt and stains of the fight in the field and the bloodied knuckles of the soldier on Honeyman's right. "You caught this man?"

"Yes, sir."

"What made you think he is a Tory?"

"He's been delivering beef to the Hessians for months. We seen him. That receipt proves it. That's what he was doing today."

Slowly Washington laid the incriminating receipt in the center of his desk as his eyes narrowed. "Leave him here. I want to talk to him alone."

The major gaped. "You want us to leave you here alone with this man?"

"Yes. If he comes out of this room before I call for you, shoot him."

The astonished major squared his shoulders. "Yes, sir." He led the captain and the two soldiers into the austere hallway and closed the door, eyebrows still arched in surprise.

Washington waited until he heard boots fading in the hallway, then quickly stood and circled the desk where he untied Honeyman's hands. Honeyman began rubbing the circulation back into his wrists.

"Are you all right? Hurt?"

Honeyman shook his head. "All right."

"We haven't much time. What have you learned?"

"Do you have a map of Trenton?"

Washington hurried to his side of the desk, unrolled a large map and anchored the four corners with leather pouches filled with buckshot. Honeyman leaned over it, studying for a moment before he began.

"The British have men camped here"—he pointed and shifted his finger from place to place as he spoke—"at Perth Amboy, Brunswick, Princeton, Trenton, Bordentown, Burlington. Fourteen hundred at

Trenton under Colonel Rall. Johann Gottlieb Rall. He has a couple of officers in his command, one named Knyphausen and one named Loss-berg. A Colonel von Donop is down here at Bordentown and has com-mand of all the troops south of Princeton, including Rall's command at Tenton, and they're all Germans. Hessians."

He paused for a moment. "Rall's a fighter, but he's no commander. He parades every day but hasn't turned one shovelful of dirt to dig trenches or build fortifications to defend Trenton. I saw only two can-non in town, both right in front of his headquarters, here on King Street"—he pointed—"and he has his men parade them to the top of King Street every morning with fife and drum as a show of force."

Again he paused to shake his head in disgust.

Washington interrupted. "How do you know about their troop placements and the numbers and commanders?"

"Saw them on a big map while I was waiting for my money in Rall's anteroom last Thursday."

Washington nodded and Honeyman went on.

"Rall's a heavy drinker and his men know it. He drinks late at night and sleeps it off in the mornings. Sometimes he's still in bed at ten o'clock. His troops condemn him for it. Morale's low. The Hessian sol-diers don't know why they don't cross the river right now and take your camp and get it over. They're looking forward to the German Christmas celebration—a day free of duty—drinking—gambling—anything to break the monotony."

Honeyman stopped to wipe at his mouth with a dirty sleeve. "Rall's opinion of your army could not be lower. He can't find a reason to do anything in Trenton to defend it because it's ridiculous to think you could cross the river, and if you did, he'd wipe you out in half an hour."

"How did you learn about Rall's opinion of us, and his troop's opinion of him?"

"Spent three hours last Thursday night in the Oak Tree tavern. It was filled with Hessian regulars. After their second pint of dark beer tongues were loose."

Washington cleared his throat. "Any boats?" He scarcely breathed, waiting for the answer.

"None. Not one on the river from below Assunpink Creek clear up to the road to McKonkey's Ferry. None in town, none being built anywhere I could see. No boats."

Washington drew a great breath of relief and asked, "Where are his cannon emplacements outside the town?"

Honeyman stared into Washington's eyes and slowly shook his head. He had been forced to serve with the British during the French and Indian wars. He had been there when the British fought the French in the classic, ironclad European rules of engagement that required the opposing armies to form up in ranks, or squares, and stand out in the open and blast each other with everything they had. He knew the sick devastation cannon and grapeshot could wreak on formations of soldiers, cutting down troops in great swaths. He had fought the Indians who crouched behind anything that could hide them, and he knew the terror that cannon struck into them when the blasting started and the grapeshot came whistling, shredding trees, stumps, brush, and whining off of rocks. Commanders in all armies in the civilized world knew the critical, decisive role of cannon in ground warfare, and they knew that the strategies of most battles were centered around the cannon. What Honeyman did not understand was how Colonel Rall had failed to build one single cannon emplacement to defend the village entrusted to him, regardless of his contempt for the American army.

"No cannon emplacements." Honeyman waited for Washington's response.

Washington was incredulous. "None? Anywhere?"

"None. Not in Trenton, not on any road approaching Trenton. The cannon are over there somewhere, maybe inside barns and sheds. But there are none visible."

Washington shook his head in utter disbelief and Honeyman went on.

"About three hundred Hessian troops are here in the Old Barracks, and the rest are scattered throughout Trenton wherever they could find a place. No particular order, no heavy concentrations, except at the Old Barracks. They got one hundred eighty-eight horses in the pens behind the barracks."

"Have they built more bridges across the Assunpink?"

Honeyman shook his head. "None. Only one bridge. The old one, at the foot of Queen Street."

Again Washington shook his head. "Any outposts watching the roads into Trenton?"

"Here, half a mile or so north of Trenton on the road just below where the Pennington Road and the old Scotch Road join. A Lieutenant Wiederhold has a few men there. It's the home of a cooper—makes barrels—named Richard Howell. He has his shop right there in the building." He moved his finger. "And here, on the River Road, just northwest of town. The Hermitage—Dickinson's home. They've got a patrol there. Those are the only two outposts I saw on the big map at headquarters. There're still some Hessians camped across the river from here but Rall's going to order them back to Trenton any day. They're usually out on patrols during the day."

For a moment Washington pondered in amazement. "No cannon, no boats, no bridges, and nearly no one watching the roads?"

Honeyman shrugged. "His opinion of American soldiers couldn't be worse."

Washington studied the map for several seconds. "Who's in command at Princeton?"

"Grant. General James Grant. Cornwallis was given leave to return to England. His wife's ill."

Washington's eyebrows arched in surprise. "Cornwallis is gone?"

"Yes."

For half a minute Washington's finger traced the critical positions on the map while he committed to memory the vital information he had just received. He raised his eyes back to Honeyman.

"Is there anything we've missed?"

"Yes. The Hessians speak almost no English, and read none of it. They can't tell a Tory from a Patriot, and they've looted and pillaged every place they've been, Tories and Patriots alike. The result is, the Tories are as afraid of them as the Patriots. The British don't like it but can't stop them."

Washington glanced at the large clock on the mantel and opened a desk drawer to draw out a large key. He handed it to Honeyman.

"You're going to be locked in a building at the north end of camp. About two o'clock in the morning a fire will break out at the south end of camp, not far from a munitions magazine. Everyone will be running, and in the uproar, use the key to let yourself out. Be sure to take the key with you. From there, you will have to manage on your own. Our troops will be under orders to shoot you if they can. I'm sorry, but there's no other way. Head north, then cross the Delaware any way you can and drop the key in the river. Turn yourself over to one of Rall's patrols. Tell them you were captured but escaped and that you saw conditions here. They'll take you to Rall, and you tell him what you have seen here—how it is with us in this camp. I don't believe many more than half my men are fit for duty. Tell him the truth, because he knows some of it, but not all."

Honeyman listened intently. "I understand."

"A few months from now someone will deliver fifty pounds in British coin to you at your home. Use it to take care of your family and to continue in the cattle business, supplying beef to the British. Keep up appearances as a Tory Loyalist. We may need you again."

Honeyman nodded.

Washington hesitated, then spoke one more time. "I can't tell you why, but I can tell you that what you brought me today is possibly the most critical information I've received in the past year. Most people will never hear of it, but you and I, and the Almighty, will know what you've done for America and liberty. As I am standing here now, I know He is watching."

For a moment a feeling seized both men and they stood there gazing into each other's hearts, and they knew, and it was enough.

Honeyman thrust the key into his pocket. "I'm ready."

Washington tied his hands once again, then strode to the door and opened it. "Aide!"

The major led the captain and two troopers into the room where they stood at attention, waiting.

Washington stood behind his desk. "You've done well. This man has given me much information. Give me the names of the two soldiers who brought him in. I will write letters of commendation." He looked at Honeyman. "I've searched the man and he has nothing. Take him to the servant's house at the north end of camp and lock him in. Post a guard, and if he tries to escape, shoot him. We'll deal with him tomorrow. Any questions?"

"Shall we leave his hands tied, sir?"

Washington reflected. "No, not in this cold. And give him something warm to eat. We have not yet descended to the level of the Hessians." He drew a breath, then finished. "Thank you. That is all."

They walked Honeyman the length of the camp and his heart fell. Soldiers huddled together around fires, summer clothing in tatters, shaking in the bitter cold. A few had broken and worn-out shoes tied on with cord, while most others had wrapped their feet in worn-out blankets or hides of animals. The blankets had absorbed water during the day and were now frozen. The hospital tents were overflowing with the sick and dying. Faces gaunt and bearded, arms and legs shrunk, hair long and matted, the men stared at him from sunken eyes, and he felt the hatred coming from them like something alive.

They shoved him into the small, plank-walled building, and the captain held a lantern while the major untied him. They left him with a blanket in the pitch-blackness of the barren room and one picket with a musket and bayonet outside the door. When their footsteps faded, he felt his way to the door and silently slipped the key into the door lock to be certain it fit, then shoved it back into his pocket. Five minutes later the two officers returned and thrust a wooden bowl at him with a watery gruel made from wild cabbage and fish, with a crust of dark bread.

"That's more than our troops had for supper," the major growled. "I hope you find it to your Tory taste."

Honeyman gagged on the steaming gruel and set it uneaten on the floor in the corner nearest the door while he worked the stale bread. He felt his way into a corner away from the door, wrapped himself in the blanket and sat down, shaking, waiting for warmth. It came slowly and the shaking stopped. For a time he listened to the faint sounds outside before he heard a quick scratching scurry somewhere in the room, then another, and then the clatter of a spoon on the floor loud in the silence, and he realized rats were into the hot gruel.

He slapped the flat of his hand on the floor and for a moment there was quiet, and then the rats continued. He listened to the sounds of them lapping at the greasy broth and tearing at the chunks of bitter cabbage and old fish. The sounds stopped and once again he slapped his hand on the floor, then stomped his foot several times. He heard the scurrying, and then silence. The picket outside worked with his key and opened the door, holding a lantern high with one hand, his bayonet ready with the other.

"What's going on in here?" he demanded, peering into the dimly lit room.

"Rats," Honeyman answered from the corner. "Rats ate my supper. I scared them away."

"Stay away from the door and be quiet." The picket closed the door and Honeyman heard the lock working. He pulled the blanket tight around his shoulders and once more settled with his back in the corner, legs crossed before him. The shaking slowly left as the warmth came creeping, and his thoughts went back to the brief, intense meeting with Washington, and he forced his mind to repeat the orders Washington had given him. A fire—use the key—move north out of camp—they will come after you shooting—get across the river any way you can—throw the key in the river—find a Hessian patrol—don't tell anyone—not Hannah—not the children—he reached to pull Hannah close—then the children—Janey throwing her arms about his waist—hugging with all her strength—the rich smell of Hannah's cooking—the warmth of the kitchen—

"Fire!"

Honeyman started and jerked and his eyes opened wide in the pitch-blackness. He shook his head, disoriented for a moment, unable to come from the warmth of his own kitchen to the frigid blackness of a locked room where he was being held prisoner.

"Fire by the powder magazine!" The shout came again and then a few voices raised and then a hundred frightened voices and the pounding of countless feet. Honeyman threw back his blanket and scrambled across the floor to the wall, and he felt for the door and kicked at it and pounded with both fists.

"Open up! You can't leave me here!"

There was no response and again Honeyman pounded with his knotted fists and shouted with all his strength. "Open this door! You can't leave me here!"

The turmoil outside dwindled and Honeyman waited until it was quiet before he pounded once more and listened for ten seconds. There was no sound. Cautiously he worked the key in the lock, swung the door open six inches to peer outside, then opened it two feet to thrust his head out while he jammed the key back in his pocket. He saw the great orange glow in the night sky at the south end of camp and heard the distant, frantic shouts. He threw the door wide, darted outside, and sprinted north, dodging, avoiding firelight, not looking back. A patrol coming in from the north was suddenly before him and he plowed into them, scattered them, knocked them rolling in his headlong charge for the darkness of the brush and willows thick along the riverbank. He heard the angry shouts behind, but he did not pause to look back. The first musket ball came whistling four feet over his head and he ducked as he heard the cracking bang and then three more came, one on top of the other. He felt a tug at his right hip and he veered left and onward into the night. Underbrush tangled his feet and he went down and bounded back up, legs pumping, scrub oak branches clawing at his face and he raised his arms to shield his eyes, and then he was in the blackness and the shouts from behind were fading.

He angled towards the river and was soon hidden in tall willows. He plowed on, holding his arms before his face, finally slowing when he broke out onto the ice of the frozen river. He stayed on the river, trotting, slipping, working north on the ice. Minutes passed before he stopped, fighting for breath, vapors rising in a cloud. He waited until his breathing slowed, and he held it as he closed his eyes and concentrated to listen. There was only a faint sound in the distance in the direction of the camp. Once again he set out at a careful trot on the river-ice near the bank, moving north. Half an hour later he stopped and again listened, and there was no sound. He worked his way back into the willows until he was hidden from all but the stars overhead, and he stopped and sat down. Slowly he caught his breath, and he wrapped his arms about his knees for warmth against the raw, freezing cold, and waited. An hour later he stood to work the cramps from his legs and beat circulation back into them, and once again sat down to wait.

The first streaks of gray divided the earth from the heavens to the east, and he stood and once again flailed his arms and worked his legs. He looked down to see what the musket ball had done to his hip. His coat and trousers were torn, and there was a dirty streak on his skin, but it had not drawn blood.

In the gray of a frozen dawn he once more ventured out onto the ice and peered up and down the riverbank, searching, but there was no boat, and his eyes narrowed as he studied the river. Four hundred yards wide, frozen most of the way, with an open, flowing channel, heavy with chunks of ice, and shrouded with a low fog. He glanced east, where the sky was bright with a sun not yet risen, and he made his calculations.

The American patrols are already on their way—no time.

He didn't hesitate. He broke into a hard run for the far shore and didn't stop until he felt the ice beneath his feet begin to sag. At the first crack he threw himself down feet first, sliding, legs spread wide. He nearly reached the open channel before the ice crumbled beneath him and he gasped at the bite of the black water and then he was swimming among the ice chunks, head held high, gasping as the water numbed him. He kept his arms and legs working by sheer will, eyes locked onto the far side of the channel—thirty yards away—twenty—ten—and then he was there. He smashed through the thin ice, driving forward until it thickened and he could not smash it with his flailing arms. He reached as far onto it as he could and kicked with all his strength and got one leg up and worked until the other one was up and he was on the solid ice, laid out flat. He inched forward until it was thick enough, and then stood, dripping, ice crusting on his clothing and in his long hair and three-day beard stubble. He flailed his arms against the numbness and forced his legs to work as he stumbled towards the New Jersey shore.

He reached the willows and remembered, and it took two minutes for his numb fingers to fumble the key from his pocket and he threw it skittering across the ice and watched it drop into the black water. Then he turned and worked his way through the riverbank willows, out past the scrub oak and underbrush, into the open. His coat and shoes were frozen stiff. His hair was a solid mat. His face showed white spots, and he could not feel his ears or his fingers. He stumbled on through the frozen snow, falling, struggling to rise, until he reached the Hessian outpost. The breakfast fires were still warm but no one remained in camp; they were all out on morning patrols. He walked on to the road and turned east towards Trenton.

He didn't know how long he stumbled on. He only knew that he finally fell and got back to his hands and knees, doubting he could rise one more time when he heard the sound of horses' hooves on the frozen ground. He looked up the road towards the morning sun and saw the silhouettes of four mounted riders wearing the tall hats of the Hessian army—a patrol returning to their camp. They surrounded him and dismounted and he repeated his name to them, but they only shrugged.

He forced his frozen jaw to work. "Rall. Take me to Rall. Colonel Rall."

They recognized the name of their commanding officer and after a terse discussion, three of them lifted him onto the horse of the fourth man, who scrambled up behind Honeyman to hold him on, and they turned their horses towards Trenton at an easy lope.

They carried him into the Old Barracks and sat him beside the huge, potbellied stove at one end of the main floor. When his frozen clothing had thawed enough, they stripped him, bundled him in blankets, and draped his clothing on chairs next to the stove. They brought steaming coffee and he held the mug with both hands and sipped at it while his color slowly returned. At one o'clock in the afternoon he ate boiled carrots and crisped sow belly. At three o'clock he put his dry clothing back on and the Hessians noticed the rip made by the musket ball and the black streak where it had creased his hip. At three-thirty they walked him north on King Street to Rall's headquarters and waited until the aide led them down a hallway and rapped on a door. Two minutes later Honeyman was facing Colonel Johann Gottlieb Rall, sparse, long-nosed, thin-lipped, with faded eyes. He remained seated behind a large desk in a library. A civilian was seated to his right.

Rall spoke in German and the civilian translated. "You are John Honeyman, who has contracted beef with us?"

Honeyman nodded. "Yes."

"One of my patrols discovered a large horse northwest of here yesterday. Saddled and bridled in a field."

"That was my horse."

"For what reason was it in the field?" Rall leaned forward, eyes narrowed, waiting.

"I left the horse to catch one of my cattle that escaped. I was captured by an American patrol. They took me to their camp across the river."

Rall nodded faintly. "So I understand. You escaped?"

"Yes."

"How?"

"There was a fire down by the munitions magazine. I broke free while they were putting it out."

"You crossed the river in a boat?"

"No. Swam."

One of the soldiers spoke. "Sir, we discovered him this morning with his clothing wet and frozen stiff. He had fallen and could not rise. There is a place on his hip where a bullet tore his clothing and left a welt."

Rall spoke to Honeyman. "They shot at you?"

"When I escaped."

"Did you see their camp? Their condition?"

"Yes. All of it."

Rall leaned back and his face relaxed. "Good. Take a seat. Tell me. Are their soldiers in good health? Good food? Good clothing? High morale? Do they have enough men and arms and ammunition to come here and attack us in Trenton?"

Notes

John Honeyman was an Irish emigrant who had unwillingly served in the Seven Years' War as General James Wolfe's bodyguard. The novel's description of Honeyman's actions in his critical and heroic role as a spy for George Washington before the battle of Trenton is accurate (see Ketchum, *The Winter Soldiers*, pp. 239–42; Leckie, *George Washington's War*, pp. 317–18). In addition, Washington did indeed provide a letter of protection for Honeyman's wife and children.

The dismissive attitude of Colonel Rall towards the American army and the uncivilized actions of the Hessian troops in Trenton are accurate (see Ketchum, *The Winter Soldiers*, pp. 229–30, 234–35).

The College of New Jersey was established in 1746 and ten years later was moved to Princeton, where the entire college was contained in Nassau Hall. One hundred and fifty years later, British North America's fourth college adopted the name Princeton University (see "About Princeton" at **www.princeton.edu**).

Germans traditionally celebrated Christmas over a two-day period, December 25 and 26 (see Smith, *The Battle of Trenton*, p. 17).

CHAPTER IV

★ ★ ★

A stiff southeast wind arose before dawn to whip whitecaps choppy on the black water in the channel of the Delaware. By noon the sun was a dull glow through the gathering clouds, and by four o'clock the wind had died and the Continental army camp was in a frozen overcast that shut out the setting sun. In the eerie twilight soldiers gathered around campfires, shaking from the cold, cooking whatever they could scavenge for supper.

Billy sat on a log, wooden bowl on the snow between his spread feet, hands thrust towards the fire, watching the wispy steam rise from the cooking pot set on rocks in the flames. At noon Eli had returned to camp with a porcupine the size of a dog. Skinned, it looked much like a pig. Cut into strips and thrown into the stew pot, with the head and flat tail following, it had cooked down to a greasy gruel. Billy had added salt from a natural salt lick they had discovered west of camp, and Eli had dug frozen bulbs and roots from the forest and washed them in river water before he split them and dropped them into the steaming morass. Twenty other men had stopped long enough to see the porcupine pelt and most had moved on. Eight remained, silent, the dancing flames reflecting in their eyes and off their hollow, bearded faces. They sat with dripping noses, waiting with their bowls in their hands.

Next to Billy, Eli raised his eyes to track an officer riding a black gelding west, away from the river, and his brow wrinkled. "That's the sixth one in the past hour," he said quietly, "and I didn't recognize three of them."

Billy wiped his hand across his mouth. "Neither did I. They're headed for Washington's headquarters. Must be something heavy."

"They better be finding a way to get some beef or mutton in here, and some flour." Eli's eyes swept the circle of staring faces. "This bunch won't last in this weather without it." He reached to stir the pot and raised a stringy strip of meat for a moment. "Almost ready."

Suddenly Billy raised his head and turned, peering southwest into the gloom. Eli caught the movement and glanced at him, then turned his head to track with Billy's eyes. "See something?"

"I thought so. Out there in the trees." For ten seconds they watched before Billy shrugged. "Shadows. Nothing." They turned back to the stew pot and Billy raised the large wooden spoon smoking and blew on it before he gingerly sipped. "Ready."

The men took turns holding their bowls over the pot while Billy dipped the steaming mixture; they settled back down to sit, clutching the bowl with both hands while they sipped at it and felt the warmth settle into their middles. One minute later Eli casually stood and walked to the edge of the firelight and stopped, facing southwest, sipping at his bowl. Ten seconds later Billy followed to stand silently at his side.

"You were right," Eli said softly. "Someone's out there."

"Patrol?"

"Wrong direction."

"See them?"

"More like sensed it."

"Do we go?"

"I'll leave in a minute. Get a lantern and put out the light and follow."

Billy walked slowly back to the fire, working at his bowl, and settled back onto the log. Eli finished his and scrubbed the bowl with snow and leaned it against the hot rocks, and a moment later was gone in the darkness. A minute later Billy picked a lantern from a tree, turned the wheel to put it out, and disappeared into the woods. Two minutes later he was moving southwest through the trees, waiting for a signal from

Eli. He had gone another hundred yards when Eli was suddenly beside him.

"There're tracks. Light the lantern."

Billy struck flint to steel and half a minute later a yellow circle of lantern light cast shadows while they stood close, shielding it, then dropped to their haunches to study the tracks at their feet. Eli studied long and hard, then rose and walked ten feet farther and again dropped to his haunches, his long Pennsylvania rifle in one hand as he bent low to peer intently.

He rose and Billy put out the lantern as Eli turned to him and spoke. "Fresh. Ten minutes. Thirteen of them, most sick, two hurt bad. Two old, three young. The two moving strongest got knapsacks, food I think. Blood spots in six sets of tracks—they aren't traveling fast. Headed downriver. Maybe Philadelphia."

Billy drew and released a great breath. "Deserters."

"That's what I think."

"Orders are to shoot them on sight."

"That what you want to do?"

"No. I'd rather try to bring them back."

"I doubt there's much fight left in 'em. I think we can bluff."

Billy pondered for a moment. "Let's give it a try."

"You keep moving in a straight line with these tracks. Try to catch up and then stay close behind. I'll try to get ahead and when they come to a clear place I'll stop 'em. When I call to you, you answer. Make 'em think they're surrounded. We'll get their muskets and take 'em all back. Something goes wrong, we'll meet back at camp."

Billy nodded, and five seconds later Eli had disappeared silently while Billy took a bearing in the dark and moved ahead. After one hundred paces he stopped to hold his breath in the frigid air, listening for any sound that would tell him they were laying an ambush. There was nothing but the far distant howl of a wolf, and then the raucous bark of a farm dog, and then silence. Billy moved on. Six hundred paces later he stopped and ahead he heard the sound of men moving through brush and trees, and the soft sound of wrapped feet in crusted snow. He pushed on and ten seconds later he heard the labored breathing of sick men struggling, and then their muted gasping in the freezing air. He slowed to peer in the dark, but there was no light. He listened, then followed, trying to keep his interval by sound.

Four hundred yards later the trees thinned and suddenly he was in a small clearing with the sounds of men moving just ahead. He heard Eli's voice strangely clear in the darkness. "Stop where you are and lay down your muskets."

All sound stopped and then Eli's voice came piercing again. "Lay down your muskets and surrender or there'll be shooting. A lot of you dead in the snow."

Again, silence, and for the third time Eli called. "Corporal, you back there?"

Billy raised his voice. "Waiting orders."

Instantly rough voices broke out, then dwindled and one answered. "Who are you? British or American."

"American."

There was a pause, then muffled talk, and once again the voice came in the dark, but too loud, too hot. "What's the idea? We're on patrol."

"South? Patrol what? Philadelphia? The British are northeast, across the river. You got two disabled. You're no patrol, you're deserters. Corporal, you ready?"

Billy's voice rang loud in the dark. "Ready."

Eli's voice came strong. "You men got five seconds to lay down your muskets and get away from them before the shooting starts."

There was a pause. "We'll surrender if you agree we won't be shot."

"We won't shoot, but I can't speak for General Washington. You got two seconds."

Billy counted two and his thumb locked onto the big hammer on his musket when the voice came.

"How many are you?"

"Enough. Time's up. Corporal, open fire."

"Stop! We're laying down our arms. Show yourselves."

"Lay down your muskets and move this way until I say. Do it now."

Billy heard sounds moving away from him and he followed, then called, "I'm going to strike a light and gather the muskets." He held his breath, listening and heard Eli's voice.

"You men sit down where you are."

With numb fingers Billy struck flint to steel and nursed a spark in the tinder, then lighted the lamp wick and set the chimney. In the yellow light, he gathered and counted ten muskets, eight with bayonets.

"Only ten. Any more over there?"

"No."

"Give me some time." Quickly Billy twisted the bayonets from the muskets and laid them in the snow, then opened the pan on each musket and dumped out the gunpowder. "The pans are empty, and I got the bayonets separated."

Eli answered. "All right. Keep the lantern lit." He spoke to the men sitting in the snow. "Who's your leader?"

One man stood.

"Stand over here, near me. You others on your feet." He waited while they stood, the able helping the crippled. "Corporal, bring your lantern over here so they can see."

Billy walked around the group and stopped by Eli, the lantern swinging from his raised hand, throwing its yellow light onto the group who stood staring, unsure what to do. Billy raised the lamp high while he and Eli looked at them.

Their clothes were in tatters, feet wrapped in rags and blanket strips. Blood spots showed black in the snow where they had walked. Their faces were gaunt, bearded, filthy, and their eyes stared from sunken sockets. Two were either wounded in battle or had frozen feet, and stood with legs slightly bent. One man had his arm about the shoulder of the man next to him. Billy glanced at Eli and Eli's mouth was clenched, and for a moment his eyes dropped to the snow in the lantern glow.

For the first time the men saw Eli and Billy, and for a moment they stared at Eli. He wore his wolf skin coat, parka over his head, legs wrapped below the knees, beaded moccasins showing. A leather strap was tight about his middle, with his tomahawk shoved through and his belt knife attached.

Their leader, standing closest, recoiled and gasped, "Indian!"

Eli swung the muzzle of his rifle to the chest of the leader, drew his tomahawk and slipped his wrist through the leather thong. He spoke to them all, the long rifle in one hand, the tomahawk dangling from his other wrist.

"There's just two of us. Billy's going to get out ahead with the lantern, and you're going to pick up your muskets and bayonets and knapsacks and follow him. Those two hurt men go first with someone up there to help them along, then the rest of you. Your leader is going to be back here with me, with my rifle right in the middle of his back. One of you makes a break, your leader goes down first, then whoever is moving gets the tomahawk."

The eyes of all thirteen men were riveted on the tomahawk, dangling loosely on its thong, black, deadly, lantern light glinting off the iron head. For a moment they raised their eyes to Eli's face, and in the shadow of the parka they were seeing an Iroquois Indian with the weapons of his own people, in the dark of a freezing night in a strange country. They understood and could accept the musket and cannon— weapons of the white men—but the tomahawk and the scalping knife struck fear into their hearts.

Billy led and they followed the moving, dancing lantern glow, plowing through the snow-covered brush and trees. They saw the blood spots in their own tracks as they struggled on, half-carrying the two injured men. Once their leader turned his head and Eli was there, rifle steady, tomahawk on his wrist. They moved on, Billy and Eli hating what they had to do. The thirteen deserters stumbled on with terror in their hearts at the image that burned bright in their minds of being stood before a line of men, and watching the smoke and flame blast from their muskets, and feeling the shock of the huge musket balls ripping. Minutes ticked by too fast and too slow as they watched for the first points of campfire lights through the trees ahead.

Three miles northeast, at the army camp, an officer worked his way west, away from the river, through the fires and the trees, peering ahead for the dull lights behind drawn drapes in a building. On December fourteenth, Washington had accepted the offer of William Keith to use his large, square, two-storied stone home nine miles north of Trenton, on the Pennsylvania side of the Delaware, just west of McKonkey's Ferry, for his new headquarters. Yesterday Washington had sent mounted messengers with sealed, handwritten orders to some of his officers in the ravaged, scattered Continental army to gather at his new headquarters that evening. The invitation was mandatory: let nothing detain you.

They had begun to arrive at McKonkey's Ferry as the wintry sun dropped below the western rim, to work their way west through the freezing, starving soldiers huddled around the fires. The troops had sat sullen, shaking in the cold, not rising, not saluting as the officers rode their horses past them, looking for the building in the fast fading light.

The last officer dismounted his horse, handed the reins to a stable sergeant, and strode to the rear entrance of the stone building. He stamped snow from his boots and rapped at the door. An aide showed him down the hall and into the spacious library, now serving as a conference room. The officer entered, removed his hat and cape, and rubbed his hands together as he walked towards the big fireplace against the east wall, nodding curt greetings to those already assembled.

The aide spoke perfunctorily. "I will tell General Washington you're all here."

Silence hung prickly in the air like something alive as the officers assembled around the large, maplewood conference table. They glanced at each other, guarded, uneasy that each had received the blunt, unexpected, written order signed by General George Washington.

The sound of boot heels came hollow in the corridor and all heads swung around as Washington opened the door and entered. The instant they saw him—tall, full uniform, mouth a thin line, face set like granite—they knew. His eyes were of one who had offered himself on the altar of the Almighty and faced his devils in the cauldron of his own Gethsemane. The white heat had burned out the dross, purged him, sanctified him, brought him low, then raised him up to emerge as pure, tempered steel, dedicated in his soul to the cause of liberty. They watched him as he took his place at the head of the table and for a moment his eyes worked around he table, checking. Arnold, Greene, Stirling, Glover, Knox, de Fermoy, Gates, Mercer, Stephen, Sullivan.

"Thank you for attending. Please be seated."

Chairs scraped on the polished hardwood floor as they sat down and their breathing slowed as they waited. Washington remained standing and there was an edge in his voice.

"What we discuss now will not leave this room for any reason." It was an order, not a request.

"To set matters before you correctly I must recite a brief chain of events for foundation. Some of it you know, some of you do not. Bear with me."

He opened a ledger and for a moment glanced at it, then raised his face.

"Philadelphia is essentially deserted. The residents were afraid of what would result if General Howe led his British forces to take it, and most of them have evacuated." He cleared his throat before he continued. "Some of our leaders there have defected to the British. Congressman Joseph Galloway of Pennsylvania has deserted, and it is rumored that Congressman Dickinson will refuse to run for reelection. The Allen family of Pennsylvania—powerful in politics—has gone over."

He drew a great breath. "Congress abandoned Philadelphia nine days ago. They were concerned they would be hanged without trial if they were taken by the British. I don't know where they are, or when they'll reconvene. Perhaps in Baltimore, soon. In the meantime, we have no way of getting support for anything from Congress."

A buzzing broke out around the table and died.

"In the meantime, the British may try to take Philadelphia. If they do, there is little we can do to resist. The loss will tend to discourage the Patriots, but as a practical matter Philadelphia has little strategic value to us."

He glanced at his notes, then raised steady eyes.

"I confirm to you that the British have captured Major General Charles Lee."

To a man, the officers straightened, then leaned back in their chairs as open talk broke out. Washington waited for silence and continued.

"He was taken mid-morning on Friday, December thirteenth, asleep at an inn owned by a Mrs. White at Basking Ridge, three miles outside of Morristown. A young British officer named Banastre Tarleton and six or eight others were part of a single British patrol under the command of Lieutenant Colonel William Harcourt that drove him out of the inn half-dressed."

Again he paused while the officers surrounding the conference table stared in utter disbelief. Incomprehensible! A Major General in the heart of enemy-held territory, asleep at ten o'clock in the morning at an inn three miles from his command, without enough pickets to raise an alarm and make a fight of it? Never! Not in their wildest imaginings!

"I had delivered written orders to General Lee three times before his capture ordering him to bring his command here. He did not do so and the results have been disastrous. General Sullivan has brought Lee's troops here to reinforce us. I am aware that Lee's capture was a matter of the greatest celebration to the British, and a profound shock to everyone engaged on our side, most of all to Congress."

Washington waited while exclamations erupted. Every man at the table was aware that General Charles Lee had all but launched a public campaign to persuade Congress and the American people that he was the man to replace George Washington. His military credentials included lifelong service in the British army, with the battlefield combat experience that Washington lacked, and he was considered by some, both British and American, to be the most able military mind in the American forces. All that being true, how was it he allowed himself to be captured under circumstances more readily associated with the bumbling foolishness of some new, raw, green recruit? Whatever bright future General Lee may have once had with the United States was gone forever.

Washington waited for the talk to subside and moved on.

"General Cornwallis has left for New York to return to England to be with his wife, who is gravely ill."

The officers looked at each other, eyebrows arched in surprise. General Charles Cornwallis was the most beloved and respected general in the British military service by both his men and his peers, and one of the most feared by the enemies of England. His absence would make a difference, bad for the British, good for the Americans.

"General Grant has assumed his command in his absence." Washington paused for the impact. It was Major General James Grant, fat, dour, despised, who had been so loud, blatant, insulting in his contempt for American soldiers. At the battle of Long Island he had nearly overrun General Lord Stirling, who with a vastly smaller force had nonetheless stubbornly, heroically, stalled Grant's entire column to cover the retreat of a company of Americans on the Gowanus Road, and then sought a Hessian officer to receive his surrender, rather than surrender to the detested General James Grant. The officers facing Washington said nothing. New battles were coming. They would remember Grant.

"General William Howe declared the British campaign for 1776 concluded on December fourteenth, and departed for New York for his winter quarters. It seems he has a yen for the holiday and social season in that city, and for one Mrs. Loring."

The men about the table shook their heads, well aware of Howe's considerable appetite and notorious reputation for the high social life.

Washington closed the ledger and set it aside, then unfolded a map that covered half the tabletop. He waited for thirty seconds while the officers silently studied the details of the Delaware River and the land on both sides, from Lambertville on the north to Dunk's Ferry on the south, from Princeton on the east to the Neshaminy River on the west. His face shone in the lamplight as he spoke.

"Each of you will have a part in what we now discuss. On pain of court-martial and a firing squad, not a word of this can leave this room."

He paused and the officers stared into his hard eyes, glanced at each other, and then looked back at the map.

"Before General Howe declared his troops into winter camp, he established a string of command posts beginning at Staten Island, and curving down here"—his finger moved, pointing—"Perth Amboy, Brunswick, Princeton, Trenton, on down to Bordentown, and Burlington."

The room was locked in dead silence as he continued.

"Hessians are stationed from here, Trenton, on down to Burlington with General Carl Emil Kurt von Donop in overall command."

He moved his finger back to Trenton. "Here, Colonel Johann Gottlieb Rall has command of about fourteen hundred. His subordinate officers are Knyphausen and Lossberg. Rall was given this post because of his performance at White Plains and Fort Washington. His men are disciplined, well-fed, ready to fight. I will come back to Colonel Rall."

He moved his finger down the Delaware. "General von Donop intended setting up his command headquarters here, at Burlington, but some of our cannon on gondolas could reach him, so he moved a few of his men away from the Delaware to Black Horse and Mount Holly and then moved his headquarters back up the river to Bordentown, here. He has about fifteen hundred men down there, scattered from Bordentown to Brunswick, wherever they can take housing. General von Donop has at least a modicum of respect for American soldiers, enough to be a little cautious." He paused and his face took on a caste like granite. "Now I move back to Colonel Rall at Trenton."

He cleared his throat and his eyes became flinty.

"Our army is a matter of profound contempt and disgust to him. He has not turned one shovel of earth to build barricades, trenches, fortifications, or gun emplacements. He stays in bed until past nine each morning. His patrols are haphazard, minimal. His men have grown resentful, boastful, disgusted. He has pulled in his outposts and there is nearly nothing and no one on any road leading into Trenton to give him advance warning of anyone approaching. He has openly said he doesn't need to do any of these things because if we come, he will simply show us the bayonet, and we cannot stand the bayonet."

A few of the officers around the table moved, and Washington let them settle before he went on.

"The German Christmas festival is coming Wednesday and Thursday. I expect their officers will let their men stand down sometime in those two days, and I expect they will issue a healthy ration of rum or beer. If they do, the command will be a little less attentive to their duties sometime during those two days, probably the twenty-fifth.

"Now I will point out where our forces are." He moved his finger. "The building we are meeting in is here, at McKonkey's Ferry, nine miles north of Trenton. In the past ten days I have gathered some of our forces here with me." He moved his finger south, down the

Delaware. "General Ewing and a force under his command are posted here, just below Trenton, on this side of the river." Again he moved his finger farther down the west side of the Delaware. "General Cadwalader has a force down here, at Dunk's Ferry, well below Bristol. So as you can see, generally, our forces are spaced about equally with the Hessians, us on this side of the river, them on the other."

He straightened and his finger left the map. "There are a few other critical facts. We have every boat within forty miles in both directions hidden on our side of the river. We can cross the Delaware, but they cannot, although I am unable to explain why the British haven't built more boats. They have lumber stacked at Trenton, already cut and cured, and engineers, carpenters, and boat builders. It appears they don't mean to cross, at least until the ice is thick enough to support horses and cannon, or until next spring."

He cleared his throat and went on. "You will recall the big Durham boats we acquired from the iron mill up at Riegelsville, above Lambertville—the ones we used to cross the Delaware to reach this side earlier this month. We still have them, hidden and ready."

Every man at the table slowly leaned back in his chair, eyes wide in stunned disbelief at what was emerging, minute by minute. Washington continued.

"The enlistments for most of our troops expire at midnight, December thirty-first. Nine days from tonight. Unless something is done, on January 1, 1777, we will have no more army."

There it was! Out on the table, raw, brutal, final. Since their devastation at New York and their humiliating, headlong run across New Jersey to escape total annihilation, the officers had lived with the terrible question riding them black and ugly every moment of their lives. What becomes of the Continental army at midnight, December thirty-first, when almost all enlistments end? Beaten, sick, starving, freezing, filthy, badly armed, dressed in rags, looking across the half-frozen Delaware at British and German troops who are warm, fed, well-armed, confident, simply waiting for winter to kill the Americans—who among the enlisted would stay one day longer than their enlistment? Only fools! Only fools!

The officers had awaited a miracle that would save the army, but none had come. Congress had thought General Charles Lee might be their savior until his unbelievable stupidity in getting himself captured had sent that illusion crashing. Then who? What? Unless the Almighty sent lightning from the heavens, on January 1, 1777, the dream of liberty, of a free America, would become but a footnote in some obscure British history book, hardly noticed by the second generation.

The officers leaned forward in thick silence, scarcely breathing, hoping against hope that Washington was going to reveal the miracle that would turn the British, save them all, secure their shining dream. Washington looked into their faces, and once again reached to tap the map with a long finger.

"Sometime during the Christmas celebration we're going to cross the river and take Trenton."

There was a sharp intake of breath around the table, and then talk erupted among the stunned, astonished officers. Washington raised a hand and slowly the room quieted.

"One at a time."

General Horatio Gates leaned forward. Large, paunchy, born and raised in England, a major in the British army by training, Gates had come to the colonies as a younger man. When the break came with England, he had offered his services to the fledgling Continental army and was considered by some to be one of the two finest military minds in the American forces, certainly the finest now with General Lee captured. The room fell silent in tense anticipation.

Gates spoke with a half-smile and his voice was restrained. "Sir, you're proposing to move what's left of the army across the Delaware with the intention of engaging the Hessians at Trenton?"

Washington's eyes bored into him. "Yes."

"In those Durham boats, I presume?"

"Yes."

Gates shook his head. "Boats that large and slow make excellent targets for cannon. Not one will survive if a Hessian patrol sees them before they reach the New Jersey shore."

"We cross at night."

Every man in the room stopped and stared at Washington in disbelief.

Gates continued. "Cross with what? We have no trained army. Only citizens who have picked up musket and ball. For the past half-year they've moved but one direction—away from the enemy as fast as they could. On the far side of the Delaware are several thousand of the finest trained Hessian soldiers in the world. Sending our so-called army across the river to engage them would amount to mass suicide."

Washington's expression did not change. "They'll stand and fight."

Gates dropped his eyes for a moment and shook his head. "The rule of engagement is one cannon per fifty soldiers." He glanced down the table at Colonel Henry Knox, short, rotund, twenty-six years old, commander of cannon. "That would suggest we need about one hundred twenty cannon. We have eighteen. The Hessians will shred us with grapeshot and canister long before we are in musket range."

"We will be in musket range before they are aware of us."

"Surprise? You think to catch them by surprise?"

"Yes."

"Professionals?"

"Yes."

"How?"

"Attack at five A.M. after the night crossing."

Gates leaned back in his chair, laced his fingers across his paunch, and stared at the ceiling.

General Sullivan spoke. "What happens if hard weather sets in?"

"We've seen hard weather before."

"If the river freezes four inches of ice out in the channel it won't support men or horses or cannon, but it will stop boats. Then what do we do?"

"The river won't freeze over between now and the time we cross."

The officers exchanged baffled glances, struck by what appeared to be Washington's blind innocence.

General Mercer interrupted. "They had a hard freeze last week on the river about one hundred miles north. A foot or more of ice. It could happen here."

"It won't."

Sullivan continued. "There's a storm gathering right now. If we get a northeaster wind, we'll be in a blizzard in the next thirty-six hours."

"So will they."

General Stirling lifted a hand. "How do we move men from here down to Trenton, nine miles south? Durham boats?"

"No. March them."

Stirling gaped. "In their condition? Nine miles at night? Half of them can hardly walk. They're boiling the inner bark from trees now for something to eat. No shoes, no winter clothes—how can they march that far in this weather and then fight when they get there?"

"I'll get food. I've sent a message to Robert Morris to get money. The nearby farmers will sell food to us."

"You'll get food in time for all this?"

"The men will be strong enough."

Gates leaned forward once again, and the room silenced. "With enlistments up in less than ten days, how are you going to force men to do all this? They have simply to refuse for nine days, and go home."

Washington's voice remained controlled, disciplined. "They'll obey."

Gates raised both hands, palms facing outward, in a gesture of defensive resignation. "Do you have the particulars worked out as to what each of us will do to effect this . . . uh . . . attack?"

"Generally, yes. We will meet again in the next two days to work out the details and I will have written orders."

He paused and waited until each man was settled, waiting, then leaned forward on stiff arms, palms flat on the table. "In the next two days, each of you shall have every man in your command check the flint in his musket and be certain he has a second one in his pocket. Check their powder to be sure it's dry. Count their musket balls. We will need more doctors, and I have sent a request to all surrounding towns in Bucks County to get them. Have your men prepare cooked food for three days and pack it in a blanket or a knapsack."

He straightened. "Each of you will be notified in writing of our next meeting, when we will address the details. Until then, what has transpired here tonight must remain in this room. Discuss it with no one. No one." He watched until he knew each officer understood.

"Thank you for your attendance. If you wish, you are invited to remain here for the night. My aide has prepared quarters. You are all dismissed."

They stood while General Washington collected his ledger and map, then strode from the room and the echo of his boot heels faded down the corridor. The officers reached for their capes and hats, minds foundering as they grappled with the shocking plan of their commander in chief. Talk was sparse, disconnected as each struggled with his own inner vision of boats trying to carry a sick army across an ice-choked river in the night, then walk nine miles undetected to do battle with an enemy that had already beaten them into near extinction five times in four months. They saw it in their minds, and they trembled.

Those who were staying the night waited while Washington's aide showed the others to the door. They filed out into the freezing night and walked, crunching in the ice and snow, to the place the livery officer had their horses saddled, waiting, nervous, vapor rising from their nostrils. They lifted foot to stirrup and reined their horses around, each to go his own separate direction, when they heard distant, loud voices and then hard words coming from the camp four hundred yards east. They held their horses in for a moment, peering at the pinpoints of campfire light in the black woods, trying to understand what was becoming an uproar. Three of them shrugged and tapped spur and disappeared into the night, riding for their own command. The remaining four, General John Sullivan among them, raised their mounts to a canter and headed due east towards the lights and the sounds.

They came in just north of the ferry, horses prancing in the cold, and slowed as the men opened a path. They reined to a stop twenty feet from a large fire and sat facing a group of thirteen men standing in rags and tatters, filthy, beaten, eyes downcast, two clinging to the man next to him to keep from toppling over. On one side of the group was a stout, sandy-bearded man carrying a musket and wearing a blanket coat. Next to him was a small man, bearded, hollow-cheeked, sunken eyes reflecting the firelight. On the other side was a tall man clad in a wolf skin coat, parka thrown back, with a long-barreled Pennsylvania rifle in one hand and an Iroquois tomahawk dangling from the wrist of the other. The officers saw the leggings and the beadwork on the moccasins.

"I'm General John Sullivan. What's going on here?"

The response surged from a dozen angry voices. "Deserters! All of them."

Sullivan's eyes widened as he stared at the men in the huddled group who refused to meet his eyes. "True? Are you deserters?"

No one spoke or moved.

Sullivan looked at the gathering of men. "Who says they're deserters?"

Half a dozen fingers pointed to Billy and Eli, and Sullivan spoke to Billy.

"Who are you?"

"Corporal Billy Weems. Boston Regiment."

"Do you accuse these men of desertion?"

"We caught them four miles south, headed for Philadelphia. They said they were deserting. We brought them back."

"Who is we?"

"Myself and Eli Stroud." Billy pointed. "He's a regimental scout."

Sullivan straightened in his saddle. "You two brought back thirteen?"

"They didn't resist much."

"Which one is their leader?"

Billy pointed.

Sullivan's eyes bored into the man. "Is Corporal Weems telling the truth?"

The man turned his face full to General Sullivan, eyes defiant. "Yes, sir."

Sullivan's eyes dropped and his shoulders slumped for a moment. He slowly shook his head, suddenly detesting war, and sick, freezing, starving men, and the evil duty of standing thirteen of his own before a firing squad.

He raised his eyes to Billy. "Is your commanding officer here?"

"Since Long Island I haven't known who he is, sir. No one has said. Sergeant Turlock is here." Billy pointed.

"Sergeant, can you find the regiment these men belong to and get an officer to lock these men up for the night? We'll handle it in the morning."

"Yes, sir."

For a moment longer the four officers sat their horses staring at the deserters in the dancing firelight. None of them had ever seen one of their own men made to stand and be shot by another of their own men, and each was struggling in his heart with the grim fact that military rank came with soul-wrenching realities. They swallowed dryly and reined their horses around and raised them to a canter.

"All right, you lovelies," Turlock said. "What regiment are you from?"

"Connecticut, mostly."

"Where in this camp?"

"South, maybe three hundred yards."

"I'm going to find an officer so you stay here until I'm back. Corporal, any of them makes a move you don't understand, you and Eli shoot." He turned to the crowd that had gathered. "The rest of you lovelies go on back to your fires. There'll be no mobs starting something here."

He stared them down, and they broke away from the fire in two's and three's, mumbling as they walked away into the darkness. Turlock waited until they were gone before he spoke to the prisoners.

"You take any food when you left?"

One man nodded and pointed to two knapsacks stacked near their blankets, muskets, and bayonets.

"When did you last eat?"

The man shrugged. "Sometime yesterday. I can't remember."

Turlock wiped a grimy sleeve across his mouth. "Get the knapsacks and sit by the fire and eat something while I'm gone."

The man's eyebrows raised. His companion picked up the knapsacks, and sat on a log around the fire, fumbling with numb fingers to open the buckles, and then with trembling hands he passed out moldy, wormy hardtack with bits and crumbs of cheese, and a few hard rinds of fried pork skin.

"You steal that?" Turlock asked.

"Saved it."

Turlock glanced at Billy. "I'll be back." He turned and started south through the trees, looking for the Connecticut Regiment and an officer. For several minutes Billy leaned on his musket, watching the ravenous men work at the frozen hardtack and pork rinds, then turned to Eli.

"I'm going to get a cook pot."

Five minutes later he returned and filled a black stew pot with snow and set it in the coals of the campfire, adding more snow as it melted until the pot was half-filled, then handed a wooden cup to the leader and set the pot before him. The man stood for a moment, surprised, before he dipped the cup and handed it to one of the disabled men, still seated. He waited, then dipped for the second disabled man, and then the others took turns before they returned to gnawing their frozen bits of food.

Billy spoke quietly to the leader. "Care to give your name?"

The man considered for a moment. "Bertram Pratt."

"Those two men hurt bad?"

Pratt looked at them for a moment. "Feet froze. Had to cut two toes off one, three off the other. They was black, going rotten. We were tryin' to get them to a hospital in Philadelphia when you caught up with us."

"Known them long?"

The man raised pained eyes. "Old one's my uncle. Young one's my cousin."

Billy closed his eyes as the pain settled in.

The man shrugged. "Couldn't find a doctor while we was runnin' across New Jersey. Nothin' to do but keep movin'. The pain was bad so we took off those toes and the pain went away for a while. I figure they'll be all right if we can get a doctor and some food and a warm bed for them. If we don't, one may lose a foot. Maybe worse."

"Didn't you tell your regiment officers?"

"Every day. Didn't pay no attention. Too busy tryin' to stay ahead of the redcoats. Didn't have no doctors anyway."

"Been with General Washington long?"

"We was at Long Island. Been with him since."

Billy turned troubled eyes to Eli, and Eli stared back at him for a moment before he dropped his eyes to the ground and shook his head.

All their heads pivoted at the sound of feet crunching in hard snow and of voices coming in from the south. They watched Turlock lead a seven-man squad to the fire. One wore a black tricornered hat with gold braid and had a saber dangling from his side while the other six were armed with muskets. The bayonets gleamed yellow in the firelight. Four of the men had a large coil of rope over one shoulder.

"All right, you lovelies. This is Lieutenant Upton from the Connecticut Regiment. He'll take you back to your camp. On your feet."

Billy and Eli took a step back as the six men with muskets took positions around the destitute group while they struggled to their feet. Billy and Eli saw the black blood their feet left in the snow.

Upton's face was young, voice high, strained, too loud as he blurted orders to his squad. "Tie their feet."

The four men with ropes leaned their muskets over a log, uncoiled their ropes, and knotted it around the left ankle of each man at five foot intervals, three men to a rope. Upton watched until they finished. "Very good. Now move these men down to our camp." He turned back to Turlock. "Someone will return for their muskets and luggage."

They shuffled away from the fire, the stronger helping the disabled, while Billy, Eli, and Turlock studied the tracks in the snow. There was black blood in half of them.

Billy spoke. "It's hard. Shooting them for trying to get a doctor."

Turlock turned to him. "A doctor? What's that about?"

For three minutes Billy and Eli talked in the firelight while Turlock listened intently. They finished and fell silent, and Turlock sat down on a log and stared into the flames for a long time before he raised his eyes.

"If that's true, you're right. It's a hard thing."

Eli spoke. "Was it General Washington gave the order to shoot deserters?"

Billy nodded.

"Then he can change it."

Turlock looked at Eli. "Yes, he can."

They said no more for a time, sitting near the fire, palms towards the warmth, each lost in his own thoughts. Eli broke the silence.

"Maybe the court-martial won't convict them. Maybe they'll let them go."

Turlock quietly said, "I hope so."

Billy turned to peer west through the trees into the darkness beyond, straining to see the lights of Washington's headquarters in the Keith House, five hundred yards distant. "The General had most of his officers at his quarters tonight, from clear down below Burlington. Must be important. Maybe we can write something for him to read in the morning that will explain about those men."

Eli looked west into the darkness. "Maybe we can. With all those generals over there, I wonder what was going on tonight."

For several moments all three of them looked west, pondering, sensing something of terrible import was stirring, but not knowing what.

Inside the Keith House, behind the closed door and drawn drapes of his second-floor private chambers, Washington sat at his corner desk, unaware he was rolling a quill pen between his fingers. His buff-and-blue officer's tunic lay on the bed where he had folded it nearly an hour earlier. He had paced the floor, eyes downcast, not caring about the time. He had finally sat down at his desk and, by force of will, pulled his raging emotions and racing thoughts under control.

Gates was right—no army, just citizens with muskets—sick, starved, frozen, no shoes, counting hours until their enlistments are up—they won't rise to it—crossing at night is impossible—impossible—surprise is out of the question—no chance against the Hessians—no chance—no chance—eighteen cannon against their many—grapeshot and canister will chop us to pieces five hundred yards before musket range—Gates was right—he was right.

He stared unseeing at the quill while he continued to roll it between thumb and fingers.

They all sensed it—know it—when the orders are given what will they do—will they obey—will they balk—will they argue? If the men sense weakness in the officers it's all over—we've lost—beaten before we start.

Slowly he laid the quill on the desk before him, and he leaned forward, elbows on the desk, face buried in his hands for a long time. Then he straightened in his chair, rose, and walked to sit on his bed, next to his tailored, folded tunic.

No choice—our last chance—if we sit here we lose the army in nine days and it's all over. We turn it around here and now, or not at all.

His head dropped forward and he studied the round braided rug on the floor without seeing it, and then suddenly his head came up.

We've come too far—paid too high a price. He will not turn His back on us now. He will not. This is His *work—not mine! If I fail, He will find another way and He will* not *fail. Gates will be wrong and He will be right!*

He was aware that an unexpected feeling had crept into the room. He felt his arms and face begin to tingle. His breath came short and he looked about the room as though expecting the presence of another being, but there was no one. Slowly the feeling faded and then it was gone.

He could not remain seated and he suddenly stood. His mind was crystal clear. His resolve was immovable. Never had his vision been more pure. He strode to his desk, seized the quill, squared a piece of paper, and began to write.

An hour later he laid the quill down and for thirty seconds stared astonished at the stack of folded, sealed papers. Before him was the finished plan, and the written orders for every officer, by which the Continental army was going to take Trenton.

Outside, in the frozen blackness, a passing breeze stirred the barren branches of the oak and maple trees and then the breeze stiffened. Ten minutes later the northeaster wind was singing through the thrashing trees, and then the first stinging ice crystals and snowflakes came slanting.

Notes

Washington had begun to formulate a plan to attack Trenton as early as December 8, 1776 (see Ward, *The War of the Revolution*, vol. I, p. 292), but it wasn't until December 22, 1776, that Washington held a council of war at his headquarters in the Keith House and revealed his plans for Trenton (see Smith, *The Battle of Trenton*, p. 16; Ketchum, *The Winter Soldiers*, pp. 222, 236). A second war council was held on December 24, 1776, where Washington made specific assignments to his generals (see Ward, *The War of the Revolution*, vol. I, pp. 292–94; Ketchum, *The Winter Soldiers*, pp. 245–46).

While General Gates is portrayed in the novel as opposing Washington's plan, historical records are silent on the reactions of Washington's generals to his plan for Trenton. However, Gates's points are well-taken and accurately describe the precarious situation of the Continental army at that time. It would not be too surprising if confidence in Washington's plan was low. With the enlistment of nearly all the soldiers expiring at midnight, December 31, 1776, the very foundation of the Revolution was in jeopardy (see Ward, *The War of the Revolution*, vol. I, p. 290). Congress had abandoned Philadelphia on December 13, 1776, for fear of the British taking the city (see Ketchum, *The Winter Soldiers*, p. 213). Several prominent Patriots had abandoned the Revolution to join the British, among them the powerful Galloway and Allen families (see Ketchum, *The Winter Soldiers*, pp. 205–6). The conversation between Gates and Washington closely follows the fictional dialogue on pages 89–91 of Howard Fast's book, *The Crossing*.

Washington's information about the number and placement of both the Hessian and the American troops as described in the novel is accurate (see Ketchum, *The Winter Soldiers*, pp. 225–26, 243–44; Ward, *The War of the Revolution*, vol. I, pp. 289–90, 296).

The capture of General Lee by the British officer Banastre Tarleton on December 13, 1776, is detailed on pages 214–19 of Ketchum's book *The Winter Soldiers*.

Colonel Rall was indeed scorned by his own men for his bad habits. He was also woefully lax in his preparations for an American assault. He boasted, "Let them come! We want no trenches! We'll go after them with the bayonet" (as quoted in Leckie, *George Washington's War*, p. 317).

John Cadwalader spent most of the war with the rank of lieutenant colonel. However, Washington temporarily promoted him to brigadier general so he could effectively command the force of Americans at Dunk's Ferry (see Ward, *The War of the Revolution*, vol. I, p. 293). Cadwalader is simply referred to as "general" throughout the novel for consistency.

Bertram Pratt and the twelve other deserters in the novel are fictional; however, desertions from the American army were frequent (see Higginbotham, *The War of American Independence*, pp. 399–403).

For additional information on matters depicted in this chapter, see Higginbotham, *The War of American Independence*, p. 166, and Leckie, *George Washington's War*, pp. 315–21.

CHAPTER V

★ ★ ★

*T*he raging inferno that swept from the Hudson River water-front through the southwest section of New York City the morning of September twenty-first left the wharves and warehouses and business buildings and homes in charred ruins. The streets were littered with wreckage from the Battery to St. Paul's Church between Broadway and the Hudson River to the west. The ruins that had fallen or been thrown into the narrow streets were shoved up against the scorched walls of buildings on either side. Inside, the broken hulks of the beams and timbers of the collapsed roofs lay jumbled like the blackened bones of some great animal, while empty windows stared dead-eyed at all who passed. October rains and the storms of November and the snows and frosts of December had crumbled the charred remains, and the runoff had seeped from the burned-out buildings into the streets carrying ashes to fill the cracks between the cobblestones, and then cover them. It clung to the shoes and boots and clothing of all who passed, and to the wheels of vegetable wagons and milk carts, and the hooves of the horses and the feet of the dogs that pulled them.

Before the smoking embers had died, both British Loyalists and American Patriots pounced on the disaster with mindless fury in their wild struggle to blame the other for the holocaust. Stones flew and clubs swung with neither side knowing or caring how the disaster had started, or who was responsible. They had found the excuse they needed to rise against each other to vent the anger that had been too long building and festering. With British and Hessian troops marching daily in the streets with their muskets and gleaming bayonets visible and ready, there was never a question as to which side would win, or which would lose, in this city divided against itself.

In open daylight, British soldiers and Loyalists smashed down the doors of King's College. They stripped the great library of its priceless collection of books, the natural history building of its irreplaceable scientific instruments, and the art building of its paintings of the great European masters. Frenzied mobs ripped down the gates and smashed the entry doors into the homes of many known Patriots to ransack them of the furniture, paintings, silverware, everything of value. Within days the plunder began to appear in the pubs and inns and door-to-door, offered for sale or barter by soldiers, Tories, or hired women for whatever price they would bring.

In the filth and grime of the streets and the burned-out warehouses and shipping offices of the waterfront, thieves, looters, army deserters, runaway slaves, and women of the night tacked together cast-off lumber and half-burned canvas sailcloth to build hovels where they slept and ate while they were not prowling the streets, stealing anything they could find to sell for a bit of food, or wood for heat, or a blanket against the storms of fall and winter. The waterfront district quickly came to be known as "Canvas Town." For the price of a bottle of whiskey, or rum, or a block of cheese, or a smoked ham, one could find a dozen assassins who would commit murder, and no one came inquiring of the bodies found in the charred hulks, or in the dirty streets, or floating face down in New York Harbor at daybreak. Only those with business in Canvas Town ventured into the squalid streets, and should their business be at night, they came in groups, with lanterns, armed with sword and pistol.

The most rabid of the Tories formed into mobs to roam the streets of central New York City with chalk and buckets of paint and brushes. They branded the doors of known Patriots with a great "R," marking them as the despised rebels. Those who trembled behind the locked doors knew the unending terror of windows shattered in the night by burning torches.

Churches attended by the Patriots were seized by vengeful Tories. The benches and pews, pulpits and sacrament tables were chopped into firewood and the buildings stripped to the walls. Captured American soldiers were herded like cattle into some, given a blanket, and held as prisoners of war behind the bolted doors, without heat, fed a starvation meal twice a day, and forced to exist in the stench of their own filth. Other churches were jammed with cots and turned into hospitals for the wounded, sick, and dying. When space ran out, the worst injured were put on blankets beneath the cots to die. Patriots volunteered, or were forced at bayonet point to serve as nurses or as aides to surgeons who used crude instruments to amputate arms and legs from screaming men. Nurses held the writhing men on blood-spattered wooden tables and forced rags into their mouths to shut out the sounds, but they could not, and they found themselves waking sweat-soaked at night to the echoes of their own cries as the scenes of carnage returned again and again bright in their sleep.

When the churches were filled, the British sent red-coated officers with swords and troops with bayonets to seize the mansions on the northern limits of town, among them the great three-storied Flint mansion with its six-column portico, and eight blocks away, the Broadhead mansion. The Flint stables were stripped of the prized Percheron draft horses, the saddle mounts, wagons, carriages, tack, and gear. The magnificent furnishings in the mansions were hauled out under armed guard and never seen again, while hospital cots were jammed to the walls in every room. Overnight they were filled with wounded and dying American soldiers. The Flint and Broadhead families were ordered either to abandon their estates or live in the cellar.

Gray-haired Rufus Broadhead, a widower, tall, slender, aging, proud, shrugged into his heavy winter coat and scarf, and walked the frozen ground to the Flint mansion, where a small, sparse British picket stood with vapor rising from his face, arms wrapped around himself, shoulders hunched against the cold. Broadhead stepped up the two steps and the picket stopped him between the two towering columns that framed the great entryway.

"'Ere, yer can't go inside. This 'ere building is now a hospital."

Broadhead pulled himself to his full height, eyes blazing. "I have come to see my daughter. She's being held a captive nurse inside."

"No visitors. There's fever inside."

"I know what's inside. It's urgent that I see my daughter."

The picket shook his head. "Move on."

Broadhead held his temper. "May I speak to your superior officer?"

"You may dig the wax out of your ears and listen. Move on. No visitors." The picket raised his musket.

Broadhead kept a tenuous hold on his rising anger. "I will see my daughter or you will have to use your bayonet!"

The picket eyed Broadhead's tailored coat with the deep blue velvet on the collar and lapel facings. His lip curled in contempt. "One of those rich American Patriots that figgers to tell the world wot's wot, eh? Well, yer money won't do you no good 'ere. My orders is clear. No visitors. Now remove yerself before I 'ave to do it meself."

Broadhead bristled and raised an extended arm, his finger pointed into the face of the picket. "I am Rufus Broadhead. Your army plundered my home half a mile from here and turned it into a hospital. I was ordered to live in my own cellar. Before I submit to that I will leave all I own, but not until I have spoken with my daughter, Mary Flint. She married Marcus Flint and lived here with him until he was killed, and she remained here to nurse his widowed mother. Now she's being held inside as slave labor. I will speak to her before I leave, or you will have to kill me where I stand."

A sneer crossed the picket's face. "As you please, only I doubt killin' will be required. Just a good bash on yer bloomin' 'ead with ol' Bess, here, and then you can talk to yer daughter all you want while yer inside recoverin'. Or dyin'."

Broadhead took two steps forward, and the startled picket raised the iron-plated butt of his Brown Bess musket to start his stroke as Broadhead closed with him. Broadhead caught the stock of the upraised weapon with both hands and wrenched it towards himself with all his strength. Caught by surprise the picket was jerked forward, off balance, and Broadhead released the musket to catch the man by both lapels, and he again jerked the man forward. He shifted his feet, twisting to half throw the man from the portico, down the two steps, sliding on the ice and patchy, frozen snow as the musket dropped clattering to the stairs.

Broadhead picked up the musket, jerked the cover of the powder pan open and shook the gunpowder onto the walkway. He threw the musket thirty feet into the bushes lining the front of the portico while the stunned picket scrambled to his feet. Without another look at him, Broadhead strode to the great double doors and banged on them with the flat of his hands.

"'Ere, you can't do that," the picket shouted and started forward.

Broadhead turned to meet him just as the big door swung open, and Broadhead turned back to face a round-shouldered man with rolled up shirtsleeves. He was wiping his hands on a soiled towel. He lowered his face to peer over wire-rimmed spectacles with tired eyes as he studied Broadhead. There was irritation in his voice as he spoke.

"What's the clatter out here?"

The warm air within the home spilled out over Broadhead, reeking, overpowering with the smell of unbathed bodies, human excretia, rotting flesh, carbolics, and in the dim light Broadhead heard the sounds of dying men, and men in pain.

He did not flinch. "I am Rufus Broadhead. I have come to speak with my daughter, Mary Flint. You have her inside under restraint, serving as a nurse. May I know your name, sir?"

"We have several nurses inside . . ."

The picket stopped beside Broadhead and reached to grasp his arm. "Yer under arrest fer—"

The man in the entryway shook his head and wearily raised a hand. "Stop that. Just stop."

The picket turned surprised eyes. "But sir, I'm under orders. No visitors. I told 'im—"

"Where's your musket?"

The picket pointed. "Over there, sir, in them bushes. This 'ere intruder jerked it away when I wasn't lookin' an' threw it."

"How did your clothing get soiled?"

"'Im, sir. 'E threw me down."

The man sighed. "Brush yourself off and get your musket."

He turned back to Broadhead. "I'm Doctor Otis Purcell. Colonel in His Majesty's Fifth Northumberland Fusileers. What's this about your daughter?"

"Her name is Mary Flint. It's urgent that I speak with her."

"Flint? Wasn't this the Flint mansion?" He glanced over his shoulder.

"It was."

The doctor removed his spectacles and pressed a thumb and forefinger against his eyes to rub them before settling the spectacles back on his nose.

"You don't want to come in here. Half a dozen contagious diseases. Fever. Stench." He shook his head sadly. "I'll see if I can find her. You can talk with her out here."

"I would be happy to come in."

"No. We have enough sickness spreading in town. Wait here." The doctor walked back through the heavy door and closed it behind. Broadhead turned his head to watch the picket work his musket out of the bushes. The man brushed at frozen mud and ice stuck to his knees and elbows and down the front of his heavy coat. He walked back to the entryway, glancing darkly at Broadhead before he resumed his position at the side of the door.

Five minutes later the door opened, the doctor stepped aside, and Mary Flint emerged from the dimness within, a heavy gray woolen shawl over her head and clutched tightly about her. At the sight of her father she gasped and threw her arms about him and he held her close for a time. The doctor closed the door and Broadhead led his daughter off the portico and stopped on the broad brick path to the street.

Mary turned her face up to his and by force of will he did not let his own expression change as he looked at his once beautiful daughter. Her dark eyes were shadowed and sunken, her cheeks hollow, face pale. He reached to touch her cheek tenderly and spoke quietly.

"You're ill. You need good food and to be in bed."

"I'll be all right."

"Where are you sleeping?"

"In the cellar."

"The wine cellar? Dry? Solid floor and walls?"

"No. The storage room. Dirt."

"Heat?"

She shook her head.

Anger and pain rose in his heart and he struggled for control. "Judith Flint?"

"Fever. Delirious. She's been talking to Edward and Marcus the last two days."

"How long has Edward been gone?"

"Eight years. Thirty-two years of marriage. She sees him as though he is standing in front of her."

"Will she be all right?"

Mary's gaze dropped and she shook her head, but said nothing.

Broadhead cleared his throat. "They took our home. I will not remain there under their rule. I have to go."

She caught and held her breath. "Father! You're going?"

He nodded and suddenly she could no longer control herself. She dissolved into tears and buried her face in his chest. For a time he wrapped her inside his arms while she shook and trembled with the wrenching sobs. Slowly she brought herself under control and wiped at her eyes with a corner of the shawl as he spoke.

"Can you come with me? I've packed what little the British left in a carriage."

"Where? Where will you go?"

"Boston. There's no fighting there. I will leave a message at the mayor's office when I have a house. Will you come?"

"I would if I could, but I'm not free. The British have pressed me into servitude."

"They can't do that. You are not a prisoner of war."

She reached to clutch his arm. "I tried to leave once. At night. I was over five miles north—half a mile from the Murray house—when they caught me next afternoon. For three days they kept leg irons on me. I can't go with you, but you leave. Please. I'll come as soon as I can."

A south wind came in off the harbor and rattled the barren limbs of the oaks and maples of the estate, and Mary shivered.

Broadhead raised his head to study the picket for a moment, standing sixty feet away by the door, and he slipped his hand inside his coat and drew out a leather purse with the drawstrings tight and tied. He carefully laid it in Mary's hand.

"There are eighty pounds in gold coins, and some of the family jewels—most of what I could hide when they took the house. I kept forty pounds for myself and the two servants I am taking with me. You take this and use it to buy your way north to Boston. Promise you will do that."

She raised concerned eyes. "I can't. You keep this. I'll be all right. I will come when I can, I promise."

He folded her hand closed on the purse. "Put it inside your shawl now, before the picket sees. You'll freeze out here. I'll take you back inside."

For a moment they stood in the bitter cold, facing each other with the queer, undefined sense they would never see each other again. Neither dared put it to words, while a thousand remembrances flooded.

In that brief moment, Broadhead saw Mary wrapped in her swaddling blanket, held to her mother's breast—the two year old with the great, brown, wide-set eyes and brown hair that curled about her face—the gangly eight year old with a great gap in her smile while she waited for two new front teeth—the thirteen year old trembling on the brink of womanhood—the confident seventeen year old who was hopelessly in love with Marcus Flint—the nineteen-year-old bride, breathtaking in her white wedding dress—the glowing, expectant mother. The frightened, white-faced woman in a bed soaked with her sweat as she labored for twenty-two hours to deliver a baby that was hopelessly twisted in its own cord—the doctors taking the baby to save Mary. Marcus at her bedside weeping, holding her, rocking her back and forth in his arms—the call for him to come to the waterfront where they had to have a militia officer to unload a munitions ship—the great cannon lifted out of the hold of the ship in the net—the paralyzing moment the two-inch hawser snapped—the great gun falling—Marcus looking upward too late, too late—the two-ton gun driving his body onto the massive timbers of the wharf—the three officers at Mary's bedside with downcast eyes—Mary turned her face away from them while they listened to her shriek, and then sobs they hoped never to hear again as long as the Almighty allowed them to remain in mortality.

Standing in the freezing wind that swept the vapor from their faces, staring into the hawkish face of her father, Mary saw him twenty years earlier—tall, eyes glowing with pride as he bent to pick her from her crib and hold her close—the smell of costly clothing and expensive pipe tobacco—the supreme security he brought to her little world—the shock on his face when he realized his brown-eyed little beauty had become a full, beautiful woman—the devastation he bore alone when Mother had died—his pride at her marriage—his joy at her announcement of a child coming—the deep sorrow as he stood at her bedside after the birth of the stillborn child—the agony in his eyes when he learned of the death of Marcus.

The memories came and faded in the few moments they studied each other, memorizing the lines of the face, the expression in the eyes. Once more Mary reached to hold him and he closed her inside his arms, her cheek against his breast, and they stood there for a time, giving and receiving the strength, the love, the empathy.

Mary pulled back. "You go. I'll follow when I can. I love you, Father."

He looked deep into her eyes and nodded his head once and whispered, "I love you, Mary." Then he turned on his heel and walked away into the wintry wind without looking back.

Shivering, Mary pulled the shawl tightly about her head and shoulders and watched him out of sight before she turned back towards the massive pillars and the entryway into the Flint mansion, clutching the leather purse. The sentry swung the door open and she braced herself against the stench and the sounds as she entered. She worked her way through the confusion of cots and men to the library where Doctor Purcell had set up his office, and she knocked.

"Enter."

She pushed the door open. The doctor sat at the heavy oak desk seized from the Flint family, sorting through hopelessly disorganized piles of medical records. Medicines, medical books, surgical instruments, boxes of bandages, stacks of papers, and some clothing belonging to the doctor were jammed onto the polished oak shelves that lined three walls of the spacious room. In one corner away from the windows, a rumpled blanket and pillow were draped over an army cot where the doctor rested when exhaustion overtook him. The windows were covered by army tarps and blankets; the costly draperies that once graced them had long since been torn from their rods and disappeared, to be sold for what they would bring down in Canvas Town or on the East River waterfront.

Mary spoke as the doctor raised his head. "I want to thank you for letting me talk to my father. He's gone. I'm going back down to Mrs. Flint."

The doctor eased back in the leather-covered, overstuffed chair and drew a great, weary breath.

"I'll need you to change bandages in half an hour." He settled the bifocals back onto his nose. "Ever kept medical records?"

"A little. Enough to know what they contain."

He pursed his mouth for a moment and leaned forward, fingers interlaced on the desktop. "You're not well, Mrs. Flint. You shouldn't be working with your mother-in-law, or those poor souls out there." He gestured and she saw the revulsion in his eyes against war and what it could do to the arms and legs and bodies of men. He continued, eyes sweeping the piles of paper on his desk. "Somehow I'm supposed to keep these records accurately while I tend the injured. I don't have half enough staff to take care of the wounded, let alone all the paperwork. I would consider it a great personal favor if you would help with these records. There's a small room in the attic with a lock on the door where you can take quarters. You can take your meals there, or here in my office, as you choose. I need you healthy, and you are not going to get well sleeping in a damp cellar and working with the diseased."

Mary's eyes widened. "You want me working on records?"

"It won't be permanent—only until the records are in some sense of order, and you've had time to regain your strength. One thing I want clear. This has absolutely nothing to do with any personal matter or thought. I'm old enough to be your father and I look upon you much as I would if you were my own daughter. You need have no fear—I pose no threat. Am I understood?" His eyes were steady, clear.

"I understand, sir. When do you want me to begin?"

"We'll change the bandages out there, and then I'll have someone clean out the attic room and help move your cot and bedding there."

"May I make one request?"

"What is it?"

"May my mother-in-law be moved up with me?"

"I doubt there's room."

"I'll make room."

He studied her long and hard. "What is her full name?"

"Judith Draper Flint."

"As you wish."

At half past six, with the bitter south wind rattling branches against the library window, Mary stood before the desk while Doctor Purcell spoke and pointed.

"That stack should be records of incoming wounded. That one, those who died. That one, those still here. That one, those who were transferred to other hospitals, or the ships in the harbor. That big stack is the personal records—medicines and diagnoses and treatment—for all who have been here, whether they're still here or not. They all have to be sorted and put into alphabetical order and then assigned numbers. I have a table and chair set up in the corner for you. Can you handle it?"

"Yes. It will take time."

"When can you start?"

"Now."

At half past seven Doctor Purcell interrupted Mary's work to place a tray on her table with a steaming bowl of beef soup, a slice of heavy brown bread, and a cup of steaming coffee. At fifteen minutes past nine o'clock he opened the door, walked to his desk, and slumped into the chair.

"Your mother-in-law was able to accept a little of the beef broth, and she chewed some bread." His eyes dropped and for long moments he was silent before he raised his head. "She has a high fever. Pneumonia in both lungs."

Mary slowly straightened in her chair and turned to face him as she took charge of herself. "She's dying?"

He nodded. "There's nothing anyone can do. I'm sorry."

Mary folded her hands in her lap and lowered her face, and her shoulders shook silently. Doctor Purcell waited a long time before he spoke again. "You've done enough for today. Go up to your room and get some rest."

A little past midnight the wind died. At two-thirty Mary jerked erect on her mattress, jammed on the floor between the wall and the low bed where Judith Flint lay. Starlight through the tiny window showed only vague black images in the small room and Mary opened her eyes wide, searching for what had awakened her. She started at the sound of Judith's voice wheezing in the darkness.

"Edward, do you hear me? There's something bothering the horses. Can you hear it? A fox. It's a fox. I can hear a fox barking."

The effort was too much. A deep cough came welling up from her chest and suddenly she shook with a coughing spasm, fighting for air. Mary fumbled with flint and steel and struck a light for a lantern, then held it high while she raised onto her knees. She rubbed hard between Judith's bowed shoulder blades, then poured a tin cup of water from the porcelain pitcher on the stand in the corner. She cradled Judith in one arm while she patiently worked the cup a little at a time while Judith tried to swallow. Mary saw the flecks of blood on her chin and around her mouth, and her heart ached as she wet a cloth and wiped them away.

Suddenly Judith sat bolt upright in her bed, staring at the far wall. She did not blink when Mary held the lantern close to her thin, emaciated face.

"Edward, you'd better go. The mare will be nervous with the new foal."

Mary passed her hand directly in front of Judith's face, but Judith did not blink or change expression.

"Edward! Are you there?"

"I'm here," Mary said. "I'll go tend the horses."

"Good. Thank you, Edward." Judith laid down, turned to curl up on her side, closed her eyes, and was asleep almost instantly. Mary tucked the blanket about the thin, bony shoulders and left the lantern burning, until she was certain Judith was sleeping soundly. She twisted the wheel on the wick and the room was plunged into blackness until Mary's eyes adjusted and once again she could see the dark shape of the bed.

Soon. She'll join Edward and Marcus and the baby soon.

For a long time she lay on her mattress with her blanket pulled up against the cold and her eyes fixed on the small window, high on the wall. It was a clear moonless night, and she studied the stars framed by the window while her thoughts ran unchecked.

Gone—all gone—everything gone—all I knew—all that was supposed to be forever. Home—Mother—Father—Marcus—our baby—my home—my town—my friends—my clothes—all gone.

She slipped a hand from beneath the blanket to rub tired eyes.

If God blesses the righteous and punishes the sinners, what did I do—what did my father do—to bring down His wrath on everything I knew and loved? What? Wealth? Father worked hard—earned it—shared it with the poor—taught his family to work. What monstrous crime have I committed? I remember committing no great crime. Then why? Why am I in a small attic room, held against my will by an army from around the world, tending the last member of my dead husband's family in her final hours? Why? How?

She wiped at a tear that trickled cold from the corner of her eye.

I can endure it all if only the Almighty will whisper the reason to me. I only ask that I be allowed to understand—know why the destruction and the killing and the loss of my family and my home was necessary. Is it asking too much? Surely He will not deny me that.

She did not know when she drifted into an exhausted sleep filled with disjointed images of forgotten things from her childhood. Marcus was there, and then a lifeless baby, and her father weeping, and she moaned in her sleep.

The wintry sun had risen to cast a bright shaft of light through the small window when the knock came strong at the door. She jerked awake and sat up, clutching the blanket to her throat as the familiar voice came from outside.

"It's Doctor Purcell. Are you all right?"

"Yes. I was sleeping. I'm sorry. I'll be right down."

She listened to his fading footsteps, then reached for Judith. Her forehead was hot, the skin on her face transparent and tight, and Mary quietly withdrew to let her sleep. She washed herself as best she could with cold water from the large porcelain basin in the corner, dressed, brushed her long hair and tied it back, then stepped out into the narrow attic hall and closed the door. The stench and sounds from below washed over her and she held her breath for a moment to adjust, then hurried to the steep stairway.

At half past nine she carried thin corn mush and hot coffee upstairs, wakened Judith, and patiently spooned tiny amounts into her mouth, wiping at the corners as she worked it and then labored to swallow. She held the coffee cup for her with a small hand towel beneath to catch the spills, watching as she sipped. She washed the frail, emaciated body with cold water, fastened a fresh diaper into place, worked a clean nightshirt onto her, brushed her hair briefly, then settled her back onto her pillow.

She looked into Judith's frightened eyes, and smiled. "You'll be all right. I'll be gone for a while but I'll be back later with something to eat. You rest. Sleep."

The pale mouth opened to speak, but could not, and Mary reached to touch her cheek. "No need to talk. Just rest."

She left the room and returned to the library where she took her place at her table. She continued with the painstaking work of sorting the confusion of medical records into stacks, ready to be sorted alphabetically and then assigned a number before being entered into a master reference ledger.

At noon she carried fish soup and a small amount of strained apples upstairs and raised Judith upright on her arm while she held a spoon to her mouth. The pale gray eyes opened but there was no recognition and Judith raised one trembling hand to push the spoon away. Mary laid her back onto her pillow and for a time sat listening to the rapid, shallow rattle of her breathing before she tucked the blanket around the curled body and made her way back downstairs.

Just before five o'clock Mary started at the sound of the library door opening, and she turned to watch Doctor Purcell slump into his chair, head down, palms flat on the desktop. Slowly he raised his face to meet her inquiring stare, and in that instant Mary knew.

He spoke quietly. "Judith Flint has gone to join her husband."

Mary closed her eyes, bowed her head, and slowly the air went out of her, but there were no tears. She sat in silence for a time while Doctor Purcell waited.

He finally spoke. "I left her in her bed. I didn't know if you wanted to prepare her for burial, or would allow me to do it."

"Thank you. I will."

"Is there a family burial plot on this estate?"

"Yes. Just north, in a grove of maples. Edward and Marcus and my son are there. There's a place for her beside Edward."

"You get what you need to prepare her. I'll assign a carpenter to construct a coffin and assign a detail to prepare the gravesite. Is there anyone I should notify to be at the funeral?"

Mary shook her head. "No, there's no one left but me. I don't know where her family is. She's the last of her immediate family. My father is gone."

"There's no military chaplain available to conduct the service. I'm sorry."

Mary did not hesitate. "I remember enough to say the words. I will take care of it."

"May I have the privilege of joining you?"

"It would be an honor."

At eight o'clock the following morning, under a leaden sky with snowflakes and ice crystals stinging on a southwind, Mary stood in her black dress, coat, hat and veil, alone at the head of the mounds of black earth hacked from the frozen ground, staring down at the plain oak coffin. To one side, his heavy army coat blowing in the wind, Doctor Purcell worked his hat in his hands, eyes downcast. Fifty feet to the west half a dozen red-coated troopers waited with heavy army coat collars upright and scarves pulled up across their faces and shovels clutched in their stiff hands, waiting for the brief graveside service to end.

Mary spoke from memory.

"The Lord is my shepherd; I shall not want. He maketh me to lie down in green pastures: he leadeth me beside the still waters. He restoreth my soul: he leadeth me in the paths of righteousness for his name's sake. Yea, though I walk through the valley of the shadow of death, I will fear no evil: for thou art with me; thy rod and thy staff they comfort me. Thou preparest a table before me in the presence of mine enemies: thou annointest my head with oil; my cup runneth over. Surely goodness and mercy shall follow me all the days of my life: and I will dwell in the house of the Lord for ever."

She stopped for several moments before she went on.

"Our Father which art in heaven, Hallowed be thy name. Thy kingdom come. Thy will be done in earth, as it is in heaven. Give us this day our daily bread. And forgive us our debts, as we forgive our debtors. And lead us not into temptation, but deliver us from evil: For thine is the kingdom, and the power, and the glory, for ever. Amen."

Doctor Purcell murmured, "Amen."

Staring into the open grave, Mary finished. "Dust to dust. Good-bye, Judith. Good-bye until we meet again." She cast a frozen clod onto the coffin.

Mary left the head of the grave and Doctor Purcell came to her side and together they ducked their heads and hunched their shoulders into the storm to walk back to the house. They closed the massive doors and paused to knock the snow and ice from their coats.

"Mary, you are excused for the balance of the day."

She squared her shoulders. "It would be a blessing if I could work—get my mind away from what's happened."

The doctor nodded and hung his overcoat on the peg beside the door as Mary worked her way through the cots to the stairway up to her quarters.

The storm held. By noon the south side of every bush, tree, and building was plastered white. By three o'clock the wind died and the snow came straight down. By five o'clock, in rapidly fading gray twilight, New York was blanketed. At half past six Mary stopped long enough to eat boiled cabbage and fish at her table and to drink black coffee, then steadily continued sorting the unending medical records.

At eight-fifteen Doctor Purcell entered the library and sat down at his desk. "We'll have more wounded arriving from Sugar House in the next two days. I have no idea where we'll put them. Maybe we'll have to send some down to the hospital ships." He shuddered involuntarily at the remembrance of the putrid conditions at the Sugar House infirmary and the inhuman conditions in the hospital ships anchored in the harbor and further south off the Long Island shores.

Mary glanced at him and kept working.

"Don't you think you've done enough today?"

Mary shook her head and read the name on the next record. Hans Conrad Gerhardt. She sorted it into the "G" section and picked up the next one. Josephus Tanner. She dropped it on the "T" section and picked up the next one, but froze as the remembrance came flooding.

Tanner! Josephus Tanner!

Her thoughts leaped. Eli Stroud! Tall—dressed Iroquois—unloading the munitions wagon on Manhattan Island before the great battle—the night passage from Manhattan Island to Long Island with the army—riding beside her in the driver's box, talking—orphaned and taken by the Iroquois at age two—leaving them at age seventeen to find his older sister—Josephus Tanner at the Fort Washington infirmary—saying he had heard of a family that knew of such a girl—Eli's excitement—Josephus Tanner taken a prisoner of war by the British when Fort Washington fell—no way to trace him.

Mary spun on her chair, clutching the record, and Doctor Purcell raised startled eyes, waiting, as she strode to the front of his desk.

"This man," she exclaimed. "Josephus Tanner. Have you heard of him? Do you know if he is still here?"

Doctor Purcell straightened in his chair, startled. "Is he family? A friend?"

"No. But he may know something that a friend needs desperately. Do you know anything of him?"

Doctor Purcell took the record and quickly scanned it. "No, I don't have any recollection of him. Judging from this, I imagine he's either passed on, or sent to one of the hospital ships in the harbor. This record indicates he was dying over two months ago."

Mary spun on her heel and in a moment was back at her table. She set aside the single record of Josephus Tanner and forced herself to slow her racing emotions and think. She straightened the finished stacks of sorted documents and then began the process of going through the thousands of remaining sheets one at a time, seeking the crucial name: Josephus Tanner.

At eleven o'clock Doctor Purcell returned from his rounds and stopped at her table. She was asleep on her arms, a medical record still clutched in her hand, the lantern glowing in her face. He shook her gently. "Mrs. Flint, go to bed. You've done all you can today."

At seven-thirty the following morning, in a world of dazzling white and bright frigid sunlight, Mary and the doctor and four other nurses braced themselves for the wrenching work of removing bandages from stumps of arms and legs, and from holes in human bodies where bayonets or musket balls or grapeshot or cannonball fragments had ripped and torn and penetrated. The cloth came away heavy with black blood and gray stinking matter. They threw the rotten bandages into a sack, washed the area of the wounds with hot water and soap where they could, worked carbolics into a fresh bandage and bound it in place. They looked for the dreaded, telltale pink lines creeping from the wounds towards the armpit or groin, pressed the nodules at both places for pain, and made notes on charts if the wounded winced. If blood poisoning had set in, it would kill them unless the remainder of a destroyed arm or leg were removed at once.

By eight-thirty Mary was back at her table, methodically moving through the stacks of records, sorting them, eagerly watching for the name of Josephus Tanner to again appear. She stopped at one o'clock to eat mutton strips and boiled carrots, then continued. At ten minutes before four o'clock, with the late afternoon dusk beginning to settle, she gasped and sat bolt upright in her chair clutching a sheet of paper. The name Josephus Tanner appeared at the top of a transfer record and she held her breath while she scanned it, then bolted from the room to find Doctor Purcell. She met him walking back towards the library, and she thrust the record to him.

"Doctor, I found this. Josephus Tanner was transferred."

He took the paper and sat down while he settled his bifocals on his nose and carefully read the document.

"Yes, he was. Two weeks ago. Out to the *Dolphin*. That's a prisoner of war hospital ship anchored in the harbor." He drew and released a great sigh, then shook his head. "I don't see how he can still be alive. This says he had a fever above one hundred three and was dying of dysentery and the plague." He closed his eyes to block out the images of misery and death in the holds of the hospital ships. "I'm sorry."

She leaned forward on stiff arms, intense, palms flat on the desk. "There's a chance," she exclaimed. "He might still be there. I've got to know."

The doctor looked at her, puzzled. "What's this all about?"

She straightened and felt her face redden as she fumbled for words. "There is a man who was kind to me when I needed help. He was orphaned as an infant and stolen by the Indians and raised by the Iroquois as one of them. He came back two years ago to find his older sister. Josephus Tanner may know where she is. If he does, it would mean more than you know."

"Who's the man?"

"Eli Stroud."

The doctor's eyes narrowed as he racked his memory. "I don't recall the name."

"Doctor, I beg of you. May I go try to find Josephus Tanner?"

Doctor Purcell's mouth fell open and he clacked it shut. "To the *Dolphin*? Child, you have no idea what you're asking. Those hospital ships are a death sentence. Things are bad here, but you have no idea what exists in the holds of those ships."

"I want to try."

The doctor leaned forward, face drawn in disbelief. "Does this Mr. Stroud mean something to you? More than a friend?"

She had never allowed herself to face the question, and now it was before her squarely, plainly, to be answered. She opened her mouth to speak but her thoughts came confused, unclear, undecided, and she stammered.

"No. I don't know." It caught in her throat and she felt her chin trembling on the brink of tears. She cleared her throat and shook herself to regain control. She started again. "Yes. In a way. He's known such pain. His family was killed before his eyes, and he was raised as an Iroquois Indian. His sister is gone and now he's trying to find what was taken from him when he was two years old. If I can help him find his sister, I will. If I have to go onto the *Dolphin* to do it, I will do that too. Please, Doctor, help me."

For long moments he studied her, slowly realizing that she did not know her true feelings for Eli Stroud. He pursed his mouth for a moment, then spoke, eyes locked with hers.

"Below decks on a prison ship is perhaps the closest one can come on this earth to being in purgatory. The ceilings are low, rooms small, no lights, no ventilation, no sanitation, no water, no toilet facilities. Ten men are stacked where there is scarcely room for five. Every disease known is down there. The air is poison. Each morning the dead are carried onto the deck and thrown overboard. The last morning I spent on one of those ships we dropped seventeen dead bodies into the sea. I have no idea how I avoided death."

He stopped, and she watched a shudder tremble his body at the remembrance. Once again he raised his eyes to hers. "You wish me to help you go onto one of those ships? A young woman of your quality? I will not have that on my head."

"It will not be on your head. It will be on mine. I won't be on the ship for more than a few minutes. Only long enough to inquire of the doctor on board if Josephus Tanner is still alive. That's all."

"I can't take the risk."

"There is no risk. I will not go below decks, I promise. Doctor, you *must* do this."

Her intense urgency reached to touch him like something physical and he lowered his face to study his hands for a moment.

"Let me think on it."

He stood abruptly and paced from her, torn between a deep wish to help this young woman for whom he felt such empathy, and his duty as a British officer, hating the rising feeling that either way he decided, he would feel regret. He drew a resolute breath and turned back to her.

"You go change to warm clothing while I write orders for the captain of the ship." He stopped and brought his eyes directly to hers. "I must have your solemn promise that under any circumstance you will not go below decks on the ship."

"Yes. Of course."

His voice became quiet, penetrating. "Listen to me carefully. This hospital has a longboat tied to a wharf to transport men to the ships. You will have to go there to get it, and there is no place in New York more dangerous than the waterfront—Canvas Town—in the dark of night. Men hide there who will cut your throat for the coat on your back. Do you have any concept of what I'm trying to tell you?"

"Yes. I do."

"In the name of Heaven I hope so. I'll arrange for four armed soldiers to escort you from here in my carriage. Two will row the boat out to the ship while the other two guard the coach. They will be under strict orders to take you to the ship and return you here, and nothing more. Their muskets will be primed and they will shoot to kill the moment anything threatens. Go directly there and return directly here. Do you understand?"

"Yes."

"Go put on your winter clothing."

She changed into a dark, heavy woolen skirt and jacket in her tiny room, then shrugged into her heaviest, ankle-length winter coat. She swept her bonnet from its nail on the back of the door and started to turn the lamp down when she stopped and turned, looking at the small bed. The purse given her by her father, filled with the gold coins and the remaining family jewels, was hidden under the mattress. For a few seconds she pondered before she knelt on the bed and lifted the far edge of the thin canvas sack of straw to grasp the heavy leather drawstrings, and she held the purse in her hands, staring while she made her decision.

If I have to bribe the captain of the ship, I will.

She thrust the heavy purse into her coat pocket and flew down the stairs to the library where the doctor was waiting beside his desk. He handed her a paper, folded and sealed.

"Deliver that to the captain on the ship. He will do all else that is necessary."

She nodded as she thrust it into the pocket of her coat with the leather purse.

"Outside is my carriage and four soldiers. Sergeant Hastings is in charge. They'll be with you at all times."

Again she nodded.

He dropped his glance to the floor for a moment, then looked her in the eye. "I have misgivings in doing this." She saw fear in his eyes, and a need she had never seen before as he struggled with his words. "My wife died giving birth to our daughter, and the baby died seventeen days later. She was a dark-eyed beauty, much like you. Be careful."

She stood rooted, stunned for a moment, then without thought she stepped to him and reached to kiss him on the cheek as she would have her father. He jerked rigid with shock, then slowly raised his arms to grasp her shoulders and gently push her back.

He followed her to the front door and watched as the two armed soldiers escorted her to the carriage hitched to a high-headed gray gelding, heavy with long winter hair, vapors rising from its nostrils into the still, frigid night air. Two of the uniformed regulars helped her into the passenger compartment of the coach then entered to sit opposite her while the remaining two mounted the driver's seat. The driver clucked to the horse and the carriage swung into motion and was gone in the gathering dusk.

The only sounds were the creaking of the carriage, the clatter of the wheels, and the horse in the empty street as the driver worked his way east towards the shipyards below Catharine Street on the East River. In full darkness he reined in at the office of the harbormaster, with the night lights of more than twenty ships dotting the blackness south of the wharves. Inside, the rotund little man on night duty studied his great scale drawing of the harbor, then tapped a stubby finger on a small circle that lay in deep water four hundred yards south of the Battery on the southern tip of New York.

"There she is. The *Dolphin*. A plague ship if ever one sailed the high seas." He raised his face defiantly. "And she's coming no closer to this island than she is right now." He shrugged into his great overcoat. "Follow me and I'll point out her lights."

Five minutes later the driver reined the horse around and the iron horseshoes struck sparks from the cobblestones as he worked his way southwest in the blackness, past the high-walled Battery, then angled west to stop at the first of the wharves. Canvas Town began two hundred yards further north.

Under a moonless black vaulted heaven lighted only by starlight, the two soldiers climbed from the driver's seat while the two inside the carriage stepped down to help Mary to the cobblestones. The tides were high and rising, and the boats tied to the wharf were undulating on the incoming sea swells. The only sounds in the darkness were the rapid breathing of the horse and the lapping of the black, frigid seawater against the pilings as Sergeant Hastings shivered and gave his orders.

"Shouldn't be much more than 'alf hour. Watch the buggy and horse sharp and keep a keen eye. Never can tell about those bloody criminals in Canvas Town. 'Alf a dozen men in there would cut all our throats fer the price the doctor's 'orse and carriage would bring."

The soldier facing him hunched his shoulders against the biting cold. He pointed north towards the blackness that hid Canvas Town. "It's not to my likin' to be standin' in the dark 'ere on this bloody wharf fer very long knowin' wots over there ready to take everythin' we've got and leave us floatin' in the bay. Don't stop fer tea out there on that ship."

"Don't strike a light and they'll never know you're here."

"They know. We sounded like a regiment of artillery comin' in, with the 'orse an' carriage on those bloody cobblestones."

The sergeant turned to Mary. "Ma'am, if you're ready, we'll move down the wharf to the doctor's boat."

Together the three walked twenty yards before Hastings stopped and pointed. "Ma'am, that's the doctor's boat. If you're ready, we'll help you."

One soldier steadied the boat while Hastings held Mary's arm. She took her place on the plank in the bow, and they both followed to sit at the midsection of the boat and drop the oars thumping into the locks.

Moments later the men were straining at the oars, moving against the incoming tide. The longboat moved steadily southward, past two great men-of-war to the west, holding a course for the lights of the *Dolphin*, which rose and fell rhythmically on the incoming sea swells.

Sergeant Hastings hailed the night watch on the decks of the ship, looming high above them, and two seamen dropped a ladder rattling against the side of the ship. Five minutes later the two soldiers and Mary stood on the decks, facing the two armed seamen and a young ensign who held a lantern, wide-eyed when he recognized Mary to be a woman.

"Identify yourselves," he demanded.

"Sergeant Hastings, his Majesty's Fifth Northumberland Fusileers. Under orders of Colonel Otis Purcell, medical doctor, to deliver this young lady here. I believe she has written orders for your captain, sir."

"Written orders to do what? This is a hospital ship and no lady has business here."

"The orders are for your captain, sir."

The young man turned on his heel and returned minutes later with a scowling captain.

"I'm Captain Worley. What's this about orders from Doctor Purcell?"

Mary handed him the sealed document and he stared at it for a moment before he broke the seal and turned it to the lantern to read it.

"Josephus Tanner? You're looking for a man named Josephus Tanner?"

"Yes, sir."

The captain turned to the ensign. "Tell First Mate Bolling to bring the ledger of both the incoming wounded and those who are no longer with us."

While they waited the captain turned to Mary. "I regret I cannot invite you to more appropriate accommodations than this freezing deck, ma'am, but this is a hospital ship and it would be folly to invite you below decks."

"Your concern does you credit. I understand. I'm fine."

Three minutes later a disgruntled First Mate Bolling appeared with two heavy ledgers. "You wanted these, sir?"

"Yes. Ensign, bring the light. Mr. Bolling, can you find the name of Josephus Tanner in either ledger?"

Bolling's eyes widened. "Now, sir?"

"While we wait."

"Yes, sir." With the books cradled in one arm, Bolling began a methodical search in the incoming ledger, moving his finger slowly down the pages, silently mouthing the names. Three minutes later his finger stopped. "'Ere, sir. Josephus Tanner came on board December fourteenth. It was a Saturday, sir. Saturday afternoon."

"Very good. Is he still aboard?"

Bolling shifted the books and again searched. Two minutes ticked by while they stood on the gently rising and falling deck and Bolling steadily moved his finger down all entries after December fourteenth, then checked it again. He closed the register and raised his head. "No, sir. No record I can see of him leaving. 'E must still be down there."

The captain faced Mary. "You have your answer, ma'am. That is all Doctor Purcell requested of me. My men will assist you back into your boat."

The captain took one step before Mary reached to grasp his arm, her face pale in the yellow lantern light. "Sir, may I see him? For less than one minute. He has a name that I must know. It is urgent."

The captain's brow furrowed. "I cannot allow you below decks under any circumstance, ma'am. I'm sorry."

"Then can you bring him up here?" She stood firm with her feet spread slightly.

"Ma'am, this uh . . . visit . . . is highly unusual to say the least. You have no idea what you're asking. That man is dying or he wouldn't be here. To identify him from among the three hundred sixty-eight men down there would take time and to bring him up here on this freezing deck would be extremely difficult."

"Captain, please. Please. You've no idea what it would mean to get that single name from him. I'm begging. Please let me talk with him for one minute. No more than one minute, I promise."

The captain's face turned to a dark scowl. "The sick are settled for the night. It's unthinkable to go prowling among them looking for one man."

"Captain, I can pay. I have gold coin. Any amount."

The captain's chin rose. "Are you suggesting bribery?"

Mary's face clouded and for a moment she stared at the deck. "I'm sorry I insulted you, sir. I didn't mean it that way. I only meant I would pay for what I want. Is there no way?"

Sergeant Hastings interrupted. "Sir, is it possible your—"

He stopped at the sound of a single musket shot that came rolling across the black waters, queerly loud from the shore a quarter mile distant. Every person on the deck turned their face north, peering into the blackness, waiting, watching for the yellow streak of flame and the cracking bang of another shot, but there was nothing. Hastings looked at the soldier by his side and they both looked once more at the shore, fear rising in their breasts. Hastings continued. "Sir, is it possible a surgeon or a nurse would have a list of where the men are down there?"

The captain turned to Bolling and growled, "Go ask Doctor Dunphy."

Five minutes later Bolling returned. "Josephus Tanner is on the third deck, amidships, sir."

The captain clasped his hands behind his back and growled, "Bring him here."

Twenty minutes later Bolling appeared back on deck leading four men who bore a stretcher covered high with blankets with only the bearded, emaciated face of a dying man exposed. Sores oozed a thick yellow discharge. The young ensign lowered the lantern while Mary quickly knelt.

"Josephus Tanner, can you hear me?"

The eyes fluttered open and in the dim lantern light she saw the life slipping away. She leaned close. "Do you remember me? Last fall we talked at Fort Washington about a little girl. A little blue-eyed girl from New Hampshire whose parents were killed a long time ago. She was given to a minister. A reverend. Do you remember?"

The eyes closed and Mary placed her hand on the blankets covering his chest and shook gently. "Do you remember?"

The eyes slowly opened once more and his mouth tried to move. The man licked his dry, cankered lips and his head nodded almost imperceptibly.

Mary realized he was seeing things that only the dying could see. "Do you remember the reverend's name?"

His mouth began to work and she brought her ear close. Above her the circle of faces became silent, holding their breath as they waited.

She closed her eyes and concentrated, her ear only inches from the foul smell of the beard, and slowly the word came.

"Fielding."

"Fielding? You said 'Fielding'?"

The head nodded faintly.

"What other name? Fielding what? From where?"

The body began to tremble and she watched him gather his ebbing strength and once again his mouth moved.

"Cyrus. New Hampshire."

"Cyrus Fielding of New Hampshire?"

The head nodded one more time before the eyes closed.

She touched his chest. "Thank you. Oh, thank you."

The four men lifted the stretcher, and the others watched as they carried it back to the stairway, down into the bowels of the ship, their hard leather heels clicking hollow.

Captain Worley fixed Mary with a stare. "Was there anything else?"

"No, sir. I scarcely know how to thank you."

He nodded curtly. "My men will assist you to your boat."

Sergeant Hastings descended the wooden rungs of the rope ladder and steadied it while Mary climbed down into the boat. Moments later they swung the bow of the longboat north with the two soldiers stroking strong.

Hastings spoke to the man next to him. "I got a bad feelin' about that musket shot."

The other man said nothing as they bent their backs and strained against the oars.

They nosed the longboat into the wharf, tied it in its berth, and both soldiers cocked their muskets, clicking loud in the darkness before they walked rapidly towards the head of the wharf, Mary between them. They peered wide-eyed, searching to locate the carriage and the horse in the darkness but there were no dark shapes, no sound. They quickly came to the place where they had left it and there was nothing—no sign, no trace.

Hastings felt the hair on his arms and neck rise as his thoughts leaped. He barked frantically, "To the right, back to the harbormaster's office. *Run!*"

Their pounding footsteps sounded too loud on the cobblestones as they ran east along the waterfront, then followed the curve northward. They had not covered fifty yards when Mary became aware of movement in the shadows to her left, among the black buildings and her breath caught in her throat. Hastings slowed and the soldier to Mary's right slowed with him, and she saw many black shapes moving, hunched over, dodging among the discarded shipping crates and barrels left in the street.

Hastings stopped and raised his musket and shouted, "'Ere, get out and show yerselves! I'm Sergeant Randolph Hastings of His Majesty's Fifth Northumberland Fusileers and I got with me an armed squad and we're going to fire if you don't—"

A musket blasted a three-foot flame from five yards to his left and another musket roared ten yards directly in front of him. He grunted and threw his arms high and went down backwards, his own musket clattering in the street. The soldier to Mary's right fired his musket at the muzzle flame and in that instant three more muskets blasted from straight ahead and the soldier buckled over forward and went to his knees before he toppled over.

Instantly Mary turned on her heel and sprinted back the way they had come, her only thought: *run, run, run!* She passed the wharf where the doctor's boat was tied, legs driving, not caring where she was going, aware only that behind her were men who would kill her if they caught her. She reached the near limits of Canvas Town and pounded on without thought until she was gasping and battling for breath. Only then did she slow and crouch behind a jumbled heap of charred roof timbers left jammed against the side of a burned-out warehouse. She struggled for seconds to control her breathing, then held it while she listened. From the pinpoints of ship lights out on the black harbor came the clanging of brass bells as the eight o'clock watch was changed. She heard the sounds of invisible men running on the cobblestones, their guttural voices growing stronger as they came closer.

"Couldn't tell for certain, but it looked like a woman. Can't be far." Sounds of abandoned barrels and crates being overturned and thrown into the street became louder.

In wild desperation she forced her mind to think.

Can't go farther into the streets of Canvas Town—can't hide in the buildings— too many robbers—too many traps. Only way is the harbor—the water.

Quickly she pivoted to her left, hunched low, and ran across the street onto the frozen snow where the dirt joined the heavy timbers of the wharf. She slowed to work her way soundlessly across the wooden beams to the far edge, where the longboats were moored, each in its berth. She jerked the rope knot that tied a longboat to the big iron ring on the wharf and set it adrift. Then she sucked in her breath, set her chin, and carefully lowered herself into the water, gasping as her skirt billowed upward in the water and the terrible numbing bite hit her legs. It reached just past her waist before her feet touched bottom. She threw her weight against the bow of the longboat and pushed it away from the wharf with all her strength and watched it move out, slow, and stop.

Then she turned in the water, arms held high, and moved back between the great pilings supporting the wharf. She felt floating trash and debris bump and then she ducked her head and shoulders as the water became more shallow, and then she was on her knees in a foot of water and could go no further under the wharf. She remained there in the muck and slime and the floating trash, battling to control her breathing, making no sound.

She heard a rustle and a movement to her right, and then another, and realized she was among rats, coming to investigate what had washed up under the wharf. Her gorge rose sour in her throat and she swallowed and shuddered, trying to control her wild revulsion, trying not to scream or retch.

The sounds of feet in the streets came, faintly at first, then closer, and then the voices, low and harsh.

"Got to be here somewhere."

"Maybe she's hiding in one of the buildings or dodged up a street."

"Not likely, the way she was runnin'. Maybe down in the boats. Maybe gone in a boat."

She bit down on her panic and remained perfectly still, hardly breathing while her feet and legs became numb, like sticks of wood. The sound of feet thumping on the wharf became louder and then they stopped directly above her head. She could hear their breathing, heavy from their run, and hear their growled cursing as they peered into the pitch-blackness, pausing from time to time to listen.

"There's nobody here."

"No? There *was* somebody here. See the longboat there, floatin' on the tide? That wasn't no accident."

"Think she's hidin' inside? Fetch it."

"*You* fetch it. That water's freezin'."

"I'm not goin' into no water lookin' for no woman. Besides, there's no time to go fetchin' a boat from the harbor. Them musket shots is goin' to have the army down here directly, lookin' for them four we done in. They was wearin' British uniforms an' one of 'em was a sergeant. And that horse and carriage didn't belong to no farmer. No sir, I ain't goin' swimmin' after that boat, not with the British army comin'. We got us a good haul from our night's work an' I'm gettin' out of here while I can."

They stood on the wharf a moment longer with Mary directly beneath their feet, mouth clamped shut, not moving. There was a muffled sound by her head and in the next instant something heavy and scrambling landed on her shoulder and brushed her cheek. She jerked and reached and felt the wet fur and the twisting, squirming body of a huge rat. She slapped at it and it hit the water splashing, and she jammed both hands over her mouth to hold in a scream.

"Hear that? There's something under there."

"If it's that woman, she's keepin' company with the wharf rats, and that isn't likely." For a split second the voice fell silent, and then came a hissed, "*Listen!*"

Far to the east came the faint shouts of angry men and the sound of feet pounding on the cobblestones.

Above her head one of the voices blurted, "That's British soldiers. I'm leavin'."

Running feet sounded loud for a moment and then they were off the wharf into the street going west, and then they were gone, disappeared in Canvas Town.

Mary moved three feet away from the mud of the shore, still on her knees, and the water rose around her. Silently she bowed her head and closed her eyes and strained to hear. The shouts of the oncoming soldiers grew louder and she could hear their boots hitting the cobblestones, and then they stopped. There was faint talking and then the sounds of the soldiers began to fade and were quickly gone.

They're going back! They can't! I'm here! They must come here!

For a moment she battled an overpowering need to scramble up onto the wharf and run shouting after them, "Come back, come back!" but she dared not—not in Canvas Town where men and women alike were found every week, face down in the streets and in the harbor, dead for the clothes they wore on their backs.

She huddled in the water, afraid to make a sound, afraid to leave. Seconds became minutes and still she waited. Her feet and legs lost all feeling and as minutes became half an hour, her shivering became uncontrollable and she began to shake violently. She waited until her knees began to buckle before she took charge of herself and faced her terror.

If I stay here I will lose both legs. If someone is waiting for me, so be it. I will remain here no longer.

Her legs were like sticks detached from her body, her mind. She gave commands but they would not move. She reached into the water with her hands, bent over, to lift them and force them forward, and it took minutes for her to move fifteen feet from beneath the wharf into the waist-deep water where the longboats were tied. With a strength born of desperation she pulled herself into a longboat and for a time lay panting, exhausted. Then she forced herself to sit up and reached to massage her legs. Her soaked skirts and petticoats were slick with ice as she pulled them back and began to work her legs with her hands, massaging, working the great muscles. She felt nothing—no pain, no cold—and in panic she began to pound them with the flat of her hands, squeezing them with all her strength, anything to make the blood circulate and return some sense of feeling to them. Slowly they responded and minutes later it was as though a thousand needles were piercing her legs. Silent tears ran freezing down her cheeks as she continued working. She reached for the gunwales of the boat and tried to stand. She could make it to her knees, but she could not force her legs to support her. She sat down on the boat seat and once again pounded and massaged her legs while the needles came and then she could move her feet, and finally could move her toes inside her frozen shoes.

She moved to the bow of the boat and pulled herself up onto the wharf on her hands and knees, and then raised her right knee to try to stand. Two minutes later she took her first step and groaned at the pain while she forced her left foot to move forward. Slowly she moved back towards the street, legs throbbing as feeling came creeping back.

The hospital! I've got to make it back to the hospital—Doctor Purcell!

She stayed away from the doorways and the windows of the burned-out buildings near the wharf until it was behind her, then moved steadily towards Broadway, then north. Her water-soaked clothing froze stiff as she forced herself onward. She worked her hands together to keep circulation, and began counting the blocks, then her steps, to distract herself from the pain and the fear.

She pushed on, slowly losing reality. She could not remember making the last turn towards the great lawn of the Flint estate covered with snow and ice, but suddenly she was there and she stumbled towards the huge pillars supporting the portico. Her foot caught in the frozen hem of her dress and she pitched forward onto her hands and knees and she could not rise. Her arms began to tremble and then gave way, and she settled onto her side in the snow, working her legs, still trying to rise.

On the portico, the picket huddled over the small metal box with draft holes, filled with glowing coals, shivering while vapors rose from his face. Movement towards the street brought his head up and suddenly he stood, head thrust forward, peering into the darkness.

He muttered, "Wot's that layin' out there in the snow? Was that there 'alf an hour ago? I'm thinkin' it was not."

He turned back to pick up his musket from where it leaned against the wall, then walked to the edge of the portico.

"Who comes there?" He waited, head thrust forward, peering. "I say, speak up or I'll 'ave to shoot. Who comes there?"

There was no sound or movement.

Cautiously he descended the two steps to the broad brick path, musket held at waist level, bayonet thrust forward, and slowly walked down the bricks, eyes never wavering from the dark form in the snow. Suddenly he jerked upright.

"May lightnin' strike me if it isn't a woman!" He slipped his musket strap over his shoulder as he trotted to Mary's side and peered into her face.

"I know this one!" he exclaimed.

He scooped her up into his arms and moved as fast as he could on the slippery ground to the big entry doors and banged with his foot. The heavy door swung open and Doctor Purcell gasped when he saw the dark form bundled in the picket's arms.

Two minutes later they had Mary on the doctor's cot in the library behind a thick portable curtain. The men waited while two women nurses removed the frozen clothing, rubbed her briskly with large towels, worked a heavy nightshirt onto her, and covered her with blankets. They pushed the curtain back and Doctor Purcell came to her side and dropped to one knee to place his hand on her forehead.

"Can you hear me?"

The wide-set dark eyes fluttered open and tried to focus, then closed. "Yes," she whispered.

"Can you tell me what happened?"

Slowly she formed the words with her eyes still closed. "Horse and carriage stolen. Shooting on the wharf. Soldiers gone. Hid under he wharf. Walked back. So sorry. So sorry."

Doctor Purcell wiped as tears came at the corners of her eyes. "You're safe now. Rest. We'll take care of everything."

She swallowed and roused and her eyes opened for a moment. "You have to write. Get paper. You have to write a letter."

"It can wait."

She stirred and tried to raise on one elbow and fell back. "No. Let me have a paper. Got to send a letter. Can't wait."

Quickly the doctor stepped to his desk and returned with a pencil and paper. "Go ahead."

With her eyes closed, fighting against unconsciousness, she began: "To Eli Stroud. Boston Regiment. With General Washington. Your sister was given to a reverend named Cyrus Fielding of New Hampshire. Cyrus Fielding."

She swallowed and for a moment her eyes opened and she looked into Doctor Purcell's face. "Did you write it?"

"Yes. Eli Stroud. Cyrus Fielding."

"Send it today?"

"I will."

She closed her eyes and her face settled as she yielded to the unutterable fatigue that reached to draw her into the warm blackness.

Notes

The northwest quarter of New York City was burned in a tremendous fire just after midnight on September 21, 1776 (see Johnston, *The Campaign of 1776*, part 2, pp. 118–19). The destruction was severe and eventually the district became known as "Canvas Town." People still lived there, though in hovels patched together from the burned wreckage. Many people of dark and evil designs—soldiers and roving bands—roamed New York City, entering homes, churches, and schools, including the King's College, pillaging and stealing whatever they desired, then selling the plunder on the open market. Some churches and other large buildings were converted to hospitals for the wounded (see Ketchum, *The Winter Soldiers*, pp. 179–80).

For additional history on the New York City fire see Leckie, *George Washington's War*, pp. 281–82.

The *Dolphin* is a fictional ship used to represent the horrific conditions of the prison and hospital ships of the time (see Leckie, *George Washington's War*, pp. 182–83).

Mary Flint, her father Rufus Broadhead, and Doctor Otis Purcell are fictional characters.

CHAPTER VI

★ ★ ★

*T*he call came unexpected in the twilight of thick, gray storm clouds and the quiet hush of thick-falling snow.

"Weems and Stroud!"

Billy and Eli paused from lacing cut pine boughs to the slanted wall of their lean-to and peered west, searching through the trees for movement. The call came again and Billy raised an arm to point at incoming men, picking their way through the thick woods, and he raised his voice. "Here! Weems and Stroud are here."

They studied the burly sergeant and two armed corporals as they approached, hair and shoulders covered by snow, vapors rising from their gaunt, bearded faces. They were dressed in filthy, tattered coats, feet wrapped in canvas.

The sergeant walked to the fire to face them, and spoke, surly, demanding. "You Weems and Stroud?"

Billy studied the three men for a moment, searching his memory for recognition but none came. "Yes."

"You the two who brought in those thirteen deserters yesterday?"

"Yes."

The sergeant hooked a thumb over his shoulder. "You're wanted at the court-martial."

"What court-martial?"

The sergeant was impatient. "Over at headquarters. They got one going over there to decide when we shoot 'em. Been at it half the day. Can't finish without you two telling what you done."

"When do they want us?"

"Now."

"Whose orders?"

"Colonel Broderick, Connecticut Regiment. Same as the deserters."

Billy looked at Eli, and Eli shrugged, then picked up his rifle while Billy reached for his musket. "We'll follow you."

The sergeant turned on his heel and retraced his steps back through snow that sifted through the trees to the forest floor, and then they were out onto the open field with the lights of the Keith House, five hundred yards due west, glowing yellow in the gathering gloom. The great, silent snowflakes drifted down soft, gentle, to stick to their hair and eyebrows and tattered coats. No human hand could hope to fashion the intricate shapes and designs that nature gave so freely, to be treasured by human eyes but for the moment and then gone forever. They followed the deepening trail through the snow, lost for a moment in the profound beauty of a white, silent world, and then they were passing the stables and the carriage barn. The sergeant spoke to the two pickets standing at the rear entrance of the great, two-storied stone house.

"Sergeant Culhane coming in with witnesses for the court-martial."

The pickets nodded and stepped aside as he climbed the two steps to the large landing and turned to Billy and Eli.

"Get what snow you can off your feet and come in. You'll have to wait in the coatroom, just inside the door. I'll let them know you're here."

They stomped their feet hard, then the sergeant opened the door and he and his two men walked into the large coatroom, followed by Billy and Eli. They used a broom to clear the rest of the snow from their feet, and the sergeant gestured to open pegs lining one wall. "Hang your coats there. I'll come get you when they're ready."

They listened to the sound of his wrapped feet moving up the hall, then a knock, and a door opened and closed. The two men left behind gestured, and Billy and Eli took off their coats, shook them before they hung them on pegs. They straightened their shirts as best they could, and ran their hands through their hair to get out as much snow and water as they could, and smooth it. They stood in the lantern light, waiting, and their noses began to drip in the heat. They wiped at them with their sleeves while the ice in the wraps on Billy's feet and in the wolf hair on Eli's knee-length moccasins began to melt and leave small puddles on the hardwood floor. Billy glanced at Eli's wolf skin coat. In late November Eli had gone out for eight nights to bring back four wolf pelts. He had wrapped them around heated rocks to dry them, then carefully cut them, and sewed the pieces together with a sliver of bone and dried gut to fashion a coat with a parka, and moccasins that reached his knees.

They heard a door open up the hall, and seconds later the sergeant was there, pointing. "Follow me."

They left their weapons in a corner by their coats and walked rapidly behind the sergeant up the long, austere hallway. Eli still wore his weapons belt with the black tomahawk thrust through. The sergeant stopped at a large door on the left and rapped. A lieutenant opened it eight inches and the sergeant spoke.

"Corporal Weems and Private Stroud are here."

The door opened wide, Sergeant Culhane stepped aside, and the young, smooth-cheeked lieutenant motioned them into the large room, Billy leading, to face a long, plain table ten feet in front of them. Seated behind the table was a colonel with a major on either side, all hunched forward, studying notes. Crowded to the left stood the thirteen men accused of desertion, with ten armed men standing loosely around them, muskets and bayonets ready. To the right was a stone fireplace with a fire crackling. The room was hot, stuffy, the air rank with the smell of wet clothing and wet hair.

The colonel was paunchy, red-faced, thinning gray hair. He raised his head and peered at Billy and Eli for a moment, then spoke. He was direct, curt, and it was obvious that he hated being there, hated the duty that required him to sit in judgment on thirteen of his own men, loathed the thought of entering an order that would put all thirteen of them before twenty-six men who would shoot them dead and bury them in unmarked, shallow graves.

"I'm Colonel Broderick, Fortieth Connecticut. Who are you?"

"Corporal Billy Weems, Boston Regiment, Company Nine."

"Eli Stroud. Scout."

Broderick looked at the Iroquois hunting shirt and the wolf skin moccasins, and his eyes fixed on the weapons belt with the ominous black tomahawk, and his forehead wrinkled. "Scout? What unit?"

"Same as Corporal Weems. Boston Regiment."

Broderick cleared his throat and dropped a finger to a paper in front of him, then raised his head. "This court-martial was convened to hear the charge of desertion against these thirteen men. I'm told you two are the ones that brought them in. Am I correct?"

A hush fell over the room as everyone stared at Billy and Eli, waiting, and Billy answered. "Yes, sir."

"Last night?"

"Yes, sir."

"All right. Start at the beginning and tell me the story."

"Not much to tell. At dusk I saw movement in the trees to the south. Eli went after them and I followed in a few minutes. He got ahead of them and stopped them, and I came in behind. They didn't fight. We brought them back." Billy shrugged. "That's all."

There was a moment of silence before Broderick spoke again. "You're saying the two of you braced thirteen men in the dark? Thirteen deserters who knew they could be shot? And there was no trouble? No one tried to escape? fight? Did they have weapons among them?"

"Yes, sir. Ten muskets, eight with bayonets. We brought them back with us."

"Food?"

"A little in knapsacks. They ate it back in camp while we were waiting for the Connecticut officers to come get them."

"Did they know there were just two of you?"

"Yes, sir."

"How?"

"We told them."

"What else did you tell them?"

"That if they tried to escape or fight, the first man down would be their leader." Billy turned his head to look at them. "I believe his name was Pratt. Bertram Pratt. We told them that after he was down we would take them as they came. I led them back to camp with Eli at their rear with his rifle in the middle of Pratt's back. They didn't fight."

"Did you accuse them of desertion?"

"We did."

"What did they say?"

"They said they were going to Philadelphia to get help for two of them. Their feet were frozen and going bad and they were afraid they'd lose a foot or a leg—maybe die. They'd already cut off some toes that had gone rotten."

Broderick hunched forward to peer intently at the notes on the paper before him for half a minute, traced a line with an index finger, then raised his head.

"We have that in the record. Did you tell them there were other men in this camp in the same condition?"

"No, sir."

"Anything else?"

Billy paused for a moment. "Only that some of them are kin to each other."

Broderick eased back in his chair. "That's in the record too." He turned to Eli. "Anything to add?"

Eli looked Broderick in the eyes. "One man's the uncle of Pratt. A younger one's his cousin. Pratt was looking out for his kin." He paused for a moment, arranging his thoughts. "They were on Long Island when we got overrun and they came on through all the other trouble after, clear down to here. If they were truly deserters I think Billy and me would have had a fight on our hands out there last night. They had ten muskets among them when I told them to stop, and if their hearts had been bad, some of them would have made a break in the dark, but none did. Once we got their muskets, those who could helped the crippled ones and they came on in peaceful. I don't think they meant to be deserters. I think they meant to get their kin to Philadelphia for help."

Eli stopped for a moment and the room fell silent while he finished. "Has anybody asked them if they would have come back once they got the sick ones to a hospital?"

Broderick's eyebrows arched. "No." He turned to the prisoners. "Sergeant Pratt, you heard the question. If you had gotten help in Philadelphia for the disabled, would the rest of you have come back?"

Pratt's eyes lowered and he stood still, not moving. For a long time he stared at the floor, searching his soul. "I never thought that far, sir. I only knew how bad I wanted to try to save the feet and legs of my uncle and my cousin. How hard it would be back home trying to work their farm without legs. I didn't mean to run out on no duty, or no battle. I was at Long Island, and then New York and White Plains, and on through Fort Washington and Fort Lee, and then across New Jersey, runnin' the whole time, tryin' to keep the company together. We all got our feet froze on night guard, and it was me had to cut off the toes when they went putrid. If you're askin' me now would I have come back when I got them to a hospital . . . I can only tell you I been waitin' and watchin' for a chance at a fair fight with the British where we can show 'em we can do somethin' besides run. I didn't come all this way to quit. I think I'd have come back. I think all of us who could, would have." Pratt stopped and for ten seconds the only sound was the crackling of the fire.

All eyes shifted to Broderick. His shoulders slumped and he raised a hand to rub weary eyes, then gathered his papers. "That's all. This hearing is concluded. The court-martial panel will reconvene and announce its decision tomorrow morning."

"Sir, may I say something?" Billy stepped forward.

Broderick sighed. "Make it brief."

Billy licked his dry, cracked lips. "Eli lost his family to Iroquois when he was two, except for a sister that he thinks is still alive. The Iroquois raised him and seventeen years later he left them to go find her. She's the only kin he has. I doubt there's a man in this room who knows what Eli does about the pull kin can have. Sometimes it's stronger than duty. I believe Pratt would have come back once he got his kin to a doctor. I believe that, sir."

Broderick leaned forward on his elbows, eyes narrowed. "Are you defending what these men did? Arguing in their favor?"

"No, sir. I'm just saying I don't think it would be right to shoot these thirteen men for what they did. I think they'll do their duty if they get a chance. I would not be afraid to fight beside them."

Broderick gathered his papers. "That's all. This hearing's concluded. We'll have our findings in writing by morning."

The snow had stopped and the clouds overhead had thinned to show patches of the black velvet heavens, studded with diamonds, and an almost full moon hanging just above the southeastern skyline. The trail left by Billy and Eli and the three soldiers was but a faint trace in the fresh-fallen snow. The two men walked east from the Keith House into the great open field in the strange, hushed wonderland with only the sound of the snow squeaking beneath their feet as they passed. An unexpected sense of awe settled over them and they slowed to look about.

Ahead four hundred yards were the woods that gave partial shelter to the Continental army, and in the trees they saw the campfires, small points of light in the darkness. Behind them the lights of the Keith House were yellow behind drawn blinds. Around them the white blanket of new snow turned the blackness to a deep, soft gray that transformed the world into a thing of beauty and deep, quiet peace. They said nothing as they moved on, each humbled by his own sudden awareness of the wonder of life, of the earth, of his own being, his smallness, and each let his own thoughts run. In the deep quiet, new feelings arose inside Billy.

So vast! Limitless. Nature knows the secret—peace—that's the secret—peace. Who are we? So small in the vastness—unable to find the way—forever looking—never finding. Why can't we learn peace? We learn war—killing each other—thirteen men back there—will they be shot in the morning? shot in the name of seeking peace? No one speaks of the foolishness in shooting men to make peace—is peace the opposite of war? Maybe—in part—but that's not the peace each man yearns for—peace in his heart. Lord Jesus had it right—peace not as the world—my peace, my peace—that's the secret—Jesus knew—nature knows.

They came to the woods and then their own lean-to, and they blew on the embers of a fire nearly dead and added twigs, then logs. They sat on the pine-bough floor of their lean-to with their hands to the fire, staring silently into the dancing flames. Billy was still lost in the unexpected impressions that had overcome him as they walked through the great field of snow in the dark of night.

There was a sound and both of them turned their heads to peer as the diminutive form of Sergeant Alvin Turlock took shape in the darkness. He walked to their fire and Billy moved to make room for him under the lean-to. He sat on the pine boughs, sensing the quiet between the two men, and he waited for a time before he spoke.

"You were at the hearing?"

Billy nodded.

"They going to shoot those men?"

"They'll decide by morning."

"You tell 'em those men fought from Long Island on through?"

"They know."

"They know they was only tryin' to save family?"

Billy glanced at Turlock and for the first time realized that beneath the tough crust of the little man, he yearned to belong to a family. Billy answered, "We told them."

Turlock reached with his sleeve to wipe at his nose. "If they decide to shoot 'em, I think it's got to go to General Washington for approval."

Eli spoke quietly. "General Washington? If it goes to him, I'll talk to him."

Turlock's eyes widened in surprise. "The general know you?"

Billy answered. "The general knows Eli."

Turlock did not inquire.

Morning came clear and the bright sun glistened off the white blanket that smoothed and covered the flaws of the world. By nine o'clock the first drops of melt were making tiny holes in the snow beneath the barren tree branches and faint wisps of steam were rising from places where direct sunlight bore down warm. At ten o'clock Billy raised his eyes to study the skyline north and east as he walked with Eli from drill towards the lean-to.

"Storm clouds a long way over there," Billy pointed.

"Heavy. We get a northeast wind, we'll have more snow."

They dropped to their knees to wrap their weapons in an old piece of cast-off canvas under cover of the lean-to, then stood and Billy led out, walking towards the camp wood yard. Turlock's high, nasal voice stopped them, and they turned to wait for him, trotting to catch up.

His eyes were bright, words coming fast. "Heard about those thirteen men?"

Billy shook his head.

"The court-martial decided. No one's getting shot. Four was declared disabled and they got a doctor looking at their feet. The other nine have to stand night picket for one week for punishment when they're able."

Billy rounded his mouth and blew relieved air. "Who said?"

"That sergeant that came to get you. Culhane? Was that his name? I seen him at drill."

Eli looked at Billy, relief flooding.

Turlock shrugged. "Thought you should know." He glanced at the nearby wood yard. "Got wood detail?"

"Got to cut and split three cords."

Turlock's eyebrows raised. "Not the usual two?"

"The cooks got some sort of special orders. They need three today."

Turlock was instantly focused. "For what?"

"No one said. I only know a couple wagons rolled in from the west and unloaded in the night. No one said what."

Turlock scratched his scraggly beard for a moment, then shrugged. "I got to get back to the cannon. Orders are to clean 'em, plug the muzzles and touchholes, and grease the axles with anything we can find. Sounds like something's stirring. I just come to tell you about those men."

"Glad you did."

"See you later." He turned and strode away.

The camp wood yard, a one-hundred-yard-square clearing carved out of the center of the deep woods rang daily with the sound of axes and the grinding of six-foot crosscut saws as men sweated in the cold to keep ahead of the forty cords of wood that fed the cook fires each day. For half a mile in all directions, whips cracked and men barked orders to mules that dragged windfall trees into the clearing where the animals stood with steam rising from their hot hides while soldiers unhooked the chains from the trees and swung the mules around to go back into the snow for the next load. Yellow wood chips and sawdust lay in a scatter on top of the fresh snow.

The two men walked into the wood yard among twenty others working with axes and saws. Each picked up a broadaxe and went to the nearest pine tree lying in the snow. They started at opposite ends, lopping off the dead branches and piling them nearby. Forty minutes later the stripped tree had been cut into seven sections, six feet long. They carried the first section to the nearest cross-armed sawhorse, laid it in the "V's," and with one man on each side, began the rhythmic pull on the six-foot crosscut saw, back and forth while the teeth dumped sawdust on both sides.

With the tree cut into fourteen sections, three feet long, they laid the saw aside and took a section to the nearest chopping block to set it upright. They picked up their broadaxes, took a deep breath, and began the work of splitting each three-foot section into quarters for kindling.

At one o'clock they stopped to wipe sweat while they drank a bowl of hot, thin, greasy gruel, then sat down on the stacked firewood to gather themselves for the effort of working with saw and axe until dusk. A little before four o'clock, with the sun reaching for the woods on the western skyline, both men stopped, sweat dripping from their chins and noses, breathing heavy, and raised their heads at the sound of a horse cantering west, thirty yards away, and they squinted to watch a horse and rider disappear into the woods.

"Was that a colonel?" Billy asked.

"Looked like it."

Two minutes later they turned at the sound of another horse, paced at a trot, working its way west through the trees at the far end of the wood yard. The rider wore the gold braid of a brigadier general.

Eli wiped at his face. "That's two in two minutes. Wonder what's going on over at the headquarters building?"

Billy shook his head. "Two wagon loads of something got here in the night, we're cutting extra wood for the cook fires, and Turlock's cleaning and plugging the cannon while officers are gathering." He wiped sweat from his forehead. "Something's stirring."

To the west, five hundred yards into the huge open field, shadows were slanting long as the officers reined their mounts to a stop at the stables in the dooryard of the large, two-storied house owned by Samuel Merrick, where General Nathanael Greene had been invited to set up his quarters. One hundred fifty yards north and west, the Keith House, where General George Washington had his quarters, glowed golden in the setting sun. White snow clung to the long winter hair on the legs and bellies of the horses and vapor rose rhythmically from their belled nostrils as they breathed, moving their feet, anxious to be free of saddle and bridle and in a stall with feed and water.

While soldiers led the horses to the stables, the arriving officers walked in the paths shoveled through the snow to be met at the door by Samuel Merrick, aging, portly, kindly, dedicated to the overthrow of the British.

"Welcome, welcome," he exclaimed. "Do come in and let us take your cloaks and hats. General Greene is expecting you just down the hall in the library. General Washington will be along directly for dinner. You'll find wines and nutmeats in the library for your pleasure while we're waiting."

The house was filled with warmth and the rich, pungent aroma of roasting ham, beef, stuffed fowl, puddings, custards, and mince and fruit pies. The officers cleaned the snow from their boots and made their way down the hall, boot heels clicking on the hardwood floor while servants disappeared with their cloaks and hats. They entered through the double doors where General Greene was waiting in the library. Two walls were lined with oak shelves and books, a great stone fireplace with oaken mantel covered a third, and large windows with drawn shades filled the fourth. General Nathanael Greene rose from a maple table surrounded by matching upholstered chairs.

"Gentlemen, you are most welcome." He gestured to a table in one corner. "Wines and dainties are there. There are a few more officers yet to come, and General Washington will be along directly."

They gathered to pour red wine into crystal goblets and take nutmeats from engraved silver bowls, then sat down at the table while warmth from the fireplace reached every corner. Talk flowed, but contrary to their expectation a sense of restraint, of uneasiness, crept in. Each had received sealed, written orders from General Washington to attend, but the curt message had said nothing of the purpose of the meeting or who would be in attendance. The feeling of slight tension grew as others arrived, including the Reverend Alexander MacWhorter of the Presbyterian Church in Newark, New Jersey. A confirmed Patriot, the reverend had opened his church to the Continental army as it passed through Newark, then packed a knapsack and left his duties to his subordinates while he traveled with the army through their darkest hours, and remained with them in the camp on the Pennsylvania riverbank.

In deep dusk Sam Merrick excused himself to answer a knock at the door. Minutes later he returned to the library and stepped aside while General George Washington entered. Instantly talk ceased and every man came to his feet facing the general, waiting. He towered over everyone in the room, and his face was set like stone while his eyes swept the room, missing nothing.

He laid a large leather valise on the table, then spoke with a sense of disciplined dignity. "I thank you all for your attendance. Please continue with your conversation until dinner is served."

Ten minutes later a servant rapped at the door. "Madame Merrick invites you to the dining room."

As the officers took their places at the dining table, their faces were those of boys, wide-eyed at the feast spread before them. Half a dozen engraved silver candlesticks with great, scented candles were spaced up the center of the table. Gleaming china with polished silver and embroidered linen napkins sparkled at every chair. Platters of smoking ham, beef, and fowl were mixed with bowls of steaming carrots, turnips, potatoes, and cabbage, with small silver bowls of pickles, relishes, jams, jellies, and garnishments of every kind tucked between.

General Washington, leaned his leather valise against the leg of his chair, nodded to Reverend MacWhorter, who bowed his head and in a firm voice gave thanks to the Almighty for the bounties of the table and the blessings of life. The ravages of war and the bitter winter faded from their minds as they raised their heads in anticipation, and for a time the only sounds were those of eating and asking for the platters and bowls to be passed once again, while Mrs. Merrick hovered nearby, ecstatic at the utter joy she saw in her guests. The eating slowed and pies and custards were wheeled in on wooden carts with ornate designs carved on the sides and handles.

The big clock on the dining room mantel showed half past eight when the men wiped their mouths on their napkins and General Washington stood and bowed to Samuel Merrick and his wife.

"Accept my thanks and gratitude for this sumptuous dinner. I cannot recall the last time I was privileged to sit at such a table."

Samuel shrugged. "It was the least we could do." His wife dropped her eyes becomingly, blushed through her broad smile, and said nothing.

Washington continued. "May we trouble you for the use of your library for the evening?"

"It would be an honor. General Greene mentioned it."

Merrick led them back to the library, and while the officers were taking their seats, General Washington shook his hand warmly. "Your service tonight will not be forgotten."

"It was nothing. I shall take my leave now. You gentlemen have the library and the first floor of our home to yourselves. Should you need anything, I will be upstairs."

Washington did not speak until the footsteps in the hall faded and died and there was total silence.

"Reverend, would you seek the guidance of the Almighty?"

At the opposite end of the table, the Reverend Alexander MacWhorter stood with bowed head and pleaded with all the strength of his soul for the Creator to allow His Holy Spirit to touch the men and grace their minds with light. They said their "Amens" and, as they raised their heads, every man in the room felt the first faint tingle in his heart.

Washington unbuckled the valise and drew out a folded map and laid it on the table before him, then rose. His blue-gray eyes quickly probed the circle of faces peering at him expectantly. He spoke with quiet authority.

"Gentlemen, tonight we are convened as a council of war to put in final form the details for the taking of Trenton. If we succeed at Trenton, then we shall consider going further east to take Princeton and on to Brunswick if possible."

Each man slowly straightened in his chair and their breathing slowed for a few seconds as their minds leaped forward, groping with the impossibility of what was coming. He had previously talked of Trenton, but he had never suggested that success there would result in a second plan to move on Princeton ten miles further north where General Grant and a strong British garrison was quartered, and a third strike against Brunswick beyond that.

With steady deliberation Washington unfolded the map, three feet square, and laid it near the center of the table. It was a detailed, close-to-scale drawing of the Delaware River, from Lambertville to the northwest to five miles below Dunk's Ferry at the southwest. Both the Keith House and the Merrick House were marked, west of the woods where the army was camped. He waited until the officers were satisfied and had settled back into their chairs.

"We covered some of this in a general way in our council of a few days ago. I choose to repeat it now as foundation for the detail of each of your assignments. It is the detail we will be discussing tonight, and the detail of each of your assignments is absolutely critical to the success of the attack that is planned."

He drew the map closer to himself and began, pointing as he spoke.

"Our forces are camped here." He tapped the map at McKonkey's Ferry, with Taylor's Island, long and narrow and heavily wooded, thirty yards off the riverbank.

"Colonel Johann Rall holds Trenton with about fourteen hundred Hessians, here, about nine miles south." Again he tapped the map, then moved his finger, following the course of the Delaware south, then westerly where it curved back west past Bordentown, further, past Pennsbury, then Bristol and Burlington, and he tapped the map again.

"General von Donop has his force of about fifteen hundred here, at Black Horse and Mount Holly, near Dunk's Ferry, about twenty miles southwest of Trenton. All Hessian forces are on the New Jersey side of the river."

He paused for a moment. The men broke their intense concentration to look up at him, ready to move on.

"To take Trenton, we must isolate Rall's garrison from any chance of getting reinforcements from von Donop. That means we must do two things. First, we must have a body of our troops cross the river just below the Trenton Ferry to seize and hold the bridge over the Assunpink Creek and control the road leading down to Bordentown to stop any of Rall's men from carrying messages down to von Donop. Second, we must land a force across the river just above von Donop's troops to cut them off from coming north, up the river to relieve Rall. Our troops will have to engage them vigorously and hold them there."

He had said it twice. Americans were going to cross the river at two separate places. Every man at the table had watched the river like a hawk each day since John Glover and his Marbleheaders moved the army across the night of December seventh with the British dogging them like death. None of them had any illusions about the fact that if the ice froze thick enough to support cannon and cavalry, or if the British built boats, the Continental army was doomed and the Revolution with it. There was no sound in the room as they waited for Washington to reveal the miracle by which he proposed moving two forces across the river to attack the Hessians in their own quarters.

Washington cleared his throat, then dropped an index finger on the map. "Across the river from where we now are, the Bear Tavern Road is the first of three main roads leading to Trenton. It travels nearly due south, down to Birmingham, here, about five miles northwest of Trenton."

He tapped the map and waited until he knew each man was tracking with him, then continued.

"At Birmingham, the Bear Tavern Road splits. One branch heads east, here, for about a mile, then turns south on the second main road, the Scotch Road. The Scotch Road eventually joins the third main road, the Pennington Road, and together the Pennington Road runs into Trenton, here at the north end."

Again he paused, watching their eyes before he went on.

"After Birmingham, the Bear Tavern Road is called the River Road.

It continues southeast, generally parallel to the Scotch Road and comes into the south end of Trenton. The River Road is less than one hundred feet from the riverbank."

He waited until the attention came back to him, then moved on.

"See this mark below where the Scotch and Pennington Roads join? That is the home of a man named Richard Howell. He runs a cooper business there. The Hessians have occupied it with an advance post with sentries and a small company of infantry, perhaps ten or fifteen men. It's less than half a mile from Trenton. They use that building to control the Pennington and Scotch Roads."

He moved his finger along the River Road. "This mark? That's the Hermitage. It's a large home owned by Congressman Philemon Dickinson. The Hessians have confiscated it and have an advance post there, perhaps fifty men, to control the River Road. The home is also less than half a mile from Trenton."

Some of the men shifted in their chairs and Washington waited until they were settled.

"Now turn your attention to the town of Trenton. There are but three main streets running north and south. King, Queen, and Quaker Lane. They all end here, within fifty yards of one another, where the Pennington Road comes in from the north and meets the Princeton Road coming in from the east."

Again he waited until he saw they understood.

"At the south end, the Trenton streets come together at Queen Street, which is the only street that crosses the Assunpink bridge." He moved his finger back to the north. "Starting at the north end of town, the streets running east and west are Fourth Street, Third Street, Second Street, and Front Street, nearest the river, here."

He paused for a moment. "On the east side of town is an open area with an apple orchard. The Assunpink Creek runs just east of the orchard, essentially forming the southern boundary of the town."

He traced the Creek with his finger. "The Creek is fairly wide and deep. If one does not cross at the bridge, there are very few places it can be crossed by cavalry or infantry without trouble, and no place to cross with cannon at this time of year."

Piece by piece, the picture was materializing, and the officers again moved on their chairs while they waited for the most critical piece to drop into place: how did Washington plan to cross the river?

"Within the town, these are the critical points." He put his finger on the map. "Rall has his headquarters here, on King Street, in a two-story home owned by a Tory named Stacy Potts. Rall usually has cannon deployed in front of it. On the corner of Queen and Third is a Methodist church with a tall white steeple." He moved his finger down two blocks. "The greatest concentration of Hessian troops is here, on King Street, in the Old Barracks. It's thick-walled, built of stone, and houses about three hundred soldiers. Behind it are pens for their cavalry mounts and cattle for food. Here, on Second Street, between Queen Street and Quaker Lane, one of Rall's officers, Lieutenant General Knyphausen, has a small command billeted in eight buildings."

He stopped and raised his head. "Considering their rank, it's odd that Colonel Rall has command over Lieutenant General Knyphausen. It seems that distinction was given to Rall because of his outstanding performance when his command stormed one of the walls at Fort Washington."

Washington stopped, and for a moment he could not surpress a rare smile. It flashed and was gone and the men at the table caught it, and in their faces he saw their need for an explanation of what could draw a smile from a man notorious for not smiling, considering the desperate matters now before them.

"Gentlemen, I share with you a strange peculiarity for which General Knyphausen has become notorious." Again the smile came. "It seems he has the habit of buttering his bread with his thumb."

Raucous laughter rang off the walls and Washington said and did nothing to stifle it. He stood with his shoulders shaking silently as he contained his own laughter and gave his officers free rein for their spontaneous outbursts of hilarity. A minute passed before they settled and Washington pulled them back to the agenda.

"There's a third officer named Lossberg who is billeted with his men along King Street with Rall. The balance of the Hessian forces are disbursed throughout the town in the homes or barns or buildings, wherever they can find housing."

He waited while the men studied, then continued. "You will recall the Germans celebrate the twenty-fifth of December to honor the birth of Jesus. Traditionally it is two days of food and drink and festivities. I anticipate that Rall will somewhat relax the daily routine among his troops and provide additional rations of rum. By the evening of the twenty-fifth it is probable their thoughts will be quite far removed from battle, and by midnight a fair number of them will be incapacitated by their indulgence in rum and wine. By five o'clock the next morning, December twenty-sixth, Rall's command will be as vulnerable to attack as they're ever going to be. That's when we will strike."

Murmuring broke out once more, and Washington raised a hand to still it. Then he continued speaking.

"One more matter weighs heavily in this decision. About three weeks ago I sent a message to Congress setting forth the dates on which enlistments expire for our various regiments. Nearly all of them end at midnight on December thirty-first. I am lately informed that the message was intercepted by the British and delivered to General Howe."

The officers gasped as one and burst into agitated conversation. Some hit the table with clenched fists. Again Washington raised his hand to command silence, and again he waited until the room was quiet.

"I agree, gentlemen. At first it would appear to be a catastrophe for us, but it might be a blessing instead. If General Howe does indeed have the document, he will probably conclude that he need only keep us trapped here until the thirty-first, at which point the soldiers will leave as their enlistments expire. The Continental army will dissolve, and he can crush the Revolution and recapture the colonies for Britain because there will be no armed force to resist him. If he thinks along those lines, that will strengthen the likelihood that neither he nor his forces will be thinking in terms of battle. Rather, they will have greater inducement to do what they ordinarily would have done anyway—remain where they are, starving and freezing us out until our army dissolves at year's end."

He paused. "With that in mind I have concluded that a third large force of our men will cross the Delaware here, at McKonkey's Ferry, then turn south and march to Birmingham, here. There, the force will split. One command will continue south to take the River Road down past the Hermitage, to the south end of Trenton. The other command will go due east to the Scotch Road, then directly south down to join the Pennington Road, past the advance post there."

Talk arose and subsided.

"These two commands will arrive at Trenton at the same time, five o'clock in the morning. The one on the River Road will hit the Old Barracks and move on past to seal off the Assunpink Creek bridge and hold the south end of town. The command traveling down the Scotch Road will set up artillery at the north end of town, commanding a clean field of fire down both King and Queen Streets, and at the same time storm Rall's headquarters. That command will also continue east to cut off access to the Princeton Road. By that time, part of those at the south end of town will have continued east, and the two commands will then move to meet each other to close the gap on the east side. When they meet we will have Rall's garrison in Trenton surrounded, with Generals Cadwalader and Ewing cutting off any hope of rescue from von Donop."

There it was! Three separate commands of starving, freezing men, a few poorly trained, most not trained at all, were to cross the ice-choked river over a spread of twenty miles, each at a different place and a different time, at night, and arrive on schedule. One command was then to march nine miles, and at exactly the right moment the three commands together were to attack three thousand of the best trained, best armed, most feared soldiers in the world. The officers sat straight up with eyes narrowed as they waited for Washington to complete what sounded like an impossible plan.

Washington leaned forward on stiff arms, palms flat on the table and his eyes were like flecks of blue diamond as the men settled and did not move.

"The command assignments will be as follows."

The only sound in the room was the fire crackling in the fireplace.

Washington turned his eyes to Colonel John Glover. "Colonel, you and I met to discuss this matter two days ago, but only in the abstract.

Now I put it to you directly. Can you move our forces across the Delaware in the Durham boats tomorrow in the late afternoon and night, troops, cannon and horses, in time to attack Trenton at exactly five o'clock the morning of Thursday, December twenty-sixth?"

There was the quiet sound of breath suddenly drawn, and then silence.

Glover studied his commander's blue-gray eyes, and he reached inside himself and the faint tingle every man had felt when the Reverend MacWhorter invoked God's blessing on the council was suddenly there, growing, filling him, rising above the voice that screamed out the insanity of the plan. Every eye in the room was on Glover, and tension hung like something tangible.

The little man nodded and spoke quietly. "Yes, sir. I've thought about it. We can."

For an instant Washington's breath caught while every other man in the room exhaled and moved, then settled once again.

Washington continued. "I have sent orders to General John Cadwalader who will command the force that is farthest south. He will cross the river here, at Dunk's Ferry, north of the Hessians commanded by General von Donop, and he will engage them and hold them there to cut off any attempt to come north to relieve Rall.

"Likewise, General Ewing will command the force that crosses just below the Trenton Ferry to cut off any escape by the Hessians in Trenton across the Assunpink bridge, and to capture any messengers Rall may send south to get help from von Donop."

Washington tapped the map and looked at Major General John Sullivan. "General Sullivan, you will command the force that follows the River Road south from Birmingham. You will take care of the Hessian outpost at the Hermitage, here, then move down to hit Trenton—half your men above the Old Barracks, half below—and move into the east-west streets of Trenton."

General Sullivan stared at the map, then raised his eyes and nodded firmly.

Washington turned back to Glover. "Colonel Glover, after your men have moved the army across the river, they will accompany General

Sullivan to become the section of his command that goes into Trenton south of the Old Barracks, near the river. Move across the Assunpink bridge and set up cannon and lines along the creek so you cover both the field and the orchard to the north, and the Bordentown road coming in from the south, where von Donop will appear if he gets past Cadwalader and Ewing. Colonel Stark and his New Hampshire regiment will be with you."

"Yes, sir."

Washington looked at Major General Nathanael Greene and for a moment their eyes locked. "General Greene, you will lead the command down the Scotch Road. Your subordinate commanders will be Generals Stirling, Mercer, Stephen, and de Fermoy." As he spoke their names, Washington looked at each man in turn. Finished, he turned to General Stephen.

"General Stephen, you will be the first across the river as the advance guard. You will need to clear the Hessians from Howell's outpost, here, outside of town, then continue for about five hundred yards, where you rejoin the command." He tapped the map at various places as he spoke, and he turned his eyes from one officer to the next as he said their names.

"General Mercer, you will lead your force to the rear of Rall's headquarters, here, and take it, then continue on through Trenton on the east-west streets, driving the Hessians out as you go." He moved his finger north. "The balance of your command will move across the north end of the town. Colonel Knox will stop here, at the head of King and Queen Streets and set up his cannon facing south to sweep King and Queen Streets and Quaker Lane. Generals Stirling and Stephen and de Fermoy will be with me waiting to see where they are needed. If all commands are successful, we will have Rall's garrison trapped."

With deliberation he once again opened his valise and withdrew several documents, each bearing his wax seal. He read the name inscribed in his own handwriting on each document, and as he did, he handed it to the officer named. Each man received his packet and laid it on the table, still sealed.

"Those are your individual sealed orders. They are identical to the plan I have laid before you tonight. Take them with you and memorize them, then burn them. It will be a court-martial offense if any of those documents fall into hands other than your own."

Washington straightened and for a moment rubbed his jawline. "We'll pause for a few minutes. Feel free to move around. If you have to leave the room, go in pairs and do not speak one word of this to anyone. Refreshments are in the corner."

For a full five seconds no one moved and then each man picked up the sealed document on the table before him and carefully unbuttoned his tunic, placed it in the inside pocket, then re-buttoned his tunic, patting his breast to be certain the orders were safely inside. Then each straightened, pushed back from the table, and stood, and open talk filled the room.

Ten minutes later Washington rapped the table and they took their seats. Washington drew a small piece of paper from the valise and waited for complete silence.

"Does any man here not understand his assignment?"

Heads turned to look up and down the table, but there was no sound, nor did any hands go up.

Washington nodded approval. "Now there are some general orders that apply to each command." He glanced down at the piece of paper. "First, I will be with General Greene's command until we reach Birmingham. After that I will be where I'm needed most. Next, the time and the order in which your commands will get into the boats is written in your orders. It is imperative that each of you be across the river and ready to execute your orders by five o'clock Thursday morning because the main attack force coming down the Scotch and Pennington Roads will have no way to know if you're in place, and they'll begin the attack no matter what happens. Be absolutely certain you are not late."

He glanced at the paper. "Each of you will leave behind the sick and disabled in your command to take care of your camp. Tomorrow those fit will be allowed to rest from all usual activities to be well rested. No drill, no wood detail. With help from Robert Morris, food has arrived before dawn this morning and the cooks are cooking it, as you know. Each man is to have three days of cooked rations, a blanket, and forty rounds of ammunition. I have sent an express rider to Doctor Shippen at Bethlehem asking him and his entire staff to come give us medical help during this campaign. I believe he will come."

He slowed and his voice became intense.

"Excepting only yourselves, no one in any command is to know the details of this attack until we are gathered on the riverbank ready to cross."

He paused to let it settle in. "The commands of Generals Sullivan and Greene will be met on the other side of the river by local Patriots who know the land and will act as our guides, and will put out all lights at Birmingham and proceed on south in full darkness and absolute silence." Again he paused. "Anyone breaking the silence will be sent back under arrest. Anyone leaving ranks will be executed."

He stopped and for a few moments ran his finger down the paper before him, then spoke again.

"Are there questions?"

General Hugh Mercer spoke. "What fortifications can we expect at Trenton? Trenches, breastworks, redoubts, cannon?"

Washington shook his head. "None."

Mercer's eyes widened. "Rall has done *nothing* to defend Trenton? On what information are we to believe that?"

"The most reliable. I can say no more."

St. Clair leaned forward. "What about weather?"

Every man at the table looked at Washington. Crossing the ice-laden river at night was fearful at best. To do it in a storm was unthinkable.

Washington set his jaw for a moment, then turned to Glover and waited in silence.

Glover did not hesitate. "The regiment's seen bad weather before. We'll get across."

Every man at the table stared in surprise. The answer had come instantly, quietly, without reservation. They moved in their chairs, then settled as St. Clair spoke once more. "That storm coming in looks like a bad one."

Glover nodded. "Looks like it is. A nor'easter."

St. Clair was startled at the ease with which Glover spoke. "What happens if it doesn't hit? We get a hard freeze instead?"

Glover shook his head. "I doubt that will happen. But if it does, we'll deal with the ice any way we can." There was no bravado, no arrogance in the little man. He spoke quietly, calmly.

Washington drew a large stack of papers from his valise and methodically divided them into three stacks. "Tomorrow, while your men are waiting to board the boats, have your officers read the marked article aloud to them."

He pushed the three stacks down the table to Greene, Stirling, and Sullivan. Each read the words in bold print at the top of the first sheet, then looked at Washington in surprise. The document was a newspaper article entitled *The American Crisis I* taken from the Philadelphia newspaper, *Pennsylvania Journal.* Each officer remembered well General Washington's orders that they read it within minutes of its arrival by special messenger December nineteenth. Most knew "Common Sense" was a pen name for Thomas Paine and that Paine had joined them and stayed doggedly with them in their headlong retreat across New Jersey.

Washington drew his watch from his vest pocket. "Gentlemen, it is imperative that our timepieces are coordinated. Would you please set your watches with mine." He waited until each had his watch in his hand, stem drawn to set the hands. "In five seconds it will be ten-twenty-two."

Each man instantly set his watch, wound the stem, checked it, then inserted it back into his vest pocket.

"This is the last time we will meet as a war council until this is over. If any of you have questions, or reservations of any kind, voice them now."

He watched their eyes. None of them spoke, and few of them would return his direct gaze. For a moment a hollow, cold feeling rose inside, and he felt the deep loneliness known only to those in command who must take on their shoulders the crushing weight of ordering men into the black abyss of battle where they must kill or be killed. By force of iron will he straightened his spine and pushed past the pain, and in that moment a feeling surged through him that drove out the dark clouds of doubt and fear and filled him with a bright certainty. This was not his work, but that of the Almighty.

"Before we separate, there are two things remaining. I would count it a privilege, gentlemen, if you would honor me by allowing me to shake the hand of each of you with my deepest hope for your good fortune."

He went around the table slowly, silently shaking each man's hand. Every man drew strength from the firm grasp of his hand and the resolve of iron determination that flowed from him to embrace them, lift them.

He stopped for the last time at the head of the table. "Last, I give you the password for this operation. You will give it to your men as they board the boats. I have thought long and hard about what words would capture the moment. History is waiting to see if our dream of freedom lives to light the world, or dies on the banks of the river."

He stopped and for a second battled for control.

"I pray to the Almighty that we will not fail Him. I have pledged Him my life in this effort."

He waited until the room was silent before he finished. "The password is 'Victory or Death.'"

Notes

The court-martial of Sergeant Bertram Pratt and the others is fictional, but it is included to illustrate how rapidly accusations of desertion were handled (see Higginbotham, *The War of American Independence,* p. 401).

Washington held his final war council regarding Trenton on December 24, 1776, at the home of Samuel Merrick. Supper was served before the room was cleared of all persons save for the officers who would be responsible for the attack on Trenton (see Ketchum, *The Winter Soldiers,* p. 245). The plan to take Trenton included dividing Washington's forces into three separate sections, each to cross the Delaware River at a different time and place in the night. The battle plan, including the placement of the Hessian and American troops, as laid out in the novel is accurate, but for additional summaries, descriptions, and maps, see Ketchum's *The Winter Soldiers,* pages 246–48, 257;

Ward's *The War of the Revolution*, vol. I, pages 293–94; and Smith's *The Battle of Trenton*, pages 20–21, 32. An excellent source for the specific details of both the American and Hessian positions before the Trenton engagement is Stryker's *The Battles of Trenton and Princeton*, pages 84–85, 92–97, 112–15.

A cartoon of General Knyphausen buttering his bread with his thumb can be found on page 154 of the 1973 edition of Ketchum's *The Winter Soldiers*.

All officers set their watches by General Washington's timepiece and the password selected by Washington was "Victory or Death" (see Ketchum, *The Winter Soldiers*, pp. 247, 252).

CHAPTER VII

★ ★ ★

tuck here in this forsaken hole called Princeton—army strung out for near two hundred miles—what? eight outposts? ten? We're wasting time—rations—men—horseflesh—sending the Germans down to deal with Washington—Hessians—thieves—brutes—one thin cut ahead of outright barbarians—they stay much longer our own troops will fight them.

General James Grant, crude, dour, short, stocky, set his teeth on edge while he jammed the heel of his officer's boot into the notch of the bootjack and heaved upward. His foot loosened and then came free and he raised his knee high to let the stiff, black leather topple over sideways to the chill, hardwood floor of his quarters. He shifted his feet to set the second boot in the notch, heaved upward once more, and let it topple. He leaned to pick them from the floor and toss them to the foot of his bed, then stood in his heavy gray woolen socks to work with the gold buttons on his white officer's vest. While his thick fingers fumbled he glanced at the clock on the fireplace mantel and drew a weary, irritated breath.

Thirteen miles—he's down there just thirteen miles—his whole army more dead than alive. They'd last about ten minutes if we'd just gather up all our troops from these ridiculous outposts and go down there after him—all over—go home to England.

He tossed his vest on the bed beside his British officer's tunic and sat down to pull at his socks. He paused for a moment to listen to the moan of the freezing wind at the windows.

Men bored out of their minds—starting to show—and where's our leader? New

York—chasing wine and women—one woman—the respectable Mrs. Joshua Loring—
Elizabeth Loring—chasing her while he's conveniently sent her husband as far away as
he can in his government job—chasing her and waiting for that new red ribbon to be
hung around his neck—waiting for the sword to touch him on both shoulders and make
him a knight. King George ecstatic with Howe's report—told only we won in New
York—no one told him we could have ended it twice but Howe wouldn't—dawdled
around—equivocated—wouldn't finish Washington when we had him trapped—rather
keep this insanity going for another year or two—be sure he'll have a place in history.
He'll have a place all right—the general who wouldn't finish.

He had one long wool sock in his hand when he heard the rapid
footsteps in the hallway and then the sharp rap on his door. He
scowled, his shoulders slumped, and he barked, "Speak!"

His adjutant's voice was too high, too excited. "Sir, that gentleman
is downstairs. Says it's urgent."

Again Grant looked at the clock. Twenty minutes before ten o'clock.
He exhaled through ballooned cheeks, battling the need to tell the man
to get out and come back tomorrow, knowing he could not. "That gentleman" was one of his most effective informants, and by Grant's direct
orders, his name was never spoken. His appearance at nine-forty at
night gave Grant pause.

"I'll be down in five minutes."

"Yes, sir. I'll have him wait, sir."

He pulled his sock back on, then his vest, and buttoned the bottom
four buttons, but did not put on his officer's tunic. He padded down
the hall, then the stairs to the lower floor, and into the parlor where his
informant stood, nervous, eyes quick, darting. He still wore a long black
overcoat with a gray scarf looped and knotted around his neck.

Grant spoke abruptly. "What brings you here?"

The man did not sit. His eyes flitted to the adjutant, then back to
Grant. "Sir, is there someplace we can talk?"

Grant turned on his heel and the informant followed, heels clicking
up the stairs and hall. Grant closed the door and faced the man, waiting.

"Sir, I believe the rebels are planning a troop movement. Probably an
attack on Trenton, and I believe it will be in the next one or two days."

"What have you seen?"

"General Washington held a council of war two days ago. Then wagons came into camp with flour and salt meat and the cooks are cooking it to hand out, three days of rations to each man. Forty rounds of ammunition. Tonight the same council of officers met again and were still meeting when I left there at seven o'clock. It all points to one thing. They're planning to attack, probably at Trenton."

While he spoke, he was working his hat with his hands, pointing, gesturing.

"How will he cross the river?"

"He has boats. The big freight boats from Riegelsville."

Grant shrugged. "He's had them for three weeks."

"He's been saving them until now. He plans mischief. I know it."

Grant stared at the man for several seconds in silence while the wind worked at the windows. He reached to scratch his jowls. "I'll send word to Rall at Trenton, tonight. Tell him to be ready. If Washington sends men over, Rall will be waiting with cannon and bayonet."

The man's head bobbed and Grant opened the door. The man hesitated and Grant said, "Tell the adjutant to give you a gold piece, to cover the, uh, use of your horse."

The man bobbed his head once more and hurried down the hall while Grant closed the door and padded to his bed to sit down, shoulders rounded while he considered. Ten minutes later he moved to the corner and sat for several minutes at his desk before he took quill and paper from the drawer and scrawled a terse message to Colonel Johann Rall.

24 Dec 1776

Herr Colonel Rall:

I am reliably informed Americans may be preparing to attack Trenton. Take all appropriate precautions. Be prepared, ready at all times.

General James Grant

Finished, he folded it twice, sealed it with hot wax, and opened the door far enough to call for his adjutant. The man bounded up the stairs two at a time and trotted down the hall to stand at rigid attention. "Yes, sir."

"Deliver this to the duty officer at once. Tell him to dispatch a messenger to carry it to Colonel Rall at Trenton, now, tonight. Urgent."

The man's eyes widened. "Tonight, sir?"

"Tonight."

"Yes, sir!"

The duty officer had to be wakened. The reluctant messenger was playing cards in his underwear. The stable sergeant was hunched over a small iron stove in one corner of the barracks. The picket at the stable door had his back turned against the howling, freezing wind, stamping his feet, hugging himself for warmth. The horse was feisty, hating the bit forced between his teeth and the bite of the saddle-cinch in the bitter cold. It was after eleven o'clock before the messenger led the animal outside into the wind and the stable sergeant and picket grabbed the cheek straps on the bridle to hold the horse while the messenger mounted. The mount bogged his head down between his front knees and buck-jumped twice, and the messenger desperately grabbed a handful of mane to hold his tenuous position in the saddle while he jerked the reins to the left and kicked the animal in the ribs. It spun two quick circles and then straightened, throwing its head as it lined out towards the Princeton Road leading to Trenton.

The road was rutted, covered with patches of snow and ice and mud frozen solid. The horse was shod with standard military flat-plate shoes that would not grip and hold, and the messenger dared not let the animal run. A slip and fall, and a thirteen-hundred-pound horse rolling on him in the pitch-black could break his leg or back, or kill him. He held a tight rein while the horse pranced, wanting to run, wanting to have the night's business finished and be back in the stable with oats and water.

At four-twenty A.M. the picket at the front door of Rall's headquarters heard the unmistakable sound of a horse walking on a frozen road and watched a big brown mare materialize from the dark. Instantly he brought his musket to the ready and shouted into the wind whistling through the skeleton trees, "Who comes there?" first in German, then in badly accented English.

The answer came in English. "Friend. Messenger from General James Grant in Princeton. Urgent message for Colonel Johann Rall."

The picket understood but four words. *Grant. Princeton. Johann Rall.* He stood with his coat blowing in the wind, unable to think of what to do next, when the messenger reached inside his coat and drew out the message, to hold it low where the picket could see it.

"Message. For Colonel Rall," he called above the wind, and pointed at the building.

The picket bobbed his head and reached for the document and the messenger withdrew it, shaking his head. "Rall. Only Rall." Again he pointed at the building.

The picket stood for a moment in indecision, torn between duty and fear of waking Colonel Rall at four o'clock in the morning. Finally he turned back to the large door and rapped heavily. Twenty seconds passed with no response and he took off his heavy mitten and banged with the flat of his hand and waited. A light flickered dull on the drawn blind at the window and half a minute later the door opened six inches to throw a narrow shaft of light onto the ground in the darkness.

Lieutenant Jacob Piel, young, eager, adjutant to Colonel Rall, barefooted and hair awry, squinted against the lantern light. Piel's own quarters were next door, but tonight he had chosen to sleep in a spare downstairs bedroom in the headquarters building after working late. "What is it?"

"Messenger with a writing from General Grant to Colonel Rall."

"The colonel's asleep."

"He will not give it to me—only to the colonel."

A sour look crossed Piel's face at the thought of waking Rall, but he drew a breath and said, "Bring him in."

Ten minutes later Rall stumped down the stairs in his stockinged feet, wrapped in a robe. The messenger came to attention and Rall spoke. "Ja. What is it?"

The British trooper thrust the paper to him. "From General Grant. Urgent."

Rall looked at Piel, who translated, and Rall responded. "Ja? What is so urgent this time of morning?"

"I was not told."

Piel translated, and Rall grunted. He spoke to Piel. "Tell him to go to the barracks and tend his horse and rest until after breakfast and then come back here. I may have a message to send back. I'll need you to come to my quarters to translate."

Piel turned to the messenger as Rall walked down the hall to his sleeping quarters. He sat on his bed, leaned forward to break the seal, and opened the message in the light of the lamp to peer at the words written in English, trying to understand. Piel knocked at the door, entered, and Rall handed him the message. Piel read it silently to himself, then read it aloud to Rall in English, then once again, translating it to German.

Rall listened intently, waited until Piel handed him back the paper, then tossed it onto his night table beside the lamp.

"Attack? What attack? Take appropriate steps? Be on guard? For what? The Americans are not going to attack. It is impossible. He thinks he knows more about Trenton than we do, him sitting ten miles away?" He shook his head in disgust. "Four-thirty in the morning. What nonsense!"

He raised his face to Piel. "Write a message to Grant in English and send it back with his messenger. Tell him I am ready for any attack. If the Americans come, we will show them the cannon and the bayonet. They cannot stand the bayonet. That is all. Do not speak of this to anyone. Do you understand?"

"Yes, sir."

Piel turned on his heel and walked out, closing the door while Rall shrugged out of the robe and tossed it on the foot of his bed, then sat to pull off his socks. He cupped his hand over the lamp chimney to blow out the flame, and settled into bed muttering, "Attack? Nonsense."

The wind died a little before six o'clock and dawn broke clear and calm. By seven o'clock the temperature had risen well above freezing and the icicles in Trenton were smoking, dripping from the eaves of the buildings and the limbs of the trees in the unseasonable warmth. By eight o'clock the streets were a morass of puddled water and mud, with the blue-coated Hessian troops hurrying to finish the necessary morning business of mess, care for the livestock, roll call and inspection, flag raising, parade the cannon with the fifes chortling and drums pounding, and finish the morning report on those fit for duty and those in the infirmary.

This was Christmas Day! Orders were posted! After the necessaries were finished, the men could rotate short duty on necessary patrols and pickets, and then stand down. Christmas trees in the barracks. Extra rations of rum. Cards. Singing. Gaming. Women. Barracks talk flourished while raucous greetings were shouted in the streets with abandon and banter and laughter flowed.

At nine o'clock Colonel Rall threw back his thick goose-down comforter and swung his bare feet out onto the cold hardwood floor. He swallowed at the morning taste in his mouth, then looked with surprise at the bright sunlight on the window shade. He walked to the window, toes curled up from the cold hardwood, tugged the shade back six inches and squinted outside at the sunlight reflecting dazzling off the melting snow, the black mud in the streets, and the troops moving, waving, hallooing. He had missed the parading of the cannon and the flag raising, but no matter. The officer of the day had seen to it.

At nine-forty Rall had finished his bath and dressed and five minutes later settled onto the chair behind his desk in his office to glance over the morning report and the officer's summary of the patrols. Piel rapped at the door, then entered with a silver tray which he set on the desk. Rall reached for the mug of steaming black coffee, then the knife and fork and began working on the fried German sausage and eggs. At ten o'clock a rap came at the door and Rall called "Enter" through a mouthful of toast. Piel opened the door and stepped into the room while Rall swallowed, finished the last of the coffee, and wiped his mouth on his sleeve. "What is it?"

"Sir, another message just arrived from General Grant."

"What message?"

Piel handed it to him. "All it says, sir, is that General Lord Stirling might be in the vicinity. You should watch for him."

Rall shook his head and pointed at the patrol reports. "Our morning patrols are back and not one word about Americans, least of all Stirling." He tossed the message to one side. "There will be no reply."

"Sir, one more thing. Major Friederich von Dechow of the Knyphausen Regiment is here to see you."

"Dechow? About what?"

"He didn't say, sir."

Rall shoved the tray towards Piel. "Take this and send Dechow in."

Two minutes later Dechow entered and stood at attention, waiting for Rall to acknowledge him.

Rall spoke. "Ja, what is it you want?"

"Sir, some of the troops spoke of a messenger from General Grant who arrived in the night. He took morning mess with them before he left for Princeton."

Rall bobbed his head. "Go on."

Dechow's eyes narrowed. "May I inquire, sir, what the message was about? There is some concern among my men."

Rall leaned back, eyes wide. "Concern? What concern? There is no concern."

"Is there any word we might be moving south to take Philadelphia?"

Rall dropped a palm flat on the table. "Foolishness! No such word. General Howe is in New York. The campaign is finished until spring."

"Is Grant expecting an attack from the Americans?"

Rall's voice rose. "Grant said be ready. Take precautions. That is all. We are ready. We have taken precautions. What is the concern?"

"There have been incidents lately, sir, over the past ten days. American patrols have shot at our pickets. Wounded a few, killed two. We have no trenches, no breastworks—"

Rall broke in loud and caustic. "You know that yesterday I myself led two patrols. One hundred men each. We moved far up the Pennington Road and caught a band of rebels sneaking back to their boats. We shot at them and wounded many and then the American artillery across the river fired on us and we came back. There is no force of Americans on this side of the river. Only small patrols. Nothing. I have seen to it myself. Tell your men."

Dechow cleared his throat and gathered his courage. "Sir, may I suggest that it would be wise to move our extra supplies and equipment and ammunition away from Trenton to keep it from rebel hands? The food and blankets we have here would be of great benefit should they seize it."

Rall leaned forward, palms flat on his desk. "To seize it they must take Trenton, and to take Trenton they must cross the river and defeat us. You've seen the reports. Their condition." He stood abruptly, arm raised, finger pointing at Dechow, face flushed, anger rising. "I would welcome it! The war will be over in one-half hour if they attack us here!" He suddenly caught himself, lowered his arm, and sat back down. When he spoke again, his voice was restrained, quiet. "Let this talk of attack stop here, now. Tell your men. Let them enjoy Christmas."

Dechow did not move a muscle until Rall finished. "Yes, sir." He turned on his heel and walked out.

As the door closed Rall exhaled and all the air went out of him.

First Grant, now Dechow. What's wrong with these men? Do they really think the Americans can cross the river and take Trenton? Insanity! I have the reports. It's all there. They could not cross the river and defeat us even if a voice from the heavens commanded it.

He impulsively seized the stack of reports on his desktop and sorted through them, once again glancing at the critical figures and conclusions in the summary at the bottom of each page. He put them back in their basket.

It is all there. The matter is finished.

He strode to the door and was twisting the handle when the first faint sense of disquiet rose nagging in his consciousness. He released the brass knob and slowly walked back to his desk and sat down. For a time he sat in silence, working with the growing feeling inside that there was something around him to which he was blind. He nursed it, nudged it, tried to define it, to push it out into the open where he could see and understand its origin, its shape and size, but he could not. He moved and licked dry lips and lapsed into tense silence once more but it would not emerge from the shadows into the light.

Then suddenly his own words came reaching and his eyes opened wide and his breathing slowed.

They could not cross the river and defeat us even if a voice from the heavens commanded it.

The words came again and his face blanched with the thought. He dared not ask the question, and then he could not withhold it.

A voice from the heavens? Has a voice from the heavens commanded them?

The hair on his neck and arms stood on end. He leaned back in his chair, frozen, staring at the far wall but not seeing. He did not know how long he sat before he suddenly shook himself and thrust out his bulldog chin and took control.

Utter nonsense! Wars are not won by voices from the heavens. They are won by voices from officers who command better trained, better prepared, better armed troops than the enemy. They are won by facts.

He looked at the stack of daily reports and bobbed his head.

Facts. They are there, and they say we will win.

He rose and marched to the door and threw it open and called down the hall, "Adjutant." He heard Piel's running footsteps and then Piel was trotting down the hall to stop before Rall.

"Yes, sir."

"Have my horse saddled and ready in fifteen minutes and one for yourself and two other officers."

"Yes, sir. How long will we be gone?"

"Two hours. Maybe three."

"Yes, sir."

The horses sensed it, and stepped frisky. The warmth of the sun, the drip of ice and snow melting from the roofs and eaves, the troopers grinning, calling, splashing uncaring through the mud as they hurried about their duties, anxious to finish and return to the warmth and levity of rum and song and the long-awaited celebration. Rall reined his sorrel gelding north up King Street with Piel beside him and two young, blue-caped lieutenants behind. He raised his mount to an easy lope, splashing, throwing mud behind and the two lieutenants instantly fell back sixty feet. Rall smiled and pulled his mount down to a trot and the two riders closed the gap.

At the north end of town, at the junction of King and Queen Streets with the Pennington Road from the north and the Princeton Road from the east, Rall reined to a stop facing the two pickets patrolling the intersection. When they understood who he was they snapped to rigid attention, waiting.

"Report," he ordered.

"Calm all morning. No enemy sighted. Nothing out of the ordinary to report, sir."

Rall bobbed his head. "Carry on."

He drew rein left, east on the Pennington Road and held a brisk canter for a time, then slowed to a walk as the stone house occupied by a detail of men under the command of Lieutenant Wiederhold came into view, partially hidden in the thick, snow-filled woods. As Rall approached the two pickets at the front door came to attention.

"Report."

"Calm. No enemy sighted since daybreak. Nothing unusual, sir."

"Is Lieutenant Wiederhold inside?"

"Yes, sir."

"Get him."

Wiederhold emerged into the bright sunlight in full uniform and came to attention.

"Is all well with your command?"

"It is, sir."

"Have you seen any Americans today? Patrols?"

"None, sir."

"Any gunfire?"

"None."

"Carry on."

"Thank you, sir."

Rall continued north onto the Scotch Road for a quarter mile, then turned west, for four hundred yards on a trail leading through the snow and the woods to the River Road, just above the home of Philemon Dickinson where a patrol was billeted. On the River Road he reined south, towards the huge stone house and stopped facing the pickets.

"Report."

"Calm since daybreak. No enemy sighted. No patrols."

"Carry on."

Rall reined his horse around the house, down the slight incline seventy feet to the river and he sat for several minutes, peering upstream, then downstream, then studying the shore ice, and finally the open channel in the center. The hard freeze of two weeks earlier, eighty miles north, had thawed with the unexpected warmth of the day, and great slabs of ice were coming down, jamming the channel. The river was running fast and full, with the grinding of the huge chunks echoing through the trees and off the banks. Rall drew his telescope from his saddlebags and extended it, then stood in his stirrups to study the river upstream as far as he could see. There was no end to the ice chunks filling the river.

He replaced his telescope, then wheeled his horse around to the River Road and turned south, back towards the lower end of Trenton and the Old Barracks building. The pickets snapped to attention as he passed and he raised a hand to his hat brim and turned north once again, up King Street to his headquarters.

Still mounted, he spoke to Piel. "Make out a report. Where we stopped, what we asked, and the answers. No one has seen an American or an American patrol today. I want it in the records."

"Yes, sir."

Rall shifted his weight to dismount when one of the young lieutenants behind spoke.

"Sir."

Rall settled back into the saddle and turned. "What is it?"

The young man pointed northeast. "Sir, those clouds have been gathering on the horizon for two days. They're piling up. Could mean a storm coming in."

"We've had storms before."

"A storm could cover troop movements."

"Theirs? You think they could cross that river in a storm?" Rall shook his head in contempt. "You saw the river."

The lieutenant's face flushed and he diverted his eyes and fell silent.

Rall dismounted and Piel asked, "Will the colonel be needing his horse again today?"

"Yes."

Rall walked into the building as Piel dismounted to tie both horses to the iron rings sunk into the marble pillars in front, and the two young officers wheeled their mounts around to return to their duties at the Old Barracks.

Rall took lunch in his office at two o'clock. At three o'clock Piel delivered a two-page report on the morning's ride. Rall scratched an extra line onto it with his quill, signed it, and put it on top of the stack. At four o'clock he buckled on his heavy blue cape and with his hat under his arm walked to the foyer, where Piel stopped filing papers and waited.

"Come with me."

Forty-five minutes later Rall dismounted in front of headquarters and handed the reins to Piel. "Stable the horses and make another report. The sentry posts we inspected and the answers we got. Troops in good spirits. Celebrating Christmas with great enthusiasm. No Americans. No Stirling. Nothing but mud and snow and a storm gathering in the northeast."

"Yes, sir."

At five-fifteen Rall ate a piece of dark German bread spread with braunschweiger and drank a stein of beer, then rose, restless, and walked up the stairs to the second floor to rap on the door of his host, Stacy Potts, who owned a tannery and a small ironworks in town.

Potts opened the door and smiled. "Merry Christmas, Colonel Rall. I trust you're enjoying the celebration."

Rall nodded. "All is well. A game of checkers would be nice."

Potts stepped aside. "As you wish. Please do come in."

Five minutes later the two were hunched over the checkerboard. At six-twenty a tray of steaming roast beef, potatoes, and carrots with mince pie and black coffee was delivered to them. At ten minutes before seven the combatants put their twelve checkers on the opposing black squares to begin their fourth game, and by seven o'clock were locked in deep concentration with the wind beginning to sigh through the trees and down the chimney.

At five minutes past seven both men jumped and their heads jerked up as the unmistakable sound of gunfire shattered the stillness and echoed through the streets. A heavy, sustained volley, then scattered shots, then silence. Instantly Rall was on his feet, jolting the checkerboard, and he spun and was out of the room running. He pounded down the stairs to his quarters to grab his cape and hat, then back out through the foyer with Piel coming behind, out into the street. He snapped his cape into place and jammed his hat on his head while he shouted to the pickets in front of his building.

"Which direction?"

"There, sir," they answered, and pointed north, up King Street. Rall peered up the street but could see nothing, then pivoted to look down King Street towards the Old Barracks where his own regiment was the duty regiment, dressed and ready to move if necessary.

Inside the barracks building the troops slammed down their rum glasses and cards went flying as they ran to grab their overcoats, hats, and muskets. They came running out the door into the street to follow the point of the pickets north, sprinting while they struggled to get their coats and hats on. The moment they reached Rall he ordered them into ranks and led them north at double time, watching everything, waiting for movement.

They slowed as they came into the big intersection of King Street, Queen Street, Princeton Road, and Pennington Road, and for a moment Rall could not see the patrol stationed there on guard. Then he saw movement and he turned as a bewildered young lieutenant advanced from the shadows.

"What happened?" Rall demanded.

"I don't know, sir. One minute there was nothing and then there was heavy musket fire and then it stopped. We fired back and we heard them running in the dark and we followed but they were gone."

"How many?" Rall held his breath, waiting.

"From the musket flashes, maybe thirty-five, forty."

"Soldiers? Did you see any officers?"

"No, sir."

"Was their volley controlled or wild?"

"Wild, sir. They were scattered all over, not concentrated like soldiers in ranks."

"Casualties?"

"Six wounded. None dead."

"Serious wounds?"

"Two."

"Did you hit any of them?"

"I don't know, sir. Too dark."

"What unit are you?"

"Major Lossberg's, sir."

"Get your wounded down to the infirmary and make out a report." Rall turned to the men behind him. "You, captain. Take the first fifty men and proceed up the Pennington Road towards McKonkey's Ferry. Watch sharp. Those shots may have been intended to draw our men up the road in the dark into an ambush. At the first sign of trouble get your men off the road behind cover and send two runners back for help. If you find no one, come back. Understand?"

"Yes, sir." The captain barked orders, the first fifty men fell into ranks, and he led them north into the blackness at a trot. Rall held up his hand for silence and they all listened as the sound of feet faded. For ten more minutes Rall held his command silent as they listened for shouts or for musket fire, and there was nothing. He turned back to his men and they came to attention.

"Go on back——"

He was cut off by Dechow, who appeared directly in front of him with both hands raised, and Rall stared at him in silence.

"Sir, the units in town have formed outside their buildings, ready. I urge you, sir, send out patrols on all roads—Princeton, down to the ferry, the road to Bordentown. The gunfire may have been intended to draw us off north while they come in from the south or the east."

Rall shook his head violently. "No. That was the attack Grant warned about. It was nothing—just a mob of farmers out to make trouble. By now those farmers are all home, frightened out of their wits at what they did. There is no danger. It's all over. Take your command back to their quarters and let them finish the Christmas celebration."

"But sir——"

"Do it!"

Rall gave orders to the rest of his command. "It's all over. Go back to your quarters and your celebrations."

At nine-thirty Piel rapped on Rall's office door and entered on command. "Sir, the captain is back from patrol."

Rall stood instantly. "Bring him."

The man entered and stood at attention, face red from the wind and the cold.

"Report."

"Sir, we proceeded more than two miles up the road towards McKonkey's Ferry and there was nothing."

"You heard nothing? Saw nothing?"

"We frightened two horses behind a fence and they snorted and ran. A farm dog came barking. That was all."

"No shooting?"

"None. Either side."

Rall nodded. "That's what I thought. Write out a report. Have your command stand down. Continue their celebration."

"Thank you, sir."

Two blocks southeast, Dechow paced in his quarters, hands clasped behind his back, forehead drawn.

Something's wrong—I can feel it—something's going to happen—Rall's closed it out—won't listen.

Suddenly he could take no more. He quickly hooked his cape over his shoulders and thrust his hat onto his head and bolted out the door. He trotted from house to house where every man under his direct command was billeted and gave the same order: "You will stay inside and remain fully dressed in battle gear until further orders. Each of you will take your turn at standing guard outside this door until morning."

He walked back to his quarters with the rising wind billowing his cape behind, the temperature dropping below freezing, and scudding clouds moving south to cover the stars. He sat down on his bed, unable to stop or control his unexplained nervousness, and he began watching the clock, counting off the minutes and hours until morning.

At ten minutes before ten Piel again rapped on Rall's door.

"Sir, I have the lieutenant's written report about the shooting."

Rall reached for the paper as he spoke. "What about the wounded?"

"Four are slight. One has a bullet hole in his leg and will recover totally. One has a broken shoulder. He will be in the infirmary for a time."

Rall nodded his approval. "Then send out word. I have no special orders for the night. The men will remain in their quarters but are at liberty to continue whatever they're doing."

"Very good, sir. I'm sure they will appreciate it."

Rall grunted, "Tell them."

Piel turned to leave when Rall stopped him. "I'm going to Abraham Hunt's home. Do you know him?"

"Yes, sir."

"He has a party going on and sent me a written invitation. If you need me I'll be there. I'll return sometime after midnight. I'll let myself in, so there's no need for you to stay here waiting."

"Thank you, sir," Piel nodded and left.

Rall snapped his cape around his shoulders, tucked his hat under his arm, turned the wick low on his lamp, and walked out the front door of his headquarters into the freezing wind. He walked south to Second Street and the tall, six-gabled home with lights glowing in every window and the sounds of a harpsichord tinkling and of singing and laughter.

Abraham Hunt was the United States Postmaster for Trenton, a highly successful merchant, and a lieutenant-colonel in the local American militia commanded by Colonel Isaac Smith. He was also a notoriously gregarious soul, open and cheerful, famous for miles for his warmth and hospitality. He made it a point to be cooperative and highly receptive to the British and Hessians and held his home open to them any time, any day, entertaining both the officers and troops with lavish dinners from the day they marched into town. The result was that neither the British nor the Americans were able to decide on which side his true loyalties lay, and consequently neither side interfered with his home or businesses.

Overhead, clouds hid the heavens as Rall approached the front door and rapped. He wiped a hand across his mouth in anticipation of the feast within while he waited, and he felt the first sting of sleet on his face as Abraham himself answered the knock.

Hunt's face beamed as he grasped Rall's hand. "Colonel, how good of you to come. Do come in out of the storm. Here, let me take your cape and hat. Fire's warm in the parlor and library, and there are wines or rum—whatever you like—and meats and pies and custards for the taking. Cards in my den. Singing around the harpsichord. Oh, what a celebration we're having. So good of you to come."

The hot buttered rum was sweet and smooth, and the warmth spread through Rall. He felt the tensions of the day draining away and his muscles relaxing as he mellowed. He exchanged brusque greetings with other officers, bowed low to Mrs. Hunt, and for a time sat in one corner listening to the tinkle of the harpsichord and the robust blend of voices singing German Christmas carols and English folk songs. He sipped at his hot rum and found himself wishing his life had allowed him to learn at least the rudiments of music and singing. But it had not. The system in his birthplace of Hesse-Cassel for selecting boys for a life in the army was rigid, brutal, unforgiving, and allowed no time for the nonsense of art or music or a thousand other things he had secretly yearned to do and to know.

It was nearing midnight when he made his way through the revelers to the den where men sat at two tables, intent on the cards they held in their hands and those in the discard. Each man had a small heap of dried white beans before him, and a larger pile was in the center of the table. Crystal goblets partially filled with red wine were at the elbow of most of the players. Rall watched for several minutes before one man gestured to an open chair, and Rall dug a handful of beans from a nearby bowl and sat down. He set his mug of rum to one side, carefully set his beans on the table, and waited for the dealer to collect the cards, shuffle, and start the next hand.

The game was commerce, and it cost each player two beans to sit in. The dealer quickly dealt three cards to each player, they held them close to their chests to study them and make their decision to either hold what they were dealt or discard up to two cards. Then the dealer went around the table again, filling each hand to three cards.

The betting began. The pile of beans in the center of the table grew while those before each player diminshed. By midnight Rall had drunk three goblets of the rich, red wine, and won a few more beans than he lost. Hunt was standing nearby, the ever present gracious host, watching the games when one of his servants came to his side and spoke to him quietly.

"Sir, there is a visitor at the front door insisting he see Colonel Rall."

For one second, unnoticed by all but the servant, Hunt's eyes narrowed and his entire demeanor subtly changed as he reached inside himself and made an instant decision. He brought his mouth close to the servant's ear and whispered, "Colonel Rall cannot be disturbed. Have the man write the message and bring it to me."

The servant nodded and left the room. He walked down the hallway to the front door where a Tory farmer stood outside, black felt hat in hand, wrapped in a heavy coat wet with the sleet that had come on the wind.

"I'm sorry, sir, but Colonel Rall cannot be disturbed. Please write the message and I will deliver it to Colonel Rall at once." The servant held out a pencil and paper to the man.

The man stepped over the threshold to spread the paper on a nearby table and, with fingers still numb from the cold, slowly wrote out his message. He read it once, then folded it, and gave it to the servant. "Colonel Rall must see this immediately."

"I will deliver it to him now."

The man nodded and walked out the door into the storm while the servant quietly moved back into the den and passed the note to Hunt's hand unnoticed. As Hunt's fingers closed on the paper he neither looked at it nor did he move towards Rall. Smiling, ever the warm, affable host, he stood nearby, nodding, chatting, and he waited. The dealer dealt a new hand. Beans were pushed to the center of the table. The men concentrated and then discarded. Hunt watched Rall push two cards away and hold up two fingers, attention focused intently on the dealer.

As the two new cards came sliding towards Rall, Hunt leaned close and thrust the note near Rall's free hand.

"Sir, this note was just delivered by a visitor at the front door."

Without moving his eyes from the dealer, Rall grasped the note, quickly stuffed it into his vest pocket, and reached for the two new cards. He looked at them and leaned back, holding a straight face as he added the two nines to the one already in his hand, and he sorted out twenty beans as the betting worked its way around the table.

Two blocks away, at his quarters, Dechow sat in the yellow lamplight at his table fully dressed, listening to the wind drive the sleet and snow murmuring against his window. Nervous, indecisive, he rose to open the door, and the yellow light caught the ice crystals driving in the freezing wind. He closed the door and stood with his head down for a few moments, then resolutely straightened and quickly threw his cape on, set his hat firmly on his head, again opened the door, and strode out into the storm. Two minutes later he stopped at the shouted voice of the sentry at the nearest home where twelve of his command were billeted.

"Who comes there?"

"Major Dechow."

"Advance."

Inside, chairs scraped as men instantly came to their feet when he opened the door. They were fully dressed except for their heavy overcoats and hats laid on their bunks with their muskets nearby.

Dechow spoke rapidly, curtly. "My prior orders are rescinded. You may stand down from duty until morning. There is no need for a picket outside your door. You may continue with your celebration. Carry on."

There were perfunctory smiles as he finished and walked out the door and sent the picket inside. Dechow stood silently outside the door long enough to hear the raucous comments and laughter as the men shed their tunics and heavy boots and set the rum and wine flasks on the table. Dechow strode to the next home where a picket again challenged, and Dechow delivered his message to the ten soldiers inside. It was approaching one A.M. when he finished delivering his message to his entire command. He reentered his own quarters, shook the rain and melted sleet from his hat and cape, hung them on the back of the door, and settled down to his own fire, his own wine.

By twenty minutes before three o'clock Rall had finished six goblets of wine, lost more beans than he had won, and was having difficulty with his concentration. He pushed his chair back, nodded to the other players, dropped his few remaining beans back into the bowl, and made his way out into the hall.

Hunt was by his side instantly. "Let me fetch your cape and hat, sir." He hurried away and returned to help Rall fit his cape on his shoulders and fasten the catch at his throat, hand him his hat, and he reached to grasp Rall's hand warmly.

"Sir, it has been an honor to have you here. Thank you for coming. Can I have a carriage take you to your quarters? The storm is fierce out there."

Rall shook his head. "The walk will do me good. Thank you for a good evening."

Hunt held the door for him and Rall walked out into the wind and the sleet, now mixed with snow, slanting on the wind. Hunt watched him walk unsteadily to the front walk, then turn north, and he was gone in the darkness. Hunt was aware the note remained in Rall's vest pocket, forgotten by Rall. He closed the door and stood in deep thought for a moment, then returned to his guests in the library.

At ten minutes past five o'clock, a tiny buzz began in the slumbering brain of Jacob Piel and at five-fifteen he opened his eyes in the blackness of his quarters. Wind and sleet and snow hummed at the window and sighed in the chimney. For a time he lay still, burrowed beneath the down comforter, listening in the dark, letting his thoughts run.

We should have put candles on the tree—like home—like Mother did—so far away. How are they? Mother? the children? Is Aunt Hilda alive for the celebration? so old—frail. How many pies did Mother make this year? how many sausages? What gifts did she make for the children? What did they make for her?

He threw back the comforter and made his way across the cold floorboards to the fireplace. By feel he lifted the leather bellows from its hook and carefully blew on the banked coals until they glowed. At the first lick of flame, he added shavings, then sticks, and finally kindling, waiting while the chimney began to draw and the warmth reached him and crept into the room. In the dancing light he looked at the clock. It was half past five o'clock, December 26, 1776.

At six o'clock he put on his boots and overcoat, hurried next door, up the stairs, and silently opened the door to Colonel Rall's quarters far enough to hold the lamp high and peer into the shadows. The colonel lay unmoving in his bed, breathing slow and deep. The slightly sour smell of last night's wine and rum reached Piel and his nose wrinkled as he closed the door and returned to his own quarters next door.

By seven o'clock Piel had heated bathwater and bathed and shaved, and was standing at the stove cooking griddle cakes and sliced ham. At seven-thirty he finished cleaning the dishes and walked to the front door of the building, opened it, and for a moment watched the wind drive the snow to the southwest, singing in the trees and gusting around the corners of the houses. He glanced up and down the street, and there was not a picket in sight. His forehead wrinkled in puzzlement as he shivered, then shrugged, closed the door, and walked to the small desk beneath the window of the west wall. He rubbed his hands together for warmth, then squared a piece of paper, reached for a quill, and carefully began to write.

My Dear Mother:

He started, and his head jerked up at the sound of more than twenty muskets blasting above the howl of the wind, and he stood stock-still with the first sense of fear rising within. Two seconds later a second volley blasted and then individual shots cracked sporadically. Piel dropped the quill, spun on his heel, and darted out the door, sprinting across the street to the home where the duty detail was billeted. He pounded on the door with both hands until a sergeant answered, still in his underwear, eyes red with drink and reveling, hair askew.

Piel gaped. "Are you the duty patrol?"

"Yes, sir."

"Were you on duty this morning?"

"No, sir. Major Dechow gave orders for us to stand down last night."

Piel recoiled back one full step in disbelief. In the entire town of Trenton, not one building, not one of the barracks had a picket out. The town was totally without a warning system.

Piel's voice rang loud. "There was heavy firing up on the Pennington Road five minutes ago. What was it?"

The sergeant's face went ghostly white. "I heard no firing. I don't know."

Piel fairly shouted, "I'm ordering you and your patrol out in three minutes to proceed at double time north up Pennington Road to Wiederhold's post and then return at once to report on the gunfire. We could be under attack."

The sergeant turned and shouted in the dark room, "Fall in! Fall in! Dress and fall in! There's shooting." Two seconds later the room was a bedlam as bare feet smacked onto the floor and frightened troopers grabbed for socks and pants.

Piel turned and sprinted back across the street to Stacy Potts's home where Rall was still sleeping, and pounded on the front door with both hands. The house was as dark and quiet as a tomb. Piel pounded for thirty more seconds, then stepped back two steps and cupped his hands about his mouth to shout with all his strength towards the window in the second floor.

"Colonel Rall! Colonel Rall! There's shooting outside of town and we have no pickets out! Colonel! Wake up!"

He shouted three times before the second floor window was thrown open and Rall's head appeared, hair whipping in the wind and sleet, eyes bleary. It took Rall a moment to focus well enough to recognize Piel down in the street and he called, "What is it?"

Piel shouted, "There's gunfire at the edge of town, near the Pennington Road. There are no pickets out. There is gunfire. Do you understand?"

Rall shook his head to drive the cobwebs from his wine-addled brain, swallowed sour, and called out, "I'll be down in a minute." The window slammed and Piel stood alone before the big house, waiting in the raging storm for Rall, not knowing what to do next. Movement from his left caught his eye and he turned to see a troop of Hessians buttoning their overcoats as they spilled out of a nearby church jerking the sleeves off the poles with the regimental colors, trying to unfurl them in the storm. They trotted into the street as Lieutenant Colonel Scheffer, weak, fevered, arisen from a bed where he had lain sick for over a week, appeared from an alley, mounted on a frightened horse, and began shouting orders to get the men into rank and file, while some of the men led rearing horses up King Street towards the cannon in front of the headquarters building.

Beyond Scheffer, Piel saw faint silhouettes of men nearly hidden in the storm, running from west to east across the lower end of King Street, towards the Assunpink Creek, and he started when he realized they were Hessians. One second later he peered north, up King Street, and a look of puzzled wonder crossed his face. Two blocks to the north, where King and Queen Streets formed the big junction with the Pennington and Princeton Roads, through the driving snow and sleet, he could make out the dark forms of mounted men hauling skidding horses to a stop while other men running on foot instantly unhitched four cannon and swung the muzzles to bear down both King and Queen Streets.

Piel narrowed his eyes to peer intently, and the scene was burned into his brain forever.

Americans were swarming around the cannon. Scarecrow men with long wet hair flying in the wind and sleet, dressed in rags and tatters, some bare legged, feet wrapped in burlap or animal hides or anything they could find, beards dirty and filled with ice and snow. They clutched muskets, or swords, or axes, or pitchforks, or anything they could swing, and they were shouting like wild men. Terrified at a sight that could only have come straight from the depths of purgatory, Piel gasped and reached for the doorknob just as Colonel Rall opened the front door of the house and stepped out into the storm, still latching his cape, and started for his horse.

At that instant the first deafening cannon blast thundered from the head of King Street, and Piel stood in horror as twenty-eight pounds of American grapeshot shredded limbs and ripped shrubs and shattered windows and splintered housefronts as it swept down King Street, knocking over Hessian soldiers as far as Piel could see.

Notes

The chronology of December 24–26, 1776, is important to understand because the sequence of events illustrates how the events favored the Americans.

During the day of December 24, 1776, Colonel Rall personally patrolled the area surrounding Trenton, but had seen nothing to cause him alarm. Late that evening, General James Grant in Princeton received a Tory visitor who informed him of Washington's previous war councils. During the next forty-eight hours, General Grant twice advised Colonel Rall to beware of an attack, possibly from General Stirling's forces, who had been rumored in the area, but because of Rall's personal patrols and his own personal arrogance, he discarded Grant's warnings (see Ketchum, *The Winter Soldiers*, p. 236).

Christmas Day brought a change in the weather. The bright morning sun caused a thaw, but late in the day, storm clouds began rolling in from the northeast (see Ketchum, *The Winter Soldiers*, pp. 237, 246–47). The storm eventually broke around eleven P.M. and continued throughout December 26.

The morning of December 25, Major Friederich von Dechow of the Hessian Knyphausen Regiment urged Rall to evacuate their main stores of supplies and munitions to prevent them from falling into American hands. Rall hotly refused because, again, repeated patrols were not turning up any immediate threats (see Ketchum, *The Winter Soldiers*, p. 237).

Around seven o'clock that night, Colonel Rall played a game of checkers with Stacy Potts, but gunfire interrupted their game. A band of about thirty Americans, thought to be farmers, had attacked the pickets at the junction of Pennington and Princeton Roads, wounding about six Hessians under Lossburg's command. Rall concluded this must have been the attack Grant had written about (see Ketchum, *The Winter Soldiers*, pp. 237–38).

Major Dechow was extremely concerned at this turn of events and when Rall refused to have any pickets stand guard anywhere in Trenton, he posted his own men (see Ketchum, *The Winter Soldiers*, pp. 237–38).

About 10:00 P.M. on December 25, Colonel Rall left for Abraham Hunt's party. Hunt was an American militia officer with a peculiar ability to remain on good terms with both the Americans and the Hessians and so was trusted by both sides (see Ketchum, *The Winter Soldiers*, p. 238). In the early-morning hours of December 26, while Rall was playing cards, a Tory messenger arrived at Hunt's house and left a written message for Rall, which Rall pocketed but never read. The message warned of an American attack (see Ketchum, *The Winter Soldiers*, p. 238).

The storm still raged in the early-morning hours of December 26 and Major Dechow finally called in his pickets, leaving Trenton without a warning system of any kind (see Ketchum, *The Winter Soldiers*, p. 258).

Lieutenant Jacob Piel arose about five o'clock on December 26. Rall was still asleep when Piel heard musket shots two hours later. Piel woke Rall who stepped into the street just as Colonel Henry Knox's cannon fired the first shot from the head of King Street (see Ketchum, *The Winter Soldiers*, pp. 258–59).

Additional information and summaries of the events covered in this chapter can be found in Higginbotham, *The War of American Independence*, pp. 165–68; Leckie, *George Washington's War*, pp. 316–21; and Mackesy, *The War for America*, p. 112.

CHAPTER VIII

★ ★ ★

*D*ecember 25th, 1776

McKonkey's Ferry, Pennsylvania

My Dear Brigitte:

Yesterday General Washington had a long meeting with some officers. This morning we were given fried corn mush with brown sugar and crisped pork, our first good breakfast in weeks. General Washington relieved us of usual duties until one o'clock this afternoon, and each man received three days cooked rations to save in a blanket or knapsack. At two o'clock we are to form with our units with the cooked rations, one blanket, and forty cartridges to receive our orders. We are left to guess the reason for all this, but I believe General Washington intends to attack Trenton. By the time you receive this letter, you should know the reason as well as I.

The weather has been harsh, but this morning the sun is out and there is a thaw. However there are storm clouds to the northeast and a wind is rising from that direction and we are expecting bad weather by nightfall. The Delaware River lays between our camp and Trenton, and if we are ordered to attack, we will have to cross it. It is wide, and large pieces of ice are starting to fill the channel. I believe there has been a heavy thaw up north.

I have been assigned to a regiment commanded by General

Hugh Mercer who is a brave and fine officer. He fought well at Long Island and is much admired and trusted by his men. If we do attack Trenton, I am certain Colonel John Glover of Marblehead will be assigned with his regiment to move the army across the Delaware to the New Jersey side. His men are mostly fishermen and have given fine service as soldiers as well as moving the army across two rivers under difficult circumstances.

I am well, except I have lost weight. Food is scarce, indeed, we have learned many lessons about food, viz., that porcupine is quite tasty when roasted properly. My clothing has fared badly and I am dressed from whatever I can find, but am generally warm and protected. Our army is poorly, but spirit remains strong; however, we have desertions daily. My friend Eli Stroud and I brought back thirteen deserters three days ago and were much relieved when they were not shot. Soldiering is not as expected, and I would discontinue if I did not know this is the work of the Almighty.

The life of a soldier is uncertain, and should I go to battle and not return, I want you to know you are in my mind daily with tender thoughts. I ask you to give my warmest greetings to your mother and the children, and remember me to Matthew when next you write to him. Please share the contents of this brief letter with my beloved mother and sister.

God bless you all,
Billy Weems

The sounds of dripping snowmelt were all around in the warm, bright noon sunshine as Billy sat cross-legged in the lean-to and carefully reread the letter. Once again felt the rise in his heart as he saw Brigitte in his mind, honey-colored hair, blue eyes, heart-shaped face. He folded the paper and slipped out of his coat made from doubled layers of old gray blanket. Carefully he opened the slit through the inside layer and drew out the thin oilcloth packet. He unfolded it and placed the pencil with the pad of paper on it, then added the folded letter to the other five he had carefully written by firelight in the bitter cold of the past four weeks but never mailed. He rewrapped them all and slipped the packet back through the slit. He was working his arms back into the coat when he heard the call of his name from behind.

Eli dropped to his haunches beside Billy. "Another letter?"

Billy nodded.

"The girl?"

"Yes."

"Going to send this one?"

Billy closed the coat and tied it with the cord around his waist, and said nothing.

Eli shook his head. "Why write if you never send them?"

Billy shrugged. "Never can tell. Might send them some day."

Eli wiped at his beard. "We're supposed to form ranks about two o'clock, right after we eat. Someone wants to read something to us."

Billy raised questioning eyes. "I heard. Read what?"

"Don't know. Someone said from a newspaper." He glanced northeast, across the river. "Storm coming."

Billy nodded. "Before night. Seen Turlock?"

"Yes. He's assigned with Glover."

They stood in line for boiled beef and cabbage that was greasy and old and steaming coffee that was strong, but they fell silent and ate with grateful reverence. They went back to receive a thick slice of brown bread smothered with blackstrap molasses, and they returned to their own campfire to sit down and eat slowly, savoring the heavy sweetness while the breeze stiffened and began to rattle bare tree branches overhead.

East of them, General Washington sat his horse on the riverbank, eyes narrowed, mouth pursed as he studied the channel. For two days, freezing weather had cleared out the floating ice without freezing solid from shore to shore. Then the unexpected thaw had set in during the early-morning hours and now great chunks of ice were once more grinding their way south to the Atlantic. For a long time Washington watched and gauged and then rubbed weary eyes with his fingers. The ice was gaining and if the thaw held, the channel would be choked by nightfall.

He drew and released a great sigh, then reined his horse around at the sound of an incoming rider. Major James Wilkinson loped his black mare up to the general and pulled her to a stop, then thrust out a sealed letter.

"General Horatio Gates asked me to deliver this to you, sir."

Washington looked at the paper for a moment, unable to make sense of Gates sending him a letter when Gates was supposed to be in camp helping the army prepare to cross the river.

"What a time to be handing me a letter! Where is he?"

"I left him in Philadelphia early this morning, sir."

Washington's forehead wrinkled in stunned surprise. "Philadelphia? What's he doing in Philadelphia?"

"I understood him to say he's on his way to Congress, sir."

For an instant Washington stared, then opened the letter and scanned it before he shoved it inside his tunic, sickened by what was now so clear.

Gone to Philadelphia! to Congress to report this as a failure before it's begun. He doesn't want to be part of this—wants to replace me!

Without another word he tapped spur to his mount and moved away from the riverbank at an easy lope, Wilkinson following.

At twenty minutes before two o'clock, orders rang out and the army moved west through the woods one mile into the open fields, out of sight of the New Jersey riverbank. At two o'clock the general officers handed out sealed, written orders to the regimental officers, who opened them and stood silent, unmoving while they read them. At ten minutes past two the officers stood before their men and each read their orders aloud. Not a man moved or spoke as the concise words and phrases came clearly in the cold December air.

Cross the Delaware—march south in two columns—total silence—do not get separated from your officers—cannon—advance patrols. Hit Trenton hard and fast at five o'clock in the morning—Sullivan's command at south end of town—Greene and Washington at north end—surround the town—storm the streets—do not stop until Trenton is taken.

The officers finished reading, and quiet, shocked murmuring broke out while men glanced sideways at each other, faces white, eyes wide.

Cross the Delaware and take Trenton at night?

The voices of the officers cracked out once more. "Attention to the orders of General Washington until they are read in full!"

As the men came back to attention Billy glanced up and down the ranks. Not one soldier was dressed in anything faintly resembling a uniform. Their heads were bare except for the few that were covered with scarves tied under their chins to keep ears from freezing. Coats, trousers, shirts, shoes, made of anything they could find to wrap and tie around their bodies. He could not remember the last time any man had shaved or bathed. Eyes and cheeks were sunken and hollow; half the men could not stand straight because hunger cramps had buckled them in half for so long. They could not remember a time they weren't starving. The single exception was Eli, standing next to him, dressed in his wolf skin coat and parka and knee-length moccasins, from all appearances an Iroquois Indian. The rest stood there in silence with the wind in their faces and tiny ice crystals beginning to sting as they came slanting.

Billy wiped his sleeve across his mouth, trying to control the fear that rose within.

"You will stand at attention for the reading."

Billy straightened and waited and the officer's voice came strong.

"Written by Common Sense, published December nineteenth. 'The American Crisis, number one.'"

He paused and then continued.

"'These are the times that try men's souls. The summer soldier and the sunshine patriot will, in this crisis, shrink from the service of his country; but he that stands it NOW, deserves the love and thanks of man and woman. Tyranny, like hell, is not easily conquered; yet we have the consolation with us, that the harder the conflict, the more glorious the triumph.'"

The officer stopped and the only sounds were the great black ravens circling the nearly deserted camp back by the river, scavenging for food crumbs. Billy felt the hair on his arms rise and from the corner of his eye he saw Eli stiffen as the officer read on.

"'What we obtain too cheap, we esteem too lightly—'Tis dearness only that gives every thing its value. Heaven knows how to put a proper price upon its goods; and it would be strange indeed, if so celestial an article as FREEDOM should not be highly rated.' "

The words struck into Billy's heart. " 'Britain, with an army to enforce her tyranny, has declared, that she has a right (*not only to* TAX) but "*to* BIND *us in* ALL CASES WHATSOEVER," and if being *bound in that manner* is not slavery, then is there not such a thing as slavery upon earth. Even the expression is impious, for so unlimited a power can belong only to GOD.' "

The hush held while the officer read. When he finished, the men stood still, held by a feeling that had begun in each of their souls and slowly grown to fill them. They swallowed and finally glanced around, aware something rare was happening, something that was lifting them above themselves in their clarity of purpose, their resolve. It caught and held and bound them together, and they did not speak of it directly, but as they looked at each other they knew.

The officer concluded. "That is all. You will move over to the river behind Taylor's Island to begin loading in the sequence called out in your orders. You will be given the password for this operation before you load into the boats. Good luck. May the Almighty be with us."

For a time there was low murmuring as the power of Paine's words sunk deep into them. Billy glanced at Eli. "Did you feel it? When he read?"

Eli nodded. "I felt it. Strong. I don't see any summer soldiers here."

It was enough. They said no more as the men began to move back towards the woods and the river, slowly, steadily, in the sequence called out by their orders. General Stephen's regiment was in the lead, followed by a light cavalry command and some infantry under Captain John Flahaven and Captain William Washington, a distant relative of General George Washington; both commands had orders to lead the attack on the Hessian pickets on the two roads into Trenton. As they moved through the trees towards the riverbank, the rising northeast wind drove clouds to blot out the blue sky, and then the sun, and the temperature began to fall.

The officers rode beside their men, watching, gauging mood, calculating their strength, their endurance, offering a word here, a hand there.

Major James Wilkinson worked his mare through the trees, twisting in the saddle to avoid the bare branches, watching as he rode. He glanced back at those behind and studied them and his eyes dropped to the ground, and suddenly he reined his horse to a stop. For long moments he sat, peering down at the tracks where his men had walked shuffling in the snow, and he murmured, "The snow. Tinged with blood. Their feet."

An old soldier raised his bearded face. "What was that, sir?"

Wilkinson looked away for a moment and cleared his throat before he dared look at the man. "Nothing. Carry on."

He looked ahead at the long line of tattered men waiting their turn to cross an impossible river and attack the Hessian army, then Wilkinson turned to look back into the silent, gaunt, bearded faces of those yet coming, and suddenly an overpowering pride welled up inside and he reined his mount away from the column for a moment while he wiped his coat sleeve across his eyes.

The army gathered on the frozen bank of the river near the stately three-storied stone home of William McKonkey and the ferry, and the officers called their commands to silence. "Men, General Washington has given us the password, and we give it to you now. If for any reason you are challenged while we are carrying out our orders on this operation, you run the risk of being shot if you cannot deliver the password. It is this."

They waited until the only sounds were the ice in the river and the wind. " 'Victory or Death.' 'Victory or Death.' Remember it."

The men quietly repeated it to themselves, then again, and they fell silent for a moment as they pondered it and realized that General Washington meant to take Trenton or give his life in the effort. They heard the voice of Colonel John Glover rise above the wind, and they looked in his direction as he gave orders to his regiment.

"Move forward and launch these boats, and load."

With efficiency born of untold years of experience, Glover's fishermen tipped the big, black Durham boats booming onto their bottoms, and hands toughened by summers and winters of salt water grasped the gunwales while they heaved their backs into it, legs driving, sliding the boats down the icy incline of the riverbank to smash through the shore ice on the leeward side of Taylor's Island, out of sight of the New Jersey bank of the river. Some held the flat-bottomed craft steady, broadside against the bank, while others began the task of loading men.

"Keep moving. Don't stop moving."

The fishermen grasped hands and arms to help the soldiers step from the snow-covered bank over the thirty-inch gunwales into the blunt-nosed vessels.

"Step high. Move on to the front. Keep moving. Don't stop."

They hit a rhythm and it caught, and the lines began to move a little faster with each minute.

"Keep coming," the fishermen called. "Step high. Move to the front."

In fading light, Colonel Glover called, "Stop the line. The first load is aboard."

His fishermen stepped into the boats and crowded the soldiers together away from the gunwales to make room to man the poles along the sides. Loaded, the gunwales rose a scant twelve inches above the water. The soldiers in the boats stood white-faced, watching the fishermen, and they drew comfort from the look in their eyes and the set of their chins.

On Glover's signal they pushed off. Once clear of the riverbank, they turned the boats to run with the current until they were clear of Taylor's Island, then they set their poles, turned the tillers, and the bows swung left, straight into the main channel, running high and full with the unexpected thaw and choked with ice cakes, some the size of cannon. Every man on shore stood stock-still, shivering, some holding their breath while they watched the heavy boats swing as they plowed into the suck of the swollen river current and they heard the hollow boom as the first of the huge ice cakes slammed into them. They saw the fishermen turn the bows upstream at an angle, and those in the front of the boats began taking the ice chunks as they came, pushing them away with their poles, giving none of them a chance to take the boat broadside. Then they were in the middle of the river, then past it, and then in the fast gathering gloom they were smashing their way through the shore ice on the New Jersey side. The bows of the big boats rammed into the bank and the fishermen leaped ashore to hold them while the men unloaded.

They watched the fishermen work the empty boats, riding high, back through the channel, then the shore ice to thump hollow against the Pennsylvania bank and the fishermen jumped over the bow to hold them while the next regiment of waiting soldiers began to load.

The horses were being held bridled and saddled with the girths loosened at the north end of camp, and on command the soldiers led them through the mounting wind and thin sleet down the icy slope to the river. The fishermen swung the boats around broadside to the bank and held them steady as the horsemen lighted lanterns. Some of them stepped into the boats, holding the lanterns high to cast a small circle of light inside the boat.

"All right, bring the first ones."

One man led the first horse down to the gunwale on the near side of the boat with one man on either side while inside the boat the fishermen held their lanterns high. The man stepped over the gunwale, into the boat, and the animal stopped, eyes glowing wine-red in the feeble lantern light while the man on the bridle gave his mount time to peer inside the boat and understand what it was. Then he pulled steadily on the bridle reins while those on either side of the frightened animal grabbed the saddle skirt with one hand and joined their other hand behind the horse's hindquarters and heaved forward. The frightened horse tossed its head against the pull of the bridle and settled back on its haunches against the pressure on its rump and then it lifted one front leg over the gunwale, then the other and as the front hooves hit the bottom of the boat clattering it buck-jumped its hindquarters in and instantly spraddled out its legs against the sudden unsteadiness of the undulating boat. Quickly the man on the bridle tucked a piece of ragged tarp under one cheek strap, pulled it across the horse's eyes, and tucked it under the other cheek strap and, blindfolded, the horse dropped its head and settled, hooves set and braced. The man on the bridle talked to the animal, reassured it, patted it on the neck until the quivering stopped, then slowly walked it to the bow of the boat and let it once again spread its feet and settle. He nodded to the next man, who led his horse forward with a man on either side, and he stopped to let his horse peer inside the boat to satisfy itself of what was inside before he stepped into the boat and pulled the bridle reins.

Downstream one hundred yards, the fishermen swung five more boats broadside to the bank and nodded to Colonel Henry Knox. Short, rotund, heavy jowled, Knox's deep, resonant voice boomed as he gave orders for loading his beloved cannon. Each battery commander, young, wiry Captain Alexander Hamilton among them, supervised his own crew in loading his gun, while Knox strode up and down the slippery riverbank overseeing the work, fretting himself into a high state of nerves at the thought that one of his cannon would be damaged, or worse, lost in the black waters of the river. The soldiers rigged ropes and pry-poles and strained with all their strength to lift the guns and carriages, ranging from one to two tons, over the thirty-inch gunwales and set them down inside the boats, then block the wheels and tie them down.

Colonel Glover walked among them repeating, "Gently, don't crack the bottoms of the boats," while Colonel Henry Knox was vociferous in his commands, "Handle those guns with care—do not damage the guns."

Fifty yards downstream, towering over his men, General Washington stood in the freezing, sleet-filled wind with a lantern held high above his head, watching his men load. Like them, he was soaked to the skin, water dripping from his nose and chin as he moved among them, giving a word of encouragement here, advice there, patting a man's shoulder as he walked by. In the dim lantern light they looked into his face, and in the blue-gray eyes and the set of his chin they saw a commitment beyond anything they had ever known. It struck awe into their hearts, and they knew their leader would be there with them until they were victorious, or dead. They looked and slowed for a moment, and they drew strength and hurried on.

Washington paused, turned his back to the wind and hunched forward to draw his pocket watch from his vest pocket near the lantern. It was after eight o'clock. He slipped the watch away and for a moment looked into the blackness downstream.

Ewing and Cadwalader. They should be loading. Are they all right? Will they succeed?

Nine miles to the south, Brigadier General James Ewing stood on the bank of the river three-quarters of a mile below the Trenton Ferry, soaked, shivering. His eyes were narrowed against the wind and the sleet and his mouth was clenched shut as he stared into the blackness and listened to the grinding of the ice and the whistling wind. He shifted his weight from one foot to the other in frustration, indecision. He turned to one of the officers standing behind him with a lantern.

"At last light the channel was high and fast and jammed with ice. I doubt we could have crossed. That's been two hours. Do you think we can cross now?"

The officer shook his head. "I don't know, sir. Only way to find out is to send out a boat and see what happens."

Ewing hunched his shoulders. "Risk some men?"

"I can't think of another way, sir."

For a moment Ewing paced. "All right. Ask for some volunteers."

The call went out and thirty men stepped forward. Ten minutes later they pushed away from the shore with one small lantern in the stern, and Ewing and his officers watched the tiny light grow smaller in the blackness and the driving sleet as his men poled the heavy boat out. Suddenly the pinpoint of light veered downstream and Ewing exclaimed, "The current caught them," and he sucked in air as he watched the light dance eerily as it swept downstream.

Ewing trotted along the icy bank southward, holding his single lantern high so those in the boat could see it, slipping, stumbling, trying to keep the light in the boat in sight. Above the wind he heard the shouts of frightened men, and then slowly the light in the boat became larger and then he could make out the black silhouette of the boat as it came in and hit the frozen bank. They were two hundred yards downstream when Ewing and his officers reached to hold the boat while the shivering men leaped over the gunwales onto the snow and ice.

The sergeant in charge came to attention and Ewing faced him. "Ice? Current?"

"Both, sir. We couldn't hold her. Maybe Glover's fishermen can do it, sir, but we'll lose some men if we try it without them."

"Glover's men are assigned with Washington and Sullivan. We have to do it ourselves or not at all."

The sergeant wiped a wet sleeve across his wet beard. "Then, sir, we'll lose about half our men in the river. Maybe more."

With shivering fingers Ewing drew out his watch, then pushed it back into his vest pocket. "We've got a little time. Maybe the freeze will help clear the channel. We'll wait."

One hour later the shivering, soaked men once again lifted their wrapped feet high to clear the gunwales and once again pushed away from the frozen riverbank while Ewing and his staff watched the light in the stern move away. The boat had not gone twenty yards before the light reversed itself and came straight back, and once again the men inside returned to the frozen riverbank.

"Sir, the ice is worse, not better. I don't want to be responsible for what happens if we put boats out into that channel. I doubt any of them would reach the New Jersey side."

Ewing felt the grab in his midsection. *What about Washington? If we can't cross, can Cadwalader get across? If Cadwalader can't cross to engage von Donop to the south, and if we can't cross to seal off the bridge road and cut von Donop off if he gets past Cadwalader, what about Washington? Von Donop will have a clear field to come up on his flanks, or his rear, and catch him by surprise. And even if von Donop does not come up to Trenton, our failure to seal off the Bordentown Road will leave a wide-open escape for Rall's troops in Trenton—they can run south across the bridge and down the Bordentown Road with no one to stop them. Washington will lose what he's trying so hard to gain.*

By strength of will Ewing forced his stampeding thoughts into some semblance of reason, of order.

With Glover's regiment handling the boats, Washington might get across. If he does, he'll have to take Trenton with his forces alone, no help from me or from Cadwalader. He can do that. If Cadwalader gets across, likely he will be able to slow Donop enough for Washington to get away, but even if he doesn't, Cadwalader will send a rider to tell Washington Donop's on the way. And, unless someone from Trenton gets to Donop to tell him Trenton's under attack, he will not know to bring his command north anyway. Some of Rall's troops might escape south across the Assunpink Bridge, down the Bordentown Road, but better we lose a few Hessians than most of my command.

Ewing straightened his shoulders and made the only decision he could. He hated it, loathed it, but knew every battlefield commander lived with the possibility that one day such a decision may rest on their shoulders. He turned back to his staff.

"We will not sacrifice this entire command until we know it is absolutely necessary. I believe General Washington can handle Trenton. I doubt von Donop and his Hessians will hear about it until it's too late. So I doubt it will make much difference if neither our troops nor Cadwalader's get across. If some Trenton Hessians escape down the Bordentown Road, we'll just have to accept that—better they escape than we lose most of this command."

He paused and his men saw the agony in his face and heard the pain in his voice as he gave his final orders. "We will stand down and wait for morning, or until the river clears enough for us to cross. Tell the men."

They turned and disappeared in the darkness, and none of them heard him say quietly, "If I'm wrong, may the Almighty be with Washington." He lingered to stare downstream for a time, trying to see Cadwalder in his mind, facing the river in the blackness, and it rang in his head, *What will Cadwalader do?*

Sixteen miles south, General John Cadwalader stood on the frozen riverbank at Dunk's Ferry with his staff by his side, his command behind, watching the first boat pole its way into the black waters of the river. The single lantern hung from the tiller at the rear of the boat, out of sight of the New Jersey shore, swinging in the whistling wind. The men squinted against the pelting sleet until the tiny light disappeared, then stood motionless, straining to hear, fearful the boat had gone down. Two minutes stretched to five, then ten, and still they waited. Suddenly the light was there, this time at the bow of the boat, and they heard the hollow sound of ice floes plowing into the side of the hull, and then it was nosing in towards shore. The riverbank rose nearly four feet sheer from the water, then angled steeply back for twenty feet before it leveled off. Cadwalader stood on the brink of the four-foot drop to hold his lantern high and quickly count the men. Thirty had gone. Ten had poled the boat back. Twenty were safely on the New Jersey shore.

The unbearable tension went out of Cadwalader and he reached to help the men scramble up the steep bank. "You made it?" he exclaimed. "It can be done?"

The sergeant answered. "It can be done right here, sir. The channel broadens here and flows a little slower than upstream."

Twenty minutes later twelve boats shoved off the Pennsylvania bank and slowly disappeared into the broad expanse of black water and ice. One hour later the bows drove into the bank at Cadwalader's feet and he turned to those waiting behind.

"Load the cannon."

Willing hands seized the trails of the huge guns at the top of the sharp incline while others drove six-inch timbers through the wheel spokes to lock them. They eased the two-ton gun over the edge of the incline and set their feet to hold it back when one man on the trails slipped on the packed snow and went down, knocking the feet out from under the man ahead of him. The six men left standing could not hold the cannon back and it careened down the incline while the men shouted a warning. The great gun cleared the four-foot drop-off and cartwheeled into the waiting Durham boat. The hull held as the cannon slammed into the far side and drove it down into the water. The near side rose high out of the water, and as the terrified men on shore watched, the huge black boat seemed to balance on one edge for a moment and then it rolled on over. The eight men inside leaped clear before the gunwale came down and for a moment there was spray everywhere as the cannon hit the water and sank out of sight.

For a moment those on shore stood rooted in the dim light of four lanterns and then the eight men in the water came up fighting, and those on shore plunged down the incline to thrust the long poles out to them and drag them ashore, gasping, water flying.

Cadwalader shouted over his shoulder, "Build fires! They'll freeze!"

Twenty minutes later Cadwalader called his staff away from four small, hidden fires, around which the eight men huddled, shaking uncontrollably, ice in their beards and hair, the freezing wind and sleet cutting into them.

Cadwalader spoke. "Can we load the cannon without ropes?"

The officers looked at each other and finally one spoke. "I doubt it, sir. There's no way to hold them back once they start down the incline. We'll be risking both the boats and the guns if we try."

Cadwalader shook his head in frustration. "The incline on the bank runs for more than two miles both directions, and either way we go, the river narrows and the channel would be impossible."

"Yes, sir. Either we get ropes now, or we wait for morning."

"Where do we get ropes?"

"Bristol, sir."

"Too far. We couldn't get there and back before morning with enough ropes to load the cannon."

"We could try to engage von Donop with just the men, sir."

For a time Cadwalader stared across the blackness of the river before he spoke. "We'd lose most of the command if we went at him on the flatland over there, with no fortifications and no cannon." He turned his back to the wind and his shoulders slumped. "Get that capsized boat righted and send all the boats to get the men back from the other side. We can't leave them there. We'll have to get the cannon out of the river at daylight—I don't know how—and hope von Donop doesn't learn about the Trenton attack until it's too late."

"Yes, sir." The officers walked away and for a time Cadwalader stood alone, staring north into the wind and sleet, trying to drive from his brain the image of Washington being caught by surprise between Rall's command in front of him, and von Donop's command suddenly on top of him from behind. For a moment he was back on Long Island, once again seeing the terror on the faces of the Americans when ten thousand British soldiers with cannon came through the Jamaica Pass and trapped them, Hessians in front, redcoats on the rear and side, with no way out but the Gowanus swamp and the East River. The screams of the doomed men echoed in his head and he shook himself and walked away, back to his command.

Twenty-five miles to the north, up the Delaware, the wind quickened. In sleet and blackness so thick lanterns could hardly be seen at twenty feet, Glover's fishermen held their rhythm. Soaked, water running from their beards and brims of their black, flat-topped seaman's hats, taking their bearings from an inner compass, they kept the big black boats moving steadily back and forth across the ice-choked river. It was after eight o'clock when General Washington and Colonel Knox took their places in one of the boats. On the New Jersey side, someone set a summer beehive box on the slick bank and Washington sat for a time, watching the men assemble into their regiments as they arrived. It was after eight-thirty when the fishermen beckoned to Billy and Eli and their company, and they stepped over the gunwales to take their position near the bow of the boat, clutching their weapons, feet spread for balance. Minutes later they felt the thrust of the poles as the boat broke free of the bank.

The wind came quartering in from their left and they felt the fishermen change the angle of the boat in the water to compensate for the wind drift, and then they hit the main channel. They heard two of the fishermen grunt as they rammed their poles into a two-ton ice floe and heaved with all their strength. The bow of the boat swung violently downstream and the soldiers on board lurched, then caught their balance and steadied as they heard the great chunk of ice grind down the side of the boat and then slip free. The fishermen set their poles and bent their backs into it and slowly brought the bow back on course, battling the larger chunks, with the smaller ones making an unending hollow sound as they slammed into the side of the boat.

Billy and Eli felt the heavy boat thump into the frozen riverbank and waited their turn to step high over the gunwale onto the ice and snow, and silently sought out the soldiers of Mercer's command. They turned their backs to the wind, and hunkered down for the long wait.

At eleven o'clock the sleet turned to snow. The temperature dropped and the wind raised to a howling blizzard.

At midnight Washington tucked a lantern inside his cape to check his watch. The battle plan called for Washington to have his entire force landed by midnight and begin their march nine miles south to Trenton. They were to arrive in Trenton at five o'clock and begin the attack in the dark. Washington pursed his mouth for a moment, replaced his watch, and began moving among his men, silently giving his support, encouragement. He said not one word of criticism nor did he mention the fact they were hours behind schedule.

At two o'clock the troops were all on the New Jersey bank. It remained only to move the rest of the horses and the last six of Knox's precious cannon. At four o'clock Glover's men unloaded the last horse. The entire command of twenty-four hundred men was in marching order, and without hesitation Washington gathered his officers.

"The guides are here. Follow their directions. Move among your men and keep them silent. And tell them in the name of heaven to stay with their officers. Stay with their officers."

The officers huddled with the guides, then gave hushed commands and the leaders started south with the wind at their backs for the first time. Thomas Rodney wiped dripping water from his face and murmured, "As fierce a night as ever I've seen," as they trudged on, moving by the sound of the man in front of them. Five minutes later the artillery officers lighted lanterns, locked the small glass gates against the wind, and mounted them on the rumbling gun carriages to dance eerily in the storm, casting a feeble circle of light in the driving sleet and on the ice-covered road; the column worked south like a great, invisible snake.

Washington and most of the general officers were everywhere on their mounts, watching, giving hushed orders, commending. "Press on, boys, press on," Washington kept repeating, as if the men were his own sons. Alexander Hamilton, small, delicate, rode his bay gelding beside the cannon, stopping now and then to give a hand when needed, or to use his mount to pull a stuck gun from time to time. Men saw him pat the barrels of the big guns as though they were a close and beloved personal friend.

At five-thirty Washington turned his horse to the column and shouted above the roaring wind. "Halt! Take ten minutes. Get off your feet if you can."

The men sat on anything they could find, or the ground, heads down against the raging storm, and did not move. Washington counted the minutes off his watch then gave orders to move on. Two men in one company could not get up. Their officers knelt beside them, shook them, slapped their faces, but they could not be roused. The officers moved them off the road and propped them against an oak tree for what shelter it provided, and left them. There was no other choice.

At ten minutes before six o'clock the snow changed to great hail-stones and the wind mounted, driving the huge balls of ice hammering into the men and animals, piling up on the road and in the fields.

At six o'clock Washington pulled his horse to a stop where the road forked at the tiny hamlet of Birmingham and shouted above the wind. "This is where the two commands separate. No more lights. General Sullivan, straight ahead on the River Road. General Greene, with me to the east, and down the Scotch Road. General Sullivan, sometime soon stop for ten minutes to let General Greene come parallel to you, since he has more distance to cover. Then, just before you take the Hermitage, stop for another ten minutes to rest your men. I'll do the same with Greene's column just before we take the cooper shop. That's all. Let's move."

The army split, Sullivan moving his column ahead while Greene moved his east to the Scotch Road, then south. Washington loped his horse back among the troops in the dark on the treacherous, slick road and his horse stumbled and went down on one front knee. Washington instantly reached to grasp a handful of mane and heaved back and one startled soldier struggled with the impression Washington had lifted the horse back to its feet while sitting in the saddle.

At six-fifteen, on the River Road, an anxious lieutenant came panting up to General Sullivan.

"Sir, the men in my company just found out the powder in their musket pans is soaked. Most of the muskets won't fire!"

Sullivan groaned, then gave the hushed order to halt the column. Quickly he moved back twenty yards, knocking the frizzens on the muskets upward to inspect the powder in the pans and he felt a sick knot in his stomach at the realization it was wet. Most muskets could not be fired. In despair Sullivan turned his face east towards the Scotch Road, trying to force a decision. Then he jerked open his coat and drew out pencil and paper and scrawled a note: Powder in musket pans wet, most will not fire. Await your orders.

He folded it and thrust it to a captain sitting his horse.

"Cut cross-country to the Scotch Road as fast as you can and deliver that to General Washington. Wait for an answer."

The man grabbed the note, reined his horse left and drove his spurs home. In three jumps the gelding was moving at stampede gait over unfamiliar ground in the black of night. The captain nearly overran Greene's column in the storm before he brought his horse to a sliding stop.

"General Washington. Where is he?"

"There."

"Sir, General Sullivan sent this message. I'm to wait for an answer."

Washington took the note, lighted a lantern under a blanket, and read the terse message. Without a moment's hesitation he dug his own pencil from beneath his coat and wrote a return message on the same paper: Use the bayonet. I am resolved to take Trenton.

He jammed the note back into the captain's waiting hand and in two seconds the man was swallowed up in the darkness as Washington listened to the sounds of the running horse fade and die. Five minutes later the officer reined in his heaving mount and handed the note back to General Sullivan. The general struck a light inside his coat to read it, stared, read it again, then shoved it in his pocket. He turned back to his men and issued the order. "Mount bayonets. Keep moving."

Back on the Scotch Road, General Washington rode steadily at the head of his column, shoulders hunched against the storm pounding his back. Slightly behind and to his right rode General Stephen at the head of his small detachment whose orders were to take the Hessian outpost at Howell's cooper shop. Behind Stephen's command, General Hugh Mercer rode his chestnut gelding, leading his regiment with orders to storm the north end of Trenton when they arrived, giving Colonel Henry Knox covering fire as Knox and his command dug in with cannon at the head of King and Queen Streets.

Directly behind General Mercer, in the first rank of his command, Billy and Eli held their position, setting the pace, listening for any sound above the howl of the storm, heads moving from side to side straining to see anything that moved in the deep purple of early dawn. Movement among the trees and then in the field to the east caught Billy's eye and he jerked his head around, squinting in the driving hail and snow, and in the gloom made out shadowy figures coming straight at the column. Instantly he raised his arm to point and shouted, "Men coming from the east!"

Eli pivoted as General Mercer hauled his horse to a halt and shielded his eyes from the storm, peering eastward. Then he turned his head and shouted ahead, "Men coming in from the east," as Billy and Eli and a dozen others stepped clear of the ranks and went to one knee, muskets leveled, ready.

Instantly Washington swung his horse around and stood tall in the stirrups with a hand shielding his eyes against the storm, battling the grab in his breast at the thought that somehow the Hessians had learned of his coming and he was leading his army into an ambush. The incoming men were a scant thirty yards away before Billy and Eli saw they were Americans, and Billy shouted, "Friendly," and rose from his knee. The others who had knelt with him stood and raised their musket muzzles, watching.

At the same moment Washington recognized them as a small body of Virginians coming at a trot. He waited while they slowed, eyes wide when they realized they were approaching their own army, and he tapped spur to horse to meet them coming in. His eyes were blazing, voice harsh as he peered down at the officer in charge.

"Who are you? What are you doing here?"

The young officer looked up in disbelief when he realized who was addressing him, and stammered, "I—I—I'm Captain Richard Anderson, sir, Virginia Regiment. General Stephen sent us out yesterday to reconnoiter. We got surrounded by Hessians and had to hide. We're just now coming in, sir." He took courage with his next statement. "Sir, we hit a Hessian outpost a while ago and shot a picket."

For a moment Washington's temper flared. "You *what?*" His arm jerked up to point south towards Trenton. "We've risked the entire Continental army to hit Trenton by surprise, and now you could have sprung the trap!"

Anderson's mind went numb and he fumbled for something to say, but no words would come.

Washington caught himself and settled down and softened. "Did the Hessians exchange gunfire with you? Did any leave the outpost for Trenton?"

Anderson shook his head. "No, sir. We got one picket and the rest of them barricaded themselves inside a barn. We waited half an hour to see if they'd come out and fight, but they wouldn't."

Washington exhaled in relief and nodded. "You must be exhausted. Go back to General Mercer's command and tell him I assigned you with him. Tell him to find some bread and fried pork for your men."

Gratitude surged in Anderson as he looked up into Washington's face. "Yes, sir. Thank you, sir."

"Carry on."

With the purple turning to gray in the howling storm, Washington loped his tall bay gelding to the head of the column and the two guides turned at the sound, then came trotting back.

"Sir, we're about one mile north of Trenton." They pointed. "Back in the trees about eight hundred yards around the bend is Howell's cooper shop. There's a Hessian patrol there."

Washington nodded and for a moment settled back into his saddle and took a deep breath. He glanced over his shoulder into the faces of the men following him and a sense of deliberation settled over him and shut out all thoughts but one.

The running is over. The time is here.

Half a mile ahead, hidden by the bend of the place where the Scotch Road joins the Pennington Road, Lieutenant Andreas Wiederhold, twenty-four years old, bright, ambitious, critical of his superior officers and absolutely certain of his own opinions on any subject, paced near the black, potbellied stove inside Richard Howell's cooper shop. His morning patrol had returned an hour earlier, and while they shook the snow and ice from their heavy Hessian overcoats they had reported there was no activity of any kind in their sector. All was quiet. Now, an hour later, true to his nature, Wiederhold was convincing himself that he could not trust his men—the only opinion he could trust was his own. He buttoned on his overcoat, jammed his hat on his head, tugged on his mittens, plucked a musket from the rack, and opened the door. Behind his back, his men shook their heads in disgust as he stepped out into the roaring storm. Outside he hunched his shoulders against the wind and made his way towards the road, a few yards away, carefully watching where he put his feet on the slick, frozen snow and ice.

Eight hundred yards north of him, General Washington rode his horse around the slight bend in the road with General Stephen right behind, and Stephen's command following at a high walk. Through the storm and the gray dawn they made out the black shape of the building, and then the shaft of yellow light as Wiederhold opened the door, and they saw him carefully making his way towards the road. Washington pointed, Stephen turned and called orders, and his entire command surged forward at a silent run. They left the road and cut a straight line through the snow for the house, muskets at the ready, while Mercer, right behind, ordered his command to a run down the road, to the right of Stephen. Billy and Eli leading in the first rank.

Wiederhold was two paces from the Pennington Road when movement to his right caught his eye, and he turned his head and squinted. His jaw dropped and he clacked it shut as he distinguished vague forms running across the open ground towards him in the pelting storm. He waited only long enough to judge there were about sixty of them and that they were Americans before he spun on his heel. Three seconds later, he threw open the door of the cooper shop and frantically shouted at his men, "Rebels. To arms!"

Twenty seconds later his command of twenty-one men barged out the door, muskets in one hand, jerking their overcoats on with the other. He pointed and shouted, "Form ranks and fire on command." The men fell into a straight line facing the incoming Americans, still two hundred yards distant, and waited with their muskets at the ready and the hail and snow blowing straight in their faces.

With the Hessians drawn up in a battle line, there was no need for silence, and General Stephen let out a howl, "Come on, men, they're ours!" Instantly his command mounted a battle cry as they charged onward, emerging out of the storm soaked, ragged, wet hair matted and flying, screaming like insane men. Some fired their first volley at too great a distance but they didn't care. They lowered their bayonets and ran on while others fired the second volley and then the third, their shouts riding the high wind into the faces of the Hessians while the distance closed. One hundred yards—eighty—fifty—while Wiederhold coolly held his fire.

At forty yards, he shouted "Fire!" Twelve of the twenty-one Hessian muskets with dry powder blasted into the storm to whistle harmlessly over the heads of the Americans.

"Reload!"

One of his men suddenly stopped, gasped, pointed towards the road and shouted, "Sir!"

Wiederhold spun to look and his whole body jerked backward. Mercer's men in battalion formation were running down the Pennington Road with the wind, cannon, and horses in their midst, paying him no attention. For a moment Wiederhold's mind locked and then Stephen's men fired their fourth volley. Wiederhold was jerked back to reality as musket balls kicked ice and frozen dirt all around his men and he felt a tug at his shoulder and realized one ball had ripped through his overcoat, and it was only then that his numb brain realized the impossible was happening.

The rebels are attacking Trenton!

He turned back to shout orders to his men but he was too late. They had already turned and were running hard towards Trenton, all thoughts of trading volleys with the Americans vanished. Wiederhold took one more look at the wild mob coming at him and pivoted to sprint after his men.

The first shot had been fired at exactly eight o'clock, three hours behind schedule. At the crack of the musket, Washington's mind leaped to Sullivan's command a mile west on the River Road.

Did he make it? There's been no gunfire. Will he hit the south end of Trenton at the same time we hit the north end? He must! He must!

To the west, on the River Road, Captain John Flahaven, commanding the lead regiment in General Sullivan's column with orders to take the Hermitage, suddenly jerked his horse to a standstill and turned his ear to listen.

Gunfire from the east! Greene and Washington are taking the cooper shop on Pennington Road!

He peered down the stormy road, and three hundred yards ahead, set in the trees on the left side, he could make out the black silhouette of the huge stone home owned by Philemon Dickinson, who had been left in the American camp on the Pennsylvania side of the river. Without hesitating, Flahaven turned to his command.

"There it is, boys! Remember Long Island. Remember New York. Let's go."

The men surged forward at a run, shouting as they ran, muskets ready. They came on the first Hessian pickets one hundred yards from the building and the Americans fired as they came, shouting all the way. The pickets pointed their muskets into the wind and fired without aiming, then turned and ran for the building.

Inside Dickinson's home, Lieutenant Friedrich Wilhelm von Grothausen's head jerked up at the sound of the gunfire and without a moment's hesitation he shouted orders. "To arms! Outside! Form ranks."

His command threw on their coats and spilled out the door into the wind just as the stampeding Hessian pickets ran past. Grothausen barked orders to Corporal Franz Bauer to stand fast with his company of ten men while Grothausen and twelve of his own men ran for the sentry post thirty yards north of the house.

Bauer stood in the road before the Hermitage watching the backs of Grothausen and his men fade into the storm, then turned to his ten men, pointing, shouting. "Take cover. Trees. Fences. Take cover and do not fire until I give the order!"

The little band scattered behind anything they could find to hide, studying everything to the north that moved, and suddenly from out of the storm they saw the black shapes of men one hundred yards ahead running at them. In two seconds they realized there were hundreds of them, and Bauer swallowed, terrified, unsure of whether he should try to reach Grothausen to support him, or stand fast where he was, or retreat to save his ten men.

At that moment the ground shook and the world was filled with thunder. Flame leaped from half a dozen places around him and the air was filled with smoke and frozen dirt and snow and ice. Tiny fragments came whistling, stinging his face, and he threw his arms over his eyes and dropped to the ground, and then the sound of blasting cannon came rolling across the Delaware to echo in the woods.

With debris still falling, Bauer raised his head, dazed, unable to understand whose artillery was blasting, and whether they were trying for him or the Americans. The third barrage came ripping and once again the world was filled with sound and flame and whistling pieces, and this time Bauer could make no mistake.

The river! The Americans are firing from across the river! They intend killing all of us!

He leaped to his feet, shouting, "Fall back. Fall back. Save yourselves."

All ten of his men broke cover at the same time and ran as hard as they could south, heading for Trenton. Behind them, Grothausen and his twelve men came sprinting past the Hermitage, stopping for nothing as they caught up with Bauer's command and passed them in their headlong run for Trenton.

Across the river, Philemon Dickinson lowered his telescope, then raised it again and studied what movement he could make out among the trees around his home. He saw the Hessians in their long dark overcoats break for Trenton, and he turned the glass north slightly, and again studied the movement until he saw the Americans running down the road two hundred yards behind the Hessians.

Shivering, soaked to the skin, he wiped a hand across his mouth as he lowered the glass. He turned to the men who had helped him move six cannon south from the main camp in the middle of the stormy night and set them up opposite his own home. They were men declared too sick for active duty and were under doctor's orders to remain in camp. With their help, Dickinson had planned to blast his own home to rubble if necessary, to drive the Hessians out into the open.

"Men, I believe we did it. The Hessians are on the run and Flahaven is past the Hermitage."

He reached to shake the hand of the man in command of the crew who had moved the first, and heaviest gun, set it up, and led in the firing order. "Sergeant Pratt, thank you."

Sergeant Bertram Pratt of Connecticut, with his small command of sick and disabled men from Connecticut, bobbed his head. "No thanks necessary."

Across the river, past the River Road, at the Pennington Road, riding at the head of Mercer's regiment with Wiederhold's routed command in sight ahead and Stephen's men right behind them, Washington heard the first faint sound of musket shots from Flahaven's command as they stormed the Hermitage, and then the far distant boom of two volleys from heavy cannon, and the thought flashed in his mind:

Flahaven took the Hermitage right on time—we'll hit both ends of Trenton at the same time. The cannon were too far—across the river—had to be ours.

There was no time to ponder it. Ahead, Wiederhold's terrified men sprinted past a tiny outbuilding where a company of Hessians under the command of General Lossberg were quartered. Inside the building, Captain von Altenbockum turned his head quizzically to listen to the sound of gunfire, then barged out the door to recoil in shock at the sight of Wiederhold's Hessians in full, panic-driven retreat past his building. Altenbockum squinted into the wind-driven sleet and gasped at the sight of hundreds of Americans in full battle cry, wet hair streaming, wind whipping their tattered rags, feet bound like bundles of meat, charging headlong. Instantly he turned and shouted orders to his men and they spilled out of the building struggling into overcoats as they ran to join Wiederhold's men in their run for Trenton. A few men paused behind a tree or a shed or a house to fire their muskets when they could to try to slow the rout to a controlled retreat.

It was ten minutes before eight o'clock. The heavens were sealed by the thick, dirty gray storm clouds, and the wind was whistling, driving the snow and sleet and hail nearly horizontal as the men leading Mercer's column first caught sight of the outskirts of the north end of the village of Trenton.

Billy broke into a trot, Eli beside him, and without realizing it he raised a fist into the air and shouted, "There it is! Come on." He broke into a full run and behind him the voices of the entire regiment rose above the storm with their battle cry as they surged forward. Altenbockum's and Wiederhold's terrified commands reached the main junction of Pennington and Princeton Roads and King and Queen Streets and sprinted around the corner down King Street without looking back. Thirty seconds later Billy and Eli hit the corner and pulled up short, and Mercer's regiment stopped to wait for the cannon. Colonel Knox was right on their heels, jerking his mount to a stiff-legged stop as his deep, resonant voice boomed orders to his cannoneers.

"Halt! Turn those guns! Two down King Street, two down Queen, and fire!"

His men hauled the horses to a sliding stop, swarmed to the cannon to unhitch them from the teams, and swung the trails to the north, gun muzzles to the south. In five seconds they lined up the guns down King and Queen Streets, point-blank, and in ten seconds they had forty-eight pounds of grapeshot jammed down the muzzle of the two covering King Street just as the door to General Rall's headquarters burst open and Rall walked out, facing Lieutenant Jacob Piel who had wakened him five minutes earlier.

Rall stood rooted to the spot, head turning, first up the street to Altenbockum's and Wiederhold's commands running like rabbits down past him, then down the street to see his command, one hundred fifty yards south, come boiling out of their billets buttoning their overcoats. Others soldiers were running up the street leading draft horses to hitch them to the cannon near his headquarters. Then Rall jerked his head around to look up the street one more time and through the raging storm made out the shapes of Americans and horses at the head of the street, and he froze, mind swamped, unable to comprehend what was happening.

At the head of the street, the American cannon loaders reached to whack the man with the linstock on the shoulder, and dove clear as he smacked the smoking punk onto the touchhole and the big guns bucked and roared. Flame leaped ten feet out the muzzles as each blew twenty-four pounds of American grapeshot screaming down King Street, shredding shrubbery and shattering trees and windows, and leaving great black streaks on the buildings as it tore past Piel and Rall into the Hessians running south, and beyond them, into the oncoming horses and the men from Rall's command running north, up the street. Two huge draft horses stuck their noses into the ground and cartwheeled, hindquarters coming high over their heads, and they did not get up as the grapeshot slammed into Hessians who grunted and staggered and went down.

Before the smoke cleared, Billy broke into King Street and dodged down the right side at a run, while Eli sprinted to the left side, both men using doorways and trees and shrubs for cover, staying away from the center of the street to give Knox's cannon a full field of fire. The ranks leading Mercer's column didn't hesitate. In full-throated battle cry, they followed at a run, waiting to come within point-blank musket range before they fired. At the same moment, the men at the rear of Mercer's column came swarming off Pennington Road one hundred yards above the road junction where Knox's cannon were reloading, in behind Fourth Street and Rall's headquarters, where bewildered Hessians had taken cover from the deadly cannon blasts and the insane Americans charging down King Street. Too late the Hessians turned to see them and one second later the American muskets ripped loose. Before the storm blew the smoke past the Hessians, the Americans were on top of them, bayonets lowered, screaming, running like wild men. For one stunned moment the Hessians hesitated, then turned and broke for King Street, back into the bedlam, the Americans right behind them.

On the street, Billy and Eli fired, and then the Americans behind them fired their first full volley and a dozen of the nearest Hessians tumbled. Instantly the Americans grabbed fresh paper cartridges and ripped them open with their teeth, reloading. Billy saw Rall mount his horse and start south down King Street, towards his own command, shouting to his men, trying to rally them.

"Form ranks! Form ranks!"

Eli's eyes narrowed as he saw Rall, and while he slammed the ramrod down his rifle barrel to seat the .60-caliber ball, he marked in his mind how Rall was dressed, his horse, how he sat the saddle.

Rall's men formed in the center of the street and Rall met them and turned his horse to lead them back up King Street, to the north, towards Knox's deadly cannon. Eli tapped powder into the pan of his rifle, slammed it shut, and raised his head, looking for Rall.

At that moment the Americans who had come in behind Rall's headquarters came swarming past the building onto King Street driving the Hessians before them. In one glance they saw the dead horses and Hessians felled by Knox's first cannon blasts, and Rall's command starting north, up the street, and instantly understood what had happened. They didn't hesitate. From doorways and behind trees and bushes and barrels and anything they could find, they cut loose with their first full volley at point-blank range into the side of Rall's startled command and Hessians all up and down the line staggered and went down.

The Hessians still on their feet slowed and turned to look at the Americans, scarcely fifteen yards away, and they gaped in astonishment, unable to conceive where they had come from. Dumbstruck, they understood but one thing: King Street had become a scene from purgatory. Some of them broke ranks and started east on Third Street, towards Queen Street, away from the holocaust.

Billy saw it and turned to look up the street, desperately hoping the cannon were reloaded, just as the deafening blasts came roaring. Grapeshot kicked ice and snow up and down King Street, and once again Hessians and horses toppled and went down as Rall's command began to dissolve, men running both south and east, not heeding Rall's shouted commands.

Miraculously still mounted, Rall looked back to see only one of his cannon was still able to function. Scheffer, the lieutenant colonel in charge of that gun opened his mouth to shout an order when his horse screamed and dropped from under him, dead. Scheffer, sick for the past five days with a fever of one hundred three degrees, called for another horse and turned command of his men over to Major Johann Matthaus.

Matthaus shouted to Lieutenant Engelhardt. "Clear out those guns at the head of the street."

With American musket balls spanging off the cannon and knocking splinters from the carriage and tearing into his crew, Engelhardt got off one shot, then shouted orders to hitch two of the horses still on their feet to move the cannon closer, and he started north, up King Street to fire back at Knox.

Eli studied the cannon crew for one split second, then lowered his rifle and got off his shot. The man carrying the linstock went over backwards and did not move. Eli reloaded, once again looking for Rall.

It was then Billy heard the gunfire from the south end of King Street and he rose to a crouch, hoping, peering through the storm to see who was shooting at the south end of town as the Hessians spilled onto King Street.

Grothausen and Bauer had pounded from the River Road into the south end of town with their terrified men following and barged through the back door of the Old Barracks shouting for reinforcements, only to find the barracks nearly empty. They grabbed what men they could and ran back out to meet the oncoming Americans coming hot behind them from the River Road and stopped in their tracks, transfixed. They had thought the Americans were only a large patrol. What they now saw sweeping at them through the storm were hundreds upon hundreds of them in a swarming mass with their bayonets lowered, shouting like fiends. Without a second look every man with Grothausen and Bauer, and every man they had just commandeered from the Old Barracks turned on their heels and ran up King Street only to be raked with musket fire from the north and west. They stopped, confused, and ran east into Front Street and Second Street.

Billy turned to his men and pointed. "They're running! Come on!"

On the other side of King Street, Eli caught the signal and shouted to those behind him, "Move up! Move up! They're breaking ranks!"

Both men started forward, staying away from the center of the street to avoid the grapeshot coming from Knox. They fired their muskets and leaped over the Hessians that were down, charging with bayonets into those running, giving them no quarter, no chance to collect their wits or get set. With no bayonet on his long Pennsylvania rifle, Eli was waving his tomahawk as he shrieked out the Iroquois battle cry and plowed into them, face-to-face, hand-to-hand. No Hessian had ever seen a man dressed in a wolf skin coat and wolf skin moccasins, screaming like a madman, knocking men left and right with a black tomahawk. In terror they turned on their heels and threw down their muskets and sprinted east through yards, past houses, down the streets, headed for the open field and orchard on the east side of town.

Behind them, Lieutenant Engelhardt moved his cannon forward to get a clear shot at Knox at the head of King Street. He had to run back to get the linstock from the man Eli had shot, then returned to open fire, loading and firing as fast as his crippled crew could work.

Knox, enraged at the thought of someone trying to damage his beloved cannon, was watching like a hawk and when Englehart's gun began blasting he turned and shouted orders. "Weedon! Can you get some men down to that gun?"

Colonel George Weedon was not a soldier by trade—he had been a tavern owner in Fredericksburg, Virginia—but he took one look at the cannon and bobbed his head. Pivoting, he shouted to Captain William Washington, Lieutenant James Monroe, and Joseph White, a tough Massachusetts sergeant. "Let's go!"

With General George Washington watching from the high ground behind Knox, holding the regiments commanded by Stirling, Stephen, and Fermoy in reserve, Weedon, Monroe, William Washington, and Joseph White broke cover and sprinted down King Street with White shouting in the wind, "Run right on over the gun. Get that crew!"

Billy and Eli saw them coming and both broke cover from their side of the street to join them, running, dodging, shouting. Engelhardt's crew kept loading and firing as they came and what remained of Rall's confused command fired their muskets at them at nearly point-blank range.

Monroe felt the hammer blow on his left shoulder and spun out of control, went down, and bounded back up, his left arm numb, useless as he stormed on. William Washington felt the hit and the burn, first on the back of his right hand, then the palm of his left, as Hessian musket balls drew blood from both hands. He ran on. Billy and Eli fired at the same moment and two Hessians with muskets staggered backwards and went down and did not move as Billy and Eli charged on, Billy with his bayonet, Eli with his tomahawk swinging over his head. Lieutenant Engelhardt's eyes widened and he could take no more. He turned on his heel and sprinted south, then turned to run east into an alley.

Joseph White had no musket, only his sword, but at a dead run he leaped the cannon with the sword raised over his head, clutched in both hands, aimed at the head of the lone Hessian still standing behind the big gun. The Hessian had had enough. All White saw of him was his back as he sprinted headlong east, looking for anything he could find to hide behind.

"Come on," Eli shouted. The six of them lifted the trails and turned the cannon muzzle east, up the nearest alley where Hessians had disappeared, and James Monroe picked up the smoldering linstock with his good right hand. He slapped it onto the touchhole and the gun roared. The cannonball ripped into the alley, bounded off the wall of a home and exploded among the running Hessians.

Billy grabbed the eight-foot-long handle of the sponge and had it halfway down the cannon barrel to reload when from his right came the sustained blasting of muskets and the feral sounds of men's voices raised in mortal combat. He and the other five men surrounding the cannon stopped to look.

At the south end of town, Grothausen and Bauer and the survivors of their men from the Hermitage were still on Front and Second Streets in full, disorganized chaos, trying for the Assunpink Bridge in a futile hope to break free of a world filled with Americans and blasting muskets and bayonets.

Eli started down the street at a run, Billy beside him, when they both saw the Americans right behind the Hessians, swarming, shooting, shouting.

"Glover!" Billy shouted, and stopped. "Glover's got them."

Eli squinted in the driving snow. "No, that's Stark!"

Tall, broad-shouldered, large hawked nose, chin like granite, Colonel John Stark of New Hampshire was leading, sword raised high, voice booming. At the battle of Bunker Hill eighteen months earlier it was Stark who had stood atop the breastworks with British cannonballs ripping everything around him to shreds while musket balls tore into the dirt and whistled past. He had paced back and forth, cursing the redcoats, waving his sword, shouting orders to his New Hampshiremen to load and fire, and nothing the British could do gave him the slightest concern. His fellow officers begged him to get into the trenches, and he had ignored them. No soldier in the Continental army equaled his bravery and no officer equaled his iron nerve when the air was filled with flying cannonballs and musket fire.

Coming into Trenton, Stark's command had been just behind Glover's, who was in Sullivan's column, but when the first sounds of heavy fighting reached them as they came in from the west on River

Road, there was no power on earth that could hold Stark and his wild New Hampshiremen back.

"Follow me," Stark had shouted, and broke out of line in the column and came storming past Glover's command without even looking sideways.

Mixed with Glover's fishermen, Stark's command surged around the Old Barracks, into King Street, and plowed headlong into the Hessians who were still standing there, confused, waiting for orders that never came. The Americans ran over the top of them, hot on the heels of Grothausen and Bauer and those who were trying for the Assunpink bridge and freedom. They cut them off, turned them left, back into the lower end of town. Stark's command surged right behind them, firing, charging into the side streets, routing them out of houses and barns and from behind sheds and trees, clearing the streets, pushing them further and further to the east.

Glover turned his command right, across the Assunpink bridge, and at a high run his men wheeled their cannon two hundred yards down the creek before Glover shouted, "Stop. Set them up here!" Two minutes later the cannon were pointed north, across the Assunpink Creek, where they could command a field of fire at the bridge, the south end of the town, and the fields and orchard east of town.

Back in the middle of King Street, Eli shouted to Billy, "Stark and Glover got the south end of town sealed off. We got 'em in a pocket. Let's drive 'em out in the open on the east side of town."

Instantly they reloaded their weapons and shouted to the Americans around them, "Let's go! Push them east!" They charged into Third Street and the Hessians crouched there behind trees and houses took one look and struck out east, legs driving as hard as they could go.

More than forty Hessians took cover in an alley, Rall among them still on his horse, floundering, disoriented, not yet able to grasp what was happening all around him. Then suddenly the mouth of the alley was filled with shouting Americans as Billy and Eli led the charge, firing as they tore into the nearest Hessians, Billy with his bayonet and Eli with his tomahawk. Fifty men were right behind them, firing, shouting, swarming all over the Hessians.

Rall shook himself and for the first time gave a clear, rational order.

"East!" he shouted. "Out to the orchard. To the Princeton Road. We can fight our way out on the Princeton Road." Instantly he reined his mount east and jammed the spurs home. The horse broke into a run up the alley while Hessians from every command in Trenton ran to follow him, ignoring Knyphausen, Lossberg, Wiederhold, and Grothausen who were shouting at their men to break off and form with their own companies.

With Rall leading anyone who would follow eastward through the streets of Trenton, Knyphausen's command at the south end of town sprinted north to join him. John Stark saw them streaming past him running east on Second Street, paying him no attention. Instantly Stark shouted to one of his officers, "Frye, go get 'em."

Captain Ebenezer Frye was a huge, beefy man with a face round as a melon. He didn't hesitate. "Follow me," he shouted to the nearest New Hampshiremen, and sixteen of them fell in behind him as he lumbered straight into the side of Knyphausen's regiment in their headlong plunge east on Second Street. He was swinging his sword over his head while his men had their muskets blasting, bayonets working. In less than five minutes Frye emerged back out of Second Street with sixty Hessians before him, their hands high, his prisoners captured so fast most of them did not yet know what had happened.

Despite himself, tough old Johnny Stark grinned when Frye made his report.

Rall galloped across Queen Street, then Quaker Lane, out into the open field next to the orchard on the east side of town with Hessians running to follow him. At the head of Queen Street, Captain Joseph Moulder was in command of two of Knox's cannon. As the Hessians came surging across Queen Street in their desperate run to follow Rall, Moulder shouted, "Fire!"

The American cannon blasted grapeshot the length of Queen Street and cut a swath through the fleeing Hessians. As fast as they could load, they fired again, and again Hessians were knocked rolling.

Billy and Eli burst out of the alley behind Rall's men, leading parts of Mercer's men mixed with Sullivan's command into the field after Rall when Billy raised an arm and shouted in alarm, "They're going to try for the Princeton Road."

At that moment, on high ground at the north end of town, General Washington stood in his stirrups and watched as the Hessians stampeded into the open field to rally around Rall, and suddenly Washington saw the weakness. Instantly he shouted to Generals Stirling, Stephen, and de Fermoy, who he had held in reserve to his right, and pointed.

"Cut off the Princeton Road! Throw up a double line clear across to the Assunpink Creek."

Five seconds later the three generals had their men running due east. Minutes later a double line of infantry formed across the road and ten minutes later they were at the Assunpink Creek. Washington blew air and settled back into his saddle. With the Princeton Road cut off, and the double line just formed by the three generals, and with Glover and Stark covering the south end of town, the Hessians were surrounded. Washington sat tall, intense, studying every move, waiting to see what the Hessians would do when they saw there was no way out.

When Rall realized the Princeton Road was now cut off and Americans were on all sides pouring musket fire and cannon shot into his command, he once again sat his saddle slumped, disoriented, groping to understand what he should do. One of his officers shouted, "We have to retake the town or we'll all be killed where we stand."

Rall blinked and then shouted the order. "Form into ranks. Ranks. Prepare for a bayonet charge to the west, back into Trenton."

Knyphausen heard the order and shouted to Rall, "Shall I march my command about left?"

Rall shouted back, "Yes."

Whatever Knyphausen meant, or whatever he understood Rall to have said in the howling wind and the thunder of muskets and cannon, Knyphausen did exactly the wrong thing. He did not march his command about left, west, rather, he marched them off to the south, towards the Assunpink bridge and within two minutes St. Clair's command stormed into them, cut them off from Rall, surrounded them, took them clear out of the battle.

Once again Rall lapsed into indecision. He had been trained his entire life in the classic European theory of battle: form your men into ranks, march them into the enemy, and annihilate them by brute force. From the moment he stepped out the front door of his headquarters into the raging storm where the American cannon had thundered to clear King Street of his command, he had been given no quarter, no moment to form his command, or any command, into ranks. In a world where wild, screaming, scarecrow Americans were shooting from every house, alley, street, tree, and bush, there had not been one minute for him to do the only thing he understood. And now, sitting his horse in the middle of an open field with his men dropping on all sides from a world filled with American musket fire, he was unable to break his mind out of the mold.

He simply sat bewildered.

To the southwest, Eli jerked the ramrod out of his rifle barrel, held the pan close to his chest out of the wind, loaded it with powder from the powder horn, slapped the frizzen shut, and squinted into the storm, the wind in his face while he sought to find Rall in the chaos before him. Billy glanced at him and understood, and ten seconds later Billy shouted, "There, Eli! There!" He raised an arm and Eli followed his point. Two hundred ten yards away, far out of musket range, in the midst of the Hessians, with half a dozen officers still mounted around him, Eli recognized Rall.

He spread his feet slightly to steady the long rifle, instinctively made adjustments for distance and the head-on wind, and squeezed off his shot. The wind whipped the rifle smoke away and Eli held his breath.

Rall jolted as the big .60-caliber ball punched into his right side. He sagged and grabbed for the horse's mane to stay mounted, and started to tumble when men around him reached to hold him up.

Major von Hanstein saw and heard the hit and was instantly at Rall's side. "Are you hit, sir?"

"Not bad. I'm all right."

"Sir, you're bleeding."

"I'm all right. Get these men moving."

"Where, sir?"

Lieutenant Piel, white-faced, shouted, "Sir, the only way out is the bridge. We've got to try for the bridge."

Rall was incapable of forming his own decision, and nodded. "Go see if it's clear." He turned to von Hanstein. "Move these men to follow Piel. We've got to cross the bridge."

At that moment Eli was slamming the ramrod down his rifle barrel, seating another musket ball against the patch, his eyes never leaving Rall.

Piel sprinted away, certain that Knyphausen's command had reached the bridge and was holding it. He was thirty paces away before he could make out some of the details of the men dug in beside the creek and he tried to stop, sliding to one knee in the wind and snow, eyes wide in disbelief as he stared at St. Clair's command.

Those are Americans! Not Knyphausen's men.

Piel turned and sprinted as the musket balls came whistling. He ran across the open field to the Hessians clustered about Rall, and he pushed his way through, panting, wild-eyed.

"Sir, the bridge is held by Americans."

Two hundred yards southwest, for the second time, Eli shook gunpowder into the pan of his rifle and slapped the frizzen to close it.

Beside him, Billy shouted, "There," and once again Eli followed his point to locate Rall, and went to one knee to steady the long rifle.

The right side of Rall's coat was black with blood and he was beginning to ride too loose in the saddle. He licked his lips and gave one more order to Piel and von Hanstein. "Turn the men around. We'll have to take cover in the orchard. We can fight from the orchard."

As the words left Rall's mouth Eli squeezed off his second shot and watched as the ball ripped into Rall, inches from the first hit. Rall's head dropped forward and he pitched headlong from his horse. Strong hands caught him and set him on his feet but he could not stand and they lifted him to carry him west through the hail of gunfire. The American lines opened to let the two men carry him through, towards the Methodist Church on Queen Street.

The remaining Hessian officers turned their swords on their own troops, slapping them on the back with the flat of the blade as they shouted, "To the orchard! Take cover in the orchard! We can ford the creek above the orchard!"

Slowly the devastated Hessians moved north until they reached the orchard where they stopped. Their shoulders slumped as they peered into the raging storm. Americans were appearing from every tree, every ditch, running, firing, shouting, and musket balls were tearing into the Hessians from the entire northern quadrant of the compass. Generals Stirling, Stephen, and de Fermoy were mounted, leading their men forward, swords pointed, coming at them shooting. And as they came, they were shouting for the Hessians to surrender, first in English and then in very bad German. Crushed, beaten, the Hessians stood where they were until the Americans were forty paces away and charging them with bayonets.

Then Scheffer raised his hands, sword held high, one hand clutching each end in the universal sign of surrender, and the Americans leading the charge slowed and stopped. The firing slackened and then stopped, and a hush fell over the battlefield, save for the shrieking storm.

"Quarter! We ask quarter!" Scheffer shouted. "I request to speak with an American officer."

Billy exchanged a glance with Eli. The Americans lowered their muskets, waiting, watching, struggling to grasp the fact that more than two-thirds of the Hessian garrison was surrendering. And in that moment, in their minds, the Americans were once again seeing these Hessians as they had seen them four months earlier, on August 27, 1776, on Long Island. In their hearts and souls the unspeakable horror once again came surging at the remembrance of being surrounded, and trying to escape the bloody chaos by retreating through the Gowanus swamp and the woods. These Hessians had caught then waist deep in the muck of the swamp, unable to move, to load their muskets, to defend themselves. The Americans had raised their hands and shouted out their surrender, but with cold precision, the Hessians had shot them and bayoneted them like cattle.

Now, with these same Hessians surrounded in a frozen field, helpless, at the mercy of the Americans and their cannon and muskets and bayonets, Billy and Eli and eight hundred of the Continental army struggled with the overpowering need to turn their cannon and muskets loose on them, and to bayonet those who tried to break out of the trap—to watch the terror in their eyes and hear it in their screams. They struggled, and then they slowly realized they could not slaughter defenseless men, no matter the justification, and they rose above it. They waited for the officers to come to terms of surrender.

George Baylor, one of Washington's aides with General Stirling's command, smacked his spurs home and brought his horse in at a run, hauling him to a skidding stop before the beaten German officers. "I'm an American officer."

"I am surrendering my command."

"You will wait here while I inform the general."

Baylor loped his horse back to General Stirling. "Sir, the German officers wish to surrender."

Stirling nodded. "I accept. Let's go." Stirling reined his horse beside Baylor and the two of them cantered back to Scheffer and von Hanstein and stopped.

Stirling spoke. "I am informed you wish to surrender."

"Yes."

"Very well. Lower your colors. I shall accept your swords."

With military flourish, Scheffer and von Hanstein handed their swords to Stirling, hilt first. They turned and shouted orders for the Rall and Lossberg standards to be lowered; several Hessian officers removed their hats and stuck them on the tips of their swords and held them high to signal the surrender.

Stirling watched, then said to Scheffer, "Your men will ground their arms."

Scheffer gave his last order and the Hessians began stacking their arms in the snow.

Billy wiped his soaked coat sleeve across his bearded mouth and turned wide eyes to Eli. "They surrendered. The Hessians surrendered."

Eli nodded once, said nothing, and reached for his powder horn. "There's still some down by the creek."

Without a word Billy reached for a fresh paper cartridge as they both started south towards the Assunpink Creek. Twenty yards to their right, Joseph Moulder and his cannoneers were moving his two cannon at a trot down towards the creek, and Billy and Eli angled over. The cannon crews made room for them and they grasped the trails with their free hands to help.

Six hundred yards ahead they saw the remnants of the Knyphausen regiment under the command of Major Friederich Dechow moving slowly towards the bridge, muskets blasting. A few of the men were up to their knees in muck, struggling with a cannon that had sunk nearly to the axles in snow and sleet and freezing mud that bordered the creek. The cannon's muzzle pointed to the sky, cocked at a crazy angle.

At the bridge, Glover's fishermen waited patiently behind rocks and trees, and bridge pilings until the Hessians were fifty paces away and then Glover shouted, "Fire!" Fifty musket balls slammed into the Hessians. Dechow twisted sideways in his saddle, his hip shattered, and the huge musket ball lodged in his bowels. He slowly slipped from his horse, unable to remain mounted. His men helped him to a fence and he leaned against it, feeling the first hint of light-headedness as he shouted to Captain von Biesenrodt.

"Take command. Rall has surrendered. You surrender these men to save them." Then he sagged and a corporal grabbed him and started back towards Trenton half-carrying him while another soldier hastily tied a white handkerchief to an eight-foot spontoon and thrust it into his hand for safe passage. They nearly reached King Street before Dechow's head tipped forward and his body went limp; the corporal gently laid him in the snow and covered his face.

Biesenrodt saw Dechow go down and turned to the few remaining officers, most of them wounded. "I dispute the order to surrender. I say we go upstream and find a place to ford the stream and fight our way to freedom on the Bordentown Road. Are you with me?"

They started east along the bank of the Assunpink, and a few of them were seized by panic and plunged into the half-frozen, fast running creek. With water to their chins they battled to get across. Some succeeded, some did not, and those who did clamber up the far bank, water spraying, ice forming in their long overcoats, were last seen staggering south in the storm, looking for the Bordentown Road.

The bulk of the Knyphausen survivors broke into a trot upstream, desperately looking for a shallow ford that would give safe passage across the swollen creek. They had not gone fifty yards when the officers in the lead came to a dead stop. They were facing Glover's fishermen, who had gone up the far bank of the creek, crossed, and were waiting for the Hessians behind rocks and trees and bushes, muskets cocked and aimed.

Biesenrodt stood bolt upright, white-faced, groping for what to do next, and only then did he look to his left to see Joseph Moulder forty paces distant, standing in the driving snow. One pace behind Moulder were the two cannon he had used to clear Queen Street, loaded, with the crew waiting, the linstock smoking. Billy and Eli cocked their weapons and steadied them against a cannon wheel and brought them to bear on the third large button of Biesenrodt's great overcoat.

Biesenrodt's breathing constricted for a moment when the realization struck into him. *We are surrounded. All sides.*

Then suddenly Major James Wilkinson walked out of the storm and Biesenrodt shouted at him, "Do not come closer or we will shoot." His Hessians cocked their muskets and brought them to bear on the Americans as Biesenrodt turned to Lieutenant Andreas Wiederhold. "Go talk with the American."

Tension was nearly a physical thing as Wiederhold walked steadily across the open ground between the cocked muskets of the Hessians and Americans, and Wilkinson came to meet him. Every man on both sides was breathing lightly, hair on their necks straight up as they waited for someone—anyone—to make the mistake that would set all the muskets thundering in an instant.

Wilkinson stopped and Wiederhold stopped facing him.

"I am Major James Wilkinson. General St. Clair is behind me with our cannon. He has instructed me to inform your commanding officer that he is to surrender."

Wiederhold struggled for a moment to understand, then spoke in broken English. "I will tell my commander. Wait."

He carefully, steadily walked back to Biederholdt.

"The American General St. Clair demands our surrender."

Biesenholdt's chin went up. "No. I will not surrender."

Wiederhold nodded and turned on his heel and retraced his steps to Wilkinson, while St. Clair walked out and Wiederhold waited for him.

"You are General St. Clair?"

"I am."

"My commanding officer refuses your demand to surrender." The words were badly accented and St. Clair struggled for a moment before he understood.

"Tell him he is surrounded. He has no chance. If he chooses to fight, his command will be destroyed."

Wiederhold's face clouded for a moment while he struggled with the English words, then he nodded. "He knows he is surrounded. That does not matter to him."

St. Clair felt his temper rising. "Tell him Americans hold every bridge, every road, every ferry, every ford. Trenton is surrounded." Then St. Clair paused, his head thrust slightly forward, and no one could mistake the anger in his voice. "Tell him if he does not surrender immediately, I will blow you all to pieces! Tell him!"

Wiederhold stared into St. Clair's eyes and he knew one thing. St. Clair would do exactly what he had said. He nodded and turned on his heel and once more walked back to face Biesenrodt.

"Herr Commander, I am told to tell you the Americans control Trenton." He paused for a moment, pondering the wisdom of finishing the message, and then continued. "He said you shall surrender immediately or he will blow all of us to pieces. Right now."

Biesenrodt stared into Wiederhold's eyes and Wiederhold did not flinch.

Biesenrodt's shoulders slumped and all the air went out of him. "I will talk with St. Clair."

Both commanders ordered their men to stand down and two hundred muskets clicked off cock as the two men walked to meet each other in the open ground.

"I will surrender if you will allow my officers to keep their swords and their baggage."

"Done."

In full sight of both commands the two men reached to shake hands.

It was over.

Wilkinson turned to St. Clair. "I'll inform General Washington."

St. Clair handed Wilkinson the reins to his horse, then drew his watch from his pocket and stared at it. It was not yet half past nine o'clock in the morning. ●

Notes

This lengthy chapter covers two of the most important events of the Revolutionary War: Washington's crossing of the Delaware River and the subsequent battle at Trenton. The actions and events depicted in this chapter are as accurate as possible and are based almost exclusively on pages 248–65 in Ketchum's *The Winter Soldiers*, which provides an excellent outline and summary of the historical events. The battle was fought in a howling blizzard and was one of the wildest scenes recorded in the Revolutionary War.

This chapter also touches on some additional points of interest.

Before the American soldiers embarked on their journey across the river, Thomas Paine's *The American Crisis* was read to them (see Ketchum, *The Winter Soldiers*, p. 248). Paine's stirring words helped warm the hearts of the men preparing for battle.

Traditionally, historians have reported that Major James Wilkinson delivered a letter to Washington from General Gates the day of the crossing informing him that Gates had departed to Philadelphia. However, Gates's reasons for leaving Washington at this critical juncture have been debated for years afterward. Some accuse Gates of going to Congress to gain favor in hopes of replacing Washington (see Ketchum, *The Winter Soldiers*, p. 249), while other defend his motives, proposing that Gates left the army due to poor health (see Nelson, *General Horatio Gates*, p. 77 and Chase, *The Papers of George Washington*, vol. 7, p. 418). In addition, many historians doubt the reliability of Wilkinson's memory, as it was several years before the major recorded the incident and by then had developed a deep animosity towards Gates (see Nelson, *General Horatio Gates*, p. 76 n. 34). The debate remains unresolved.

The day of the Delaware crossing was clear, though the skies grew darker and the storm clouds moved in throughout the day. By eleven o'clock at night, a heavy storm finally broke, pelting the American army with snow, sleet, and eventually hail. The storm persisted, adding to the delay in Washington's schedule (see Ketchum, *The Winter Soldiers*, p. 252).

Some of the lines of dialogue in this chapter are variations on dramatic and descriptive quotations from the men who experienced the events firsthand. James Wilkinson made famous the observation that the snow was "tinged here and there with blood from the feet of the men who wore broken shoes" (as quoted in Ketchum, *The Winter Soldiers*, p. 248), and Thomas Rodney recorded that the night march to Trenton was "as severe a night as I ever saw" (as quoted in Ketchum, *The Winter Soldiers*, p. 252). Washington did scrawl a note to Sullivan, ordering him, "Use the bayonet. I am resolved to take Trenton" (as quoted in Ketchum, *The Winter Soldiers*, p. 253).

Brigadier Generals Ewing and Cadwalader attempted to cross the river as portrayed in the novel, but inadequate boats and an approaching storm motivated Ewing to cancel the crossing and hope for the best. Not so with Cadwalader. Being unable to cross at Bristol, Cadwalader's men ferried the boats farther south to Dunk's Ferry, where they attempted a second crossing. Cadwalader had managed to cross most of his men but was unable to ferry his artillery. He recalled his troops and was about to attempt a third crossing the next day when word reached him that Washington had secured Trenton (see Ketchum, *The Winter Soldiers*, pp. 268–69).

The battle in Trenton was every bit as fierce and frenetic as the novel illustrates. In a raging storm that made muskets an unreliable weapon, men fought with bayonets while violent cannons fired grapeshot through the streets. The remaining Hessian pickets from the outlying posts retreated into Trenton and Rall's command quickly turned to chaos and confusion; Rall never did manage to gather his troops enough to effect a counterattack. The Americans managed to force the Hessians into the orchard on the east side of town, where Rall was hit twice and then moved to the relative safety of Trenton proper, while Scheffer and Biesenrodt surrendered to the American army (see Ketchum, *The Winter Soldiers*, pp. 258–65).

Part Two

★ ★ ★

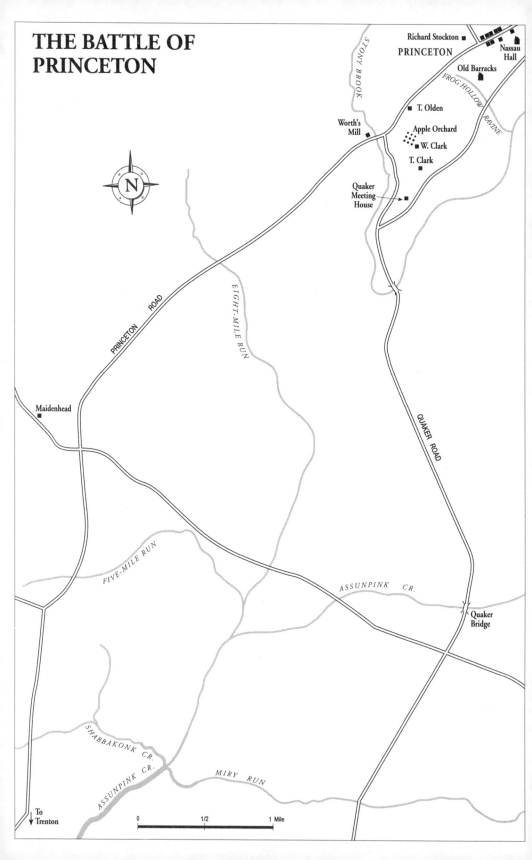

THE BATTLE OF PRINCETON

Richard Stockton

PRINCETON

Nassau Hall

Old Barracks

STONY BROOK

T. Olden

Worth's Mill

Apple Orchard

W. Clark

T. Clark

FROG HOLLOW RAVINE

Quaker Meeting House

N

PRINCETON ROAD

EIGHT-MILE RUN

QUAKER ROAD

Maidenhead

FIVE-MILE RUN

ASSUNPINK CR.

Quaker Bridge

SHABBAKONK CR.

ASSUNPINK CR.

MIRY RUN

To Trenton

0   1/2   1 Mile

Trenton, New Jersey
December 26, 1776

CHAPTER IX

★ ★ ★

A strangeness comes stealing over a battlefield after the guns have fallen silent. Hills, or streets, or valleys, or breastworks where men clashed in death struggles are no longer so high, so wide, or so unattainable. Magically they have become ordinary, normal, vulnerable. Places where men fell have lost their terrible, bright fascination and are once again just places, like a thousand others. Fallen comrades somehow seem diminished, smaller. Fallen enemies become ordinary men, no longer great and fierce and unconquerable.

Billy and Eli hunched their shoulders against the howling northeast wind that drove the sleet stinging in their faces and walked into the open field north of the Assunpink Creek. They silently picked their way through the litter and the dead towards fifteen hundred men who milled among the black craters where unnumbered cannonballs had ripped the frozen, black earth. Eight hundred stone-faced Americans with cannon and loaded muskets and leveled bayonets had surrounded seven hundred blue- and green-coated Hessians, hands held high, and they were coming out in small groups on command to stack their arms in the wind and snow.

Billy and Eli narrowed their eyes against the wind as they searched for the tall, dark shape of General George Washington in his black cape, sitting his bay horse among the silent soldiers. He was not there, and Billy and Eli turned west, trotting towards the town. They came into Trenton on Fourth Street and crossed Quaker Lane in silence, wind nearly at their backs, peering wide-eyed at the destruction and the dead and wounded as though it were all new to them.

A young Hessian moaned and Billy turned to look. The smooth-cheeked boy sat propped against the door frame of a small home, black blood frozen on his coat front and on the flagstones to his left side. The door had been blasted off its hinges by grapeshot. His long, blonde hair blew in the wind as he turned pain-glazed blue eyes to Billy, licked parched lips and tried to speak, but could not. He lifted his left arm towards Billy and Billy gasped and bit off a groan. There was no hand extended from the empty sleeve. It had been blown off above the wrist.

Billy knelt beside the young man and pushed back the coat sleeve and shuddered. Eli handed him his belt knife and Billy cut a piece from the rope he used to tie his coat at his waist and quickly fashioned a tourniquet, while Eli pulled the cork from his canteen and held it to the dry, fevered lips. Billy moved the boy inside the doorway, out of the wind, and propped him against the wall as best he could, then placed the boy's good right hand on the stick of wood he had used to twist the tourniquet. He looked into the blue eyes until the young German understood and his fingers tightened to hold the twisted rope tight while tortured eyes peered up at Billy.

Billy said, "I will send help." He repeated it, waiting to see if the boy understood.

The head nodded once, and then the face dropped as the boy looked at the stump of his left arm. Billy stood and for a moment stared down and swallowed, then turned back out the door into the wind, Eli beside him. They walked west to Queen Street and paused to look up and down at the trees and homes shattered by cannon fire. Hessians in their great winter coats lay dead and dying where they had fallen. The carcasses of a dozen horses lay on the frozen ground, some still hitched to the cannon they had been pulling when the American grapeshot came whistling. One horse was patiently scraping the street with a front foot, trying to rise, unable to understand why its hind legs would not work. Eli looked and saw the broken spine just ahead of the hindquarters. He shot once in the middle of the forehead and the animal's head dropped.

Behind them Americans began filtering into the town, systematically going through each home, business, building, searching out the stores of food, blankets, medicine, powder, and ammunition the Hessians had laid in for winter. Ten yards to his right Billy saw a Hessian officer, bareheaded, coat open, hands smeared with blood, moving south, pausing at each body to feel for a pulse, then move on. Beside him a young lieutenant carried a bag.

Billy stopped the man and spoke. "Are you a doctor?"

The man puzzled for a moment. "Doktor? Ja."

"There's a man up there with a hand gone. Do you understand?"

The doctor shook his head.

Billy took him by the arm and with Eli, led him trotting back down Fourth Street and pointed to the vacant doorway. The doctor paused, then suddenly his eyebrows arched and he nodded his head violently. In a moment he was through the doorway with his assistant.

Billy and Eli traveled west on Third Street to Queen and they could see Rall's headquarters on the far side of King. The once graceful home of Stacy Potts was streaked with black marks left by grapeshot. Windows were shattered and the walls broken where a dozen cannonballs had punched halfway through the house. Third Street was littered with smashed tree limbs, parts of houses and buildings, abandoned cannon, dead horses and Hessians. The two men moved north staring tight-lipped, silent.

Ahead they saw Major Wilkinson emerge from Fourth Street onto Queen. From the west, they saw mounted soldiers riding down Third Street towards them. In the instant of seeing they recognized the tall black shape of General George Washington on his big bay horse, and at the same moment they saw a group of Hessians carrying someone to the entrance of a church. Washington and his cluster of officers stopped and Washington dismounted to follow the enemy soldiers inside the small, white building while his officers waited.

Inside the church, Washington removed his hat and held it beneath his arm as he walked to the group of Hessian officers, who pulled back to give him entry. Before him Colonel Rall opened his eyes and squinted in the dim light until he recognized the tall figure standing over him.

Washington peered down at him, and it was Rall who spoke first, slowly. "General, I surrender my command."

An aide translated the German to English, and Washington nodded. "I accept."

"Will you treat my soldiers humanely? They are good men who have served well."

"I will, colonel. I will."

"I thank you, and I congratulate you on your victory."

"I wish you well."

There was little else to be said, and Washington stood for a moment, staring into the eyes of the defeated, dying officer before he straightened. He bowed slightly from the hips, then turned. The other German officers stepped back to give him passage and he strode from the room, out into the wind, closing the door behind.

Inside, Rall's officers began removing his clothing to get to the two wounds in his side when one of them discovered the folded note in his vest pocket. Puzzled, he read it, then passed it to Rall. In an instant Rall remembered the late night card game at the home of Abraham Hunt— the written message he had not taken time to read—and he forced his eyes to focus as he read.

"The Americans are coming tonight to attack Trenton."

His eyes closed and his head rolled back as his hand lowered, and the note fluttered to the floor. He opened his eyes and spoke to those hovering over him. "If I had read this at Mr. Hunt's I would not be here."

Outside, Washington remounted his horse and turned west down Third Street as Wilkinson rode up and both men halted. Billy and Eli stopped five yards behind Wilkinson.

"Sir," Wilkinson said, "I have come to report the last of the Hessians down by the creek have surrendered. Trenton is ours."

Washington leaned to shake Wilkinson's hand. "Major Wilkinson, this is a glorious day for our country." For a rare moment Washington allowed himself the luxury of a smile while he savored the moment of this impossible victory. Then, with the wind at his back, he once again shouldered the crushing load.

"Major, would you carry a message to the general officers east of town handling the surrender. Tell them to turn those proceedings over to the junior officers as soon as possible. I need them at Rall's headquarters. Tell General St. Clair I will need a report on our own casualties, and those of the Hessians, immediately."

Wilkinson saluted and reined his horse around and raised it to a lope, then turned east on Third Street. Billy and Eli watched him until he disappeared, then turned back to Washington, and moved out of the street to let him and his aides and officers pass.

Washington did not move. He stared down, studying them. He peered at Eli's wolf skin coat, and suddenly spoke. "Don't I know you? What is your name and regiment?"

"Eli Stroud. Scout."

Washington's expression did not change. "Didn't you carry a message for me recently?" He did not speak the name "Honeyman" or "Griggstown" and Eli understood.

He nodded. "I did."

The officers at Washington's side looked at Eli, then at Washington, waiting for the general to demand that he be addressed as "Sir." He said nothing as he turned his eyes to Billy. "What is your name and regiment?"

"Corporal Billy Weems, sir. Originally Company Nine, Boston Regiment, lately assigned to General Mercer."

Remembrance was instant. "Do I recall you and Mr. Stroud guiding Colonel Glover to stop General Howe in the wheat fields south of White Plains?"

"Yes, sir, we were with the colonel."

"Have you seen him today? Is he all right?"

"Yes, sir. We were with him half an hour ago when he and Colonel Stark took the last of the Hessians down by the creek. He was fine then, sir."

Relief showed in Washington's face. "Good. Stay close to your regiment. I may need you later."

Eli nodded. Billy answered, "Yes, sir."

Washington tapped spur to horse to move on down to Rall's headquarters when Billy spoke again.

"Sir, may I inquire?"

"What is it?"

"Wasn't that Colonel Rall the Hessians took inside the church?" He pointed.

"Yes."

"Is he alive?"

"He is dying. There is nothing we can do for him. I left him the dignity of being with his own officers."

Billy glanced at Eli and Eli wiped his hand across his mouth and remained silent.

"Thank you, sir."

Washington nodded and moved down the street to stop at the graceful home Stacy Potts had given to Colonel Rall as his headquarters. Washington tied his horse and walked in through the splintered door, his aides and officers following.

Billy turned his back to the wind and pointed to the ragged Americans entering every house. "They're starting to pile supplies in the street. We better go on down to the Old Barracks and see if the horses and wagons are still there."

Eli nodded. "And the cattle. Enough meat there for a month."

The thick, ugly clouds overhead continued to lock Trenton in a pall of gray, and the wind held, driving the sleet nearly horizontal. There was no great celebration among the Americans of their miraculous victory, rather they anxiously searched the town in silence, desperate for the food and clothing they had been so long denied. They paused in kitchens only long enough to cram a loaf of bread inside their tattered shirts, or stuff a biscuit in their mouth as they carried anything they could eat from the pantries or root cellars to stack near the street.

They broke into a warehouse and stood openmouthed at the sight of hundreds of blankets in bundles, half a dozen crates of boots, a thousand pairs of thick wool socks, shipping crates with trousers, shirts, and heavy Hessian overcoats. They called to those behind and the word spread. The tattered, shivering Americans came to silently strip their rags and pull on new trousers, shirts, warm socks, boots, and button the heavy overcoats tight against the storm, reveling in the luxury of warmth.

They battered down the double doors of the town livery and stopped, stunned as they counted eighty barrels of flour, sixty barrels of dried beef, and eighty barrels of salt pork. The piles of stores in the streets grew, and Billy and Eli sent wagons hitched to teams of horses and mules up King Street where men loaded the stores in the big, springless Hessian freight wagons.

Inside Rall's headquarters, General Washington's officers started fires in both of the great stone fireplaces and set coffeepots to boil. Twenty minutes later General St. Clair and a dozen other general officers tied up their horses in front of the building and entered. One of Washington's aides pointed to the library when they entered, and General Washington gestured them to upholstered chairs surrounding a large maple table. The wind moaned through one hole in the south wall made by an American cannonball that had crossed the room to knock rock chips from the fireplace. An aide poured strong, smoking black coffee into Stacy Potts's china cups and the officers took their places. Washington stood at the head of the table and wasted no words.

"Has anyone heard from either General Ewing or General Cadwalader?"

The officers looked at each other, startled that in the chaotic battle none had thought of either Ewing or Cadwalader. They shook their heads in silence.

"Then we do not know what lies south of us. A strong force of fresh Hessians under General von Donop could be coming this way, if word has reached them. They can be here in four hours."

For a moment he studied the tabletop in deep thought.

"There is a large force of British in Princeton under General Grant, and they could be here in two hours." Again he paused. "Our men are at their limits of exhaustion. In the last thirty-six hours they've given about all they can. So the question is, what is our next move? Princeton? Brunswick? Bordentown? Or back to our camp to let our men regain strength before we make our next attack?"

Knox's reply was instant. "Princeton. Just ten miles. We have our cannon and horses here and we can be there in three hours. Surprise is still in our favor."

Sullivan leaned forward. "Our men can't march that distance in three hours. Some of them are falling asleep in the snow right now."

Stirling interrupted. "What about the prisoners? We could have as many as a thousand. We can't take them to Princeton and we can't leave them here."

Greene raised a hand. "The initiative is ours. If they are no better prepared for an attack in Princeton than they were here we could take it before nightfall."

Washington turned his face to St. Clair. "Did you assign someone to get a damage report of losses?"

"Yes, sir. Should be here any time."

Thoughtfully Washington dropped his eyes and the room grew silent as he pondered. Then he raised his head.

"Gentlemen, today we've won more than a battle. Much more. We have given our country, our people, their first cause to rejoice in more than a year. In my judgment the news of our taking Trenton will go through the states like wildfire and become a rallying cry. Yesterday it appeared certain the Continental army would dissolve at midnight on December thirty-first when the enlistments expired. Today it is nearly certain this victory will inspire most of the men we have, and thousands of new volunteers, to take up the cause of liberty."

The only sound in the room was the wind outside, working at the hole in the south wall.

"That is worth more right now than taking Rall's entire garrison. I will not risk this victory by engaging the British in a second battle that could end in our defeat. It is my judgment—"

He was interrupted by the sound of a door, then rapid footsteps in the hallway, and then a knock at the door.

"Enter."

An aide stepped inside and stood at attention. "Sir, one of our captains is here with a message for General St. Clair."

"Bring him in."

A bearded man, soaked from the storm, entered and stood at attention. "Sir, I have the damage report requested by General St. Clair." He held out a paper.

General Washington gestured to St. Clair, who stood and strode to the man to take the paper. "Thank you. Would you wait outside."

Every eye in the room stared at St. Clair as he opened the folded paper where he stood, his eyes sweeping the page. His eyebrows arched, and he slowed and silently read the very brief report again, word for word. Then he raised incredulous eyes to General Washington.

"Sir, we have taken nine hundred eighteen Hessian prisoners, including thirty-two general officers. We're still counting those who fell in the streets, but it now appears the Hessian dead and wounded will be in excess of one hundred."

Washington's officers looked at each other, but Washington's eyes never left St. Clair's as he waited for the count of American dead.

"Sir," St. Clair said hesitantly, "it appears that we did not lose one man in the fight. We have two officers reported wounded, and two privates. That's all. No dead!"

Washington's eyes closed for a moment while audible gasps broke out, followed by an outburst of voices loud in disbelief. He waited until the talk quieted.

"Is the report on our losses confirmed?"

"This says it is, sir."

"Would you call the captain back into the room?"

Thirty seconds later the captain stood at rigid attention as Washington spoke to him.

"Captain, is the report of our losses confirmed?"

"Yes, sir, it is. The officers in every regiment report all men accounted for. The report is accurate."

"Thank you. Dismissed."

The captain turned on his heel and was gone.

Washington turned to St. Clair. "Does it identify the officers who were wounded?"

"Yes, sir. One was James Monroe. An eighteen-year-old lieutenant from Virginia. A musket ball in his left shoulder. Fairly serious but even after taking the wound he continued to help capture a Hessian cannon out there in King Street and fire it at the Hessians. He will survive it, sir. The other officer was your cousin, William Washington. He was wounded slightly in both hands when they stormed the Hessian cannon."

In that moment a sudden sureness surged in the hearts of every man in the room and they were awed, humbled with the overpowering certainty.

We were not alone out there!

They stared at each other in silence as the feeling gripped them, and then it faded and was gone and they began to breathe again. No man spoke of it because they could not find words to describe the rare, powerful impression. They moved, shifting their feet, and waited for General Washington to continue the council.

"Gentlemen, I cannot risk this victory by engaging the British immediately in a battle we might lose. We'll go back to our camp and give our men time to gather their strength. In a few days they'll be ready. We have enough food and provisions from the Hessian stores to feed and clothe them."

He waited while murmuring broke out and died before he turned to General Sullivan. "Assign a detail of men to go through this building as soon as possible and gather every document, every letter, every map they can find. Find the quartermaster's office and collect all the money and valuables and documents there."

"Yes, sir."

"Each of you take charge of your commands. As soon as we've gathered all the food and supplies we can transport, we'll go back to McKonkey's Ferry and move across the river to our own camp. Bring the Hessian prisoners. Same marching order as we came. We'll use the Pennington Road."

By mid-afternoon the columns were beginning to form at the big junction at the head of King Street. Sergeant Joseph White paused beside the cannon he and his crew had manned, pain showing in his face. A Hessian cannonball had cracked the thick oak axle and the big gun was sagging to one side, muzzle pointed upward. White shook his head sadly and tenderly laid a hand on the wet, cold barrel. A voice from behind startled him and he turned.

"Sergeant, that gun is beyond repair. You'll have to leave it."

White squinted against the storm, up at Colonel Knox on his horse. "She's not hurt bad, sir. Maybe I can fix it."

Knox shook his head. "No time. Leave it."

White nodded. "Yes, sir." He watched Knox canter his horse away, then turned once more to his beloved cannon. He went to one knee, studying the widening crack in the heavy axle and a stubborn resolve formed in his heart. He rose and called to two soldiers standing nearby awaiting orders.

"You two. I was on the gun crew that used this cannon to clear King Street. She got hurt in the fight, but she can be fixed. You two game to give me a hand?"

With the storm still raging, White hailed two more soldiers. An hour later, in the fading light of late afternoon, White straightened. "All right. Let's wheel her around and see if she holds."

Five pairs of hands grasped the trails and swung them around while White held his breath and watched the cracked axle. A broad grin formed in his wet beard. "She'll hold, boys! If we're careful we can get her back."

Two hundred yards ahead the nine hundred eighteen Hessian prisoners were assembled on the roadway and General Sullivan called for Colonel Glover.

"Can your regiment hold these men in line and keep them moving?"

"Yes, sir."

In approaching twilight the great column began its journey nine miles north, straight into the teeth of the raging northeaster. Glover's regiment was split, one half on each side of the Hessians, Billy and Eli among them.

By eight o'clock they had passed Howell's cooper shop. It was past midnight when they reached the turn towards the river. It was one A.M. when the leaders stopped on the frozen banks of the Delaware. The storm was still howling, sleet driving in from the north.

It was approaching two A.M., December 27, 1776, when the first boats pushed off towards the Pennsylvania riverbanks.

It was breaking dawn, gray and bleak, with the wind still driving the sleet when the last boats loaded, and it was full morning when their bows thumped into the banks near the American camp and waiting hands grasped frozen hawsers to hold the boats steady while the half-frozen men clambered ashore. The last to climb over the gunwales were Sergeant White and his tiny group, who strained and lifted until they got the big gun ashore where White, grinning proudly through his frozen beard, warmly shook hands with those who had helped save his cannon.

Billy and Eli waited until the last man was ashore before they tied the ropes to stakes driven into the frozen ground and were turning to go to the nearest fire, when they slowed and stopped near a huddled group of silent men gathered around something lying on the ground. They worked their way in and stopped short.

Sergeant Turlock glanced at them and they saw the pain in his eyes. At his feet were three bodies, covered with new Hessian blankets. Turlock walked to Billy and Eli and spoke quietly. "They didn't make it. Froze. Just sat there in the boat and froze without a word."

Billy knelt beside the bodies and tenderly touched the nearest blanket, then rose back to his feet. Eli stared down, then shifted his eyes. He said nothing as he reached to wipe the wet sleeve of his wolf skin coat across his mouth.

Notes

Rall was carried off the battlefield and taken to the Methodist Church on the corner of Queen and Third streets before finally being moved to his headquarters in the Potts's home on King Street (see Stryker, *The Battles of Trenton and Princeton*, p. 192). For narrative purposes, the author has chosen to deviate from the historical record slightly and allowed Washington to occupy Rall's headquarters while Rall remained at the Methodist Church. While Rall's officers were tending to his wounds, they found the note Rall received during Hunt's party the night before. When he finally read the warning—too late—he remarked, "If I had read this at Mr. Hunt's I would not be here" (as quoted in Ketchum, *The Winter Soldiers*, p. 270).

Washington did visit the dying Rall and they had a brief conversation where Rall officially surrendered and begged Washington to treat the captured

Hessian troops with kindness. Washington agreed and left a few words of consolation and compassion for the Hessian soldier (see Stryker, *The Battles of Trenton and Princeton*, p. 192).

Colonel Knox and General Greene were in favor of pressing on to Princeton, but Washington recognized that the Continental army had won a major psychological victory as well as a physical victory that day and he was not willing to jeopardize either by advancing into another battle prematurely (see Ketchum, *The Winter Soldiers*, pp. 265–66).

The casualty reports for both the Hessian and American armies are accurate: over a thousand Hessian troops were either killed, wounded, or captured, while only four Americans were wounded (see Ward, *The War of the Revolution*, vol. I, p. 302). James Monroe eventually became the fifth president of the United States (see Leckie, *George Washington's War*, p. 321). The only other American casualties were the three men who froze to death on the return trip across the Delaware (see Ketchum, *The Winter Soldiers*, p. 266).

Sergeant Joseph White repaired a broken cannon and, with the help of four men, transported the cannon back to the American camp. As he told Colonel Knox who asked why he bothered dragging a broken cannon away from the battlefield, "I wanted the victory complete" (as quoted in Ketchum, *The Winter Soldiers*, p. 267).

Indeed, the American victory at Trenton was total and complete and marked a turning point in the war. "This was a long and a severe ordeal, and yet it may be doubted whether so small a number of men ever employed so short a space of time with greater or more lasting results upon the history of the world" (as quoted in Ward, *The War of the Revolution*, vol. I, p. 303).

CHAPTER X

★ ★ ★

*M*argaret Dunson stopped by the great fireplace in the parlor and closed her eyes to listen for the sound of the front gate closing, but it did not come. She glanced at the clock on the heavy mantel, then walked quickly to the front window to hold back the curtain with anxious fingers while she peered out past the white picket fence to the street. For two days a strong northeaster had raged, whistling at the windows and howling in the chimney, but had quieted in the night. By noon the first rifts had appeared in the thick storm clouds, and now shafts of sunlight came slanting from the west to cast shadows of trees stark and bare on the snow in the frigid afternoon. She watched people hurry past in the streets, bundled to their noses, vapor trailing behind their heads.

She turned back to the fireplace and reached with a brass poker to swing one of the four arms outward from the banked fire, and with a hot pad lifted the lid on the kettle hanging from the hook at the end of the arm. The diced mutton and vegetables were simmering and she reached with a wooden spoon to dip some broth. She blew on it, then gingerly sipped at it and worked it in her mouth, testing for flavor.

Salt. And a touch more sage.

She walked to the kitchen to return with the salt bowl and a small pewter box of sage, and added a pinch of sage to the smoking mix and enough salt to make a small white mound in the palm of her hand. She stirred with the wooden spoon, dipped more broth, blew, sipped, and nodded her head in satisfaction before she returned the spices to the kitchen cupboard. She paused at the black kitchen stove to open the oven door and peer inside at the four loaves of bread and the single pan of cinnamon rolls, fully risen and beginning to brown on top. A smile came creeping at the thought of the children reaching for the thick, steaming slices with eyes wide and faces beaming in anticipation of heaping butter on, and that first soul-warming mouthful. She closed and latched the oven door, gave the grate in the firebox one shake, then glanced at the woodbox.

Takes so much wood to keep a family through the winter. Caleb will have to fill it before supper, and the fireplace box too.

At the thought of Caleb she once again walked to the front window and leaned to peer up and down the street, and suddenly in her mother's heart she knew something was wrong. Her breathing constricted for a moment and she straightened and stood still to allow the premonition to settle.

Caleb's in trouble.

She turned to the coat-tree near the front door and reached for her heavy winter coat, then stopped at the sound of the front gate closing. She threw the door open as Brigitte came striding toward the house where Caleb had shoveled a path in the snow, scarf wrapped about her head, face white from the cold. She came through the door and Margaret closed it and waited while Brigitte unwound the scarf and began working with the large buttons on her ankle-length winter coat. Brigitte was watching Margaret's eyes, sensing her deep concern.

"The children have not come home from school," Margaret exclaimed.

Brigitte slowed and stopped, looked at the clock, then frowned.

"It's Caleb," Margaret said. "Something's wrong. I know."

Brigitte's shoulders slumped. "Caleb again? Do you want me to go looking?"

"We'll both go."

Margaret reached for her coat as Brigitte buttoned hers back up over her long dress. Her shoes still had light dustings of flour from her day's work at the bakery. She wound the long, deep blue wool scarf back around her head and waited while Margaret buttoned her coat. Margaret swung the supper kettle away from the fire, and the two of them shook the four loaves of bread from their pans and set them on the cupboard covered with a towel to cool, with the pan of cinnamon rolls beside, before they walked out the front door.

They were one block from the school when they saw the twins with Caleb behind them. The twins came running, their nine-year-old legs pumping as they ran on the icy path.

"Mother, Mother," Adam shouted. "Caleb got in a fight and there's blood!"

Priscilla slowed as she approached, panting, wide-eyed, frightened. "Mother, it was awful! Caleb and Robert Simmons and Elijah Beaman. Rolling on the ground and hitting!"

With Brigitte beside her, Margaret paused to pull Prissy to her while Adam stopped in front of her, serious eyes upturned, waiting for Mother to make everything all right. Margaret spoke calmly. "It's all right. We'll take care of things."

Adam exhaled in relief and turned to watch Caleb who slowed at the sight of Margaret and Brigitte, then resumed a steady pace towards them. There was blood around his mouth and chin and flecks on his coat front, along with snow and ice and frozen dirt ground into the heavy wool. His right cheek was bruised and his left eye was partially closed.

Margaret was aware of those in the street who slowed to watch, but as Caleb approached, her facial expression did not change. She said quietly, "Come along. We'll settle this at home." Margaret and Brigitte turned and started for home without so much as a glance at the proper Bostonians who stopped to stare at two grown women stoically marching two children and a rather tall young man with a battered face and dirty coat up the cobblestoned street.

Caleb pushed through the front gate, then into the house without pausing to hold either door open for the women and children, and was on his way to his bedroom when Margaret's voice stopped him.

"You'll tell me what this is all about." It was not a question.

He did not turn to face her. "Not now."

"*Now.*" There was iron in her voice.

Slowly he turned, face a blank, a slight sneer forming on his mouth. "Nothing. There was a fight."

"The third one in six weeks. Who?"

"Simmons and Beaman."

"Simmons and Beaman who?"

"Robert Simmons. Elijah Beaman. Nobody. Just two boys."

"I know Robert Simmons, but not Elijah Beaman. Robert's two years older than you. Who started it and what was it about?" She waited, holding her breath. Brigitte stood beside her, not moving, watching his eyes and face. The twins stood to one side, staring at Caleb, waiting. None of them made a move to take off their winter coats.

Caleb shrugged and shook his head. "Nothing."

Margaret blurted, "You're bloodied and dirtied over nothing? You'll tell me now or we'll go to Robert's home and he'll tell us."

Hot rebellion flashed in Caleb's eyes and Margaret straightened in shock and held her breath while she waited. Slowly Caleb relaxed his clenched jaw.

"They said getting liberty was worth the war. I said it wasn't." His face went dead, expressionless as he waited for Margaret's explosion.

"Caleb!" Her voice was high. "Your father gave his *life* for liberty. Matthew is gone now and so is Billy, fighting for liberty! You think you know more than them?"

His eyes and voice were without expression as he spoke. "I know Father is dead. I know Matthew is gone and you're here alone, and you and Brigitte are working yourselves to death to keep us all. I know Brigitte and I tried to take bullets and food to help our army and we got eleven people killed by our own soldiers. Nearly got killed ourselves. For what?" His voice was rising, his eyes coming alive. "Our army got beat down at New York and they're clear over in Pennsylvania right now, nearly starved and frozen to death. We don't know if we'll ever see Matthew or Billy again. All in the name of liberty! Much more liberty and we'll *all* be dead!"

Margaret raised a warning finger. "Don't you *dare* say such a thing!

Not in this house. Not with the price we've paid doing the work of the Almighty!"

Caleb's voice rang loud off the walls. His eyes were flashing, defiant. "The Almighty? Where was He when Father was killed? when our own soldiers killed those people with Brigitte and me? when the British killed half our army over at New York? Where was He then?"

Margaret's voice was shrill, nearly cracking. "Caleb! Don't you *ever* pass judgment on the Almighty. Do you think you know His mind? Can you see what He sees? Do what He does? Until you can, don't you *dare* speak against Him!"

Brigitte took one step towards Caleb, hands cocked on her hips, and there was fire in her eyes. "Stop it! You've made enough fool of yourself! Standing there dirty and bloody acting like you're smarter than everybody else and talking back to your mother. You hold your mouth, young man, and get to your room and clean yourself up. Then we'll—"

Caleb cut her off, his voice booming. "You! Listen to yourself! You—the one who saved a British soldier and now you want to marry him! If we're doing the work of the Almighty, then what are you doing helping the enemy?"

Brigitte's hand flicked upward and her open palm smacked loud against Caleb's cheek, and his head twisted sideways. By pure reflex his right hand cocked and he had started to swing before he caught himself and stopped. Adam took a step backwards and Prissy began to wail as Caleb lowered his hand, then reached to touch his cheek where Brigitte's handprint was coming red.

Margaret reached to pull Prissy to her, and Adam came to her side while Caleb and Brigitte stood in silence, both shaken, white-faced at what they had done, frightened, silent, not knowing how to undo it. Then Caleb turned on his heel, strode to his bedroom, and closed the door hard.

Margaret spoke quietly, holding Prissy against her side. "Come on. We'll go to your bedroom and change. Adam, you too." Brigitte followed. The tapping of their heels on the hardwood floor of the hallway was the only sound in the house, and in silence they went to their rooms to change from their winter clothing.

In the fading light of a sun already set, Margaret silently walked out the back door, down into the root cellar for a jar of butter, then returned to set it in the kitchen next to the loaves of bread. Brigitte opened the cupboard to gather dishes and cups and began setting the table. Adam and Prissy sat on the sofa, backs rigid, hands folded in their laps, watching every move of the two women, studying their faces for a sign of whether the explosive anger was past.

Margaret stopped beside the kitchen woodbox, thought for a moment, then shrugged once more into her long winter coat.

Brigitte glanced at her. "That's Caleb's job."

Margaret did not answer. She walked out the back door to the wood yard and returned with her arms loaded with split kindling. Brigitte put on her own coat and followed her back out. Each made two more trips to fill the two woodboxes and then both hung their coats back on the coat-tree by the front door. Margaret swung the iron arm out from the fireplace and removed the lid from the kettle and the rich aroma spread. While Margaret filled a large bowl with the smoking stew, Brigitte cut the warm bread and arranged it on a platter, then set it on the kitchen table.

Margaret turned to Prissy. "Go knock on Caleb's door and tell him supper is ready."

Prissy's lower lip trembled and Margaret knelt beside her. "Caleb didn't mean those things. None of us did. It just happened. He loves you—all of us. You go tell him. He'll like that."

Hesitantly Prissy walked down the hall and rapped softly on Caleb's door. There was no sound inside, and she put her mouth close to the door and said, "Caleb, Mother says supper is ready." She waited in silence, then spoke again. "Caleb, please come. I want you to come."

She heard a chair scrape, then footsteps, and the door opened slowly. Prissy looked up into Caleb's red eyes and knew he had been crying; she reached to put her small hand in his big one, and they walked out to the supper table together.

They knelt by their chairs as always, Margaret nodded to Brigitte, and she offered grace. They sat at their places in awkward silence while Margaret dipped steaming mutton stew onto their plates and Brigitte passed the bread platter. Supper became painful as they avoided each other's eyes and spoke in low tones only long enough to pass or receive the food.

Finally Margaret rose and walked into the kitchen to return with the pan of warm cinnamon rolls. She deftly sectioned them out of the pan onto their plates with the raisins still warm and plump, and the children began to unroll them one piece at time, savoring them with cold milk.

Caleb finished and pushed his chair back, but before he could rise Margaret raised her face and spoke.

"Caleb, I'm sorry."

All motion at the table stopped. In the tense silence they could hear the clock ticking.

Caleb did not look at his mother. "I'm sorry, too." For a moment longer he sat in the silence, then rose and walked back to his room. For half a minute no one at the table moved, and then Margaret pushed her chair back, stood, and said with finality, "Well, these dishes won't wash themselves."

Margaret washed and Brigitte dried while the children got into their heavy flannel nightshirts. Brigitte brushed out Prissy's hair and braided it loosely for the night, and Margaret called them all to her big bed for evening prayers. Brigitte brought the twins and they waited until Margaret realized Caleb was not coming. Without a word she strode down the hall to his bedroom and rapped on the door. She was reaching to rap again when he opened the door.

"Time for prayers."

His eyes were distant, face a mask. "I'll have my own."

Margaret did not move or speak. She stood as she was, eyes locked with his, waiting. Seconds ticked by, and finally Caleb glanced down at the floor for a moment, then stepped towards her and followed her back to her bedroom to kneel beside the twins. After Margaret had offered their evening prayers, Brigitte followed her to tuck the twins in and they left the door partially open for the night. Caleb's door was closed tight and there was no light in his room.

Margaret walked down the dim hall, through the arch, into the parlor, and settled into her rocking chair. She brought her hands into her lap and began working them together, looking at them without seeing, while she faced her worst fears. Brigitte quietly sat on the sofa and for a long time they remained silent, each lost in her own thoughts in the yellow lamplight and the dancing flames in the fireplace. Finally Brigitte glanced at the clock.

"Time for bed."

Margaret nodded but did not move, nor did she speak.

Brigitte spoke again, subdued, quiet. "Mother, I'm so sorry for what I did—for what happened. I never expected . . . there seems to be so much anger and hatred in Caleb lately. I should never have lost my temper, I know."

Margaret shook her head. "It wasn't all your fault. He said some terrible things."

"He defied you."

Margaret did not raise her eyes as she continued to slowly work her hands together, studying them. "He spoke against the Almighty. I would rather be dead than have him turn on God. I'm terrified. I don't know what to do."

"Won't it pass? Won't he grow out of it?"

Slowly Margaret shook her head. "I don't know. I know I cannot give him what he needs most."

"Love?"

Her voice was low, thoughtful. "I can give him all my love but it's not enough. He needs the love of a good father. Matthew could have helped, or maybe even Billy, but the war has taken all of them away from him. Deep inside he senses what was taken from him and now his need is turning to anger, even hatred. If it has a chance to get deep enough for long enough, I don't know if he'll ever rise above it."

She was still working with her hands, and her expression did not change as a silent tear trickled down her cheek. Brigitte watched the tear and her heart ached.

Quietly Margaret continued. "I don't know which is worse. To take a musket and go out to kill the enemy or be killed, or to stay here at home and try to carry on with our men gone. Caleb's becoming hateful, bitter. You want to marry a British captain. All of us working from dawn to dark to stay alive. We don't know if we'll ever see Matthew again, or Billy." She slowly shook her head. Her voice was flat, dead, emotionless. "Sometimes I think it would be a relief to be on the battlefield, where you know who you're fighting and the rules are simple. Kill or be killed. Here, your body keeps walking around while inside you're dying from watching everything you ever knew slowly crumble and go away and you don't know how to stop it."

For the first time she raised her eyes to Brigitte's and they stared into each other's souls in silence.

"Mother, I didn't plan to fall in love with Richard. I don't know . . ."

Margaret raised a hand to stop her. "Matters of the heart pay no attention to country or station. My only fear is for you. If he lives through the war and your feelings for him don't change, you will have to make a decision that will bring you the greatest joy and the greatest pain. Him and England, or someone else and here. And no one can decide it for you. I can only pray you decide right for you."

As never before, Brigitte sensed in her young heart the awful, eternal truth. For a true mother, unspeakable joy and unbearable pain are the twin handmaidens that come with each child. Inherent in one is the possibility of the other. It is the price a woman pays to fulfill the measure of her creation.

Margaret heaved a great sigh, then stood. "Tomorrow's Saturday. We have our chores and they won't wait. We better go to bed."

Inside her room, in her nightshirt, she sat on the edge of her bed in the feeble yellow light of one lamp for a long time. She turned to look at John's pillow, still in its place because her heart would not let her put it in the closet with the other bedding. She reached to touch it, smooth it tenderly with her hand.

What should I do, John? How do I save him?

A strange feeling rose inside and she slipped to her knees on the floor and bowed her head, hands clasped before her. She did not know how long she poured out her heart to the Almighty. She only knew that when she finally said her quiet "Amen" she was empty, and there was a wet spot on the sheet where her tears had fallen. She turned the wheel on the lamp wick and slipped into bed in the darkness. She reached to touch John's pillow once more and her eyes opened wide in the blackness with the sure conviction that he was near. She did not remember drifting into a troubled sleep.

Her eyes opened suddenly in the early dawn and she lay in the gloom of nearly full darkness for a moment before the remembrance of yesterday's events came flooding. She sat up and swung her feet to the floor, then slipped into her robe and her thick, felt slippers and silently padded out to the chill parlor where she used the bellows to raise sparks from the coals she had banked. She fed shavings, then small kindlings to the coals until the warmth reached into the room. The firebox in the kitchen stove was cold and she carried two sticks of burning kindling from the fireplace to rekindle it. Minutes later a pot of water was heating for oatmeal porridge and coffee. She walked to the front window to peer outside at the gray preceding sunrise. The skies were clear and there was no wind.

Brigitte walked into the parlor with her arms folded, holding her robe tightly about her, and she walked to the front window to glance outside before she sat down at the large dining table.

"Oatmeal?"

"Yes. Cold outside."

"I had bad dreams about last night."

"So did I."

"Caleb up yet?"

"No. Let him sleep a while. He has about a cord of kindling to split."

"I won't be going into the bakery today. It's closed for the holidays."

"Good. You can help with supper."

The sun rose cheerless over a frozen world while Margaret and Brigitte made their beds and washed up for breakfast. Margaret measured coffee into the coffeepot, then added boiling water from the kettle on the stove and set the pot on the black top to simmer. She shook oatmeal into the boiling water remaining in the kettle and stirred, then replaced the lid and slid it beside the coffeepot to steam. They sliced yesterday's bread and Margaret set butter and a jar of plum jam on the table.

Prissy walked through the archway digging sleep from her eyes. "Oatmeal?"

"And bread and jam. Is Adam up?"

"I don't know."

"Go peek."

Prissy returned in a few moments, still yawning. "He's awake."

"Tell him breakfast will be ready in fifteen minutes. Get changed. You both have to straighten your rooms."

"Before school?"

Margaret smiled. "It's Saturday."

Prissy's eyes widened for a moment before she grinned at the thought of a day without school. "Oh! I forgot."

Margaret went back to the kitchen for heavy pewter porridge bowls and called to Brigitte, "Better wake Caleb."

Ten seconds later Margaret jerked to a stop at the frantic shout from Brigitte in the hallway. "Mother! Caleb's not here!"

Margaret dumped the bowls clattering on the table and ran through the archway, down to Caleb's room and dodged through the door where Brigitte stood white-faced. The moment Margaret entered Brigitte spun to her.

"Did you send him somewhere? An errand?"

"No. I thought he was here."

"Did you hear him leave?"

"No."

Margaret jerked the closet door open and in seconds checked his clothing, then his shoes. "He's run away. Taken a change of clothes and run away."

Brigitte gasped, then clapped her hand over her mouth and began to sob. "I slapped him and he ran away. I did it. I did it."

Margaret's face became stern. "Nonsense. Get hold of yourself. He ran away because he's become hateful. What we have to think about is where would he go and how do we get him back?"

Brigitte dropped her hands and wiped at her eyes and tried to force a sense of order into her thoughts. "I can't think where he would go. Not to Dorothy's. The church? Silas?"

Margaret shook her head firmly. "No. He'd go to join in the fighting, and to do that he has to either walk out through the Neck, or cross on the Charlestown Ferry, or get on a boat going towards New York."

She spun on her heel. "Quick. Get your coat on and go down to the Neck as fast as you can. Maybe someone there saw him. I'll leave the twins at Dorothy's and go on down to the docks. If he got on a boat, or crossed on the ferry, maybe someone will remember." She paused for a moment. "If you find him bring him home, but no matter what, be home before dark."

Five minutes later Brigitte threw open the front door and ran to the front gate to disappear running west down the street, past the white fences and tidy homes, towards the narrow neck of land which connected the peninsula on which Boston was built to the mainland. People stopped at the unseemly sight of a young lady sprinting through the frozen streets of Boston on a Saturday morning, but Brigitte paid no heed as she ran west towards what was called the Barricades at the narrowest section of the Neck, where soldiers could control whoever passed through. If any American soldiers remained at the Neck, they would know if Caleb had passed through in the night, or early morning.

Margaret shoved the porridge and coffee off the stove onto the cold oven top, then trotted to bank the fire in the fireplace while she called orders to the twins.

"Get into your heavy coats. You're going to Dorothy's for the day."

Three seconds later Prissy walked through the archway, eyes wide, lip trembling, sensing something was tragically wrong.

"Where's Caleb?"

Margaret shook her head and made the hard decision. "We don't know. We're going to find him. Don't you fret. You'll be at Dorothy's with Trudy and you'll be fine."

Margaret gave the twins no time to whimper. She marched them to their rooms and with deft fingers thrust their arms into their heavy coats and buttoned them tight, then jammed Adam's knit cap down over his ears and tied Prissy's winter bonnet under her chin. Two minutes later she had her own coat buttoned and threw the front door open, seized the children by their hands and strode out, stopping only long enough to close and lock the door before she walked rapidly up the street, the children trotting beside to keep up. Three minutes later she pushed through the gate to the small, neat, austere home of Dorothy Weems and stopped at the door, vapor rising from her face, while the children panted beside her. She rapped sharply and the door opened almost instantly.

"Margaret!" Dorothy Weems, short, blocky, plain, stood with eyebrows arched, hair covered with a scarf for her Saturday work. "Come in! It's cold out there. I'll set coffee."

Margaret shook her head violently. "I can't stop. Can I leave Adam and Prissy here for a while?"

Dorothy read the pleading and the fear in Margaret's eyes. "What's wrong? Something's wrong."

"Caleb. We can't find him."

Dorothy caught her breath. "For how long?"

"Sometime in the night."

Dorothy reached for the hands of the twins. "Of course. I was just setting breakfast. How long will you be gone?"

"I'll be back before dark."

The sound of running feet came behind Dorothy and she turned as Trudy slowed and stopped, wide-eyed at the sight of Margaret and the twins. Stocky, plain like her mother and her brother Billy, Trudy turned green eyes to Dorothy, silently inquiring, afraid to hope the twins could spend the day.

Dorothy spoke. "Set two more places for breakfast. The twins are staying."

Trudy gasped. "Honest? All day?"

Dorothy nodded and Trudy squealed and reached to grasp Prissy's hand and lead her inside. Adam frowned and followed.

Dorothy turned back to Margaret. "What can I do to help?"

"You'll be doing enough to watch the twins."

"Did he say anything? Leave a letter or note?"

Margaret shook her head and her eyes dropped. "We talked last night after supper—he and Brigitte and I. He said some hard things against the Revolution. We argued." Margaret paused and considered for a moment. "Brigitte slapped him."

Dorothy clapped her hand over her mouth, then dropped it. "Go find him. I'll have supper waiting here for all of you. Go on." Impulsively Dorothy stepped out into the freezing air and threw her arms about Margaret and for a moment they stood in the frigid sunlight in the embrace of old and understanding friends. Then Margaret turned on her heel and trotted back to the gate.

She turned northeast on Cornhill, then due east on Ann Street, towards the docks on the east side of Boston. A forest of masts stood undulating in the bay where creaking ships were anchored, rolling gently on the incoming tide, waiting their turn at the wharves where other ships were already tied, loading or unloading cargo coming from or going to ports all over the world. Their sails were furled, lashed to the great arms, with icicles hanging and beginning to melt in the brilliant winter sun. The heavy salt tang in the air carried a hint of dead things washed up under the docks on the rocks, while men of every nationality and dress moved about on the unending business of the sea. Startled ship officers paused to tip their hats at the strange sight of a handsome, middle-aged woman striding on the docks, while the seamen and dockhands stopped to stare, then continue with their work while they covertly watched her come and go.

Margaret walked directly to the gangplank of the nearest ship and stopped facing a young officer who was intently studying a manifest. He raised his eyes, instantly recoiled wide-eyed, and stammered, "Uh, ma'am, uh, do you, uh . . ." He recovered enough to jerk his knitted cap from his head. "Uh, DeLoy McCallister at your service, ma'am. Is there something I can help you with?" The words were strong with a thick Irish accent.

"Are you with this ship?"

"The *Galway?* Yes, ma'am. Third mate."

"I'm looking for my son. He's close to six feet tall, slender, blue-eyed, brown hair. He may be wanting to sign on to a ship to get down to New York."

"That would not be the *Galway*, ma'am. We passed New York five days ago. We're about loaded to leave for Calais, ma'am. France. That's our next port of call."

"Have you seen a boy such as I described?"

"No, ma'am."

"Thank you." She turned to go when the young man touched her sleeve. "Uh, ma'am, might I suggest that you, uh, be aware while you're on these docks. It would not be good for a comely woman such as yourself to be hereabouts after dark, if you know what I mean." His eyes dropped and his face reddened.

Margaret smiled. "Thank you for your concern, sir."

"Not at all, ma'am." He bowed slightly at the waist as Margaret strode further north on the docks, heels clicking a determined cadence on the great, heavy, black timbers. She turned her head constantly as she walked, peering everywhere, studying the crews on the docks and on the ships, watching, waiting for anything that might lead to Caleb.

Two miles west, Brigitte slowed and stopped on the frozen, icy road at the Neck, face white from the cold, vapor billowing as she panted from her run. The Barricades were still there, but they were no longer patrolled by soldiers, either British or American. The road through the narrow passage was trampled by hundreds of feet and the hooves of countless horses and oxen, ruts cut by unnumbered carts and wagon wheels bringing farm produce to market in Boston. She leaned against one of the waist-high barricades, legs trembling, while she struggled to catch her breath.

To the west a quarter mile she saw the moving black shape of a horse and cart moving on the road in the white world. She waited as the laboring horse with long winter hair hanging from its belly approached, head rising and falling with each stride. The owner walked at the side, handling the reins and talking his horse along while a shy, spotted dog trotted at his heels, tongue lolling out. The round-shouldered, gray-bearded man squinted at Brigitte as he came into the Barricades, and pulled the horse to a stop. It stood with one hind leg cocked, moving its head, trying to understand the reason for stopping where it had never stopped before. The old man stared at Brigitte inquisitively, waiting.

"Sir, I'm looking for a young man—my brother—nearly six feet tall, slender, blue eyes, brown hair. Have you seen such a boy west of here this morning?"

He shook his head. "No. A soldier?"

"No."

"He in trouble?"

"No."

"Lost?"

Brigitte's face fell as she spoke. "Ran away."

The old man nodded. "How old?"

"Fifteen."

"I haven't seen him. Why did he run away? To join the army?"

"Maybe. We don't know."

The old man pursed his mouth in his heavy gray beard. "Might just let him go. He'll be back when he learns about war. Anyway, there are others behind me. Maybe one has seen him."

"Thank you."

He nodded and slapped the reins on the rump of the horse. Its iron shoes dug into the snow and ice as it heaved into the horse collar, and the cartload of dried corn creaked into motion. Brigitte squinted one eye to look at the sun and guessed the time as approaching eleven o'clock. She shaded her eyes with one hand to peer west at another incoming black dot nearly a mile distant, and settled in to wait.

On the east docks of Boston, Margaret picked her way through the piles of freight and the working dockhands to the plain, weathered door with the peeling black lettering, "Josiah Worley & Sons." The old brick, two-storied merchant's countinghouse stood among the many that faced the wharves and the sea beyond. Margaret drew a deep breath, turned the brass knob, and pushed into the austere office. For a moment she stood still, waiting for her eyes to adjust to the dim light.

A tall, balding clerk in a white shirt and dark vest raised his eyes, then gaped as he realized a woman had entered a man's world. His chair squeaked as he stood behind his desk. His movements were quick, his voice high and nervous.

"Yes, ma'am. What is it?"

"I'm looking for a young man. Not quite six feet tall, slender, blue-eyed. He may have been here earlier looking for passage, perhaps to New York."

"Picking crews is up to the ship captains. We don't handle that here."

"Do you have any ships leaving soon for New York, or even further down south?"

"Not New York. The British have New York shut down. The nearest friendly port to New York is Philadelphia."

"Do you have a ship going there? Philadelphia?"

"Yes. Tomorrow."

"What name?"

"The *Angela.* Tied up right now in front of the countinghouse. She'll finish loading sometime tonight and leave on the morning tides."

"What is the name of the captain, and how do I find the ship?"

"Paulo Serian. Right out the front door, second one to the left."

"Thank you." Margaret turned and reached for the doorknob when the high voice came once more.

"Relative? The boy you're looking for?"

"Son."

"The *Angela* doesn't take passengers."

"We are not looking for passage."

A knowing look crossed the man's face. "Runaway?"

"Not if I can help it."

He shrugged.

Margaret walked back into the frigid air with its smells and sounds of a busy harbor, once again aware of the stares and the slowing of work as she passed by the men. The second ship was more than one hundred yards north, and she stopped to read the name *Angela* in tall, carved letters on the bow of the large, three-masted schooner sitting low in the water, nearly loaded. The gangplank was down, and the yardarm was swinging a huge net loaded with barrels over the railing towards the black opening of the great hatch on the main deck. Sailors worked with guide ropes to hold the load stable, then position it directly above the black, gaping hole, and control it as the yardarm settled, lowering the net until it disappeared in the yawning hole.

Margaret approached the man at the end of the gangplank, who was intently counting, making marks on a sheaf of papers as seamen who were bundled against the cold moved crates and barrels up the gangplank. He raised his eyes and slowed as she stopped in front of him. She saw a controlled irritation in him at having his work interrupted by a woman.

"Ma'am. You wanted something?"

"Are you the captain of this ship?"

"No, ma'am. First mate."

"I'm looking for a young man."

"There's a lot of them around. Any special one?" He continued marking the paper, watching the sailors move the cargo on board.

"Yes. Caleb Dunson. Just under six feet tall, slender, blue eyes, brown hair. He would have been here sometime early this morning, perhaps before sunrise."

"Relative?"

"Son."

He made more marks, then spoke to one of the sailors carrying a ten-gallon barrel marked "Lime Juice" on his shoulders. "Tell the bosun I need Cap'n Serian here."

The sailor did not stop. "Aye, sir."

Five minutes later a small, wiry man in a heavy black coat, wearing a black officer's cap strode into view on the deck. He was swarthy, snapping black eyes, trimmed beard, and an aura of total control, total confidence moved with him like an invisible cloud. The loading stopped while he walked down the gangplank and eyed Margaret for a moment, then spoke to the larger man. "Mr. Orton, the bosun said you needed me."

"Yes, sir. This lady is looking for a young man who answers the description of the one we took on this morning as your cabin boy. She wishes to speak with you."

Margaret started, and Serian turned to appraise her. "I see." He turned back to Orton. "First, there is another matter. Can we be loaded and have the hatches closed by ten o'clock tonight?"

"Possible, sir."

"A storm is coming from the north. It might move inland, but I don't want to take the chance of being locked into this harbor while it blows itself out. I would like to be clear of the harbor entrance before midnight. The tides won't yet be running strong, but we can make it if we cast off about ten o'clock. Can we do it?"

"It will be close, sir."

"See to it, Mr. Orton." His voice was resonant, his words tinged with a Spanish accent, strong with the ring of authority.

"Yes, sir."

He turned to look at Margaret and bowed stiffly from the hips. "Ma'am, I am Captain Serian of the *Angela*. It is unusual that we have a visitor such as yourself. I would invite you on board but some members of the crew have superstitions about women coming aboard. Could we discuss your son over here?"

Margaret returned the bow. "Thank you, sir." She followed him twenty feet, away from the flow of sailors and cargo and they stopped, facing each other.

"I am Margaret Dunson. I am looking for my son, Caleb."

"Could you describe him."

"Young, tall, slender, blue eyes, brown hair."

"Is his older brother a navigator?"

Surprise showed in Margaret's face. "Matthew. Yes. How did you know?"

"Such a young man approached me this morning and offered to serve as my cabin boy for passage to Philadelphia. Claimed his older brother was a navigator and he wished to become the same. I accepted."

"Is he still on board?"

"Yes."

"May I see him?"

Serian raised a finger to stroke his beard as he pondered. "Is there something wrong?"

"He should be home."

"Did he run away?"

"Yes."

"You are certain you wish to have him back?"

"Yes."

"Wait here. I will bring him and you can talk."

Serian made his way back and again the sailors with sacks of fresh potatoes on their shoulders opened a way for him as he strode purposefully up the gangplank to the stern of the ship, and Margaret watched him disappear towards the captain's quarters. Five minutes later the work on deck slowed as Serian came striding back, heels clicking on the hardwood deck. Behind him, head down, Caleb followed.

They came into view and Margaret's hand flew to cover her mouth as she tensed and gasped. Orton glanced at her, then back at Serian as he descended the gangplank. Serian stepped onto the wharf and turned to wait for Caleb, who followed him to where his mother stood silent, waiting.

Margaret did not move to touch him.

Serian spoke matter-of-factly. "I presume this is your son."

"He is." Margaret looked into Caleb's eyes and spoke quietly. "Come home."

Caleb could not meet her steady gaze. "I can't."

Serian stood still, eyes narrowed as he studied the two of them.

Margaret did not take her eyes away from Caleb. "You can. We need you."

"I only make trouble."

"You didn't make the trouble. It came on its own, to all of us. We didn't make it."

"No, I don't fit anymore. Anyplace. Not home, not school. Nowhere."

"You fit at home. That's where you belong."

Caleb shook his head. "I'm going to New York."

"To join the fighting?"

"Yes. Isn't that what everyone wants me to do?"

"There's time for that later. You're not ready. Matthew was nineteen. So was Billy, and he was nearly killed. Your father had been in the war, and he was killed."

"I know all that. I'm going anyway."

"Caleb, you're throwing away everything in your life that has meaning. Can't you see that?"

"I can see that how I think only makes trouble at home."

"We can talk."

"We did that last night. It made things worse."

"Caleb, I'm begging. Come home. This family has lost enough. It will kill me if I lose you."

"I'll be all right."

Serian shifted his feet but remained silent, watching, listening intently.

"You thought that when you and Brigitte took the wagons. Only three of you got home. Don't you see what you're getting into?"

Caleb shrugged. "What difference does it make?"

"It means everything to me."

Caleb shook his head in resignation and started back towards the gangplank. Margaret took one step, then stopped, terror in her face.

Serian cleared his throat and turned towards Caleb. "Mr. Dunson, may I ask what is your age?"

Caleb stopped and turned back. "Fifteen, sir."

"Did you report that to Mr. Orton when you came to him?"

"He didn't ask."

Serian nodded. "I see. A mistake. I believe the law of the sea and this commonwealth is that unless you are sixteen you must have the written permission of your father before you go to sea. Very dangerous work. Do you have his written consent?"

"He's dead."

Serian turned to Margaret. "Ma'am, I'm sorry."

"It's all right."

He turned back to Caleb. "Then you must have the written permission of your mother or of a court. Do you have either?"

Caleb's face grew red with anger. "No. You know I don't."

Serian clasped his hands behind his back. "I could be arrested for taking you on as my cabin boy. This ship could be seized. Do you see my position?"

"I see you're sending me home."

"I am a man of my word. I took you on as my cabin boy because you showed promise. I am also obedient to the laws of my profession, and they prevent me from keeping you on." He dug coins from a purse and thumped them into Caleb's hand. "There are two shillings—a week's pay—and a lesson to me for not asking your age. As to whether or not you leave with your mother is entirely up to you. You may find other captains on these docks that will risk taking you on without the proper papers, but I will not. I wish you well."

He stood with his feet slightly spread, and turned his eyes to Margaret, probing, waiting to see if she understood. She returned his frank stare and realized he had purposely forced Caleb from his ship. Her nod was perceptible only to Serian, and he turned his eyes to Caleb's, waiting.

For ten seconds Caleb stood staring silently at the two small silver coins in the palm of his hand, not knowing what else to do. Then Margaret moved to his side and slid her arm inside his. She said nothing as she started walking, and slowly Caleb took his first steps to go with her.

Serian watched them move away and called, "Ma'am, I will leave his sailor's kit of clothing at the office of the harbormaster."

Margaret paused long enough to turn. "Give the clothing to a needy sailor." Her voice wavered and cracked as she finished. "God bless you, sir. God bless you."

In silence the two of them walked slowly, steadily back west on Ann Street, then angled southwest on Cornhill, on down to where the white picket fences and the prim white houses lined the cobblestoned streets. Their feet crunched on the snow and ice, and their faces were white from the cold as they came to the gate at the home of Dorothy Weems. They entered the yard and Margaret rapped at the door. Dorothy opened it and relief flooded as she saw Caleb.

Margaret spoke. "I can take the twins. Thank you so much."

"Oh, no," Dorothy exclaimed. "I've set out ham for supper. Please stay."

"We can't. Brigitte is down at the Neck and she's due home soon. I think it would be best for the family to be together tonight. I don't know how to thank you."

"Don't thank me. It was my blessing."

The two women bundled the twins in their winter wraps, and Trudy said her good-bye to Prissy as Margaret led them back towards the gate. The twins held a respectful silence as they walked on home, through the gate, to the front door. They waited while Margaret twisted the key, then entered and began working with their mittens and heavy coats. Margaret fed kindling to the banked coals in the fireplace and the firebox in the kitchen stove while Caleb walked to his room and closed the door.

A stark, colorless winter sunset passed, and the gray of twilight was settling over Boston when Margaret glanced at the clock. It was twenty minutes past five o'clock. She went to the front window and moved the shade to peer outside, searching for Brigitte in the street. She returned to the kitchen to finish the deep-dish beef pies when she heard the gate close. She trotted to the front door and threw it open as Brigitte stomped snow and ice from her heavy shoes.

She raised her eyes to Margaret's, holding her breath, waiting.

"He's home."

Brigitte's eyes closed as utter relief surged within, and her head dropped forward for a moment. "Oohhhh." The sound was quiet, spontaneous.

She stepped into the house and unwound her scarf from her head, then quickly unbuttoned her coat. "Where is he?"

"In his room."

Brigitte started for the archway and Margaret grasped her arm. "Give him time. Go about getting the table ready for supper. Have you been at the Neck all day?"

"Yes."

"You must be starved. We have beef pies baking. Help the children get washed for supper. They can help set the table. Act normal. I'll take his supper to him in his room. He needs time. He has to find a way to get back to us and at the same time save his male pride."

"Where did you find him?"

"Aboard a ship. Cabin boy."

"You went on the ship?"

"No. The captain brought him off." Margaret paused. "The captain was a good man. He's the one who got Caleb to come with me. I shall forever be grateful to him."

The mantel clock read half past six when they knelt beside their chairs and Brigitte said grace over supper. They ate in silence, the twins afraid to ask why Caleb's chair was empty, Brigitte and Margaret lost in their own thoughts. While the twins helped clear the table, Margaret set a beef pie, sliced bread, and a glass of milk on a tray and walked to Caleb's door. She stood in the hallway but did not knock.

"Supper's here." She waited, but there was no sound. "Caleb, are you there?"

"I'm here."

"I have your supper."

"I'm not hungry."

Her shoulders slumped. "I'll leave it by the door."

She waited for a few moments, but there was no sound. She set the tray on the floor beside the door and silently walked back to the parlor.

"Time for bed."

The twins quickly went to their rooms, relieved to be away from the tension and the mystery of where Caleb had been and why he had not come to supper but was still in his room with his beef pie growing cold in the hall. Brigitte helped them into their nightshirts and they came to Margaret's room to kneel for prayer. Margaret walked them to Prissy's room and sat them on the bed, wide-eyed, fearful.

"Caleb needs time to think about some things. You were both good today, the way we had to go and leave you at Dorothy's. And you were good tonight when you didn't ask questions. Just be normal around Caleb."

She leaned to hug them, and then tucked them into their beds, turned the lamp down, and left the door open a few inches as she walked back into the hallway. Brigitte was waiting on the sofa in the parlor and Margaret sat in her rocking chair.

"Did he take his supper?"

Margaret shook her head. "It's still in the hall."

For a time they sat in silence, each lost in her own thoughts, and then Margaret suddenly turned her head to the fireplace and sat up. "There's not enough firewood for tomorrow." She sat for a moment, then rose. "Boston would never recover if we were seen splitting kindling on the Sabbath. I'll have to do it now."

Brigitte stood. "It's freezing out there. Let me. I'll do it."

Margaret shrugged into her coat. "I'll do it. I need to do something."

It was after nine o'clock when they lighted two lanterns and Margaret walked out to the wood yard by the back door and set the lights on the stacked logs. She jerked the axe handle upward to loosen the blade from the chopping block, set the first log upright and swung hard. The axe bit deep but the wood did not split. She lifted the axe blade with the wood hanging, and slammed it down hard and the wood cracked. Two more times and it split into two pieces. She set half of it back on the chopping block and split it, then split each piece one more time, and reached for the other half of the log while Brigitte gathered and stacked the kindling sticks.

In the yellow glow of the lanterns the women hit a rhythm. By nine-thirty the stack of white sticks of split pine was growing, and they traded jobs: Brigitte swinging the axe, Margaret gathering. At nine-forty the back door opened and they both straightened to look as Caleb, dressed in his heavy work coat, closed the door.

He walked to the chopping block and without a word took the axe from Brigitte. He set the next log on the chopping block and swung the axe angrily, with a vengeance. The wood split, half on each side of the chopping block, and he reached for one half, split it, split the quarters, and Brigitte reached to gather it. He pushed her aside, then grasped the axe and set the other half of the log on the chopping block and turned his face to Margaret.

"I'll do it. You go inside."

Without a word Margaret gave Brigitte a head signal and they walked back into the house. Margaret unbuttoned her coat.

Brigitte spoke. "I want to help him."

"No. He needs to be left alone, and he needs that work. Get ready for bed." She walked down the hall to return with the tray and slip Caleb's beef pie back into the oven.

For a long time they sat in silence, listening to the muffled sounds of the axe, and then the kindling being dumped onto the stack. They said nothing, nor did they move, each deep in their own thoughts, their own fears. At eleven o'clock Brigitte went to her room, closed the door, changed into her nightshirt, blew out the lamp, and slipped between the sheets.

At midnight Margaret quietly stole to the back door and listened for a time. There was no letup in the steady sound of the axe and the stacking of the kindling. She returned to the parlor to sit in her rocking chair and began rocking gently back and forth, listening to the sounds from the wood yard. She did not remember slipping into sleep. At fifteen minutes before one o'clock she suddenly started, and turned her head to listen. The sounds of the axe and the stacking of kindling continued, and she settled for a few moments, then rose to walk to the kitchen stove. She opened the oven door and lightly tapped the top of Caleb's beef pie. It was cooling, and she gave the firebox grate a shake to revive the coals, then added two more sticks of kindling. At one fifteen she again stood at the back door, listening. She heard the axe thump into the chopping block, and then the sound of kindling being gathered and stacked, and then silence.

Quickly she set the steaming beef pie on the dining table with the milk and bread, and had barely passed through the archway to the bedroom wing when the back door opened and she heard Caleb work his feet on the mat, then walk to add kindling to the woodbox in the kitchen. He made three more trips to fill the kitchen woodbox and the fireplace woodbox before he hung his work coat on the wall peg beside the door. Margaret stood by her bedroom door in the darkness of the hall and held her breath, hoping desperately, and then she heard a chair scrape at the dining table, followed by the sounds of a spoon working with the beef pie.

She silently entered her bedroom and sat on her bed in the total blackness, listening and waiting. Fifteen minutes later she heard quiet footsteps in the hall and then silence. She waited for a time, then lighted a lantern and silently stole back to the dining table. The beef pie and glass were gone. She stepped into the kitchen, lantern held high. The dirty dishes were carefully stacked on the cupboard. She opened the back door and held the lantern over her head to peer at the wood yard. More than a cord of freshly split kindling was stacked against the back wall. She walked back to her bedroom, cupped her hand over the lantern chimney to blow it out, then slipped into bed. For a long time she lay staring into the blackness before her eyes closed and she slept.

In the gray before sunrise, a fresh pork roast with carrots and potatoes was already simmering in a pot on an arm in the great fireplace, and a custard was already set in the root cellar before Brigitte walked into the parlor with her robe wrapped tightly about her. She walked to the back door and opened it to lean out into the freezing air to look at the wood, then closed the door and turned to Margaret.

"Did you see what Caleb did last night?"

"More than a cord cut and stacked. He was up past one o'clock."

"Is he awake yet?"

"I don't know. Help me with breakfast."

At twenty minutes before ten o'clock Margaret gathered Brigitte and the twins at the front door for the required Sunday morning inspection before leaving for church. She straightened Prissy's winter bonnet and nodded approval at Adam.

Hesitantly Prissy asked. "Is Caleb coming?"

"He has some things he wants to think about. He might come later."

Adam narrowed his eyes in doubt. "What things?"

"Young man things." She opened the door and Brigitte led the twins out into a gray, overcast world with a heavy breeze moving storm clouds to the west. Margaret remembered Captain Paolo Serian's remarks to First Mate Orton—a northeaster coming—might move inland—and she wondered if his ship had made it clear of Boston Harbor before the wind set in. For his sake she hoped he had succeeded.

Brigitte led them north to the church, up the brick walkway with the snow shoveled to either side, into the chill air inside the old building. Without sunlight, the high, stained-glass windows were dull, and the heavy overcast outside provided little light inside the church. The Dunson's took their usual bench and waited in the gloom. At ten o'clock Reverend Silas Olmsted, sparse, hawk-nosed, round-shouldered, entered from the door behind the pulpit and took his place. His black robe somehow seemed too large and hung too loosely from his pinched shoulders.

Olmsted's high, nasal voice reached out over the congregation. "We shall sing from page four of the hymnal."

Brigitte lifted the worn hymnal from its pocket in the bench ahead and opened it and they sang, Margaret joining in without thought as she worked with growing apprehension of what Caleb was doing at home. Silas's sermon was lost on her as she struggled to rise above her worst fears that Caleb would be gone when they reached home. She rose with Sila's "Amen" still echoing in the high ceiling and was out the door and in the breeze and overcast walking rapidly down the street, the twins following at a trot, Brigitte behind. She pushed through the gate without slowing, then the front door and breathed with relief at the sounds of Caleb in the kitchen.

At half past one, Margaret turned to Brigitte. "Tell the children to come to dinner." They had knelt at their chairs to say grace when they heard the quiet steps in the hallway and Caleb entered to kneel beside his chair and bow his head. Dinner was quiet, subdued, with only brief exchanges of conversation that were conspicuous in their avoidance of the single question that filled the thoughts, the hearts of everyone at the table: What's happening with Caleb?

A knock came at the door while Brigitte was washing, Margaret drying the dishes in the kitchen. Adam trotted to the door. Margaret glanced at Brigitte in surprise, then laid the towel on the cupboard and walked to the door as Adam swung it open. She slowed slightly at the sight of Reverend Olmsted standing in the door frame, hat in his hand, his heavy winter coat reaching nearly to his shoe tops.

"Reverend Olmsted," she exclaimed. "What a surprise. Do come in from the cold."

"Thank you." He stepped inside and Adam closed the door.

"Can I get you some dinner? We still have some warm pork roast."

"Thank you, Margaret, but I do not intend to stay. I've come to see Caleb. Is he home?"

For a moment Margaret stared. "Caleb? Yes, he's home. Is something wrong?"

Olmsted pursed his mouth. "I don't know. I noticed he was not with you in church today. Is he ill?"

"No."

"May I speak with him for a moment?"

Margaret nodded. Two minutes later she returned from the hallway with Caleb following. Silas studied him as he approached, searching for an impression, a feeling, and it came.

He did not waste words. "Caleb, could you come visit me at the church?"

With narrowed, accusing eyes Caleb glanced at Margaret, and she looked steadily back at him.

Silas continued. "Your mother didn't know about this."

Caleb stood silently while a sense of defensive withdrawal crept into his eyes.

Silas smiled as though nothing were happening. "In half an hour? Would that be all right?"

The wind had died and deep dusk had settled before Caleb walked out the door, buttoning his heavy winter coat as he pushed through the gate. Lights came on dull behind drawn shades as he walked east towards the church, shoes crunching the frozen ice and snow. He walked to the rear of the church and rapped on the door of the entrance to the living quarters of Silas and Mattie Olmsted. Minutes later he was seated in the small, square, spartan room, yellow in the light of two lamps, where Silas conducted much of his private counseling. He came directly to it.

"Thank you for coming. You missed church with your family this morning. You aren't sick. Is something happening?"

Caleb shrugged but did not raise his eyes. "No."

"You're getting on with your mother? Family?"

Caleb hesitated. "Well, yes."

Silas saw the opening. "What's the trouble at home?"

For the first time Caleb's eyes came to Silas's. "What trouble?"

"I'm asking you. You aren't getting along with your mother. Why?"

"She told you that?"

"She hasn't said a word."

"How did you know?"

"You told me. What's wrong?"

Caleb straightened. "I told you?"

"Yes. That's unimportant. Caleb, come to it. What's wrong?"

"Nothing. We argued. It was nothing."

"Argued about what?"

"The war."

Silas paused to peer intently at Caleb's face, at the discolored place by his right eye. "How did you get hurt?"

Caleb's hand darted to touch his cheek. "At school."

"How at school?"

"A fight."

"The war?"

"Yes."

"Tell me about your argument with your mother about the war."

Caleb took a deep breath and his resentment surged. He released the breath and spoke, too loud, too high. "Mother thinks this war is something holy—God's war. I don't. My father's dead. My brother's gone and we don't know if we'll ever see him again. Billy's gone. Brigitte and I tried to do something good and we got eleven people killed. Nearly killed us. Our army got beaten so bad at New York that they're hiding clear over in Pennsylvania." He was gesturing, then pointing an accusing finger at Silas. "God's war? Where was He when all this was happening? If this is His war, then how come we're the ones getting killed and beaten?"

Silas sat unmoving, waiting, while Caleb stopped and lowered his hand. Then he spoke quietly. "Anything else?"

"Yes. Mother and Brigitte are working themselves to death to keep the family, and I'm working at the printer's helping with his newspaper when I can. How come? Mother and Brigitte never did anything wrong to anyone."

Silas looked into Caleb's eyes and waited for the hot anger, the passion to dwindle, and then Caleb dropped his eyes, embarrassed. Silas quietly began to rub his hands together, studying them, sorting out his thoughts in silence, waiting for something to tell him what to say. Caleb waited in the quiet, and finally shifted his feet.

Silas raised his eyes to Caleb's. "I don't think I can answer your questions, Caleb."

Caleb reared back in his chair, wide-eyed with surprise.

Silas paused for a moment and then continued to speak softly, thoughtfully. "I've had a question like that one for thirty years. I prayed about it every day, every night. I never got an answer. I don't know why. After awhile I wept over it, nearly every day."

His lip quivered and he closed his mouth hard and sat for a time, staring at his hands while he struggled to hold back tears.

"I didn't think I was asking too much. If He couldn't grant my prayer, I thought at least He could let me know why. But He didn't." Silas paused and his voice quivered as he finished. "I'm old now. I'll be gone soon. Then I'll know why He didn't answer."

Caleb saw the muscles in Silas's old, weathered jaw flex as he worked with his emotions. He had never supposed this little old bent man who had been his reverend since the day Caleb had been born ever had a human emotion. That he would share such a thing was beyond Caleb's wildest imaginings. He yearned to know, to blurt out the single question—"What did you ask of God?"—but he could not. He sat silent, eyes pleading to know.

Silas looked him in the eye. "I asked God for children. More than anything in this world, Mattie and I wanted children—our own family. She knitted little things for years. I built a cradle. It's all stored and maybe someday someone else will get to use those things. I watched the light in her eyes die one day at a time for twenty-five years, and then she was too old. I still pray about it. In the Old Testament God gave Isaac to Abraham and Sarah when they were old. He can still do that for Mattie and me if He will. Or maybe he will find a child from someone else that Mattie and I can raise. He can do it, you know."

Again he paused for a time, then raised his eyes back to Caleb. "Was I asking too much? Having children?"

Caleb looked into the pale blue eyes and he saw the deep yearning and he felt the unanswered question that this little man had held silently in his own heart for thirty years: *Why has God denied me and my Mattie the one thing we wanted most in this mortal life? Children!* Caleb saw the old eyes begin to glisten and Silas raised a hand to wipe the single tear that started down his cheek. Silas did not try to hide it, nor did he apologize. He sat in silence, waiting for Caleb's answer to his question.

Caleb tried to speak, but could not. He choked and swallowed hard, and once again raised his eyes to Silas's face and tried to speak, but could not get the words out. Finally he cleared his throat and shook his head.

Silas sighed and dropped his eyes to study his hands for a time before he spoke, quietly. "I don't know why God wouldn't send us children. And I don't know why He has refused to let us know why. I know I will go on praying for the answer as long as I'm alive, and I know that if He doesn't answer, I'll learn the reason when I'm gone. Then I'll understand, and it will be all right."

He stopped, and a strange spirit crept into the room. Caleb felt the hair on the back of his neck rise as he sat there, and for a long time neither man spoke or moved while the spirit possessed them, and then it faded and was gone, and once more Silas looked at Caleb and spoke softly.

"I can't answer your question about where God was when your father was killed, or why your family has been separated. I can't even answer the single question that means more than anything else to me. I wish I could, but I can't. I only know that I will not quit praying about it as long as I live."

It was over. The old man stood, and then Caleb stood, and they faced each other in silence for several moments before Silas opened the door.

"I will tell no one what we've said, not even your mother. You can tell her what you think best. I wish I could be of more help, but I can't."

Suddenly, impulsively, Caleb thrust out his hand, and the gnarled old hand reached to seize it. For a moment the two faced each other, aware that their time together had brought forth something rare, precious. They both knew it would be locked in their hearts forever, to be brought out in quiet moments to be remembered and pondered, and that neither would ever speak of it again to anyone, or to each other.

The old man stood in the yellow light of the doorway while Caleb raised the collar on his heavy coat against the cold and walked away. The snow crunched under his feet as he turned the corner and started west towards home. He glanced upward, and there was no light, no moon, no stars. The heavens were still sealed away by a thick, chill, heavy overcast.

CHAPTER XI

★ ★ ★

*G*eneral William Howe faced himself before the full-length mirror in his second-floor bedroom of the Jacobson mansion and raised his chin to work patiently at finishing the knot in his cravat. Tall, slender, he paused to turn slightly while he studied himself, judging whether his apparel would draw the desired side-glances and guarded remarks at the great banquet and ball to convene at nine o'clock in the grand ballroom of the huge Murdock mansion in northwest New York City.

It was not by chance that he had ordered the British army into winter quarters December fourteenth and arrived in New York City December eighteenth at the height of the winter social season, when the rich and powerful filled the calendar with social events each more grand than the last. The day following his arrival, the Americans loyal to the Crown had hand-delivered a beautifully scrolled invitation to him to lead the grand march for the gala event of the socialite season at the Murdock mansion. The following day he had ordered Joshua Loring out of town to inspect American prisoners in New Jersey, and then arranged for Loring's wife, Elizabeth, the beautiful, blond, charming social butterfly, to attend the grand ball as his consort. After all, the appointment of Joshua Loring to the undemanding position of British commissary of prisoners, and the providing of an extremely lucrative stipend for his services had not been a result of Loring's competence or skills, but rather to accommodate the fancy that Howe had taken to Loring's vivacious wife. Joshua loved his power and purse, Elizabeth loved her meteoric rise to the top of New York society, and Howe loved Elizabeth; happy with the arrangement, they turned a deaf ear to the expressions of shock and outrage that rumbled through the city. Howe had humbly, graciously accepted the invitation to preside at the fete and sought the services of the finest tailor in New York to create appropriate attire.

The tailor had fawned over him for an hour, spent another hour taking measurements, then proposed that a gown be created for Mrs. Loring appropriate to the elegant suit the general was to wear: a shirt of the finest snowy-white linen with lace at the cuffs and cascading down his chest, silk vest trimmed in gold, white velvet breeches, silk stockings to match the vest and which fastened below the knee with gold closures, and white ballroom slippers edged in gold. The coat was of sky-blue velvet, long tails, gold at the broad lapels and four-inch cuffs. Elizabeth's gown was of the same luxurious sky-blue velvet, white lace and gold at the throat and cuffs.

Howe again proudly surveyed his attire. His usually saturnine expression cracked as a smile of approval flickered. In his mind he was seeing himself and Elizabeth together, suit and gown matching, him dark, her blond, the two of them the utter envy of every woman and the disgust of every man in attendance. For a moment he visualized how stunning it would be with the crimson sash of knighthood beneath the velvet coat once the king had formally tapped him on each shoulder with the sword to make him a knight of the realm, as the king had promised. It was a pity it had not happened earlier; it would have electrified everyone in the ballroom. He turned to the lightly powdered wig on the dresser and sobered. His dislike for the wig was the price he had to pay for the pleasures he anticipated. He would wait for his aide to assist in fixing it on his head.

A rap came sharp at the door and Howe flinched, then glanced at the clock on the ornately carved mantel above the great stone fireplace. Five minutes before eight o'clock. A flicker of concern crossed his face as he called, "What is it?"

The voice of his aide came through the door, and Howe could not miss the man's distress. "Sir, there is a lieutenant downstairs who insists that he see you."

Howe's forehead creased in puzzlement. "Lieutenant who?"

"Jacob Baum. From the command of Colonel Johann Gottlieb Rall at Trenton. Sent here by General Grant at Brunswick, sir."

"*What?*" Howe exclaimed. He strode to the door and jerked it open. His aide recoiled one step back, fearful, waiting for Howe's anger. Howe's voice was loud, demanding. "There's a German officer here from Trenton? At eight o'clock on a Saturday night?"

"Yes, sir."

Howe was incredulous. "For what?"

"He has not said, sir. He says he has an urgent message and insists on talking to you."

"Get the message and bring it here."

"It is not written, sir."

"Then he'll have to wait. I have important matters in one hour. Billet him for the night and I'll see him in the morning." Howe started to close the door and his aide took one step forward.

"Sir, might I suggest you see him. He says he has slept only four hours since December twenty-sixth. He's ridden two horses half to death on orders of General Grant to deliver a critically urgent message."

"All right, all right! I'll be down in a few minutes."

Howe slammed the door closed and turned and stopped, his mind leaping with the possibilities of what catastrophe would drive General Grant to send a man from Trenton to New York in two days to deliver a message on the eve of the most glittering social event of the season. He began to shrug out of his velvet coat, stopped, reconsidered, and walked back to the door. He was not going through the tedious labor of changing out of his ballroom attire into his uniform, then immediately change back, simply to satisfy protocol before a German lieutenant. He strode down the hall and stairs, his ballroom slippers quiet on the hardwood floors.

His aide met him. "In the library, sir."

Howe pushed through the French glass doors, sensing the faint aroma of sweet pipe tobacco that lingered in the library, aware of the walnut shelves that lined the walls, filled with books from every civilized country in the world. Lieutenant Jacob Baum stood in the center of the room before the massive mahogany desk. He gaped for a moment at Howe's dress, then came to attention.

Howe stopped in his tracks, shocked. Lieutenant Baum's greatcoat was smeared with dirt and blood, filthy, torn, his boots caked with mud. His high, pointed Hessian hat was gone and he held a dirty, ragged scarf in his hand that he had wrapped about his head to keep from freezing. He had not shaved for three days and his face was covered with grime, nose running from coming out of the freezing cold into the heat. He was fatigued, beaten in both body and soul, eyes dead, flat, and he was not steady on his feet as he waited for General Howe to speak.

"Lieutenant, I am General Howe. I am told you have a 'critically urgent message' for me."

A strong German accent tinged Baum's English. "I have a message from Herr General Grant at Brunswick, sir. With the General's permission may I ask to be seated?"

Howe carried a plain wooden chair from the corner and placed it facing his desk next to the expensive, upholstered one, then walked to a small table in the corner for a crystal decanter of whiskey and a matching goblet. He filled the goblet and set it before Baum, then set the flask down and took his place in the great chair behind the desk. Baum raised the goblet and drank deeply.

"Thank you, sir. I am to report to you that the Americans have taken Trenton. The entire garrison is gone."

Howe's mouth fell open for a split second and he jerked forward in his chair, eyes narrowed in utter disbelief. "*What?*"

"Two days ago. In the morning the day after Christmas. There was a storm and they came from the west. They had cannon at the ends of the streets and the American soldiers came into the streets and they drove the garrison out into the field and the orchard on the east. The entire garrison was killed or captured, except for a few of us who escaped."

Howe's face turned pasty-white. He sat without moving for several seconds while his mind reeled, groping. "The Americans now hold Trenton?"

"Yes, sir."

"How many of them?"

"I do not know. Many. Perhaps five or six thousand. They came so fast I did not have time to gauge their numbers."

"Is Colonel Rall captured? His officers?"

"I think Colonel Rall is dead. I saw him hit once and then I ran with my own regiment down to the Assunpink Creek where most of us were captured. I know Major von Dechow is probably dead, along with four other officers. Two other officers and I and about fifty soldiers got into the water and we waded upstream for a distance and then got out and went further east before we turned towards Princeton. Some of us escaped but some were too weak and did not."

"You reported this in Princeton?"

"To General Leslie. He sent me on to Brunswick to tell General Grant. He sent me on to report it to you, because I could speak a little English. I slept four hours yesterday in a barn because I could go no further. I changed horses once. I have eaten almost nothing since the morning of December twenty-sixth."

Howe's eyes narrowed and he leaned forward, focused, intense. "Do you know who the American commander was?"

"No, sir."

"General Washington?"

"I never saw. All I know is the terrible storm was in our faces and there were cannon shooting and American soldiers with muskets and bayonets everywhere."

"Where did they cross the river? How?"

"I only know they did not cross at Trenton. They came in from the west, so they must have crossed somewhere up the river."

"Coryell's Ferry? McKonkey's Ferry?"

"I do not know. They came down both the River Road and the Pennington Road and into both ends of town at the same time."

"How long did the battle last?"

Baum dropped his eyes to consider. "I estimate about one and one-half hours. Maybe less."

Howe jerked erect. "They took Trenton from Rall in an hour and a half?"

Baum raised pained eyes. "I estimate that is true. Yes."

"Did Colonel Rall try to escape across the Assunpink bridge and go on down to Bordentown for help?"

"No, sir. They had cannon down there and a strong force of foot soldiers. I saw them myself. It was impossible."

"Do you know where the Americans are now? Are they coming towards Princeton? Brunswick?"

"I do not know. I was not allowed to rest at Princeton or Brunswick. I have ridden for two days to get here."

"Is there anyone else who can confirm this report?"

"At Princeton. Three or four of us reached Princeton. I am the only one they sent on to report to you."

By force of will Howe slowed his fragmented, racing thoughts. He leaned back in the great chair and stared unseeing as his thinking clarified and the decisions began to form. Moments passed in silence before he rose, strode to the door, and opened it to call down the hall to his aide, "Captain MacKenzie!"

The officer ran to the library and burst through the door. "Yes, sir."

"First, find another officer and bring him here to me as fast he can move. Then take this man to the nearest place where officers are billeted and get him hot food, a hot bath, dry clothes, and a bed. Then report back here for further orders."

"Yes, sir." The man nearly stumbled over his own feet as he pivoted and ran from the room. Instantly Howe went back to his chair and slid ink, quill, and paper into place and wrote a hurried message. He was setting his seal in the hot wax when MacKenzie returned with a captain who followed him into the library wide-eyed, half frightened.

MacKenzie announced, "This is Captain Jonas Welch, sir."

Howe did not hesitate. "Captain, General Lord Charles Cornwallis is presently quartered at Number One Broadway, down near the waterfront, and he's planning to leave for England immediately. Find him and deliver this message to him as fast as you can. Wait for his answer and bring it to me. Not one word to anyone. Do you understand?"

The captain exhaled, relieved to know he had not been ordered to appear before General Howe for some infraction. "Yes, sir."

Howe handed him the written document and the captain turned on his heel and fairly trotted from the room.

MacKenzie hesitantly asked, "Is there anything else, sir, or shall I escort Lieutenant Baum to his quarters now?"

"Go ahead, but report back as soon as you can." Howe listened to the click of the boot heels in the hallway while he took a deep breath and leaned back against the edge of the heavy desk working with his thoughts, forcing conclusions, and the beginning of a plan. *So he's on this side of the river and he took Trenton from the Hessians. My reports said his army was so weak that would be impossible.*

He shook his head in disbelief. *This will go through the colonies like wildfire! Washington will become the overnight symbol of the American cause. When this reaches Germain—Parliament—the king . . .*

He sobered, staring at the floor. *Someone will answer for this, and it is not going to be me.* He rounded his mouth for a moment and blew air.

Rall's the one. He had everything in his favor. I ordered him to build breastworks, redoubts, trenches. He's the one who will answer.

He walked around the desk to the chair, took up his quill, and began making notes. *Rall quit his post. Went on the attack, did not defend the town. Disobeyed my orders to build breastworks, redoubts, trenches. Had he obeyed me, he would not have lost his post.*

He did not mention that he himself had strung outposts clear across the state of New Jersey, from Perth Amboy to the Delaware, and down nearly to Philadelphia. He omitted that in doing so he had divided his command into units small enough to become targets for precisely what had happened at Trenton, nor did he mention that General Henry Clinton had hotly advised him against it months earlier. He folded the notes and was placing them in a desk drawer when the front door slammed and boots clattered to a stop. He rose and moved quickly down the hall.

Captain Jonas Welch, gasping for breath from the two-mile run on horseback, came to attention and thrust a paper to him. "Sir, General Cornwallis sends his answer."

Howe took the message, broke the seal and read the message twice, and spoke to Captain Welch. "That will be all. No one is to know about this."

"Yes, sir." Welch stepped back out into the freezing night and Howe returned to the library to wait. Minutes later the front door opened and he heard the aide trotting down the hall.

"Sir, Lieutenant Baum is provided for. Is there anything else?"

"Yes. General Lord Cornwallis will arrive here sometime around midnight. When he does, make him comfortable. I will return here just after midnight."

"Yes, sir. Where will you be?"

"At the ball. No sense wasting the evening entirely. Get my carriage. I'm late."

At ten minutes past nine o'clock, General Howe extended his arm to Elizabeth Loring. She laid her hand on his and with the orchestra playing grandly, side by side they led the procession down the center of the great ballroom with Mrs. Loring radiant in her new sky-blue gown. Behind them Governor Tryon and his lady held their chins high and followed. Overhead three thousand candles on three gigantic chandeliers lighted the ballroom floor, while buntings of royal blue tastefully graced the eighteen marble columns supporting the ceiling.

A little past ten o'clock General Howe became aware that too many officers were glancing his way while they spoke quietly among themselves. It was ten-forty-five when Governor Tryon casually stopped beside him at the table with the crystal punch bowl and the five hundred cut crystal cups.

Tryon poured, picked up his punch cup, and sipped for a moment before he spoke. "Have you heard?"

"Heard what?"

"The officers say soldiers arrived from Princeton. There's a rumor the Americans crossed the Delaware and took Trenton." Tryon stopped and watched Howe's eyes intently.

"I heard."

"If they did, it's the worst news we could receive."

Howe shrugged and sipped his punch. "Why? A trifle. We can retake Trenton when we wish."

Tryon shook his head. "I'm not talking about retaking Trenton. I'm talking about the fact the American army was beaten, ours for the taking. With this victory, Washington is going to become a shining star who will be able to gather an army as never before. Mark my word."

Slowly Howe set his punch cup back on the table and studied Tryon's eyes, and then he walked to the place where Elizabeth and Mrs. Tryon were talking, gesturing. They stopped as he approached and Elizabeth smiled at him expectantly. Howe bowed slightly to Mrs. Tryon.

"May I take Elizabeth away from you?"

"Of course."

Howe extended his hand and Elizabeth took it and he walked her away from the milling throng and spoke quietly. "Something has come up that requires me to leave. I'm sorry."

"Now? Leave now?" Disappointment was thick in her voice and eyes.

He shook his head. "I'm so sorry. You'll soon understand."

Little was said as the carriage worked its way to the Loring home, where the general took her to the door, bowed, said his good night, and strode quickly back to the coach. The driver raised the team of matched black geldings to a trot as he worked his way through the narrow cobblestone streets and pulled them to a halt before the portico of the Jacobson mansion at midnight. Five minutes later Howe was in his second-story bedroom changing into his uniform. At twenty minutes past midnight Captain MacKenzie strode down the hall and rapped.

"What is it?"

"General Lord Cornwallis has just arrived, sir."

"I'll be right down."

Three minutes later the men faced each other, seated on opposite sides of the large, dark desk in the library, and Cornwallis, large, round-faced, fleshy, spoke.

"My apologies, sir, for taking time, but half of my baggage was already aboard the ship bound for England when I got your message. I had to go identify it so it could be unloaded. I'm afraid the captain was not pleased."

"I'm sorry for the tremendous inconvenience to you, and the disappointment you must feel in being denied the opportunity of seeing your wife. I trust her health is improved."

"She remains ill."

Howe leaned forward. "Let me come directly to it. A German lieutenant named Jacob Baum arrived about five hours ago with a message. He had ridden for two days, with no food and only four hours sleep, on orders from General Grant at Brunswick to tell me the American army crossed the Delaware the night of December twenty-fifth and on the morning of December twenty-sixth took Trenton. They killed or captured nearly the entire German garrison."

Cornwallis froze. For ten seconds the only sound in the room was the crackling of the fire in the fireplace and then Cornwallis spoke, his voice nearly a whisper. "The Americans took Trenton from Colonel Rall? Impossible!"

"The news is in the streets right now. I heard it in the Murdock ballroom two hours ago."

Cornwallis swallowed, battling to recover from the worst shock he could remember. "What of Colonel Rall?"

"Baum thinks Rall's dead, along with Dechow and some other officers."

"Who led the Americans?" In his heart Cornwallis already knew.

"The messenger didn't know. I think it had to be General Washington himself."

"How many Americans?"

"The messenger estimates between four and five thousand."

Cornwallis shook his head. "I doubt it. Last report, he had less than half that with him at McKonkey's Ferry."

"I know. The question is, what do we do now?"

Cornwallis eased back in his chair, mind beginning to work with the facts. He began shaking his head slowly. "When this reaches England there will be a reckoning. A terrible reckoning."

Howe nodded and remained silent.

Cornwallis pursed his mouth for a time, forcing his thoughts, reaching for a conclusion. "We have no choice. We mount a force large enough to retake Trenton regardless how large Washington's forces are, and we destroy the American army." He paused and leaned forward, intense, focused. "And we do it now. Starting tonight."

Howe eased back in his chair, uncertain whether Cornwallis had just delivered him the worst insult of his military career, or was doing what he could to prevent further damage to Howe's reputation before Germain, Parliament, and the king. Or both. Howe was keenly aware of the vicious murmurings that were rampant among his own officers, accusing him of having formed a plan to use the war with America for his own gain by purposely winning a series of small victories while refusing to end it by simply crushing Washington in one all-out battle. After all, Howe had already held Washington in the palm of his hand at Long Island, Brooklyn, Manhattan Island, White Plains, and again on the banks of the Delaware, each time to dawdle and delay and refuse to end it just long enough to allow Washington and the Continental army to escape. His officers were angry, then enraged when the king rewarded Howe with the promise of knighthood! Why, they fumed, should Howe change his tactics when refusing to end the war had gained him knighthood?

However, of one thing Howe was certain. The man seated across his desk was one of the most able generals in British history, and the most beloved by the men he led, and Germain, Parliament, and the king knew it. Howe chose to pass over Cornwallis's inference that delay was no longer to be tolerated.

"I agree. I want you to take command of that operation." He waited for Cornwallis to react.

Slowly Cornwallis drew in a great breath and he felt deep pain in his heart. More than his military career, more than anything else in the world, Charles Cornwallis loved his wife, and she loved him. It had been suggested by some physicians that her failing health was the result of a heart broken by her husband's absence. When Cornwallis learned of it, he instantly requested to be relieved of his duties in America to be at her side. Nothing else in the world would have driven him to turn away from his duty to his beloved England. Seated across the desk from Howe, he bowed his head for a long time while Howe waited, barely breathing. In his heart, Cornwallis was torn between his love for his wife, and his sworn oath as a British officer to the Crown. Never had he been so torn between love and duty.

He raised his head. "I must see your maps showing the present locations and strengths of our troops, and who our officers are, and where their troops are located and who is in command."

Howe began to breathe again. Three minutes later the two men were standing, leaning over the desk, while Cornwallis traced the string of outposts with his finger, ending at Bordentown on the Delaware River. He then backtracked and tapped the map.

"How many men here, at Brunswick?"

"About a thousand."

"Who's in command?"

"General Grant."

"I thought he was at Princeton."

"He left General Leslie in charge at Princeton. He went to Brunswick to take charge personally of moving our supplies and money to other locations in case the Americans take Brunswick."

"How many men at Princeton?"

"Perhaps six thousand."

"And here, at Perth Amboy?" He tapped the map on the New Jersey coast opposite the southern shores of Staten Island, less than two hours from New York by longboat.

"I've ordered one thousand over there, prepared to march."

"Do you know where General Washington is now with his forces?"

"No. His arrival in Trenton was a total surprise. Where he has gone from there has not yet been reported." Howe paused for a moment and Cornwallis peered at him, waiting. "There is one thing that could become critically important to your planning."

Cornwallis straightened. "What is that?"

"We intercepted a letter written by General Washington himself to their 'Congress.' That letter sets out the date that the enlistments expire for nearly every soldier in the Continental army." Howe paused and the room became silent. "Midnight, December thirty-first. By morning of January first, I expect General Washington will have almost no army remaining."

Cornwallis stared in silence for a few seconds before he spoke. "Are you certain?"

"I have the letter. Would you care to read it?"

Cornwallis shook his head. "Not if you are convinced it's true."

"I believe it's true."

"Do you think the soldiers will reenlist?"

"I doubt it. I anticipate General Washington will lose most of them."

"I hope that occurs. However, I must assume I will still be facing his army as it is now."

Once again Cornwallis leaned over the table to study the maps. "I propose that I take the men here at Perth Amboy and march them to Princeton. While we're marching, send orders to General Grant in Brunswick to march his men to Princeton, and send orders to General Leslie to prepare his command in Princeton to march, while he waits for General Grant and myself to arrive. That will give us about eight thousand seasoned, fresh soldiers with three generals to march on to Trenton. I have no question that such a force can do whatever is necessary to retake Trenton and destroy Washington's rabble altogether. That accomplished, it is my conclusion we will be in a position to demand the unconditional surrender of the Americans."

"Artillery?"

"We take nearly all of it from Perth Amboy and leave only enough at Brunswick and Princeton to defend the towns in event of attack. The rest of it comes with us. When we engage General Washington, I want everything we can reasonably spare. I plan to end this war."

"When do you plan to start?"

"The minute I leave here. I'll go directly to Perth Amboy and I'll have that garrison with artillery marching for Princeton by noon tomorrow, provisioned and with their artillery. I believe we can be in Princeton with eight thousand men and our artillery within seventy-two hours and on down to engage Washington at Trenton the next day. I'll send messengers ahead advising Generals Grant and Leslie of the plan, and to be prepared."

"Washington will have scouts out. They'll know about this in time to vacate Trenton."

"Let him. We'll have scouts out too, and there is no place he can run that we cannot follow. I am convinced our army is better prepared for a winter campaign than his, and sooner or later he will have to stand and fight, or surrender. Either way, the outcome will be the same. And the terrible stigma of this Trenton disaster will be largely erased and forgotten."

Howe folded the maps and set them aside as he pulled paper, ink, and quill before his chair and sat down. He wrote thoughtfully for several minutes, sprinkled the salts to dry the ink, dumped the residue into the basket by his knee, folded the document and sealed it with hot wax impressed with his seal. He handed it to Cornwallis.

"Those written orders should provide you with whatever you need." He stood. "The German lieutenant who brought the news is billeted nearby. His name is Lieutenant Jacob Baum. If you wish to speak to him my aide can take you. Is there anything else?"

Cornwallis slipped the sealed orders inside his coat. "If you have talked with Lieutenant Baum I do not need to. May I have those maps?"

Howe quickly handed them to him. "Anything else?"

"Nothing I can think of at the moment. If something arises, I'll send a messenger."

Howe nodded and a look of interest bordering on humor crossed his face. "Do you intend going to Perth Amboy from here and rousing that command in the night?" He could not believe Cornwallis intended rousting an entire command out of their beds without notice, before four o'clock on a winter's morning.

The answer was instant and firm. "Yes. They'll be finished with morning mess by eight o'clock and marching with full provisions and artillery by noon."

"In the dead of winter?"

"In whatever weather the Almighty sends."

Howe reached to shake the thick-fingered hand. "Thank you."

"I shall keep you advised of developments." Cornwallis bowed slightly, turned on his heel and walked steadily out of the library, down the hallway, and out the front door into the frigid night air. Howe followed him to the door and stood in the rush of frigid air to watch him mount his waiting carriage. The armed escorts closed the door and the driver slapped the reins on the rumps of the four horses as the whip cracked, and the carriage lurched into motion with vapor billowing behind the horses' heads.

The carriage disappeared in the dark and Howe stood for a moment, pensive, thoughtful, listening to the clatter of horse hooves on cobblestones as the sounds faded in the night.

Had he done it right? If he had personally left New York to take command of the forces preparing to march to Trenton to destroy the Americans, would it be seen by Germain and Parliament and the king as an admission that the Trenton disaster was the result of his own unforgivable mistake? By handling it casually, sending a subordinate officer to clean up the mess, would they believe it was only a minor interruption, not worthy of the personal attention of the commanding officer? that it was one of those insignificant incidents so common to an otherwise successful campaign?

He did not know. Shivering, he stepped back inside the mansion, closed the door, and slowly made his way back to the library. For a time he sat in his chair, searching his memory, pondering.

The night of December twenty-fifth? There was a storm that night—a bad northeaster. Did Washington cross the Delaware in that storm? horses, cannon, his army? If he came into Trenton from the west, where did he cross? His army was nine miles away at McKonkey's Ferry. If that's where he crossed, he marched his men nine miles in a blizzard after they were on the New Jersey side, and he caught the Hessians by total surprise. How? How did he do it?

A strange unsettling feeling crept over him.

If that's what he did, what else is he capable of? Is it possible he will find a way to beat Cornwallis? eight thousand of our best? He shook his head. *He might have caught the Hessians by surprise, but there is no way under the sun he's going to surprise Cornwallis.*

He rose and turned off the lamps in the library and made his way upstairs to his luxurious bedroom. His aide had hung his new ballroom suit in his closet and as he hung his uniform beside it, he paused to touch the beautiful sky-blue coat.

I wonder if Elizabeth will ever forgive me.

Later, in the darkness, as the warmth of his bed settled in, he saw once again in his mind Lieuteunant Jacob Baum, professional Hessian soldier: dirty, exhausted, beaten, able to recall little more than the blasting of American cannon and American soldiers with muskets and bayonets running over the top of the Hessian garrison. The thought crept back into Howe's consciousness.

If Washington could do that with what was left of his army, could he find a way to beat Cornwallis? And if he does somehow beat Cornwallis, what will be the result?

In the darkness his eyes opened wide.

The Americans will have all they need to raise another army. And Parliament, and Germain, and the king, will have all they need to convene a hearing at Whitehall. And if they do, I will be the one standing before them.

For a long time he lay in silence before he drifted into a troubled sleep.

Notes

With the British campaign closed for the winter of 1776, General William Howe now had the luxury of enjoying the company of his favorite "lady": Mrs. Elizabeth Loring. Their affair was common knowledge, even by Joshua Loring, who had accepted Howe's promotion as commissary of prisoners with the understanding that those duties would frequently take him away from the side of his lovely wife (see Ketchum, *The Winter Soldiers*, pp. 182, 202).

Word of the Trenton defeat reached General Howe shortly after December twenty-sixth. Lieutenant Jacob Baum escaped Trenton across the Assunpink Creek and traveled almost nonstop for days as he followed orders to deliver the disastrous news to Generals Leslie, Grant, and Howe (see Ketchum, *The Winter Soldiers*, p. 268).

After Baum's report, Howe immediately sent for General Charles Cornwallis, revoking his leave to England to visit his wife, who was seriously ill, and assigned Cornwallis the command of 8,000 troops with orders to march immediately on Trenton, retake the town, and destroy Washington's army. Cornwallis set out that night, marching one thousand troops from Staten Island, through Perth Amboy on the New Jersey coast, and heading for Princeton (see Ketchum, *The Winter Soldiers*, pp. 283–84).

CHAPTER XII

★ ★ ★

*I*t's the waitin' that's hard. Knowin' they're obsessed with revenge, and comin' with more men and more guns, but not knowin' when or from where."

Sergeant Turlock paused for a moment in the bright noon sun with his smoking bowl cradled in his hands. "We stung 'em good over there at Trenton, and you can believe they got an army of men marchin' this way right now with cannon and cavalry, and only one thing in their minds. Find us and bury us. All of us."

He paused to raise the bowl of beef soup and sipped at it gingerly.

Billy Weems broke a piece from his thick slice of heavy, dark bread and dipped it in his soup, then thrust it into his mouth to chew it thoughtfully as he looked about the wood yard where half the Massachusetts Regiment were seated on logs, stacked wood, or chopping blocks with steaming soup bowls in their hands. Following breakfast they had been given thirty minutes to gather around the Reverend Alexander MacWhorter for his usual Sunday-morning sermon, and then the regiment had moved out to its assignments. Billy's company had gathered at the wood yard to swing the axes and push the saws, and now white wood chips and sawdust from the morning's work lay heaped and scattered in the snow for fifty yards in every direction. More than twenty cords of kindling wood were stacked at random in the clearing, ready for the fires that must be endlessly fed to cook and to keep men from freezing to death.

At noon, each man had received his ration of beef soup and bread, made from the cattle and flour they had seized from the Hessian stores three days earlier at Trenton, and now they sat quietly, savoring the strong, salty beef soup and the taste of solid, heavy bread. A few of them wore clothing taken from the Hessian stores, though most still wore the rags and tatters remaining from their summer clothing. With some new Hessian blankets to cover themselves at night, they had cut their old blankets into strips and wound them about their feet and legs, then tied them with cord. At least their feet were warm. With steaming soup in their hands, the men were remembering.

Two days ago, when Colonel Glover's Marblehead Regiment rammed the last of the big Durham boats into the frozen Pennsylvania bank of the Delaware and unloaded the cannon, General Washington had written an open letter to the army and required his officers to read it to their commands. In silence the men had dressed ranks and listened in surprise to the unusual warmth of Washington's words as he praised them for their "spirited and gallant" service in taking Trenton. He promised them they would share in the food, stores, and medicines they had seized from the Hessians, the most needy first, and he had kept his promise. That day they had slaughtered ten of the forty-five cattle they had brought back, and roasted them on great spits until evening. In the twilight they had cut large chunks of beef into their bowls, with bread and boiled potatoes and strong black coffee, and sat on logs near the fires. For more than an hour they had eaten in silence and sipped at their steaming coffee. They had used the last of their bread to wipe every sliver, every shred of beef and grease from their bowls, and then they had stared into the dancing flames as it settled in their stomachs, and they felt the strength working into their systems. The following morning the officers had begun handing out the blankets and clothing to those who were suffering the most. The others watched in silence, then went on with their duties. They had slaughtered more beef that day to make stew, and today they had added more beef to make thick, strong soup.

Eli wiped his bowl clean with the crust of his bread and chewed, then sipped at the last of his coffee. He set the mug in the snow beside his bowl and raised his face in the bright, frigid sun to peer south across the river, searching for moving dots on the road to Trenton that would be the British army coming with enough men and cannon to wipe the Continental army from the face of the earth.

Turlock glanced at him and raised a pointing finger. "See what I mean? It's the waitin'. Every man on this side of the river's looked down there a dozen times this morning just like you're doin', watchin', wonderin' when the redcoats are goin' to show up. Pretty soon their nerves are goin' to get bad, and then they're goin' to start wishin' the British would get here just so they could get it over with, one way or the other."

Eli said nothing and continued peering across the river.

Billy set his empty bowl down. "I wonder what the plan is. Are we just going to sit here and wait? Let them come to us?"

Turlock shook his head. "I doubt it. Too much at stake. What General Washington did at Trenton is going to shock the whole British army. Provoke 'em. They got to get him quick or run the risk of havin' this whole war take a strong turn in our favor. What that means is, Washington's done the impossible once, and he better figure a way to do it again or lose what he's gained. He better come up with another plan like the one at Trenton, and that don't include sittin' here waitin' for them to make the next move."

Billy thought for a moment. "The officers met all afternoon two days ago at Washington's headquarters. Any idea what they decided?"

"No. I been waitin', but so far no one's give any orders about a move. Like I said, the waitin's the worst of it."

Eli sensed movement to his left and turned his head as a captain wearing the green sash that identified him as an aide to General Washington strode into the clearing and his voice rang through the wood yard.

"Attention to orders. Attention to orders. The general has ordered all regiments to be prepared to cross the river tomorrow morning starting at daybreak. We're to form up on the New Jersey bank ready to march to Trenton."

Dead silence held for two seconds before talk erupted from soldiers all over the wood yard and into the great encampment in the woods, down to the riverbank.

Turlock shook his head and turned to Billy. "There she is. The general's plan. We're goin' back across to finish what we started."

Billy started to answer, then stopped and rose to his feet as the captain with the green sash came striding and slowed to a stop. He eyed Eli and his wolf skin coat for a moment before he spoke.

"You must be Stroud. Eli Stroud."

Eli came to his feet. "I'm Stroud."

"General Washington wants you at his headquarters as soon as you can get there. You and Billy Weems." He turned to Billy. "Are you Weems?"

"Yes, sir."

"You two know where his headquarters are?"

"Over in the clearing?"

"Yes. The Keith house."

"We'll be right there."

The officer nodded and handed a paper to Billy. "Here's a pass. Show it to the guard on duty at headquarters." He turned on his heel and was soon lost in the mix of men as they stood and worked with stiff muscles for a moment before they once again picked up their axes and crosscut saws.

Billy put the paper inside his coat and looked at Eli. "Wonder what it is this time?"

Turlock interrupted. "That doesn't take much of a guess. He needs to know where the British are comin' from and how many, and to get that he needs scouts. You two are it."

Eli shrugged, then reached for his rifle. Billy scooped up his musket, then spoke. "We'll be back when we can."

Turlock pulled a sour expression. "Take yer time, take yer time. Cuttin' this wood's so much fun I'll likely get resentful if you get back too soon."

Eli picked a path already formed in the snow and Billy fell in behind as they moved silently west towards the large, stately Keith house, five hundred yards west where Washington had established his headquarters. They walked in silence, each pondering what the general had in store for them. They approached the back entrance and stopped as the picket challenged them, eyes narrowed as he studied Eli's coat.

Billy replied. "I'm Corporal Billy Weems and this is Scout Eli Stroud. An officer ordered us to report here to General Washington. Here's the pass he gave us."

The picket read the document, nodded, handed it back to Billy, and opened the door. They entered a room, cold and unheated, with wall pegs for winter wraps, and the picket gave orders.

"Leave your weapons here and hang your coats and clear your feet of snow. I'll tell the general you're here."

They leaned their guns in the corner, Eli unbuckled his weapons belt and hung his knife and tomahawk on a peg, and they shrugged out of their coats and hung them over their weapons. They stood in the chilly room, waiting until the picket reentered and held the door while warm air from the house flooded around them.

"Follow me. The general's waiting."

The picket's boots clicked on the hardwood floor while Eli's moccasins and Billy's wrapped feet made little sound as they walked down the hall. They stopped at the first door and the picket rapped.

The familiar voice came from within. "Yes. Who is it?"

"Corporal Billy Weems and Scout Eli Stroud, as ordered, sir."

Ten seconds later the door opened and the three men faced General Washington. He was in full uniform, tall, calm, reserved. He appeared weary except for his eyes. They were alive with an inner fire. The picket stepped back as Washington spoke.

"Thank you for coming."

They entered the small private room and stood facing a square, plain desk with papers folded on one side. Washington stood on his side of the desk, picked the top paper from the stack, unfolded it, and spread it on the desktop before he raised his head and spoke. There was a sense of impatience, and he wasted no words.

"Gentlemen, I anticipate the British are moving, probably towards Trenton. Tomorrow morning we cross the river and move down to meet them. Until I know their numbers and which direction they are coming from I will not know where to place our men, or in what numbers." He gestured to the paper covering the desktop. "This is a map of the area north and west of here. Let me show you."

In that instant both Billy and Eli knew what was coming, and they felt a grab in their chests as their breathing slowed. They moved to the leading edge of the desk as Washington began.

He tapped the map. "This is Trenton." He continued to speak as he moved his finger south down the Delaware River naming the towns. "Bordentown, Bristol, Burlington." He paused before moving his finger back to a point above Trenton. "This is Princeton, ten miles northeast of Trenton. There are two main roads between the two towns. The Princeton Road, here, and to the east is the Quaker Road, here." His finger traced the two roads, each of which connected the two towns, but separated from each other to form an elliptical shape with the roads about three miles apart at the center of the ellipse.

"The Princeton Road is the better road, and I expect it is the one they will use if they come from Princeton."

He paused a moment to allow them time, then again moved his finger northeast from Princeton. "This is Brunswick." He lifted his finger and moved it due east a considerable distance. "Here is Perth Amboy, about fifty miles northeast of Princeton, on the New Jersey coast, very close to Staten Island."

"Now observe," he continued, moving his finger. "Moving from Princeton towards Trenton on the Princeton Road, Stony Brook is here, Eight Mile Run here, the road to Pennington here, Five Mile Run here, and the Shabbakonk Creek, here. There are bridges across each creek."

He shifted his finger to trace the Quaker Road. "Coming on Quaker Road, there is Stony Brook here, Assunpink Creek here, Miry Run here, and a branch of the Assunpink Creek here, all with bridges." He pointed once more. "Here, on the Quaker Road, just north of the branch of the Assunpink, about two miles from Trenton, are about five homes. The settlement is called Sandtown."

Again he paused for several seconds as both men intently studied the map. Then he asked, "Does this give you a general idea of the area?"

Billy answered, "Yes, sir. I remember some of it from when we passed through coming from Fort Lee."

Washington looked at Eli, who said, "I remember." He did not mention the names of Griggstown or Honeyman, and Washington nodded silent approval. Then Washington straightened and for a moment locked eyes with Eli, then Billy, and the two young men saw the iron determination and the need in the stoic face as Washington spoke.

"I want you men to go over there immediately and do whatever is necessary to find out where the British are coming from, and in what numbers. If you can, find out which officers are in command." He drew a breath before he continued. "And be certain to get a count of their cannon. I must know how many, and from which direction they're coming." He stopped, and for five seconds the room was locked in silence before he put the question directly before them.

"Can you do it?"

Neither man hesitated. Eli shrugged and Billy nodded. "Yes, General Washington."

"Good. I must give you a few details about what to expect over there. I have ordered Colonel Joseph Reed and a squad of Philadelphia light cavalry to ride up the Princeton Road until they make contact with the British, and then report back. General Cadwalader is on the New Jersey side of the river now. Most of his men are at Bordentown, but he has patrols out somewhere between there and Princeton. I've also sent orders to General Heath who remained north of Brunswick with a small command to stir up as much trouble as they can north of Princeton, as a distraction. General de Fermoy is going to be north of Trenton with a small command, too. I tell you all this so you'll know we have people over there and generally where they are."

Eli's eyes narrowed as he put the information in its place, and Billy nodded his understanding.

"Now perhaps you'll understand what I am about to tell you. You will have to use your own best judgment as to where you go and what you do, bearing in mind that I am depending on you to get critical information back to me as quickly as possible about the British numbers, artillery, and their officers as best you can. That's why I'm sending two of you. If in your judgment you run into something that is critical, one can return instantly while the other continues with your assignment."

Both men remained silent, aware of the unspoken reason

Washington was sending both of them. If either of them were killed, the other could continue. They accepted it and moved on.

"I cannot be more specific because I lack the information I need to do so. Do you have any questions?"

Eli asked, "Who is General de Fermoy?"

"A French general approved by the Continental Congress. He was with us at Trenton."

Billy spoke. "May we take a telescope, General?"

"Yes. I'll get one for you before you leave."

Eli gestured at the map. "Do you have a copy of that?"

"No. I'm sorry."

Eli shrugged. "Will it make any difference if we're seen over there?"

"No. We'll have several patrols over there and so will they."

Billy asked, "Is there any reason we should not shoot if we have to?"

"None. I anticipate there will be skirmishes that will get worse until the heavy battle begins."

Eli asked, "When should we be back here?"

"No later than dark on January first. But within the next two days I would like a report on what you've learned. One of you can bring it back, or send it back with one of the other American patrols you might find coming this way."

Billy leaned over the map to point at the coastal town of Perth Amboy, fifty miles to the northeast. "Do you expect British troops to be coming from here?"

Washington paused to consider the question of how much critical information to reveal to a private and a corporal. For a moment he studied the two men before him and made his decision. "Yes. Let me explain." He paused to search for words. "When we took Trenton we inflicted an unforgivable humiliation on the British, and they simply cannot let it go unavenged. I fully expect General Howe to send enough men and artillery to annihilate us altogether, and I expect them to come from every place he has troops. He has a large garrison on Staten Island, and if he sends them, they'll come through Perth Amboy. They'll probably go to Princeton first, and gather there with other British forces to march on Trenton. Right now there are no patrols out towards Perth

Amboy, and it is critical to know if the British are sending troops from there."

Billy glanced at Eli, then back at Washington. "When should we leave, sir?"

"Immediately. Go back to your camp and stop only to get enough food for a few days and some ammunition, and then go. I'll send a written order with you to have Colonel Glover get you across the river."

Once more Eli pointed at the map. "Could I take time to make a rough copy?"

"Yes."

Five minutes later Eli folded a piece of paper and stuffed it inside his shirt and waited while General Washington sat down at the desk and wrote briefly, then folded and sealed the message and handed it to Billy.

"Give that to Colonel Glover. He'll get you across the river."

Billy nodded and tucked it inside his shirt. "Anything else, sir?"

"Yes." He raised his voice to call, "Major Harrison," and ten seconds later a uniformed officer was standing ramrod stiff before his desk.

"Major, would you go immediately to my quarters and get a telescope from the desk in the corner?" Two minutes later the major handed the scarred, black leather case to General Washington.

"Thank you." The young man was on his way out when Washington handed the telescope to Billy. "You should find it to be excellent."

Billy looped the leather strap around his neck. "Thank you, sir."

Eli drew a deep breath. "Anything else?"

Washington paused to look at each man. "Yes. Good luck."

Eli nodded and Billy answered, "Thank you, sir."

The two men walked out the door and the aide led them down to the waiting room where they gathered their weapons and put on their coats, then walked out, squinting in the bright sunlight reflecting off the white snow. They stopped at the wood yard and Turlock leaned on his axe handle as they approached, and spoke above the sound of axes ringing and saws grinding.

"What's happening?"

"Looks like we'll be gone for a day or two," Billy answered.

"I figured."

Eli grinned. "Take care of things here."

Turlock shook his head and looked sour. "Anything to get out of work." The two young men started on towards their lean-to and Turlock called after them, "You two be careful, hear? I'm savin' four of them biggest logs for you to cut when you get back."

Twenty minutes later Billy handed the sealed order from General Washington to Colonel John Glover who opened it and studied it for a moment, then led them to two of his bearded sailors. Five minutes later the two sailors were thirty feet from the snow-covered banks of the Delaware, and the four men grasped the gunwales of a longboat and tipped it over, booming hollow, onto its bottom. They put their backs into it and skidded it down the slight incline onto the shore-ice of the Delaware, and drove it hard until the ice began to give beneath their feet, then they all leaped inside and rode it sliding until it broke crashing through the ice. The sailors quickly set the oarlocks into their holes and settled the big, flat-bladed oars into place and dug deep into the black water to drive the boat forward, cutting their own path through the thin ice that covered the main channel. The bow drove crunching into thicker ice as they approached the New Jersey side of the river, and Billy and Eli straddled the gunwales at the bow and kicked down hard to break through the ice on both sides while the sailors continued to stroke with the oars. Five minutes later the boat ground to a stop and Billy and Eli leaped from the bow and ran hard to thicker ice, then stopped to turn and wave at the sailors. The Marbleheaders waved back, then pushed the boat into the channel, reversed their seats, and began pulling for the Pennsylvania shore.

The wintry sun was still an hour high when the two turned southeast on the Scotch Road and set out at a trot, avoiding the ruts cut deep in the frozen mud three days earlier by the cannon carriages and wagons of the American army going to and coming from Trenton. They slowed to a walk for a half mile to catch their breath, then resumed their trot. They stared in silence as they passed the dark, deserted outpost building near the junction of the Pennington Road, remembering Lieutenant Wiederhold ordering his small command of Hessian pickets outside in the howling blizzard to form a battle line to engage the horde of charging Americans, only to break and run in a wild panic to Trenton.

They slowed again as they entered the big junction of the four roads at the north end of the town and they stopped in awe as they looked south down King Street, then Queen Street. Not one thing moved in the freezing shadows cast by a sun half-set. Litter and wreckage lay everywhere, just as it was when the battle ended. For a time they stood transfixed, staring, as scenes flashed in their minds from what now seemed to be a battle fought in a dream world in a time far past. They could see no smoke rising from any chimney in town. Open doors hung crazily on their hinges, splintered by cannonballs, and shattered windows stared like dead, accusing eyes.

Without a word the two moved on past Trenton to the orchard east of town, angled through the open field to the Assunpink Creek and followed it nearly due north for a time, then crossed on the ice where it narrowed, and angled nearly due east to the Quaker Road. They followed Quaker Road to the bridge where it crossed the branch of the Assunpink, and beneath a nearly full moon high in the freezing night, they slowed as they came to Sandtown.

One dim light showed in one house, and the two silently came in behind the largest of the two barns. Inside, they talked low to settle the two horses in their stalls, then leaned their weapons against the wall and sat down in wheat straw piled in one corner used for cattle bedding, and waited for their eyes to adjust to the darkness. They chewed dried beef and drank water from their canteens, then covered themselves with the straw and drifted into a dreamless sleep.

The sun rose on a world sparkling with a thick covering of frost and found them seven miles northeast of Sandtown traveling through open, undulating farmlands, wet to the knees from the snow and frost in the fields and woods. They stopped long enough to break a frozen biscuit on a rock and chew at it until it softened and drink from their canteens water so cold it hurt their teeth.

Eli raised a hand to shield his eyes from the rising sun as he squinted due east. "About forty more miles to Perth Amboy. Should be getting close by nightfall."

Billy nodded and glanced to the west. "Right about now Glover's putting the first boatloads ashore on the New Jersey side. That's going to be a hard crossing."

Eli's rare grin showed in his beard. "I wonder if Turlock got all that wood cut?" He sobered. "Getting across the river will be hard enough, but the worst of it is going to be getting the army to stay after they get there." He turned his eyes west and stared thoughtfully for several seconds. "Their enlistments are up tomorrow night. I don't know how much more Washigton can ask of them—how much more they can give. He's crossing the river today to get ready for the next battle. That might be a little hard if he's left there all alone to fight it."

Billy shoved the plug into the neck of his wooden canteen. "We better finish and get back."

Eli looked at him. "You and me and Washington against half the British army?" He shook his head. "Of course if Turlock stays, that would just about even things up."

Billy grinned, then became thoughtful. "I wonder what he's doing right now."

The two picked up their weapons and turned their faces into the rising sun and once again settled into the swinging, ground-eating trot, while Billy turned his head to peer once more back towards Trenton.

Twenty miles behind them, to the west, Sergeant Alvin Turlock and the Continental army stood on the frozen banks of the Delaware at McKonkey's Ferry in morning sunlight that caught the thick frost crystals to turn every tree, every bush into a great glowing jewel in the dazzling white world. Vapors billowed from the faces of the soldiers in the still, freezing air, the coldest morning they could remember since Glover brought them across so long ago. Six inches of crusted snow crunched beneath their frozen feet, and the horses threw their heads and moved their legs, nervous, sensing what was coming. Wood smoke from a hundred cook fires rose three hundred feet into the still air, straight as a string.

Glover's fishermen had skidded the fifty-two great, dark Durham boats from the frozen banks onto the river-ice in the gray before dawn and broken them through to the water. Washington had ordered a

Delaware regiment to board first, and with the first arc of the sun throwing long shadows to the west, the Marblehead fisherman shoved off the Pennsylvania shore and heaved into the long poles, driving the boats, loaded and riding low in the water, for the New Jersey shore, five hundred yards distant. The muted sound of released breath came from those waiting their turn on the Pennsylvania side when the big boats thumped into the inclined bank on the New Jersey side and soldiers jumped over the gunwales onto the snow, grasping the stiff, frozen hawsers to hold the boats steady. They unloaded quickly and the officers shouted their companies into rank and file to prepare for the march south on the River Road to Trenton, while Glover's men poled the boats back into the wisps of steam rising from the open channel to return for the next load.

"Massachusetts Regiment next," came the shouted order, and twenty minutes later Turlock was crouched in one of the huge boats, watching the Marbleheaders settle into their rhythm with the long poles, listening to the ice chunks slam jolting into the side of the boat as it moved steadily across the black water. To the north, General Washington and more than twenty of the officers were in another boat, and the three boats north of them carried their saddled horses, blindfolded, heads lowered, legs spraddled out to take the roll of the boat and the shock of the ice chunks plowing into the side.

The boat thumped into the New Jersey riverbank and Turlock leaped ashore to grasp one of the heavy hawsers and back up, holding it taut as other men did the same, and they held firm as the boat rose in the water until it was empty. Turlock quickly coiled the rope and cast it back to the waiting Marbleheader as others set their poles and pushed off. He stopped to peer upriver where General Washington and his officers were waiting to finish unloading their mounts. Downriver, the Delaware Regiment had landed first and was already in rank and file, waiting for marching orders.

"Massachusetts Regiment, fall into rank and file!" The order echoed along the riverbank and into the woods as Turlock looked for his officers and followed their point to take his position at the left end of the leading rank and wait for the others to form on him. While the soldiers worked into their proper places, Turlock came to attention as General Washington cantered his tall, bay gelding past, tossing its head, wanting to run in the cold. Behind came a dozen officers, each holding their horses in as they followed Washington down past the Delaware Regiment. Washington paused at the head of the regiment long enough to give orders to the officers, and within two minutes the Delaware column was moving down the River Road towards Trenton.

Washington reined his horse around and spurred back and Turlock watched him pull the horse to a stop facing the officers of the Massachusetts column. He could not hear the orders, but within ten minutes the column was moving south in the tracks of the Delaware Regiment. The men were glancing north and east from time to time, watching for the first flash of red in the brilliant sunlight that would signal the arrival of the British regulars. Every man in the army knew they were coming; the single unanswered question that hung over them was, *when?*

An hour later they passed the tiny hamlet of Birmingham, and forty minutes later the road turned slightly to run parallel with the river, thirty yards to their right. With the sun climbing to its apex they stared as they passed the Hermitage, the vacant home of Philemon Dickinson where Hessian Lieutenant Grothausen and his small command of pickets had fled in terror four days earlier after General Sullivan's command had suddenly materialized out of the raging blizzard and the cannonballs had come whistling from across the river.

It was shortly past noon when they marched past the Old Barracks at the south end of King Street and stared north in silence at the vacant town, still strewn with the wreckage and destruction of the battle. They crossed the Assunpink on the Queen Street bridge and continued south more than a mile to stop short of where the Delaware Regiment had halted with their backs to the Delaware and a small rise in the ground before them as they faced east. Three minutes later they peered back north at the sound of incoming horses as General Washington loped his mount past them, followed by most of his general officers. Turlock paused to study them as they came.

The general rode with eyes narrowed, focused intently on something ahead. The officers riding behind looked neither left nor right as they passed the Massachusetts Regiment and pulled their horses to a stop five yards short of the first file of the Delaware Regiment and gathered about Washington. Turlock was in the first file of the Massachusetts Regiment and less than fifty feet from the cluster of officers, watching the expressions on their faces, listening to their every word. Washington spoke.

"I'm going to speak to them. Remain here."

His officers nodded and remained mounted as Washington reined his horse around and trotted twenty yards further south, brought it to a halt, and turned. He was facing the Delaware Regiment, their backs still towards the Delaware, his back towards the slight ridge. The big bay mount stood in six inches of snow in the still, freezing midday air, vapor rising from its muzzle and wisps of steam from its hide. Washington was tall, dark in his winter cape as he studied the bearded, expectant faces of the men in the ranks. He began to speak and a strange hush fell; Turlock leaned slightly forward on his musket, watching, listening intently as the usually quiet voice was raised to reach every man in the Delaware company.

"My countrymen, it is my great privilege to pay to you that praise and tribute which you have so abundantly earned, both from myself as your commanding officer, and from your country. The service you rendered four days ago in the battle at Trenton was a great tribute to your courage and your dedication to your country. News of your victory is reaching out to cities and people both here and abroad. Those who would rob us of our liberty will know that your dedication is undimmed. Your fellow countrymen will rise to new heights of support for the cause."

He paused and for a moment he stared at the ground, searching for words.

"I frankly confess my inability to speak with the power of Thomas Paine, but I do know that you are the soldiers of whom he wrote. You are not the summer soldiers who shrink in the trials of winter. You have so nobly suffered unbearable hardships ,and deprivations in silence, and finally have risen in impossible conditions to defeat a powerful enemy. For these things I, and your countrymen, are indebted to you forever."

Again he paused and Turlock saw him struggling to form what was coming next.

"Were it in my power, I would send you home when your enlistments expire tomorrow with my greatest blessings for yourselves and your families. But I cannot. Our victory at Trenton will surely bring the wrath of the British empire down upon us, and unless we meet them and somehow turn them, we will have lost all we have gained at such a terrible price. I put the question to you: can we allow that to happen? We cannot. For that purpose I am here before you today to beseech you to consider the opportunity that fate has now delivered into your hands. You can deliver to your country a service that may never again be within your power. As a reward, I am offering every man of you who will remain with the army for another few weeks, a bounty of ten dollars. It is little enough for what you have done and what you will yet do for your country."

He stopped and Turlock saw him ponder for a few seconds while he tried to judge if he had said enough. Then Washington reined his horse back to his right and loped it to his group of officers and stopped. Four of the officers tapped spurs to their horses and rode back to stop, facing the Delaware Regiment, and one raised his voice.

"You have heard General Washington. You know what you have done and you know what you can yet do for your country. You have heard the bounty offered for those who will remain with the Continental army for a few weeks past your enlistments."

The officer stopped and drew in a great breath and Turlock knew what was coming next. His breathing slowed and he straightened, waiting.

The officer concluded. "Each man who will remain with the army after your enlistment has expired tomorrow, step forward."

Turlock turned his head slightly to watch for movement in the ranks of the Delaware Regiment. Five seconds passed. Ten. Twenty.

Not one man moved in the awful silence.

The officer stiffened in his saddle, shocked, unable to gather his shattered thoughts. He reined his horse around and trotted back to Washington without saying a word. General Washington was less than fifty feet from Turlock as the officer reined to a stop facing him. The officer's face was white as the snow. Turlock saw the shoulders of the tall Virginian slump for one split second, and then something happened.

Washington straightened in his saddle and he squared his shoulders. He raised his face, and his jaw was set like granite. The pale blue eyes were points of light as he reined his horse around and once again rode the fifteen yards and stopped, back straight as a ramrod as he faced the men once again.

As Turlock watched, the expression on Washington's face softened. A tenderness crept into his eyes that Turlock had never seen in the eyes of any officer. The hard lines around his mouth disappeared, and his brows peaked as in one moved by seeing the deep suffering of another. He looked down into the faces of the men with a sense of understanding, of compassion that Turlock never supposed Washington possessed, and Turlock felt the hair on his arms lift, and stiffen on the back of his neck. A feeling crept into his breast like none he had ever known before and it spread silently to touch the men rank by rank. Their eyes dropped and they glanced at each other for a moment, then stared at the ground.

Washington spoke. It seemed his voice was subdued, quiet, yet it reached every man in the Delaware Regiment.

"My brave fellows, you have done all I asked you to do, and more than could be reasonably expected; but your country is at stake, your wives, your houses, and all that you hold dear. You have worn yourselves out with fatigues and hardships, but we know not how to spare you. If you will consent to stay only one month longer, you will render that service to the cause of liberty, and to your country, which you probably never can do under any other circumstances. The present is emphatically the crisis which is to decide our destiny."

He stopped. He raised a hand as though to speak further, but there were no words he could think of that would add strength to what he had already said. He slowly lowered his hand and reined his horse to the right and raised it to a trot, back towards his officers and Turlock.

Turlock did not know how long he stood without moving, without breathing, aware Washington had been touched by a power not of any man, knowing that at that moment, somehow, the course of the world's history hung in the balance. He waited and watched.

Washington reined in his horse, and the officer next in command licked dry lips, then spurred his horse out before the Delaware Regiment. He stopped, facing the ranks, and he cleared his throat before he raised his voice.

"All those who will remain after their enlistments expire, step forward."

The spirit that had gripped every man in the Delaware Regiment began to slowly recede, and then it was gone. The officer sat his horse in the dead silence, waiting. Turlock's heart rose to his throat, and he did not realize he had shouldered his musket and was preparing to stride out before the Delaware Regiment and declare himself the first volunteer, regardless of the fact he was not in the Delaware command.

Then, from the second rank, an old, bearded, hollow-eyed, hollow-cheeked veteran, dressed in rags, with blanket strips tied to his feet, shuffled forward and faced the officer. His voice was high, scratchy. "I can't go home if my country needs me."

From the first rank came another. From the second rank a young, smooth-cheeked boy stepped forward to stand beside the old veterans. Then another and another. Turlock reached to wipe at his eyes, and then glanced at Washington. The face was once again that of the rigid commander, but the eyes were too shiny. Turlock looked back at the men stepping forward and soon it was half of them, and then it was all except those who were too sick, too exhausted, too feeble, too naked to march one more mile.

General Washington waited for a few moments, then spun his horse and started back up the riverbank. He had an army to take care of, and the burden of command gave no time for him to pause to taste the sweetness of the moment. He locked it away in his heart to be retrieved in some quiet time when he could savor the rare, unforgettable moment.

In the late afternoon the officers received their orders. They were to bivouac where they were for the night. In early dusk the men had cook fires burning, and had cleared places in the snow for their blankets. They were sitting near the fires with steaming mugs of coffee and slices of warmed mutton and bread when the call came.

"Mail. Mail."

Turlock sat cross-legged near his fire, sipping his coffee, watching others walk to the rider who had come in from Philadelphia with the large canvas sack and was calling names from letters in the firelight and handing them out to eager hands. One thing he knew. There would be no mail for Sergeant Alvin Turlock.

The rider called, "Eli Stroud," and Turlock's head jerked up in surprise. Quickly he set his coffee mug to one side and rose to trot to the man.

"Stroud? You called Stroud?"

"Yes. Here." The man thrust a letter towards Turlock. "You Stroud?"

"No. He's on scout. I'm his sergeant. I'll take it."

He strode hastily back to his blanket and dropped to one knee to turn the letter towards the firelight. He read the address, and then he peered close to read the name of the sender.

Colonel Otis Purcell. Medical doctor. Northumberland Fusileers, His Majesty's Royal Army. New York City.

Turlock's forehead creased in puzzlement and he stared at the letter for a long time, pondering before he carefully slipped it inside his tattered coat.

Notes

Though General Washington had achieved a remarkable military victory in the streets of Trenton, perhaps his more personal victory came on the banks of the Delaware River December 30, 1776. Washington's officers read a prepared speech praising the "spirited and gallant" soldiers (see *The Papers of George Washington*, vol. 7, p. 448) without whom the Revolution would have faltered and died countless times over.

On December 30, 1776, fully aware his soldier's enlistments would expire at midnight the next day, General Washington delivered one of his most notable speeches to his men on the New Jersey banks of the Delaware River. His first attempt at influencing his men to remain included a promise of a ten dollar bonus to each man who would stay. General Washington knew he was not empowered by Congress to make such a promise, but he did so anyway.

Making the promise gave him great distress, since by doing so he had essentially usurped the powers of Congress to himself, a military commander. From the beginning of the Revolution, Washington had adamantly opposed ever vesting such powers in any military commander, because his personal conviction was that power over military affairs must remain in the hands of Congress and the people, not military dictators.

Washington agonized over what he had done, only to find out later that since Congress did not know when they would be able to convene again to conduct the business of the war, they vested such powers in him for a short time before they fled Philadelphia. Washington's relief at finding out he had not exceeded his congressionally granted authority was monumental. The act of Congress granting Washington such powers was a tremendous tribute to the integrity and character of Washington, since by so doing they essentially entrusted the entire war into his hands. When he discovered this fact, he immediately wrote them, advising he would never abuse the power, and would relinquish it back to Congress at the earliest opportunity, which he did. Few events portray the high principles and character of Washington as clearly as this incident, which history has largely passed over (see Ketchum, *The Winter Soldiers*, pp. 279–81, 333–34).

General Washington appealed to Robert Morris to raise money to pay the soldiers. Morris did so and, on January 1, 1777, sent Washington a canvas bag which included "410 Spanish milled dollars, 2 English crowns, 72 French crowns, 1,072 English shillings" (see Ketchum, *The Winter Soldiers*, pp. 279–80).

When the ten dollar bounty failed to rally the troops, Washington offered a second, heartfelt and personal speech, the text of which is quoted in this chapter and also appears as the epigraph of this volume (see Commager and Morris, *The Spirit of 'Seventy-Six*, pp. 519–20; Freeman, *George Washington*, vol. 4, pp. 332–33 n. 44, 45). After Washington's words, almost every able man answered the call for volunteers (see Ketchum, *The Winter Soldiers*, p. 278).

For the battle that was coming, General Washington had 1,200 veterans and 3,400 untried militia to engage General Cornwallis, who had 8,000 seasoned soldiers, some of the finest in the British army (see Ketchum, *The Winter Soldiers*, pp. 283–84).

CHAPTER XIII

★ ★ ★

*T*here!"

In deep dusk Billy dropped to one knee in the drifted snow, arm extended, pointing, voice excited, low.

Instantly Eli crouched, balanced, and his head snapped around to peer northeast along Billy's point. Across a shallow valley, more than a mile distant, pinpoint fires glowed in a long, narrow stand of oak and maple trees in the open, gently rolling farmlands of eastern New Jersey. "That has to be them," he breathed. "Can you see their flag?"

Billy fumbled with the stiff leather case and drew out the telescope General Washington had given them. He forced numb fingers to extend it, then raised it to his eye. For thirty seconds he studied the double lines of campfires strung out for more than half a mile, then concentrated on the center of the line. His eyes narrowed for a moment as the firelight caught the blue-and-white crossed lines on the red background of a flag on a pole.

"The Union Jack. British."

"How many fires?"

Billy moved the glass slowly, counting the individual points of light in the double rows. "Eighty. About eighty."

For a moment both men made mental calculations before Eli quietly spoke again. "About eight hundred soldiers? Maybe a thousand?"

"I'd guess about one thousand."

"Can you see horses? Cannon? Tents?"

Billy raised the telescope again. "I can see where they are, but I can't count them."

"Can you tell which direction they came from?"

Seconds passed while Billy studied the camp through the telescope. "No."

"If they came from the east they have to be from Perth Amboy, headed for Princeton, or maybe Brunswick." He stopped to study the fires while he worked with his thoughts. "I think they're going to join Grant and Leslie to attack Washington and retake Trenton. This is what Washington wanted to know." He settled onto one knee in the crusted snow, pondering.

Billy spoke. "We need to know how many they are, and how many cannon. And if we can, we need to find out who's in command." He stopped to gather his thoughts. "I think we need to talk to someone over there—probably an officer."

Eli nodded. "That's what I think."

Billy collapsed the telescope, returned it to its case, and rose to his feet. "Let's go."

The deep purple dusk turned to black of night as the two worked their way through the crusted snow, moving due east, then angling back north in a great circle. They stopped every three hundred yards to listen and peer into the night, searching for British pickets or patrols. Far to their right the lights of a farmhouse glowed, and on a distant rise to the north was a cluster of lights from a tiny hamlet that was not on their map. A great distance to the west a wolf pointed its nose into the starry heavens to mourn the world, and another answered the lonesome call.

The full moon had risen above the eastern horizon when Eli suddenly dropped to his haunches with a warning hand silently raised to Billy. Instantly Billy dropped and waited in the stillness, vapor rising from his face in the bitter cold. West, from their left, came a whisper of sound and then muted voices.

"Patrol," Eli hissed.

Neither man moved as they waited, balanced, ready to move hard and fast if they had to. The sounds of moving men came stronger and then they could hear the squeak of the frozen snow beneath boots as the patrol came towards them in single file, dark shapes in the faint silvery light of the moon. The patrol passed forty feet south, and neither man moved until the sounds had died. They placed their feet carefully until Billy stopped and went to both knees in the snow, hunched forward as he peered hard at the ground. Eli dropped to one knee and reached to touch the hard-crusted snow, then look east, to his right. Billy rose and in three strides was beside him.

"The tracks of the column," Eli whispered, "they came from the east."

"Perth Amboy."

Without a word they continued north until they were a quarter mile past the camp, and then turned west. Hunched low, moving slow, pausing every thirty seconds to listen, they stopped behind a thicket of scrub oak with their backs to the north, facing the center of the camp. For five minutes they studied the lay of the tents, the movement of troops, and the location of the fires. They saw the horses picketed in the trees at the west end of camp, eyes glowing wine-red in the yellow firelight.

Billy nudged Eli and whispered, "Cannon?"

Eli shook his head. "Maybe near the horses."

"How many men?"

They silently counted the tents, then made the calculations.

"One thousand," Billy whispered.

Eli nodded.

Fifty yards to their right an owl hooted, and in the quiet they heard the rush of wings. Eli raised a warning hand, and both men turned their faces away from the moonlight to remained motionless, listening. Ten seconds later a six-man patrol came plowing through the snow traveling east on the far side of the thicket, their silhouettes sharp and clear against the campfires. Neither Billy nor Eli moved until the patrol was gone.

Eli pointed west and they moved on, stopping, listening, circling south until they were at the west end of the camp, two hundred yards from two pickets stamping their feet for warmth in the bitter cold. For long moments they watched, using the telescope to gather the detail. Eli raised a hand to Billy, and Billy nodded his understanding and settled into the snow as Eli looped the telescope around his neck, hunched low, and disappeared in the darkness, moving directly towards the campfires. Minutes stretched into half an hour while Billy watched and listened, but there was no sudden shout, no gunfire. He rose and worked his legs, and a million needle points pricked them as feeling returned. He reached for his musket.

I'll give him five more minutes and then I go in after . . .

"I'm coming in." Billy jumped at the sudden whisper to his right and Eli was there, a tall, silent, dark shape in the night. Billy settled back as Eli dropped to his haunches beside him, pointing as he spoke in whispers.

"About fourteen or fifteen cannon at this end of the camp—I couldn't see them all. Just over sixty horses next to them tied on rope lines. Pickets about every hundred yards. Two officers' tents are in the middle, a big one for the commanding officer and his bunch, a smaller one beside it for the other officers. I don't think they're expecting anything."

He paused to consider. "In there right behind the officers' tents are about six horses saddled and ready to go. I expect that's so the officers can get mounted in a hurry if they have to." He paused to arrange his thoughts. "We got to get an officer and a horse."

"A horse?" Billy asked.

"Once the officer tells us what we want to know one of us has to ride back to Washington to tell him. The other one goes on up towards Princeton to look."

Billy nodded.

"I saw the pickets south of the officers' tents. They're about one hundred yards apart. When everybody's asleep, I figure I can take out two of those pickets right behind the officers' tents and get one of those saddled horses and an officer."

"How about patrols?"

"One passes there about every thirty minutes. We'll have to watch and wait."

"Let's go."

Slowly they made their way, to stop crouched in the bed of a tiny, frozen stream one hundred yards south of the officers' tents, waiting until the drum-rattle of tattoo rolled out over the frozen snow to echo off distant trees. The lamps in the tents of the enlisted men winked out, and then those in the officers' tents. The pickets allowed the campfires to burn low except for one at each end of the camp, and the big one just north of the officers' tents. For more than half an hour Billy and Eli waited, memorizing the intervals of the patrols and the pickets. When the next patrol passed between them and the officers' tents, Eli handed his rifle to Billy, Billy nodded, and Eli slipped silently out of the streambed and was gone.

Five minutes later Eli was crouched ten yards behind the picket east of the officers' tents, waiting for the man to move or make a sound. One minute later the man threw his arms about himself, pounding for warmth, and stomped his feet. He heard the rush from behind one split second before Eli reached him; he was turning when the flat of Eli's tomahawk blade struck the crown of his head and he sagged. Eli caught him and his musket as he fell, and silently laid him out full-length in the snow, musket across his chest, then crouched and waited. There was no challenge, no sound.

He moved back twenty yards towards Billy, then turned west. Five minutes later he was crouched five yards behind the second picket, waiting. Seconds ticked into minutes and the picket did not move. Silently Eli scooped up snow and fashioned a large snowball. Slowly he drew his arm back and underhanded the snowball twenty feet rattling into the frozen, bare bushes east of the picket. The man whirled and raised his musket, and in the moment of his turning Eli lunged. The startled picket recovered enough to open his mouth before Eli's tomahawk once again flashed down, and the flat of the blade slammed hard into the heavy felt hat. The picket buckled. Ten seconds later he was laid out in the snow, musket across his middle.

Eli didn't hesitate. Quickly he trotted east back to the officers' tents and slowed as he came in on the west side and worked his way to the front, where the saddled horses were tied to a rope strung between two trees. He moved in slowly, crooning low to the horses as they moved their feet and turned to face him, ears pricked, vapor rising from their nostrils. None whickered in the brittle cold as he gently caught the lead rope to the nearest horse and worked on the knot. It was wet, frozen, and he could not loosen it. In one easy movement his belt knife was in his hand and the lead rope was cut. He worked up the rope until he could touch the horse on the cheek, and he caught the bridle reins just below the bit and tugged gently. The horse, trained to obedience in battle, day or night, did not resist and slowly Eli walked it away, silent in the snow, south past the tents, into the darkness. Five minutes later he was on his haunches beside Billy.

"I'll be back," he said as he handed the lead rope to Billy. "I think the saddle girth is loose."

Billy spoke quietly to the horse as he raised the stirrup and reached for the lock ring on the saddle.

Minutes later Eli once more eased up to within ten yards of the horses. He dropped to his haunches to listen, but there was no sound except the occasional popping of a knot in the fire before the officers' tent. He lowered his face and gave the bark of a fox. It rang loud in the silence, and the horses brought their heads around, eyes glowing in the firelight, ears pricked as they searched. Again Eli uttered the bark, quick, piercing, and the horses moved their feet. Two of them blew, snorting, nervous, stuttering their feet.

A light came on inside the nearest officers' tent and muffled voices broke the silence. Then the tent flap fluttered as someone inside worked with the tie strings, and it opened. An officer stepped out, bareheaded, clad in his nightshirt, heavy overcoat and boots, and a heavy wool scarf dangling. He stepped out into the night, head turning from side to side as he peered into the night, searching for what had bothered the horses. He walked to them and spoke, trying to settle them, when he suddenly realized there were five, not six. Quickly he moved to the end of the line and reached to feel where Eli had cut the lead rope. He was turning to call to the others inside the tent when the black tomahawk arced in the firelight. Eli caught the falling officer and held him on his feet for a moment while the horses settled, then hoisted him over one shoulder and silently moved away, south.

He laid the limp officer next to Billy and spoke. "They're going to be coming in a minute. Help me get him up on the horse, and then we've got to move west fast."

They made no effort to cover their tracks in the snow as they pushed west, Billy leading the horse at a trot while Eli held the unconscious officer draped across the saddle, arms and head flopping. They had covered half a mile when they stopped to look back. All the campfires were burning brightly, but there were no points of light moving towards them in the blackness. They came to the west end of the small valley and paused at the crest of the low rise, and Billy used the telescope.

"There are two lanterns coming this way. Nearly a mile."

They settled back into their trot, and half a mile later, with the British camp and the pursuing patrol out of sight on the far side of the rise, Eli called a halt.

"We're far enough. Give me a hand with this officer."

They sat the man on the ground and Eli rubbed his face with snow, then slapped his cheeks until his eyes fluttered open. In the light of the full moon he stared at Eli, unable to understand where he was or how he got there.

Eli grasped his coat lapels and spoke. "Can you talk?"

The man nodded.

"What regiment are you with?"

"Fourth Brigade, Seventeenth Infantry." The man shook his head to clear the cobwebs and suddenly realized what was happening. He stared at the dim shape of a man hunched over him dressed in a wolf skin coat, head covered by a parka, face invisible. "Who are you?" he asked. "How did I get out here?"

Eli ignored him. "What rank?"

"Who are you?" the man demanded hotly.

Eli's hand was a blur as he swept his belt knife from its sheath and brought it to the man's throat. "We don't have much time. Answer and we won't leave you out here with your throat cut. Lie once and I'll come see you again. Now, what's your name and your rank?"

With the cold steel against his throat, the man settled. "Sturgill. Alexander Sturgill. Captain."

"From Perth Amboy?"

"Staten Island. We came through Perth Amboy."

"Headed where?"

"Princeton."

"To do what?"

"Join General Grant and General Leslie to march on Trenton."

"How many in your column? Officers and all."

"One thousand regulars, twenty-two officers."

"Who's in command?"

"Cornwallis. General Charles Cornwallis."

Eli heard Billy's sharp intake of breath.

"How many cannon?"

"Sixteen."

"Horses?"

"Sixty-eight."

"When are you to arrive in Princeton?"

"January first."

"Have they heard about what happened in Trenton four days ago?"

"Yes. Yes. That's why we're marching."

Quickly Eli jerked the scarf from around the man's neck and wrapped it once through his mouth, then down behind his back to tie his hands, and left him sitting in the snow. He drew Billy fifteen feet away and asked, "Do you believe him?"

"Yes."

"Take the horse. Go half a mile south, then turn west and ride hard for Trenton. You can make it by daybreak. Tell Washington what you heard and then head north to Princeton. South and a little east of town is a swampy place some call Bear Swamp. It's frozen now, but there's a lot of cattails and marsh grass there. Find it and I'll meet you there sometime around noon tomorrow."

"What are you going to do?"

"Drop back and slow down that British patrol that's following our tracks in the snow. Then go take a look at Princeton."

Billy hesitated. "What about the officer?"

"He'll get free in about ten minutes."

Again Billy hesitated. "If anything goes wrong, there's these letters in my coat. Would you—"

Eli cut him off. "I'll deliver them, but nothing's going to go wrong. Watch for British patrols and stay away from farm lights where the British might be sleeping."

"You do the same."

Billy vaulted into the saddle, Eli tossed his musket up to him, and Billy wheeled the horse due south. Eli waited until the sound of the trotting horse faded, then turned back and started east, directly towards the two moving lanterns just over half a mile distant. He passed the officer still tied in the snow and dropped down to wait. The tiny, dancing lights grew and then Eli could hear the crunching of the snow in the clear, freezing air, and then the labored breathing and guttural cursings of the men. He waited until the nearest lantern was less than twenty yards away, and then went to one knee to steady the long rifle.

The crack echoed for miles in the night and the big .60-caliber ball smashed the nearest lantern, shattering the glass and splattering the burning oil onto the overcoat of the man carrying it. Instantly the entire patrol dived into the snow while the man cursed and stripped off his overcoat and tromped it into the snow to kill the blaze. The other lantern went out instantly and Eli sprinted ten steps north, then stopped and jerked out his ramroad to reload.

Three seconds later the patrol fired a volley at the place they had seen the muzzle flash of Eli's rifle and Eli listened to the musket balls sing past, forty feet away. Thirty seconds later Eli fired again at the place where the musket flashes had been and heard a man grunt and then curse. Again he ran to the north and stopped.

There was no more musket fire, and no more sounds, nor did the second lantern relight. Eli reloaded and sat in the silence for a time before he backed up fifteen paces, then turned northwest and began the swinging trot towards Princeton.

Dawn broke stark and clear on a frozen world as Billy reined in the weary horse, hide steaming, breath making clouds of vapor. He stood tall in the stirrups and raised the telescope to peer west along the creekbed he had been following. In the distance he counted two houses and three barns clustered close.

Sandtown. Trenton's about two more miles.

With the sun a frigid golden ball one hour high in the east, he reined the horse down to a walk at the Continental army camp strung out for more than three miles along the south bank of the Assunpink Creek, east of the Queen Street bridge. He moved through the camp, watching for the Massachusetts Regiment, when a voice from his side came high.

"All right, you lovely, you're back. Where's Stroud?"

Billy turned towards Turlock. "Headed for Princeton. Where are General Washington's headquarters?"

Turlock pointed west. "Down there half a mile. You two get into any trouble?"

Billy shook his head. "Not much."

"Whose horse did you steal, ours or theirs?"

"Belongs to a British officer." He smiled. "He said we could take it."

"Better climb down and get some coffee. It's ready."

"No time. I got to report to the general."

"Come back when you're through."

Billy turned the horse west and five minutes later stopped in front of the big command tent of General Washington. He dismounted and the picket challenged him.

"I'm Corporal Billy Weems, here to report to General Washington on a scout."

Two minutes later he was inside the tent, standing across a plain table from General Washington who rose to meet him, intense, focused.

"Report."

"There's a column coming from Perth Amboy to Princeton to join Generals Grant and Leslie, and they intend coming here. They've heard about what we did here. One thousand men, twenty-two officers. Sixteen cannon, sixty-eight horses. They'll arrive at Princeton sometime January first."

"Who's in command?"

"General Charles Cornwallis."

Washington's eyes dropped for a moment. "How did you get this information?"

"Captured one of their officers, a captain."

"Where's Mr. Stroud?"

"Gone up to Princeton. I'm going up to meet him."

"Is he all right?"

"Yes."

Washington slowly took his chair, working with his thoughts. "General Howe knows about Trenton and has sent General Cornwallis to retake it. It appears we've provoked Howe. The remaining question is how many men has Howe committed to his plan? One thousand with Cornwallis, but how many from Grant's command, and Leslie's command? How many can we expect to arrive here, and when?"

Billy nodded. "Eli's up around Princeton trying to get some of those answers, sir."

"Good. You've done well. You'll need food and rest."

"With due respect, sir, I need to get up there and find Eli. He might need some help."

"You two work together?"

"Pretty much."

"As you wish. Do you need a horse?"

"I have a British cavalry horse outside. I'll trade him for a fresh one."

Washington looked amused. "You appropriated a British horse?"

"Yes, sir. I had to use the horse hard to get here overnight."

"I'll arrange for the trade."

"Thank you, sir."

Washington worked with pen and quill for a moment, then walked to the door and called an aide.

"Take Corporal Weems to Major Summers and arrange for a fresh saddle mount." He handed the paper to the aide and turned back to Billy. "Thank you for your report. I trust I will receive further information as it beomes available."

"Yes, sir."

Billy followed the young aide back into the bright sunlight, gathered the reins to the jaded horse and walked with him fifty yards west to where the horses were held in a rope pen. Mounted, Billy headed east riding a fresh, big-boned, brown gelding through the camp, noticing for the first time that some of the men were rolling their small gathering of worldly possessions into their blankets and tying both ends. He came to Turlock's fire and Turlock rose and walked to meet him with a mug of steaming coffee in each hand. Billy dismounted and followed him back to the fire, where they both stood near the warmth and worked at their coffee.

"Some of the troops are leaving?"

"Yep. Mostly the ones that can't go farther." He sipped at his coffee. "It got testy yesterday. Washington himself talked to the Delaware Regiment. At first not one of them was going to stay, so he talked to them again." Turlock's face became thoughtful. "I never heard him talk like that—never knew he could."

Billy lowered his coffee mug. "What did he say?"

"It wasn't so much what he said, it's where it come from. Right out of his heart. He told them this army, right here, right now, has a chance to do something for this country and liberty that we won't have the chance to do ever again, and we better think that over before we fail." Turlock turned his face to Billy. "I never before saw anything like the look in his eyes that was there when he spoke."

"What happened?"

"One old soldier stepped out and then another one and then a boy, and pretty soon everybody who could walk was out there with him. The other regiments seen it and it wasn't any trouble at all when it came their turn. Somethin' a man won't never forget."

"How many finally stayed?"

"Don't know. We got more comin', though. Cadwalader, Arnold, Mifflin, and maybe some others. We lost most of Glover's command."

Billy gaped. "Glover left? Why?"

Turlock shrugged. "Depends on who you listen to. Some say his wife was ailing and he wanted to be near her. More people are saying he wanted to go privateering. I know he talked with Washington, but I don't know what they said. Whatever his reasons, he's gone."

Billy's coffee was cooling as he sipped at it. "I got to go meet Eli up north near Princeton. I better get going."

"You two run into any British last night?"

"Yes. They were coming from Perth Amboy to Princeton."

"How many?"

"One thousand."

"Who's in command?" He held his coffee cup poised, waiting.

"Cornwallis."

Turlock's eyes widened and he rounded his lips and blew air. "The best they got. If he joins up with the troops in Princeton and Brunswick he'll have enough to make real trouble." He glanced at the Delaware River behind them. "If they catch us here, it'll all be over quick."

"Washington plans to stay here?"

"Don't know. Didn't say. But if he does, the only thing we got in our favor is that little ridge to the north. If they cross the Assunpink further up the north and come down with troops on our right, and then come over the top of that rise, we're trapped. We got the river out there behind us, but with the big boats still up there at McKonkey's Ferry we can't get out."

Billy studied the rise to the north, then the Assunpink and the single bridge crossing to the left, then the open country to the right, and he felt a rise of concern. "I doubt Washington intends staying here."

Turlock shrugged. "We'll see."

Billy handed him the empty coffee mug and gathered the reins to his horse. "The coffee was good."

"Hadn't you better sleep for an hour or two?"

"I'm all right. Eli might need help."

"Got anything to eat?"

"Yes. In my coat."

"You two be careful."

Billy nodded and swung onto his horse when Turlock raised a hand to stop him, then dug inside his coat.

"I nearly forgot. I got a letter here for Stroud. Came yesterday."

Billy stared. "A letter for Eli? From who?"

"A British doctor in New York. Purcell." He drew the paper from his coat. "Want to take it to him?"

Billy pondered for a moment. "Maybe I better. Can't tell what might happen in the next day or two."

Turlock handed it up to him and Billy tucked it inside his coat, then turned his horse back towards the single bridge that crossed the Assunpink. The horse's hooves thumped hollowly as they crossed, and Billy turned north up King Street, still strewn with battle wreckage, deserted, quiet, eerie. North of town he raised the horse to a gentle lope traveling east for a mile and a half, then turned north on the Quaker Road.

Billy held the pace for two miles, then slowed the horse to let it blow before he raised it to a canter, then back to a walk, pacing it as he worked north the ten miles to Princeton. He passed the low, flat place to his left that he remembered marked "The Barrens" on the map, and pushed on. At the halfway point the horse clattered across the Quaker bridge where it crossed the frozen, winding Assunpink, with Billy watching ahead for anything that moved, but there was nothing in the bright, frigid sunlight. He pushed on, feeling the rhythm of the horse's stride and breathing, slowly covering the frozen miles, until he clattered across the bridge spanning Stony Brook two miles south of Princeton.

Coming off the bridge Billy caught the first flash of movement ahead to his left and instantly reined the horse off the road to the right into a stand of maple and pine, and dismounted. He grasped the reins beneath the bit and held the horse steady, wishing he had the telescope that still hung around Eli's neck. He narrowed his eyes against the bright snow, waiting, and then there was movement again. He saw the black dots strung out in a line in the white world, and twenty seconds later they became mounted cavalry half a mile away. They were moving at an angle that would intercept the Quaker Road about two hundred yards north of where Billy was hidden. Billy's breathing slowed.

British or American?

The horse moved its feet and Billy spoke low to it and it stopped, blowing vapor from its belled nostrils. Billy went to one knee in the snow, eyes nearly closed to cut out the sun's glare, and he studied the riders intently. They were less than a quarter mile away when he suddenly recognized they were Americans. He pivoted and swung onto the brown gelding and spurred him back onto the road heading north at a gallop. Instantly the small column of cavalry stopped and spread while the men unslung their muskets and brought them up to cover Billy. He came into them with the reins in his left hand, his right hand raised and his fingers spread. He reined the brown in and covered the last twenty yards at a walk and stopped before the officer in charge, who had studied him intently as he rode in.

"Sir, I'm Corporal Billy Weems, Boston Regiment. I'm here on scouting assignment by orders of General Washington."

The officer nodded. "I think I've seen you before. I'm Colonel Joseph Reed. The patrol with me is the Philadelphia light cavalry."

"I know, sir. General Washington told us we may find you up here."

Reed straightened in his saddle and quickly looked around. "We? Who's with you?"

"Eli Stroud, sir. Scout. I'm to meet him at noon over at Bear Swamp, somewhere to the east."

"You didn't come together?"

"We left together yesterday, sir, traveling east to see if British were coming from the coast. We found them and I took the information back to General Washington while Eli came this way."

"Are they coming from the east?"

"Yes, sir. One thousand from Staten Island under General Cornwallis."

Reed froze. "Cornwallis?"

"Yes, sir."

"How do you know that?"

"We captured an officer, sir."

Reed eased back in his saddle while his thoughts raced. *Cornwallis! I heard he was on his way back to England! Howe must have stopped him and sent him here to take command. If he brought one thousand regulars with him, when he joins Grant and Leslie he will have a force of about eight thousand!*

Reed exhaled slowly as the sure knowledge struck home. *We won't have half that many! If I were Cornwallis, I would annihilate Washington right there on the banks of the Delaware! When we took Trenton away from Howe, he lost too much. He's trying to reclaim his honor and his position.*

Reed twisted in his saddle to point nearly due east. "Bear Swamp is over there about a mile or so." He lowered his arm. "I'm going to take my command straight on towards Princeton until I make contact with the British. You may hear shooting when we do." He turned in his saddle one more time to point southwest. "If you go back on the Princeton Road, know that General de Fermoy has a command of men just south of the bridge at Five Mile Run, about halfway back to Trenton. They're to slow the British if they come. They have two cannon, so if you have to use that road, stay in plain sight and go in slow with your hands high until they recognize you. General de Fermoy is French, and his rules of war are a little different."

"I'll remember, sir."

Billy saluted. Reed returned the salute and wheeled his horse around as he called orders to his patrol and led them north up Quaker Road. Billy watched them for a few moments, then reined his horse due east, off the road, into the drifted, crusted snow, watching for snow-covered cattails, reeds, and tall grasses that would mark the frozen Bear Swamp.

Behind him, half a mile to the north, Reed slowed his patrol at the first farmhouse and came into the farmyard at a walk with every man watching everything that moved. A milk cow stood in a small pen beside the clapboard barn, eyes closed in total disinterest, chewing its cud. Nine weaner pigs clustered around a sow in a low pen beside the barn, and chickens stepped daintily in the snow inside the chicken coop to take beady-eyed aim on kernels of grain before their beaks struck with deadly accuracy. The house was silent.

Reed dismounted and strode to the front door and pounded with the flat of his hand. Moments later the door opened less than one foot and a man peered out through the crack, suspicious.

"I'm an American officer," Reed said boldly. "I need information regarding the British and the town of Princeton."

The man opened the door wide. His wife stood behind him with an infant clutched to her as the man spoke. "We don't care for the British, so we've stayed away from Princeton. I don't know much about what they're doing there."

Reed studied him briefly. "Do you know how many are there?"

The man shook his head. "No. I only know that when they came they took two of my cattle and half my sheep and grain and winter meat, just like they did at the other farms around here."

Reed could hear the anger in the man's voice. "Do they send patrols out this way?"

The man shrugged. "Once in a while."

"Have you heard about what happened at Trenton?"

A light came into the man's eyes. "We heard. Were you part of that?"

"Yes."

"You really shocked them. There's talk about them coming back to Trenton."

"I know. We're here to find out how many, and when. Anything we can."

"Wish I could help more, but I can't."

Reed nodded. "Thank you." He turned on his heel, remounted, led his patrol out of the farmyard at a brisk trot, and raised them to an easy lope north. Twice more he stopped at farmhouses, and each time the taciturn, reluctant farmers repeated what he already knew. He moved steadily north to the open country with a growing sense of frustrated apprehension.

Where are they? After Trenton, they should have patrols swarming. Have they seen us and are drawing us into a trap? Ambush?

With Princeton a scant two miles ahead, he reined in his horse and the patrol stopped while Reed sat quietly in his saddle for several seconds. The only sound in the frigid world was the squeak of saddle leathers as the horses labored with their breathing. He made his decision, turned to his patrol, and his words came loud, clipped, in the rising tension.

"We're going right on towards Princeton until we make contact. Watch sharp both right and left for the first sign of a trap or an ambush." He turned his horse and once again his patrol followed him at a canter, moving ever closer to Princeton.

More than two miles east of the patrol, Billy brought his horse down to a walk and sat tall, eyes squinting against the sparkle of sunlight on the frozen snow, watching for the dark form that would be Eli's wolf skin coat in the white glare. Blackbirds with one red patch on the leading edge of each wing darted scolding among the brittle cattails and the tall, gray clumps of frozen marsh grasses as he moved east through Bear Swamp. He had gone four hundred yards when Eli rose from a tangle of grass and cattails thirty feet ahead and trotted to him. Eli wasted no time.

"You report to Washington?"

"Yes. You been to Princeton?"

Eli nodded, and Billy saw the heavy concern as he spoke. "Things are happening that Washington needs to know."

"What things?" Billy swung down from the horse and faced Eli.

"Grant and Leslie are waiting in Princeton for Cornwallis to get there tomorrow. With those he's bringing, he'll have about eight thousand fresh troops spoiling for a fight, and they'll have sixty cannon and maybe a thousand mounted cavalry. I think they'll be at Trenton two days from now."

Billy made instant calculations and his breathing slowed. "We've got about half that many, and they're exhausted, worn out. Right now they're just east of Trenton sitting on the bank of the Delaware, and if Cornwallis comes in on them from the north and east at the same time, there's no way out."

Eli stopped. "Washington can't cross the Delaware?"

"The boats are up at McKonkey's Ferry."

"We've got to get back and tell him."

For long seconds Billy remained silent while his mind leaped, and suddenly he pointed west. "I met Colonel Joseph Reed's patrol over there, headed into Princeton to find out what you already know. He told me General de Fermoy has a force over on the Princeton Road at Five Mile Run to slow down the British when they come." He paused for a moment, then concluded. "If we can find Reed, maybe he can take word back to Washington while you and I wait to see what happens and then go on over to Princeton Road to tell de Fermoy what to expect."

For a moment Eli pondered. "I think you're right. Let's go."

Eli handed his rifle up to Billy as Billy drew his foot from the onside stirrup and Eli swung up behind him. The brown horse accepted the double load as Eli reached to take his rifle, and Billy raised the mount to a gentle lope following his own tracks back to the Quaker Road.

Three miles to the northeast, Joseph Reed pulled his horse to a stop and the patrol halted behind him, puzzled, sensing the bafflement that was now plain on Reed's face He pointed straight ahead at trees less than a mile distant.

"The College of New Jersey is just past that stand of trees. I can't understand why we haven't seen the British." Slowly he turned his head, first to the right, then the left, and then he twisted in his saddle to peer south, behind the patrol. There was nothing.

He drew a great breath. "So be it. We ride until we make contact."

"*There!*"

Every man in the patrol started at the urgently hissed word from a private at the rear, and every head jerked to follow his pointing arm, finger extended towards the west at a farmyard two hundred fifty yards away. The man walking from the barn to the house was wearing the unmistakable crimson coat and crossed white belts of a British regular, sparkling bright in the sun and the white world. The soldier continued steadily on towards the house and entered.

Reed released held breath. "He didn't see us." Instantly he gave hand signals and commands. "The first six, to the left, the second six, follow me to the right. We surround the house one hundred yards out and come in on foot from all sides at once. Try to get there without being seen or heard. I'll handle things at the door."

Half the patrol swung a quarter mile south, the other half a quarter mile north, formed a circle, and turned their horses towards the house. They rode in at a trot, silent in the snow, and dismounted one hundred yards out, hiding behind anything they could find—trees, bushes, ditches, fences. They dismounted and came in at a run, dodging, running, until they were all within ten feet of the house.

The yard was silent. No curtains moved at the windows, no door opened, no one challenged. Reed trotted to the door with sword drawn, and stopped dead in his tracks. With his nose wrinkled he turned to his aide and whispered, "Mince pies?"

The aide's eyes grew large as he nodded. "Mince pies."

Reed signaled to the six men behind him, grasped the door latch, jerked it up, raised his sword above his head and bolted from the bright sunlight into the dim room, his men hot behind him, muskets at the ready. Instantly Reed realized he was in the kitchen, and that the room was crowded with red-coated British regulars who were standing around a table, too startled to think or move.

Reed thundered, "Surrender or die!" as his six men slammed into the nearest redcoats and jammed them against the wall. In the wild confusion the British tried to reach their weapons leaning against the far wall. Reed's men swung their musket butts cracking against British heads, and the first three redcoats went down. The others stopped dead in their tracks. Reed still had his sword poised above his head and he faced the nearest British officer as the remaining six men of the American patrol came storming through the door to fill the kitchen.

With his sword high Reed shouted in the face of the stunned British officer, "Do you surrender or die, sir?" He backed the man up until he hit the wall.

The officer stammered, "Surrender. We surrender."

Reed lowered his sword and gave hand signals to his men. Thirty seconds later they had all the British muskets, pistols, and swords gathered, and the British crowded against one wall of the kitchen, hands high. Movement at the archway into the parlor caught Reed's eye and he pivoted, sword poised before he realized the man was not in uniform and there was a wide-eyed, terrified woman behind him silently weeping as she clutched two small children to her skirts. Reed lowered his sword and faced the man and spoke loud, demanding.

"I'm Colonel Joseph Reed, Continental army. Who are you, sir?"

"Jared Wilson. This is my farm."

"Were you harboring these British soldiers?"

The man shook his head. "No. They broke in. They were stealing my wife's mince pies."

Only then did Reed remember the strong, pungent smell of sweet mince pies, and turned to look back at the table. There were eight of them, still warm. Four had been cut and partially eaten. He looked back at the soldiers against the wall. Some of their red coats were stained by the rich brown mince drippings. For a moment Reed puzzled, then turned to their officer.

"It seems you were so anxious to steal Mrs. Wilson's mince pies, no one thought to put out a picket."

The officer's face flushed and he looked at the floor and refused to speak.

Without warning a laugh rolled out of Reed and startled everyone in the room. He brought himself under control and turned to Mrs. Wilson.

"Ma'am, may I say your mince pies have just received the highest of compliments. I doubt there is anything else in the world that would have prompted a British patrol to forget basic military discipline and get themselves captured. I, and the Continental army, are indebted to your mince pies."

He sobered and turned back to his men. "Take them outside."

They stood their twelve prisoners in a line in the dooryard and Reed strode to the officer in charge.

"Your name, rank, and command, sir."

"Gerald Ballantyne. Major. Sixteenth Dragoons."

"What are you doing out here?"

"Patrol."

"Who is your commanding officer?"

"General . . ."

"Sir," came an urgent voice from his men, and Reed turned to look. A private was pointing. "Someone's coming."

Two hundred yards south a brown horse was laboring through the snow, and as it approached Reed saw it was carrying double; he recognized Billy. Four of his men brought their muskets to the ready as the horse slowed and stopped. Eli slid to the ground and Billy dismounted and walked to Reed, leading the horse, studying the twelve red-coated soldiers as he came.

"Sir," Billy said, "you might remember me from this morning." He gestured to the soldiers. "Prisoners?"

"Yes they are." He glanced at Eli. "Is this the scout you were looking for?"

"Yes, sir. He's been to Princeton. Maybe he can help."

Reed looked at Eli for a moment, aware of the wolf skin coat and the knee-length moccasins, and the tomahawk and knife in the weapons belt.

"When were you in Princeton?"

"Last night."

"Do you know how many British are there and who is in command?"

"Eight thousand when Cornwallis gets there tomorrow. Grant and Leslie are waiting for him. He's coming in from Perth Amboy with one thousand men and sixteen cannon. He'll take command of those already in Princeton and they intend coming right on down to Trenton."

Reed turned back to the Major Ballantyne. "Sir, is he correct?"

Ballantyne's face turned white. "I don't know."

Eli smiled. "He knows."

Reed spoke once more to Ballantyne. "Who is your commanding officer?"

"General Grant."

"Is General Leslie in Princeton with his command?"

Ballantyne stood silent.

Reed paused for a moment. "I haven't got time to waste. We'll take these men back to General Washington. They'll talk to him." He turned to his patrol. "You six go get your horses and return."

The first six men left at a trot as Mrs. Wilson came out of the house with a shawl drawn tightly about her head and shoulders.

"Sir, I have cut some mince pie for yourself and your men and I have milk. Do you have time?"

Reed glanced at his men, ringed around the British with their muskets ready. They swallowed and raised a hand to wipe at their mouths. He bowed to Mrs. Wilson. "Ma'am, we didn't come to eat your food."

"I know that, sir. I offer it as a gift."

Again Reed glanced at his men and in their eyes he saw the unbelievable thought of eating warm mince pie on this frigid day.

"It would be most appreciated, Mrs. Wilson."

When the first six men returned with their horses, Reed ordered them into the kitchen where great slices of warm mince pie were on the table with a pitcher of milk and glasses. In silent reverence the men cut chunks with their forks and closed their eyes as they slowly chewed the spicy sweetness and swallowed. They drank cold milk and wiped their mouths when they finished.

"Ma'am, we never hope to eat better mince pie. There's no way to thank you enough."

They walked back into the bright sunlight and the other six men came inside for their share. Colonel Reed gave Billy and Eli a wave and they followed him inside where Mrs. Wilson stood quietly by, glowing at the sight of the bearded, ragged soldiers eating her mince pies with expressions that said more than words. They finished and wiped their mouths and walked back out.

Colonel Reed was the last to leave. "God bless you, Mr. and Mrs. Wilson. God bless you both." He walked out squinting into the bright sunlight where Billy and Eli were waiting.

"Do you two want to come with us?"

Billy shook his head. "No, sir. We'll stay here to see what General Cornwallis does."

Reed nodded. "I'll tell General Washington."

With the horses gathered, Reed ordered his patrol mounted and watched while the British soldiers scrambled up behind his men to ride double. He took his position at the head of the column with the British officer riding double behind his aide to his right. Before he ordered the column forward he stood in his stirrups and turned to the prisoners.

"If anyone attempts to escape, I will shoot Major Ballantyne." He raised his pistol, then shoved it inside his coat. "All right. Follow me."

He led them out of the farmyard at a canter, and as they passed Mr. and Mrs. Wilson standing in their doorway, each man nodded his respects to them, and then they were out onto Quaker Road moving south.

Eli glanced at the westering sun. "We can go around Princeton and be on the north side yet tonight if we leave now. I figure that's where Cornwallis will come in."

Billy nodded and they both walked to the Wilson family, still standing in the doorway, and Billy spoke. "None of us will forget your generosity. We surely do thank you."

Mrs. Wilson blushed and Mr. Wilson nodded as Billy and Eli mounted the brown gelding and left the dooryard, traveling east. They rode in silence, watching intently for any movement, any dots moving on the snow-covered roads, any body of horsemen that could be British cavalry. An hour later they turned north, and another hour passed before they turned west.

The sun had set stark and cold and lights were winking on in the distant, scattered farmhouses when Eli raised his hand to point at a stand of pines and oak clustered about a barn, two outbuildings, and a small, square home less than one mile north of the small town of Princeton. Billy reined in the weary horse to peer in the gathering dusk. The house was dark and the barn door partially open. There was no movement, no cow waiting to be milked, no one feeding livestock at the end of the day.

Eli spoke. "I stayed there last night. It's abandoned. I figure whoever lived there left when the British came. There's still some hay in the barn and the well's good."

They came into the dooryard slowly in the darkness, listening, watching, but there was no one. They entered the barn and unsaddled the jaded horse in a stall and carried loose hay from the corner. While Billy struck flint to steel in a second stall, Eli walked to the well and returned with two steaming, dripping wooden buckets with rope handles. He set one in the stall with the brown horse and waited a moment while the animal sunk its muzzle into the sweet water and the sucking sound began. He took the second bucket to the stall where Billy had a small fire going and set it down, then sat down cross-legged opposite Billy.

"Got to keep that fire low."

Billy nodded as they both dug inside their coats for the dried fish and fried pork, and the hard biscuits wrapped in canvas.

"Wish we had coffee," Eli said.

They sat with the yellow firelight reflecting off their faces and making faint, ghostly shadows inside the barn. They gnawed chunks of hard fish and pork and biscuit. They drank from their canteens and refilled them from the water bucket, and as they stared into the low, dancing flames and worked at their meat, a strange, unexpected, reflective mood settled over them. The warmth of the tiny fire reached them and they wiped at their noses as they began to drip. For a long time they sat in silence, each lost in his own thoughts.

Billy spoke low, his words echoing in the empty barn. "Ever think about dying? whether God has appointed a time for each man to die?"

Eli didn't raise his eyes from the fire. For a time the only sound was the grinding of the hay by the horse in the next stall. "You worried?"

For a moment Billy hesitated. "I think about it. We've been through some bad battles with men killed all around us. We could have been dead half a dozen times. It seems like after awhile we've used up all our chances, and the balance tips the other way, and it's our turn to go. I wonder if God decides all that."

"I've thought about it."

"Do you think He decides?"

Eli's forehead wrinkled and he reached to wipe at his mouth, then settled. "It seems like there's more to it than that. I think God sees things different because He sees more than just us. Your Bible says He made everything in the heavens, and if He did, He sees us as part of all that. His plan is bigger than ours."

Eli paused and Billy held his silence, waiting. Eli raised questioning eyes. "In His plan, do you think we decide anything, or does God decide it all?"

Billy's eyes narrowed for a moment, then grew wide at the thought. For a time they sat in silence before Billy answered. "We decide some things. I decided to join in the fight for liberty. So did you."

"Why?"

"Something inside. I know I have good thoughts and bad ones, and I can decide which ones I follow."

Eli raised his face. "Remember I told you the Iroquois teaching about the Twin Brothers. The Good Twin and the Bad Twin?"

"I remember. I think they're the same as Jesus and the devil in the Bible."

Eli suddenly leaned forward, focused, intense. "You think your Bible says they were twins? Brothers? Jesus and the devil?"

Billy reached into his memory. "I've heard it taught that way."

Eli didn't hesitate. "If they're brothers, and if Jesus said He is the Son of God and that we're all God's children, then we're all one family. God, His son Jesus the good brother, the devil the bad brother, and all of us."

For a time neither moved as the power of the thought reached deep inside them. Finally Billy shook his head. "I don't know. I wish I did."

Eli shook his head. "I'd give a lot to know." Once again he raised his face to Billy. "You asked if God decides when we die. I doubt it, at least for most of us. It seems like He set us here free to decide most things for ourselves. If we stay to fight with the army we're more likely to be killed than if we went home. I think we decide that. And even in battle, experience and good sense make a difference."

Billy added more sticks to the fire. "Maybe we decide most things. Right and wrong, good and bad."

A knot popped in the fire and a tiny column of sparks spurted and settled.

Eli asked quietly, "Don't most things finally come down to right or wrong?"

Billy shook his head. "I'm not sure."

Eli drew a weary breath. "Neither am I. We'll have to wait. Maybe someday . . ."

They drank cold water and rewrapped what was left of their meat and biscuits. Billy was working his small packet back into his coat when he touched the envelope Turlock had given him, for Eli. Quickly he jerked it from his coat and thrust it towards Eli.

"Turlock gave me this. A letter for you."

Eli looked at him in disbelief. "Me? From who?"

"A British doctor."

"A *what?*"

He broke the seal, unfolded the paper, and turned it to the firelight.

He read the scrolled lines, then reread them, and lowered the document, eyes wide in surprise.

"This is from Mary Flint! She had a doctor write it. She was a nurse in his hospital. She says the reverend who got my sister a long time ago was named Cyrus Fielding." He paused to look directly into Billy's eyes. "The doctor says Mary's sick. She was nearly killed getting the name of the reverend. She was in this doctor's hospital in New York when he wrote this."

Billy gaped. Eli rose, nervous, pacing in the stall, needing to do something. "Someone's got to go help her," he exclaimed, and his words echoed.

Billy waited while Eli slowed before he spoke. "If she's in the hospital now, she's getting help."

Eli stopped and slowly sat back down. "I guess you're right. I hope she gets well. I surely do." He read the letter once more, then his head dropped forward and his shoulders slumped as he stared at the cold dirt floor of the stall. In his mind he was seeing the dark, brave eyes and the dark hair, and he was feeling the pain she had endured from the loss of her infant and her husband and all a woman holds dear. He felt the soul-wrenching ache as though it was his own, and he wished he could take it from her, but he could not.

Billy checked the horse, then walked to the loose hay scattered in the corner of the barn. He pushed it into a pile as Eli came from the stall. They burrowed into the stack for warmth, and in the dim light of the dying fire Eli spoke quietly.

"The British have some wagons loaded with gunpowder and about two hundred horses at their camp. If we get there in the morning before it's light we can likely cause them some trouble. Slow them down. Give Washington a little more time."

"We'll do it." Billy waited a few moments. "She's all right. You'll see her again."

Notes

Many, perhaps most, of the Marblehead Regiment under Colonel John Glover chose to leave the Continental army when the enlistments expired. Most historians agree that some of Glover's men turned their attention to privateering. During this period of time, General Washington was issuing "Letters of Marque" to civilian ship owners, granting them authority to take British ships on the high seas. Some historians also indicate that a possible motivation for Glover leaving the war was because his wife was ill and his personal businesses were failing (see Ketchum, *The Winter Soldiers*, p. 279; Freeman, *George Washington*, vol. 4, p. 333; Billias, *General John Glover and His Marblehead Mariners*, pp. 129–31).

General Washington sent Colonel Joseph Reed and twelve soldiers towards Princeton to scout out the strength and position of the British forces. Nearly within sight of Nassau Hall, Reed captured twelve British Dragoons at the Wilson farm where the British had stopped to eat Mrs. Wilson's mince pies. The prisoners were interrogated by General Washington and they confirmed that the British would have about 8,000 prime troops available to march on Trenton. General Cadwalader had obtained the same information from American spies and had drawn a rough map for General Washington (see Ketchum, *The Winter Soldiers*, p. 283).

General Washington ordered the French General de Fermoy to take a small command of soldiers to the bridge spanning Five Mile Run that intersected Princeton Road, and to send word when the British marched. Among the men under de Fermoy's command was a small company of Pennsylvania riflemen led by Colonel Edward Hand (see Ketchum, *The Winter Soldiers*, p. 288).

CHAPTER XIV

★ ★ ★

Y ou have a slight touch of pneumonia still lingering."

Doctor Otis Purcell leaned from his chair beside the bed to tuck the thick, down-filled comforter under Mary Flint's chin, and he smiled into the serious, dark eyes. "Your fever's gone. Another week of rest and strong soup and vegetables and you can get up and around for an hour or so each day, but for now you remain here in your bed." He reached to touch her cheek tenderly, as he would a beloved child. "It's late. You go to sleep."

Mary smiled up at him. "Thank you. How can I ever repay you?"

"Get well. That will be pay enough."

He turned down the lamp on the table beside her bed. "I'll be back to check on you in the night. If you need anything, call."

"I will."

He picked up his lantern, walked from the small room on the third story of the Flint mansion, left the door ajar three inches, and silently walked down the hardwood floor of the hall with his lantern high, casting a giant shadow behind him. The stairs creaked once as he descended to the ground floor, and he made his way to the French doors into the library where he had set up his office, and entered. He set his lantern on one corner of his desk, then turned up the lamp on the other, and glanced at the mantel clock above the huge, stone fireplace.

Twenty minutes past nine o'clock. Wearily he slumped into the leather upholstered chair behind his desk and ran a hand through his rumpled hair, then leaned back to rest for a few moments in the yellow light.

Night rounds. One hundred sixteen men. Maimed and crippled and sick because the human race cannot rise above war. He closed his eyes for several moments. *Every monarch, every military officer should be forced to spend one month in a makeshift hospital like this one. Try to heal these men—save them. Amputate some arms and legs. Hear the screams. Listen to men rant in fever deliriums. Watch their eyes when they die. Every officer. Might help end wars.*

He rose exhausted and rubbed eyes weary from peering intently at too many wounds, making too many critical decisions. He picked up the lantern and quietly walked from the library feeling old and drained. Amid the moaning of men in pain, the rattle of rapid, fevered breathing, and the heavy, oppressive stench of carbolics, medicines, gangrene, and human refuse, he paused at the bedsides of the wounded and sick and dying to hold the lantern high while he leaned over. He laid his hand on foreheads, and held a cup of cool water to parched lips, and whispered encouragement to those who turned questioning eyes to him in the dim light. Where there were no beds, men lay on blankets arranged on the floor, and he knelt briefly to arrange pillows and straighten blankets before he listened to their breathing and felt for fever.

He finished his rounds on the first and second floors, then silently stole up the stairs to Mary's small room on the third floor where he had ordered his staff to arrange a good bed, away from the crowded rooms and the heartbreak below. He silently pushed the door open and held his lantern high while he peered inside. In the dim light he saw her dark head on the white pillow, with the comforter drawn to her chin, and he listened to her deep, regular breathing for a time before he swung the door nearly closed and returned to the stairway at the end of the hall. On the ground floor he stopped at the small storage room he had converted to an apothecary and briefly checked the scant stock of medical supplies remaining. Four of the five one-gallon bottles of alcohol were empty, the fifth one half gone. He closed the door and walked on to his office in the library.

The mantel clock read ten minutes past eleven as he dropped into his chair, bone tired in mind and body. He unbuttoned his vest, then leaned back in the chair to close his eyes while he allowed himself the luxury of shutting off his mind for a few precious minutes. He started at the sound of the French doors rattling and he sat upright, trying to focus.

"Sorry, sir. The lights were on. I wouldn't of bothered if I'd known you were asleep."

Purcell cleared his throat. "It's all right, corporal. What's the matter?"

"Nothing, sir. I just wanted to know if there was anything else I could do before I go to bed."

Purcell dug his knuckles into his eyes for a moment while he forced his mind to once again accept the grinding burden of running a makeshift military hospital in a foreign land. He sighed as he looked at Corporal Victor Welles. The lantern light added lines to the man's already aged face, and his brows seemed too large in the yellow light. His right hand was lightly bandaged while it finished healing from having three fingers blown off by an exploding British cannonball. The blast had left Welles a little addled, sometimes disturbed in his thinking and judgment. His thumb and index finger were free, and the old soldier had begged to help in the hospital while his hand finished healing. He knew nothing of treating the sick, nor was he capable of learning, but he had faithfully followed orders in doing what he could and was helpful in cleaning and scrubbing and carrying out the soiled bandages to burn each day.

"Nothing tonight, corporal. But in the morning would you fill the alcohol bottles from the barrel in the cellar?"

"Are they empty again, sir?"

"Four of them."

"Yes, sir. I'll do it."

"Good night, corporal."

"Good night, sir."

Purcell turned down the lamp, shrugged out of his vest, dropped it on his desk, and sat down on the cot he had long ago arranged against one wall. He took off his shoes before he lay out full-length on his back, one arm across his eyes, and he felt the unending tension begin to drain from his muscles, and then his mind, as he slipped into deep sleep.

Corporal Welles quietly made his way to his own cot in one corner of what had once been the grand dining hall and sat in the shadows for a few moments.

No reason I can't fill those bottles tonight. It'd please the doctor. With the bottles filled I could do something else in the morning.

Proud of his reasoning, he lighted the lantern he kept beneath his cot to answer any call he may get in the night and made his way to the makeshift apothecary where he took the first empty bottle from the shelf. Holding the lantern high he worked his way to the kitchen door leading to the cellar, and carefully descended the stairs into the chill, dank air. He turned into what had been the cement wine room and walked to the far wall where four twenty-five gallon kegs of alcohol had been placed on the rack that had once held six kegs of nine-year French wine. He placed the lantern on the cement floor by his feet, jerked the stopper out of the bottle, raised the neck to the spout on the wooden spigot with his left hand, and turned the spigot handle with the thumb and index finger on his right.

The stream of medicinal alcohol hit the bottom of the bottle, it began to fill and the acrid fumes rose and reached into the room. Welles wrinkled his nose against the bite and turned his face away as his eyes began to water, and as he did his grasp on the bottle slipped. He made a desperate grab with both hands for the tumbling bottle and missed, and it shattered on the cement floor. The splashing alcohol drenched his shoes and the lantern by his feet, and there was a *whump* as the alcohol caught. The spigot to the twenty-five gallon barrel was still wide open, spewing a steady stream of alcohol onto the floor. With his shoes and trouser legs on fire, Welles staggered backwards away from the keg, frantically pounding at his blazing pant legs. The alcohol running from the spigot was rapidly spreading and it caught and the flames came licking at Welles. He turned and ran from the room, raced up the stairs, burst into the kitchen and slammed the door just as the keg in the cellar exploded.

The blast shattered the rack and the other three kegs dropped crashing to the cement floor where they split and instantly exploded.

The concussion blew every door in the basement to pieces, ripped the kitchen door off its hinges, and shattered every kitchen window outward into the black of night. Welles was thrown headlong against the far kitchen wall and slumped to the floor, unconscious, clothing still smoldering. An instant later the entire basement of the proud Flint mansion was a holocaust of blue and yellow alcohol flames, reaching up the stairs into the kitchen, filling it with thick, choking, black smoke.

The first muffled explosion and instant tremor reached deep into Doctor Otis Purcell and a quiet, faint urgency arose in his sleep-locked brain as the second, heavier sound came rolling and the floor of the library shook. Bottles rattled on the desk and the cot shuddered as the voice inside Purcell's head rose demanding. His eyes opened wide in the darkness while he tried to force his fumbling brain to identify what had wakened him. He swung his feet off the cot and lunged for the large French doors and threw them open. The rank stench of burning alcohol struck him like something physical and he recoiled, bewildered, unable to grasp what had happened. He threw one hand over his nose and mouth and started down the dark hall where smoke and flames were billowing from the kitchen door when the first frantic cries erupted from the sick and wounded in the huge room adjoining the entryway. Five seconds later the first floor was plunged into a chaotic bedlam of sick and wounded men, shouting, screaming, scrambling from every room in the dim light for any door or window through which they could escape the stench of burning alcohol and the smoke that was strangling them.

"Stop! *Stop!*" shouted Purcell, and he grabbed the man nearest him. "Maintain order! We can all get out if we will maintain order!" The man wrenched free and plunged on towards the two great front doors, pushing his way, stumbling over cots, heedless of the men underfoot who had fallen and could not rise. Purcell seized another man and screamed, "Stop! Order!" but he could not be heard in the roar of terrified voices. The man struck Purcell's hands away and was gone in the mindless stampede for the doors.

"Useless! Useless!" Purcell cried, and turned towards the corner near the great entryway where the broad, graceful, curving staircase led to the second floor. Smoke was filling the room and flames were leaping from the kitchen down the hallway towards the entrance when Purcell reached the base of the stairs. He leaped them two at a time and was halfway to the second floor when an avalanche of panic-driven wounded came pounding downward, sweeping him aside in their headlong plunge for the nearest door or window on the ground floor. In the smoke he could hear windows being smashed as men threw cots, or tables, or chairs, crashing through them.

The amputees! They left them behind. Four of them! Purcell flattened himself against the high, polished oak bannister until the mob coming down thinned, then battled to the second floor, on to the first door and threw it open. In the master bedroom four men with either one or both legs missing were struggling to rise from their beds. Two had rolled out onto the floor and were trying to crawl to the door. Instantly Purcell seized the arms of the nearest man and jerked him upward. "Stand on your good leg!" he shouted, then turned his back to the man and drew both arms over his shoulders, crossed them over his chest, and leaned forward.

"I'm taking you down," he shouted, and turned to the other three. "I'll be back."

He had gone five steps back towards the top of the stairway when a man came running from behind, and Purcell stopped him.

"You carry this man down and out of this building or I'll have you shot!" he shouted. The man blinked in the smoke, hesitated for one moment, then reached to take the disabled man on his own back, and was gone. Purcell darted back into the room for the second man. Ten minutes later he staggered out onto the frozen portico with its six great columns, and slumped to his knees into the snow. He released his hold on the crossed arms of the man on his back and the man, the fourth one, slumped to one side, unconscious, while strong hands lifted him to carry him away.

Purcell was vaguely aware that a company of British cavalry had arrived. A major he had never seen before was shouting orders and the regulars were moving in to try to restore a sense of sanity and order. Most of them were stripping off their heavy winter overcoats to wrap about the shoulders of the sick and disabled who were scattered all around the building in the snow.

Still on his knees, Purcell turned to look. The first floor of the mansion was an inferno. The floor joists in the basement had burned nearly through and the floor was sagging, threatening. The great staircase was ablaze, impassable. Flames were leaping upward to the second floor to show bright orange in the windows. The thick smoke was trapped on the third floor. The fire could be seen from the Hudson River to the East River, from Canvas Town to the slopes of Fort Washington. It lighted the three-hundred-foot high granite face of the New Jersey Palisades, west across the Hudson.

People began arriving on horseback, in buggies, wagons, carriages, or on foot, to stand in silent, wide-eyed awe at the rare spectacle, aware there was nothing anyone could do to save the landmark building. The major in command of the mounted troops moved among the arriving citizens with eight armed regulars behind him.

"Sir, I'm very sorry but we must have the use of your carriage. You will take as many of the wounded as you can to the warehouse on the wharves of Catharine Street, on the East River. These two men will escort you. When you have safely left the wounded there, you will return for more. Do you understand?"

Staring at two mounted regulars with slung muskets, the citizens understood. Carriages and wagons and buggies began leaving, loaded with wounded, with one red-coated cavalryman leading, another following, their horses' hooves clacking down the icy cobblestone streets.

Purcell rose from his knees shivering in the cold. A regular came in from the side and draped his heavy overcoat around Purcell's shoulders and moved on. Purcell walked slowly back towards the burning building, putting the overcoat on, buttoning it. An ache came in his left arm and he paused to work it slowly up and down as he stared.

So fast. Too fast. It started in the basement, in the alcohol. I smelled it. I wonder what happened. I wonder how many got out.

The nagging ache came again in his arm and he flexed it, worked it for a moment. The clatter of incoming horses and military wagons came from behind and he glanced back to see soldiers drive a dozen big wagons drawn by teams of heavy horses onto the estate and stop near the clusters of waiting wounded. Regulars jumped down and turned to catch bundles of blankets and pass them out to the shivering victims.

I must go to the Catharine Street warehouse. They'll need me there.

He turned, looking for the major, when a thought struck terror in him and stopped him dead in his tracks.

Mary! The third floor!

Frantically he sprinted to his left, calling her name, searching to see her face among those still waiting, but she was not there. He stopped and forced his racing thoughts to slow.

She may have already gone to the warehouse but I can't take the chance. And I don't have the time to look at everyone still here.

He looked one more time at the building. Flames were coming from every window in the second floor, scorching the white outer walls, but the fire had not yet reached the third floor. Half a dozen third-story windows were broken with black smoke billowing outward, but none of them yet showed the orange glow from inside. Purcell sprinted around the building, to the rear, where a steep exterior stairway had been built from the ground to a narrow door on both the second and the third floors as an emergency escape. The fire on both the first and second floors had blackened it, but it was still in place, intact.

He raised an arm across his face against the heat and ran to the ground landing and started up. A dozen soldiers shouted at him to stop, and two tried to catch him, but he took the stairs two at a time, legs driving as he bounded higher, one arm across his face, the other grasping the banister. The second floor exterior wall was so hot it was smoking as he passed it. He reached the small landing on the third floor and grasped the doorknob and jerked. It would not turn, nor would the door budge. He put his back against the banister and kicked with all his strength, again and again, until the panel in the door splintered. He kicked it out and the smoke came billowing to blind him, choke him. He took a deep breath, stooped to pass through the hole, and once inside dropped to his stomach.

By feel he worked his way down the hall to the second door and reached up to grasp the handle. It turned and he rose to his hands and knees and threw the door wide, then crawled into the room, blind and choking in the smoke. By feel he located Mary's bed and reached to the pillow, and she was there.

Instantly he rolled her in the comforter and laid her on the floor. Still on his hands and knees he dragged her out of the room, down the hall, and out onto the landing where he gulped great draughts of fresh night air. When he could, he stood, lifted Mary still wrapped in the comforter over his shoulder, grasped the banister to steady his wobbly legs, and started down. On the ground fifty people stared upward in the dancing firelight and raised hands to their mouths as they held their breath, watching the dark figure against the white wall, moving steadily down the narrow, steep stairway. He passed the second floor, and then he was on the ground and shouts of relief flooded as the soldiers and a dozen citizens rushed forward to grasp Mary from his shoulder. He sagged to his knees and strong hands lifted him and walked him away from the building.

His face was black and his eyes were bloodshot and watering as he spoke to the two who were carrying him.

"Is she alive? Stop. I must see if she's still alive."

They stopped and he ordered them to lay the comforter on the snow while he opened it. He gently slipped two fingers under her jaw and closed his eyes, praying in his heart. It was faint and irregular, but the heartbeat was there. A sob caught in his throat as he raised his face. "She's alive! Quick. Wrap her and follow me."

He led them to the front of the building and climbed to the driver's seat of the nearest military wagon. He ordered the soldiers to hand her up to him and he held her on his lap, clutched to his breast as the driver took up the slack in the reins. Suddenly from behind came a great cracking groan, louder than a cannon shot, and the driver hauled back on the reins as both men turned to look back. The thick floor joists in the basement of the great Flint mansion had burned through and the entire first floor had collapsed, crashing into the basement. With all support gone from below, the second floor had followed. The exterior walls were buckling outward, and with nothing inside the building for support, the monstrous ridge-beam that supported the massive roof had cracked and the roof was sagging. While they watched, a second great cracking sound came from the building as the ridge-beam splintered. The roof dipped in the center, then collapsed into the raging inferno below. A pyre of sparks shot five hundred feet into the frozen night to reflect off the few clouds overhead and light New York City for ten seconds. Everyone around the building gasped and instinctively stumbled backwards, away from the building as though it were a living thing in the final agony of its death throes. For a time no one moved, mesmerized by the spectacular, awful scene before them.

Then Purcell turned to the driver. "Move!"

The soldier slapped the reins on the rumps of the horses and shouted and they lunged into the horse collars. The wagon lurched forward, slipping, swaying on the snow and ice as it clattered on the cobblestones of the narrow street leading west towards the wharves and docks on the East River and Catharine Street. The driver hauled the running horses to a halt before the warehouse and Purcell carefully handed Mary down to the waiting arms of a soldier and jumped down to follow him inside.

In the light of one hundred lanterns, a crowded, confused mix of red-coated regulars and citizens moved about feverishly setting up cots and dropping folded blankets on them while others brought the sick and wounded to lay them down and cover them. A loud undercurrent of moans and commands and talk echoed in the cavernous building. Purcell walked to the nearest officer, a colonel.

"I'm Colonel Otis Purcell. I'm a doctor. I want this person in a bed in a private room immediately. Is there an office in this warehouse?"

The colonel stared at his blackened face and bloodshot eyes for one moment, then pointed.

Purcell walked across the crowded floor and pushed open the door into a small office. He shoved a scarred desk against the wall, waited while a soldier erected a cot, then quickly spread a blanket on it. The man carrying Mary carefully lowered her onto the cot and Purcell covered her. She lay unmoving, dark eyes closed, barely breathing, hair awry, face dirty from the smoke. A tiny stove in the corner drove the chill from the room as Purcell knelt beside the cot. Once again he felt for her heartbeat, then turned to the soldier and the man who had carried Mary.

"Could you bring cold water to drink, and hot water to wash?"

They left and returned. Purcell poured water from a canteen into a cup and gently lifted Mary to hold it to her lips. She coughed and he moved the cup back, then once again worked some into her mouth. She coughed again, and then swallowed, but her eyes did not open. He set the cup down and turned to the steaming porcelain basin on the desk to soak a cloth, and tenderly began wiping away the smoke stains on her face.

He turned grateful eyes to the soldier and the man standing nearby in the lamplight. "Thank you both. Go back out and help with the other wounded."

They nodded and closed the door behind them as they left the room.

Half an hour later Purcell drew a battered wooden office chair up beside the cot and sat down. Mary's face was as clean as he could get it, and he had smoothed her hair back. She was warm under the blankets, and as he looked at her he felt the tension draw to a knot in his stomach.

That's all I can do. For now, we wait.

He had given no thought to his own appearance. He sat on the wooden chair beside her bed still wearing the heavy military overcoat that reeked with the smell of smoke. His face was black, cheeks streaked by watering, bloodshot eyes. He felt the wheeze deep in his lungs from the smoke he had inhaled, and he heard the same sound in Mary's lungs when he held his ear to her back.

He sat quietly, driving every thought from his mind while he waited for movement or a sound from Mary, or for her to open her eyes and recognize him. Utter fatigue settled over him like a pall as he sat in the quiet of the small office. Without realizing it he once again flexed his left arm against the slight, nagging ache, and then settled against the back of the chair to wait. His eyes closed and his head tipped forward as sleep came.

He jerked awake in the middle of the night and gently touched her throat. The heartbeat was steady and stronger. He brought his ear close to her face and listened to breathing that was deep and even. The smell of hot coffee was faint in the room and he softly walked out into the warehouse where the sick and wounded were lying on cots in orderly rows with soldiers and nurses working among them. Hot coffeepots smoked on the top of several of the black iron stoves, and he walked to the nearest officer, a major.

"Sir, I'm Doctor Purcell. Could you tell me who's in command?"

The major eyed him dubiously for long moments. "You're a doctor?"

"Northumberland Fusileers. I was at the Flint mansion when the fire started."

Understanding rose in the major's eyes. "You were there?"

"I was. Who's in charge?"

The major pointed. "General Hollins. Over there."

"Thank you." With his heels tapping hollow on the cement floor, Purcell walked to the General. "Sir, I'm Colonel Otis Purcell, medical doctor. I was there when the fire started."

Hollins paused to stare for a moment. "You could use a bath and some rest, doctor. What can I do for you?"

For the first time Purcell considered his own appearance. "I apologize, sir. I haven't had much time to consider how I look. Do you know how many of the patients made it here?"

"Eighty-one. How many did you have over there? The records were burned."

Purcell's shoulders slumped. "One hundred sixteen. That means thirty-five are missing. Could some of them be at private residences?"

"A few, but not many. The building burned to the ground. Any idea how it started?"

Purcell shook his head. "None. It started in the basement. We had medicinal alcohol stored down there. It exploded."

General Hollins shook his head sadly. "A tragedy. Could it have been sabotage?"

Purcell shrugged. "I don't know. I doubt it." He squared his shoulders and asked, "Do you know what time it is?"

The general drew out his pocket watch. "Half past three o'clock."

Purcell gestured to a coffeepot steaming nearby. "Could you spare some coffee?"

"Certainly. Cups are there. Help yourself."

Purcell clutched his steaming mug of coffee with both hands and made his way back to the small office and closed the door. He sat down once again beside Mary and raised the cup to sip gratefully. He finished his coffee and set the mug on the desk, then settled back onto the chair to wait, unconsciously working his left arm and shoulder against the ache that persisted, and the numb feeling that was creeping. His eyes closed and his chin settled onto his chest.

The rap came loud at the door and Purcell started from deep sleep. He opened his eyes and stared, groping to understand where he was. Then the bright images of the fire and the smoke and the wounded fleeing in panic, and of the mansion collapsing in on itself in the black of night came rolling back, and he closed his eyes for a moment when the rap came again. He walked to the door and opened it to face General Hollins. Behind the general, morning sunlight was streaming through the few windows on the far wall of the brick warehouse.

Hollins spoke. "You have a patient in this office. Who is he?"

"Mary Flint. My assistant. She has pneumonia, and was nearly asphyxiated by the smoke last night."

"I see. Will she survive?"

"She has a good chance. I'll examine her again in a few minutes."

"Good. We have hot water and soap on a bench against the back wall, and hot coffee if you'd care to avail yourself. When you finish I need to talk with you about last night."

"Do you know the time?"

Hollins drew out his watch. "Ten minutes before eight o'clock."

"Thank you. I'll come find you directly."

Hollins paused for a moment. "You survived a terrible ordeal. We heard about the four men you brought down from the second floor, and the person from the third floor."

Purcell swallowed. "Have you located any more of the thirty-five we couldn't account for?"

Hollins shook his head.

Purcell raised a grimy hand to wipe at his black face. "I'll be along shortly."

Hollins nodded and turned on his heel as Purcell closed the door and returned to Mary's side. He pressed two fingers against her throat and closed his eyes to concentrate, then lowered his head to listen to her breathing. Satisfied, he turned her onto her side, covered her, and walked to the door.

The water was hot, the soap strong, and Purcell stripped to the waist to wash himself. Finished, he poured hot, bitter black coffee and walked to a window to peer outside at the new day. The sky was clear and blue and the world was drenched by dazzling sunlight. Icicles that hung long and ragged from the eaves were dripping holes in the snow, and puddles of steaming water were forming on the docks and in the streets. Ships tied to the wharves undulated slowly on the incoming tide. British soldiers in their sparkling red tunics and crossed white belts, and sailors in light coats and shirtsleeves moved about on the docks with a sense of buoyancy at the rare, unexpected break in the freeze that had gripped New York for weeks.

Purcell finished his coffee down to the dregs, set the mug on the bench, and walked across the cement floor to the small office. Inside, he went to Mary's side and once again sat to feel her pulse and listen intently, then slowly relaxed in giddy relief.

In time she will recover. I'll get a woman to come in and bathe her and change her clothing. He blinked and straightened. *She has no clothing! She has nothing—no money—nothing! Lost it all in the fire.* He pondered for a moment. *No matter. I'll buy new for her.*

He started to rise when a wrenching seized his chest. His left leg buckled and he went to his hands and knees on the cement floor. He tried to rise but his left arm and leg were numb and would take no weight. Instantly a grab of white hot pain struck beneath his sternum and he tipped onto his side, writhing, reaching to grasp at his chest with his right hand as the sure knowledge flashed in his mind.

Stroke! I'm dying!

There was no panic, only the instant decision of what he must yet do. He tried to call out but the pain in his chest would not let him draw enough breath into his lungs. He tried to drag his body to the door but there was not enough strength left in his right leg and arm. He rolled back towards the desk, then gathered his right leg beneath himself and reached with his right hand to pull open the single middle drawer until it fell spilling onto the floor. He slumped back into a sitting position and quickly sorted through the confusion of small office things that scattered, and seized a paper pad and the stub of a pencil, then pulled the drawer onto his lap. Spots were dancing before his eyes as he positioned the pad on the drawer and forced the fingers of his right hand to pick up the pencil. Sweat was forming on his forehead and lip as he began to write, his useless left arm dangling. By force of iron will he moved the pencil clumsily to form one word at a time. The searing pain struck inside his chest again and he lost consciousness for one moment, shook his head, and focused his eyes once more, and finished the brief writing. His right hand relaxed and the pencil dropped onto the pad as his head tipped forward, and warm, friendly blackness came reaching for him.

At twenty minutes past nine o'clock General Hollins rapped on the office door, waited, rapped again, then opened the door to peer into the small room. He gasped, recovered, and a look of sadness crossed his face as he took two steps forward and knelt beside the body of Colonel Otis Purcell.

He was still sitting, head dropped forward, chin on his chest. The upside-down drawer was across his lap with the pad centered, the pencil lying beside it. His right hand was curled near the pencil, his left arm hanging limp, left hand on the cement floor.

Hollins gently laid the body on the floor and removed his own tunic to respectfully cover the face. Then he reached for the pad to read the few scrawled words.

Jan 2 1777. I am Otis Purcell. I am dying. I leave all my worldly possessions to Mary Flint. Signed, Colonel Otis Purcell.

CHAPTER XV

★ ★ ★

*T*he temperature had risen thirty-five degrees the previous afternoon, and in the evening, gray storm clouds had rolled in to seal the heavens. Through the night, a soft, warm rain had fallen steadily, quietly, then slowed and stopped. The storm clouds that had hung heavy through the night were thinning, and stars were showing, dull pinpoints in the swirling overcast. The snow on the ground was turning to slush, with pools of melt-water gathering in the low places as Eli stopped in a grove of maple and oak trees. Billy stopped beside him, and reached to grasp the cheek-strap of the brown gelding to hold it quiet. The silence was broken by the steady drip of countless icicles melting in the leafless tree branches all around them.

Both men were wet to the knees, and wet snow had packed and balled inside the horseshoes of the gelding. It stood beside Billy, moving its ears nervously, irritated at having been taken from a warm stall with hay and water in the middle of the night for no reason it could understand. Billy spoke to it softly and it settled. Both men listened intently for a time, but the only sounds were the dripping of the ice and the breathing of the horse as they silently picked their way north to the edge of the grove and again stopped.

The small town of Princeton lay half a mile farther north, ghostly in the light of the partially hidden quarter moon, the town lights showing behind the drawn curtains of a few scattered homes. On the near edge of town more than a hundred fires burned at spaced intervals, showing the orderly rows of the white tents of the British camp before them.

Eli spoke. "The British generals and high officers are in homes in town. Most of the soldiers are in those tents. Some captains and lieutenants are in the big ones." He raised his arm to point. "Over there at the east end of the camp they got about two hundred horses, some tied to ropes between trees, most held inside a rope pen." He shifted his point. "At the west end are eight wagons filled with kegs of gunpowder. They got pickets out watching both the horses and wagons."

He paused and turned to Billy. "I think I can get to the gunpowder and set some of it off. If I do, that ought to draw enough attention to let you get to the horses at the other end of camp. Cut the ropes and lead the whole bunch running through the middle of camp and make all the noise you can. I'll be waiting in the woods out past where the explosions will be. Pick me up and we'll ride double down to Five Mile Run and join de Fermoy and the ones Washington sent there."

Eli paused and scratched at his beard for a moment. "That ought to slow the British down some. Got any better ideas?"

Billy pondered for a moment. "How many pickets at the wagons?"

"Eight."

"Can you get past them and set off the gunpowder?"

Eli shrugged. "If I get there before it's too light and catch them by surprise. You got the worst of it. After the powder blows, everybody's going to be wide-awake and watching. It won't be easy to get to the horses."

Billy weighed his chances. "Maybe. I think they'll be looking west, where the fire and smoke are. One thing's certain. If we're going to do it, we better get started."

Eli took a deep breath. "When I go west, you go east. Keep the gelding quiet." He paused for a moment. "If something goes wrong, will you find Mary? Tell her I surely do wish her well."

Billy heard the urgency in Eli's voice. "I will. You better get moving."

Eli turned westward and was gone. Billy paused to tie the right leather bridle rein around the muzzle of the brown horse to stop any chance of a whicker or call, then turned east and threaded his way through the trees, leading the horse by the left rein.

The eastern sky was still black when Eli dropped behind a low growth of scrub oak at the west end of the sprawling British camp. He was less than one hundred yards from the nearest wagon, silhouetted by the fires two hundred yards further east, high and unreal in the night. He opened his mouth to breathe silently while he watched and listened for the pickets. One passed, then two, their boots making sucking noises in the slush and mud of the melted snow. He moved fifty yards north, facing the wagon farthest north in the line, and once again stopped to wait, watching, again counting the pickets.

Still eight. I have to get the first four to reach the wagons.

Hunched low, rifle in his left hand, tomahawk in his right, placing his feet carefully for silence, he came in fast. The first picket was turning when the flat of the tomahawk struck the crown of his head and he went down silently in a heap. Eli paused only long enough to be certain the picket was not moving, then turned towards the next one, forty yards away, near the second wagon. Eli groaned out loud as he moved away five yards and stopped, crouched low, waiting.

The second picket unslung his musket and came at a trot calling, "Robbie? What's wrong? Robbie?"

The last thing he heard was the sound of a footstep behind him in the mucky snow before the flat of Eli's tomahawk slammed down in the center of his hat. His knees buckled and he pitched headlong into the snow and mud less than eight feet from the first picket. Again Eli paused only long enough to be certain the men were not moving, then moved away quickly and once again dropped to the ground, waiting.

No one came in the silence, and Eli cupped his hand around his mouth and called, "Robbie? Where are you?"

Ten seconds later two pickets came charging, muskets at the ready. One stumbled over the two men on the ground and went to his knees cursing while the other one tried to stop too quickly, slipping in the snow and mud. The one on his knees started to rise, looked down, exclaimed, "They're both here."

For a moment both pickets stared at the black shapes on the

ground, unable to understand how they got there. Realization hit them both at once and one opened his mouth to shout an alarm just as Eli's tomahawk arced in the dull moonlight, and the man went down. The other one frantically grabbed for the hammer on his Brown Bess musket, then threw his arm upward over his head as the tomahawk flashed downward one more time. Lights exploded in his head as the flat of the blade smashed into his hat and he went down.

Four!

Eli left the pickets where they had fallen and sprinted towards the high-walled, heavy wagon. He vaulted into the box, seized the first keg of gunpowder and swung his tomahawk with all his strength. The wooden top splintered and Eli shook all the gunpowder out, spreading it at random over other kegs and onto the wagon floor. He threw the empty keg aside and smashed the tops out of the next two, again shaking the gunpowder out all over the remaining kegs. More than one hundred yards to the south, the remaining four pickets raised their heads to stare into the darkness, puzzled at the unexplained sounds, and they started north at a trot.

Eli seized a fourth keg and knocked the bung out of it, spilled out some of the powder, then set the keg down on its side. He crouched in the wagon box, cocked his rifle, held the powder pan low to the spilled gunpowder, raised the rifle muzzle to clear the end of the wagon, and pulled the trigger.

The rifle crack echoed in the darkness as the powder flared in the pan. The flash caught the gunpowder spilled in the wagon box and ignited it. The orange flame blossomed and hissed, and instantly Eli leaped from the wagon box, sprinting eastward hard for sixty feet before he dived headlong into the mud and rolled into a ball with his hands over his ears and his back to the wagon.

Inside the wagon box, the fire spread quickly through the spilled powder and reached the keg with the bung knocked out, and the hissing flame burned into the open hole. The keg exploded and ruptured four others clustered around it, and they exploded, and all the others blew. Flame and splintered wood were blasted three hundred feet into the air, lighting the night sky for miles. The wagon box was shattered, the axles splintered, the spokes blown out of the six-foot wheels, the hubs thrown outward sixty feet. Eli felt the sharp jolt as the concussion wave struck him in the back and rolled over him. The four pickets running towards the wagon were knocked sliding backwards thirty feet in the mud, stunned, disoriented. Tents at the near end of the camp were thrown down, and those at the far end of the camp were set flapping as the wave passed, into the open countryside. Windows in Princeton rattled, and seconds later lights came on in town.

Eli rolled onto his feet and watched as the remaining four pickets, all on the west side of the wagons, rose dripping from the mud, and came trotting north towards the scattered, burning wreckage, trying to force their numb minds to work. Eli, on the east side of the line of wagons, waited until he counted four pickets moving north, then spun on his heel and sprinted south to the last wagon. Once again he leaped into the wagon box and smashed three kegs and scattered the gunpowder over everything, then knocked out the bung of a fourth one and set it down. He quickly filled the pan of his rifle from the spilled powder, slapped it shut, cocked the hammer without loading either powder or ball in the barrel, lowered the pan to the heaped gunpowder, and pulled the trigger. The powder in the pan flared and ignited the gunpowder on the wagon floor. The moment it caught Eli leaped over the side and once again sprinted, this time eighty feet to the west, towards the trees and brush, and dived. He rolled into a ball, hands over his ears, back to the wagon.

At the east end of camp Billy crouched in a shallow ditch eighty yards from the rope pen holding one hundred eighty horses. To the right of the rope pen, twenty-two horses owned by the officers were tied to a rope line stretched between two trees. Billy held a firm hand on the cheek-strap of the bridle on the brown horse, and watched the pickets, black silhouettes against the glow of the campfires farther west. The British horses were settled, standing still, knees locked, dozing in the unseasonable warmth that had turned the ground inside the pen to a morass of mud and horse droppings six inches deep. He counted the pickets once more—ten of them—and cast an anxious glance at the moon, white in the black of night.

Where is he? Did they catch him? Catch Eli in the dark? Not likely. Then where is he?

The great flaming mushroom leaped into the sky at the far end of camp and Billy gasped, wide-eyed. The brown gelding jerked back against Billy's hold on the cheek-strap, ears pricked, eyes white-rimmed with fear, feet stuttering in the soft snow and mud. Billy caught the reins just below the bit and pulled hard, talking low to the horse, when the shock wave came rolling past.

The horses in the rope pen reared back away from the fireball in the heavens, and when the concussion wave hit them, they turned to run. They hit the rope, and the pickets shouted and waved their arms to hold them inside the enclosure. Slowly the herd backed away, milling, snorting, prancing in their fear while the pickets continued to wave and talk to them, trying to settle them.

Billy untied the muzzle of the brown and swung up into the saddle, musket held across his thighs.

One more. Come on, Eli. One more.

He heard the bits and pieces of splintered wagon and powder kegs begin to rain down on the camp, and he saw the British soldiers come boiling out of their tents, stunned, half dressed, peering west at the glow of the burning remains of the wagon. The officers burst from their tents to stare dumbstruck.

One more. I've got to have—

The second blast lighted the dark heavens almost two hundred yards south of the first one, and instantly the terrified horses in the rope pen reared back away from the great mushroom of flame and turned, snorting, whickering, prancing, ears working back and forth. The pickets closed in against the pen, screaming at the horses, waving their arms to keep them from running through the rope, and the horses turned around, heading west.

In the chaotic bedlam, Billy shouted and kicked the frightened brown gelding in the flanks and it bolted out of the shallow ditch and into a high run straight at the rope pen. At that moment the second concussion wave slammed into the horse herd. Their hooves dug into the wet muck and they turned once more, confused, terrified, and started for the east side of the rope enclosure at a run. The frantic pickets shouted and waved their arms, then fired their muskets into the air to turn them. In the face of the blasting muskets and the muzzle flame, the leaders set their front legs stiff and dropped their hindquarters to stop, and those coming behind plowed into them, then slowed. Slipping, stumbling, the herd turned to the right and ran along the rope with those behind following.

None of the pickets saw Billy racing in from behind. Hunched low over the neck of the racing brown, he swept past them, moving the same direction as the horses in the enclosure. The herd hit the rope on the west side of the pen, sliding, slipping, trying to stop, and began to pile up. Billy hauled the brown to a sliding halt and leaned from his saddle with his belt knife in his hand. In one stroke he cut the taut rope circling the tree trunk and the herd came streaming through the opening. Shouting, Billy slammed into the leaders and broke through to the front, and the herd fell in behind him, strung out, following as the brown raced west. There was no time to get to the twenty-two horses tethered nearby, and Billy didn't try. He glanced over his shoulder once and the one hundred eighty horses were there, running behind, following his lead. He spurred the brown to a stampede gait, straight down the thirty-foot-wide gap that divided the two rows of military tents, the herd thundering right behind.

The British soldiers standing between the tent rows staring west at the fires and the great clouds of smoke felt the ground shudder, heard the pounding of hooves from behind, and turned to see the wild-eyed horses stampeding straight at them. They tried to dive to one side; some made it, others did not. The horses behind the leaders could not see ahead and they stampeded to the right or left only to get tangled in the tents and the tie-down ropes, and they went down head over heels, ripping the tents from their pegs. They tore past the two big command tents with mud flying, and half a dozen horses plowed into the canvas sides, jerking the pegs and tie-down ropes out of the ground in their blind run. The great tents collapsed in on themselves, covering the officers and the horses in one great terrified, writhing mass.

Billy's brown gelding held the pace, legs driving, neck outstretched, ears laid back, and forelock flying while Billy shouted with all his strength as he crouched low in the saddle and gave the horse free rein, kicking it in the flanks at every stride with the wind whistling in his ears. They flashed past the tents and the campfire at the center of the camp, and then they were three-quarters of the way through. Then the last tents whipped past and they were running free towards the shadowy light of the burning wreckage of the two wagons, with the six remaining wagons between. Billy straightened in the saddle to take the slack out of the reins and brought the brown horse under control.

The pickets near the burning hulks of the two wagons swung around at the sound of the oncoming herd and stood still, baffled by the sight of more than half the horse herd streaming west in the night. They saw a mounted rider leading, but in the darkness could not identify who—friend or foe—and they watched the horses run thundering between the six wagons, out into the open field beyond, where they began to scatter. None of the pickets raised a musket as they watched the animals disappear in the darkness.

Billy pulled the brown down to a controlled run, angling west, standing tall while he peered into the black tree line.

Where is he? Where is he? He's got to be here!

Fifty yards to his left a dark shape broke running from the trees and Billy held his breath for a moment until he saw the arm waving. He turned towards the oncoming figure and then hauled back solid on the reins and brought the brown to a stiff-legged, sliding halt, mushy snow and mud flying. Billy kicked his left foot free of the stirrup as Eli tossed his rifle to him. Eli jammed his left foot into the stirrup and swung up behind Billy, and Billy raised the brown to a controlled run, turning southwest to stay out of the trees. He held the pace for three minutes, feeling the steady reach and gather of the brown's legs as it ran, then came back on the reins and brought it to a stop. The horse stood spraddle-legged, mud-splattered, sides heaving from its run. Eli slid to the ground and ran five paces away from the gasping of the winded horse, where he turned his head and closed his eyes to listen for two full minutes. Billy stood tall in the stirrups, eyes searching to the north for any pinpoints of light that could be the British following with lanterns. There was no sound of pursuit, and no lights followed.

Eli walked back to Billy. "See anything?"

"No."

"I doubt they're following."

"If they intend marching on Trenton, they'll be coming this way with daylight."

"Probably so. I figure they'll take the Princeton Road, west of here. It's better than the Quaker Road, but they're going to have trouble with the cannon in this mud." A wry smile crossed his face. "I expect they'll get a late start, with their horse herd scattered and two powder wagons gone."

"Likely. We better get over to the woods west of the Princeton Road and wait. General Washington needs a count on how many are coming."

Billy dismounted. "I ran the horse pretty hard. I'll lead him for a while." He turned southwest and Eli fell in beside him, slogging through the mud and melting snow in the dim light of the partially obscured moon.

Suddenly Eli asked, "Where's your musket?"

Billy's eyebrows arched in surprise. "I guess I lost it somewhere back there."

"Did you get those twenty-two horses on the tether rope?"

"No. No time. When those powder wagons blew things happened pretty fast."

"No matter. They'll be a while gathering the ones you scattered."

Dull moonlight sifted through the trees as the two men moved southwest, across the narrow bridge spanning Stony Brook, past Worth's Mill on their right. There the Princeton Road ran southwest through land that flattened into gently rolling hills with fields divided by heavy woods. Small streams worked their way to larger ones, all eventually joining the Assunpink to flow into the great Delaware River. Two hundred yards past the Stony Brook bridge they moved west of the road into a thick stand of trees and settled to wait in the patchy snow and mud, listening for the first sounds of fife and drum, and horses and marching men slogging through mud, and cannon rumbling in the night.

Minutes passed, and they lost track of time. The horse moved its feet impatiently in the soggy snow and soft layer of forest mulch beneath, uneasy, sensing the tension in the men. The eastern sky changed from black to deep purple, then gray. A light skiff of clouds appeared above the skyline, and both men watched as the sun, not yet risen, turned the undersides to deep crimson, then rose and yellow.

The temperature was rising. The woods were filled with the steady drumming of water dripping from icicles melting in the barren trees, drilling holes in rotting snow. Dark patches of hard earth appeared, then turned to mud, and in the low places puddles grew. Snow and ice that had lain six inches deep on the Pennington Road disappeared to expose the brownish-red clay, and then turn it into a sticky quagmire.

Eli glanced up at the pale sky, then loosened his coat. He looked about at the snow and ice, melting so rapidly it seemed the countryside was changing while he watched.

Don't remember it ever being this warm early in January. Not natural.

The thought bothered him. Everything he had learned taught him that all things in life finally came to rest on nature—what was natural. And when unnatural things happened, it unsettled him.

Eli broke the silence. "Maybe they decided to come on the Quaker Road."

Billy started to answer, then stopped, and turned his head to listen. The unmistakable sounds of chortling fifes came faintly on the clear air, and then the steady rattle of drums. Thirty seconds later the red coats, crossed white belts, and white breeches of mounted British officers flashed bright and proud as they rounded the gentle bend in the road approaching Stony Brook. The red, white, and blue of the Union Jack, and the regimental colors of the marching men sparkled in the brilliant light of a sun just rising. Behind the officers came the first rank and file of the regulars, followed by a company of green-coated Hessians jaegers, the elite German troops with their tall hats sparkling in the early light.

Billy drew the telescope from its case and studied the oncoming column for a full minute, then handed it to Eli, his face grim.

Eli waited until the British appeared at the turn coming into the Stony Brook bridge. He raised the glass and began the count.

More than twelve mounted officers led in a file. The one in front was fair sized, portly, with more gold on each shoulder and on his hat than Eli had ever seen before. He sat a tall, heavy-boned sorrel with four showy stockinged feet, and rode erect, head high, resolute, determined. The officers crossed the narrow bridge, followed by the first company of regulars. The sound of their fifes and drums was a steady, throbbing beat that was growing by the minute. The second company crossed the bridge, then the third, and Eli's breath came short.

Eli lowered the telescope and looked at Billy. "The main force. That officer in front must be Cornwallis. Leslie and Grant have to be there somewhere." Eli reflected for a moment. "One of us should go on down to Five Mile Run to tell them Cornwallis is coming, while the other one waits to see how many men and cannon are following."

"I think you're right." Billy raised the telescope and for a time watched and counted before passing it back to Eli. Billy pursed his mouth for a moment. "I'll go on down to Five Mile. You take the horse and see who's coming behind. I'll meet you there."

Eli nodded, and Billy handed him the reins to the horse. Eli said, "Stay out of sight. You don't have a musket."

Billy nodded as he turned, and Eli watched him move through the trees west to a streambed, then angle southwest, following it through the woods at a trot.

Eli continued the count as the column moved steadily southwest in the mud of the Princeton Road, which was growing worse with each passing minute. Horses were sinking halfway to their knees with each step. Soldiers' boots were sticking above their ankles in the soft brownish-red clay. Officers shouted orders and some companies left the roadbed, hoping for more solid footing, only to mire down in muck worse than what they had left. The column struggled on, mud splattered to their hips, angry, frustrated, cursing.

Eli held his place, telescope raised, counting intently. The commissary and ammunition wagons passed, sunk halfway to their axles in the sticky red clay, the horses straining into the horse collars to move them at all. Orders were shouted and men came with more horses, and the column stopped while they hitched them to the wagons, and once again the column moved on.

Sun glinted off brass and iron, and Eli swung the telescope back to peer as the first cannon came rolling onto the bridge. Their carriage wheels were clogged with mud, their crews covered with it as they grasped the spokes and bowed their backs trying to make the thick, six-foot wheels turn.

The sun was climbing in the east before Eli saw the last company cross the bridge and mire down in the ruts and thick morass of mud.

Close to eight thousand men. Twenty-eight cannon. They're fresh now, but they won't be after they've marched to Trenton in the mud.

He collapsed the telescope and shoved it back into its case, his thoughts leaping.

They got twice the number Washington's got in Trenton. The men at Five Mile Run don't have a chance against a force this size.

He was reaching for the reins of the brown when movement to the northeast caught his eye, and he raised a hand to shade his eyes as he studied Stony Brook bridge and Worth's Mill, beside it. A regiment of regulars had left the main column on the Princeton Road and were marching east, towards Quaker Road. Instantly Eli jerked out the telescope and extended it.

Two more regiments followed the first. The three of them marched one hundred yards from the road, where an officer stopped his horse, pointed, and the troops formed in an open field, near a stand of oak, maple, and pines. The mud-spattered regulars shrugged out of their knapsacks to leave them on the soggy ground while they began setting up their nine-foot iron tripods and hanging cook pots from the chains.

Eli stared in puzzlement. *Setting up camp? Within a mile of Princeton?*

He buckled the telescope back into its case, untied the reins to the brown, and quickly led it west through the stand of trees, away from the road and the three-quarter-mile long column struggling southwest through the quagmire. The trees thinned, and then Eli was out in an open meadow. He mounted and turned the brown southwest, parallel to the British column on the Princeton Road. He raised the horse to an easy lope, soft mud flying twenty feet in the air behind. Within minutes the brown was splattered from its chest to its hindquarters, and Eli's moccasins were covered.

Still half a mile west of the British, he caught up with the head of the main column as it reached the bridge spanning Eight Mile Run. While the leaders crossed the bridge, Eli put the brown down the slight embankment into the shallow creek, and stopped to let it bury its muzzle in the clear, flowing water to drink. A minute later he eased back on the reins and the horse raised its head, water dripping, munching at the bit. He reined it up the far bank, then on southwest, maintaining his half-mile interval with the column as it struggled on.

The sun was climbing when the column reached the bend in the road that turned due south, four hundred yards north of the place where the Princeton Road intersected with a northwest road that led to the town of Pennington. Eli stopped the brown and once again drew out the telescope to study the movement of the column. Suddenly he sat tall, watching intently as a section of the main column pulled out of line and left the road to continue on southwest across open farmland towards the tiny village of Maidenhead, just a few hundred yards west of the Princeton Road. Eli sat still as he counted.

Nearly fifteen hundred headed for Maidenhead. What's at Maidenhead?

He shifted the glass. The main column was relentlessly moving on towards the bridge at Five Mile Run. He replaced the glass in its case and made an instant decision.

That leaves five thousand five hundred with twenty-eight cannon, headed for Five Mile Run. I have to get there first.

He kicked the brown to a high lope, mud flying, and he held the pace as he passed Maidenhead and the road to Pennington. He reined left, towards the Princeton Road, and half a mile ahead of the British main column he came onto the roadbed with the British officers pointing at him, exclaiming. There was no musket that could reach him, nor could the short German rifles, and it would take five minutes to pull a cannon out of the column, load, and fire it. The frustrated British realized he had scouted their strength and position, and believed he was headed for Trenton to report to General Washington. The red-coated officers shouted obscenities and shook angry fists at him, but could do nothing more as they watched him ride out of sight, plowing through the mud on the Princeton Road.

Five Mile Run was a branch of the Assunpink Creek and all traffic on the Princeton Road traveling between Trenton and Princeton had to cross the Five Mile Run bridge, or ford the stream.

One hundred yards south of the bridge, Billy crouched in a stand of trees with ten soldiers under the command of General de Fermoy, eyes locked onto the bridge and the curving roadbed beyond, waiting for the first sign of an incoming rider, or marching British soldiers. The forest floor beneath their feet, thick with fallen leaves and pine needles, was spongy with the melting snow, and their hair, shoulders, and faces were wet with the dripping from the barren branches overhead. They held their hands over the powder pans of their muskets and waited in silence. Billy squinted up at the sun, moved his feet to relax cramping leg muscles, then settled.

He's had enough time. Too much. Where is he?

A bearded soldier beside him spoke quietly without turning his head. "Maybe they crossed over to the Quaker Road."

Billy shook his head. "Not likely. Too much mud."

The soldier wiped a wet sleeve across his mouth and resumed his silent watch, when suddenly his arm jerked up to point. "There! A horseman!"

A quarter mile past the bridge, at the place where the road turned southwest around a grove of trees, a mounted rider plowed steadily towards them, mud flying high behind the loping horse. The ten men each brought up their long, beautifully hand-tooled Pennsylvania rifles, ready, then glanced at Billy, waiting for his word as to whether the incoming rider lived or died on the bridge.

Billy's breath came short as he waited. The big-boned brown gelding came on, spotted with red-brown mud from shoulders to flanks. The rider raised his right hand and Billy saw the buckskin hunting shirt trimmed with Indian beadwork, then the face.

"Hold your fire. It's him."

Billy broke from cover as the horse's hooves rang hollowly on the bridge. He trotted out of the trees onto the road, waving, five of the soldiers following. Eli pulled the horse down to a walk, then a stop as he closed with Billy and the men behind him. He dismounted from the winded brown as Billy spoke.

"You all right?"

Eli nodded and wasted no time. "There's between five and six thousand British soldiers with twenty-eight cannon behind me, and they're primed for a fight. How many men you got here?"

"Eleven of us here. More back in the woods."

"With de Fermoy?"

Billy glanced at the man next to him for a moment. "General de Fermoy left a while ago. Headed back to Trenton alone. We've got about six hundred men here."

Eli's head thrust forward in disbelief. "De Fermoy *what?*"

"He's gone. Never said why. Just left."

"Then who's in command?"

"Colonel Edward Hand. We're part of his Pennsylvania regiment."

For the first time Eli paused for a moment to study the men gathered around Billy. They were bearded, tanned from summers in the sun and winters in the snow, dressed in buckskins and moccasins, long hair tied back, and each carried a long Pennsylvania rifle with an engraved walnut stock worn smooth. Their eyes were calm, disciplined, steady as they silently watched him, judging. He realized they had noticed his buckskins, his tomahawk, and knife as he rode in and had taken him to be an Indian, only to discover that he was a white man.

He could only guess how they were silently explaining it to themselves, but one thing became clear. These men had come from the deep woods of Pennsylvania where they had learned from the Indians to clothe and feed themselves from the land in all seasons. From the worn look of their buckskin bullet pouches and engraved powder horns, they knew that their lives depended on their rifles and their ability to use them with deadly accuracy over long distances. Instinctively Eli knew they would fight like Indians—remaining invisible while they struck, then disappearing instantly without a trace or sound to lay another ambush, strike, and disappear.

In the few moments of silent exchange, an odd feeling of acceptance, understanding, took root between Eli and the men facing him borne of their intuitive sense that they had all been forged and formed by the same laws of nature, and nature's God. Without a word passing between them, they understood and trusted each other.

"We haven't got much time. Where's Hand?"

Billy and those with him turned on their heels and set off at a trot back towards the woods, slogging through the mud and snow; Eli followed, leading the brown. They passed through the stand of trees that had hidden them, into a small clearing, where they stopped. There were moccasin tracks in the snow and mud, but nothing more. Then, in the surrounding trees, Eli sensed movement, and suddenly men silently walked into the clearing. They were clad in buckskins, and each carried a rifle, loose and easy, as they came to Billy and those with him.

There was no question which man was in command. Colonel Edward Hand stood over six feet tall, lean, tanned, broad in the shoulders, dressed exactly like his men. His long brown hair was tied behind his head. The aura of natural leadership and authority surrounded him like a great, invisible cloak, and in his eyes Eli saw the rock-solid determination, the compassion, and the respect that had made Hand a legend among his own men. They would follow him wherever he led.

Hand's voice was gentle, soft, and he did not waste words. "I'm Colonel Hand. You're Stroud?"

"Yes."

"Are the British on the Princeton Road?"

"Yes."

"How many?"

"Altogether, about eight thousand of them. But about fifteen hundred stopped at Maidenhead, and another thousand are back at the south side of Princeton. The main column has five thousand men with twenty-eight cannon."

"Know who's in command?"

"Cornwallis."

For a moment Hand pursed his mouth as he considered.

Eli spoke. "What happened to de Fermoy?"

Hand lowered his face for a moment. "I don't know. A little while after Weems got here and told us about the British coming, General de Fermoy left for Trenton. Didn't tell us what he had in mind." He raised smiling eyes to Eli. "Seems he drank about a gallon of rum before he left. Sure hope he can see straight enough to get back to Trenton. Be a shame if he wound up in Brunswick, or maybe New York."

Every man within earshot grinned, and Eli found himself grinning with them.

Hand paused for a moment. "Our orders were to wait here to see how many British are coming, and to slow them down to give Washington more time to dig breastworks and gun emplacements."

"How many men you got?"

Hand gestured as he spoke. "Some Pennsylvania Germans over there with a few Virginians, and my Pennsylvania riflemen, about six hundred. Captain Tom Forrest has two cannon."

"What do you figure to do?"

"Break up into two groups, one on each side of the road, east and west. Whichever side of the road has the best clear shot hits 'em with one group, then falls back to reload while the other group hits 'em from the other side. They haven't got a musket or rifle that can reach as far as ours, and it'll take 'em too long to set up cannon. General Washington wants us to slow 'em down until dark. Hand paused long enough to look Eli in the eye. "What do you think?"

"Good. We better get at it. What about the horse?"

Hand eyed the brown. "It'll be in the way. Turn it loose. It'll go home." Then he squinted upward at the sun, calculating. *About mid-morning, maybe ten o'clock. We've got to slow them down for about six hours.*

While Eli stripped the bridle from the brown and tied it to the saddle, Hand called out the names of two lieutenants and one captain, and with his small command gathered about, gave short, abrupt orders, pointing as he spoke. Eli led the brown ten yards away, then slapped it on the flank and it trotted away while Eli cached the saddle beneath a pine tree and joined Billy. Within seconds the force was divided into two groups, Hand leading one with a lieutenant second in command, the captain leading the other with a lieutenant beside him. Each group had one cannon.

"Any questions?"

There were none.

"Let's move."

One of Hand's soldiers handed Billy a rifle, bullet pouch, and powder horn, and the two groups moved north to within eighty yards of the bridge, one on each side. Billy and Eli remained with the group on the east side, and within two minutes the Americans had disappeared behind bushes or trees or in small streambeds to wait.

A mile north of them, General Charles Cornwallis spurred his horse ahead and came quartering in beside Major Donlevy Furman, commander of the first fifteen hundred infantry in the main column.

"Major, move your command ahead of the column and form an advance line at once."

"Yes, sir." Furman turned and shouted orders, and his infantry struggled to a trot in the mud, cursing as it splashed to cover their black boots, then their white breeches, and speckle their crimson jackets. Their fifes and drums fell silent as they opened a gap and left the main column behind.

Behind Furman's advance line, Cornwallis and his staff of officers rode horses caked with mud to their bellies, leading the main column as it plowed through the ruts and muck, struggling every step of the way to keep the heavy commissary and munitions wagons, and the cannon moving.

Furman's infantry rounded the gentle bend where the road turned to the southwest, and the Five Mile Run bridge came into view. Every eye in the line squinted in the bright sun, watching, waiting for anything that moved. Beside Major Furman rode a proud Hessian jaeger officer, green coat speckled with mud, long, waxed mustache stiff, high hat sparkling in the morning sun. He scowled, impatient with an army mired by mud, disgruntled that they were being sent to crush a ragtag army that should have been annihilated months ago on Long Island.

The bridge was clear. Beyond, nothing appeared in the barren trees or the bushes. They moved on, muskets at the ready, bayonets gleaming. As they came onto the bridge, they formed into a column, four men abreast, boots clumping on the heavy timbers as they crossed and moved on in the mud.

The whack and the grunt came at the same instant, and the German officer threw his hands high as he pitched headlong from his horse, towards Furman riding next to him, dead before he hit the muck in the road. Major Furman drew rein on his horse to stare down at the body, confused, momentarily unable to understand what had happened. A split second later the flat crack of a Pennsylvania rifle that had killed the German officer rolled past Furman. Instantly he hunched forward in his saddle as a second .60-caliber rifle ball whistled past his ear, followed by the cracking bang of a second distant, invisible rifle.

He jerked his horse around and shouted orders as the blasting sound of a complete volley reached him. Whistling rifle balls ripped into the officers around him and into the first ranks of his command; men grunted and groaned as they buckled and went down. With the first rifle volley still echoing, fourteen pounds of cannister shot came tearing into the column, followed by the blast of the cannon.

"Return fire!" screamed the British officers, and watched as those still standing in the first three ranks raised their muskets and looked for a target. But they could see nothing more than a faint showing of white smoke hanging in the trees two hundred yards past the bridge. Rattled, frightened by an enemy they could not see, they fired their muskets blindly into the trees and listened as the heavy .75-caliber Brown Bess musket balls smacked harmlessly into the tree trunks and branches. Then the leading ranks turned and those behind them gave ground as the entire advance command began a retreat back across the bridge towards the main column.

Behind them, Cornwallis heard the two, quick rifle shots followed by the sustained volley, and then the deeper sound of a British musket volley. He raised his hand and shouted, "Halt!" The main column stopped in the mud while Cornwallis's mind raced.

Who's up ahead shooting? Have we met the main army?

While he sat his horse forcing his thoughts, an officer beside him pointed excitedly. "There, sir! It looks like our advance command is returning."

Quickly Cornwallis had his telescope extended to peer at the oncoming soldiers. "Major Furman's command. Perhaps they ran into Washington's army."

They waited while the mud-spattered, grim-faced regulars retreated; Furman distanced his men and reined in his horse, breathing hard as he reported. "An American force at the Five Mile bridge, sir. Rifles. They fired at a distance too great for our weapons to match."

"How many casualties?" Cornwallis asked.

"Perhaps fifty, sir. Maybe more."

"Re-form your command fifty yards ahead of the main column. I will order additional troops to replace your losses. We will move on to the bridge."

"Yes, sir."

With another company of men to bolster their number, Major Furman once again called orders and the advance command moved south, with the main column a scant fifty yards behind. They rounded the slight bend, sighted the Five Mile Run bridge, and moved on to the scatter of red- and green-coated bodies lying in the mud, arms and legs thrown at odd, grotesque angles.

Cornwallis sat his horse, incredulous, making calculations of the distance from the trees where the rifle had cracked to the place where the German officer lay face down in the mud. *Over three hundred yards! Dead on the first shot!*

He raised anxious eyes. *They must know we're here. If it was Washington's main body, and they meant to engage us, then where are they?*

He spun his horse to shout orders to the advance command. "Major Furman, cross the bridge and take those woods at once!" He shouted at an artillery officer, "Bring up two cannon."

With Major Furman leading, the fifteen hundred infantrymen moved towards the bridge at a trot, while the artillery officer shouted orders to the first two cannon crews. Five minutes later two teams of horses trotted briskly past Cornwallis and the officers at the head of the main column, then turned sharply to swing their cannon around, muzzles pointing at the woods. The crews swarmed onto the big guns, two ramming powder, packing, and then the cannonball down the barrel before an officer shoved the sighting and elevation quadrant into the muzzle to take a hasty reading of angle.

At that moment the running feet of the first regiment shook the bridge as they swarmed past onto the open ground leading to the trees. They paused only long enough to form into their standard long lines with muskets loaded and lowered, bayonets thrust forward. On command they charged the trees at a trot. Behind them the cannon crews stood with linstocks smoking, ready to fire at the first Americans to run from the trees.

The cannon crews waited, eyes narrowed. Cornwallis extended his telescope to study the action. Furman's infantry closed with the tree line—fifty yards—thirty—ten—and nothing moved. They hit the tree line at a trot and picked their way into the grove. Some jays scolded, and a flock of blackbirds rose noisily from the treetops to circle above them, cawing their displeasure at the interruption.

Major Furman plunged on, dodging through the trees, sword held high. His command followed, their proud, straight line breaking as they worked through the trees. The major reached the far edge of the grove and ran into the small, open clearing beyond, shouting, waving his sword, intent on leading his command in a head-on charge to flush out the hidden American riflemen and annihilate them.

There were no Americans. Nothing moved except the birds. He slowed, then stopped as his men peered into the trees surrounding the clearing. There were no dark shapes slipping away, only the tracks of Indian moccasins and boots in the mud, leading southwest.

In frustrated rage Furman turned to his soldiers, shouting as he pointed with his sword. "They have fled to the far edge of the clearing. Form ranks and follow me."

He waited while they rapidly formed into the long lines once again, then led them trotting southwest towards the tree line on the south edge of the clearing, boots slogging, faces grim, expectant. He was past the center of the clearing before he saw the first movement in the trees ahead and realized it was men hiding behind trees and bushes, bringing the muzzles of their dreaded, long Pennsylvania rifles to their shoulders.

He opened his mouth to shout "Halt," when white smoke erupted in the trees and in the next instant it was as though a mule had kicked him in the chest where the two white belts crossed over his heart. He felt the hot, searing pain as the rifle ball punched deep, and then numbness as he tipped backwards off his horse, landing on his shoulders in the sticky red-brown mud. His last clear impression was one of wonderment as he turned onto his side and did not move again. He never heard the cracking blast of the volley that killed him and thirty-three of his men behind.

The British captain behind him gaped at his fallen commander for a moment before he could rally his shattered thoughts enough to shout the command, "Halt!" The regulars stopped, waiting, and he barked his second command. "First rank, kneel and prepare to fire!" The soldiers in the first rank went to one knee and brought their heavy muskets up as the captain opened his mouth to shout "Fire," when the second American volley erupted from the trees. The captain was the first British soldier to drop, dead from a bullet through his head, and behind him, twenty-one of the kneeling regulars grunted as the whistling musket balls knocked them over backwards. Some groaned and a few moved before they all laid still.

The young lieutenant who was next in command stood white-faced, brain numb as he stared at the major, the captain, and fifty-four men from the first rank, all dead in the mud within one minute. Around him the ranks of regulars began to back up, away from the trees from where the deadly rifle fire had come. The young lieutenant raised a hand and his voice cracked as he tried to shout his first command when the third volley rolled from invisible men in the trees. The lieutenant dropped where he stood, and sixteen of the regulars behind him stumbled and went down.

Those still on their feet spun on their heels and in an instant the remainder of the fifteen hundred British advance command was in a full, panic-driven rout. They plunged back across the clearing, into the woods, heedless of the tree limbs tearing at their faces and tunics.

East of them, on the far side of the Princeton Road, the second group of hidden Americans held their positions, watching, waiting, listening. They had counted three volleys, and then silence.

North, across the bridge, Cornwallis held the entire British main column at a standstill, waiting for the first regiment to return and report on how many men they were facing and where they were. From his position fifty yards behind the front ranks, he had heard the sounds of battle, followed by the ominous quiet. He licked his lips as he maintained his iron-willed control of his racing thoughts.

Those were American rifles, not British muskets. Why are we not firing back at them?

At that moment the first flash of red showed through the trees, and Cornwallis stood tall in his stirrups to watch the regulars of the first regiment break into the open. Most had lost their hats in their blind stampede through the trees, but they did not care. They ran on towards the Princeton Road, sweating, mud flying.

Eighty yards east of the road, Colonel Edward Hand calmly watched as the British regulars running nearly directly towards him reached the road. To his right were Eli and Billy, and to his left, twenty-two of his Pennsylvania riflemen. Hidden twenty yards south of them was the balance of his command, and Captain Tom Forrest with one cannon. All were hidden, invisible to both the sprinting regulars and General Cornwallis across the bridge.

Hand raised his left arm far enough for his men to see, and quickly pointed, first to Billy and Eli and three other men next to him, and then across the bridge at the two cannon Cornwallis had placed in front of his main column, each with a three-man crew. He shifted his arm and pointed at the balance of his three hundred men, then turned to point at the regulars who were plowing directly at them through the mud twenty yards west of the roadbed. Silently his men raised their long rifles and picked their targets.

Hand waited until the running regulars were five yards from the Princeton Road, then turned his rifle north and squinted down the gunsight. He settled the thin blade of the foresight into the center of the man holding the smoldering linstock behind the first cannon across the bridge, and squeezed off his shot. Instantly Eli, Billy, and the other three riflemen Hand had selected squeezed off their shots, and the six men handling the two cannon at the front of the British main column all crumpled and dropped.

The running British regulars just reaching the roadbed stopped so abruptly that half of them slipped to one knee in the mud. Stunned, wild-eyed, they saw six Americans eight yards east of the roadbed appear from nowhere, calmly drawing their ramrods to reload. The British regulars fumbled to bring their muskets to bear and in that instant nearly one hundred Pennsylvania rifles thundered and the leading ranks of the regulars staggered and went down.

Those behind had had enough. They broke for the bridge as hard as they could run, and had not gone four paces when the remainder of Hand's group cut loose from twenty yards south. More than thirty of the fleeing redcoats dropped into the mud, dead, just as Forrest touched off his cannon and its load of cannister came ripping. The survivors of the first regiment did not look back at their fallen comrades as they ran headlong to be free of the deadly fire that came from nowhere to cut their ranks to pieces.

The leaders were on the bridge when the American riflemen on the west side of the road fired their next volley, and the British dead piled up two and three deep on the wet, muddy planking. In a blind panic, those behind leaped over the bodies, stumbling, falling, rising to scramble on towards the mesmerized British main column waiting on the north side of the bridge at Five Mile Run.

Cornwallis sat his horse in angry astonishment. He had just been an eyewitness to the deaths of close to two hundred of Major Furman's vaunted infantry, and from the moment the first American rifle cracked to knock the German officer off his horse nearly one hour ago, the only Americans they had seen were the six who purposely stood up just past the bridge to reload.

He shouted hot orders over his shoulder. "Bring up five more cannon and two extra crews to replace the ones we lost. Move all seven cannon down within fifty yards of the bridge and rake those woods with cannister until I give further orders."

Minutes later five teams of horses came at a trot, dragging mud-caked cannon. As they passed the two big guns previously in place, the crews stared down at the six men who were still lying in the mud, unmoving, dead. The two fresh crews grabbed the reins of the horses still hitched to the two guns, and fell in behind the other five cannon, to follow them to within fifty yards of the bridge. Hunched low, using the horses and guns as shields, they loaded them before they wheeled the carriages about to bring the gun muzzles to bear south.

The moment the guns were lined past the bridge, point-blank on the trees on both sides of the road, the gunners jammed the linstocks onto the touchholes and the big guns bucked and roared. The crews peered through the smoke to watch the one-inch lead cannister balls rip into the grove of trees, tearing limbs and branches to pieces. Frantically they reloaded and touched off the second barrage, then the third, fourth, and fifth, watching as the trees were reduced to shattered stumps and the limbs blown to shreds, lying helter-skelter on the wet, spongy ground.

"Cease fire!" Cornwallis shouted, and the big guns fell silent while heat waves rose from the brass barrels. Cornwallis raised his telescope, and for three long minutes he glassed the trees, searching for anything that moved. There was nothing. He shoved his telescope back into its leather case strapped to his saddle as a look of grim satisfaction crossed his face.

There isn't a man left alive in those trees. We've cleaned them out.

Once again Cornwallis shouted orders. "Major Alexander, take command of Major Furman's advance infantry. Search those trees and return with a count of the American dead and wounded."

He watched while a white-faced Alexander led the shattered advance command through their own dead on the bridge, then divided, half to the left, half to the right. They disappeared into the devastated woods, and for five long minutes Cornwallis sat still, watching, listening. Then the regiment reappeared, trotting to the roadbed, back across the bridge. Alexander stopped his horse facing Cornwallis.

"Report."

Alexander licked his lips. "Sir, there are no Americans in those trees, either dead or wounded. Only tracks leading south. Mostly moccasins."

Cornwallis's shoulders sagged for a moment. *So that's their game. Delay.* "How many? A large force?"

"Sir, it's hard to tell. About six hundred, half on each side of the road."

Cornwallis shook his head. *Six hundred men, and they cut the advance command to pieces and stopped this main column for more than an hour.* For a second he felt a grudging admiration for the Americans. Then he straightened his spine and spoke to Major Alexander.

"Form the entire first regiment in front of the cannon as a skirmish line. At first contact with the Americans, fire a volley immediately, then move your troops out of the way to give the cannon an instant, clear field of fire." He called ahead to the officers in charge of the seven big guns. "Load the cannon with cannister and keep them at the front of the main column, twenty yards behind the skirmish line. Fire when the first regiment separates to give you a clear field of fire." He turned to a colonel. "Recover our dead and wounded and place them in the ambulance wagons as we cross the bridge and continue south. We move on at once."

Six hundred yards south of the bridge, hidden in a stand of pine trees, Colonel Edward Hand and his command waited while one of his bearded backwoodsmen descended from the top of the tallest pine, dropped to the ground, and handed the telescope back to Hand.

"They scouted the trees where we were and went back to the main column. They have another fifteen hundred infantry in front as a skirmish line. Just behind they've got seven cannon."

For a moment Hand considered. "They counted our tracks in the trees and they know we're only a small force. They intend on using that command in front to draw our fire, and then use the cannon to get us when they know where we are. We've got to keep them from reaching Trenton before sundown. Here's how we're going to do it."

The small band of Americans gathered about, Billy and Eli beside Hand, as he spoke first to his officers then to his men, pointing as he explained his simple plan. Then he took a deep breath and his eyes traveled around the circle.

"Any questions?"

There were none.

"Let's get to our positions."

Half a mile to the north, Major Alexander marched the advance regulars across the Five Mile Run bridge four abreast, then re-formed into a skirmish line with forty men abreast, laboring through the soft mud on both sides of the road, silently watching for any movement in the trees. Behind them the cannon formed into a single file to cross the bridge, with the iron shoes of the heavy horses striking hollow on the thick planking. The officers followed, then the main column came slogging.

Major Alexander, the officers leading the advance, and the men behind in the first rank marched in silence, tentative, knowing that each step could be their last. They did not know the name of the officer who led the small American command that had struck with such devastating precision, nor did they know from where the small band of men had come. What they did know was that many of the hidden Americans wore moccasins. If they wore moccasins, then they were from somewhere deep in the wooded mountains, where they had learned the art of war from the Indians whose cardinal rule was to strike hard from hiding, then disappear. And necessity had taught them to feed themselves and their families with those accursed long Pennsylvania rifles. Any man among them could hit a squirrel at one hundred yards and bring down a running deer at two hundred. Given a rest over which to steady the long barrel, they could put five consecutive shots on a seven-inch paper disk at three hundred yards, and five out of seven shots on the same paper at four hundred yards.

Worst of all, when fired from a distance, the whistling bullet reached its target before the crack of the rifle. In an ambush of more than one hundred yards, the first sound was of the bullet hitting, followed by the flat bang of the rifle that had fired. Many of the British officers and men who had died back at the Five Mile Run bridge never heard the sound of the rifle that killed them.

The first rank of Major Alexander's advance command marched on with the growing conviction that this would be their last day on earth.

Behind the advance regulars, the seven cannon with their crews, the British officers, Cornwallis among them, rode in silence, tense, watching the woods ahead. They stared as they passed the place where their canister shot had blasted the trees to splinters, and marched on southward between the woods and the open meadows that embraced the road.

Three hundred yards—four hundred—five hundred—and no Americans had moved in the trees. The main column trudged on amid the sound of thousands of boots and hundreds of horses' hooves plunging into the mud and the sucking noise of being drawn out.

The white-faced regulars licked dry lips, and dared let their thoughts run. *Maybe our cannon scared them away. Maybe they're gone. Maybe.*

Cornwallis wiped the sleeve of his tunic across his mouth. *They're not gone. They're still out there, waiting. I know it. I can feel it. Stubborn. Who are they? Who's that commanding officer? I wish he were on my staff. Him and a hundred more like him.*

Overhead the warm sun moved west in its undeviating path. Birds dressed in their winter plumage darted and flitted and scolded. Running water could be heard in the small draws and gullies as the snowmelt answered the eternal pull of lower ground. With each passing minute the frightened regulars eagerly drew an increasing measure of comfort from the workings of nature so abundant on all sides.

Cornwallis narrowed his eyes and made calculations. *The Shabbakonk Creek should be about half a mile ahead. One more bridge to cross, then on into Trenton. If we can just clear that last bridge before they—*

Without warning, rifle balls came smacking into the advance infantry, followed by the blasting of a volley from each side of the road, two hundred yards ahead, as more than fifty red-coated regulars dropped in their tracks, dead. The sound of the cracking rifles had not died when two cannons fired and twenty-eight pounds of cannister shot ripped into the leading ranks of Alexander's infantry. The regulars in the ranks behind fired their muskets south without aiming, then leaped from the roadbed to give the British cannon behind them a clear field of fire on the smoke drifting from the trees ahead.

The cannon crews stood dumbstruck for a moment before they lunged for the reins of the horses to turn the guns around. The moment the cannon muzzles came to bear on the faint remains of the distant rising smoke they rammed the linstocks onto the touchholes and once again the big guns blasted cannister shot that ripped through the bare branches of the trees. Hastily the crews loaded and fired a second, then a third volley before Cornwallis shouted orders.

"Cease fire. Gather our casualties. Regroup and keep moving."

A major mounted beside him turned in surprise. "Sir, aren't you going to send a patrol to assess the damage done by our cannon?"

"No. That's exactly what they want us to do—waste more time. Delay us until dark. They were gone before the cannister reached the trees."

Once more the terrified advance command closed ranks and moved forward, silent, hesitant, white-faced. In the distance they saw the dark line of tall, dead cattails and willows marking the banks of the Shabbakonk Creek. They groaned with the realization that once more they would have to form into a narrow column to cross the bridge, and in so doing they would be prime targets for five minutes, with almost no capability of returning a heavy field of fire.

They marched on, jittery thumbs locked over the hammers of their muskets, ready to cock and fire at anything that moved. The mounted officer leading the regiment bowed his head for a moment to plead with the Almighty for his life, and when he raised it he reined his horse to a sudden halt. He pointed as he shouted over his shoulder, "Halt! They've pulled down the bridge! Wait here while I ride to get orders from General Cornwallis."

He spurred his horse back to where the general waited impatiently. "Sir, they took the bridge down."

Cornwallis did not hesitate. "Ford the stream, at once."

"Where, sir?"

"Straight ahead."

The officer swallowed, wide-eyed. "Yes, sir."

He loped his horse back to his regiment. "Form into a skirmish line and follow me. We're going to ford the stream."

There was loud murmuring as the officer put his horse sliding down the muddy bank and jumped it belly deep into the swollen stream, then kicked it, lunging up the south bank. Behind him the first rank of the skirmish line skidded down the slick red-brown mud of the bank into the water and waded across, muskets held high, then clambered up the far side to level ground. The second rank followed and emerged on the south bank five yards behind the first.

The third rank was halfway up the north bank when once again the rifle balls came whistling, three hundred strong, raking the regulars on the level ground above the creek bank, knocking them backwards, rolling down the creek bank, taking those still climbing up back into the water in a tangle of the living, dying, and dead. Seconds later the two American cannon blasted, and grapeshot tore into the ranks in the water and those just descending the north bank.

From a narrow ravine one hundred fifty yards south of the creek, Colonel Hand studied the main column with a telescope. The British officers were frantically shouting orders while the devastated advance command ran pell-mell back towards the main column. The British cannon crews grabbed the reins of their frightened horses and jerked them forward towards the creek, then wheeled them sharply around to bring the seven heavy guns to bear south, towards the traces of rifle smoke filtering upward through trees and from the ravine where Hand and his men were hidden.

Hand gave a signal and his men backed away from the lip of the shallow draw and trotted west, then south, following the ravine out of sight of the British as the first volley of cannister came ripping into the trees and brush behind them. Three more cannon volleys blasted out before the Americans heard the red-coated regulars splash through the creek and charge into the woods and the ravine where they had been, followed by the distant cursing as the British once again found only tracks in the mud and snow.

Hand paused long enough to squint upwards at the westering sun and make time calculations. Then he gathered his command about him, Billy and Eli beside him on his right.

"Just about three hours of daylight left. Up ahead, about half a mile this side of Trenton, is Stockton Hollow. You know the plan. Let's go."

With Hand leading the single file column, his command followed the ravine until it flattened out into an open meadow. They stayed in the trees, skirting the open ground as they worked south. They emerged into Stockton Hollow where the road led downward into a natural, open draw, forty feet lower than the surrounding ground and more than one hundred yards wide.

Entering the Hollow from the north would be easy for the British, but once on the low ground, the Americans would have the high ground on the south side and the British would have a sharp incline to climb to reach them. The tremendous imbalance of six hundred Americans facing more than fifteen hundred British in the advance guard would be lessened, but none of the Americans had illusions that they could do anything more than slow the British.

Hand led his command down the north incline to the floor of the Hollow, across the bottomland, and up the south bank before he stopped to give orders. They divided the force, one half on each side of the road, each with a cannon hidden in the trees where they commanded a cross fire the length and breadth of Stockton Hollow. The Pennsylvania riflemen picked their places and vanished behind rocks and trees and in the brush overlooking the incline down to the bottomlands.

Minutes later they heard the distant sounds of officers calling orders to men marching in mud, and they remained motionless, waiting for them to appear on the road approaching the far lip of the Hollow.

The red coats of the weary, demoralized advance command appeared as distant dots and then grew until they were marching soldiers. They came on, and silently the Americans brought their rifles to bear, and waited in the warm, west sun. Hand had his telescope resting over a rock, studying the British, waiting to see in what formation the leading ranks would descend to the bottomlands in the Hollow.

They did not descend. Thirty yards short of the rim, the front ranks halted and marched off the roadbed. All twenty-eight cannon came straight on through, then divided, half on each side of the Princeton Road, spaced five yards apart. Calmly their crews placed their sighting quadrants in the muzzles, adjusted the screw elevations on the rear of the big guns for distance, and took their positions near the touchhole, awaiting orders.

Hand's breathing slowed. *Cornwallis is taking no more chances. He intends to rake this rim with cannister, then send his infantry through the Hollow with the cannon covering them.*

Instantly he called orders. "Get the cannon crews first, then the officers. Fire when you're ready!"

The distance from the line of hidden Americans to the British cannon was just over two hundred yards. The moment they got Hand's orders, the riflemen steadied their long weapons over a tree limb, or a rock, adjusted for range, and squeezed off the first volley. Of the eighty-one men in the twenty-seven cannon crews, seventy-three went down in the mud. At the same instant, the two American cannon blasted. One British cannon was blown completely off its carriage, another slumped and jammed the muzzle into the mud as the right wheel shattered.

In the forty seconds it took the Americans to reload, fresh British cannon crews sprinted from the ranks to snatch up the smoking linstocks and touch off the big guns. The air across Stockton Hollow was suddenly filled with whistling cannister shot that threw mud, snow, and bits of trees and brush thirty feet into the air all around the Americans. Several staggered and sat down in the mud.

Instantly the regulars in the British main column came charging like a great, red horde. They poured over the north rim, down onto the lowland, stomping through the mud and rotting snow, their shouts swelling, echoing.

Hand gave signals and the two American cannon crews depressed the gun muzzles and touched off their second volley. Grapeshot cut huge gaps in the oncoming British, but they closed ranks and kept coming. The American riflemen fired their second volley and the leaders in the red-coated mass went down. Those behind leaped over the bodies and kept charging. While the Americans were reloading, the second British cannon volley came ripping across the Hollow, over the heads of the regulars, to once more rake the American lines. Down in the bottomlands, the British soldiers were beginning to take cover behind anything they could find, running forward in short sprints to more cover, others following behind.

Hand made the hard decision. "Fall back! Fall back!"

Hard hands seized the trails on the two American cannon and men threw their weight into moving them back, one hundred fifty yards from the rim, where they quickly leveled the muzzles, reloaded, and covered them with tree branches and brush. The riflemen formed a line and the

Americans waited for the first wave of British regulars to come over the rim.

A red-coated soldier dodged into sight and took cover in a tangle of trees, and instantly there were hundreds of them charging forward. The Americans held their fire while Colonel Hand made calculations of the distance. Eighty yards—seventy—fifty—thirty.

"Fire!"

At nearly point-blank range the American rifles blasted and not one rifle ball missed. The leading British ranks folded and went down. Those behind came running, when the two American cannon roared. Twenty-eight pounds of lead balls coming in a cross fire tore a wide swath in the British lines. The British behind slowed, then stopped, and then began a controlled retreat, while the British cannon on the south side of the Hollow fell silent. Unable to see the Americans, and knowing their own infantry was closing with them, they dared not fire.

The British officers barked orders. "Cannon crews, advance and close with the enemy."

The gun commanders turned the big horses around, mounted the one on the left while the crews rode the trails, and fell into a column. They kicked the horses into a run, down the incline, across the bottomlands, and up the steep south slope, mud flying, the guns slipping, sliding, tilting crazily as they bounded over rocks and gullies in the road. All twenty-six of the undamaged guns cleared the rim and continued until they came to their own red-coated soldiers crouched in the trees, waiting. Instantly they formed a new line and the crews scrambled to load.

The moment they were loaded, the gun commanders shouted, "Fire!" Once again the cannister shot blasted trees and brush to shreds and threw snow and mud high in the air. Six Americans buckled and went down and did not move.

Colonel Hand took one quick glance at the sun, which was settling onto the western skyline. The junction of the Princeton Road and King and Queen Streets leading into Trenton was a scant six hundred yards behind them

One more hour. We've got to hold for one more hour.

"Fall back!"

Two hundred yards further south the Americans dug in once more, cannon separated, hidden, the riflemen crouched behind anything that afforded cover. The setting sun was casting long shadows eastward as the British once again wheeled their mud-caked cannon and crews into a long line and loaded.

Again Hand timed it to the second before he shouted, "Fire!" The American riflemen knocked the British gun crews backwards into the mud. Again fresh British crews surged forward, and again Hand shouted, "Fire!" The two American cannon blasted grapeshot in a cross fire that ripped into the fresh British gun crews. While yet a third wave of fresh British cannoneers were running forward, the American riflemen were desperately reloading. As the British gunners raised the linstocks to touch off another volley, Hand's men fired a hasty volley, and again the British gunners staggered and fell, while yet another line came surging forward to man the cannon.

They reached the big guns and before the American cannon could finish reloading, the British got off their volley. Mud and brush flew all up and down the ragged American line, and Hand gritted his teeth as men buckled and went to their knees. One entire American cannon crew was down, dead or wounded, and three of the nearest riflemen leaped to finish loading.

We've got to hold!

"Reload and fire when ready," Hand shouted.

The Americans held. They reloaded and kept firing, ducking when the British cannister came whistling, picking their targets, firing quickly, reloading frantically. The British edged forward slowly, dodging from tree to tree, firing blindly when they could not see an American for a target.

The sun slipped behind the western skyline while the cannon and rifles and muskets blasted. The distance between the American line and the advancing British was seventy yards when Hand again shouted the order to fall back. The Americans began a stubborn, dogged retreat— firing, moving back, firing—as the sun set. They reached the junction with King and Queen Streets, and the American cannon fired their last volley before starting down King Street. From behind houses and buildings, alleys and doorways, the Americans maintained their steady stream of rifle fire, refusing to run, determined to stall the British until full dark.

Suddenly the unmistakable sound of a cannonball whistling overhead stopped Hand in his tracks. Instantly he heard the blasting boom from behind, towards the Delaware River, and it flashed in his mind.

That was our cannon! Washington! He's coming—giving us cover!

The British and their cannon had reached the gentle rise on the north end of Trenton, and the American cannon under Washington's command were dug in on the rise on the south side of the Assunpink Creek. With the gray of dusk falling, the big guns traded shot for shot, volley for volley, the cannonballs whistling over the town.

From behind Hand's command came a surging battle cry from five hundred voices as Americans from Washington's command came pounding up the muddy streets, muskets blasting. They reached Hand, and with his small command in their midst, the Americans all began a slow, steady retreat, back towards the Queen Street bridge. The British followed, musket and rifle fire hot from both sides.

Two mounted riders appeared among the men, shouting encouragement, and Eli glanced to see Generals Nathanael Greene and Henry Knox mix among the men, shouting them on. They backed onto the Queen Street bridge with musket balls whistling, and Billy and Eli went to one knee to aim and fire while the remainder of Hand's command crossed. Billy and Eli jerked out their ramrods to reload as they backed across the bridge when Billy turned to peer into the dusky shadows behind, and his eyes widened.

In the fading light he saw the tall form of General George Washington sitting on his white horse at the other end of the bridge, waiting for the last man to clear. British musket balls were singing everywhere, and cannonballs were blasting mud and brush all up and down the Assunpink Creek bank. Yet, Washington was sitting as calm and erect as though on a summer's evening horseback ride.

Eli saw Billy's stare, and glanced backwards, then stopped to look before the two of them backed across the bridge, past the general, to the safety of the American trenches and breastworks. They joined Colonel Hand with his command and waited for further orders when the sounds of heavy gunfire reached them from up the Delaware to the west. They waited and listened, and thirty seconds later a rider came charging into camp.

"They tried to cross up there on one of the fords. We stopped 'em."

Hand said quietly, "This isn't over yet. I think they'll try the Assunpink bridge one more time before dark."

No sooner had he spoken than the sounds of British infantry running through Trenton reached them, and in the dwindling light they saw the red-coated regulars of the advance command swarm towards the bridge. Sergeant Joseph White, with the cannon he had repaired and saved after the battle of Trenton, was on a rise overlooking the bridge. With fifteen other cannon crews, he brought his gun to bear point-blank on the bridge.

From beside him came a calm, high, nasal voice. "All right, you lovelies, hold your fire until I say."

Sergeant Alvin Turlock watched the red-coated infantry reach the bridge, shouting as they came. He waited until the leaders reached the south edge of the heavy wooden structure before he shouted, "Fire!"

Wood shards, mud, and water flew. When the smoke cleared, not one British soldier was standing on the bridge.

"Reload," shouted Turlock, and sixteen gun crews scrambled as the second wave of British infantry came swarming. They leaped over their own dead in their second attempt to take the bridge, and again Turlock let them reach the near edge.

"Fire!"

In the deep twilight, orange flame leaped fifteen feet from the muzzle of every American cannon, and again the British on the bridge were lost in a cloud of wood splinters, mud, and creek water. When it settled, the British dead were stacked two deep on the bridge and more than twenty were in the water, not moving. Their regimental colors and their Union Jack, which had fluttered so bravely in the shimmering light of sunrise, were shredded, their poles splintered. They lay stained, trampled in the mud.

"Reload," shouted Turlock one more time as the British made their last charge. When the smoke cleared, the bridge was heaped with the dead. Bodies were scattered on the creek banks and in the water. The groans of the dying could be heard for a hundred yards. The British remaining on the north side were retreating to disappear into the dark streets of Trenton.

For a few seconds, Turlock watched and listened, then turned to the cannon crews. "Cease fire. It's over for now."

Notes

On January 2, 1777, General Charles Cornwallis marched out of Princeton with 8,000 men, among them some of the best British and German soldiers in the world. With orders to retake Trenton and eliminate the Continental army, Cornwallis left Colonel Charles Mawhood with 1,000 troops as a rear guard for Princeton, and another 1,500 men under the command of General Alexander Leslie at Maidenhead for reserves. Both Mawhood and Leslie were to bring their commands to Trenton the following day (see Ketchum, *The Winter Soldiers*, pp. 286–87).

Cornwallis's efforts to march to Trenton were seriously hampered by an unexpected turn in the weather. The previous day had warmed well above freezing and a warm rain had fallen, turning the dirt roads and the countryside into deep mud. Horses, wagons, cannon, and men were mired down and unable to find solid footing (see Ketchum, *The Winter Soldiers*, pp. 286–87).

General Washington had anticipated the move by Cornwallis, and had sent about six hundred men under the command of General de Fermoy to meet the British at Five Mile Run and delay them until nightfall. However, de Fermoy abandoned his command without notice or explanation and returned alone to Trenton, leaving Colonel Edward Hand in command of the trained Pennsylvania riflemen to engage the British column at Five Mile Run. The first shot knocked a Hessian officer from his horse. General Cornwallis ordered out an advance guard of 1,500 men to clear the Americans from the woods. Though the novel portrays an advance guard constantly totaling 1,500 men, historically there was only one command of 1,500 soldiers, whose losses ranged from 100 to 500 men (see Ketchum, *The Winter Soldiers*, p. 290). Hand, highly skilled in fighting in the woods, laid ambush after ambush at Shabbokonk Creek and Stockton Hollow, was slowly forced to give ground as the vastly superior British force struggled on (see Ketchum, *The Winter Soldiers*, p. 289).

At dusk, General Washinton's cannon south of Trenton commenced firing over the town and into the oncoming British, giving Hand and his men cover while they stubbornly held their ground as the dusk deepened. Amid whistling musket and cannon fire, Washington sat on his horse by the Assunpink bridge until all of Hand's men had reached safety (see Ketchum, *The Winter Soldiers*, pp. 289–90).

Three times the advance British guard attempted to cross the bridge, and each time the American cannon and musket fire stopped them. Sergeant Joseph White recorded, "such destruction it made, you cannot conceive. The bridge looked red as blood, with their killed and wounded, and their red coats" (as quoted in Ketchum, *The Winter Soldiers*, p. 290).

It was full dark when Cornwallis's main column finally reached Trenton. Unwilling to make a night attack, the British and Hessians were forced to make camp and wait for morning (see Ketchum, *The Winter Soldiers*, p. 291).

CHAPTER XVI

★ ★ ★

*T*he deep gloom gave way to the black of night as the big guns fell silent. The weary, hungry American army gathered wood for fires and sat on rocks and logs in small groups to heat coffee and salt beef, and gnaw on hardtack. Sounds drifted from Trenton across the Assunpink Creek, where British soldiers were roaming the streets, working systematically through the wreckage of the shattered and burned buildings, taking what they wanted.

North, towards the bridge, they heard General Henry Knox call orders to three cannon crews. "Fire a volley into Trenton every few minutes until further orders. Keep those redcoats jumping!" Thirty seconds later, flame leaped fifteen feet from the cannon muzzles. The flash lighted the creek's banks for a hundred yards, and the exhausted soldiers turned their faces away while the concussion rolled past and the echo faded in the night.

A young soldier seated across the fire from Billy held his steaming coffee cup with both hands, nursing it as he sipped. In the firelight, Billy could see the deep doubt and concern in his eyes as he spoke.

"Seems to me we got ourselves in a fix," he said. "The British army's just over the creek. We can't back up because of the river and we can't move up or down the river 'cause they'll be right on top of us. Yes, sir, we got ourselves in a fix." He turned troubled eyes to his lieutenant. "Lieutenant Bridges, sir, isn't that so? We're in a bad fix?"

The eleven men in the circle stopped all motion, all talk, and turned their eyes to Lieutenant Bridges. Young Stephen Olney had voiced the single question that was riding each of them like a great black cloud.

Had General Washington led them into a trap from which none of them would escape?

Lieutenant Bridges looked at the anxious, young eyes of Stephen Olney for several moments, aware of the silence as the men waited for his reply. He stared into the fire, searching for words, then said thoughtfully, "I don't know." He raised his eyes and quickly glanced around, face calm, voice steady as he finished. "The Lord will help us."

The unexpected answer caught everyone by surprise, and for a few moments a hush held them. Then the cannon by the bridge blasted out a second volley and all the men flinched, recovered, and continued sipping at their scalding coffee.

Billy broke the silence. "General Washington won't let us get trapped here."

Eli raised his eyes. "Did you see him? At the bridge? Sitting that white horse until we were all across? British musket balls and cannon shot all around, and none hit him?"

Billy turned towards Eli. "I saw."

Eli sipped gingerly at his steaming cup. "That Indian might have been right, back there about twenty-two years ago. Maybe Washington can't be killed by musket or cannon. Maybe he will live to be the father of a new country."

The men raised surprised eyes and Turlock asked, "What Indian?"

"Back when Washington was with the British, and Braddock got killed. An old Indian chief saw his best warriors try to shoot Washington so close they couldn't miss, but they did. He said Washington couldn't be killed by a bullet or cannonball, and he would live to become the father of a great nation."

Turlock's eyebrows arched. "First I heard of it. Who was the Indian?"

Eli shook his head. "I never heard. But the Indians remember it. I wanted to see Washington, to judge whether the story is true. That's partly why I came to join his army."

Turlock squinted one eye and sipped at his coffee. "What do you think now?"

Eli pondered for a moment. "After what I saw at that bridge, it might be true. If it is, he's special. Time will tell."

An involuntary shiver ran through Turlock and he murmured, "Chill coming in."

Eli said, "It was too warm today. The thaw sure slowed down the British. Looks like a freeze might set in just in time to let Washington move the army out."

Olney's head swung around towards Eli. "You figure the Lord's doing things with the weather?"

Eli sipped at his coffee. "The weather's been acting unnatural, in our favor. That old Indian I mentioned might say the Almighty was watching over the general. Bridges, what do you think?"

Bridges stared into the fire and repeated himself. "The Lord will take care of us."

The cannon by the bridge roared again, and all eyes turned northwest to watch the orange flashes as the cannonballs exploded in the streets of Trenton.

Billy lowered his coffee cup for a moment. "Cornwallis is over there somewhere. I wonder what he's thinking by now."

Eli wiped his sleeve across his mouth. "After that mauling his column took today from Hand, I imagine he's a little vexed. He's likely getting his entire army ready for one big push to get us all."

Turlock raised his eyes to stare thoughtfully into the darkness across the Assunpink Creek. "If he comes with a night attack . . ." He didn't finish the sentence. All eyes in the circle turned northwest for a moment, then the men resumed working on their steaming coffee cups.

"Weems and Stroud." The call came loud in the dark. Billy and Eli both turned to peer up the creek bank. A mounted rider was coming, shadowy in the low cook fires on the sloped creek bank.

Billy and Eli both set their coffee cups on a log and stood, and Billy called, "Here. Weems and Stroud are here." They watched him come in, a small, wiry man, riding a jaded bay mare with vapor trailing from her nostrils. Her eyes glowed wine red in the firelight as he reined her to a stop. The flames reflected from the gold on his tricornered hat and his shoulder epaulets.

"You're Corporal Weems and Private Stroud?"

Billy answered. "Yes, sir."

"I'm Major Harrison. General Washington wants you at the command post. Do you know where General St. Clair made his headquarters?"

Billy nodded. "Yes, sir. That big house west of here."

"That's the place. You're to come now."

"Yes, sir." Billy reached for his musket as Eli picked up his rifle. Before they started along the creek bank, both men paused for one moment to look northwest, across the creek at Trenton, deserted and quiet except for the British soldiers still lingering in the dark streets, lighted only by the smoldering fires started by Knox's cannonballs.

"He's over there," Eli said quietly. "Corwallis and his army. I'd like to know what they got in mind."

Across the Assunpink, on the low hill just past the major road junction at the north end of Trenton, General Cornwallis silently cursed the mud as his aide held back the flap of a hastily erected tent. Cornwallis ducked to enter, and his staff of general officers immediately rose and came to attention until he was seated.

His jowls shook slightly as he spoke. "Be seated. Gentlemen, we have little time to make a difficult choice. The best information I have is that most of Washington's forces are just south and east of Trenton throwing up breastworks and entrenchments along the banks of the Assunpink Creek. They have about thirty cannon. Their force is composed of perhaps four thousand six hundred troops, of which three-quarters are absolutely green militia. The decision which we must make immediately is whether we conduct a night attack or wait until dawn. I am open to suggestions."

Sir William Erskine, the quartermaster general of Cornwallis's command, spoke instantly. "Sir, in my opinion, the decision is obvious. At this moment, the rebels are still set back on their heels in an entirely defensive posture. The critical momentum is all in our favor. We cannot allow them to recover and regroup."

General James Grant, taciturn, stubborn, still filled with nothing but contempt for the entire Continental army, shook his head violently.

"I disagree. Our forces have just concluded a ten-hour march through mud—under fire most of the way—and they need time to gather strength. We are on unfamiliar ground. How do we cross the Assunpink? Ford it? It's swollen from this cursed thaw. And what lies across the Assunpink? How far east do Washington's lines go? How well entrenched are they? How many men will we lose needlessly if we try to storm their breastworks in the dark, on ground they know and we do not?" He shook his head again. "Wait until morning."

Erskine dropped his palm smacking on the table. His face flushed as he turned hot eyes towards Grant. "Are you certain he will be there in the morning? Have we forgotten his overnight evacuation from Brooklyn across the East River, when General Howe was certain he had him trapped? And again at White Plains? If Washington is the general I take him to be, his army will not be found there in the morning!"

Grant grunted. "Nonsense. He's trapped. He has no boats to cross the Delaware to the south, and if he moves his army east or west, they'll be strung out for miles, and at our mercy when we catch them. He has to stand and fight where he is, and that will be the end of him."

Erskine's voice was brittle, his eyes glowing like flecks of obsidian. "Mark my word. He will not be there if we wait until morning."

Cornwallis intervened. "Thank you, gentlemen. Taking circumstances as they now exist, it appears to me we will experience fewer losses if we storm the rebel positions in daylight. Our troops are exhausted. They need rest. I can see no way out for Washington. He has no boats to cross the river, and he cannot march his army east or west and fight at the same time." He leaned forward in his chair and said matter-of-factly, "We've got the old fox safe now. We'll go over and bag him in the morning."

Von Donop raised a cautionary hand. "Sir, may I recommend that patrols be sent east to probe Washington's right flank throughout the night? We need to know his location, and where the rebels are moving."

Cornwallis eased his back against his chair to consider. "We'll keep patrols on the southern limits of Trenton to be certain he does not move during the night. That should be sufficient." He waited while von Donop settled before he finished. "I will send written orders by special runners to both General Leslie and Colonel Mawhood to bring their troops to join us immediately. With their added strength the battle should be over very quickly."

As the British officers left the tent, each slowed to peer south across the big road junction. The sounds of their own soldiers prowling the streets of Trenton drifted to them on the night air, and each of them reached to turn up his overcoat collar against the north breeze that was becoming steadily colder. They slogged through the hardening mud to their horses with one unspoken thought in each of their minds.

Will he be there in the morning?

South and east of them, across the Assunpink, out of range of the British cannon, General Washington stood at the head of a long conference table in the library of the two-storied home where General St. Clair had established his headquarters. Before him sat his general officers, keenly aware that Washington was impatient with the late arrival of Brigadier General Arthur St. Clair. They sat in silence, tight-lipped, eyes diverted, waiting.

Nothing could be more clear to them than the fact General Washington had brought the Continental army to a place that had become a death trap. With a powerful British force at the other end of Trenton, poised to crush them to oblivion at any moment, each officer was harboring dark questions about the judgment of their commander in chief. They turned at the sound of horses approaching, and moments later a sturdy rap came at the door.

General Washington spoke. "Enter."

Major Robert Harrison, a new officer on his staff, opened the door to announce, "Sir, General St. Clair has arrived."

"Show him in."

St. Clair took the empty chair on the near side of the table and turned towards Washington, waiting, and Washington did not hesitate.

"We have little time. General Cornwallis and most of his force is camped on the small rise at the north end of Trenton. He has five thousand five hundred seasoned troops with about twenty-eight cannon, and two thousand five hundred more men in reserve, all of them ready to fight. We have twelve hundred seasoned troops, with about three thousand four hundred green militia who have never seen battle." He paused to let the information settle into the officers.

"Cornwallis is going to attack. The only question is, when? Should he attack now or in the next few hours, we will be hard-pressed to survive."

He stopped to unfold a map and spread it on the table, and nodded to General John Cadwalader. "General Cadwalader made this map based on information received from reliable spies. It shows all of the roads between here and Princeton, and how the British were disbursed until this morning when General Cornwallis marched out. Take a little time to make yourselves familiar with it."

He stopped. The clock on the mantel ticked steadily in the silence as the officers intently studied the rough drawing. Then, one by one, they leaned back in their chairs and turned once again to General Washington.

"We must decide. Shall we remain here? Or shall we retreat down the Delaware and hope to cross into Pennsylvania somewhere? Or shall we try to find a way to take the initiative—to attack them?"

Dead silence settled. Sullivan leaned forward. "Sir, did I understand you correctly? You're suggesting we attack them?"

"That has been in my mind for some time."

St. Clair interrupted. "Surprise them at Brunswick or Princeton? They would never expect it."

Washington nodded. "I've had a patrol of Philadelphia Light Horse and two scouts around Princeton for two days reporting on British strength and movement. General Cornwallis didn't leave much of a force behind to defend Princeton. There are substantial stores kept there—food, clothing, munitions.

He paused and an intensity came into his being that struck an awe into the officers. "Our victory at Trenton shocked the British, but far more important, it lifted the spirit of our countrymen beyond anything we could have hoped. An attack now would not only avoid the appearance of a retreat, it would add to what is already a tremendous surge of commitment to the cause of liberty."

Again he paused, and no one moved or spoke as he went on. "Let me direct your attention to the map." He laid a forefinger on the spread paper. "We are here, with Trenton just across the creek, here." His finger shifted as he spoke. "North of Trenton is the Princeton Road, which is the one used by General Cornwallis to get here today. Over here to our right, east of us, is the Quaker Road. It also connects Princeton and Trenton. Princeton Road is the better of the two roads, but Quaker Road is passable. It runs here, easterly past Sand Town, then angles north here, across Miry Run and past the Barrens. It crosses a road here, and then crosses the Assunpink here, before it angles westerly a bit, on towards Princeton, where it crosses Stony Brook, here."

He paused in the silence and waited until every eye was on him. Then he tapped the map.

"The single most critical factor in any assault we may make on Princeton is right here."

Each man half-rose from his chair to pore over the place where Washington's forefinger had come to rest.

"About nine hundred yards after Quaker Road crosses Stony Brook, you see that the road forks, here. The left fork continues on nearly due north, parallel to Stony Brook, to connect with the Princeton Road, here, just north of Worth's Mill." He retraced the road, back to the fork. "The right fork of the road, here, angles off to the northeast, and proceeds behind three prominent farms, across Frog Hollow Ravine, and on into Princeton. The farms are owned by Thomas Clark, William Clark, and Thomas Olden."

Once again he paused for a moment. "Now, notice. By coming behind these three farms, the road is also behind all the fortifications, all the breastworks, all the gun emplacements built by the British, and there is a large stand of trees that hides the road from almost everything to the west. This road will allow us to bypass most of the British defenses and troops undetected, and still reach Princeton."

The officers raised their heads, eyes narrowed as the stunning realization reached into them.

He intends to attack Princeton!

"In the past few days I've talked with Colonel Joseph Reed, Philemon Dickinson, and General St. Clair about the feasibility of using the route I've just shown you to reach Princeton. Each of them is familiar with the area, and agreed it could be done."

General St. Clair nodded his head once.

"I've also asked a few of the local residents to be here tonight to answer questions about the idea." He turned to his aide. "Major Harrison, are they here?"

"Yes, sir. Waiting."

"Show them in."

They entered the room hesitantly, five civilians in a military world, keenly aware of their lack of proper military protocol. They felt the tension in the room, and stood with nervous eyes darting from one officer to another, finally settling to stare at General Washington, wishing they were home among their own.

"Thank you for coming. I have asked you here because we need some critical information you may have about the nearby countryside. Perhaps the best way to proceed is to let my staff of officers pose questions."

They began immediately. What are conditions on Quaker Road at this moment? Will it support cannon? wagons? What obstructions? Is it flooded at any place? Have you seen any British soldiers on Quaker Road today? yesterday? Are the bridges passable? Is the road east of the Clark and Olden farms shielded by trees?

One at a time the local farmers answered. Quaker Road was muddy when we came in this evening. Cannon and wagons will have trouble with the mud unless the weather changes. It is not flooded. There were no British soldiers on the Quaker Road today, or yesterday. The bridges are all passable. The road behind the three farms is not generally visible from the west.

The questions ceased and General Washington brought his full attention to bear on the group of farmers. "Should we decide to march to Princeton, would you consider acting as our guides?"

For a moment all movement in the room ceased. The officers turned startled eyes to Washington, stunned at what he had revealed to the civilians without first stating it openly to them. The five farmers stared at Washington while their minds went numb. *Guide the Continental army on a night march to Princeton?*

One of the farmers stammered, "Sir, uh, our wives and families—they won't know."

"I'm sorry for that. We need you."

The men looked at one another for a moment, shrugged, and turned back. "We will do it."

A sigh escaped the officers. Washington turned to Major Harrison. "Would you see to it these men receive a good supper and are allowed to rest until further notice? And bring in the two scouts."

Harrison led the five civilians out, down the hallway, to a sergeant at a desk in the parlor. Major Harrison spoke. "The general has ordered these men fed and given a place to rest until further orders."

"Yes, sir. I'll see to it."

Harrison turned and walked back down the hall to a small room next to the library, and opened the door. Billy and Eli stood as the door swung open.

"General Washington is waiting."

They left their weapons behind and followed Harrison back into the library. They both quickly glanced at the officers, then faced General Washington. The officers stared at Eli's beaded buckskin shirt for a moment.

"Gentlemen, I present Corporal Billy Weems and Private Eli Stroud. They spent the last two days scouting between here and Princeton. I have a few questions."

He nodded to Billy. "Did you see General Cornwallis march his force into Princeton from Perth Amboy?"

"Yes, sir."

"Did he disperse any of his command on Quaker Road?"

"No, sir. There were about one thousand, and they all marched on into Princeton."

He shifted to Eli. "When General Cornwallis marched out of Princeton, did he disperse any of his troops east, towards Quaker Road?"

"No. He left about a thousand on the south edge of Princeton, and another fifteen hundred at Maidenhead. None went east to Quaker Road."

Washington tapped the crude map at the fork of the Quaker Road, above Stony Brook. "Do you recognize this area?"

Eli studied it for a moment. "Yes."

"Can the right fork of this road be seen from the west?"

Eli's answer was firm. "Not right there. There's trees and a few low hills on the west side of the road. Further north there's a place or two where someone on the Princeton Road could see, but not at the fork."

For a moment Washington lowered his face to stare at the table. "What were weather conditions outside when you entered this building?"

Eli answered. "There's a cold north wind rising. The mud's setting up hard right now. If the wind holds I expect by midnight it'll be frozen solid out there."

Washington turned to his officers. "Do you have any questions?"

There were none.

A hush settled over the room for a moment before Washington spoke again. "Thank you. You are both dismissed." He turned to Major Harrison. "Would you show these men out?"

As they stepped out the back door into the chill of the rising north wind, Billy turned to Eli, eyes wide in the darkness. "He intends marching on Princeton, probably tonight!"

Eli nodded. "The way he was asking about Quaker Road, and the right fork up above Stony Brook, it sure sounds like it."

Behind them, inside the conference room, Washington again faced his officers. "Let me be blunt. We will be defeated if we remain here. We cannot cross the river. Our only choice is to move. If we move, we have only two choices. Go southwest along the Delaware and hope to find a place to cross the river, or move northeast around General Cornwallis's forces and attack Princeton. The risks are about the same no matter which way we go because we will be a marching army, which as you all know is very nearly a defenseless thing."

He stopped and for a split second his officers saw the deep anxiety in his eyes. "The question is, can we move northeast without being detected? I think we can. If we leave a small command of men here with orders to keep large fires burning all night, make a show of going out on patrol, and create considerable noise digging trenches, I believe we can deceive the British with the illusion that our entire force is still here. The men left behind will stop just before dawn and come to join us."

Again he stopped for a moment while his officers sat in rapt silence.

"If we wrap the wheels of the cannon carriages with blankets and canvas, and if the ground freezes as I expect, they can be moved quietly. The heavier baggage wagons that will make noise can be sent down to Burlington where General Putnam will cross them over to Pennsylvania and safety."

Washington waited while comments went around the table.

"There's terrible risk. If the British discover we're no longer here, or if one of their patrols happens onto us while we're on Quaker Road, they'll have cannon and cavalry there before we can set up any appreciable defenses. If we have to fight Cornwallis's entire command in open country without trenches and breastworks, we will be defeated. I want no man here to think otherwise. If we agree to do this, we could lose everything. Everything."

Washington stopped. Tall, dominant, his face was set like granite, eyes glowing like blue-gray flecks of light. A strange feeling came creeping into the officers around the table, and they eased back against their chairs, silent, vaguely aware something rare was happening. The room seemed charged with a quiet spirit. It rose above their fears, their deep anxieties, to settle their minds. They were awed by the sure conviction that powers far beyond those of men were in motion.

St. Clair broke the silence. "It's obvious we can't remain here, and if we have to move, it might as well be to attack. That's the last thing they expect. It can be done."

Washington asked quietly, "Are we agreed?"

"We are."

"Then let us work out the details of your commands, and your orders."

At midnight, over ground frozen solid by a frigid north wind, one hundred fifty baggage wagons, together with three of the heaviest cannon, rumbled away from Trenton, southwest towards Burlington. Five hundred men fed split fence rails to great fires along the south bank of the Assunpink, then bowed their backs into digging trenches with picks and shovels while the north wind whipped the vapor from their faces. With a black sky dimly lit by a few stars, the rebel army began slipping away, light infantry leading, and a company of Philadelphia militia following. The cannon, with wheels wrapped for silent travel, moved next, followed by General Hugh Mercer's brigade.

Colonel John Haslet walked beside Mercer's horse. Haslet's legs were swollen and painful from nearly freezing during the crossing of the Delaware on Christmas night. In his pocket were written orders from General Washington, relieving him from combat duty to return to Delaware to recruit a fresh regiment. Haslet had requested permission to stay with the army for just one more battle, and Washington had consented.

Behind Mercer's brigade marched St. Clair's brigade, then General Washington, followed by the bulk of the army. Three companies of Philadelphia Light Horse infantry brought up the rear. So silently had the army left the banks of the Assunpink that some of the American rear guards and sentinels were unaware when they passed.

On the north side of the creek, a British patrol crept close to the Queen Street bridge to peer south at the American fires in the freezing darkness. The sergeant watched for a time, then moved his patrol east more than a hundred yards along the creek bank and whispered to his corporal, pointing.

"See 'em diggin' over there in the firelight? Hear 'em? Won't do 'em much good in the mornin' when we come marchin'."

In full, freezing darkness the civilian guides led the Americans past the five log buildings of Sand Town and moved on northeast, then angled north to cross the bridge that spanned Miry Run. One mile later they marched past the wastelands called the Barrens, then continued on to cross the Quaker Bridge over a branch of the Assunpink Creek. Yesterday's mud was frozen solid as rock. Strips of blankets wrapped around feet were soon torn loose and unraveled. Once again blood lay in the places where the soldiers walked.

Where the road had been cut through groves of trees, the stumps were invisible traps. Cannon wheels thumped to a halt when they struck a stump, and the men who followed, unable to see either the stump or the stalled gun, stumbled into them. The soldiers fell time and again, but rose wearily to back the gun up to work past the stump, hoping to see the next one in time.

Horses slipped on the icy ground. Some fell. Two broke legs and threw their heads, voicing their pain. Instantly soldiers were all over them, clamping their muzzles shut to silence them while others quickly cut each suffering animal's throat; they dared not fire a musket to end the pain more quickly. They stayed on the animals until they were no longer moving, then moved on.

Men marching a short distance from the column broke through ice on small ponds and in low places. They thrashed on through, soaked sometimes over their heads, and continued the march, clothing freezing stiff as they went.

Colonel Edward Hand's command had fought the delaying action against Cornwallis the entire previous day, and with no rest was marching, exhausted. Cadwalader's command, along with Mifflin's command, had endured a forced march the previous night, and were now in their second night of marching with no sleep. Fatigued, bone weary, they plodded on. When a cannon jolted to a stop against a hidden stump, men fell asleep in the few minutes it took to free the gun. Nearby soldiers lifted them to their feet and helped them stumble on.

Sergeant Joseph White, who had rescued his beloved cannon from the battle at Trenton, was walking beside his big gun with Captain Benjamin Frothingham at his side. Three times in one hour, White fell asleep while walking, and tumbled to the frozen ground. Each time, Frothingham set him back on his feet. "Sergeant, you are the first person I ever see sleep while marching."

Just before three A.M. a whispered rumor spread like wildfire. "We're surrounded by the British!" Sixty raw militia in Mifflin's command gasped in terror, and without a word broke from the column, pounding off into the frozen countryside running east, then back south, hoping to reach Philadelphia before the redcoats or the dreaded Hessians caught them. Those remaining in the column listened until there was no more sound, then turned their faces north and continued their struggle in the night. Those who fled were never seen again.

With the first gray of morning, Washington tapped spur to his mount and loped it forward beside the column, and reined in beside Mercer. He drew him to one side and quietly issued orders.

"The bridge across Stony Brook isn't far ahead. When we're across and come to the fork in the road, take your command on the left fork. Go west to where the Princeton Road crosses Stony Brook and destroy the bridge. That should slow Cornwallis when he comes, and at the same time stop anyone from Princeton escaping to the south."

Mercer bobbed his head. "Yes, sir."

Washington rode back to his place beside his staff with deep concern nagging. *How far behind is Cornwallis? Did he find out we were gone in the night? There should have been British patrols, but there are none. Why? Are we marching into an ambush?*

Doggedly he moved on with his column, every nerve singing tight as daylight came creeping. He drew out his watch and drew a deep breath.

Past six A.M. Two hours behind schedule and we haven't reached Stony Brook. We'll have to take Princeton in broad daylight! Where's Cornwallis?

He slowly let out his held breath, but showed no outward sign of concern as they moved on.

The sun broke above the eastern skyline clear and bright in a cloudless sky. A thick frost covered every blade of dried grass, every barren tree, every fence post and rail, sparkling in the brilliant light. The Americans crossed the Stony Brook bridge, and nine hundred yards north, General Hugh Mercer and his three hundred fifty men separated from the main column, marching left at the fork, while the army continued straight towards Princeton on the right fork of the road. General Washington watched Mercer's men until the trees cut them off from view, then turned his horse and studied the roads south, watching for any movement that could be Cornwallis coming to trap them.

There was nothing.

Where is he? He has to know by now.

At that moment, nine miles south, General Charles Cornwallis paused at the flap of his tent to be certain his gold-trimmed hat was cocked at the proper attitude, tugged briefly at the sleeves of his heavy overcoat, squared his shoulders, and stepped out into the early shafts of golden sunlight. Frost crystals glittered everywhere, and for a moment he paused, struck by the beauty of the winter's morn. His staff joined him as he strode to the crest of the hill and extended his telescope. He moved it slowly across the ridge of the Assunpink Creek at the south end of Trenton, lowered it, and the most peculiar expression his staff had ever seen crossed his face.

Quickly he raised the telescope and once again glassed the enemy lines for more than a minute. Again he lowered the glass, and turned to General James Grant.

"There isn't an American cannon or a soldier in sight! Where have our patrols been all night?"

"They've reported every hour. The rebels have been digging the entire night."

"Send a mounted patrol down there immediately. Have them report back to me. We'll all wait."

They watched ten mounted cavalry race their horses the length of King Street, east to Queen Street, pound across the Assunpink Bridge, and wheel left, holding their racing pace for five hundred yards. The sergeant in charge pulled his mount to a sharp, sliding halt on the frozen ground, wheeled around, and returned to pull up before General Cornwallis. He was breathing heavily from his frigid run, his horse blowing hard.

"Sir, they're gone. Not a man, not a cannon, not a wagon in sight. Only fresh mounds of dirt all up and down the creek bank and fires still smoking. Their tracks go east to the Quaker Road."

Cornwallis threw both hands in the air. His face went white as the frost, then flushed red as he stammered for words that would vent his wrath. Beside him, Grant stared at the sergeant in disbelief, then barked, "Gone? What do you mean—gone?"

"Gone, sir. There is nothing down there."

Cornwallis could hardly contain his fury. He clamped his jaw closed against his overwhelming need to condemn them both, turned on his heel and walked ten paces away to try to bring his rage under control. For ten seconds that seemed an eternity, Cornwallis's staff stood in fearful silence, trying not to stare at him. His breathing became labored as he fought to force his brain to rise above the shock, and begin to function.

Destroyed! He has destroyed me! Never in my military career has an enemy officer humiliated me as Washington has. With the king and the cabinet and the French and the whole world watching, he has made me appear to be an incompetent, blundering nincompoop!

A life filled with the habit of strict military discipline took over. Cornwallis turned on his heel and called out orders. "Form your commands into ranks immediately for marching double time! If we catch him before he reaches Princeton, we can still destroy him. Move!"

Nine miles north of Cornwallis, on the Princeton Road south of Worth's Mill, British Colonel Charles Mawhood sat straight in his saddle, his fresh officer's uniform sparkling red and white in the brilliant sunshine of the beautiful winter's morning. His black, gold-trimmed hat was tilted slightly over his right eye. He held a tight rein on his brown mare, who was feeling the lift in the mood of the day and wanted to run in the bright, frosty world.

Mawhood felt good. The days and nights of agonizing tension following the catastrophic defeat at Trenton had ended with the arrival of an enraged General Lord Charles Cornwallis with his one thousand regulars and additional troops from Brunswick. When Cornwallis marched them all out of Princeton to pin Washington against the Delaware and destroy him and his rebel army, he had ordered Mawhood to remain behind with the seventeenth, fortieth, and fifty-fifth regiments to defend Princeton against any possible attack. With Cornwallis poised to annihilate Washington, a heady sense of relief pervaded the defenders of Princeton. Mawhood saw no need for night patrols, and had ordered them cancelled.

There was no British patrol, not one British soldier watching the Quaker Road.

Then, in the dark hours before dawn a messenger had ridden a tired horse into Mawhood's camp to deliver new written orders from Cornwallis: Leave a small company of troops behind to defend Princeton, and bring the balance of your column down the Princeton Road to join our forces in our assault on the American lines.

Mawhood had jubilantly leaped to his feet when he read the orders, and fairly bellowed, "We're going to join General Cornwallis! We'll have our moment!" He and his command were to become part of the grand battle that would end the war and be written gloriously in history books forever.

Quickly he roused his officers. "General Cornwallis has ordered us to march to Trenton to join him. The fortieth regiment is to remain here to defend Princeton. The fifty-fifth and seventeenth regiments are to have finished breakfast and be in ranks, ready to march in one hour. Have the drummers sound reveille."

There was nearly a jaunty spirit among the regulars as they finished their breakfast and packed their knapsacks for the march. Clearly, the action would be a farce! Two hours of heavy cannon bombardment, then two volleys from five thousand muskets, and a bayonet charge down over the ridge across the Assunpink at all possible fords. Overrun the exhausted, ill-equipped, untrained farmer rabble that composed the American army. End the rebellion in one final, decisive, crushing collision of the two armies. Then it would be, "Pack your knapsacks, boys, and go home to England! The conquering heroes!"

So buoyant had Mawhood been as he led his column south out of Princeton that he had allowed his two pet spaniels to follow for a distance, barking their joy at being free to run among the soldiers and nip at the hocks of the horses. Stepping lively on the freshly frozen ground, they marched southwest on the Princeton Road, past the farms of Thomas Olden, William Clark, and Thomas Clark, across the Stony Brook bridge, past Worth's Mill in the ravine, and climbed the slight rise south of the mill. Mawhood had eyes only for the road ahead, and no reason, nor inclination, to glance either to his left or right.

It was about ten minutes before eight A.M., January 3, 1777.

A little over one mile nearly due east of Mahwood's southbound column, American Major James Wilkinson, riding with General St. Clair and the northbound American column, caught a flash from his left, and turned in his saddle, eyes narrowed as he searched to the west. There!

Again! Puzzled, Wilkinson reined in his horse to peer intently. He cupped his hands around his eyes to cut the sun's glare off the patchy snow, and a moment later the flash came again.

Wilkinson's eyes popped wide. *Sunlight off bayonets! Over a mile away. Mercer? Can't be Mercer. Too far.* He studied the movement, and his breath shortened. *They're going south—the wrong way! They're British! Marching towards Trenton!*

At that moment he saw two dots break from the rear of the British column. The two mounted horsemen jumped their horses over a split rail fence, ran them down the gentle slope more than one hundred yards, and pulled them to a stop. They shaded their eyes with their hands, peering into the early morning sun. Then Wilkinson saw them spin their mounts and kick them back up the hill at stampede gait, straight for the officer leading the column.

Mawhood heard the pounding of horses' hooves at the same moment he heard the frantic shout, and turned to look. The two cavalrymen hauled their winded horses to a skidding halt and the one in the lead turned to point, arm extended, eyes wide.

"Sir, there's a rebel column moving north towards Princeton on the back road east of town."

Mawhood's jaw dropped open for a split second. "What? Where?"

"There, sir."

The entire British column had seen the two cavalrymen race their horses to the head of the column. They stopped in confusion as Mawhood shielded his eyes and peered east, into the sun, across the wooded hills and valleys until he saw the movement beyond the trees.

"How many?" he asked the two riders. "Did you see exactly how many?"

"No, sir. But it is a sizable force."

For three seconds Mawhood sat in his saddle while his mind raced. *Who are they? Washington? the rebel army? Impossible. It has to be a smaller force. But who? How many?* He peered back towards Princeton. *The fortieth is back there alone in Princeton and they don't know a force is coming at them. I can't risk it.*

He pointed at the cavalryman nearest him. "Return to Princeton now, as fast as you can. Warn the fortieth regiment. Tell them we're coming."

"Yes, sir." The man slammed his spurs into the flanks of his horse and was gone.

Mawhood stood in his stirrups to crack out orders to officers who stood wide-eyed, rooted for a moment. "Turn the column! Double-time back to Princeton! Move!"

Tough British discipline rose above their surprise as the troops turned and started back down the hill they had just climbed, moving at double time.

To the east, across the mile distance separating the two opposing forces, Major James Wilkinson called to General St. Clair. "Sir, there's a British column moving north on the Princeton Road, double time. They were headed south until they saw us."

Instantly St. Clair's head turned west, probing. "Have they seen Mercer?"

"I doubt it, sir. There's trees between him and them."

St. Clair's response was instant. "There's nothing we can do about it right now except move ahead. Mercer will take care of his command."

At that moment, General Hugh Mercer's advance skirmishers, working through the trees at the side of the left fork of the road, saw Mawhood's regulars for the first time, running across the Stony Brook bridge and up the slight incline back to Princeton. They stopped in their tracks, and Captain Markus Beebe turned to Sergeant Calvin MacHenry. "Get back to General Mercer as fast as you can and tell him the British are on the bridge, headed back towards Princeton on the double."

"Yes, sir." MacHenry spun on his heel and ran back through the trees, crouched low, paying no heed to the branches that reached to snag his clothing and face. Mercer's column, marching on the road, heard the thrashing in the trees and instantly dived from the roadbed into the brush and trees, rifles and muskets at the ready. They recognized the sergeant, and Mercer stood.

"Sir, there's a British column on the bridge right now, heading back towards Princeton on the run."

"How many? A patrol?"

"No, sir. Several hundred. Maybe over a thousand."

Mercer looked west up the road while his mind raced. *If the British are on the bridge, I can't reach it to destroy it. Sullivan and St. Clair and Washington are to the east, a British column to the west, both moving north, and they're going to collide somewhere up there. If the British get there first, they may be able to ambush our army. If I can catch the British and engage them, I might be able to hold them until Washington and the army can get set.*

"Sergeant, get back to Captain Beebe and tell him to catch up with us as fast as he can. We're going to cut straight north and try to catch the British before they have a chance to attack our column to the west."

"Yes, sir."

Mercer turned and gave hushed orders to his officers. "There's a British column on the bridge, headed for Princeton. We're going to move straight north from here to try to catch them before they have a chance to attack our column to the west." He turned to two of his scouts. "Go to the crest of that hill and try to locate Washington and St. Clair, then report back."

"Yes, sir."

Mercer led his men due north, off the roadbed to a steep bank, sixty feet high. Snow that had partially thawed the previous day, then frozen overnight, covered the ground. He turned and called orders to the two cannon crews.

"Get ropes on your guns and move them to the top of the bank."

Captain Benjamin Frothingham turned to Sergeant Joseph White. "Let's go."

Captain Daniel Neil, commander of the other cannon and crew, turned to his men. "Get the ropes."

While the men struggled, slipping, sliding on the crusted snow, moving the two big guns up the steep bank, the two scouts reached the top and anxiously turned their faces to the east, searching for Washington and the main column. Suddenly one jerked his arm upward, pointing. "There! See them? That's Sullivan's command, and Washington's right there behind."

"Let's get back down and report."

As they turned, a movement ahead and slightly to their left caught their eye and they stopped. Five hundred yards away, near an apple orchard, sat a lone British cavalryman, looking straight back at them. For a moment that seemed forever, the two Americans and the lone British soldier stared at each other before the British regular jerked his horse around and galloped off towards the home of Thomas Olden, which lay where the Princeton Road made a slight, gentle curve to the right, directly towards Princeton.

The British cavalryman caught up with Mawhood and brought his horse to a sliding halt. "Sir," he panted, "there is an American force coming up on our rear. If we engage the American column to our right we could be caught in a trap."

Mawhood's face went white. "How many?"

"I don't know exactly. Hundreds."

Mawhood's shoulders slumped. What had been simple was suddenly complex, tearing him inside. *If I turn on the Americans behind me, I leave the fortieth regiment without help to face the American column to the east, which is the bigger of the two. If I go forward to help the fortieth, I leave the force behind me untouched to attack me from the rear and give support to the Americans off to the east. What do I do?*

He set his jaw and shouted his orders. "Companies three, five, and six of the fifty-fifth, march on towards Princeton double time and support the men in the fortieth. The rest of you in the fifty-fifth and seventeenth, bring two cannon and follow me. We're going after the Americans behind us."

He turned to Captain Truwin of the Philadelphia Light Horse Company. "Take your first and second companies and engage the force coming in behind us until we can get there."

"Yes, sir."

Truwin led his men out at a high lope, into the barren fields and orchards of the farm of William Clark, then slowed to a canter, standing tall in the stirrups, watching for movement. It came suddenly.

"There! Coming into that orchard! Americans with two cannon. Form a skirmish line and prepare to dismount and fire!"

South of Truwin, Sergeant Joseph White and his cannon, with some of the advance skirmishers, was ahead of Mercer. A heavy stand of trees and a short, steep bank were between them, and they could not see each other. As White and those with him moved into the orchard, Captain Truwin shouted, "Fire!"

The first British volley tore into the trees too high. Not one American was touched. White and those with him instinctively ducked as the musket balls whistled into the overhead branches, and they paused to peer at the enemy. The bright sunlight reflected off the British muskets and bayonets, and their breastplates, and it seemed to make the red-coated soldiers larger than life, striking an awe into the crouching Americans.

The thunder of the first British volley reached Mercer and stopped him in his tracks. From his position he could not see the field of action and did not know which side had fired. Without hesitation he shouted, "Stop! Form a battle line and move forward, double time." His command came over the hill, into the orchard, shooting as they ran forward to the picket fence at the edge of the fruit trees. Captain Truwin swallowed hard when he realized he was outnumbered, and when Sergeant White and Captain Daniel Neil wheeled their two cannon into place and loaded, Truwin shouted his next order.

"Fall back. Keep firing."

Behind him, Colonel Mawhood's command came pouring over a rise, and wheeled their two cannon into place forty yards from the two guns of White and Neil.

"Fire!" shouted White, and the two American cannon blasted first.

Cannister shot ripped into the British lines as Mawhood shouted, "Fire!" The British guns boomed back at the Americans.

White smoke rose in the still morning air as the guns on both sides roared and the musket and cannister shot whistled. Mercer sat his big gray gelding, sword in hand, directing the fire of those near him while the British fire tore into the trees and brush and the American line all around him.

Captain Truwin came dodging in from Mawhood's right. "Sir, we're outnumbered. We don't have enough muskets and bayonets to hold the right flank."

As Truwin spoke, Mawhood shouted his orders. "Attack! Bayonet charge!" The entire British line, red coats and white breeches and belts bright in the sun, surged forward. In seconds they covered the forty yards separating the two lines and were in among the Americans, cursing, slashing with their bayonets, pounding with the iron-plated butts of the ten-pound Brown Bess muskets.

Outnumbered, too few muskets, too few bayonets, the American line sagged back under the onslaught, and then it broke. Still mounted on his gray horse, Mercer rode among them, shouting, "Stop! Form a battle line!" He whipped them across their backs with the flat of his sword, but they dodged around him in their blind run from the din of the muskets and their fear of the flashing bayonets.

Mercer heard the hit and felt the sick give as his big gray horse went down rolling, its right front leg broken by a British musket ball. Mercer hit the ground on his right side, his sword flying, and lay for a few moments, stunned, disoriented, shaking his head to clear the cobwebs before he struggled to his feet. He searched for his sword, then once again ran among his men, slapping them with the flat of it, shouting for them to stop and form a battle line, but there was no way to stop the rout. He was swept up with them, moving down the hill towards the William Clark farm.

The British regulars, filled with a surging lust to avenge the loss of Trenton, saw their opportunity. They ran in among the rear ranks of the Americans, lunging with their bayonets, swinging their muskets, cursing, shouting, laying waste to every American they could reach. A young lieutenant, dragging a broken leg, tried to hide beneath a wagon near the farmyard. Two red-coated regulars jerked him out and held him while others drove their bayonets through him. Lieutenant Bartholomew Yeates, bleeding from a musket ball in his shoulder, turned to face the British as one redcoat clubbed him with his musket; he went down, where others plunged their bayonets into him thirteen times before they swept on.

Captain John Fleming shouted to his Virginians, "Dress the line!" A British regular shouted back at him, "We will dress you," and shot Fleming dead.

With his sword still in his hand, General Mercer suddenly found himself alone, near the Clark barn, surrounded by shouting regulars. The British recognized him to be an officer, but with his heavy overcoat covering his shoulder epaulets, they did not know his rank. Some thought him to be General George Washington.

"Surrender, you cursed rebel!" one shouted. Mercer ignored him, braced his feet and swung his sword at the nearest redcoat, then advanced, slashing with each step. They knocked his sword from his hand, then swung the butts of their muskets at him. One crushed his head and he dropped to his knees, unconscious, and the regulars drove their bayonets into him again and again. He toppled over onto his side and did not move, bleeding from his nose and ears, and from countless bayonet wounds. The regulars backed up and looked, then left him for dead while they plunged off to storm the two American cannon that had been wheeled into place.

Captain Benjamin Frothingham and Captain Daniel Neil were frantically helping their two cannon crews load the guns and bring them to bear on the shouting mob of red-coated soldiers surging up the incline at them with bayonets lowered. Desperately Sergeant Joseph White slammed the rammer down the barrel to seat the charge of powder, jerked the rammer out, and reached for the ladle filled with grapeshot. British musket balls were spanging off the cannon amid the din of the oncoming regulars. Captain Frothingham was gauging time and distance, and he knew it was too late.

"Stop!" he shouted to his crew. "Retreat! Leave the gun! Now!"

White threw down the ladle and grabbed the two privates in his crew and shoved them ahead of him as he broke into a run. Frothingham drew his sword and waited until they were clear before he followed, sprinting to catch up.

Captain Daniel Neil heard Frothingham's shout and was giving the command to his own cannon crew to retreat when a British musket ball punched through his left arm. It twisted him sideways and backwards, and for a moment he clenched his teeth against the shock and pain. When he turned back, the first rank of charging regulars were a scant six feet from the muzzle of the gun.

Too late!

In the next five seconds, Captain Neil and his crew were dead on the ground. The regulars dragged their bodies aside and quickly swung the two American cannon around. Trained hands finished loading them, and brought them to bear on the backs of the Americans, who were running in chaotic retreat towards some woods near the home of William Clark, half a mile away. The two guns boomed and the grapeshot tore into the rebels. Colonel John Haslet, the last surviving American soldier of the proud First Delaware Regiment which had been disbanded December 31, 1776, had followed Captain Frothingham and Sergeant White in their retreat from the two cannon. In his pocket were the written orders of General Washington, relieving him of combat duty to return to Delaware to raise a new regiment.

As Haslet approached the barn on the Clark farm, he slowed and turned to what remained of Mercer's command. "Stop!" he shouted. "Form a battle line at the top of the slope! We can hold them if—"

He never ended his sentence. A British musket ball struck him in the forehead and he dropped where he stood.

Frothingham and White had reached the woods beyond the Clark farm and stopped for a moment, gasping for breath. They turned to look back at the battlefield, and stood transfixed. The Americans were in a wild, terrified stampede away from the advancing British, who were firing with every musket, bayoneting men who were wounded on the ground, and blasting grapeshot from their four cannon.

"Where's Sullivan? Cadwalader? Greene?" Frothingham cried in anguish. "They've heard the battle. Where are they?"

To the northeast about one mile, General John Sullivan had continued his hurried march towards Princeton, when his advance skirmishers came galloping back. "Sir, there's a major British force straight ahead, blocking us."

Sullivan looked north for a moment. "How far?"

"Just over one-quarter mile."

"Have they seen us?"

"I think so, sir."

"How many?"

"No way to tell, sir. They're in a battle line, like they're waiting."

Sullivan considered for a moment. "We don't know what we're up against, so we will wait for—"

At that moment the distant sound of muskets reached him as Mawhood's regulars fired their first volley at Mercer's command. Sullivan twisted in his saddle, peering back to the southwest while his entire column fell silent to listen. The firing increased, and suddenly the heavy, unmistakable boom of cannon mixed in with the musket fire, and it grew hot, held for a time, then lessened.

Sullivan's eyes narrowed as he worked with the sudden rush of thoughts and fears. *That's Mercer. What's he run into? Whose cannon are firing? Someone's in retreat—who? Who?* He straightened in his saddle to look north towards Princeton. *Who's up ahead? How many? If we're outnumbered, an attack on entrenched troops would be a disaster. Until I know how many, I have to wait.* He turned once again to peer back towards the southwest. *If I go back to support Mercer, I run the risk of the British up ahead following me and coming in on my flanks. Cadwalader and Greene are both behind me. Maybe they can go to support Mercer.*

Caught between the need to attack the British to the north, and the compulsion to go back to the southwest to support Mercer, Sullivan made the only agonizing decision he could, hating the wrenching pain inside.

"We wait right here to hold that British force ahead where they are."

Behind and west of Sullivan's command, General John Cadwalader was struggling to keep his command of raw troops moving forward as a column. They were strung out through the trees, indifferent to his shouted orders, seeing no need to form in ranks to march when they could move just as well in small groups. Behind him, Colonel Edward Hand led his group of Pennsylvania riflemen, Billy and Eli in the first rank, followed by Colonel Daniel Hitchcock and his veteran regiment. Further back, General Nathanael Greene led his command, watching to the west for the first sign of red flahses in the wooded hills.

Cadwalader, Hand, Hitchcock, and Greene all heard the eruption of musket fire, then cannon, over the hill just west of them, and jerked their mounts to a halt. Their commands stopped all movement, all sound, as they listened, wide-eyed, with the question hanging over them.

Who's beaten? Retreating?

Cadwalader's command was nearest to the fighting, and he wasted no time. Riding his horse among his men, he personally gave the orders. "Fall into ranks in marching order. We're going over that hill."

Fourteen days earlier, nearly every man in his command had been a civilian—a farmer, merchant, silversmith, baker, or shopkeeper—without the slightest hint of how soldiers conducted themselves or how battles were fought. They stared back at him, confused, hesitant. He reached down to grasp some of them by the shoulder. "You, go there. You, go here."

Quickly he shoved and pushed until he got them organized into position, then gave them the order, "Forward. Follow me."

As he started them forward, General Nathanael Greene saw Captain Joseph Moulder coming up from the rear of the column with his two cannon. He spun his horse and loped back to Moulder and pointed up the hill.

"Captain, move those two guns and crews up to the crest of that hill and commence firing as you see the need."

"Yes, sir."

Ahead of Greene, Cadwalader was having trouble holding his mount. With the incessant blasting of the muskets and cannon growing louder, the horse was prancing, throwing its head, nervous. Cadwalader held a tight rein, looking constantly over his shoulder to be certain his men were following. They rounded the hill just below the tree line, and came into the little valley.

Cadwalader shouted his next order. "Form a battle line behind that fence!"

The men spread out behind the fence, and for the first time had a clear view into the valley. The entire command stopped in their tracks, wide-eyed in horror.

Before them, in the bright sunlight of the beautiful morning, the entire panorama of a bloody, heart-wrenching, lost battle lay before them. Dead and wounded Americans dotted the land. Live Americans were in a blind, mindless stampede east, up the hill, to escape the musket balls and grapeshot and bayonets of the red-coated British. The regulars were in full battle fever, swarming after them, pausing only to bayonet wounded Americans where they lay with their hands up, shouting their surrender. Groups of the redcoats were gathering around wounded American officers to slash at them, driving their bayonets into them again and again with a hot, blood-lust to kill. The sound of British muskets and cannon was deafening, interrupted only by the shouts of the swarming red horde, and the screams of the terrified, wounded, and dying Americans.

When Cadwalader's men rounded the hill, the movement caught Mawhood's eye and he stopped for five seconds to consider.

Reinforcements! Who are they? How many? If I engage them and lose, there will be no support for the fortieth up north. I can't chance it.

He shouted his orders. "Have the drummer sound parade ranks! Get those four cannon over onto that knoll." Instantly the drummer began the familiar drumroll, and the British soldiers, scattered all over the valley, slowed and stopped, then turned to form in ranks with their commander. The four cannon, two of them the ones the British had taken from Captain Frothingham and Captain Neil, were moved up to the small knoll.

While Mawhood's men were re-forming their battle line and waiting for their cannon to get into a support position, Cadwalader's men shook themselves as though to escape from the worst nightmare they had ever seen, then turned on their heels and ran. There was no power on earth that could stop them as they crested the hill and piled into the companies coming up, turning them back, sweeping them along in the panic. Mercer's remaining men mixed with the other regiments. No one paid any heed to their shouting officers as they ran blindly to escape the holocaust behind.

With his regulars regrouped into a new battle line, Mawhood looked towards the knoll to his left. While he watched, his four cannon wheeled into position, muzzles trained on the retreating Americans. He waited for a few more moments, puzzled by what the Americans had done.

They came around the hill, looked, and disappeared. Where are they? Setting up an ambush?

Mawhood had not seen Captain Joseph Moulder wheel his two guns out on the crest of the hill to the east, load them, and bring them to bear on his poised regulars.

Mawhood drew a deep breath. *We've got them on the run and I don't intend letting them rally. We'll attack. If they've set up an ambush, we'll handle it when we see it.* He turned in his saddle, sword raised, to shout out his next order. "Follow me. We're—"

His words were cut off by the first booming blast of Moulder's two cannon. Grapeshot came whistling, knocking into his regulars, clipping branches from the brush and scrub trees. Shocked, Mawhood jerked around to stare east at the crest of the hill, fumbling in his mind to understand how the rebels had gotten guns up there and how many there were. The entire British line flinched when Moulder's guns blasted a second time and the grapeshot tore into them. They held their position, looking at Mawhood, waiting for him to give them an order that would get them out from under the muzzles of the two cannon on the ridge. Mawhood stared at the guns, unable to count them, but behind them he saw movement, and men coming forward beside the cannon.

At the guns, Moulder was all alone with his two crews. "Fire as fast as you can," he ordered, and leaped onto his horse. He galloped off to the north to where six Americans were running away. He stopped them and pointed back towards the guns. "Get on back there! Give those men some support!" The soldiers nodded, but the moment he turned, looking for others, they spun and were gone, running away. Moulder rode back to another group of men, ordering, pleading, threatening, but no one was willing to join his cannon crews. Alone, his cannon were holding Mawhood's entire command at a standstill, but one thing was crystal clear, the moment Mawhood realized there were only two cannon and very little else, he would storm the guns, cross the crest of the hill, sweep down the east side, and destroy what was left of the commands of Mercer, Cadwalader, and Greene.

A young lieutenant on the east side of the hill turned to Thomas Rodney. "Take some men and get up there to support those cannon."

"Yes, sir." Hastily Rodney gathered fourteen men, took a determined breath, and led them running to a small depression where thirty terrified Philadelphians cowered in the trees. "Come on," he shouted. "We've been ordered to go join the cannon on the hill." Hesitantly, the

Philadelphians came to their feet and Rodney led them all at a run towards Moulder's guns.

They crested the hill and British musket balls came whistling thick. One ripped through Rodney's overcoat at the elbow, another tore the insole of his shoe, and a third punched a hole in his hat. Not one man stayed with him as he plunged on to dive in behind Moulder's cannon.

Through narrowed eyes, Mawhood studied the cannon and the lack of a line of soldiers to support it, then shifted to stare hard at the woods, struggling with a hard decision.

I think we're facing just two cannon. Just two cannon! No support. And those men who came out of the woods have gone and no one has returned. If I'm right we can end this in five minutes by storming—

His thoughts got no further.

From the north, near where Sullivan's column had stopped to prevent the British fortieth and fifty-fifth companies from coming in behind the Americans facing Mawhood, General George Washington came storming on his tall white mare at a stampede gait. The general's cape was flying behind him as he leaned forward in the saddle, spurring his mount at every stride. The horse's drumming hooves were fairly flying, neck extended, ears laid back, forelock whipping in the wind. With every stride, Washington was distancing five of his aides and staff, whose mounts had no chance of staying with the horse, or the horsemanship, of the general. Behind the aides and staff came the veteran Virginia Continentals, and beside them, Colonel Edward Hand and his regiment of Pennsylvania riflemen, running as hard as they had ever run in their lives. Billy and Eli were two steps behind Hand, the entire regiment howling like men from the infernal pit.

Washington swept in from the east, behind the hill where Moulder's cannon were still banging away. He spurred his laboring horse up the slope, took one look, and knew instantly what had to be done. He spun the horse and plunged back down the slope at an angle to the northeast and hauled his horse to a stiff-legged halt in front of Hand's regiment and the Virginia Continental militia. Washington's orders were abrupt, final.

"Form up here and get ready. When I move the Pennsylvania militia up the hill, move your men around the north side of the hill and attack."

He did not wait for a response. He reined his horse around and in three jumps the mare was once again at racing stride. Washington pulled her to a skidding halt in front of a group of terrified Pennsylvania militia cowering on the east side of the hill. The men looked at him dumbstruck, unable to believe their commander in chief was before them, sitting a sweating, blowing horse. They feared what was certain to be an outpouring of his anger and wrath.

Washington stood tall in the stirrups to shout, "Parade with us! There is but a handful of the enemy, and we will have them directly!"

Astonished, a few of the Pennsylvanians stood, and then a few more. They began to fall into ranks. Some sprinted to other groups nearby, looking for their proper regiments, and within seconds the semblance of a battle line began to form.

At that moment Colonel Daniel Hitchcock led his running New England Continental militia up to Washington and stopped.

"Sir, my command stands ready to help form a battle line and lead the charge."

Washington shook his head. "Take your command up and join Hand. I'm going to lead these Pennsylvanians into battle myself."

For a moment Hitchcock's eyebrows peaked in surprise. "Yes, sir."

While Hitchcock turned his command and led them north to join Hand, Washington watched the stunned Pennsylvania militia work itself into a loose line.

"Straighten the line," he shouted. "Close it up. Tight."

Within minutes the line was straight, the ranks closed, muskets at the ready. Washington wasted no time. He stood tall in the stirrups to be seen by the entire line, whipped his hat from his head and waved it so all could see, and shouted, "Follow me!"

He led them at an angle over the hill, keeping Moulder's cannon to his left. At the crest of the hill he saw that Mawhood had shifted his battle line the same direction to escape the deadly grapeshot that Moulder was blasting into his lines as fast as he could reload and fire.

The moment Washington saw their battle line, he turned and shouted to his men, "Do not fire until I give the order!" He reined his mare to his right, positioning himself near the center of his line, with three of his aides and staff beside him, white-faced, waiting for the deadly volley the red-coated British were sure to deliver.

The long line of Pennsylvania militia, dressed in the homespun clothing they had worn from home, held the line and moved forward, slowly at first, then at a high walk, and then at a trot. Washington sat ramrod straight as he raised his horse to a trot, jaw set like granite, eyes narrowed as he gauged time and distance to the British lines.

Mawhood sat his horse dumbstruck! Who was the tall officer on the white horse, riding straight into the muzzles of his muskets without a flicker of hesitation? *Washington? Could it be General Washington himself?*

Mawhood shouted his order. "Do not fire until my command."

His men cocked their muskets.

Washington raised his mount to a canter. His green Pennsylvania militia who had been thrown into a panic-driven retreat less than an hour earlier held the line behind him, running directly at the British.

Thirty yards! That's close enough! Washington pulled his horse to a stop, turned his head and shouted, "Halt!"—and one instant later—"Fire!"

The Pennsylvanians leveled their muskets and the roar of their first valley echoed clear into Princeton. In the same second, Mawhood shouted, "Fire!" His regulars blasted out their first volley.

When the muskets roared, Major John Fitzgerald was less than thirty feet from the general. Quickly he snatched his hat from his head and covered his eyes, unable to stand the thought of seeing Washington cut down by the British volley. With the echo of the guns still rolling, he hesitantly lowered his hat and peered at the place Washington had been, knowing both the general and the big white mare would be dead on the ground.

Fitzgerald gaped.

Washington was sitting his horse as if both of them had been planted there. The general raised his arm and shouted, "Follow me!" He turned straight into the British lines less than one hundred feet away. Suddenly a few of the Pennsylvanians gave voice to a new spirit that was rising among them, and others joined. In three seconds the entire line was surging forward, their battle cry rising.

North of Washington, Hitchcock's battle-seasoned veterans followed his orders and formed a battle line as though they were on parade. On the right, Lieutenant Colonel Nixon's New Hampshiremen, three Rhode Island regiments in the center, and on the left, Lieutenant Colonel Henshaw led his Massachusetts regiment.

"Forward!" Hitchcock shouted, and the men followed him at a run. At less than one hundred yards from the British, Hitchcock ordered a halt, then shouted, "Fire!" The musket balls tore into the British as the Americans reloaded, and again Hitchcock led them forward at a run.

To the right of Hitchcock, Colonel Edward Hand halted his regiment of riflemen, and in a moment they formed a battle line, went to one knee to steady their long rifles, and fired. British officers and red-coated regulars all up and down Mawhood's battle line groaned and toppled. Hand's regiment reloaded.

Up on the hill, Moulder wheeled his cannon to his right, bringing them to bear on the shifting British line and instantly fired. Cannister shot whined through the air to cut a swath in the line.

The blasting of the American rifles, muskets, and cannon reached a crescendo that drowned out the British weapons. Washington's Pennsylvanians were closing with Mawhood's line at a run. To the north, Hitchcock's veterans were about to turn Mawhood's flank. Near Hitchcock, Hand's riflemen were cutting down officers and red-coated regulars with every shot from their dreaded Pennsylvania rifles.

Mawhood saw it coming. A few of his regulars backed up. A few more, and then most of them, and they turned and started to run.

We can't hold them! We'll lose every man!

He shouted the only order he could. "Fall back! Bring the cannon!" Even as he shouted he knew it was too late to save his big guns. Washington's militia had already reached the emplacements and stormed over them, swinging their muskets, lunging with their bayonets, and the gun crews broke and ran, leaving the cannon to the Americans.

Hitchcock saw the break in the British lines and instantly turned to his men. "Charge!" His command sprinted forward in full-throated battle cry, bayonets flashing, muskets blasting. Beside his command, Hand stood and called, "Come on, follow me!" With Billy and Eli beside him, the riflemen broke into a run after the fleeing British, pausing only to fire and reload.

East of them, the British retreat became a disorganized, fearful rout. They turned and ran in all directions, some towards the Princeton Road, some towards Stony Brook, some towards Princeton. No one looked back. They were scattered, a red-and-white horde running for their lives across the open field of the Clark farm. Hand's command was hot behind Mawhood's group as they fled west, and Hand paused only long enough to shout orders to his officers. "Take half the men back to help Washington and Sullivan. I'm going on to try to get some of those British officers."

Two companies slowed and stopped, and their commanders turned them back to the east where General Washington was leading the Pennsylvanians. Billy and Eli were in the leading rank as they ran to join the fighting.

General Washington spurred his horse forward, shouting to his men, "It's a fine fox chase, boys!" He was exuberant at the sight of the proud, vaunted British, beaten, scattered, running for their lives with the Americans in hot pursuit.

North of the battlefield, where Sullivan held his command, keeping half of the British fifty-fifth regiment in check from coming to the rescue of Mawhood, the British soldiers stared in stark disbelief at the sight of Mawhood's entire command in full, panic-driven retreat. Mawhood reached the Princeton Road and veered south, across the Stony Brook bridge, with a disorganized group of his regulars following him towards Maidenhead. Others ran north along the Stony Brook, with Hand's riflemen just yards behind them, reducing the red-coated number with each crack of their rifles. The west slope of the battlefield was littered with the British dead and wounded. Their knapsacks and muskets, thrown down in their headlong run, were everywhere.

With his head bowed, the commander of the British fifty-fifth regiment obeyed the last order he had received from Colonel Mawhood.

"Form ranks. We are under orders to fall back to join the companies of the fortieth in Princeton."

Reluctantly the regulars moved their eyes away from a sight they would never forget, and fell into ranks. They did not march west to the Princeton Road. Rather, they marched nearly due north across the gently undulating fields, down the steep incline to the bottom of Frog Hollow Ravine, then up the north slope back to level ground. As they crested the rim, the commander's eyes opened wide.

Not forty yards to the north, the fortieth regiment was formed into a battle line, prepared to engage the Americans. The fifty-fifth marched slightly to the east, turned, and set up their own battle line facing the deep ravine, and the two British regiments waited side by side.

From his position, General John Sullivan had watched the British fifty-fifth withdraw across Frog Hollow Ravine to take up their new position beside the fortieth. Relief flooded through him with the realization that his men, who had been forced to remain in place and do nothing while the battle was raging southwest of them, were about to receive their chance. At that moment, a few of Hand's command joined Sullivan, Billy and Eli among them.

Sullivan issued his orders. "Form into ranks and follow me."

He led them north at double time, their voices raised in shouts as they came to the edge of Frog Hollow Ravine. They plunged down the steep embankment, forded the small stream in the bottom, and clawed their way up the north bank. They stopped just below the rim and spread out, forming one long battle line.

Sullivan looked to his left, then his right, and in the eyes of his men he saw an eagerness, a commitment, a need to drive the British from their land, their country. He raised his arm, sword held high. "Charge!"

They burst over the rim, a flowing, shouting line, bayonets lowered, driving straight for the entrenched British. They fired one volley, loaded, ran farther, and stopped long enough to fire their second before running on.

The British had had enough. They had seen Mawhood's command shot to pieces, routed by the Americans, panic-stricken and scattered in all directions. What they now saw coming over the rim of the ravine was the same tide of shouting, shooting men who would stop at nothing.

Both the fortieth and the fifty-fifth regiments broke. They stripped off their knapsacks, turned, and bolted, some running northeast to the backroads in a desperate hope of reaching Brunswick without passing through Princeton, while others ran west, to scatter at the Princeton Road, away from the men and muskets behind them. Those in the center of the British line realized they could not escape to the east or west, and turned north, sprinting back towards Princeton.

"After them!" the American officers shouted, and the center of the American line surged forward. The British reached the outskirts of the small town and dodged through the streets and houses, pausing only to look over their shoulders at the Americans behind them, who were matching them stride for stride, gaining on them with each passing yard. In desperation the British shouted, "Nassau Hall! Regroup in Nassau Hall!"

The small town of Princeton was known for the College of New Jersey, which lay on the southeast corner of the main intersection of the small town and was housed in Nassau Hall. It was reputed to be the largest building in New Jersey. Its president, Reverend John Wither-spoon, sober, dignified, had led the town in its rise against British tyranny, and as a member of the Continental Congress, had spoken loud and strong for liberty. When the British occupied Princeton, they had billeted an entire regiment in Nassau Hall, where the regulars had stabled their horses in the basement, and stripped all the books from the great library.

Now the frantic British regulars pounded across the campus, threw open the doors of the great stone building, and crowded inside the large prayer hall. They slammed the heavy crossbar across the great double doors, then smashed the glass out of the windows. As the Americans came streaming across the campus, the regulars opened fire through the vacant window frames. The Americans in the first ranks dodged behind trees, and slowed and stopped while they studied the thick stone walls of the great hall.

Hunched down behind a low stone garden wall, Billy turned to Eli. "Where's Turlock? We'll need cannon."

"Coming up with the Massachusetts Regiment."

Both men turned to peer south, and saw mounted officers two hundred yards back leading horses hitched to two cannon. They waited while the distance closed, and then recognized Lieutenant Alexander Hamilton, small, wiry, fearless, with Captain Joseph Moulder beside him. The two officers had refused to leave the battlefield south of Frog Hollow Ravine without their beloved cannon. They hauled the horses and two guns to a halt while two officers near Billy and Eli ran back to meet them. Billy and Eli followed, listening intently.

A young lieutenant, breathing hard from his run, looked up at Captain Moulder. "Sir, they're inside," he exclaimed, pointing to Nassau Hall. "We'll need cannon to get them out."

A look akin to sheer joy fleeted across Moulder's face. "We lost track of our crews. Got anyone here who can load and fire a cannon?"

Eli interrupted. "Wait here." He sprinted away to return with a puffing Sergeant Turlock and three cannoneers who recognized both Hamilton and Moulder. When Turlock saw the big guns he turned hopeful eyes up to Moulder.

"Sir, I understand you need cannon crews."

"We do. Sergeant, get the guns loaded and aimed, ready to fire."

Turlock didn't waste a second. "Yes, sir. All right, you lovelies. Captain Moulder and Lieutenant Hamilton were thoughtful enough to bring along these guns, and we're going to use them to open up that building." He pointed to Nassau Hall, with a sense of regret showing at the thought of blasting the famous structure. "Wheel these guns a little closer and we'll clear the British muskets from those windows."

Quickly they unhitched the horses and the men seized the trails and wheels and pushed the cannon closer to the great hall. A silence fell over the Americans as they watched, while the British muskets maintained an incessant fire from the windows of the building.

"Load," Turlock ordered, and Billy seized one powder ladle, Eli the other. They dipped them full of the fine black granules from the budge barrel, inserted it down the cannon muzzles, twisted the ladles to dump them, withdrew them, and grabbed the rammers. They slammed them down the barrels to seat the powder, followed by dried grass. A second cannoneer poured eight pounds of one-inch grapeshot into each gun while the third one rammed a patch of dried grass to lock it all in place.

"Fire!" shouted Turlock, and Hamilton and Moulder lowered the smoking linstocks to the touchholes. The guns blasted and the grapeshot whistled and splattered the stone wall, splintering the wooden window frames, knocking seven redcoats backwards.

"Load."

The second volley knocked chips from the stones in the wall, and tore the wooden frames out of two windows, back into the building.

"Load solid shot this time," Turlock ordered. "We'll see about those doors."

Behind the big double doors, cross-barred from the inside, at the far end of the prayer hall, a huge portrait of King George II, father of their monarch, King George III, hung proudly above a massive oak mantel. He was dressed in his royal finery, smiling benignly down on his subjects.

"Fire," ordered Turlock.

The cannonballs blasted through the doors. One tore the length of the hall, and struck the face of King George II dead center, perfectly decapitating his head from the painting. The crouched regulars raised their heads and turned to look, and the sight of their former monarch, grand and glorious in the painting with his head blown off, struck a peculiar fear into them.

Turlock twisted the elevation screws on both cannon and lowered their muzzles slightly. "Let's see if we can break the crossbar."

Again the guns bucked and blasted. One cannonball knocked a splintered hole through the lower panel of the right door. The other one hit the seam where the doors met, ripped through, and blew the crossbar inside into two splintered halves. The heavy doors yawed open into the dim hall.

Captain James Moore, an angry Princeton resident whose home had been ransacked by the British, leaped from behind the tree where he had been crouched and started towards the shattered doors at a run.

"Come on!" Billy shouted. Eli threw down the cannon rammer and the two of them sprinted towards the big double doors, James Moore right with them. Two more of the cannon crew followed, running as hard as they could, and then a hundred more Americans came charging. Billy and Eli reached the doors two steps ahead of James Moore, just as the British troops were frantically trying to push the doors closed.

Billy didn't stop. He hit the right door at full stride with his bowed shoulder and slammed it inward. Four regulars were thrown back and Billy ran over the top of them into the great hall, straight into the startled redcoats. Eli was one step behind him with his black tomahawk swinging above his head like the sword of an avenging angel, and James Moore was one step behind Eli.

The redcoat nearest Billy lowered his bayonet to thrust, and Billy slapped it aside, caught the musket, and wrenched it from the hands of the startled soldier. He swung the Brown Bess like a scythe, knocking three regulars sideways, then threw it into the redcoats behind them. He lunged, caught the nearest regular by the lapels of his heavy overcoat with one hand, his belt with the other, lifted him high over his head and threw him kicking into a cluster of men who were backing up, fumbling for the hammers on their muskets.

Behind Billy, Eli had turned to his left towards a group of regulars who were gathering to charge. He let out an Iroquois battle cry as he leaped towards them, swinging his tomahawk. The high-pitched, warbling war whoop struck terror into the regulars and they threw down their muskets, stumbling over each other in their wild scramble to get away from the howling fiend before them.

James Moore and the twenty other Americans who had plunged into the hall swept up discarded British muskets. Moore cocked his musket and fired it into the ceiling while the others cocked their weapons and brought them level at the chests of the nearest regulars.

The redcoats threw up their hands and shouted, "We ask quarter!" Instantly the cry spread, coming from every British regular inside the hall. Billy slowed and stopped, and Eli lowered his tomahawk. A white flag appeared, and quickly another one was impaled on a bayonet and thrust out a shattered window to flutter in the bright sunlight in full view of the Americans waiting outside.

Moore waited for silence, then called out orders. "Single file. Follow me out the door and lay down your arms."

Captain James Moore led them out of the wreckage of the big hall into the bright sunlight. One at a time the British followed him with their eyes downcast. He stopped and pointed, and they laid their weapons on the frozen ground, then walked to form into rank and file. Billy and Eli followed the last man out the door and waited while he laid his musket on the stack. Lieutenant Alexander Hamilton and Captain Joseph Moulder walked from their cannon to face the humiliated, beaten redcoats.

"We accept your surrender."

The battle of Princeton was over. It was not yet ten A.M.

Notes

On January 2, 1777, in full darkness, the guns of both the British and Americans fell silent. General Cornwallis convened a war council to decide what to do. Sir William Erskine said, "If Washington is the general I take him to be, his army will not be found there in the morning" (as quoted in Ketchum, *The Winter Soldiers*, p. 291). General James Grant argued Washington could not move his army overnight, and that with a night's rest and daylight, the British troops would sustain fewer casualties. General Cornwallis settled it by saying, "We've got the old fox safe now. We'll go over and bag him in the morning" (as quoted in Ketchum, *The Winter Soldiers*, p. 291).

Washington convened a war council of his own to determine how to extract his forces from their very vulnerable and highly exposed position along the Assunpink Creek. With a map drawn by Cadwalader that showed a back road near Princeton, Washington proposed a night march around Cornwallis and the British, and an attack on Princeton at dawn (see Ketchum, *The Winter Soldiers*, pp. 293–94).

Private Stephen Olney voiced the fears of most of the soldiers to Lieutenant Bridges, to which Bridges replied, "The Lord will help us" (as quoted in Ketchum, *The Winter Soldiers*, pp. 284–85). Indeed, in what Washington called a "providential change of weather" (as quoted in Ketchum, *The Winter Soldiers*, p. 295), a freezing north wind arose and solidified the mud that had slowed the British the day before. Washington ordered the heaviest wagons to move down to Burlington, while men wrapped the cannon wheels in cloth to silence them; the army began its silent march on Quaker Road (see Ketchum, *The Winter Soldiers*, p. 295).

The night march to Princeton was extremely difficult with tree roots and stumps and rocks stopping the cannon and causing men and horses to stumble and fall. Other dangers lay beneath the thin ice on ponds and streams. In the night, a rumor spread that they were surrounded by Hessians, and some militiamen bolted, running to Philadelphia, never to be seen again (see Ketchum, *The Winter Soldiers*, p. 296). Some men fell asleep while marching, and Captain Benjamin Frothingham told Sergeant White that "you are the first person I ever see sleep while marching" (as quoted in Ketchum, *The Winter Soldiers*, p. 296).

Shortly before eight A.M., Washington's forces crossed the Stony Brook bridge and came to the fork in the road. General Hugh Mercer marched three hundred fifty men along the left fork of the road, with orders to destroy the Princeton Road bridge and delay Cornwallis's column when it came. General John Sullivan, General Washington, and the rest of the American main column proceeded toward Princeton on the right fork, angling behind the British cannon and troop placements (see Ketchum, *The Winter Soldiers*, pp. 297–98).

Two of Mawhood's British cavalrymen chanced to see Washington's column marching north, while Major James Wilkinson saw Mawhood's column about a mile to the west and marching south. Each soldier reported the sighting to their respective commanding officer. Mawhood turned his column around and marched them rapidly toward Princeton to engage the main American column (see Ketchum, *The Winter Soldiers*, p. 298). From that point, the maneuvers and clashes of the two opposing armies became complex. Richard M. Ketchum's book *The Winter Soldiers* gives an excellent detail of the battle, together with a most helpful map, on pages 298–310.

In summary, as Mawhood marched to intercept the Americans, Mercer and his small command spotted Mawhood's men and hastened to engage Mawhood to prevent an ambush of the American column. Seeing Mercer coming, Mawhood sent part of his troops back to Princeton as reinforcements for the men already stationed there, while he personally led the balance of his forces to meet Mercer on farmlands owned by Thomas and William Clark and Thomas Olden. Mercer's untested militia broke under Mawhood's attack and fled the battlefield in panic. Mercer's horse was shot from beneath him while he was trying to rally his men, and Mercer was mortally wounded (see Ketchum, *The Winter Soldiers*, pp. 298–304).

Several other fine American officers also lost their lives, notably Colonel Haslet, Captain John Fleming, Captain Daniel Neil, and Lieutenant Bartholomew Yeates (see Ketchum, *The Winter Soldiers*, pp. 303, 313).

Upon hearing the intense gunfire, Greene and Cadwalader came to assist Mercer. Greene ordered Captain Joseph Moulder to take his two cannon to the crest of the small knoll and open fire. The cannon fire surprised Mawhood, who recalled his troops until he could scout out the big guns. At that moment, General Washington came riding into the battle alone, rallying the disorganized men with his famous cry, "Parade with us! There is but a handful of the enemy, and we will have them directly!" (as quoted in Ketchum, *The Winter Soldiers*, p. 307). With reinforcements from Colonels Hand and Hitchcock, Washington led the charge that routed Mawhood's command into a wild, panic-driven retreat that scattered them in all directions. General Washington chased after them, shouting, "It's a fine fox chase, boys!" (as quoted in Ketchum, *The Winter Soldiers*, p. 308).

Meanwhile, Sullivan moved his men forward to attack the British regiments assigned to defend Princeton. When Sullivan's men charged, the British broke ranks and ran back into Princeton to barricade themselves inside Nassau Hall. Captains Alexander Hamilton and Joseph Moulder arrived with their cannon and opened fire. One cannon ball neatly decapitated a huge painting of King George II hanging inside the building. The British inside surrendered (see Ketchum, *The Winter Soldiers*, pp. 309–10).

CHAPTER XVII

★ ★ ★

*W*ith the sun past its zenith, General Washington brought his
tired mare to a stop twenty yards from the great Nassau Hall. He dismounted, turned, and handed the reins to Major John Fitzgerald of his
staff. "Have someone walk her until she's cooled out, then rub her
down, and grain her. Gather all the officers you can find for a council."

"Yes, sir." Dried sweat streaked the mare's hide, and lather had built
up around the saddle and bridle from the wild run that Washington had
made for more than one hour leading his men in their rout and chase of
the British. The Americans had fragmented Mawhood's command, then
driven the leaderless regulars in every direction until they were no longer
an army.

Fitzgerald handed the reins to the nearest sergeant, gave orders, then
swung back onto his own weary horse and looked around the campus
for the men wearing gold braid on their black, tricornered hats.

Most of the American soldiers were scattered throughout Princeton, hunting for the British stores and supplies. Some had found homes
where the British officers had just begun breakfast when the American
troops had come storming, and without a word the Americans sat down
at the tables to finish the meals, savoring every mouthful. Others found
blankets, salted pork, flour, dried fish, dried fruit, sacked potatoes, medicines, gunpowder, and munitions, and were putting them out into the
streets for the wagons to pick up.

While he waited, Washington studied the shattered windows in

Nassau Hall, then the splintered doors, and the stack of British muskets forty feet from the entry, all of which he understood immediately. As he walked, waiting for his officers, soldiers stopped to peer at him. In silence they watched at a respectful distance, while in their minds they once again saw him flying on his white horse to inspire the terrified Pennsylvania militia into action. Straight into the muzzles of the British muskets—Halt!—Fire!—the Pennsylvanians hold—the British break —"It's a fine fox chase, boys!"

They looked at him, and they dropped their eyes, and said nothing. They went back about their work, but no man who had seen it would ever forget the memory.

Fitzgerald loped his horse back to Washington and dismounted. "The officers are on their way, sir—the ones I could find."

Washington identified and counted them as they came. Sullivan, Hitchcock, Greene, St. Clair, Cadwalader, Knox, Wilkinson. They gathered near him while he peered out over the campus, searching for those who were missing.

Fitzgerald said, "That's all I could find, sir."

Washington nodded. "Come with me." He led them inside Nassau Hall, through the devastated prayer hall to an austere classroom that had an old, scarred pinewood desk, and tables and benches for the students. They pushed the tables aside and sat on the benches, facing him as he stood before the desk.

"I left General Potter at the Stony Brook bridge to destroy it, with Captain Forrest to assist. I also left scouts out to report here to us when they see General Cornwallis approaching. He can't be far."

He drew a deep breath, and every man in the room saw the fear in his face when he asked the next question. "Has anyone seen General Mercer?"

Cadwalder spoke quietly. "His aide, Major Armstrong, gave me a message. He found General Mercer near a barn on the Clark farm." Cadwalader's eyes dropped as he finished. "His skull is broken. He has more than fifteen bayonet wounds. Major Armstrong and Dr. Rush are there with him in the Clark home, but there's little hope. He's dying."

Washington's head bowed. He raised his hand to his face, thumb and forefinger digging into weary eyes. His jaw was clamped shut and those nearest saw him swallow hard. Hugh Mercer had been one of his oldest, dearest friends. A general in whom he had total confidence, total trust. He had loved the man as he would a brother.

Slowly Washington raised his face. "Colonel Haslet?"

In the silence, Greene spoke softly. "He fell trying to rally the Pennsylvania militia. A bullet struck him in the head. He felt nothing."

The air went out of Washington, and his shoulders slumped, and for a fleeting moment every officer in the room saw the searing pain in Washington's heart. They looked at the floor and they waited in the silence while he rallied. There was no time for grief, for venting the pain. Quickly he swept it aside into that place where he stored such things, to be brought out in the quiet moments when he had the luxury of time to come to terms with his own personal heartbreaks and sorrows. He composed himself and moved on.

"At best, we have very little time. Our first duty is to our wounded. Order your men to seek our own wounded first. Leave the dead. I regret it, but there is nothing we can do about it."

He paused to order his thoughts. "Order your men to get all the British stores they can find, particularly gunpowder. What we can't take, have them burn. Blow up the excess munitions. Take all the cannon our horses can pull, and spike the remainder. Leave the British as little as you can."

He turned to General Henry Knox. "When we leave here, take a detail of men to the western edge of town and find an estate called Morven. It belonged to Richard Stockton. General Cornwallis used it for his headquarters. Go through it from basement to rooftop and get all the records you can find, along with all the gold or currency."

"Yes, sir."

"As soon as each of you can, report the number of our casualties to Major Fitzgerald. Include your best estimate of the British casualties, including the prisoners."

He stopped and shifted his feet for a moment. "We have a difficult decision to make. The British have a large store of supplies and munitions at Brunswick, along with seventy thousand pounds, sterling. It is a very tempting prize. We could arrive in Brunswick before morning. What are your thoughts on that proposal?"

St. Clair shook his head. "Most of our men could not make the march, sir. Few of them would be fit for battle when we got there. They've already made the march from Trenton, and fought a battle after two nights without sleep."

Greene spoke. "It would be a tragedy to risk all we have won, and lose it, sir."

Washington heaved a great sigh. "I concur. I do not know how many British were left to defend Brunswick, but even if it were but a small force, I am hard-pressed to think our men could rise to another march and another battle. They're absolutely fatigued."

He raised one hand to stroke at his chin. "I have considered where we should go for winter quarters. It appears to me that Morristown would be our best choice. The town is small, located on a plateau at the foot of the Thimble Mountains. Nearby, on the east, is another ridge, the Watchung Mountains. They run from the Raritan River on the south to the northern borders of New Jersey. From outside those mountains, the only access to Morristown is through narrow passes that we can easily defend should the British attempt an attack. We will be just thirty miles from New York City, where we can keep a constant watch on General Howe and his movements. I recommend that we winter there to allow our men to regain their strength, and to refit the army for the spring. Are there other suggestions?"

There were none.

"Then we will march from here to Morristown. Is there anything else?"

The officers glanced at each other and shook their heads.

"Very well. When you hear the drumroll, assemble your commands as quickly as you can. We will march out immediately for Morristown. We cannot afford to have General Cornwallis catch us here."

He paused for one moment. "I extend to each of you my congratulations. You and your men performed well today. I believe what we have accomplished here will solidify the resolve of our people and will shock the British empire profoundly. I thank you all."

He stopped for a moment, forehead wrinkled as he reflected to make certain the council had handled the necessary business.

"I believe we are finished. Continue in your orders. You are dismissed."

Notes

The best estimates record the British losses after the battle of Princeton at 286 either killed, wounded, or missing, and the American losses at 44 either killed or wounded (see Ketchum, *The Winter Soldiers*, p. 313; Stryker, *The Battles of Trenton and Princeton*, p. 295; Ward, *The War of the Revolution*, vol. I, p. 316; Boatner, *The Encyclopedia of the American Revolution*, p. 894).

Two hours after the battle of Princeton, word reached Washington that Cornwallis had been seen approaching Worth's Mill and would be in Princeton shortly (see Ketchum, *The Winter Soldiers*, p. 313). Washington debated on his next course of action, but decided that it would not be possible to march to Brunswick for another attack despite the tempting cache of supplies and munitions there (see Ketchum, *The Winter Soldiers*, pp. 313, 316–17). It was time to find quarters for the winter instead. It was obvious the Continental army needed rest as "some of these boys had been on their feet for forty-eight hours, during which time they had fought two battles in the dead of winter, made a forced night march across sixteen rugged miles, and been almost without food or drink" (see Ketchum, *The Winter Soldiers*, p. 314).

The weary, but victorious Americans gathered up men and supplies and began marching to Morristown. Though this chapter does not detail the events surrounding the march to Morristown, it is well worth reading about the heroics of Major John Kelly as he and a small group of men held off Cornwallis and the British army while the Americans evacuated Princeton (see Ketchum's *The Winter Soldiers*, pp. 314–19).

The battle of Princeton marked an important development in the makeup of the Continental army. The ragged men who had fled across New Jersey only months before had now returned in strength and pride to claim their land and liberty. It was during the early months of 1777 that Washington substituted the regional and individual designations of the Continental army with the term "American," which was "the greater name" (as quoted in Ketchum, *The Winter Soldiers*, p. 319).

CHAPTER XVIII

★ ★ ★

*D*octor Benjamin Franklin sat on the delicate, velvet-upholstered settee in the richly decorated and appointed anteroom of the French Minister of Foreign Affairs, Comte de Vergennes. He leaned forward, both palms laid over the silver crown of his plain, crooked hickory cane, expression nearly bemused, eyes half-closed. He missed nothing as he studied those who passed, gauging their mood, listening to every word spoken.

The large, heavy door into the inner office opened and Monsieur Gérard of the Foreign Office stood stiffly to one side. Immaculate in his dress, the small man woodenly announced, "The Comte de Vergennes will see you now."

Franklin heaved his seventy-one-year-old body onto his feet, stood for a moment while his legs took the weight, and reached for his leather valise. He smiled humbly to Gérard, and said quietly, "Thank you," as he walked into the office.

Vergennes stood behind a massive, dark oak desk in his sumptuous office. Behind him, the large painting of young King Louis XVI· above the heavy fireplace mantel dominated the room and gave the impression the king was somehow a presence. A fire burned in the fireplace, and knots popped, throwing tiny volcanoes of sparks that died and fell back into the flames. The warmth reached far into the room.

"Please, be seated there, near the desk," Vergennes said. His smile was broad, solicitous.

Franklin bowed and sat down, his valise in his lap. "Thank you, your Excellency."

"I trust your coach was heated for your ride here."

Franklin glanced out the windows to his left. The Tuesday morning had dawned overcast in Versailles, cold, raw, with a strong wind blowing from the north. The coach ride had chilled him, despite the blanket wrapped about his legs.

He shook his head. "No, it was not heated, but no matter. I had a blanket. Somehow I survived."

"Could I have hot coffee brought in? Tea?"

Franklin raised a hand. "Your thoughtfulness is most appreciated, but that won't be necessary. My visit will be brief. I have received news from America and London that I thought would be of interest to you."

Vergennes's eyes narrowed slightly. "Good news, I presume."

Franklin did not answer the question. "It appears the American military forces have lately met the British in battle on one or two occasions. The results have been, shall we say, startling?"

Vergennes's eyebrows arched. "Lately? I understood that General Howe had ordered his army into winter quarters last December. The fourteenth, as I recall. Am I misinformed?"

Franklin smiled. "No, you understood correctly. The British did go into winter quarters, but the Americans did not." He paused to watch the expression on Vergennes's face change from bland interest to sudden consternation, then continued. "On December twenty-sixth last, American soldiers crossed the Delaware River and captured the town of Trenton from a garrison of fourteen hundred Hessian soldiers. Over a thousand Hessians were either killed or captured. Their unfortunate commander was killed. Rall, I believe. Yes, Colonel Johann Gottlieb Rall, from Hesse-Cassel."

Franklin stopped, and he read perfectly the split second that Vergennes's eyes widened before he recovered his composure. "I was not aware."

In that moment Franklin knew he was in control and he pressed his advantage. He spoke amiably, almost casually. "On January third last, the American forces again engaged the British. On that occasion they brought the British forces to a standstill at Trenton, then marched northeast and seized the town of Princeton from the British troops garrisoned there."

Again Franklin stopped, and Vergennes stood in thinly veiled shock, silent, unable to frame a casual response. For a few moments the only sound in the room was the popping of pine knots in the fireplace and the slight whisper of the draw in the chimney.

Vergennes moved his feet. "Princeton? American forces took Princeton from the British?"

"It appears they did."

"Who was the commanding officer for the British forces? General Grant?"

Slowly Franklin shook his head, then pursed his mouth. "No, it was General Lord Charles Cornwallis, under direct orders of General William Howe."

Vergennes leaned forward, palms flat on the desk, arms stiff. His voice was too high and there was no pretense of restraint. "General Washington defeated General Charles Cornwallis?" he blurted. "Impossible!"

"There was a time when I could not have agreed with you more, your Excellency, but the hard truth is that is precisely what happened. Overnight, General Washington marched his entire army north around the eight thousand British troops between Trenton and Princeton commanded by General Cornwallis and captured the entire town. All the British garrisoned there were either casualties or captured, save for those who ran every which direction and were not seen again. Remarkable."

Franklin raised his chin and casually reached to scratch at his throat, while he watched Vergennes's eyes, every instinct focused. *He's foundered. Can't grasp it.*

Franklin waited, forcing Vergennes to ask the questions that had suddenly become the most critical in his life.

"This information has surely reached London by now."

Franklin nodded and waited.

"What are the British saying about all this?"

Franklin opened his valise and sorted through several pages of newspapers. "The British are seething. Yes, here we are. I'm sure you're acquainted with Horace Walpole—sage and political weather vane for England. It seems Mr. Walpole is much in agreement with Frederick the Great, of Prussia, that it is probable the United States will maintain their independence. He writes . . . here it is . . . that Washington's march around Cornwallis and taking Princeton was a masterpiece of military genius. Seems all of England is utterly shocked by it all."

Vergennes's breathing slowed. "And the Americans? What is their reaction?"

Franklin chuckled. "Euphoric. Volunteers for the army are popping up in every state. General Washington is revered—can do no wrong. The newspapers are filled with accounts of the battles, most of them I'm afraid somewhat exaggerated. Here. I brought copies of some of the newspapers for you."

Franklin handed Vergennes several sheets of newsprint, including some translated from English to French, and printed by Franklin on his own printing press at his quarters in Passy, nearby. Franklin waited in silence while Vergennes spread them on his desk. Vergennes was instantly lost in the details of the most prominent articles.

Franklin sat quietly until Vergennes raised his head, thoughts racing. "Have the British taken steps to redeem themselves? Perhaps mounted a winter assault on the American forces?"

Franklin shook his head. "No. To the contrary, they seem to have withdrawn their forces closer to New York City and are apparently satisfied to sit out the winter there."

"And the Americans?"

"Gone into winter quarters at Morristown, New Jersey, thirty miles from New York City. It's a small town—a natural fortress protected by mountain passes. I believe the British are afraid to make a winter assault through those mountains."

Vergennes paused to stare once more at the newspapers, and Franklin's conclusions settled.

He's tempted. He wants to believe now is the time to break openly with the British and declare France an ally to America. Close, but not yet. Wait. Don't push him. Wait.

Franklin squared a large number of newspapers still in his valise and closed it. He rose, facing the smaller man across the huge desk. "I must leave. I do thank you most sincerely for allowing me to interrupt your morning without an appointment. I can only hope the information I've delivered is of value. Thank you again, your Excellency."

In an instant Vergennes was once again the practiced diplomat. "Not at all. It has been my pleasure. Your efforts are much appreciated. I want you to feel free to stay in contact with this office at any time, day or night. My thanks for coming."

Franklin passed through the luxurious anteroom, out into the hallway, and walked slowly towards the large foyer. As he passed a table on his left, and another on his right, he slowed long enough to place a copy of the newspapers, translated into French, on each. In the foyer he smiled humbly at the two men behind their desks, and as he passed, he laid newspaper copies before them. He spoke not a word, paused at the door long enough to bow to them, tip his peculiar, round hat made of the fur of a marten, and walked out into the blustery, cold north wind.

His coach was waiting. The driver opened the door for him and assisted him in taking the two steps to enter the van, then closed the door while Franklin wrapped the blanket back about his legs. The driver mounted the box, picked up the reins to the team, and clucked them into motion. The coach clattered off down the cobblestone street with Franklin seated by the window concentrating deeply on his thoughts as he peered unseeing at the people in the streets, their coats wrapped high and holding their hats on their heads.

A coach rattled past in the opposite direction, the wheels of the two carriages passing within two feet of each other in the narrow street, and Franklin glanced at the occupant in the opposing coach as it passed. The tingle started instantly, and ten seconds later Franklin gasped as recognition struck home. He banged his cane hard against the front wall of the coach. The driver hauled the team to a stop, leaped from the box, and jerked the door open.

"Yes, Doctor Franklin? Are you all right?"

"Turn around immediately and follow that coach that just passed us."

The driver looked up the street at the disappearing carriage and asked no questions. "Yes, sir."

As fast as traffic would allow, he circled back in the narrow streets, caught sight of the carriage slowing ahead, and called down to Franklin, "Sir, the coach is stopping ahead."

"At what building?"

"The office of the French Minister of Foreign Affairs. Comte de Vergennes."

"Stop here."

Franklin shifted and moved his head far enough to take a good view of the door of the carriage ahead, and waited. The driver climbed down from the box, while the doorman unfolded the three-step boarding stairs, and assisted a well-dressed man down from the van. Franklin leaned forward, focused on the man's face as he turned.

Stormont! I was right! Lord Stormont, British ambassador to France!

Franklin watched as Stormont faced the door into the building and squared his shoulders, chin high.

Franklin smiled. *Something's bothering him. I wonder what it is.* He settled back in his seat. *A little patience. Time will tell.* He called up to the driver, "You may drive on."

The doorman quickly assisted Stormont to the door and held it open for him. As the door behind Stormont closed, the two men in charge of the foyer raised their faces from devouring the articles in the newspapers Franklin had left, recognized Stormont, recoiled, and quickly opened the center drawer of their desks and jammed the newspapers inside.

The man nearest the door quickly stood, flustered, grasping for words. "Your Excellency! What a surprise. I wasn't aware you had an appointment."

Stormont stopped before his desk. "I do not have an appointment. I have just received news of the most troubling nature and I must see his Excellency, Comte de Vergennes. I will wait the entire day if necessary."

The man blinked. "I, uh, am certain that will not be necessary." He turned to his companion. "Will you inform the foreign minister that Lord Stormont requests an audience immediately?"

The man stood, turned on his heel, and nearly fled from the room.

Stormont stared at the man before him for a moment, one eyebrow raised. "May I inquire, were those newspapers you placed in your desk drawers just now?"

The answer was too quick. "Oh, no, they were, uh, reports, yes, reports, of, uh, the heads of state of the various, uh, sovereign states with which France is presently engaged, and, uh, their ambassadors and their addresses. Yes. His Excellency Comte de Vergennes insists on being informed of such, regularly."

The sounds of footsteps in the long, polished hallway echoed slightly, and then the sound of women's voices gasping, commenting. The men turned to look as two of the women engaged in the house-keeping and cooking duties of the offices and the kitchen appeared in the archway to the hall. They were engrossed in reading a newspaper, pointing, gesturing, commenting. They suddenly realized where they were, jerked the newspaper down, and one started to beg forgiveness for their disrespectful conduct when they both recognized Stormont.

Their eyes popped wide, they gasped, clapped their hands over their mouths, spun on their heels and ran from the room. Their footsteps echoed in the hall until a door slammed and a painful silence gripped the foyer. Stormont turned back to the man at the reception desk and opened his mouth to speak when the second man spoke from the archway.

"His Excellency, the Foreign Minister will see you now."

Stormont turned on his heel and followed the man down the hallway. He passed through the anteroom without stopping and into the office of Vergennes.

Vergennes bowed. "An unexpected pleasure, your Excellency. Please be seated. Coffee? Tea?"

Stormont ignored the invitation and remained standing. "I have just become privy to facts that are shocking beyond belief. I have been aware for some time that French crews are loading French supplies and munitions onto French ships flying the French flag, for delivery to America, contrary to the clear, firm understanding that England had with this office that such would not be the case. I have let it pass in the vain hope you would reconsider."

He paused only long enough to order his thoughts. "However, that is now forgotten in the latest incident indicating a hostile intent on the part of France against England. An American ship, the *Reprisal,* has brought four captured British ships to a French port, and France allowed it entry and treated it as friendly."

Stormont's face was red, his neck veins extended. "That could be construed as an act of war by France against Britain under present international conditions."

Vergennes's face was an absolute blank. He did not move nor speak.

Stormont's doubled fist slammed onto the desktop. "I demand on behalf of the British crown, that the four captured British ships be released to their rightful owners now, with assurances that such transactions shall not be tolerated in French ports again."

He paused for Vergennes's reactions, and there were none.

Stormont concluded. "Am I clearly understood?"

Quietly Vergennes responded. "Absolutely. This is the first I have heard of such actions. Rest assured, I shall launch a thorough investigation instantly. If your information is correct, I will order the release of the British ships the first moment possible and submit to your king a written apology, with assurances such shall not be tolerated in French ports again, should it come to our attention."

It flashed in Stormont's mind. *He knows about Trenton and Princeton, and what it has done to us. He knows about the four ships and he has done nothing because he is very close to an open break with us. France means to declare war on England the very moment they decide the Americans may win. I am wasting my time.*

Stormont straightened. "Thank you for granting me an audience without an appointment."

"It was a pleasure. Feel free to return at any time."

Stormont turned and swept out of the room and down the hall. In the foyer, both men and women watched him pass out the front door. The moment the door closed, he could hear their outburst of comments.

Outraged, frightened, he remembered nothing of his carriage ride back to his quarters. Later, after picking at his supper for a time before abandoning it altogether, he sat at the desk in his bedroom with quill and paper. Slowly he addressed a message to the secretary of state in London.

"It is certain, My Lord, that the general animosity against us and the wild enthusiasm in favor of the rebels was never greater than it is at present . . . That M. de Vergennes is hostile in his heart and anxious for the success of the Rebels I have not a shadow of a doubt."

───────

Notes

Though Benjamin Franklin, historically, did not inform Comte de Vergennes of Washington's success at Trenton and Princeton, Franklin was aware of the activities in New Jersey (see Clark, *Benjamin Franklin,* pp. 316–17) and the author has chosen to include the scene in the novel for narrative purposes.

News of the battles reached Vergennes on February 25, 1777—the same day Lord Stormont met with Vergennes to discuss the matter of the *Reprisal,* which was an American ship that had captured four British vessels and delivered them to a French port (see Ketchum, *The Winter Soldiers,* p. 328). Stormont was enraged at the increasingly obvious support of France to America and penned a letter which contains the quote that concludes this chapter (see Ketchum, *The Winter Soldiers,* p. 329).

With the American cause proven by the success at Trenton and Princeton, it would only be a matter of time before France would openly declare war against Britain and align herself with America (see Clark, *Benjamin Franklin,* pp. 316–17).

CHAPTER XIX

★ ★ ★

*T*he pungent smell of pines, oaks, and maples coming into their spring foliage hung sweet in the still air of the small, orderly village of Morristown. The fifty houses and three white steeples glistened in the bright sunlight, beneath a clear, brilliant, blue sky that dwarfed the green valley nestled at the foot of the Thimble Mountains.

The hills were alive with pink dogwood blossoms and white mountain laurels, and the stream was lined with green skunk cabbage. Beady-eyed red squirrels darted about, tails arched and curled over their backs, chattering as they snatched at seed pods, then sat on their haunches to pry them open to reach the fresh, growing nubs inside. Jays argued with blackbirds, robins tiptoed on the ground with their heads turned to catch the vibrations of worms and insects moving in the earth, and sparrows darted after small flying insects. The quiet hum of bees performing their miracle of gathering pollen while they insured the survival of all blossoming plants was an undertone to a world once again alive with the joy of spring.

A quarter mile from the town, near the sprawling Continental army camp, Billy, Eli, and twenty other soldiers stood knee-deep in a clear mountain brook, barefooted, stripped to their underwear. It was Monday and they were taking their rotation in washing their clothes in water so cold it numbed their feet. Every man among them was soaked, head to toe, hair and beards dripping while they grinned from the mock battles they had fought in the stream, water flying as they grappled and went down shouting, laughing.

The memories of the winter, the days and weeks and months of sickness, of soul-destroying starvation and freezing, were forgotten for a time as they romped in the water. They finished washing their clothes and hung them on the bushes to dry while they sat on the grassy banks in their underwear, reveling in the warm morning sunshine and the clean, warm air. They plucked small stones from the streambed, black, gray, white, worn flat and smooth by millennia of running water, to toss them back splashing, watching them settle in the crystal water.

Eli turned to Billy. "Any idea what the cooks got in the pots for today?"

"Turlock said mutton. Mutton and turnips."

"We'll have to go get a possum some night. A big granddaddy possum sounds good right now."

Billy grinned. "You might have to cook it."

Eli shrugged. "Simple. You just clean 'em out and bury 'em on hot rocks for a day or two, skin and all. They come out smoking, so sweet and tender they fall apart."

Food had not been plentiful since they marched into the valley and set up their army camp near Morristown. But what they did get was so much more than what they had lived on for eight months that it seemed they had arrived in the land of promise. The men had slowly gained flesh and muscle and strength. They had cut trees to build small huts chinked with dry grass and mud for protection from the winter storms, and the regiments had each taken their turn guarding the mountain passes against attack by the British. Then the barren trees had shown the first swelling of bulging buds, and green had appeared on the branches as the days grew longer and warmer. Spirits rose with each passing day.

Billy tugged his damp shirt over his head, then put on his trousers. He pulled on his socks and, with a sense of reverence, he slipped on the thick-soled, lace-up shoes he had taken from British stores following the battle of Princeton. He had never supposed that he could covet anything as he coveted the shoes. The day he found them he had cut the cords holding the tattered blanket strips to his feet, and slowly worked his feet into the stiff leather, then patiently tied them. He had sat for minutes, lost in the feeling of having shoes on his feet once again.

Something between his battered, bleeding feet and the ice and the frozen ground. He had slept with the shoes clutched in his arms, beneath his blanket, for weeks.

He finished tying the shoes and rose. Eli was beside him, dressed in his damp buckskins. Together they walked back to camp, to the small hut they shared with four others. They turned at the sound of the familiar nasal voice.

"You lovelies heard?"

Billy shook his head. "Heard what?"

"About Burgoyne."

Eli glanced at Billy, then turned back to Turlock. "Who's Burgoyne?"

"Gentleman Johnny Burgoyne. General in His Majesty's Royal Army, King George the Third. Gambler, carouser, lady's man, and all-around dandy. I heard he writes plays. Also the commander of one of the crack outfits in the British army. And he's headed here with an army."

Billy's forehead wrinkled in puzzlement. "Morristown?"

"No, Canada. And then down Lake Champlain and the Hudson River valley to come in from the west, behind us, and trap us. Burgoyne and an army of about ten thousand on the west, and Howe and his army on the east."

"How do you know?"

Turlock grunted. "Newspapers. New York, Boston, London. Cat's out of the bag. King George took it hard when we captured Trenton and Princeton. It appears he means to teach us we ought not do such things."

Eli's eyes narrowed and he stood motionless, mind racing. "Wait a minute. Canada? Where in Canada?"

"The Richlieu River, so far as I know."

"And he's coming down Lake Champlain and the Hudson valley?"

"Him and his whole army."

Eli's mouth clamped shut and Billy saw the instant intensity in his face. "What's in your mind?" Billy asked.

"He's coming right through the country where I was raised. Joseph

Brant's up there with his Mohawk, and Red Jacket and Cornplanter right along with him, and they've all taken sides with the British. Brant's one of the smartest men I ever knew, and he knows every hill and valley and stream up there. We might be able to stop Burgoyne, but if Brant joins with him, I can tell you right now, Washington's got trouble he don't even know about." Eli stopped, rounded his cheeks, and blew air.

Turlock spoke. "I've heard of Brant. Isn't he a fighter?"

"One of the best. He can likely raise two or three thousand Mohawk and Iroquois and Onondaga warriors any time he wants. And they don't fight like the British. The first notion you get they're even around is when a bullet or an arrow or a tomahawk knocks you down." Eli paused for a moment, collecting his thoughts. "When is Burgoyne supposed to be here?"

Turlock shrugged. "Left England sometime in late March. Should be here soon."

"You sure about all this?"

Turlock hooked a thumb over his shoulder. "Major Fitzgerald has the newspapers. I seen 'em." He waited for a moment. "Well, I just thought you might want to know. I better get back to the stew pots. I drew cookin' duties for the day. Servin' the noon meal soon. Mutton stew, just like for supper."

For long minutes Eli stared after Turlock, his mind working, calculating.

Billy waited, then spoke. "You got things to think about?"

Eli nodded in silence.

Billy said, "I'm going inside. Call me when you want to go for supper."

He walked into the dim light of their crude hut and sat on his bunk, then turned and laid down, hands behind his head. He glanced at his old, threadbare blanket coat, with the six letters he had written to Brigitte between the double layers, and for a moment his mind reached back to the gentle times in the warmth and security of Boston, and Brigitte's face was before him.

Eli's voice jolted him out of his reveries. "Billy, I got to go see Washington. You want to come?"

Billy swung his feet off the cot. "Washington? Why?"

"There's some things he better know."

The two walked through the camp, to the Freeman Tavern on the edge of Morristown's public square where General Washington had established his headquarters. The picket challenged them and they stopped.

Billy spoke. "Corporal Billy Weems and Scout Eli Stroud to see the general."

The startled picket stammered, "What? Who sent you?"

Eli broke in. "No one. Just tell the general who's here."

The picket shook his head. "Only if you got written orders from a major officer."

Eli spoke. "We just heard about the British sending a general named Burgoyne to trap us all. I got a few things the general needs to hear about that and there's no time to waste. If it all goes wrong because I don't get to talk to him, you might have some trouble."

Billy broke in. "We're the two the general sent to scout the British before the Princeton battle. We were with Hand when he slowed down General Cornwallis."

The picket's eyes widened. "Wait here." He was gone for one minute before he returned. "The general will see you now."

They left their weapons at the door and followed the picket into a library and glanced at the polished maple bookshelves filled with books of every description. General Washington was seated behind a small desk on one side of the fireplace. He rose as they entered, and Billy spoke.

"Corporal Billy Weems and Scout Eli Stroud, sir. We hope you'll excuse the interruption. We wouldn't have come except Scout Stroud has information that may be important."

"Go on."

Eli locked eyes with Washington. "We just heard the British are sending a general named Burgoyne with a big force down from Canada. Lake Champlain and on down the Hudson River. They intend trapping us with Burgoyne on one side and Howe on the other."

Eli stopped, waiting for a response from Washington, and the general answered. "I've been informed. Is that what you came to tell me?"

"Not all. I was raised by the Iroquois for seventeen years in those hills. Joseph Brant's up there in that country with Red Jacket and Cornplanter. They've all joined the British, and together they can raise maybe two, three thousand Indian warriors—Mohawk, Iroquois, Onondaga. They know every hill and valley and stream up there, and they know how to fight in those woods. Joseph Brant's one of the smartest men I know, and if Burgoyne gets them to join him, maybe we're going to have more trouble than we can handle."

Washington slowly sat back down on his chair. "What do you recommend?"

"I'll be a lot more help to you up there than down here watching Howe. I speak the language, and I know how they think, how they fight. I know those mountains."

"Do you know Joseph Brant?"

"Yes, and Red Jacket and Cornplanter."

"Will Brant remember you?"

"Yes. I met him once. We had just finished a battle with the French. I was part of a small party that broke the French lines and ran off their horses. He wanted to meet me. He was surprised when he saw I was white. He'll remember."

"What can you do up there that others cannot?"

"The woods are so thick up there that moving an army south without knowing the trails will likely be impossible. Brant knows those trails, and if Burgoyne takes him on to guide his army, he'll make it through. I know those trails too. I think I can slow Burgoyne down—maybe even stop him—whether or not Brant and his warriors become his guides."

"Won't Brant and his warriors be able to find you and stop you?"

"That's an interesting question, but one thing is sure. I stand a better chance of doing something to slow them down than any other man in this army."

"Are you volunteering to go up there to resist General Burgoyne?"

"I am."

"Alone?"

Eli pondered for a moment, then turned to Billy, silently asking the heavy question.

Billy turned to Washington. "I'll go."

Washington shifted back to Eli. "When?"

"When will Burgoyne land up there?"

"He will be there any day."

"Then we better leave now."

"Would you two men wait outside for a short time? I want to consider all this."

Outside, in the warmth of the midday sun, Billy turned to Eli. "You sure you want me along? I might slow you down."

Eli shook his head and said nothing; they settled into a thoughtful silence, waiting.

The picket opened the door. "The general will see you again."

Inside the library, General Washington rose to face them. He handed each of them a folded paper, sealed with wax and the imprint of his rank as commander in chief of the Continental army.

"Here are my written orders. You are to leave as soon as you can. I do not yet know who will be commanding our forces up there, but I am certain it will be either General Schuyler or General Gates, with militia. I must remain here to face General Howe. You will have to find the army up there and present these orders. Generally, you both have authority to move about as you see fit, advising our forces according to what you learn. Am I clear?"

Billy replied, "Yes, sir."

Eli nodded.

He handed them a second, smaller paper. "This is an order allowing you to draw ammunition and food before you leave. Is there anything else?"

"No."

"Dismissed."

With their weapons in their hands they walked away from the building, back to the cluster of huts and tents, saying little, lost in the new thoughts that came rushing one on top of another. They got their wooden spoons, bowls, and pewter mugs from their hut, sought out

Turlock's smoking cook pot, and stood in line with the others gathering for their noon meal. Turlock dipped mutton stew with a long-handled, wooden spoon and loaded their bowls. He spoke as they poured steaming coffee from a battered two-gallon pot.

"Did I see you coming from Washington's headquarters?"

Billy nodded. "Yes. Looks like Eli and I are going north to join the militia up there when they meet Burgoyne."

Turlock eyed Eli. "Isn't that where you come from?"

"Yes."

"Makes sense. When do you leave?"

"Today, soon as we can."

Turlock shook his head in disgust. "Amazin' what some folks will do to avoid eatin' mutton stew twice in one day." He looked them both in the eye. "You two be careful." He wanted to say more, but the words he wanted would not come. He shook the dripping wooden spoon at them. "Hear me? You be careful."

They walked back to their hut and sat on a crude pinewood bench by the front door while they spooned up the smoking stew, blowing on it before they took it gingerly into their mouths. They ate and drank in silence, washed their utensils in the stream, then went back to their hut to sit their utensils on the bench to dry in the sun.

Together they walked down to the commissary where they drew hardtack, dried corn, salt pork, coffee, sugar, and rice rations for fourteen days. At the powder magazine they got fifty rifle balls, and a one-pound canvas bag of gunpowder for each rifle. In thoughtful silence they walked back towards their small log hut. They put their food and ammunition rations on the rough, split-log table.

Eli turned to Billy. "We'll be gone a while. Anything you need to do before we leave?"

Billy reflected for a moment. "I should write to Mother. You?"

Eli shrugged. "I've got no family."

"Maybe Mary Flint would like to know."

For a moment Eli saw her face, the dark eyes and dark hair. A quiet longing he had never known before arose inside, and a faraway look stole over his face. "I wouldn't know what to say." He pushed it aside and spoke abruptly. "Want to write to your family while I go tell the captain we're leaving?" His wry smile flickered. "Wouldn't want to get shot for a deserter."

He ducked out the low door frame and strode away in the sunlight as Billy dug his stub pencil and rumpled writing pad from his coat. He smoothed the wrinkled sheets on the uneven tabletop and thoughtfully wrote:

May 5, 1777
Morristown, New Jersey

My Dear Mother and Sister:

I first assure you I am well in mind and body. Since I wrote last, I have enjoyed good food and a warm log hut. The army remains camped here at Morristown, where we are safe. Spring has arrived and the mountains here are green—the weather generally warm.

I am obliged to inform you that I am being sent north with my friend, Eli Stroud. We are to join the militia in the region of Lake Champlain where it is thought Eli can be of help in fighting the British, since he knows the country and the language of the Indian people up there. I do not know when I will return, or when I will be able to write again. You are not to worry. We are in the right cause and the Almighty favors us, as I have seen many times.

I think of you often. Trudy, I will try to bring you a surprise from the north country when I return. Obey Mother and help her in every way. You are a fine daughter and sister.

I am sorry I do not have more time. I think of you every day and you are in my prayers always. I look forward to the day when I can return. I have much to tell. Please let Margaret and Brigitte read this letter, and ask them to tell Matthew when they write to him next.

I place you all in the hands of the Almighty.

Your loving and ob'dt son and brother,
Billy Weems

As he folded the paper, troubling thoughts came to slow him. *I may be killed up north. I may never return! What would become of Mother! Trudy!*

He stared down at the letter, grappling with the sudden, startling inner acceptance of his own mortality. He could be killed! He could be one of the bodies lying face down in a field, or on a riverbank, or in the forest. A shallow grave dug by hasty hands, his body rolled in, the earth thrown on by men who did not know his name or care. A brief letter to his mother by an officer she had never heard of, and her heartbreak as she lived out her days in a world of gray loneliness.

His mouth went dry as he struggled. *What's happening to me? Battles— death all around me—how many times? How many men have I killed? How many have tried to kill me? How many times could I have been dead? I've known it—why is it different now?*

He slowly straightened, staring down at his hands, comprehending for the first time that a British cannon or musket could instantly turn them white, limp, lifeless. His breathing slowed as he stared, wide-eyed.

Suddenly an overpowering compulsion came flowing. He had to be home, safe with his mother and Trudy. Going to work at the accounts house, coming home to a warm supper, reading by the firelight in the evenings, talking with Mother, cutting firewood. Never had he felt such a powerful need to be with his family, doing the quiet, ordinary, unremarkable things of life. How precious, how wonderful they seemed as he sat there, staring. The impulse washed over him to walk out of the small hut and leave behind his weapons of war, the army camp, the war, and he swallowed hard at the lump that sprang into his throat to choke him.

From a place deep inside a new intuitive sensation rose to calm him, steady him. Without putting it to words, he knew something had happened to the foundations of how he saw the world. Somehow he had reached new depths. He was seeing what had always been there plainly before him, but lost to him as though he were blind. A tingle arose, and his hands trembled as he realized that the new, sobering vistas opening in his mind and soul would clarify only with the passage of time.

He drew and exhaled a great breath. His hands steadied as he finished folding the letter, pressed a seal onto it, then addressed it. He reached to shove his pencil and the worn pad back into his coat when he heard the soft tread of Eli at the door as he entered the hut.

"I told the captain. We ought to get our bedrolls packed."

They laid their spread coats on their bunks, placed their food rations, extra rifle balls, the gunpowder bag on them, and wrapped them tight. They rolled the coats inside their blankets, then tied their blankets with long rawhide strips, leaving a loop large enough to sling the bundle on their backs. They buckled on their weapons belts, Eli shoved his black tomahawk through his, and they each glanced about the room for a moment. Standing in the unlighted hut, with the sunlight streaming in through the open door, Billy turned to Eli.

"Which direction do we take from here?"

"The streams and river will be running high with the spring snowmelt. If we go north and then a little east from here, we'll miss the Passaic River and the Ramapo and the Hackensack, and some other small ones, and then we can cut east and come out at the Hudson River. From there we can follow it north to its headwaters, then on to the south end of Lake Champlain and follow it north from there. If Burgoyne's coming down Lake Champlain and the Hudson River valley, we ought to find them if we go up the same way."

They slung their bedrolls over their shoulders, picked up their rifles, and walked out into the brilliant day. A few soldiers slowed to stare at them as they made their way north through camp. Eli waited while Billy delivered his letter to the office of the adjutant, and they continued on, out of camp, following the wagon ruts winding north at the foot of the western slopes of the Thimble Mountains.

Eli slowed to stare silently at the spectacular colors, and listen to the sounds of birds and insects. The mountain air was so pure they could count branches on pine trees half a mile away. Billy said nothing, giving him his time, and then suddenly Billy was aware that Eli was doing more than basking in the deep beauty of a rare spring day. He was drawing a strength from the wilderness into his soul. He had been too long away from the power of the forces of nature, too long in the confused, tangled webs of intrigue of the world of white men. His inner wellsprings had been drained.

As they moved on, Billy spoke. "Will we be going near where you were born? Your home?"

"Probably not. We'll likely not get that far north."

"How far south did the Iroquois come while you were with them?"

"All down the Lake Champlain country. A long way south in the Hudson River valley. We fought battles. Hunted food."

They fell silent as they moved on, each deep in their own thoughts. The wagon road rose to cross a low knoll, and as they reached the crest, Billy stopped and turned to look back. The valley lay before them, with the three white steeples and the green trees marking Morristown, and the smoke of cook fires rising straight into the still air to show the Continental army camp. Billy stood still for a time while his thoughts ran.

Eli spoke quietly. "I been concerned since you decided to come. Your home is in Boston. You're leaving a lot behind, and no one knows when you'll ever see it again." He looked Billy in the eyes. "You belong here. Sure you want to go on? No one would fault you for staying."

Billy stood silent for a long time. "Why are you going north?"

Eli drew and released a great breath. "I believe I have a sister up there, and I learned down here that she was taken in by a preacher named Cyrus Fielding. Maybe I can find her." He dropped his eyes for a moment, then raised them. His gaze was intense as he finished. "But that's not the whole reason. I got a feeling that this country was meant to be free and it won't let go of me. That's why I'm going."

Billy dropped his eyes and for a long time stared unseeing at the dirt and growing grass and tiny mountain flowers in the wagon road, and then raised his eyes.

"I know. It won't let go of me either."

They looked back at the breathtaking beauty of the valley for a moment longer, then turned their backs. With the warm sun on their heads and shoulders, rifles in their hands, they walked over the crest of the low hill, down the north slope.

They did not look back.

Notes

Washington established his headquarters in Morristown on January 7, 1777, and the Continental army quartered in the protected valley all winter (see Stryker, *The Battles of Trenton and Princeton*, p. 303).

May 6, 1777, British general John Burgoyne arrived in Canada with a plan to proceed south down the Lake Champlain-Hudson River "corridor" and target several forts, particularly Fort Ticonderoga, which was thought to be the key to holding the northern section of the continent. From there, he would proceed further south to Albany to join forces with General William Howe and the Mowhak Indian chief, Joseph Brant. The objective was to cut off the northern colonies and end the war with a "divide and conquer" tactic. General Burgoyne was not only well known in the high society of England, he was an effective, proven officer (see Ketchum, *Saratoga*, pp. 73–76, 84–85, 88).

Selected Bibliography

★ ★ ★

"About Princeton" at http://www.princeton.edu> [5 October 1999]

Billias, George Athan. *General John Glover and His Marblehead Mariners.* New York: Holt, Rinehart and Winston, 1960.

Boatner, Mark Mayo, III. *The Encyclopedia of the American Revolution.* New York: David McKay Company, Inc., 1966.

Chase, Philander D. ed. *The Papers of George Washington.* Vol. 7, October 1776-January 1777. Charlottesville and London: University Press of Virginia, 1997.

Clark, Ronald W. *Benjamin Franklin: A Biography.* New York: Random House, 1983.

Commager, Henry Steele, and Richard B. Morris, eds. *The Spirit of 'Seventy-Six: The Story of the American Revolution as Told by Participants.* New York: Da Capo Press, 1995.

Fast, Howard Melvin. *The Crossing.* New York: William Morrow and Co., 1971.

Freeman, Douglas Southall. *George Washington: A Biography.* Vol. 4. New York: Charles Scribner's Sons, 1951.

Higginbotham, Don. *The War of American Independence: Military Attitudes, Policies, and Practice, 1763–1789.* New York: Macmillan, 1971.

Johnston, Henry P. *The Campaign of 1776 Around New York and Brooklyn.* 1878. Reprint, New York: Da Capo Press, 1971.

Ketchum, Richard M. *Saratoga: Turning Point of America's Revolutionary War.* New York: Henry Holt and Company, 1997.

————. *The Winter Soldiers: The Battles for Trenton and Princeton.* New York: Anchor Books, Doubleday, 1991.

Leckie, Robert. *George Washington's War: The Saga of the American Revolution.* New York: HarperCollins, 1992.

Mackesy, Piers. *The War for America, 1775–1783.* 1964. Reprint, Lincoln: University of Nebraska Press, 1993.

Nelson, Paul David. *General Horatio Gates: A Biography.* Baton Rouge: Louisiana State University Press, 1976.

Smith, Samuel Stelle. *The Battle of Trenton.* Monmouth Beach, N.J.: Philip Freneau Press, 1965.

Stryker, William S. *The Battles of Trenton and Princeton.* 1898. Reprint, Spartanburg, S.C.: The Reprint Company, 1967.

Ward, Christopher. *The War of the Revolution.* New York: Macmillan, 1952.

ACKNOWLEDGMENTS

★ ★ ★

Richard B. Bernstein, a constitutional historian specializing in the Revolutionary generation, made a tremendous contribution to the historical accuracy of this work, for which the writer is deeply grateful. The staff of the publisher, Bookcraft, most notably Lisa Mangum, editor, and Jana Erickson, art director, spent many hours immersed in the details of preparing the manuscript for publication. Harriette Abels, consultant and mentor, again performed her magic, and finally her approval.

However, the men and women of the Revolution, whose spirit reaches out from the pages of history to lift and inspire, were ultimately responsible for this series.

This work proceeds only because of the contributions of all those who have helped.